EUROPA
Awakenings

P. R. Garcia

DEDICATION

Dedicated to Sharron and Darlene for their reassurance to pursue my love of whale watching, their support to write this trilogy and their encouragement to pursue my dreams.

To the San Diego Natural History Museum Whalers for their love of the incredible cetaceans and other marine life that call the Pacific Ocean their home. And for their dedication to the people of San Diego and the world to see the wonder and importance of these creatures through knowledge, sharing and guidance.

And to London, a most precious gift who always brings a smile to my face.

ACKNOWLEGEMENT

I would like to acknowledge the extraordinary volunteers of the San Diego Natural History Museum Whalers and the San Diego Birch Aquarium at Scripps Institution of Oceanography for their dedication to the cetaceans and other marine life residing in the waters off southern California and northern Mexico. Both organizations have a dedicated group of volunteers who work as naturalists on the whale boats during the gray whale migration season in San Diego from late December through mid-April. The knowledge they have passed on to me was invaluable in writing this book.

The legend of Atlantis, as described in the writings of Plato from 360 BC, was the basis for the first Oonock city. Their third city is based upon legends and the ruins of Puma Punku in Bolivia, South America. The saltwater lake is modeled after Lake Titicaca, which resides on the borders of Peru and Bolivia. The Message of Holes Enok bored into the rock can be seen near Pisco Valley, Peru on a plain known as Cajamarquilla. It is known as the "Band of Holes" and consists of 6900 holes dug in a row of eight holes uniformly spread over a mile radius. Archeologists have no idea why they were made or by whom.

On October 18, 1989, NASA launched the spacecraft Galileo to study Saturn. In February of 1997, on its way to Saturn, Galileo briefly orbited Jupiter and sent back pictures of several of her larger moons, including IO, Ganymede and Europa. The images sent back confirmed the analysis that Europa was covered by a layer of ice possibly sixty miles thick under which may exist a subsurface ocean. Many scientists believe Europa's waters contain the three primary ingredients for life (water, heat, and organic compounds) and believe her waters have the best chance for containing alien life in our solar system. NASA had proposed a mission to determine if life does exist there, known as JIMO (Jupiter Icy Moons Orbiter) but the project was cancelled in 2005. However, in May of 2012, ESA (European Space Agency) announced the selection of a new mission known as JUICE (Jupiter Icy Moon Explorer) and hopes to launch in 2022

I would like to thank D. Williams, W. Cooley and M. Sixtus for their help in editing this book.

FOREWORD

Astrologists agree that there is a fantastic chance that beneath the ice shield of Jupiter's moon, Europa, lies a vast global ocean where life may exists. My interpretation of Europa is a world of lilac, salty water where ocean-floor-heat-vents spew heat, oxygen and particles of light up into the waters. Her deep oceans are filled will a diversity of life, many with the capability of bioluminescence, just as our deep ocean fish have. Thus, Europa's ocean is the complete opposite of ours – the light is at the bottom and the dark is at the top, for little sunlight reaches Europa, and her ice shield blocks any that does.

In this beautiful florescent world of light and color, lives a sentient race known as the Oonocks, an ancient race at least seventy to one hundred million years old. They are, for the most part, peaceful beings, who value family and honor above all else. They have no words such as divorce, greed, want or hate, for those things do not exist. The race consists of clans, which number from several hundred members to several thousand. Each clan specializes in two or three fields, such as fishing, farming, ship building, engineering, physics, chemistry, metal urging, aerodynamics and so forth. Each clan is governed by a royal family, usually consisting of a Lord and Lady. Together, the clans are managed by a King and Queen, to whom everyone pledges their loyalty and lives to. Every individual contributes something to the whole; those who do not partake is a specific area of study become soldiers; those too young to work attend school; and those too old teach the young. Although not a perfect society, it is pretty close.

No land exists above water on Europa, so the Oonocks are aquatic beings. They are equipped with three pairs of wings that glide them through their watery world. Their streamlined bodies are muscular and strong, tapering into a long tail with a feathery lilac end. Strings of pearl-shaped glowing lights cascade down from the top of their heads, framing a gentle, oval face with large lilac eyes and soft lilac lips. Like most creatures of Europa, they are bioluminescent and glow a soft lilac color. Their expected life span is twelve thousand years. Infancy lasts a hundred years and adulthood is not reached until one turns a thousand years old. And, as if this isn't enough to convince us of their excellence and superiority, they are blessed with a special power – the ability to transform into both land and aquatic creatures equal to or larger than themselves.

Approximately sixty four hundred years ago, this peaceful existence of the Oonock world was destroyed when the reigning king betrayed his middle son, JeffRa, devastating him beyond repair. In retaliation, JeffRa tried to assassinate his older brother, Enok, who is the future king. Once the best of friends, the two brothers became mortal enemies and civil war broke out. JeffRa and his followers are hunted down and exiled to Ganymede, another of Jupiter's moons. There he became the leader of another race called Terrians, a barbaric society who embrace cruelty, greed and war. From his place of exile, JeffRa continued to plot his brother's end, promising to never stop until ever Oonock in the universe was dead.

When JeffRa's invention inadvertently destroyed Jupiter and turned it into the gas ball it is today with its giant storms, King Enok and his mate, Queen Medaron, took twenty ships filled with Oonocks and fled Europa. Most of the ships went further out into the galaxy, but King Enok brought three ships to Earth to live. Another two settled on Mars, which, at that time, was Earth's sister planet, green with vegetation and covered with life. But JeffRa followed, searching the planets for his hated brother, consumed by his unquenchable thirst to eradicate all Oonocks. Believing his brother and family were on Mars, JeffRa attacked and reduced the thriving surface to a burnt out ball of dust and rock. JeffRa's error gave King Enok the needed warning to save both Earth and his Oonocks. Overnight, in a blaze of fire and water, he sank his golden city to the depths of the Pacific Ocean. Thus the legend of Atlantis was born. There, beneath the cloak of darkness and water, the Oonock race remained, safe and unknown, for thousands of years. Occasionally, they emerged and tried to live on land again, but for one reason or another, were always forced back to the security of the deep, causing the creation of many Earthly legends. During this time, they had no idea that JeffRa had crashed on Earth, and was still hunting his brother and wife.

Believing all danger of JeffRa was gone and wishing to live above in the light of the sun again, the Oonocks emerged once more from their Complex below and build a new city. Trying to avoid the human-interactions that occurred at their former cities, King Enok chose a location far away from their previous cities and on the other side of the world, high on top of a tall plateau in Bolivia (Puma Punku). They named her Third City. There they lived in happiness and peace, safe behind their megalithic stone walls, hidden from the world, never interacting with the indigenous natives. For several hundred years the Oonocks lived in harmony and contentment until one fateful day when the sound of marching feet broke the stillness of the air. JeffRa and his army of Terrians had found them.

The two brothers, King Enok with his Oonocks and JeffRa with his Terrians, fought a great war. Both sides suffered great losses. JeffRa was at last defeated, but the Oonocks paid a huge price. Once more they were forced to retreat to the sanctuary of the deep ocean and try to rebuild their race, but the possibility to do so seemed impossible. Queen Medaron lied in a state of deep depression over the loss of her only son whom JeffRa killed. King Enok lied in the medical ward, gravely injured by JeffRa, desperate to survive to save his people and his mate. As they and this noble race struggled to survive and rebuild, they learned a horrifying truth of JeffRa's attack: his release of a biological weapon that caused all future Oonock newborn children to die within the first few years of their lives. Later, it caused infertility, thus dooming the Oonock race. With no way to reproduce and no way to return home, they faced a dismal future; when the last Oonock died, the great Oonock race would be no more. Centuries later, something marvelous happened. Queen Medaron discovered she was pregnant with the future Queen. With the joy of a new life came the realization that, because of JeffRa's curse, the unborn female could not survive as an Oonock. To ensure her survival, the decision was made for her to be born on land as a human. To protect her, it was also decided that she would never know who or what she really was. Thus begins book one, *EUROPA: Awakenings* and the *Europa Series*.

NEW LIFE

Medaron stood in the doorway surveying the contents of her dwelling, taking in its design and colors as a remembrance for days to come. Her eyes drifted toward the now empty cage where her two pet Dumbo Octopus normally resided. Enok, her life's mate, had moved the octopus to his temporary quarters when their residence was converted to an air-breathing, lower air pressure environment to accommodate her pregnancy. She wondered how they were coping with their new short-term home. She sighed knowing once she left Enok would release her pets back into the ocean; he would not welcome a constant reminder of her absence. Of all Earth's animals the Dumbo Octopus were her favorites, probably because they reminded her of her pets back home. She would miss them. She placed her hands lightly on her belly, wishing there had been a way their child could have been born at the Complex and lived in the house where she and Enok had been happy for several millennia. But circumstances dictated the child could not survive being born in her true form and therefore made it imperative she be born in the human world. Medaron closed her eyes and sensed her fetal daughter inside her. Although only a few weeks old, Medaron could already feel her daughter growing inside her, developing lungs, becoming human. She opened her eyes, took one last look and stepped through the doorway, closing the door behind her. Tonight she would journey to the world above and leave this world behind.

As she stepped outside she saw a young human male with short curly dark brown hair and emerald green eyes standing there waiting to escort her. Medaron smiled at her son, Earon, marveling at the fact that, even in human form, he resembled his father. Medaron knew he too was committing the sights, smells and sounds of the Complex to his memory, for he was accompanying her to the world above and it would be many years before he would return. He said not a word but gave her a warm smile as he slipped his arm through hers and began walking down the path toward the Exit Chamber, gently guiding her. As they walked, Medaron stared at the glass walls on each side of the walkway wishing she could transform into her true self once more and swim through the lilac waters being held back by the glass partitions. But she knew such a transformation would endanger her unborn child. She continued to scan the lilac waters, as she neared the Exit Chamber entrance, searching for her one true love, her life's mate, Enok. She knew he would be there waiting for her on the other side of the glass where she could not reach him, waiting to say his goodbyes, waiting to stay behind, waiting for their happiness to be torn apart. Her human heart began to beat faster as she saw a soft white glow begin to appear ahead. Unaware of her actions, her feet began to keep pace with her heart beat as she rushed toward the light, watching it grow brighter and larger with each step until she stood before him. Forcing a smile onto her face she stepped forward and placed her hands upon the glass separating them; she in her transformed human body, he in his true form. In response, Enok gracefully moved through the water and placed his hands on the glass opposite hers. Neither said a word as they looked into each other's eyes, not wanting this moment to end.

"You are as beautiful in your transformed human body as you are in your true form," Europa heard Enok say inside her mind as he looked at her, noting her long wavy light brown hair encircling her oval face, her long slender neck, her strong shoulders and petite body. In addition to her beauty Enok realized she had a glow about her, something he had heard human females had when they were with child. The glow made her more intoxicating, more desirable and Enok wondered how he was going to live without her.

Continuing to look into his eyes Medaron spoke, "Nothing is more beautiful than you in your true form. Know whichever being you transform into my love for you remains constant and true. You are my life's mate, my one true love. I am yours now and forever. No separation can diminish that love, no hardship can destroy it, no vow of revenge can stop me from loving you for eternity."

"You are the reason I exist," Enok replied back, now forcing a smile onto his face. "I am your life's mate now and forever, beyond death and for all eternity. The love I have for you has no bounds and grows more each day."

"For that I am happy", Medaron said, as she drew even nearer to the glass wall. "I will miss you."

"And I you. Hopefully our time apart will be short and will pass swiftly. Just as soon as I am able to breathe above I will immediately join you, Earon and our daughter at Minnos and we will forget this time of sorrow."

"On that day I will sing a song of joy," Medaron said. Tears tried to form in her eyes but she would not allow them to. As the Supreme Monarch of their people she would not disgrace herself or her husband with such a show of emotion; she would fulfill her duty with all the dignity and responsibility required of a sovereign. The child inside her was the next female leader of their people and her survival and happiness was hers and Enok's top priority. For that reason they had agreed the child would be born above in the human world never knowing the truth of whom and what her parents were, where they originated from or of her people's existence in the deepest part of the ocean. She would be raised as a human being in the human world with no special powers or longevity of an Oonock.

"You make me proud to stand beside you as your co-monarch and your life's mate," Enok said, as he drew closer, wishing he could reach through the glass and hold his wife. Seeing Medaron was having trouble fighting back the tears he asked, "Did you decide on a name for our daughter?"

"Yes," Medaron answered, as she forced the smile to remain on her face. "I chose your first suggestion – Europa. You were right; it is the perfect name for her. She will be the last female leader of our people and therefore should bear the name of her homeland."

"I was hoping you would choose that name. She may never know of her birth rights or who she really is, but at least she will have the name." Enok moved his hand on the glass over the position of Medaron's womb. "Europa, it is I, your father. I cannot make this trip with you today but I will join you soon. Know this, My Child, I love your mother more than life itself and it was by that love you were created. You are a rare and precious jewel loved by your people, cherished by all." Enok raised his eyes to once again look into Medaron's. "Until I am able to join you please tell our daughter I love her very much."

"Every day," Medaron replied.

Earon had stood back from his parents to allow them some privacy. When he saw Enok turn his eyes toward him he stepped forward and placed his hand on the glass near his father's. "May the Waters keep you safe and bring you to us soon, Father," he said. "Our life will not be complete until you are with us again."

"May the Waters keep you safe also, Son." Enok responded back. "Know that no father has ever been prouder of his son than I am of you, Earon. As the second leader of our people you could have remained here, but you have honored me by going with your mother to watch over *you* and your sister in my absence. The sacrifice you make to live above as *your* sister's canine protector, knowing she will never know of your dedication to her, is noted. From the bottom of my heart I thank you."

"No thanks is needed, Father. It is my pleasure and honor to fill in for you. I know yours and Mother's separation will be a short one, but until the day you join us I promise to keep both of them safe for you." Earon said, delighted he had pleased his father so.

"I know this is true. The day when you can end your charade and the four of us can live as a real family cannot come soon enough. Remember to listen to Jeanip, to adhere to his and your mother's rules. They are in place to protect not only your sister but you also. I love you, My Son." Enok could say no more for he too was now having trouble fighting back the tears in his eyes. The three people he loved most in this world were leaving to begin a life outside his world and apart from him.

"I love you too, Father. I will now take my leave." Earon walked away and entered the Exit Chamber. From the look on his father's First Commander's face, time was short and Earon wanted his parents to have what time remained to say their last goodbyes. He walked over to the transportation capsule and transformed into the shape he would assume to protect his sister – the shape of a Rottweiler. He jumped into the capsule and curled up at its end. He knew he could have risen to the surface as a Moby like the others, but he did not want his mother to make the journey alone. Even though both would be asleep for the trip, he hoped his presence in the capsule would bring his mother some comfort.

Seeing they could delay their departure no longer, Jeanip walked over to where Medaron and Enok were. "I'm sorry Your Majesties, but if we plan on using the cloak of the new moon to hide our arrival we must leave now."

"Very well," Medaron whispered. She looked into Enok's eyes one last time. "Stay well," was all she could say as she turned and walked through the entrance. The tears she had fought so hard to deny now ran freely down her cheeks. She was thankful she had been able to contain them until she entered the Exit Chamber, thankful Enok had not seen them.

"Take care of them, Jeanip," Enok said, as he watched Medaron lie down above Earon in the transportation capsule. He now turned his attention to the male human in front of him, a weathered soldier who lived by the strictest code of honor and dignity. "You have always been

12

my captain, my first in command and my truest friend. You fought by my side in the Terrian war and have saved me and Medaron many times. Now I add to your duties the role of chief protector of Medaron and my family. Their well-being and lives I place in your hands."

"It is an honor I accept willingly, Sire. I will forfeit my life if need be to keep them safe," Jeanip replied, as he watched the sorrowful look on his sovereign's face. He knew this separation was not only hard on Medaron but it was tearing Enok's heart apart too.

"Are the paintings with her?"

"Yes, Sire, they are hidden in the capsule. I will make sure they are set out so she will see them when she awakens in the morning."

"Thank you."

"I will send word when we have arrived at Minnos. May the Waters keep you safe and give you long life, My Leader and My Liege." Jeanip bowed his head slightly forward and placed his right hand upon his forehead. "With your permission I will now take my leave of you."

"May the Waters give you the wisdom and strength you will need to fulfill your duty," Enok stated, as he quickly glanced at the capsule containing his life's mate. "Permission granted." He watched Jeanip turn and entered the Exit Chamber, closing the door behind him. After the lock engaged Jeanip sealed the door, listening for the familiar suction sound as the seals interlocked around the door frame. The purple light above the door signaled departure was permitted.

Jeanip walked over to the transportation capsule and gazed at the two sleeping monarchs. "Are they ready?" he asked Evonic, the medical attendant who would be accompanying them. It was necessary to bring their own medical personage not only to help with Medaron's pregnancy but for any medical matters that might arise in the future. Since the members of Jeanip's team were human only in appearance they would not be able to seek medical assistance from a human doctor if they were ever injured or ill.

"Yes, they are ready," Evonic replied. "I have the unit set and ready for your inspection."

Jeanip knelt down and brushed a lock of light brown hair away from Medaron's face. "Sleep well, Your Majesties, for when you awake you will be in the world above feeling the warmth of the sun on your face and smelling the sweetness of that world's air." After he closed the lid he leaned over to check the pressurization gauges; all were operating in the green. Jeanip pushed the status button and waited for the confirmation panel to signal everything was operating correctly and sealed accurately. Due to the enormous water pressure at such a deep depth it was necessary for Medaron and Earon to be transported in a special capsule designed to depressurize them as they ascended to the surface to prevent decompression disease. Jeanip knew any containment leak or slight variance in the water pressure could prove fatal to the sleeping monarchs. For that reason he had insisted on an extensive diagnostic sweep of the capsule before it would lock; if anything, no matter how miniscule, was out of alignment the lock would not engage. Finally, after several minutes, the display panel light glowed purple, signaling the capsule was operating perfectly and completely sealed.

Jeanip surveyed the room to ensure everyone was ready. In addition to Evonic and himself, the Minnos team consisted of Medaron's female helper Misso, Europa's female helper and second guardian Birea and four helpers; Second Guard Caption Sunam, Mintoo, Ebar and Tinderoon. Jeanip had handpicked his team himself, aware of their strengths and weaknesses since all but Evonic had fought under his command centuries before in the Terrian wars. Evonic's place on the team was decided by Medaron; she felt comfortable around him and confident in his knowledge of human anatomy. In addition to extensive military training and educated in security protocols, each team member had also lived above on land for extended periods of time, a definite necessity for this mission. All were familiar with human customs, languages, breathing with lungs in an air environment and walking upright on two legs. Jeanip was confident his team would fulfill his or her sole responsibility of protecting the royal family and keeping their identities secret from the soon-to-be born monarch.

Jeanip stood up and addressed his team. "Your attention. Let's go over our exit plan one last time. When this chamber fills with sea water transform into your true selves, then proceed to the outer chamber. That chamber will maintain an oxygen rich air supply on top. Once inside transform into a Moby and fill your blood stream with enough oxygen to sustain you for sixty minutes, then exit through the gateway. Remember, it is a long swim to the surface. Once outside, wait for the remainder of the team and we will rise together. Does everyone understand?" Jeanip looked around the room as the water began to rise in the chamber. He saw each team member give an affirmative nod. "Mintoo, Ebar and Tinderoon will exit first and secure the perimeter. Then Misso, Birea and Evonic will follow. Sunam and I will go last with the monarchs. I will signal when you may begin your accent. The new moon will help hide us but the sight of eight Mobies suddenly appearing in the bay may not go unnoticed. Therefore, as soon as you have taken in new air, transform into jumpers for your journey to the cave. I will remain a Moby in order to carry the monarchs. When we are forty yards from the cave transform into humans. Once Sunam is human he will take the monarchs from me and I will transform. We will carry the transportation capsule into the cave and remove our monarchs. Together we will enter the secret passage; I will carry Medaron and Sunam will carry young Earon. Are there any questions?" No one spoke a word. "Then we are off to our new life above."

As the inner chamber finished filling with sea water the eight travelers transformed into their true selves. Jeanip signaled to the chamber operator they were ready for departure and noticed Enok still hovering at the glass wall. He bowed slightly as he reached up and took hold of the capsule's handles along with Sunam. Enok watched as Mintoo, Ebar and Tinderoon exited, followed by Birea, Misso and Evonic. A purple tear escaped his eye as he watched Jeanip and Sunam disappear through the gateway with the capsule. The sound of the outer doors opening confirmed their departure, forcing Enok to close his eyes tightly to prevent any additional tears from escaping. Unable and unwilling to move from his location, he leaned his head against the glass, overcome with the realization his family was now gone and it could be many years before he beheld them again. He had lied to Medaron when he said the medical assistants were close to curing him and he would soon join her. The truth was they were years away from correcting his breathing problem and some feared he could never be cured. He had sent his true love above knowing he probably would never be able to share her life above, her life with their daughter. Raising his hand, he clenched his fingers into a tight fist and hit the glass wall repeatedly, cursing JeffRa for the war injury he had inflicted upon him, cursing the human race for their weak bodies, cursing himself for letting her go. He continued to take his despair and anger out by pounding on the glass wall until it finally cracked, sending shards of glass into his hand, spilling Enok's purple blood into the lilac waters. Not caring if he bled or not, he drifted down to the Complex's floor staring into the empty Exit Chamber. There he remained, too grief stricken to rise and return to his home, a home where no one waited except for two Dumbo Octopus.

Jeanip transformed into a Moby and opened his mouth allowing Sunam to gently maneuver the transportation capsule into a secured position inside. He gently closed his teeth on the transportation capsule and submerged, swimming to where the others waited outside. Sunam followed soon after. Seeing his team was ready, Jeanip gave a low grunt from deep in his throat and signaled for the group to begin their assent to the surface. Together, the eight sperm whales navigated up the side of the deep canyon wall rising steadily toward air. As they neared the surface there was no light to welcome them to their new world, no moon light to shine upon them, only the tiny dots of stars. One by one each broke the water's surface and expelled the air in their lungs before breathing in fresh sea air, breathing in life itself.

As planned, they transformed into dolphins, taking in more fresh air and positioning themselves around Jeanip as he continued toward the hidden cave entrance to Minnos. Maneuvering as silently as possible, Jeanip took few breaths fearing his loud blow might be heard on land and call attention to them. When they reached the forty-yard marker Jeanip signaled for the sea jumpers to transform into human form. Sunam and Evonic carefully slid the capsule out into the open ocean. Now free of his charge, Jeanip submerged and transformed into a human himself then, together with Sunam, guided the transportation capsule toward its destination.

They reached the secret entrance within minutes. Mintoo, Tinderoon and Ebar swam inside to secure the cave. Evonic followed, then Sunam and Jeanip with the transportation capsule with Misso and Birea bringing up the rear. Jeanip saw Tinderoon, Ebar and Mintoo had dressed and were waiting at the water's edge to assist in the capsule's removal. He and Sunam lifted the capsule so the three males could grab it and set it on the cave's floor. Evonic emerged from the dressing room and immediately checked the gauges to ensure everything had gone as needed. He turned off the pressurization, signaling to Jeanip it was safe to open the capsule's lid. Jeanip turned the lock and heard the magnetic hinges release, causing a hissing sound as the air inside escaped through the newly formed small openings. As he raised the lid he saw his peacefully sleeping monarchs lying in the same position he had last seen them in. Finally assured they were fine, Jeanip went and got dressed. He returned, bent down and scooped Medaron into his arms ever so softly, then waited as Misso slipped a blanket around her. Misso then did the same for Earon after Sunam lifted him into his arms. With Tinderoon and Ebar guarding the front and Mintoo and Evonic guarding the rear, the group ascended the stairs to the world above and their new home, Minnos. They had arrived safely and together they would await the birth of their newest female monarch, Europa.

Medaron began to stir, turning on her side to snuggle up next to Enok. The sound of meadow birds singing brought her back to the reality she was no longer at the Ocean Complex. There was no Enok to share her bed or wish her good morning. She now remembered the night before, saying good bye to Enok and entering the transportation capsule to begin her life above. Evidently her journey had been successful for she was lying on a human bed. She took a deep breath, breathing in the fragrance of the flowers from her gardens outside. As her mind cleared, she realized mixed in with the sweetness of the flowers was the tantalizing aroma of fresh brewed coffee, a smell she had almost forgotten. "I am at Minnos," she thought. Slowly she opened her eyes to see a room lit by the morning sun shining in through a large bay window draped in white curtains. The walls of the room were still the color of light lilac she had painted them hundreds of years earlier, although she could tell they had been repainted recently. New pictures of wildflowers hung on the walls and there was also an unfamiliar large dresser with a mirror across from the window. Beside her bed she noticed a new night stand on which sat the antique Tiffany glass lamp she had purchased from New York along with a pitcher of water and a glass, presumably put there by Misso. Stretching, she felt the softness of the sheets upon her skin, another sensation she had missed. She looked down and saw a large comforter in a wildflower print lying across her. Then something caught her eye on the night stand, something that should not have been there. She was surprised and delighted to see two framed paintings of her pet Dumbo Octopus she had left behind. Medaron reached out to pick one up and, as she did, a note fell out from behind the frame and onto the floor. She reached down and picked it up, tenderly opened the note and read:

My Dearest Love,

   Since neither I nor your two friends can be there to greet you each morning, I painted their pictures for you in hopes they will bring a smile to your beautiful face as you start each day. Let them be a reminder of how much I love and miss you. I am incomplete until we are together again.

   Love,

      Enok

   P.S. Forgive the crude workmanship. You were always the artist.

   She hugged the painting close to her body wondering how Enok or she were going to endure seventy to ninety years of being apart. For over seven thousand years they had been joined together as life's mates and had never been apart longer than a few weeks; never years. Each was willing to make the sacrifice for their daughter, but Medaron wondered what price would be paid in the end. She placed the painting back on the night stand, kissed two fingers on her right hand and placed the kissed fingers on the painting. Enok had been right – the paintings would put a smile on her face each morning.

No longer able to resist the tantalizing smell of coffee, Medaron stretched her legs in preparation to rise. As she stretched her legs encountered something large on the bed near her feet. She looked down at the large brown and black creature that seemed to have shared her bed last night. She smiled as she saw her son Earon still asleep, lying there in his transformed canine form.

"Minnos, I have returned," Medaron whispered to the cottage as she sat up in bed, stretching her arms toward the sky. "I have a surprise for you. I carry inside of me a human female child that will be born in the fall. Soon your halls will echo with the sounds of her laughter and her tiny feet as she runs through your rooms. Guard and protect her well, for she is the last Waters' monarch. Shield your secrets; keep them hidden from her so she may not know who and what her parents and people are. Help her live a long and happy life. Her name is Europa."

———————

Minnos was a four hundred acre estate Enok had established almost four hundred years earlier when it was determined the Terrian threat had been eliminated and it was safe once again to live on land. The land was part of the tribal lands of the local native tribe and was governed by tribal law and immune to local jurisdiction. The grounds were mostly kept feral as a sanctuary for wildlife but over the years some livestock had been added. Enok had built the country cottage as a present to Medaron in the hopes it would help her recover from the death of their son. As he hoped, the challenge of creating a utopia for the two of them brought new life into her soul and she eagerly decorated and furnished their cottage. She had Jeanip build a sitting porch, which encircled the entire cottage, and a porch swing which hung from the rafters on the cliff side overlooking the ocean, a secluded place where she and Enok could spend their evenings in each other's arms. Three large bedrooms were on the second floor, each having a balcony also overlooking the ocean. One bedroom had now been converted into a nursery with a small servant's room adjacent to accommodate Europa's second protector, Birea. Downstairs were two servant's quarters off the kitchen; one was Misso's and the other was Jeanip's quarters, containing the security and operations room along with the secret entrance to the cave. A small sitting room and formal living room graced the front of the house while an extra-large kitchen with a casual sitting room equipped with a large stone fireplace adorned the back. Several barns were on the property along with a bunk house for the male helpers. Under the bunk house was a second security room and a secret storage area for weapons, food, medicines and numerous other items which might be needed. As protection, a security system encompassed the area five miles in each direction around the cottage, monitoring anything and everything that walked, hopped, slithered, crawled or flew across the area. The remaining four hundred acres were fortified with motion detectors which were tied into an elaborate security system to alert them of any intruders, human or non. Unfortunately, soon after the completion of the cottage, it was discovered Enok's battle injury from the last Terrian War prevented him from living in an air environment; in human form his lungs could not process oxygen correctly, thus making it necessary to abandon their dream cottage and return to the Ocean Complex. In the three hundred and eighty years since they left, Medaron had only visited several times but never to live there, until last night. She had left its care to reliable caretakers and if her bedroom was any indication of that care, she knew they had taken excellent care of her beloved cottage.

Medaron swung her feet over the side and carefully put her weight on her legs and stood. The floor was cold, another sensation she had forgotten; it was such a perplexing thing to have one's feet cold while the rest of the body was warm. Not wishing her son to miss any of these wonderful experiences, Medaron reached over and rubbed the dog's head, jostling him awake. He stretched and transformed into his human form, a form he could remain in until Europa was born.

"I assume, Mother, we have arrived?" Earon said, stretching out his human arms. As he stepped onto the floor he too was amazed at the odd cold sensation in his feet.

"Yes, Earon, we have arrived. Welcome to Minnos."

"What is that unusual smell?" he asked.

"That, My Darling Son, is one of mankind's most delectable inventions. COFFEE!!" Medaron reached out and took her son's hand. Together, they wobbled down the stairs toward the delicious smell of coffee. Their lives on Minnos had begun.

A STRANGER ARRIVES

Medaron woke to the usual sound of song birds filling the morning air with their music. But today they seemed not to be singing songs of joy but warnings of something coming. She had not slept well last night and this morning her body was filled with an uneasy feeling, a feeling that something was not right. She sat up in bed trying to focus her thoughts, trying to decipher what the warning meant, but to no avail. The feeling was so vague she had no way to explore it further. Deciding she simply had a bad dream, she rose and walked down to the kitchen. The aroma of fresh brewed coffee filled the air as it had each morning for the past twenty years. Misso had risen early, as she did each day, and prepared breakfast for Medaron, having a fresh cup waiting for her at the table. As Medaron entered the kitchen she was delighted to see Jeanip was joining her this morning as he did several times a week. Crossing the floor, she looked at the solider sitting at the table noting his hair was almost entirely gray now. Even from across the room she could see the battle scars on his face and the large slash down his left arm. As she neared the table she saw him stand, observing he rose a little slower these days, his stance not as straight and tall as before. Was Jeanip beginning to feel his age? Were the years of existing in human form taking its toll upon his body? Perhaps she should suggest he return to the ocean Complex for some rest and rejuvenation. She would probably have to order him to go because he was always the soldier, always on duty, always watching over her and her children.

"Good morning, Jeanip," she greeted, as she reached the table and took her seat at the head. Misso immediately brought her a plate of scrambled eggs, bacon, toast and hash browns. She then returned to the counter for Jeanip's plate and sat it down in front of him.

"Good morning, Your Majesty," Jeanip greeted, as he sat back down. He waited for Medaron to take a bite of food or a sip of coffee, for custom dictated no one ate or drank before members of the royal family.

Medaron lifted her coffee cup and took a sip of the brew she loved. She held the liquid in her mouth for a second before letting it slide down her throat. She never grew tired of the taste of this marvelous brew. And for the hundredth time she thought "The human world may have many faults, but inventing such a marvelous drink certainly was not one of them." Medaron sat her cup back down. "And where is our girl this morning? I went by her room before I came downstairs and saw her bed was empty."

"She was up early this morning," Misso answered, pouring more coffee into Medaron's cup. "She asked me to inform you she was spending the morning with Anna, Rannie and Suzie. Since she leaves soon for college they wanted to spend some time together. They were going to breakfast, do a little shopping and then spend time down at the beach. She said to tell you she would be home for dinner this evening."

Jeanip saw the slightest look of worry on her face. "Don't worry, Medaron. She okayed it with me before she left. Birea went with her. She is well protected."

"And Triton?" Medaron asked, as she looked around to see if her son was anywhere to be seen.

"Of course. He never allows her to go anywhere without him. Why the worry this morning? Europa knows our security protocols and the importance of adhering to them."

Medaron took a bite of her scrambled eggs raising her eyes from her plate and looked at Jeanip. "Probably just being an overprotective mother, but I woke this morning with an uneasy feeling. It is nothing I can put my finger on, but something feels different, out of place, foreboding. It is almost like a feeling I used to have long, long ago. But I cannot remember what it is or what it means."

"I checked the security grid before I came in for breakfast this morning. It did not show anything out of the ordinary. Are you sure you're just not apprehensive about her leaving in a few weeks for college? Or that she is soon to be twenty?"

"That is possible, Jeanip. Twenty! Where have the years gone? It seems like yesterday we came up and began our lives here. Twenty! If we were home she would be preparing to take over the leadership from her father and me. She would be preparing to lead her people, not going off to college somewhere. Instead of a small birthday party, I would be planning a gala event that would be attended by dignitaries and clan leaders and friends."

21

"Yes, if we were home. But we're not, thanks to JeffRa and his vow to destroy our race. Europa will never know the celebration she should be having or the life she should be beginning." Jeanip looked into his queen's eyes from across the table. "She is happy, Medaron. Europa is a wonderful human with dreams of the future, a wonderful personality and a love for life. Forgive my frankness, Your Majesty, but what more can you ask for?"

"No forgiveness needed, Jeanip, for you are right. Sometimes I slip into the past, remembering JeffRa's unending lust for revenge, the lives he destroyed, the son he killed. Sometimes I forget he is gone and can no longer hurt us. Thank you for reminding me how fortunate we are that she is happy."

"Any time it is needed," Jeanip smiled. "Besides, if we had not been forced to leave our world we never would have come here and you never would have discovered coffee!"

Medaron laughed. "That WOULD have been a tragedy!"

"Now about this feeling you are having," Jeanip stated, knowing the importance of Medaron's intuition. If she was beginning to sense something than it was time to raise the security protection. "Let me know if it continues or if you get clarity on the cause. I will increase the security for a few days as a precaution and have the men double check the grounds."

"Thank you, Jeanip. As always, you protect us well. No doubt her leaving soon for college and out of our protection has me uneasy. I am sure your increase in security measures will make me feel more at ease."

"Remember, Medaron, Triton and Birea will be going with her to college. It's not like she will be on her own. Plus, she will have security measures in place to assure her safety just as she has here. She knows to adhere to her security protocols. You have taught her well."

"More coffee, Ma'am?" Misso asked.

"Yes, I think I will have one more please."

"Jeanip, would you like another?" Misso asked, as she walked toward Jeanip with the coffee pot.

"No, I best get started on my day. I will take my leave of you if you have no further need of me. Have a good day, Your Majesty."

"You too," Medaron said, as she forced a smile onto her face. Jeanip had assured her everything would be alright. Now if only she could believe that.

"Come on you guys," Europa yelled, as she ran across the sand, grabbing a raft and jumping into the ocean. The salty water surrounded her tanned legs and rose higher with each step she took. The cool sand beneath her feet felt good after the hot sand on the beach and she eagerly dug her toes into it while closing her eyes, feeling the sun's warmth upon her face. The ocean was her second home and she relished every experience it offered. "You guys are such slow pokes."

"Right behind you," yelled Suzie. She, Anna and Rannie grabbed rafts and ran into the surf. Jumping over the waves, they were soon at Europa's side.

Keeping one eye on Europa and the girls, Birea shook out a blanket and placed it on the beach. She folded the young women's clothes and placed them on the blanket along with a towel for each. Seeing the area was secure, Birea sat down on the blanket, checking to assure her weapon was ready if needed. Triton sat down beside her, watching Europa playing in the waves. Both would keep watch as long as Europa remained in the water, never taking their eyes off her. At the first sign of danger they would spring into action.

"Hey look!" shouted Europa, pointing to a section of the ocean where the surface was being broken. "The jumpers are coming to play."

"Jumpers? Why do you call them that? " asked Anna. "They're dolphins."

"I know," Europa answered in delight. 'My mother has called them that since I was little. I guess the title just stuck with me."

"Hey, did you ever wondered why they only play with us here?" Suzie asked. "I live just down the beach a ways and I've never seen them there."

"Don't you know why they only swim with us here? It's because they're in love with Europa," laughed Anna.

"So what if they are?" Europa asked, breaking into laughter at the thought. "But the truth is, I cannot remember a time when they were not here. When I was a little girl they were always waiting for me whenever Mother took me swimming. They even came when Jeanip was with me and you know how intimidating he is. I asked him about it once, why the dolphins only come to this section of the beach and he said it was because of the schools of small fish they like to eat that hide here in the shallows. He said the shallows only exist along this section of the beach. So while I wish it were true that it is my presence which attracts them, the truth is it is their stomachs."

"Who cares why they're here," Suzie exclaimed. "We get to swim and play with dolphins!"

"Look, here come Jack and Jill!" shouted Europa, as she pointed to the two bottle nosed dolphins at the front of the pod swimming toward them. The purple star birth mark on their sides made these two dolphins easily discernable. Each held a special place in Europa's heart because they were the first two dolphins to play with her as a young child. Behind the two the ladies could see several more dolphins swimming their way, bringing their total to ten. As they neared the swimmers' location they began to click and whistle, encouraging the ladies to play with them. Europa removed eight purple plastic rings from around her wrist and threw two to each of her friends. Excited by the game, the dolphins' clicks and whistles intensified. They began to swim around the girls then switched to leaping into the air and over the rafts, making their human playmates roar with laughter. One by one, the women tossed their rings far out into the ocean in different directions and watched with delight as the dolphins sped off with incredible speed to fetch them. As Birea watched from the beach she wondered who loved the game more – the girls or the transformed Oonocks.

The girls played with the dolphins, laughing and having the best time for the next hour. The time began to grow late and all too soon it was time to say their goodbyes to their sea friends and returned to the beach.

"That was the best!" Annie shouted, as she toweled dried her hair. "I could . . ." Annie stopped in midsentence when Triton jump to his feet and growled. Notified of a possible threat Birea immediately leaped to a standing position, weapon in hand. Both she and Triton immediately stepped in front of Europa forming a protective shield. At the same time, the four bathers turned to see a figure walking down the beach toward them with a bicycle that appeared to have a broken wheel. Before Europa could react, Triton took off running toward the figure in attack mode. Covering the distance in minutes, he jumped upon the startled stranger, pinning him to the ground, his barred teeth inches from his face. Birea ran toward the stranger followed by Europa and her friends.

"Triton, release," Europa shouted, as she stopped several yards away from the stranger lying on the ground, his bike laying a few feet away. Triton lifted himself off the figure but remained at his side, teeth still barred, ready to strike if necessary. "Are you okay?" she asked. By the frightened look on his face she could tell he had truly been traumatized by Triton's attack.

Weapon still in hand, Birea positioned herself between the stranger and Europa. "Who are you? What are you doing here? You are trespassing on private property."

"I'm sorry, I didn't know," the man replied, afraid to move as he kept an eye on Triton and Birea. "I had an accident with my bike just up the road. The wheel is bent and I couldn't ride it back to town. Plus, I cut my leg pretty good so I didn't think I could walk back either. I heard voices and thought there might be some one here that could help me."

"Triton, heel," commanded Europa, as she stared down at the man. Triton growled one last warning then returned to Europa's side, sitting at her feet. "I am sorry if he scared you. He is a guard dog and you came out of nowhere, making him think you were a threat."

"I can assure you, I am no threat. Is it safe to stand up?" the stranger asked, still keeping an eye on Triton.

"Yes, as long as you make no sudden moves you are safe." Birea replied. She holstered her weapon and held out her hand to help the man to his feet. "What is your name?"

"My name is Terrance Landers," the stranger replied, as he accepted Birea's hand and struggled to his feet. Terrance looked at the woman; she was probably in her late thirties, about six feet two and very muscular. Yet despite her physique her facial features were very delicate, very feminine. Her light brown hair was cut very short and he noticed the early signs of grayness in her temples. Her eyes were an unusual color, almost the color of lila,c though Terrance knew such eye color did not exist. Perhaps she wore contacts, he told himself. "I'm staying at the inn in town," he continued. "I'm sorry if I startled you."

Terrance stopped talking when he heard another voice speaking and saw Birea remove a radio from her pocket. Turning her back to the group Birea answered the call. "Yes, Sir, this is Birea. (Pause) No, no backup is needed. (Pause) A young man who is injured stumbled onto the beach. (Pause) Yes, Sir, all is secure. Triton is standing guard. (Pause). His leg, Sir. Medical attention is needed. (Long pause). No, I see no threat of danger. (Pause) Yes, we will return shortly."

"Lean on me and I will help you over to the blanket," Birea said slipping her arm around Terrance's waist and helping him hobble over to the blanket. He ungracefully plopped down, a low moan escaping his mouth. Triton quickly walked over and stood a few feet away, his gaze fixed on Terrance's face, ready to attack at the first sign of aggression.

"You wouldn't happen to have any water, would you? I lost mine when my bike flipped," Terrance asked, noticing Europa's beauty for the first time. For a moment he was mesmerized by this vision before him. She looked to be around twenty, about five feet ten with soft curly reddish-blond hair that was parted down the middle of her forehead and draped over her shoulders, still wet from her swim in the ocean. Like Birea, her facial features were delicate and feminine, but more refined. Her eyes were the color of the ocean, a soft blue that were sparkling as if they were stars. Her lips were round and firm and even without lipstick they held a tinge of warm pink. Still in her two-piece swim suit, Terrance was able to see she had a fine figure with a small waist, a long neck and a voluptuous bust line.

"I'll get it," Anna answered, intrigued by the young, cute stranger. She ran to the cooler and retrieved a cold bottle of water. "That looks like a nasty cut," she commented, as she handed Terrance the water.

"I think it looks worse than it really is," he stated, removing the cap on the water bottle and taking a long drink.

"I believe you are correct, Mr. Landers," Birea announced, as she tore open Terrance's paint leg to inspect the wound. "It doesn't appear to need any stitches. I'll clean it and put a dressing on it. This will probably hurt," she said, as she took out a small bottle of antiseptic from a first aid kit and poured it on the wound. Terrance winced in pain and clenched the blanket with his hands, biting his lip to keep from crying out. The last thing he wanted was to appear a wimp, especially in front of the cute one with the guard dog. He gulped another mouthful of water hoping it would make the world stop spinning and his nausea lessen. The water began to help just as Birea finished cleaning the wound and wrapping his leg.

"I believe that will be sufficient," Birea stated. "Just keep it clean so it doesn't get infected. Drink some extra fluids the next few days to replenish your fluid loss."

Europa stood close to the blanket staring at the man before her. She thought he was perhaps the handsomest man she had ever seen. He had light brown wavy hair with natural blond highlights running through it. The features of his face were defined and his skin was tanned. Even

26

through his tussled clothes she could tell he had a good figure, very muscular. His smile was warm and friendly, making you trust him. His eyes were the color of the sky; one could get lost in those eyes, Europa thought. And he spoke with a beautiful accent that stirred her heart.

"Hi, Terrance, my name is Europa." Europa extended her hand and smiled as she saw Terrance quickly check to see where Triton was before accepting it. "And this is Anna, Suzie and Rannie" she announced as she pointed to her friends.

"And who is the nurse?" asked Terrance, unable to look away from Europa's gaze.

"I'm not a nurse," stated Birea. "I'm Miss Europa's security guard. My name is Birea."

"Well, thank you, Birea. I appreciate your help." Terrance tried to stand but was having difficulty since he could barely bend the injured leg. Anna and Suzie rushed to his aid and assisted him to a standing position. "Do you have a phone I can use? I can call the inn and have someone come out and pick me up."

"No need," Rannie quickly answered. "We were just getting ready to head back to town. You can hitch a ride with us."

"That would be greatly appreciated," Terrance replied.

"You already have three in your car," announced Europa. "And your trunk is too small for his bike to fit. I can put it in the back of my truck and take him to the inn."

"Europa, we do not know who this man is," objected Birea. "Your mother and Jeanip would not approve of you giving this stranger a ride. Besides, I told Jeanip we would return straight away."

"Call him back and tell him I am taking this gentleman into town. I am sure he is not a mass murderer, are you?" Europa asked, looking directly at Terrance.

"No, I can guarantee you that I am not a mass murder," Terrance assured her.

"See, he is perfectly okay," Europa stated. "Besides, Triton will be with me. You may ride with Anna." Europa spoke with such a commanding voice Birea knew better than to object.

"As you wish," she answered, slightly bowing her head. "I do not approve but as long as Triton accompanies you I will allow it. I will put your bike in the back of the truck, Mr. Landers." Birea placed the broken bike inside the truck bed, securing it with a rope. She also grabbed Terrance's water bottle and a piece of the blood soaked pant leg. She slipped them into her pocket knowing Jeanip would want to run a complete background check on the stranger.

Visibly in pain as he tried to walk, Suzie and Anna helped Terrance to the truck. Doing his best not to grimace from the pain, he slid onto the front seat.

"Ready?" Europa asked, as she held the door open for Triton to jump into the back seat. As soon as Triton was settled, she hopped into the driver's seat, closed the door and started the engine. "Buckle up," she told Terrance as she drove away, Anna following close behind. She smiled to herself as she saw in the rear view mirror Triton sitting on the back seat directly behind her staring at Terrance.

"Are you sure it's safe with him in the back?" Terrance asked.

"He will not bother you as long as you do not make any sudden moves or try to touch me."

"Don't worry, I won't!" Terrance said. "Europa, that's a very unusual name. Does it have a special meaning? " he asked.

"My father chose it for me. He was an amateur astronomer who loved Jupiter and her moons. He believed the moon Europa was the most beautiful object in space. When I was born he said the most beautiful thing on Earth should have the name of the most beautiful thing in the heavens, so he named me Europa."

"Wow. I've never met anyone named after a moon before." This made both of them laugh. Remembering Triton in the back seat, Terrance quickly glanced again at the dog and was relieved to see the canine had not moved. "Thank you very much for taking me back to town."

"It is no trouble. Besides, I did not want you to get injured further by my friends fighting over you in the car. We do not get many handsome strangers crashing our beach gatherings." She blushed slightly realizing she had called him 'handsome'. She quickly glanced at him and saw him look down and smile, evidently noting the comment and feeling a little embarrassed also. "How did you say you injured your leg?" Europa asked, swiftly changing the subject.

"I'm embarrassed to say," Terrance said. "I'm in town to see my father. He's a professor at the University of Michigan teaching ancient civilizations but his hobby and passion is song birds. He heard of a colony of Red Rock Sparrows nesting in this area that has had limited human contact. He couldn't pass up the opportunity to study them. I thought I'd surprise him but, when I arrived, the inn's manager said he left the day before for the field. So I decided to go out and try to locate his camp. Knowing the importance of silence, I rented a bike which turned out to be a BIG mistake. I followed the trail the inn manager suggested, but I didn't have any luck finding him so I decided to go back to town. I came across a family of squirrels chasing each other around some trees and became engrossed in their antics. I watched them instead of where I was going and drove right into this big hole. My front tire turned and the bike flipped, throwing me over the handle bars and down an embankment onto some tree branches, cutting my leg. When I finally managed to hobble back up the embankment I found my bike's front tire bent. Fearing no one would find me on the trail, I decided to try to make it back to town along the beach. I heard voices and you know the rest."

"You are lucky you were not hurt worse than you were," Europa said. "It is pretty lonely out there. Those trails are seldom traveled and no place to be at night alone, especially if you are hurt." She paused for a moment then asked, "How long are you staying in town?"

"Probably a week, but it really depends on how long my father stays in the field. If he's not back in a couple of days I'll probably go stay at his place in Michigan until he returns. If he returns in a day or two, I'll probably stay with him until his study is done. I normally spend my summers with him since my parents divorced some years ago. I live with my mom the rest of the year in Australia."

"I wondered if that was an Australian accent."

"I was actually born in the United States, but I've lived in Australia for the past ten years. I guess I've picked up a bit of their accent and lingo. Are you a resident or are you on vacation also?" Terrance asked, wanting to learn more about his rescuer.

"No, this is home. I live up the beach with my mother on a four hundred acre ranch that is mostly an animal sanctuary. It is private property and off limits to people. But being new here I guess you did not know that when you stepped on to our beach."

"The inn manager did mention not to veer off the path."

"He probably told you not to veer off the path because that would put you onto our land and possibly endanger you."

"Endanger me?" Terrance asked. "Why would I be in danger? Oh, you mean the dog."

"Actually, Triton would have been the least of your worries. Perhaps you noticed Birea's weapon. She would have used it if you had shown any aggression toward us. And I am sure you heard her on the radio with the cottage. She was telling them we were okay and they did not need to send more armed guards."

Terrance looked at her, trying to decide if she was really serious or teasing him. By the serious look on her face he chose the first. "Are you someone important who needs armed guards to protect you?" he asked.

"To my mother I am," Europa answered, smiling. "But there is a little bit more to the story that I will reserve for another time. Plus, my mother does not like strangers stepping onto her property unless they are invited."

"Well, I won't make that mistake again." He smiled and gave Triton another glance. "Do you always travel with a guard dog?"

"Afraid so. Where I go, Triton goes. I cannot remember a time when I did not have a guard dog with me. He even attended school with me."

"You're kidding!"

"Nope. Like I said, where I go Triton goes."

"You said you live with your mother. Are your parents divorced also?"

"No, my father died when I was very young," she replied. "He was a treasure hunter and had discovered an unknown Spanish vessel deep in the ocean. While excavating it something went wrong and we lost him."

"I'm sorry to hear that."

"As I said, it was a long time ago. Well, here we are," Europa said, as she pulled in front of the inn. As Anna parked beside them Birea immediately exited the car and walked toward the truck, untied the bike and lifted it down to the street.

"You have arrived, Mr. Landers," Birea announced, as she opened the passenger door. "Europa, we need to return home."

"It was nice meeting you, Terrance," Europa smiled as Terrance slid out of the truck, being careful not to move too fast and startle Triton. "I hope you find your father."

Birea quickly climbed into the vacated seat and swiftly closed the door. Europa watched in amusement as her friends fussed over Terrance, almost knocking him to the ground as they began to escort him into the inn.

Terrance stopped and looked back at Europa. "Europa, thank you again for your help. I'd really like to repay you for your hospitality. Would you be kind enough to join me for dinner tonight? Say around six?"

"I don't think . . ." Birea began.

"I would love to," Europa announced, cutting Birea off in midsentence. "I will meet you in the lobby at six o'clock. Until then." Europa put the truck in reverse, bubbling inside with the anticipation of seeing Terrance again as she drove away. "Not a word, Birea" she stated, knowing Birea had a list of objections on why she should not meet Terrance that evening. Birea remained silent leaving the matter for Medaron. Seeing the stranger was now gone, Triton finally relaxed and fell asleep in the back seat. He too did not like the idea of Europa returning to have dinner with this stranger, but he knew she had a mind of her own. At least he would be going with her.

Medaron and Jeanip were waiting for her on the front porch when she pulled up in front of her home. Fearing they were upset with her for taking the stranger to town, she was going to remind them she would be twenty soon and capable of making sound decisions regarding the meeting of men. Birea exited the truck and walked up the stairs, passing Medaron and Jeanip without saying a word. Europa followed and walked toward them with as much strength and confidence as she could summon. Triton followed.

"The young man has been safely returned to the inn?" Medaron asked. Europa searched her face trying to decipher if her mother was upset with her or not.

"Yes."

"His injuries were not severe?" Jeanip asked.

"No, not too severe," Europa replied. "He did get a bad gash on his leg which Birea cleaned out and bandaged. And he smashed his bike up pretty good."

"I am glad he was not hurt too badly," Medaron responded, as she and Jeanip turned to go inside.

31

Europa paused for a minute wondering where the lecture was. Was she dreaming? Choosing her words carefully she said, "Mother, I hope you will not be upset if I change my mind and do not eat with you this evening. Terrance, that is the name of the young man, asked me to have dinner with him at the inn as a sort of thank you for rescuing him and I accepted."

"That was very nice of him," Medaron said, as she turned back around. "I suggest if you plan on being on time you go upstairs and get ready for your date. Since your man seems to be an honorable gentleman it will not be necessary to take Birea with you, just Triton. I will have Jeanip fed him while you get ready."

"Yes, Mother," Europa said, as a big smile appeared on her face. She ran up the stairs and kissed her mother on the cheek. "Thank you." She then hurried up the stairs to get ready.

Europa and Triton met Terrance for dinner that evening and again the following day for lunch. On the third day, they meet for an early breakfast at the inn followed by a tour of the local sights. Feeling she was neglecting her friends, Europa suggested they spend their fourth day boating on the ocean with Anna, Rannie and Suzie. But Terrance had a fear of the ocean and no coaxing by Europa could convince him boating was a safe recreational activity. As a compromise, the five spent the day together on the beach. The women swam and played in the water while Terrance firmly sat on the beach watching them. When the dolphins came to play Terrance wished he could join in the fun, but his fear of ocean predators and drowning was too strong to entice him into the water.

Upon returning to the inn later that day they learned Terrance's father still had not returned from the field. Realizing he was probably camping at one of the less familiar, more isolated rookeries, Europa offered to take Terrance the following day to the various locations. She did not want a repeat of his first attempt to find him. Grateful for her assistance, Terrance eagerly accepted her offer and they agreed to meet at sunrise.

"See you tomorrow," Terrance stated, as he escorted Europa to her truck and closed her door. "I'll bring breakfast."

"It is a date." Europa prepared to leave when she heard Terrance call her name as he stopped in front of the truck then walked over to her window. Before she realized what he planned to do, Terrance leaned in through her window and kissed her quickly on the lips. "No," she commanded, as Triton attacked. The canine obeyed and stopped, staring at Terrance and barring his teeth. "That was a dangerous thing to do. Triton still does not totally trust you. Next time you get the urge to kiss me let me know so I can prepare him." A huge smile filled her face.

Terrance looked at her, suddenly realizing how foolish his actions had been. Not wanting to break the fragile bond he and Triton had formed and still wanting to kiss Europa, he looked at Triton and said, "I would very much like to give your owner a proper kiss goodbye, if you have no objections." Triton looked at Terrance, then at Europa. Seeing no danger in a kiss he snorted, then turned and laid down on the front seat. "I believe he is saying he has no objections. So, with your permission, Miss Waters, I am going to kiss you."

"I would like that very much," Europa softly answered. Still unsure of Triton's reaction, she put her head outside the truck window and waited for her kiss. As Terrance's lips moved toward hers she closed her eyes, and then felt his warm soft lips on hers. Both became lost in their kiss, forgetting about Triton, forgetting about time itself. When the two heard Triton give a short bark. their lips untouched and both were brought back to reality, immediately looking toward Triton.

"Be careful going home," Terrance said, as he turned and practically ran up the stairs. He had kissed Europa not only once, but twice and was still alive to relish the sweetness. He turned and waved a final goodbye.

Europa waved back and began her drive home, singing to her heart's content once she had cleared town. Triton looked at her, pleased she was happy. He liked Terrance and was glad he brought such joy to his little sister.

THE ROOKERIES

Europa woke extra early the next morning and silently walked down the stairs, Triton following at her heels. When she reached the bottom she was surprised to see her mother and Jeanip sitting at the kitchen table having their morning coffee. Misso was standing at the stove preparing a small breakfast due to the early hour.

"Up bright and early this morning," Medaron quietly stated. "Early plans?"

"Yes," Europa answered. "Terrance and I are going to check out the sparrow rookeries to see if we can find his father."

"Spending a lot of time with this young man, aren't you?" Jeanip asked. Europa wasn't sure how to respond to this question until she saw Jeanip smile. She knew he was teasing her.

"Yes, I guess I have been." Europa confessed, smiling back. "I am sorry I have not been spending much time here at Minnos lately. Once his father returns from his field study, he plans on returning to Michigan and then home to Australia. Once he leaves I will still have time to spend with you before leaving."

"Plus, one never gets tired of hearing that beautiful Australian accent, does one?" Medaron commented. She saw the surprised look on her daughter's face. "You look surprised at my statement, Europa. I may be an old widow, but I can still appreciate a handsome young man with an accent. And Birea has informed me he IS very handsome. When do we get to meet this man who has stolen my daughter's heart?"

"Oh, Mother, he has not stolen my heart," Europa answered, blushing slightly. "He is someone I enjoy spending time with. He is very intelligent and a true gentleman. Besides, it is not often we get tourists my age."

"I am sure that is the reason," Medaron teased, giving Europa a warm smile. "Are you still planning on attending your birthday dinner tomorrow evening? Or has that too been forgotten?"

"Mother, you know I would not think of missing it." Europa smiled, as the grandfather clock struck six o'clock. "I have to run. We need to get an early start if we are going to check out all the rookeries."

As she turned to leave she heard her mother say, "Be sure to invite Terrance to your birthday dinner, if you have not already done so, Europa."

Her mother's words brought a flood of happiness washing over Europa. Medaron's invitation to Terrance meant both her mother AND Jeanip accepted him and were willing to trust him with her. "Thank you so much, Mother," Europa said, as she hurried over to her mother and kissed her quickly on the cheek. "I will be sure to ask him this morning."

"Don't forget the rookery on the edge of the property. People seem to forget that one," Jeanip said. "Keep your rifle with you if you go out there. Tinderoon reported spotting mountain lion signs when he was out that way last week."

"I packed a few things for you to take with you," Misso announced, as she held up a packed lunch and thermos. "There are a few sandwiches, fried chicken, coleslaw, apples, some chocolate cake and several bottles of water. There are a few eatables for Triton too. The thermos contains coffee."

"Thanks, Misso," Europa replied, as she took the items, turned and hurried to the front door, jumping down the stairs. Her exit was so swift it caught Triton off-guard. He jumped up and scampered after her, barely missing the front door hitting him as it closed.

"I believe our girl has her first big crush," Jeanip said, as they watched Europa drive away in her truck. "I must admit you are handling this very well."

"She is twenty tomorrow, Jeanip," Medaron replied. "Even if I hate to admit it, my little girl is now a woman. And one day she needs to find a life's mate so she can truly be happy in this human world we have given her. From everything Europa has told us about Terrance, and from the way he makes her feel, he seems to be a very fine young man and I can find no reason to object to them seeing each other."

"I concur," Jeanip responded. He too thought Terrance was a fine young man worthy of his young monarch's attention. And the security scan he had done with the blood sample and fingerprints Birea had supplied him showed nothing. "But I will reserve my final approval for when we meet this young man."

"As will I," agreed Medaron. "I look forward to meeting him tomorrow night."

"Has your uneasiness subsided?" Jeanip asked, still concerned about Medaron's feeling.

"No. I believe it is even stronger today. Something in the air, like before a storm arrives. You can sense it but you cannot see it or hear it."

"Still no idea what's causing it?"

"No, but I feel I should." It bothered Medaron she could not remember when she felt this feeling before. Several times she thought she remembered, but then it would slip away again just out of reach of her memory. "I know it is something I have felt before, something I should remember but cannot for some reason. But I sense Terrance is not the cause or a part of it."

"I've tightened security as promised. If anything or anyone appears out of the ordinary, the security grid will pick it up." Jeanip was still concerned over Medaron's uneasiness. In the past, her feelings had saved them from disaster so he knew better than to just dismiss the feeling. Hoping to put his monarch at ease he stated, "I am sure once tomorrow's party is over the feeling will start to subside."

"I do hope so."

The deer slunk silently along the fence line while remaining hidden amongst the trees. He stopped just before the trees ended; from here he had a good view of the entrance to Minnos. She had driven her red truck to town each morning for the past four mornings between nine and nine-thirty. If she traveled to town again this morning, he would intercept her at the bend in the road and fulfill his oath of revenge. He imagined Medaron's heart break when she learned of her daughter's death. He would leave the purple stone that powered his weapon beside her body so Medaron and Jeanip would know it was he who had killed her. As the minutes ticked by he could barely force himself to remain hidden; he so wanted to see the life drain from her eyes. He began to

36

stomp his hoofs in an attempt to alleviate some of the excitement, the anxiety that was surging through his body. Where was she? Wasn't she going to town today? Finally, unable to wait any longer, he stepped out onto the road and began to walk toward the house. He knew it was a dangerous act, but he had to know if she was still at home. He cautiously walked closer, ready to sprint out the gate if anyone came down the road. At last, he could see the house and the parked cars – her truck was not there. Somehow he had missed her. But how? Infuriated, he ran down the road to the safety of the tree line, bellowing his outrage and tearing up the ground with his antlers. After several minutes he began to calm down and was able to think clearly again. Perhaps she had gone into town earlier; if so, he could still intercept her on her way back to Minnos.

Terrance was waiting outside when Europa arrived. When she pulled into a parking spot he trotted over to the truck carrying two fresh cups of coffee and a bag containing breakfast sandwiches and several pastries. Triton quickly hopped in the back seat and sat down directly behind Europa.

"Good morning, Europa." He turned to address Triton. "Good morning, Triton. I am now going to kiss Europa good morning, so please don't attack me," He leaned over and kissed Europa.

"Good morning," she said, as she kissed him back.

"I brought breakfast" he said, holding up the bag of breakfast food and cups of coffee.

Europa held up Misso's prepared lunch and thermos. "Between what you brought and Misso sent we certainly will not go hungry today."

"Or thirsty," chuckled Terrance.

"Any thoughts of where you would like to start?" Europa inquired.

"No, I thought I'd leave that up to you."

"Well then, if you are ready, we will get started," Europa announced. "I thought it would be best to start with the one closest to town and end with the one the furthest."

Europa drove to the closest Red Rock Sparrow rookery located in the cliffs by the bay's entrance. Before starting their search they quickly ate their breakfast and drank some coffee while Triton enjoyed

37

the turkey sausage Misso had packed for him. When finished, they surveyed the grounds for signs of tire marks and foot prints, but none were found. Next they walked along the bottom of the cliff, scanning the wall above for signs of climbing pegs or foot holds. Again, they found none. Lastly, they searched the trees for signs of a blind Terrance's father would have built to covertly study the birds, but that too brought disappointment. Terrance's father had not visited this rookery. They drove over to another rookery several miles east but again there was no sign Terrance's father had been there.

"There is another rookery to the north that is on public land, but you have to cross through our property to get to it. He might have gone there not knowing he was trespassing." She hesitated for a moment thinking of the possibility. "No, that would not be possible. The security system would have sounded as soon as he stepped onto the property notifying Jeanip of his presence." Europa thought for a moment trying to think of where Terrance's father could be. "But he could have taken an old cow trail that bypasses our land. We will try there."

Terrance gave Europa a puzzled look. "You mentioned my father would have set off a security system?"

"Yes, our property is protected by a security system. It alerts the house if anyone or anything comes onto the property."

"Are you in the witness protection program or a member of some important family? You have a personal body guard and are guarded by a canine twenty-four/seven. Now you tell me your property is protected with a security system. Who are you?"

Europa realized it was time to tell Terrance who she was. "Terrance, do not freak out, but I am part of a royal family. My parents were the king and queen of a country that no longer exists. For our protection the cottage is under twenty four-hour-a-day security, as am I."

"You've got to be kidding me! You're a princess? Of what country?" Terrance asked, taken aback by Europa's announcement.

"As I said, from a country which no longer exists; it was destroyed in a great civil war. I know you have many questions, Terrance, but for now please realize it is sufficient for you to know I am of royal birth and require constant guarding. The rest I will tell you when we know each other a little better."

Jeanip was walking across the side yard when he heard Sunam call his name from the side kitchen door. "Jeanip, we've got something on the security grid." Jeanip immediately ran toward the kitchen and into the house, following Sunam to the security room. "It just showed up all of a sudden out of nowhere, this huge thing. The read out shows it's an enormous buck with massive antlers."

Jeanip quickly sat down at the console and brought up the report. "Boy, he is a big one. I didn't think there were any more like him around anymore."

"Is it possible he's not what he appears to be?" Sunam asked, fearing the worst.

"The grid would have told us if he was a shape shifter," Jeanip confirmed. "The report shows nothing out of the ordinary, but we'll keep an eye out for him just the same. Medaron's been having some strange feelings these past few days; she might be picking up something from this buck."

"Do you want me to go out and see if I can find him?"

"No, not yet," Jeanip stated. "If he shows up again on the grid then we'll do some investigating."

"Yes, Sir," Sunam agreed. After a brief pause he asked, "Are you going to tell Medaron about the deer?"

"I have been debating that exact question," Jeanip confessed. "I believe for now I will refrain from mentioning it to her. If I perceive he is a problem, I will advise her of the animal."

"Jeanip, wouldn't it be something if this deer turned out to be a Terrian after all these years?" Sunam asked, a look of worry clearly written on his face.

"Now you are beginning to sound like Medaron," Jeanip stated. "I see no indication of the possibility of a Terrian presence. But we will keep the security at high level to make sure I am correct."

It took about thirty minutes to reach the north rookery. As at the other two, there was no sign anyone had been there. "I don't think we're ever going to find him," Terrance said. "It's like he just vanished off the face of the Earth."

"I know of one more place, Terrance. Do not give up hope yet," Europa stated, taking Terrance's hand into hers and smiling warmly at him. "This other place is pretty remote. We will have to go through some rough terrain. There are no roads leading to it and we will need to walk part of the way in. It is a small rookery just at the border of our land, actually not far from the house. Since it is so close to Minnos, and on tribal ground, no one ever goes back there. Without a doubt, it is definitely the purest of the rookeries and would be the best rookery for your father to study."

Europa saw a faint gleam of hope flash across Terrance's eyes. "I bet that's where he is. That would explain why he's been out here so long. If it's that difficult and remote of a place he would remain camped there until he was finished with his studies."

Europa drove down the dirt path as far as she could then turned into a meadow. She carefully eased her way through several meadows and the forest, dodging tree trunks, branches and holes. She stopped the truck at the beginning of a rocky outcrop.

"We walk from here," Europa announced, as she leaned over Terrance and removed a revolver from the glove compartment. She then stepped out of the truck, reached behind her seat and brought out a shotgun.

"Know how to use these?" she asked Terrance, as she raised the two weapons into the air, showing Terrance his choices.

"Are those really necessary?" Terrance asked, a little concerned about their adventure.

"Like I said, this is rough country. Jeanip made sure to tell me not to explore out here without my gun."

"Maybe this wasn't such a good idea, Europa. Maybe we should just go back to town and wait for my father to return." He saw Europa give him on odd look, almost a look of impatience. "But if you really want to do this, I'll take the revolver."

Europa handed Terrance the revolver, then reached down to retrieve the food Misso had packed them. "We should have lunch before we start off. We do not want to leave food in the truck that a mountain lion or bear can smell. Whatever we do not eat we will have to bury."

"Sounds good to me," Terrance replied.

They quickly ate their lunch and washed it down with a cup of coffee. Europa peeled off some of the chicken meat from two chicken legs and gave it to Triton, along with some water in a cup. After they had eaten their fill, Europa packed up the bones, leftovers and any trash and placed them in a Ziploc bag. From behind her seat she brought out a canvas bag into which she placed the Ziploc bag. Grabbing a small shovel from beneath her seat, she proceeded to walk several feet from the truck and prepared to dig a hole where she could bury the scraps.

When he did not find her truck in town, the buck returned to the blind. He had almost reached his location when he heard the sound of a car. He froze and waited. As the vehicle came into view, he stared in disbelief as he saw not more than fifty yards away from where he stood her red truck traveling through the field heading in the same direction he was. This was an unexpected surprise and he began to quickly formulate a new plan for her demise. He knew he would have to plan carefully, for he would not have the element of surprise in the open. He saw there was another human with her, along with her guardian canine. Suddenly, his heart began to beat faster as he saw her truck stop. He waited and watched as the truck sat there. Finally, after fifteen minutes the truck doors open and she emerged carrying a bag and a shovel along with a shotgun. The other human exited from the passenger's side. Together they walked to the top of the bluff laughing while her canine protector waited in the truck. If she followed standard wilderness guidelines, she would dig a hole and bury her trash, thus giving him the opportunity he needed. While she was digging he could race across the field and attack her before she knew he was there. The only drawback of the plan was the canine. If he could get close enough before he sprinted he should be able to catch the canine off guard. And even if the canine transformed into another creature, he should be able to toss her over the bluff and still have enough time to defend himself. He felt the second human posed no threat. He began to inch closer, saliva starting to drip from his mouth as he prepared to run the moment she put her head down to dig. Keeping his eyes on her he did not see the small branches on the ground. As he stepped forward he heard the branches snap beneath his weight, shattering the stillness of the canyon. He froze instantly, hoping somehow the noise had not been heard by the two humans or her canine. He saw the one human point in his direction and he knew he had lost his element of surprise and, with it, his chance to end her life this day. Furious with himself for blowing such an idealistic opportunity, he shrunk back into the cover of the forest, his eyes glowing red with anger.

"Europa, look there," Terrance shouted, pointing to where the sound had originated. At the edge of the forest was a huge ten point buck standing motionless, staring at them. Europa signaled Triton to remain in the truck. As she watched the magnificent buck she thought for a moment she saw the deer's eyes glow red.

"I have never seen deer in this area before," Europa exclaimed quietly. "He is beautiful. Look at the size of his antlers; he must be very old." Then, in a blink of an eye, the buck turned and was gone. "Where did he go?" she asked.

"I can't believe it. We found it," Terrance shouted in excitement, as he took off running as fast as his injured leg would allow him toward the tree where the deer had been standing.

"What?" shouted Europa. running after Terrance. Triton immediately jumped down from the truck and ran after Europa, not sure if there was a possible threat or not. "What do you see?"

"Look up in the tree the deer was standing next to," Terrance shouted, as he pointed toward the tree top while continuing to run to it. "It's my dad's blind. I'm sure of it."

The three arrived at the tree at the same time. Triton remained close to Europa, surveying the area for any possible threats. Europa looked up into the canopy and saw nothing but branches and leaves. "Are you sure, Terrance? I do not see anything,"

"That's because it's a studies blind. It's build to appear as part of the tree. I've helped my dad build enough of them to know one when I see one." As they walked around to the other side of the tree, they could see wooden boards nailed into the tree acting as a ladder to the blind.

"Hey, Dad, are you up there? Dad?" shouted Terrance. No greeting was returned. "He doesn't seem to be up there. I'm going to go up and check it out." Europa saw a puzzled look come across Terrance's face as he looked around the area.

"Is something wrong?" she asked.

"This is a long way from the rookery. I don't understand why he built it here."

"Maybe he didn't want to disturb the sparrows," Europa suggested. "You said he likes to study birds that have not been influenced by humans."

"He must have a new scope camera lens and telescope then. His usual equipment is not capable of taking photographs or watching the birds from this distance." Terrance placed his foot on the first board and lifted his body up. "I guess the only way to find out is to climb up and see for myself. I'll be as fast as I can." He climbed up and slipped inside the blind. Lifting the door flap to allow light in, he surveyed the inside and its contents. Scattered around the floor were notebooks, pencils, some canned food, water and a sleeping bag. Yes, this was his father's blind with all the usual items except for one; sitting in front of a small observation hole was a state of the art, high powered telescope with a digital zoom camera. "This is new," Terrance thought, "and rather sophisticated for bird watching." He examined the telescope closer and realized it was way out of his dad's league. Next he picked up a notebook and scanned the pages. The last note written had been dated earlier that day. He breathed a sigh of relief knowing his father was okay and thought perhaps he had gone into town to get some more supplies.

"Terrance, are you okay up there?" he heard Europa call.

He stuck his head out of the blind and called down, "Yes, I'll be down in a minute." He went back inside and wrote his father a note, informing him he was in town at the inn, placing it on top of the telescope. His curiosity overcame him and he leaned down and looked into the telescope to see, if indeed, the sparrows could be seen from this distance. A confused "What the . . . ?" escaped his mouth when he saw what the telescope was focused on. It wasn't Red Rock Sparrows but a country cottage with a sitting porch surrounding it on four sides. It was Europa's cottage. But why would he be watching Europa's house? He dismissed the thought by surmising his father had simply moved the direction of the telescope when he left. But that didn't make sense either because there was no other observation hole; to observe the sparrows the telescope would have to look out the back of the blind, not the side. Something wasn't right. He walked over and picked up the note, stuffing it into his pocket. Until he knew what was going on he didn't want his father to know he had been in the blind.

"Coming down," he shouted to Europa, as he climbed back down, concealing the fact he had been up there.

"So, is it your father's?" Europa eagerly asked.

"Yes, it's his. But no one's home," he said, trying to appear excited about the find. He decided not to mention to Europa his father's telescope was aimed at her house until he talked to his father. He knew there had to be a reasonable explanation for what he saw.

"Everything okay?" Europa asked, sensing Terrance was upset.

"Just disappointed he wasn't there," Terrance lied. He quickly turned and headed back to the truck.

The ride home was quiet. Terrance said little. Europa thought perhaps he was tired or his leg was hurting. She had never seen him so quiet and withdrawn. "My mother is not expecting me for dinner, so if you would like to grab a bite to eat we can," Europa stated, as she pulled up in front of the inn.

"I'll take a rain check, if you don't mind. I'm really beat and my leg is starting to throb," Terrance responded, exiting the truck. "Plus, I'd like you to be home before dark. And even though your mother is not expecting you, I'm sure she would love to have dinner with you for a change. I have been monopolizing all your time lately."

"Speaking of my mother,'" Europa began, "she told me to be sure to invite you to dinner tomorrow night at six. It is my birthday and we are having a small family dinner."

"Your birthday? Thanks for the advance notice. How do I get you a present by then?" he laughed, winking at Europa.

"I do not expect a present from you," Europa said. "You being there and sharing the celebration with me will be more than enough."

He leaned through the window and kissed her goodnight, this time not even asking for Triton's permission. "See you tomorrow at six. Drive carefully. Call me when you get home so I know you made it safely." He stood on the inn's steps and watched as Europa drove down the street until he could no longer see her tail lights. He then turned and ran up the stairs, thrilled to be alive. As he entered the lobby he immediately noticed the manager motioning for him to approach the desk. "Your father stopped in today. He was sorry to have missed you. He left you a note." The manager reached inside the desk drawer and handed Terrance an envelope with his name written on it in his father's handwriting.

"Thanks, Mr. Everett," Terrance said. "Wouldn't you know it? The day I go looking for him is the day he comes back to town. Did he say how much longer he planned on remaining out in the field?"

"He mentioned something about leaving on Friday or Saturday," Mr. Everett replied. "He said his study should be completed by then and he needed to return to Michigan and the university."

"Thanks again, Mr. Everett," Terrance said, as he hurried to his room anxious to read what his father had to say. He quickly sat down on the bed and tore the envelope open. He read:

Dear Terrance:

I am so glad you are here, Son. What a great surprise. Sorry I have been out so long. The rookeries here are fantastic. I should be wrapping up in a couple of days, then we can go back to Michigan together. Meet you Friday morning in the dining room at ten.

Love Dad

"Friday, that's in three days," thought Terrance. "In three days we'll be returning to Michigan. But am I willing to end my relationship with Europa?"

THE UNSEEN ENEMY

Terrance arrived at eighteen minutes to six. He made sure he wasn't late, but he didn't want to appear too anxious by arriving too early either. Pulling into the driveway he had to admit he was a little nervous about meeting someone who held the title of "queen", even if technically her country no longer existed. He wondered if he should bow when he met her. Was he even allowed to speak to her? What if he made a bad first impression and she didn't like him? A thousand questions raced through his head as he parked his car. Taking a deep breath in preparation of what was to transpire, he stepped out of the car and looked at the front door. His fears immediately vanished as he saw Europa standing there waiting for him. As he began to walk toward the house, she hurried down the steps followed closely behind by Anna, Rannie, Suzie and Triton.

Europa saw he was wearing a new, pressed, light blue shirt accented with a black tie and creased pressed jeans. His hair was shorter, indicating he had gotten a haircut, probably for the benefit of her mother. She thought he looked fantastic and very presentable. She was sure her mother would be pleased.

"You are here," she smiled, as she walked to greet him.

"I told you I would be," he replied. "Did you doubt me?"

"Doubt, no. But my family can be a little intimidating."

"How's it going, Terrance?" asked Anna.

"Are you ever going to let us have Europa for a day?" teased Suzie. "Or are you going to keep her all to yourself?"

"Hi, you guys" Terrance greeted the ladies. "Nice to see you all again."

46

Europa took Terrance's hand and began to walk with him toward the house. "Are you ready for this?"

Before he could reply a very tall, muscular man stepped out onto the porch and held open the door for the group. He extended his hand toward Terrance. "Hello, I am Jeanip. You must be Terrance."

Terrance shook Jeanip's hand. "Yes, Sir, that's me."

"Welcome. Please come inside." Jeanip gestured for the group to step through the door.

The first thing Terrance noticed were the beautiful antiques. His mother collected them, so he was familiar with their value and age. He was amazed to see several furnishings that were hundreds of years old and in mint condition. Holding his hand tightly, Europa led him toward a beautiful, distinguished woman with medium brown hair speckled with gray and almost lilac eyes sitting on a purple satin sofa.

"Mother, this is Terrance. Terrance, this is my mother, Medaron Waters."

Medaron rose and took Terrance's free hand into her two hands. She looked directly into his eyes. "It is a pleasure to finally meet you, Terrance. Europa has had many good things to say about you."

"It's nice to meet you, Mrs. Waters. Thank you for inviting me." Terrance thought he felt a rush of warmth travel through his body, then recede. It was so quick he was barely conscious of it. Medaron had sent an energy burst into him to detect who he really was. When the burst returned to her body Medaron sensed honesty, truthfulness, good heartedness and a deep affection for her daughter one could almost consider as love. Medaron smiled as she let go of his hand, relieved to know he was not the source of her uneasiness. He was exactly as Europa had said.

"Please have a seat," Medaron gestured toward one of the chairs.

"You have some lovely antiques," Terrance said. "That's a sixteenth century Elizabethan china cabinet, is it not?" He pointed toward the china cabinet in the adjacent room.

"You know your antiques," Medaron replied with a smile. This young man was full of surprises.

"My father's study in ancient civilizations brought me in contact with a lot of old things over the years. Plus, my mother is a collector."

47

"Many of them were brought here by my ancestors who first settled this land and built the cottage. When we moved here I did not have the heart to get rid of them. Plus, they seem to make the cottage homier. Europa tells me your father is a professor at the University of Michigan?"

"Yes, Ma'am, that is correct."

"We were hoping he would be with you tonight. He was not able to attend?"

"No, Mrs. Waters, he's still in the field doing his sparrow study."

"That is a shame. Perhaps you two can join us one evening for dinner before you leave."

"I will be sure to extend the invitation when he returns," Terrance said politely, while thinking to himself he would never mention it to his father. The last thing he wanted to do was bring his father to a house he was spying on. Before he could utter another word a very tall, petite woman with long dark hair tied in a ponytail entered the room and stood in the archway, evidently preparing to announce dinner. Her entrance signaled the end to Terrance's conversation with Medaron, a fact he was overjoyed about. He did not wish to go into detail about his father's whereabouts.

The petite woman stood in the archway and waited until Medaron acknowledged her presence. Knowing her mother would allow her a few minutes before the announcement of dinner for Terrance to meet Misso, Europa quickly led Terrance over to her. "Misso, I would like you to meet my friend, Terrance. Terrance, this is my mother's right-hand-helper, Misso."

"Please to meet you, Sir," Misso greeted, nodding her head in acknowledgement.

"Same here, Misso," Terrance replied. "I wanted to be sure to thank you for that delicious lunch you made for us when Europa and I went out the Rookeries. It was very delicious. It was nice to have some real home cooked food for a change."

"It was no trouble."

"You may announce dinner now," Medaron said once the introduction was complete.

"Europa's birthday dinner is now served."

48

Medaron stood first, followed by the others who were seated. "Let us go enjoy this fantastic meal Misso has fixed for our birthday girl." Medaron held out her hand to her daughter. Europa let go of Terrance's hand and placed it in her mother's and walked into the kitchen.

"Jeanip, tell the men to come in for dinner," Medaron instructed. Jeanip stepped onto the back porch and rang the dinner bell for the men to come in from the bunk house. As they entered the house Europa was delighted to see that. besides Sunam and Tinderoon. they were being joined by Mintoo, Ebar and his wife and Evonic. She should have known they would attend for they had never missed one of her birthdays for the past nineteen years. Europa walked up to each and shook their hand, thanking them for coming and introducing them to Terrance. Terrance shook each member's hand as he looked up to address them, wondered if people from Mrs. Waters' homeland were all prone to be over six feet three, as were those he had already met.

Medaron stood at the head of the table waiting for the pleasantries to be concluded. Once completed, she asked everyone to hold hands and said the blessing. "May the Waters bless this food, our family and our friends who have joined us tonight to celebrate Europa's twentieth birthday. May her life be filled with joy and love." Medaron gave a nod signaling it was permissible to sit as she stated, "Let us enjoy this meal. Please, everyone, be seated."

Jeanip scooted Medaron's chair. Terrance did the same for Europa, while the remainder of the guests took their seats. Together, they began to enjoy a delicious meal of Europa's favorite foods Misso and Birea had especially prepared for her birthday. Europa looked around the table, delighted to be sharing this occasion with her family and closest friends. Since she had no blood relation other than her mother and Jeanip, the helpers had been her adopted family since she was born. It was only at special occasions. such as birthdays and holidays. that they ate as a family. Her mother had always maintained the distinction between royalty and helpers; even Jeanip did not routinely eat with them and he was Medaron's brother.

When the meal was finished all retired to the siting room off the kitchen. Misso brought coffee and tea while Birea followed with a three-tiered birthday cake with twenty candles burning and placed it on the coffee table. Everyone sang "Happy Birthday" after which Europa made a silent wish and blew out her candles.

The buck stood motionless several yards from the front gate. He knew some of the security detectors around the estate would be turned off to accommodate the arrivals and departures of her party guests. He cautiously walked up to the gate and stood just outside the entrance, surveying the surrounding area while testing the air with his nostrils. He knew he was taking a big risk coming to the estate tonight with so many visitors, but since he had missed his opportunity to end her life yesterday, he wanted to give himself a little advantage for the next time they met. He cautiously took one step, then another inside the estate, listening for any danger. As he turned a corner he saw the cottage with numerous cars parked in front of the porch. He stopped, standing perfectly motionless, turning his ears toward the house to pick up any sounds that someone could be outside. After several minutes he was assured everyone was in the house celebrating the abomination's birthday and felt it was safe to approach the vehicles. He silently walked straight over to her truck, flaring his nostrils and taking in a deep breath as the hair on the back of his neck stood up. The smell of her human stench was both sickening and tantalizing. He had never been so close to anything of hers before where he could actually smell her and it excited him. He lifted his hind leg and urinated on the truck wheels marking his territory. He then walked around to the passenger's side, lowered his head and made a long, wide scratch down the front fender with his antlers to mark the vehicle. Between the smell and the scratch he would have no problems distinguishing her truck. Suddenly realizing he had once again been distracted by the thought of her, he quickly raised his head to determine if anyone had possibly detected him. All was quiet; everyone was still in the house. He turned and silently walked down the road, breaking into a leaping run once he cleared the gate. He followed the forest line back to the tree where the blind was hidden, transformed into human form and climbed up into the blind. He spent the next hour spying on the cottage through his telescope, salivating when he saw Europa through the side window. "Tomorrow," he thought. "Tomorrow will be the day."

After cake and coffee it, was time for Europa to open her presents. Sitting beside the fireplace, she picked up the first one, announced who it was from and opened it. It was a beautiful lilac sweater from Anna. The next gift was from Suzie and Rannie. They gave her a new MP3 player filled with her favorite songs and a photo album filled with pictures of the four friends over the years.

"It's so you won't forget us when you're off to college," Rannie exclaimed.

"That could never happen," Europa answered. "Remember, you are coming to visit at least every month or so." Next she opened up her presents from Jeanip, Misso and the men. She then picked up a small box with a red ribbon around it. She looked at the tag and was surprised to see it was from Terrance. "Terrance, you did not have to."

"Did you really expect me to come without a present? What kind of gentleman would I be?" he asked. "You didn't give me much notice, so I'll apologize now if you don't like it. Your town doesn't have a huge selection of special gifts."

Europa untied the ribbon and lifted the lid. Terrance saw a gleam in her eyes as she carefully lifted up a gold chain bracelet with the charm of a red breasted bird attached to it, a small red ruby representing the breast.

"It's lovely," Europa said, as she looked into Terrance eyes, her own filling with tears. "It looks just like the sparrows we saw yesterday out at the rookeries."

"That's so you won't forget ME!" Terrance chuckled.

"Mother, look," Europa said, as she walked to her mother with the bracket dangling from her fingers. "Is it not lovely?"

Medaron took the bracelet from her daughter's fingers. She surveyed its detail, turned her gaze toward Terrance and smiled at him. "This is extraordinary, Terrance. I see besides antiques you have very good taste in jewelry also. You could not have made a better choice." She handed the bracelet back to Europa. "It is beautiful, Europa. Something to cherish always."

Europa took the bracelet and walked over to Terrance. She handed him the bracelet as she held out her arm "Would you be kind enough to do the honors?" Terrance laid the bracelet over her arm and connected the clasp. "Oh, it looks wonderful," she said, as she raised her arm to admire the bracelet. "Thank you so much."

"Europa, here is your gift from your father and myself," Medaron said, holding out a small box wrapped in lilac paper with a purple bow. Europa walked back over to her mother and took the box. "But before you open it, I have something to say."

51

Medaron rose, signaling for the others to remain seated. She took Europa's right hand into her own and turned her to face her guests. "I would like to thank you once more for joining us this evening in celebration of my daughter's twentieth birthday. In our homeland a young female monarch's twentieth birthday marks the end of her childhood and the beginning of her adulthood. She takes on the responsibility of monarch duties such as leadership, diplomatic authority and the ruling over the people. This is done by a special ceremony of the placing of the hands. Even though our homeland no longer exists, I would still like to perform the ceremony. Once completed Europa will bear the title of 'Queen' and will begin to take over the responsibilities of overseeing Minnos from me. As your new queen, you will give her the same obedience and compliance you have given to me all these years." Medaron paused briefly then said, "Europa, if you would please turn and face me."

Europa turned and stood in front of her mother, the present still in her hand. Medaron placed a hand upon each shoulder. "As reigning queen I pass my leadership, my honor, my knowledge on to you. From this day forward you will be known as the 'queen-in-waiting'. You will become, with time, the protector of Minnos and the strength of our nation. We will look to you for guidance, depend on you for protection, rely on your judgments. We pledge our lives to you and will defend you above all, even if that means forfeiting our life to do so." Medaron looked down at Europa, a tear escaping her eye and sliding down her cheek. "Europa, if you would open your gift now."

Europa opened the lilac package to reveal a golden chain with a unique amulet on it. It was a round sphere with an opaque covering of unknown substance. The inside was filled with a lilac liquid in which was suspended a dime-size purple stone.

"Oh, Mother, this is beautiful," Europa said. "It is almost identical to the one you wear."

"If you will give it to me, I will place it around your neck. Once it is placed there it is never to be removed." Europa handed the amulet to her mother, who placed it around her daughter's neck and snapped the clasp closed. "Our ancients designed these amulets to protect and aid our monarchs. They have been passed on to each new generation. Today it is passed on to Europa." Medaron looked at their guests. "I now present to you your new Queen and Monarch. May the Waters guide her in her royal duties and bring her long life."

Europa turned around and was surprised to see Jeanip, Birea, Misso, Evonic and all the workers kneeling on one knee, their heads bent down with their right hands raised to their forehead. "To you, Queen Europa, we pledge our lives in your defense and give you all we are."

Europa quickly looked at Terrance and the girls to see their reaction to such a dramatic demonstration. She could see their uneasiness in not knowing what they should do and was touched when they too knelt to acknowledge her new rank.

The formal festivities completed, everyone crowded around Europa to view her new bracelet and amulet. Everyone complimented Terrance on his excellent choice of a gift and his taste in jewelry.

"Mrs. Waters, I've never seen such an amulet. It must be priceless," Terrance softly said, then realized he had said it out loud. He hoped his comment did not offend anyone, especially Mrs. Waters.

"Mother, are you sure I should wear this. If it is priceless and irreplaceable, do you not think it would be better kept in a safe?"

"No, Europa, it was made to be worn by my daughter." Medaron answered, smiling at her. "As Queen you must wear it. Legend states it will protect and guide you."

Seeing the hour was getting late Sunam, Mintoo, Ebar and his wife, Tinderoon and Evonic thanked Medaron for the wonderful evening, wished Europa happy birthday one last time, told Terrance it had been nice to meet him and departed. Misso and Birea returned to the kitchen to finish cleaning up. Jeanip escorted Medaron into the living room with Europa, Terrance, Anna, Suzie and Rannie following. The small group remained in the living room for several hours telling stories and laughing.

"It's getting late. I should be heading back to the inn," Terrance announced. "Girls, would you like me to follow you?"

"Actually, Terrance, we're staying the night," said Rannie. "We wanted to have one more girls' slumber party before Europa leaves for college."

"Terrance, if you're going back to town be careful on the drive. That road can get a bit winding and hard to maneuver at night. Plus, there's a deer out there several people have almost hit. Seems like it likes to hang out around the curve," Suzie stated.

"My mom almost hit him the other day," Anna added. "It scared her to death. She said one moment the road was clear and the next there he was. She said it had really weird eyes, almost glowing."

"Deer's eyes glow when a car's headlights shine on them," clarified Jeanip. "Most animal eyes do."

"Yes, Sir," stated Anna. "But this was in broad daylight."

"Terrance, I bet that is the same deer we saw yesterday out at the small rookery behind the house. It was beautiful. The rack of antlers on its head was magnificent. I did not know there were still deer around here," Europa said, looking in Jeanip's direction.

"There hasn't been for years," he replied wondering if it was the same deer that had set off the security grid. "Hunters wiped them out. He might have come down from the mountains. There are still several herds up there in the deep forest."

"Did you notice anything unusual about his eyes?" Medaron asked Europa, wondering if there was more to this deer.

"I thought I did for a minute. They seemed to glow red. But then I realized it was the sun reflecting in them."

Medaron immediately looked at Jeanip. He heard her say inside his mind, "Jeanip, a deer with strange or red glowing eyes? That could indicate a shape shifter. If it is, it could be a Terrian here after Europa. That might be why I keep having this uneasiness, this feeling of dread."

"I heard, Medaron," Jeanip silently replied. "It certainly warrants checking into and I will proceed to do so. Plus, I will turn the fences on right away." He turned to face the young women. "I am sure it's just a plan old deer," Jeanip said out loud. "But perhaps, if you have no objections, Medaron, Terrance should spend the night here at the estate. The girls are right. That road can get a bit treacherous at night, especially if a fog blows in from the ocean. He can sleep in the bunk house with Sunam and Tinderoon. I know they will have no objections. He can return to town in the morning."

Europa looked at her mother, giving her a pleading look. "Yes, I agree. It would be safer for him to return in the morning. Now, if you will excuse me, I think I will retire for the evening." Medaron stood up, crossed the room to the stairs and ascended to her bedroom.

"I think it's time we all retire," Jeanip suggested. "Terrance, I need to take care of something in my room then I'll walk you out to the bunk house. You have five minutes to say your goodnights." Jeanip walked over to Europa and lightly kissed her on the cheek. "Good night, Birthday Girl. Ladies, try not to stay up all night talking about how good looking I still am for an old guy. And remember, the alarms will be on." He walked into his room to turn on the fences.

Terrance said goodnight to Europa's friends then turned to her and took her hand. "See you in the morning," he said as he softly kissed Europa. Like Europa, he too had planned for a better kiss but, with her friends watching and Jeanip back from his room, it was not possible. A small kiss would have to suffice for the moment. He turned and followed Jeanip onto the porch.

"You'll find the beds in the bunk house very comfortable." Jeanip said. "You'll need to stay inside and wait until Sunam or Tinderoon turn the alarms off in the morning before leaving the bunk house. The grounds are protected by security alarms at night."

"Alarms?" Terrance asked, a little concerned.

"Security that's not needed anymore, but something Medaron insists on. Perhaps one day I'll tell you why." Jeanip stopped half way across the yard. "Terrance, before you retire for the night there is something important I need to talk to you about. I understand Europa has told you of her royal heritage and her need for our high security."

"She told you, did she?" Terrance asked.

"Not exactly. Let's just say not much happens here on Minnos I don't know about. Anyways, with that knowledge comes great responsibility. No one outside of Minnos, except for her three girlfriends, and now you, know Europa is of royal blood. And that secret must be maintained no matter what. Please believe me when I tell you there are people from the old homeland who would love to find Europa, to end her life. Part of her protection is that her true identity is unknown. Do you understand what I am telling you, Terrance?"

A serious look crossed Terrance's face. "If word got out Europa was a princess, err, I mean a queen, her life could be in danger? And for that reason I must never tell anyone who she really is."

"That is correct. So I can count on your silence, Terrance? Or must I slit your throat tonight while you sleep to silence you?"

Terrance stared at Jeanip. He had no doubt he was kidding, but he also knew that to protect Europa he would not hesitate to end Terrance's life, if it meant keeping her safe. "Sir, I care deeply for

Europa. And I know Mrs. Waters would not have said those things tonight during the ceremony in my presence if she did not trust me. I will not break the trust you, Mrs. Waters and Europa have put in me. Europa's secret is safe with me, now and even upon my death bed."

"Then we will speak of this no more. Now off to your room. Good night, Terrance".

"Good night, Jeanip."

Jeanip returned to his room and immediately walked over to the security grid again and sat down at the console. Now concerned about this deer and what its presence might imply, he began to scan the readings across the estate looking for any signs of it. But other than the previous day's security alert, there was no sign of the deer. Remembering what Europa had said about seeing the buck at the Red Breasted Sparrow rookery closest to the property, Jeanip did a current sweep of that area and was surprised when he could not get an update. He tried several times and each attempt produced the same identical old report. Something was wrong with the security grid in that area. An uneasy feeling now began to permeate his mind, making him believe this deer could possibly be a shape shifter hunting his monarchs. There was no other explanation for the fact the security grid in that specific area was not working. He would have to take his soldiers out there first thing in the morning to investigate if his fears were accurate. He also knew that until he could confirm or eliminate those suspicions, Medaron, Europa and Triton would have to be placed on lock down and remain behind the cottage's protective walls, something he knew Europa was not going to like.

JEFFRA

Medaron tossed and turned in her bed, unable to sleep. That strange feeling had gotten stronger and was plaguing her thoughts. Plus, she kept thinking about the deer the girls and Europa spoke of, particularly about the part of it having strange eyes. That was a grave concern since it indicated a possible threat. She no longer could contribute her uneasiness to the simple fact Europa had turned twenty and would soon be leaving for college. Or would she? How could she possibly let Europa leave the security of Minnos and move hundreds of miles away with the possibility of a Terrian shapeshifter out there stalking her? Finally, emotional exhaustion overcame her and she was able to fall asleep but her sleep was not restful. Her dreams were tormented with memories of the war with the Terrians and the day Enok almost died and her son killed. All too soon she awoke, exhausted and frustrated. Knowing sleep was not attainable, Medaron decided to go downstairs and try to get some rest on the side porch. As she descended the stairs, the feeling seemed to grow even stronger, making her hold onto the railing to steady her walk. Why couldn't she remember what this feeling was? She knew she recognized it, but it was buried deep in her memory. She switched on the light as she walked into the kitchen, wondering why it was so dark and where Misso was. Then she remembered the time and the fact Misso was still asleep. She turned the coffee pot on and grabbed a Danish to eat while she waited for it to brew. When it was done she poured herself a cup, grabbed an afghan from the back of a chair and walked out to the side porch. She sat down on the porch swing, pulling her legs up on the seat and snuggled under the afghan. She closed her eyes and took a deep breath, breathing in the ocean smelis. This part of the porch overlooked the ocean and she could

57

hear the waves crashing against the rocky cliff below. This had always been her favorite spot to sit and think, probably because she spent most of her pregnancy out there so she could be closer to the ocean and Enok. She had designed this section of the porch as a place she and Enok would spend many hours together, hours which never occurred. Taking a sip of coffee, she looked out at the ocean; Enok was out there, his essence floating in the ocean's waters. She believed he could hear her thoughts when she spoke to him and wished he had a way to talk back to her, to advise her.

"Enok, I wish you were here. I need your help in protecting our daughter. Last night I learned of the possibility a Terrian still lives and Europa may be in danger. Jeanip has everyone on high alert and has increased the security grid. He assures me nothing will happen to her and I have full confidence and trust in him and his decisions. But Enok, if I lost her . . ." Medaron closed her eyes, fighting back the tears. Very quietly she whispered, "I could not survive losing another child, Enok. Losing Tiree that day almost destroyed me and it would have if it had not been for you and your love. You brought me back from the hell I was in. But you are not here to save me this time. If Europa dies I will die with her." She paused for another moment collecting herself, trying to focus on something positive. "Oh, Enok, you would be so proud of our daughter. She has grown into such a beautiful woman. I see a lot of you in her, especially her love of life and nature. She would have made such a wonderful Supreme Monarch. JeffRa stole much from her, from us. I miss you SO much, Enok. I still love you, now and forever."

"Up a little early this morning, aren't we, Your Majesty?" Jeanip asked, as he stood in the doorway to the side porch, holding a canister of coffee and a cup for himself.

"Jeanip, how long have you been standing there?" Medaron asked, a little startled but not surprised at Jeanip's sudden appearance. She should have known her early rising would not go undetected by Jeanip; nothing happened in the cottage he did not know about.

"For a few minutes. I thought you might like some more coffee and perhaps some company. Or perhaps just coffee."

"I would love some company. Please sit down, Dear Brother." Jeanip filled Medaron's coffee cup, then sat down next to her. He poured himself a cup and sat the canister on the floor beneath the swing. "Are you okay?" he asked, noting the worried and tired look upon her face. He knew Medaron was an early riser, but it was very unusual for her to have risen before Misso or himself. This uneasiness was beginning to have an effect on her. Plus, he heard what she said about not surviving the loss of Europa. He was determined she would never, ever experience that loss. He had almost lost her once; he would not chance losing her again.

"Yes I am fine. I just did not sleep well last night. For some reason I kept dreaming about the Terrian wars, particularly the day Enok was injured. And I could not stop thinking about that dang deer." Medaron noticed the concerned look on Jeanip's face. "And yes, the feeling is still there."

"An uneasiness that could probably be contributed to the fact Enok was not here to help celebrate Europa's most important birthday. That, added into the talk of that deer, made for the makings of a very restless sleep," Jeanip added, knowing how much Medaron still missed her mate.

"That too," Medaron replied. "It was bad enough JeffRa robbed her of her heritage, but the fact her father was not here to help celebrate the occasion made it almost unbearable."

"I too have concern over that deer, Medaron," Jeanip confessed, noting the concerned look appear on his sister's face. "The security grid picked up the deer on the road inside Minnos. Adding in what Europa's friends said about his eyes, I thought it pertinent to take the men out to hunt for it this morning after breakfast to determine if it is friend or foe. I am sure we will discover it is just some simply misplaced deer curious about its surroundings." He thought it best not to inform Medaron about the malfunctioning section of the security grid until he went out and determined the cause. His queen was already stressed and he did not want to contribute to her level until he had all the facts.

"Let us hope so," Medaron quietly said, trying to hide a yawn. "Might I ask a big favor of you, Jeanip?"

"Anything, Your Majesty."

"Skip breakfast with Europa this morning and take the men out at first light. I will feel better once I know the truth about that deer – be it good or bad."

"As you wish, Your Majesty."

Medaron pulled the afghan tighter around herself and snuggled up to Jeanip's shoulder. He raised his arm and placed it around her, pulling his beloved sister and monarch into the cradle of his body. Medaron rested her head on his chest and soon was fast asleep, feeling more at ease now that she knew Jeanip would track the deer down. Jeanip carefully reached over and removed the coffee cup from her hand and sat it on the swing next to him. He looked down at her, delighted in the knowledge that, at this moment, she was safe in his arms, just as she had been when they were kids, before she married Enok and became his queen, before JeffRa's reign of terror to destroy all he loved. Now more than ever, he wished he could tell Medaron the truth about Enok's existence and his death, for she needed Enok's strength. But that was not his decision to make.

The four friends had stayed up half the night talking about Europa leaving for college, boys, shopping, how handsome Terrance was and if he and Europa were an item. Even with little sleep Europa awoke early, eager and excited to see Terrance. She quietly arose and silently began to get dressed, wanting to allow the young ladies more time to sleep. As she slipped on her new birthday sweater over her head, the clasp of the necklace became caught and she became trapped in her sweater.

"Hey, can one of you guys help me? The necklace is caught on my sweater," she called out to the girls, regretting she had to wake them.

Suzie woke and came over to try to free it, but was unable to. She poked Anna with her foot, arousing her from her sleep. Anna came over and tried to free the clasp. As she tried to pull it free the clasp broke, causing the chain and amulet to fall to the floor.

"Europa, I'm so sorry. I was being very careful. It just kind of fell apart," Anna apologized, sickened by the fact the necklace had broken in her hands.

"Don't worry about it, Anna," Europa said, as she stooped down and picked up the broken chain and the amulet. She examined the clasp to see if it was repairable. "This appears to be something easily repaired. I am sure the jeweler can fix it with no problem and in a short amount of time. I will go into town later and take it to him. My mother will never know this ever happened."

"She was so excited when she gave it to you," Anna replied, still obviously shaken by the experience. "I wouldn't want her to get upset with me about breaking the clasp."

"Anna, my mother would not get upset. She understands accidents sometimes happen. Besides, it was my fault the clasp got caught in the first place, not yours. If this is anyone's fault, it is mine."

After waking Rannie, the girls went downstairs following the smell of bacon and coffee, a tired Triton following behind. He was not surprised to see Medaron and Terrance already seated at the table enjoying coffee, but did wonder why Jeanip was not amongst them. It was not like him to miss breakfast when they had company.

"Good morning, ladies. I hope you four got some sleep last night. Please have a seat," Medaron greeted the four, as she gestured toward the table.

"Good morning, Mother," Europa greeted, kissing her mother on the cheek before taking her place at the breakfast table. "Good morning, Terrance."

"Good morning,. Mrs. Waters," the three friends said in unison, as they too took seats. "Good morning, Terrance."

"Good morning, ladies," Terrance replied, as Misso began to carry plates of food to the table.

Triton looked at Medaron and silently asked, "Mother, what is wrong? Where is Jeanip? He would not miss this breakfast with Europa and her friends unless some security issue required his immediate attention."

Keeping her eyes on her coffee cup she replied, "Both Jeanip and I have some concerns about what was said last night about that deer, especially the part about his eyes. Such eye distortion could mean a shape shifter. To determine if it is one or an ordinary deer, Jeanip and the males have gone out to find it."

"A shape shifter?" Suddenly Earon realized what Medaron was suggesting. "You think it might be a Terrian! After all these years? It cannot be possible."

"Probably not, but we need to be sure, Your Majesty," Misso silently stated, as she refilled Medaron's coffee cup. "If there is to be another war we need to know so we can prepare."

"War?" Earon asked silently, as he stared at Misso, then turned to look at Medaron in disbelief. "Mother, do you really think war is coming?"

"It is always a possibility," Medaron replied. "We have only survived the pervious wars by being prepared."

Unaware of the silent conversation taking place, Europa leaned over and asked Terrance, "Were you able to get any sleep last night? Did the men keep you awake?"

"I slept surprisingly well," Terrance stated. "The bed was very comfortable and I never heard a peep out of the men."

"I am glad to hear that. You probably got more sleep than I did since these three kept me up half the night talking about you." Europa tilted her head toward her three friends sitting across the table. They gave Terrance a look of "Who, us?" "I hope my mother and Jeanip have not been giving you the third degree this morning," Europa stated, as she turned to smile at Medaron and Jeanip. It was at that moment she realized Jeanip's seat was empty. She has been so absorbed at seeing Terrance she had not noticed Jeanip was not joining them this morning.

"Is Jeanip okay? It is most unusual for him to miss a special breakfast." A look of disappointment was clearly visible on Europa's face.

"Pressing estate matters," Medaron replied. "He asked me to give you his apologies and regrets for missing breakfast with you and your friends this morning."

"I would love to stay and visit more, Mrs. Waters, but I really need to get going," Terrance stated, as soon as breakfast was finished. "My father is returning this morning from his field study and I am supposed to meet him back at the inn."

"Are you girls staying around for lunch?" Medaron asked, visibly tired.

"Actually we need to be heading out too," Rannie answered. "My mother is expecting me to watch my little sister while she goes to the doctors this morning."

"Well then, I will say my goodbyes," Medaron replied. "Thank you all again for sharing in Europa's celebration." She looked over at Europa. "I did not sleep well last night so I think I will go upstairs and take a small nap. Europa, be sure to stay inside the cottage this morning until Jeanip is able to resolve that estate issue."

"Okay, Mother."

The three friends hurried upstairs to get their overnight bags while Europa gave her mother a kiss. As she stepped back from her mother Medaron noticed Europa was not wearing the chain and amulet she had given her. "Europa, where is your amulet?" she asked, looking directly at Europa. "Did you not hear me say that once it was placed around your neck it was not to be removed?"

"Yes, Mother, I did. I did not intentionally remove it. You see, I had a slight accident this morning while getting dressed." Europa pulled the broken chain from her pants pocket and placed it inside her mother's hand. "I am sorry, Mother. While I was getting dressed this morning the chain got caught in my sweater. When we tried to unsnag it, the clasp fell apart. I planned on getting it fixed when I went into town later this afternoon."

Medaron took the broken necklace from her daughter's hand and examined it. "I purposely bought a new chain so that this would not happen. It must have had a faulty clasp. Jeanip and I will go into town later and have the jeweler replace it." She looked at Europa, who had a worried look upon her face. She reached her hand up and placed it on Europa's cheek. "Do not worry, Europa, I am not mad; at least not at you. I am disappointed the jeweler sold me a faulty necklace. And I am sorry if I sounded a little forceful. I know you do not understand, but now that you are twenty it is very important you wear the amulet at all times. You must NEVER be without it. Promise me that."

Europa looked at her mother. Medaron was right; Europa did not understand why it was so important for her to wear the amulet always. Before she left for college she would have to insist her mother explain to her the reason why. "Yes, Mother, I promise."

"I believe there is an old silver chain in the china cabinet that will suffice until I bring back a replacement." Medaron walked over to the antique china cabinet and opened one of the drawers. She picked up a worn cigar box and raised the lid to reveal several forgotten treasures inside. She sorted through the items until she found what she was looking for – an old silver chain. She slipped the amulet on to the silver chain, dropping the broken chain into her pocket. "There, as good as new." Medaron walked over to her daughter and placed the amulet once more around her neck.

"Thank you mother," Europa stated, as she felt a slight tingling sensation pulse through her body as her mother returned the amulet to its place around her neck.

Medaron heard the girls returning from upstairs. "Thank you again for coming. Remember to drive safely. And keep an eye out for that deer. It sounds like he has a habit of walking out into the road at the most inopportune moments."

"We will," the girls promised. Medaron turned and retreated upstairs to the comfort of her bed. She was so tired she forgot to remind Europa again not to leave the cottage.

"I wish your mother hadn't asked you to stay inside," Terrance stated. "I was hoping to take you with me to meet my father. It's probably the only chance you will get to meet him."

"I do not think she would mind if I went," Europa said. "Besides, she will be asleep and will not even miss me."

"I don't think you should go against your mother's request," Terrance stated.

"As of last night I am a queen and can therefore make my own decisions. I will leave her a note telling her I went into town with you and will return shortly."

"If you are sure it is okay," Terrance replied, still uneasy about Europa defying her mother. "Maybe you should let Misso know you're going."

"I see no reason to inform her," Europa said. Besides, she knew Misso would have objections to her leaving if her mother told her not to. Europa quickly wrote a note stating where she had gone and placed it next to the coffee pot where her mother was sure to see it. With any luck, she would be back before her mother awoke.

"Come on, Triton, we are taking a quick trip into town," Europa announced, as she and her guests headed toward the front door. To her surprise Triton just sat there and gave no indication he intended on going. "What is wrong with you? I said we are going, so come along." Again Triton just sat there. He knew it was not okay for Europa to leave the security of the cottage, especially after their mother had told her to remain inside. "I am going with or without you, Triton, so make up your mind." Seeing he had no way of stopping her and not wanting her to go without him, he followed behind her, huffing along the way to show his disagreement.

Europa and Rannie rode back with Terrance while Anna and Suzie followed in their car. At nine thirty-two Terrance pulled up in front of the inn, giving him twenty-eight minutes before he was to meet

64

his father. Europa gave Rannie a hug goodbye as they exited the car and she turned to walk home. She and Terrance waved to Anna and Suzie as they drove past them, then hurried into the inn's dining room, Triton reluctantly tagging along behind. Terrance surveyed the room but did not see his father; evidently they had arrived before he did. The two decided it would be best to wait in the dining room and selected a table with a good view of the entrance. After ordering coffee, they chatted about the night before and waited for Terrance's father. Terrance glanced at his watch and saw it was ten after ten.

"You know that is a pretty rough drive," Europa stated, as an excuse for Mr. Lander's lateness. "He is just a few minutes late. It might be taking him longer than he thought it would."

"Or he got caught up in his study, like he often does, and forgot about the time," Terrance said, a little annoyed his father had not arrived.

Ten minutes after they left, Medaron returned from upstairs. Misso walked into the kitchen right behind her. "Unable to rest, Your Majesty?" Misso asked.

"To many thoughts racing through my mind," Medaron said.

"Would you like some coffee, Your Majesty?" Misso asked, as she headed toward the coffee pot.

"No, thank you, Misso. I think I will call the jeweler and let him know about the clasp." Medaron walked into the living room and called the jeweler while Misso turned to go upstairs and gather the laundry. "Hi, Mr. Hatfield? This is Medaron Waters. The gold chain I bought from you must have had a faulty clasp because it broke this morning. I was wondering if I could bring it by later today and exchange it for a new one." (Pause) "Yes, the one I bought for Europa." (Pause) "Yes, thank you. I understand these things happen sometimes." (Pause) "We should be there around two." (Pause) "Oh, I see. Then I will be right down to pick up a new one. You said you will be there until noon?" (Pause) "I'll see you shortly."

Medaron hung up the telephone and walked back into the kitchen. She was glad to see Misso had returned with the laundry. "Misso, do you know where the extra keys are to Europa's truck? Mr. Hatfield has to go out of town today and will be closing the store at noon. I need to go into town right away if I want to exchange the chain."

"But, Ma'am, Jeanip isn't here to go with you. You know security protocol calls for him to accompany you whenever you leave the estate," Misso reminded Europa. "Plus, Jeanip stated you, Earon and Europa were to stay behind Minnos' walls for protection until that deer incident is resolved." She knew it was not okay for Medaron to go into town, especially by herself.

"Yes, I remember but, if I do not go now, I will have to wait until Monday. It will be too late to go when Jeanip returns. Besides, I will be fine," Medaron reassured her. "I will just run into town and come right back."

"Then I must go with you."

"You have too much to do here. I am a big girl, Misso. It may have been many years since I fought in the war, but I remember how to defend myself. Europa has the shotgun in the truck if I would need it for any reason. Do you know where the keys are?"

Misso thought of lying to her and saying she did not know, but she could not knowingly lie to her monarch. "They are in the desk drawer. Are you sure it is necessary to exchange the broken chain today? The silver chain looked very nice around Europa's neck and I am sure it will be sufficient until Monday. But if you are intent upon exchanging it today, then I cannot allow you to go alone, Your Majesty. My work can wait until we return from town."

Medaron walked over to the desk drawer, opened it and removed the keys. "Thank you again for offering, but for some reason I feel this is something I must do alone. Besides, a nice ride along the coast would be enjoyable." She saw the deeply concerned look on Misso's face. "Do not worry so, Misso. I promise to go straight to the jewelers and come right back. I will be back before Jeanip returns and he will never know our little secret, I promise. I will not be gone long," she said, as she left the room and headed outside.

Misso saw the note by the coffee pot just as she heard Medaron start the truck. She read Europa's message and quickly ran after Medaron to tell her Europa had left the estate, but she was too late. Medaron was already half way down the driveway and on her way to town. A chill ran through Misso's body as she realized both her queens and Earon were off the estate without Jeanip's knowledge while they were under a high security alert. She hoped Jeanip would return soon to resolve this situation, yet at the same time she feared how angry he would be that both monarchs left while she was on duty.

The deer entered a small grove of trees thirty feet from the estate entrance, watching as the two cars left the estate. He had no way of knowing if she was in one of the cars. While contemplating his next move he was surprised to see her truck pull out of the estate and head toward town fifteen minutes later. He calculated the time it would take her to go to town and return, wondering if he should ambush her at a different location. After considering various locations he decided his original choice of the wooded area where the road curved was still the best location for an ambush. The trees prevented much sunlight from lighting the area and both sides of the road were heavily overgrown with bushes and plants. Concealment was good there. He could surprise her before she even knew he was there. This was the chance he had been waiting for. Today would end the Water's dynasty. Today she would die and another part of his revenge satisfied.

Medaron enjoyed the thirty minute ride into town. She couldn't remember the last time she had driven alone. As her guardian, Jeanip always accompanied her whenever she left the estate. "This was nice," she thought. "I may have to do this more often." She drove straight to the jewelers and exchanged the chain, checking the clasp before she left. She said her goodbyes to Mr. Hatfield and thanked him.

She slowly drove home, enjoying the beautiful day. There was a slight breeze coming in from the ocean, bringing with it the smell of saltwater. Wildflowers of every color carpeted the landscape. She could hear seagulls fighting over a fish that had washed up onto the shore below. The sky was cloudless, the color of light blue.

As she rounded the bend in the road she suddenly saw a large antlered deer walk onto the road, not far in front of her. "This must be that deer they were talking about," she thought to herself, as she applied the brakes. Suddenly the deer's eyes turned a penetrating, glowing red as he stared at her. The strange feeling she had been experiencing flooded through her and terror filler her as she recognized it; it was the feeling she experienced when JeffRa had killed her son and seriously injured Enok. It was a feeling she had buried deep within her subconscious so she would never feel it again.

"Today I avenge my family and my people," she heard a voice shout in her mind, as she stared into the deer's red eye.

"JeffRa!" she screamed. "It cannot be."

"Medaron? Where is your daughter?" JeffRa asked, totally surprised it was Medaron in the truck and not Europa.

"For my daughter I give my life to end yours," Medaron said, as she pushed the accelerator to the floor, picking up as much speed as she could to crash into the deer and kill her mortal enemy. Not expecting the move JeffRa was not able to jump out of the way to prevent being hit. The truck struck him full force and flipped, rolling over several times. Medaron screamed as she was thrown from the truck just before it rolled down an embankment onto the rocks below, smashing and bursting into flames. Pain throbbed through her body as she hit the ground. Blood began to flow into her eyes from a severe cut on her forehead, making it hard for her to see. She quickly wiped the blood away while struggling to see where JeffRa was. At last she saw him lying in the road, still transformed into a deer. He was not moving and she could not determine if he was breathing or not. Desperately needing to know if he was dead, she dragged her broken body over to the deer carcass, picking up a piece of broken glass from the road as she went. If JeffRa was still alive, she would use the glass to cut out his heart. He had meant to kill Europa and she knew he would not stop until he fulfilled his quest. After several agonizing minutes, she reached the deer and saw his chest rising, confirming JeffRa was still alive. Summoning all the strength she had, she raised the piece of glass into the air and plunged it into JeffRa's heart. Then blackness engulfed her as she passed into unconsciousness.

Terrance, Europa and Triton continued to wait in the dining room for Terrance's father. Another hour passed and still no sign of Mr. Landers. Terrance looked down for the tenth time at his watch, becoming more frustrated and annoyed. "I don't understand where he is. He told me specifically ten o'clock. I'll go check with the front desk to see if perhaps he arrived before we did. I'll be right back." Terrance got up from the table and proceeded directly to the front desk. Europa saw the clerk shake her head negatively. Evidently Terrance's father had not arrived early. As Terrance walked back toward her a strange feeling engulfed her. It was so powerful she almost lost her breath for a moment. She didn't know what, but something was wrong, something terrible. She heard Triton whimpering and looked down to see him standing, looking toward home. He looked up into her face and whimpered again. Europa almost thought she heard him say they had to go home immediately, that something had happened.

As Terrance returned, Europa stood up and said, "I have to go."

"I'm sure he'll be along shortly."

"No, I have to leave NOW!" Europa interrupted him. "Something's wrong. Something's happened at the estate." The look of fear on her face and the way Triton was acting convinced Terrance something was indeed wrong and Europa needed to leave.

He quickly threw some money on the table to cover their coffees. "I'll just go inform the clerk to tell my father we had to leave and we'll go back to Minnos."

"No, you wait here. I don't want you to miss him again," Europa said. "Can I take your car? I can have one of the girls bring you out later to get it. Or perhaps you can come out with your father."

Terrance lifted the car keys out of his pocket. "I don't mind going with you."

"Stay," Europa said, as she ran from the inn, Triton right next to her. They jumped into Terrance's rental car and Europa sped down the road, driving as fast as possible; but even at the accelerated speed it seemed like an eternity getting to the estate.

———————

Jeanip and Sunam walked into the kitchen carrying broken parts from the security devices they had discovered while looking for the deer, which was nowhere to be found. Jeanip slipped his ring of keys from his belt and removed a red key and handed it to Sunam. "Get enough parts to fix those broken devices and put them in the back of the pickup," Jeanip instructed Sunam. "As soon as I apprise Medaron of what we found, we'll go back out there and repair the grid."

"That's strange how only certain ones were broken. It was not random, but a deliberate pattern to inhibit us from seeing that section of the land. Someone did this deliberately."

"Yes, that's what has me worried. Someone wanted the lands behind the house unsecured so we would not know he or she was out there. Add in the deer report along with Medaron's recent uneasiness, and I would say it is very possible we have a Terrian in the area."

"After all this time, do you really think at least one Terrian is still alive? And he is preparing to carry out JeffRa's vow of revenge?"

"Yes, I do, Sunam. All evidence points to it, especially the way the security grid was sabotaged. Call Mintoo and Ebar and let them know we have a problem out here and need their help. We'll get the

69

security grid out there working properly and then we'll start patrolling that section by horseback. I'll meet you in the pickup as soon as I inform Medaron of what we found." Jeanip did not relish the thought of telling Medaron there was a security breach. He was glad he had informed Medaron that she, Earon and Europa were to remain inside until he returned.

Hearing Jeanip's voice, Misso came running. Seeing the look on her face Jeanip asked, "Misso, where is Medaron?"

"She's not here, Jeanip" she answered, as she neared Jeanip. He could clearly see the fear on her face.

"What do you mean she's not here? Where is she?" Jeanip yelled, fear now starting to creep into his being also.

"The chain Medaron bought for Europa's amulet broke. She went into town to get a new chain from Mr. Hatfield."

"How? "

'"She took Europa's truck."

"By herself?"

"Yes," she replied. "She wouldn't let me go with her." Holding Europa's note in her hand she added, "But that's not all, Jeanip. I found this note from Europa stating she went into town with Terrance to meet his father after Medaron specifically told her to remain within the cottage. Medaron does not know she is gone." The look of anger that suddenly flashed across Jeanip's face almost frightened Misso more than the thought Medaron, Europa and Earon could all be in danger.

Jeanip ran out of the cottage, straight to his pickup. He jumped in and pressed the gas pedal to the floor, sending dirt and rock flying as he drove out of the yard. He headed straight for town.

Sunam was just coming out of the bunkhouse with a burlap bag containing the needed parts when he saw Jeanip's pickup racing down the road. He immediately dropped the bag and ran into the house, fearing something had happened.

"Misso, what's wrong? Where is Jeanip going?"

"He's gone after Medaron. She took Europa's truck and went into town alone. Europa's gone into town too without permission."

Sunam ran as fast as he could toward the barn, fear coursing through his body. "Tinderoon, there's trouble" Sunam yelled, as he entered the barn. "Saddle up. Hurry." He quickly grabbed the bridle and saddle from the rail outside his horse's stall and opened the gate. He saw Tinderoon running toward him, bridle and saddle in hand. They saddled the horses in record speed and took off after Jeanip. Tinderoon did not know what the crisis was and there was no time to ask. He followed Sunam, hoping by some chance nothing major was wrong.

As Jeanip neared the bend in the road a wave of dread swept over him. Somehow he knew something was wrong with Medaron. It was the same feeling he had felt when Enok was almost killed during the war. As he rounded the curve he saw her broken body lying on the road. He slammed on the brakes, stopping just inches from her motionless body. He jumped from the pickup and ran to her seeing a large pool of purple blood beneath her.

"Medaron, speak to me! Medaron!" He called to her as he dropped to his knees, gently lifting her into his arms. Her face was covered with blood, originating from where he could not tell. The position her left arm laid indicated it was broken in one or possibly two places. Her clothes were drenched in blood. He could see through the rip in her pant leg a large gash in her left leg. Blood also soaked the right leg. He placed his hand on Medaron's neck, hoping to feel a pulse. He held his breath as he searched. "Please, Medaron, don't die on me." Finally he felt a faint pulse. She was still alive.

She moved slightly, trying to open her eyes. "Jeanip?" she barely whispered.

"I'm here, Medaron. Just lie still for a moment while I wipe the blood from your eyes so you can see." He removed a handkerchief from his pants pocket and carefully wiped the blood away from her eyes. He tilted her head back slightly so that any new blood would not reflow into them. "You're going to be alright. Just lay still." He surveyed the area, suddenly realizing there was no sign of Europa's truck. He then noticed the scraped dirt and broken brush at the embankment and wondered if the truck had gone over. "What happened here?" he asked.

The silence was broken by the approaching sound of galloping hoofs on the pavement. He reached inside his jacket and quickly removed his pistol from its holster. Holding Medaron in one arm, he raised the gun and took aim with the other arm. If the approaching sound was foe it would not reach Medaron. As the horses rounded the

71

bend Jeanip saw it was Sunam and Tinderoon. They quickly jumped from their steeds, grasping their rifles from their holders as they dismounted

"Sunam, get some water for Medaron from my pickup. Tinderoon, get the rifles and bring extra ammunition."

Sunam and Tinderoon did as ordered and returned. Jeanip took the water from Sunam and slowly poured a little into Medaron's mouth. Sunam took one of the rifles from Tinderoon and laid it at Jeanip's side. Barely glancing at Medaron, the two males took positions around Jeanip and Medaron with guns raised, standing guard against anything which might come. They would allow no one to harm their beloved monarch or Jeanip.

"The deer, Jeanip. The deer is not a Terrian, it is JeffRa," Medaron whispered, terror filling her eyes for the first time Jeanip had ever seen.

"What?" Jeanip asked in disbelief.

She grasped Jeanip's hand and repeated. "It is JeffRa. He is the deer everyone has been seeing. He did not die that day he went over the cliff with Tiree."

Jeanip looked around. He saw neither a deer carcass nor any sign JeffRa had been there. "Medaron, are you sure? I don't see any sign of him."

"He was here, next to me. I was not able to kill him with the truck so I drove a piece of glass through his heart."

Jeanip looked and saw lying next to her a piece of glass covered in blood. "Tinderoon, get the blue flashlight from my pickup. I need to see if this blood belongs to a creature from Earth or a Terrian." Tinderoon ran to the pickup and quickly brought back the special flashlight. "Shine it on the piece of glass next to Medaron and the surrounding area." As Tinderoon clicked on the light, the blood on the glass and the area under it glowed a distinct sparkling bluish purple. That meant only one thing – Terrian-Oonock blood. Medaron was not mistaken. JeffRa had returned. But where was he now?

"Sunam, Tinderoon, Medaron said JeffRa was here. Fan out. See if you can find a dying deer or any other creature badly injured. JeffRa has been a Terrian for so long we can't be sure what will happen when he dies or what his transforming capabilities are. He may remain a deer or transform back into Terrian when he dies. Although unlikely,

72

there is even the chance he still retains enough Waters' DNA to allow him to flow out, so look for an unusual wet spot or pool of liquid." Immediately the two males began to search the area for their enemy, the Oonock whose life's mission was to eradicate the royal family and them.

"I found Europa's truck," Sunam called back from the top of the bluff. "It went over the bluff. It's burned and smashed to pieces. Perhaps he is under the truck. Do you want me to go down and see?"

"No, if he went over the bluff with the truck the fire would have erased any sign of him. Continue your search up here." The two continued to look but were unable to confirm if Medaron had killed JeffRa or if he had escaped once again. Returning to their guard positions around their queen, Sunam handed Jeanip an oval purple stone.

"I found this," Sunam said, as he handed the object to Jeanip.

Jeanip took the stone. He recognized it immediately and was not surprised to see an etching of Medaron carved into it. This was the power source to a special weapon JeffRa had constructed to be used solely for the purpose of killing the royal family. Staring at the stone, he stated, "I guess this confirms what Medaron said."

"JeffRa is alive and he's back," Sunam said, barely able to believe his own words.

Their thoughts were broken suddenly by the sound of another car approaching, this time from the direction of town. Preparing for a possible assault, they watched as the car neared them, slowed and then stopped. For a moment the car sat there, its driver remaining inside. Sunam and Tinderoon aimed their rifles at the car in preparation for whom or what was inside. Finally the door opened and out stepped Europa, followed by Triton. Europa looked as if she was in shock, not believing the scene before her. As much as he wanted to go to his mother, Triton stayed with Europa, surveying the area for potential threats. Even before Jeanip could give the order, Sunam hurriedly ran to her and brought her into their circle. Triton raced to his mother's side, laid down next to her and gently rested his head on her.

Medaron placed her hand on top of Triton's head and whispered, "My Son."

Tears flowing from her eyes, Europa knelt down beside Jeanip and looked at her mother being held in his arms. "Mother," was the only word she could speak.

"Europa, I'm sorry. Give me your hand". Europa did not move but just sat there staring at the broken and bleeding body of her only parent. "I need to give myself to you."

"Medaron, no. You don't know if she can take the transfer," Jeanip objected, terrified at losing Europa too. "It could be too strong for her. It might kill her."

"It must be done," Medaron said. "It is the only way to keep her safe. Please, Jeanip, I don't have much time." Hearing the desperation in Medaron's voice, Jeanip laid his gun on the ground and took Europa's hand, gently placing it in Medaron's.

Using what strength she had left, Medaron took her daughter's hand and held it tight. "I give to you all that I am. From this day on you are the Supreme Leader of our people. Ennay Benu Carif." The amulet around Medaron's neck began to glow and a soft hum could be heard. The amulet's glow grew brighter as strands of lilac began to emanate from it and encircle Medaron's body until her entire body was encased in the lilac glow. Jeanip watched as the glow of energy in Medaron's body started to flow down her arm into her hand, then crossed into Europa's hand, up her arm and into her body. In a mixture of sorrow and joy, he saw the glow in Medaron's body diminish, as the energy transferred to Europa until only Europa's body was encased in the glow. Then, it too began to fade as the strands of color receded into the amulet around Europa's neck. Europa crumbled onto the ground, shaking violently, then laid motionless. Just as Jeanip feared, the transfer was more than Europa's human body could handle. Jeanip looked down at Europa's chest to see if he could see any sign of her breathing. To his great relief he saw her chest rise as she drew air into her lungs. Somehow she had survived the transfer.

Jeanip looked down at the broken body of his monarch in his arms. "Medaron, she survived. She now possesses all you were and have been."

Medaron looked up into Jeanip's eyes. "As it should be," she whispered. She was so weak Jeanip could barely hear her. "Jeanip, take me out into the ocean. I do not wish to flow into this earth. Take me to the water so I may become one with it and Enok. Hurry, Jeanip, I cannot hold on much longer."

Jeanip carefully stood, holding Medaron in his arms. He looked down at Triton who was lying next to the unconscious Europa. "Earon, I need your help. I need for you to transform into a human for your sister needs Earon now, not a guard dog. Stay with her and protect her well.

JeffRa has returned. He has fulfilled his promise to end your mother's life, even though it was Europa's life he thought he was ending. We cannot determine if he is dead or not, although your mother says she killed him. Take Tinderoon with you and take Europa back to the cottage. I will meet you there shortly. Sunam, you come with me to keep guard while I take Medaron out into the ocean."

Without another word, Jeanip turned and carried Medaron down a small hill opposite the bluff, across the beach and into the ocean. Sunam followed, remaining on the beach keeping guard, rifle ready to fire if JeffRa returned.

Triton immediately transformed into Earon, a young human male. He quickly scooped his sister into his arms, holding her gently against his heart. "Tinderoon, if you would be so kind as to drive us home." He walked over to the car Europa had arrived in and paused for a moment, watching his mother's final minutes as a human as Jeanip carried her out into the ocean. "May the Waters take you home," he softly spoke. "I love you and I will miss you, Mother." Tears freely flowing from his eyes, he carefully climbed into the back seat while holding Europa securely in his arms. Giving the surroundings one last security look, Tinderoon slid into the driver's seat and took the siblings back to the cottage.

Jeanip waded out into the ocean until the salty water surrounded Medaron's almost lifeless body. He held her head above the water as the waves began to wash the blood away. Within moments, Jack and Jill along with the other dolphins surrounded Medaron and transformed into human beings. Crying lilac tears, they raised their hands to their foreheads and bowed deeply to their monarch as they placed the other hand upon her body.

Jeanip looked down at his beloved monarch and sister. He barely heard her whisper, "You must take her to FarCore. There she will be safe."

"I will, Medaron. I promise I will keep her safe."

"Thank you, Dearest Brother, for all . . ." Medaron closed her eyes. She did not finish her sentence. Her breathing became shallow then ceased. Jeanip and the transformed Oonocks watched as her body began to glow as she transformed back into her true self. The radiance grew brighter as her skin became transparent until all that remained was the light. Then the cohesiveness of her skin began to break down, allowing the glow to spread itself out onto the ocean waters. It spread itself further and further, until it became so thin it too disappeared. Jeanip looked down and saw all that remained in his arms were the clothes his dearest sister had been wearing. She had gone home, returned to the waters from which she came, forever a part of the salty waters of this planet.

Sunam slowly drove Jeanip back to the cottage with the two horses tied to the tailgate of the truck. When they reached the cottage, Jeanip exited the truck and slowly walked into the cottage without saying a word to Sunam. Today he felt his age and every step seemed like an eternity. As he entered the dwelling he heard Misso crying in the kitchen. Earon stood waiting for him at the bottom of the staircase.

"Is Mother gone?" Earon asked, trying to fight back his tears. "Has she returned home? Is she now one with Father?"

"Yes," Jeanip whispered. "Is your sister safe?" Jeanip asked in the voice of a beaten man as he reached out to hold onto the staircase banister to keep from collapsing.

"Yes, she is lying in her bedroom. Birea is with her." Earon replied, as he fell down onto the stairs, no longer able to contain his sorrow. He lowered his head and cried openly as grief consumed him.

"Send a message to Evonic that we need him immediately," Jeanip instructed Misso. "He will know how to treat Europa. Have the men lock the front gate and electrify the fences. No one is to enter."

Jeanip looked into Earon's eyes. He placed his hand upon Earon's shoulder, thinking how much he resembled his mother. Earon returned his gaze and feared Jeanip was going to collapse before his very eyes. Never had he seen Jeanip so distraught, so much in agony. Jeanip had always been the superior, unemotional soldier, no matter what happened – until today. Seeing Jeanip in such a condition of weakness made Earon realize his sister's assassination was a definite possibility and, for the first time in his life, he felt fear. Jeanip removed his hand and walked through the house without another word, his head hung low, his shoulders drooped as if from a tremendous weight. He went straight to his room, closing and locking the door behind him. He sat down at his desk, placed his arms upon its surface and lowered his head to rest on them. Then for the first time in almost nine thousand years, Jeanip cried. He cried for the loss of his queen, he cried for his failure to keep her safe, but most of all, he cried for the loss of his beloved sister.

76

LOCKED GATE

Terrance continued to wait for his father until one o'clock. Finally abandoning hope of his return, he rose and walked out of the dining room. Europa still had not returned with his car and that worried him more than his father not returning. He was standing in the lobby trying to decide his best course of action when he saw Anna walk by the front windows. He immediately ran out after her.

"Anna, boy am I glad to see you!" he shouted, startling her as he seemed to appear out of nowhere.

"Oh, hi, Terrance. What's up?"

"I was wondering if you could give me a ride out to Europa's? She borrowed my car to run back to the cottage after having a feeling something was wrong. She's been gone quite a while and I'm starting to get worried. I thought I'd go and check on her."

"How long ago did she leave?"

"Several hours ago."

"Gee, I hope everything is alright. I'd be glad to give you a ride. My car's right over here." Terrance practically ran to the car in his haste to return to Europa. Anna hopped into the driver's seat and sped off toward the estate. "You said she had some kind of feeling? Did she say what it was?" Anna inquired.

"No, just that something was wrong back at the estate. She said she had to get back home right away."

"Why didn't you go with her?"

"I wanted to, but she insisted I stay here and wait for my father. Remember, he was supposed to meet me this morning at the inn, but he never showed."

"I'm surprised she hasn't called you to let you know what's going on. That's not like her; she has to know you'd be worried sick about her." Anna stopped for a moment, a look of concern crossing her face. "Oh my gosh, Terrance, what if something has happened to Europa and that's why she hasn't called! I hope she's all right."

"Me too," Terrance stated, his mind imagining the worst.

As they headed for the estate Terrance kept a watch out for his car in case they passed Europa returning to town. He was upset with himself for not going with her; he should have forgotten about meeting his father. He wished Anna would drive faster. He was ready to suggest that very fact when he felt the car slow down and heard her say, "Looks like something happened up ahead. There's a large stain on the road. It appears as if an animal might have been hit. Oh, I sure hope someone didn't hit or shoot that deer."

Terrance looked at the road ahead and noticed the dirt and shrubs on the side of the road had been mangled and the large dark stain on the road. Fear gripped his heart as he stared at the scene of an apparent accident. He turned to Anna and saw, by the look on her face, she was imagining the worst just as he was. She accelerated the car and soon turned down the driveway leading to Minnos and the front gate. Terrance began to feel more at ease for he was only minutes from entering the estate, minutes away from discovering if Europa was okay, if something was wrong. But that feeling soon left when he saw the gates were closed and his car parked in front of it. Anna stopped next to Terrance's parked car when she saw the front gates was chained shut and contained a sign reading: DANGER. DO NOT ENTER. FENCE IS ELECTRIFIED. CONTACT WITH ANY PORTION OF THE FENCE WILL RESULT IN SEVERE BODILY INJURY OR DEATH.

"Do not enter? Fence is electrified?" Anna read out loud. "What's that all about? I've never known these fences to be locked during the day. And never have they been electrified. What is going on inside there?"

"I fear, Anna, something very terrible has happened," Terrance muttered, as he stared at the posting. "Even Jeanip would not go to these extremes unless something was really, really wrong." Suddenly, the thought popped into his mind Jeanip was very upset about Europa disobeying her mother and going with Terrance to town and this was his retaliation. Maybe Jeanip planned on keeping the two apart. No, that didn't make sense. Jeanip was an honorable man; he would simply tell Terrance he was no longer welcomed at Minnos and have him barred from the property. "I wonder why my car is parked out here and not up at the house? Surely if Europa made it this far she must have made it to the house. Why would they put my car outside the fence?" More bewildered and worried than ever, Terrance walked over to the car and tried the driver's door. It was unlocked. Seeing no keys in the ignition, he lifted the floor mat and, to his relief, saw them along with a note. He picked it up and read:

> *Terrance;*
>
> *Thank you for allowing Europa the use of your car. Due to a security issue Minnos has been locked down. Please leave an address at the inn where Europa can reach you if you leave before the security issue is resolved.*
>
> *Jeanip*

"What does it say?" Anna asked, hoping at last they would know what was going on.

"I don't understand," he said aloud, as he handed Anna the note to read. "What in the hell is a security issue? What has happened to Europa? Who in the hell does Jeanip think he is to tell me to leave my address at the inn?" He stopped in front of Anna hoping she had some idea of what was going on. She only shrugged her shoulders, indicating she had no clue. "This is ludicrous. I can't wait out here not knowing what has happened or if she is okay. Does Jeanip really think I could possibly leave before seeing her, before knowing SOMETHING? I have to get inside NOW." Terrance walked up to within inches of the gate. He could feel the hair on his arms tingle as they began to encounter the electrical charge being given off by the fences and gate. "Do you hear me?" he screamed toward the house with as much volume and force he could summon. "Let me inside! Turn off these stupid fences at least long enough to let me in. PLEASE!"

Terrance was so obsessed with getting inside he did not realize he had stepped closer to the electrified gate and was in danger of being electrocuted. As he took another step forward, Anna rushed up behind him and pulled him away. "You can't enter, Terrance. Stop before you kill yourself," she shouted, bringing Terrance back to reality.

"What did you say?" Terrance asked, a little confused at what just happened.

"You can't enter, Terrance. No one can. If you try to get through that gate, it will kill you. And you're no good to Europa dead, are you?" Seeing the blank look on Terrance's face she grabbed him, shaking him as hard as she could. "Don't you understand? Minnos is on lock down and no one can get in until Jeanip says they can."

"But I can't just leave her," Terrance said, as he realized the truth of what Anna was saying and how close he came to death. "What am I supposed to do?"

"I guess the only thing we can do is return to town and see if we can find someone who knows what happened out here." Anna continued to watch Terrance's reaction to determine if he was okay. She did not want him trying to walk through the gate again. "Are you okay to drive back?"

Terrance stood there a moment just looking at the gate, not sure what he should do. He didn't want to go back to town and finally decided to remain at the entrance. "I think I'll wait here for a while just in case someone comes to unlock the gate, Anna. If you find out anything, leave me a message at the inn." Seeing there was no hope in persuading Terrance his wait was futile, she returned to her car and drove back to town leaving Terrance to his thoughts.

Fearful someone would come to let him in as soon as he left, Terrance sat down in a shady spot next to his car and waited. He spent the next several hours alternating between sitting on the ground and pacing. Several times he walked up to the gate and studied the lock, trying to determine if there might be a way to disarm it. When it started to get dark he decided his quest was impossible and returned to town hoping Anna had left him a message.

Evonic came down the stairs with his medical bag and walked into the kitchen where Jeanip, Earon and Misso were waiting. He sat down at the table.

"Medaron's lucky that transfer didn't kill the girl," Evonic said. "What was she thinking? Europa lives in a human body, not a transformed Waters' body. Human bodies are too frail to handle such energy and certainly not all at once. If the amulet hadn't absorbed most of the energy you'd be planning a funeral right now."

"But will she be alright?" Jeanip asked, fearing he could lose Europa too.

"Only time will tell us that. She will need to remain asleep for three or four days while her body adjusts to the new powers and energy Medaron gave her. It's very important for her body to remain completely at rest during this transition. Otherwise, her systems may overload and her heart could be damaged or even fail. I've given her something to keep her asleep. Once I'm confident her body has healed, I will awaken her. I'll remain here until that time."

"Thank you, Evonic," Earon said.

"Hello, Your Highness. It is a pleasure to see you again. It's been several years," Evonic addressed Earon, as he bowed his head slightly and raised his hand to his forehead. "You two need to understand she's not out of danger yet. No human has ever received a monarch's transfer so I'm in the dark on how to help her. There is no procedure I can follow, no cure I can give her. I'm simply treating her human body with traditional human medicine and hoping her body can adjust to the newly introduced alien energy."

"Will there be any side effects from the transfer?" Earon asked, concerned about his sister's future.

"I honestly don't know, Your Highness. We'll just have to wait and see how she does when she wakes up. But I do know one thing. When she wakes up she's going to wonder where her mother's body is and why Triton isn't at her side."

"Yes, Earon and I were just discussing that," Jeanip said, as he walked over to the kitchen counter to pour himself a cup of coffee. "We've been trying to decide what the best course of action is. The only plan we can come up with is to tell her Medaron is already buried in the family cemetery next to Enok's grave. I'll have Sunam dig a fake grave and put a temporary headstone on it."

"As for Triton, I'll just have to transfer back and forth between the canine and myself, depending on who needs me – Jeanip or Europa," Earon stated. "It's either that or tell her Triton is also gone and she suddenly has a long lost brother."

"I wouldn't suggest the later," Evonic said. "Europa just lost her mother. She doesn't need to lose Triton too. And add in the shock that she has a brother she never knew about . . . well, she might not be able to emotionally handle that."

"That's what we were thinking," Earon said. "I'll just have to be certain to transform back into Triton right before she wakes up."

"That would be my suggestion," Evonic stated. He watched Jeanip walk back and forth in front of the counter taking a sip of coffee now and then. He had never seen him look so old, so beaten down. Not even during all the years they were at war with the Terrians had he seen Jeanip look as he did now. "Jeanip, you look exhausted. Would you like me to give you a vitamin supplement or something else before you leave? You're no good to anyone if you're unable to function."

"Leave? You are planning on going somewhere?" Earon asked in disbelief.

Jeanip turned toward Earon and saw the bewilderment in his face. He did not look forward to telling Earon where he was going and why. It seemed there was no end to the dreadful duties he had to execute this day. "Earon, I need to leave for several days. I have full faith in your ability to handle things while I'm gone. Evonic will be here to oversee Europa's medical condition and Sunam, Tinderoon, Ebar and Mintoo will be here for security. Birea and Misso will help with Europa. I will be back before your sister awakens."

"Now? You are really considering leaving NOW? Are you insane? We have to notify the authorities regarding the accident. Do you think they are not going to notice Europa's smashed and burned truck on the rocks? I can guarantee you they are going to have a lot of questions, especially when they find out Mother is dead but there is no body to prove it. What is more damn important than Europa's wellbeing and my mother's death?"

Jeanip took a deep breath and walked up to Earon. He wished there was some way he could avoid telling him what he was about to say. "I have to make the journey I prayed I would never have to make, Earon. I have to go tell your father that Medaron is dead by JeffRa's hands and he may still be alive."

"My father?" A startled look came upon Earon face. His mind raced to comprehend what Jeanip was saying, why he was leaving. Was Jeanip saying his father was alive, that he had not died as they had been told? Was he about to hear a truth Jeanip had hidden from them, from his mother? Earon looked directly into his eyes and said, "You told my mother years ago he had died. Are you now telling me he's alive? He's alive and my mother never knew it?"

"Yes, Earon," Jeanip replied as he returned Earon's fixed stare. He could hear the shock and anger in Earon's voice. "Enok is alive. He never passed as I told your mother."

"You lied to her?" Earon yelled, having trouble, even as he said it, grasping the concept Jeanip would deliberately lie to Medaron, his Supreme Monarch. "Why would you do that?"

Jeanip knew there was no easy way to explain why he had lied to Medaron about Enok's death, no way not to admit he had broken her trust. "Enok commanded me to tell Medaron he had passed when the medical team told him they could not correct his breathing problem. Enok realized he would never be able to join your mother up here on land or share in Europa's life. Their separation was tearing his heart and soul apart every day and he knew it was doing the same to your mother. Their bond was so deep, even hundreds of miles away in the deep recesses of the ocean he could feel your mother's deep sorrow and emptiness. He always blamed himself for her life of solitude and could not bring her more suffering by telling her he could not join her as they had planned. So to spare Medaron any more anguish, Enok decided she be told he had passed. He gave me the command and I followed his orders."

"But she did suffer. She never stopped grieving for him, stopped loving him. I cannot tell you how many times I saw her sitting on that damn side porch swing staring out into the ocean and talking to him. You saw her too. How could you watch her time after time sit there and long for my father, knowing all the while he was ALIVE? I thought you loved her, Jeanip. I thought she mattered to you."

A flash of anger fled through Jeanip's body as he listened to Earon's words. He jumped up, leaned across the table toward Earon and crashed his fist into the table, leaving a deep impression in the wood. "Don't you think I saw her each time she sat on that damn porch swing, Earon, suffering because of what I told her?" Jeanip screamed aloud. "Don't you think it tore me apart each and every time I saw her cry, knowing I was the reason for that pain? Don't you think I wanted to tell her the truth, to stop being a soldier for just one minute, to break my vow to Enok? All I wanted to do was to tell her that her love was alive, take my sister in my arms and kiss away her sorrow, comfort her as her loving brother. But I could not do those things. And now that she's gone that is a truth and a sorrow I have to live with every day for the rest of my miserable life." Jeanip became silent as he slumped back into his seat, drained and emotionally distraught. Remembering he was Enok's commander and who he was addressing, he kept his eyes lowered and said, "Forgive me, Your Majesty, for raising my voice to you and allowing such a display of emotions. I meant no disrespect. But I did realize the pain my sister was in."

Earon continued to stare at Jeanip, not mentioning a word about his outburst. Jeanip wondered if he had even heard what he said. "Father never should have done that. And if you truly loved my mother, neither should you have." Earon stood up from the table and stormed out of the room, climbing the stairs to Europa's room.

"I did as I was ordered," Jeanip whispered, as he watched Earon leave. "Even though I did not agree with Enok's decision and believed he was in error, I followed orders. And I did love my sister, more than you will ever know." Evonic had remained standing silently in the kitchen during Earon's and Jeanip's discourse. He now turned and looked at Jeanip in amazement. In all the time he had known Jeanip, he had never heard him say a negative word against Enok. He did not envy this commander who alone bore the weight of both his monarchs' decisions and the repercussions for carrying out their orders.

"When are you leaving?" Evonic asked softly.

"Right away. The sooner I get this horrible deed over the sooner I can get back here. As Earon said, there is still a lot that needs to be attended to." Jeanip placed his cup on the counter. "We found no evidence to verify if JeffRa was killed or not. If he is still alive he will try again to assassinate Europa. Enok is her father and now Ruling Supreme Sovereign. He must decide what to do next, how best to protect his children. These are decisions I cannot make." Jeanip looked at Evonic. "I've instructed Sunam to call the police after I leave and advise them Medaron was killed in an accident. I need you to make out her death certificate and leave it at the front gate for the sheriff. Sunam will inform him we already had a family only funeral, as our custom dictates. Ask Sunam to bring you a weapon from the storage room. Europa and Earon need all the protection we can give them now."

"You really have thought of everything, haven't you?" Evonic said, admiring Jeanip's thoroughness. No wonder Enok trusted him so much; he was the perfect soldier, always on duty, always thinking ahead, always planning every minute detail. "Do you think the sheriff will accept we've already buried Medaron?"

"Planning every detail comes with the job," Jeanip responded. "As for the sheriff, I could care less about what he thinks."

"I need to run back to town to let my office know I will be out for several days," Evonic stated. "And I need to pick up some more medical supplies. Can you ask one of the men to take me into town and back? I'll be sure to make it as quick a trip as possible."

84

"No! No one leaves the estate, no one comes in. That is why you are to leave the death certificate outside the gate along with a notice stating we will issue a statement in the next few days." Jeanip saw Evonic's look of disbelief on his face. "Security protocols demand the gate be locked and the fences electrified to ensure adequate protection. We cannot take chances with Europa's and Earon's safety, especially since we cannot confirm JeffRa's death."

"I don't know, Jeanip, if I have enough medication with me to keep Europa asleep until you return," Evonic stated. "And there may be other medicines I will need to treat her human body."

"Any human or Oonock medical supplies you may need will be in the storage shed," Jeanip replied. "We keep an updated supply of both. Sunam can take you down there if needed."

"Very well."

"I must go now, Evonic. See you in a couple of days. If you need anything, see Sunam. He is in charge of security until I return."

"May the Waters protect you and guide you on your journey," Evonic stated, as Jeanip disappeared behind the door leading into his room and the secret entrance to the cave.

Terrance rose early the next morning, showered and dressed, then tried calling Europa again But there was no answer. He couldn't understand why no one was answering the telephone. What had happened out at Minnos? He had to know. Not knowing what else to do, he decided to drive out to the gate in hopes someone would let him in. He stepped into the hallway and walked toward his father's room. Hoping his father had returned during the night, he knocked on the door but only silence greeted him. Disappointed, he walked down to the lobby and asked the clerk if his father had returned. He had not. He proceeded down to the lobby and purchased coffee and food from the dining room in case his wait at the gate was a long one.

The drive to the estate seemed extra-long this morning; possibly because he was alone and had no one to help pass the time. When he reached the bend in the road where it appeared an accident had occurred he slowed down, surveying the area. Nothing had changed; there were broken bushes, torn up dirt and grass and the spot on the road. After passing the location, he pressed on the accelerator and continued his journey toward Minnos. As he neared the entrance disappointment once again filled his heart as he saw his way still barred by the locked gate. It appeared no one had been out there since he had left. Determined today was the day he would get inside, he remained in his car, drinking his coffee and eating the donuts, watching the driveway ahead for any sign of movement. He wished he could see the cottage from here, but it was too far down the driveway to grant any sighting. As the day progressed, Terrance was torn between retuning to the inn and remaining at the gate. Rationalizing his father was already a day late, he decided to remain at the gate. Suddenly, Terrance jumped to his feet, positive he heard the sound of an approaching car. He ran toward the fence and looked down the drive but no car appeared. Believing it was his imagination, he went and sat down beneath a nearby tree and slowly ate his fruit and sandwiches. As he sat waiting he began to conjure up various scenarios of why his father hadn't returned and what had happened at Minnos to keep him barred from seeing Europa, each scenario more worrisome, more dreadful than the previous. Realizing allowing his imagination to run wild was not helping, he stood up and jogged around the tree a few times to loosen up his body. Once he tired of jogging, he tried calling the estate, but again no one answered. Why didn't someone answer the dang phone?

Finally forcing himself to face the reality that no one was coming to let him in, Terrance decided to return to town. His waiting out at the gate was serving no purpose other than making him worry more. He returned to his car and headed toward town, taking one last look at the gate as he drove away. As he neared the bend in the road he noticed police lights ahead. He slowed down, and then came to a stop as an officer stepped into the road blocking his path. Hoping the officer might know what had happened, he rolled down his window to ask when he noticed a wrecker towing something up the embankment. He stared in horror as he saw a burned, smashed red truck slide over the bluff. It was Europa's truck. Panic stricken, he jumped from his car and ran toward the embankment.

"Sir, you'll have to remain in your car" the officer said, as he grabbed Terrance's arm.

"That's Europa's truck" he yelled, trying to free himself from the officer's grip.

"Sir, you need to get back into your car" the officer repeated, this time with more force in his voice.

"But that's my girlfriend's car. Is she okay?" he asked, as he looked up into the officer's face. Didn't he understand? That was Europa's truck and it was smashed and burned and whoever was in it was probably dead. His Europa could be dead. Was that the reason the gates of Minnos were locked? No, Europa was with him when she felt something was wrong which meant someone else was in the truck. Who? Medaron? Jeanip? "TELL ME!" Terrance yelled at the officer. "What happened here? Is Europa okay?"

Feeling sympathy for the young man, the officer let go of his shoulder. "Miss Waters is unharmed," the officer replied. "That's all I can tell you. The family will issue a statement concerning the accident."

"But . . ."

"No buts, Sir. Either return to your car or I will place you under arrest for impeding an investigation. Your choice." Terrance looked at the officer, realizing by the sound of his voice he was serious.

Terrance returned to his car. He knew he wouldn't be able to see Europa once the gates opened if he was sitting in jail. He remained stationary until the wrecker pulled away with the smashed truck, escorted by several police cars.

"Okay, you can proceed now, young man" the officer told him. "Please drive carefully." Terrance followed behind the wrecker and police cars into town. He pulled up in front of the inn and sat there trying to determine what course of action to take next. He had to find out what happened, but how? Maybe Anna or one of the other girls would know, but he didn't know how to get in touch with them. He decided to go inside and ask the clerk if she knew where they lived. As he walked into the lobby he saw Anna at the front desk. Suzie and Rannie were with her. Terrance could see all three had been crying. A shiver of fear ran through his body.

"We've been looking everywhere for you," Anna said, as she ran up to him.

"I was out at the estate's gate hoping someone might open it," Terrance explained. "What is going on? I saw Europa's truck all smashed and burned. A wrecker was bringing it up from below the cliff. It looked like it went over and smashed."

"We know," said Rannie. "We heard about it a few hours ago. Evidently Mrs. Waters was driving Europa's truck and had an accident."

"Mrs. Waters? Is she alright?" Terrance asked, concerned about Medaron but relieved it was not Europa.

"I'm sorry to say she was killed," Rannie replied, having trouble holding back the tears.

"No!" Terrance muttered, as he sank into a lobby chair. He looked up at the girls. "Poor Europa. Is she okay?"

"We don't know," stated Suzie. "With the estate locked down we can only assume she's there. We've tried calling, but no one will answer the phone."

"I know. I've been trying to call all day," Terrance said. "I'm going to go back out there and scream until someone lets me in."

Anna put her hand on his shoulder. "It won't do any good, Terrance. No one is going to open the gate for you. We must wait."

"I can't stay here and do nothing."

"That's all we can do," Suzie added. "The Waters are a very private, very secretive family. And when it comes to Europa, they're almost paranoid about her security. Believe us, Terrance, there is NOTHING you can do but wait. Wait until they decide to unlock the gate."

"And how long will that be?" Terrance asked, seeing the truth in what Suzie was saying.

"Who knows?" answered Anna. "It could be a couple of days, a week, even a month."

"A week? A month? You've got to be kidding," Terrance stated in disbelief.

"Terrance," Suzie said, as she wiped away tears, "I'm sure it will be just another day or two. After all, there's a funeral to be held. Look, here's our phone numbers. Call us if you need anything, even if it's just to talk. If we hear anything we'll let you know."

"And promise us, Terrance, you won't go back out to the gate," Rannie stated. "They could perceive your presence as a threat and keep the gate locked longer."

"She's not kidding," Suzie said, seeing the look of disbelief on Terrance's face. "You cannot go back out there."

Realizing he had no options opened to him, Terrance agreed not to go back out to the gate. He would remain in town. "What about the police?" Terrance asked, jumping up from his chair. "Perhaps they can tell us something."

"Already tried," Anna replied. "They're as tight lipped as that locked gate. They wouldn't tell us anything."

"I couldn't get any information from the policeman out on the road either," Terrance stated. "All he said was Europa was okay and the family would be issuing a statement." He sank back into the seat feeling totally defeated. "A day or two," he repeated softly. "How can I wait for another day or two to find out what's going on out there?"

"We just have to," Suzie said. "Would you like us to stay with you for a while?"

"We don't mind," Anna added. "We're going to worry no matter where we are."

"Thanks, you guys," Terrance said. "But I think you should go home in case Europa tries to call one of you. I'll go up to my room and try calling again." Terrance rose and proceeded toward the stairway as the three friends began to leave. "Hey, let's plan on meeting tomorrow for lunch. Maybe by then one of us will have heard something."

"It's a date," Anna replied. "See you at noon."

Terrance proceeded up the stairway to his room while Anna, Rannie and Suzie left the inn. Each silently hoped when they met the following day someone would have more information about the accident and Europa.

ENOK

To assure no one, human or Terrian, saw Jeanip leave Minnos, he used the secret underground passage that led from his room to the cave. As he descended the stairs he thought it seemed like only yesterday he carried the pregnant Medaron up these stairs to her room. He had walked down these steps numerous times since that day but they never seemed so dreary, so dark, so long as they did this day. At last he reached the last step and stepped down into the large cavern that allowed him secret access to the ocean and Minnos. He looked around, remembering when they first built this hideaway hundreds of years ago before when Minnos was built. It contained a sleeping area for six; various change of clothing for any Oonocks who wished to come on land; food, medicines, weapons; and a large storage chamber where many of Medaron's things were stored. He made a mental note that certain things would have to be brought down from Medaron's room and stored down here until they could be taken to Saint's Isle.

Jeanip slipped into the cold, salty water of the cave, dove beneath her waves and swam out a few yards before transforming into a dolphin. Jack and Jill along with their pod soon swam alongside. Now paranoid a Terrian could be anywhere, Jeanip remained a dolphin and randomly swam outside the bay with the pod until nightfall. Once darkness arrived, he transformed into a Moby and began his dive to the Ocean Complex. For the first time in his life he wished he was not Head Commander, that it was someone else's duty to advise Enok of the current situation.

When he was close to the Complex's entrance he uttered several preselected clicks to activate the beacon which would lead him through the gateway. Once through, he followed the tunnel to the Exit Chamber where he promptly transformed into his true self. It had been a number of years since he had existed in his true form and it felt strange. It took him a moment to remember how to navigate through the water using his wings. As he passed the threshold into the outer chamber he was surprised to see Enok already waiting for him. He sensed Enok knew something was wrong and by the look of despair on his face, he already suspected the worst.

"Your Majesty," Jeanip greeted Enok, raising his hand to his forehead and bowed slightly as he floated forward.

"My Medaron, she is gone, is she not?" Enok asked, staring into Jeanip's lilac eyes. Jeanip could see Enok's body tense as he awaited the answer, fearing it would confirm his loss.

"Yes, Sire." Jeanip could barely speak the words. He watched as his sovereign crumbled to the stone floor, a loud scream emanating from deep inside his soul. Jeanip knew Enok had survived through countless tragedies over the years, including the death of his parents and his son, but he wondered how he would recover from this tragedy. He held out his hand and opened it to reveal Medaron's amulet and chain resting in his palm. "How did you know?"

"I felt her essence in the waters," Enok said in a thought so small, so soft Jeanip almost didn't hear him. Enok reached out and took the amulet from Jeanip's hand. He held it in front of his face and stared at it, trying to comprehend what the absence of its owner really meant. "I felt her kiss my cheek and I heard her voice tell me she loved me." Clutching the amulet tightly in his hand, his wings fell to the floor as a new wave of sorrowfulness washed over him.

"I have failed you, Sire. You charged me with her safety and I did not keep that charge. I do not deserve to remain your commander. I do not deserve to live." Jeanip floated down to the floor and sat beside his grieving leader. All the sorrow of that day came flooding once again into Jeanip as his body shook with grief. Together the king and soldier sat on the floor and cried until they had no more tears left to shed.

"Europa and Earon, are they safe?" Enok asked, his head still hanging down in sorrow as he returned to the present and was able to control his grief.

"Yes, Sire. Both are well and safe."

"What happened?"

"It was JeffRa, Enok."

"JeffRa?" Enok asked, jerking his head up to look at Jeanip to assure himself he heard correctly. "What do you mean it was JeffRa? JeffRa died almost a thousand years ago. Why do you say it was him?"

"We were wrong, Sire. I was wrong. JeffRa did not die that day he went over the edge with Tiree. I wouldn't have believed it except Medaron said it was him. She was certain. And there was a lot of Terrian blood at the scene. Plus, we found this." Jeanip opened up his other hand to reveal the purple oval stone bearing Medaron's likeness.

Enok reached out his hand and took the stone. He knew no one but JeffRa would have such a stone, which meant he had been there with his Medaron. "The traitor still lives?"

"Yes, Sire, it seems he is still alive."

"Were there other Terrians as well? Or just JeffRa?"

"I can't say for sure, but we believe he was alone. Medaron had gone into town without my knowledge and without a security escort. On her way back to the estate she encountered him. He had transformed into a deer and was waiting for Europa."

"Europa?" Enok asked, a more terrified look crossing his face.

"Yes. Medaron had taken Europa's red truck and JeffRa believed it was Europa driving it. Evidently, he had come to fulfill his promise of assassination. Medaron realized who he was and used the truck in an attempt to kill him. From what we can surmise, JeffRa realized at the last minute it was Medaron in the truck and tried to jump out of the way, but Medaron hit him full force. She was thrown from the truck and suffered internal injuries, but somehow managed to crawl over to JeffRa and plunge a shard of glass into his heart. She told me she had killed him but we could not verify it."

"Were you the one who returned her to the ocean?"

"Yes, Sire. Medaron asked me to take her so she could flow out and became one with you and the waters."

"To become one with me? What must she have thought when she flowed out only to discover my essence was not in the water? If only I have been there," Enok said, the guilt of not being with his life's mate when she died weighing heavily upon his heart. "She deserved so much better."

Sensing his guilt, Jeanip added, "Sire, she did not die alone. Runbee, Shanem, Graybin, Tontee and several others were there. They gave her all the respect a monarch's passing deserved."

"I am glad she did not flow out alone, that she was surrounded by those who loved her. But she still deserved better; she deserved to have me waiting there for her." Enok paused for a moment, lost in thought. "Did you know Runbee and his group decided on their own to live as dolphins so they could keep an eye on her, Earon and Europa? Over the years, they kept me informed of Europa's activities and how she was growing into a beautiful young woman. They loved swimming and playing with her."

"And Europa has enjoyed their company. Of course she has no idea they are transformed Waters from her homeland. Her friends are always trying to figure out why they only swim with her. She's the envy of them all." Jeanip saw the faintest smile on Enok's face as he imagined his daughter being envied by her friends.

Suddenly Enok's face transformed from sorrow to anger and realization. "We must assume JeffRa survived and he will try again to kill Europa and Earon."

"That was my belief also, Sire. Before I left Minnos I made sure both Europa and Earon are under high security lockdown. No one or no thing can enter the estate, no one can leave. Both wear their amulets. They are safe."

"But for how long, Jeanip? They cannot stay under high lockdown forever."

"Medaron requested I take them to FarCore."

"FarCore?" I don't believe FarCore is necessary. That would give Europa no life at all. But I do believe she and her brother should be moved to Saint's Isle." As Enok thought the words he realized all his and Medaron's sacrifices, the years apart, all the effort everyone had executed to keep Europa from knowing the truth of who she was had been wiped out by JeffRa's act of vengeance. "She will have to be told the truth of who she really is and the reason for the move; the one thing Medaron and I hoped would never happen. All the sacrifices everyone made these past twenty years to assure her a happy human life wiped away in an instance by a madman's thirst for vengeance."

"We always knew this was a possibility and is the reason why Saint's Isle was built, Enok. And you're correct; if she and Earon are going to make the move safely, she has to know the truth and understand what is at stake. But I do not have the authority to make that decision; only her father does. As her father and our Supreme Leader, I need you to tell me how to proceed."

"You said both my children are safe, but are they doing well?" Enok asked, concerned for the welfare of his children. "I assume it was necessary to inform Earon of where you were going when you left and the reason why? That means you had to inform him I was still alive?"

"Yes, Your Majesty," Jeanip replied. "I told him you were alive and well and the reason behind the deception."

"How did he handle the news?"

"As you might expect, Your Highness," Jeanip replied, not wanting to add to the Enok's distress by telling him Earon's reaction.

Enok turned and stared at his commander. He knew Jeanip was being evasive. "Like I would expect? What kind of answer is that, Jeanip? What I would expect is for him to be terribly angry, to hate me for lying to him and his mother, to spit upon my grave if I had one. Is that how he reacted? Does my son hate me? I have lost my most precious mate; have I lost my son also?"

Jeanip knew he had to tell Enok the truth, but he tried his best to sweeten it. "As you said, he was extremely angry and could not believe you would have concealed your life from him and his mother," Jeanip replied as Enok stared at the floor. "But he blames me, Sire, more than you. He believes I betrayed my sister by fulfilling your command." Jeanip reached out and placed his hand on his sovereign's wing. "But let me assure you, Enok, he does not hate you. You have not lost your son. He still loves you dearly and, with time, he will come to understand the reason for your decision. He has little knowledge of the Quanundocii and does not understand the repercussions of being separated from the one you are united with; therefore, he cannot understand why you would make such a decision. He has just lost his mother. There's an assassin hiding somewhere outside the boundaries of Minnos waiting to end his and his sister's lives. Give him some time. His anger will subside soon and he will remember how much he loves you."

"I hope you are correct, Jeanip," Enok stated. "What of Europa? How is she handling the death of her mother?"

Jeanip did not answer. He expected Enok to give him instructions on how to proceed with the young monarchs' move, not ask how Europa was handling Medaron's death. He could feel Enok staring at him.

"Jeanip, how did she react?" Enok asked again, this time with authority in his voice.

"She doesn't know."

"What do you mean she does not know? She does not know her mother is gone?" Enok asked, his voice loud, as he rose from the floor and looked down at his commander. "Jeanip, why does she not know Medaron is dead? What else have you not told me?"

"Medaron was still alive when Europa arrived at the accident scene," Jeanip began to explain. "She knew she only had minutes to live and in order to preserve who she was and keep Europa safe, she transferred her powers to Europa."

"What do you mean she transferred her powers? Without any preparation on Europa's part? She is human, Jeanip. A human cannot absorb such powers."

"I know, Sire, I know," Jeanip explained remembering that terrifying moment in time. "I advised Medaron it was too dangerous, but she would not listen to me. You, more than anyone, know how stubborn she can be and did as she pleased. Plus, she was my queen and she was dying; I could not override her decision. But, Enok, somehow Europa was able to accept the transfer."

"Her body accepted the energy? She lives?"

Jeanip saw concern cover Enok's face at the thought of also losing his daughter, the same concern he had felt when Europa collapsed after the transfer. "Yes, Sire, she is alive. The transfer was more than her human body could handle all at once; it put her into a state of unconsciousness, but it appears there was no damage to her organs or her body. Her heart and lungs are strong. Evonic has her sleeping so her body can adjust to the new alien energy that pulses through her body. As soon as I return, we will waken her and my first priority will be to tell her of Medaron's passing."

"Medaron must have been truly scared if she did such a transfer. She never would have taken a chance with Europa's life unless she felt it was necessary to keep her safe. Does Evonic say how the transferred power will affect her? Is she is any danger?"

"He isn't sure. No human has ever received our powers. But he hopes, by keeping her sleeping, the powers will go dormant and remain that way until she says the words to awaken them. So legends say."

"Legends? What good are legends here? They are stories about healings and powers that occurred hundreds of thousands of years ago on a world far away from this one. Our legends have nothing to do with humans. We did not even know of their existence when these legends were formed."

"Yes, Sire," was all Jeanip could say.

Jeanip remained seated on the floor with Enok floating above him not speaking a word. Jeanip was not sure if Enok was contemplating his course of action or still trying to process everything Jeanip had told him. He watched the gentle swirls of color in the water twirling around him, embracing him, giving him strength. Finally Enok stopped, a look of determination upon his face as he took Medaron's amulet and placed it around his neck alongside his own.

"JeffRa will not succeed in annihilating my family," Enok stated. "He will not harm another member as long as I am alive. He fooled me into thinking he was dead, but not this time. This time I will be the one to end HIS life." Enok looked at his loyal commander, a new determination in his eyes. "Come, Jeanip, we have plans to make. This time we have something JeffRa will not expect."

"And what is that, Sire?"

"MY REVENGE!"

Jeanip immediately rose and followed Enok, delighted to see a determined and energetic Enok once again. He saw in his sovereign the Enok of old, the leader of a nation, the strategist of war. This was his monarch who would stop at nothing to end JeffRa's reign of revenge. For the next two and a half days they planned Europa's and Earon's transfer to Saint's Isle, Europa's new future, what she would and would not be told and most importantly the capture and execution of JeffRa.

SEARCHING FOR THE TRUTH

Terrance met Anna, Suzie and Rannie for lunch the next day as planned. As he walked toward their table in the dining room, he hoped they would have word about Europa, but to his disappointment they too had heard nothing. Like his, their calls still went unanswered and the gates were still locked. Frustrated by their inability to ascertain the truth and deeply saddened by the death of Medaron, the four decided to cancel lunch. The girls left promising once more to keep Terrance apprised of anything they heard and he did the same. He walked the ladies to their cars, giving each one a hug goodbye. After they left he turned to go back inside and up to his room. As he entered the lobby the manager called him over to the service desk.

"Good afternoon, Mr. Landers. I understand your father has not returned yet."

"That is correct."

"That puts me in an awkward predicament, I'm afraid." Terrance could see Mr. Everett was a bit nervous and was having trouble looking him directly in the eye. "When your father was here the other day he only paid for his room up through today. He believed his business here would be concluded and he would be leaving for Michigan this afternoon. Evidently those plans have changed and he will be extending his stay. However, since he is not here to pay for his room, I cannot keep the room for him. I was wondering if you would like to pay for several more days or, if you prefer, you can move his belongings into your room. That is, if you are staying."

"Yes, I am staying for a while. I'm not sure how much longer my father will remain in the field so I think it best for me to bring his belongings to my room. If you could have someone let me into his suite, I'll remove his things right away."

"Thank you, Mr. Landers. I'll have Rita go up with you and unlock the door." The manager motioned to a young girl with dark, short hair wearing a light blue maid's uniform. "Rita, please unlock the door to room 24B for Mr. Landers. Mr. Landers, if you need help moving your father's belongings, please let Rita know and she will send Stanley up to assist you."

"Thank you, Mr. Everett," Terrance replied.

Terrance followed the young maid upstairs to his father's room, feeling confident there would not be much to move. His father usually traveled pretty light. Soon they were standing outside the room and he patiently waited while Rita unlocked the door and flipped on the light. Terrance stepped inside and quickly surveyed the contents of the room: his father's clothes, several notebooks, three books and a pile of pictures on the desk. Just as he had suspected, there was little needing to be moved; this would not take long at all. He walked over to the stack of pictures and began to thumb through them, expecting to see various snapshots of the Red Breasted Sparrows. But they were not pictures of birds – they were pictures of Europa and Minnos. He stared at them in disbelief, catching himself just before he gasped out loud. Remembering Rita was still waiting at the door, he did his best to act as if nothing was out of the ordinary. "Please tell Mr. Everett I can handle this myself. There isn't much here to pack up," he said, waving his hand across the room so Rita would see the contents. "It shouldn't take me long to pack his things."

"OK, Mr. Landers. If you change your mind, just call the front desk," Rita said. "We'll send someone right up to help you."

"That I shall," Terrance replied, as he walked over to Rita and handed her a five dollar bill. "Thank you for letting me in." Taking the five, Rita smiled and left.

Terrance closed and locked the door, then slowly walked over to the desk. Reaching down, he picked up a picture of Europa and just stared at it. "Dad, what were you up to?" Fearing Rita might return to clean the room, he decided it would be safer to look at the pictures in the privacy of his own room. Grabbing the two suitcases from the closet, he quickly gathered his father's belongings and stuffed everything into the two cases. Once he had everything in sight, he began to search the room for hidden objects; he knew his father often hid important items and papers in various locations in hotel rooms. Under the mattress he found two journals and discovered beneath a dresser drawer two large manila envelopes. The ceiling panel above the bed revealed a bag containing a hi-tech digital camera, more pictures and several photo cards. Lastly, he checked the breakfast table and its two chairs and was astonished to discover a strange weapon taped to one of the chairs' underside. He pulled the weapon free then stared at the strange object, both stunned and horrified his father would have such a thing in his possession. It was stocky on one end with something resembling a gun barrel protruding from it. There was no trigger he could discern, but it did have numerous buttons and switches on it. On top of the stocky end was an oval impression where evidently something was to be placed. It appeared to be made of some type of metal, but was surprisingly light.

"My gosh, Dad, what have you gotten into?" Terrance asked. Tucking the weapon beneath his arm, he picked up the suitcases and hurried from the room, making sure the door locked behind him. He walked as fast as he could down the hallway to his own room, occasionally looking back over his shoulder to assure himself he was not being followed. "Stop being so paranoid," he said to himself. "No one knows what you found in your father's room. You are overreacting." Finally, after minutes that felt like hours, he reached his room and quickly slipped inside, closing the door and bolting both locks plus latched the security chain.

Now feeling safe, Terrance quickly dumped the suitcases' contents onto the bed and separated the clothing, photos, notebooks and papers into separate piles. Ignoring the clothing, he quickly scanned through the papers and determined there was nothing of importance contained within them. The notebooks revealed information and drawings of the Red Rock Sparrows, again nothing of importance. Thinking perhaps he had over-reacted in his father's room, he picked up one of the journals. To his horror, he saw page after page of detailed notes regarding Minnos and its inhabitants. Now fearful of what the second journal might contain, he sat it aside. Summoning up what courage he had left, he took a deep breath and picked up the first manila envelope. His hands shaking slightly, he opened the envelope to discover a copy of the estate land title and a photo of a painting of the original occupants at Minnos. As he scrutinized the photo, he couldn't help but think how much the woman resembled Mrs. Waters. There were also several drawings of unknown machines with hand scribbled notes written in a strange language. Next he opened the second envelope and discovered it contained detailed hand drawn maps of the estate showing the locations of buildings, trees, streams, etc., in addition to a network of security devices on the property. The map showed in detail which devices were connected together and which could disable a section of the grid. In disbelief he saw in the middle of the disabled devices a big red X with the words "tree blind" written beside it.

Suddenly feeling faint, Terrance walked into the bathroom and splashed some water on his face. He looked at himself in the mirror and said, "You can do this, Terrance. You can go through your father's items and try to figure out the truth." Taking a deep breath, he walked back to the bed and sat down. He reached over and picked up the stack of photos. Of all the articles in his father's room, the pictures scared him the most. Praying the majority of the pictures would be of birds and the early pictures of Europa were harmless, he began to thumb through the stack. He stared in skepticism and alarm as he saw more pictures of Europa, along with pictures of Mrs. Waters, Jeanip, the help, the cottage, the grounds, the gate, security devices and more. Each bore a number and letter code on the back. The last picture sent chills of horror down his spine – it was a picture of Europa's red truck.

Terrance spent the evening going back through the journals, looking at the pictures, trying to make some sense out of what he found. He went through everything over and over but could not find any clue as to what his father was up to, why he was spying on Minnos and the Waters family. Exhausted and emotionally drained, he dozed off at four a.m., spread across the pictures on the bed. He was awoken by his telephone ringing at ten-twenty. Groggy, he forced himself out of bed and answered the phone. It was Anna. She and the ladies were downstairs with news and they needed him to come downstairs right away. Promising to meet them in five minutes, he quickly grabbed everything off the bed and hid it under the mattress. He then dashed into the bathroom, ran some water through his hair, brushed his teeth and put on a clean shirt. After taking a quick look in the mirror to make sure he looked presentable, he placed the "Do Not Disturb" sign on the door knob and rushed downstairs. When he stepped out of the elevator he saw Anna standing there waiting for him, but he did not see the other two friends. As he approached Anna he could see she had been crying again.

"What did you find out?" Terrance asked immediately, a little out of breath. "Did you get to talk with Europa? How is she doing? Did she tell you why the gate is locked?"

"Let's go into the dining room," Anna suggested, as she reached out and took his hand. "I'll answer all your questions once we are seated. Suzie and Rannie are already waiting at the table for us." Terrance followed Anna into the dining room thinking her news must be bad if he needed to sit down to hear it.

As he neared the table Terrance saw Suzie and Rannie had also been crying. "Tell me what you know," Terrance insisted, his voice shaking as scenarios ran through his mind. "Is Europa alright?"

"Europa has not been injured," Rannie said, as she lifted several tissues to her eyes to wipe away her tears.

"It's not good," Suzie said. "The family has released a statement which will be printed in today's newspaper. Out of respect for our friendship with Europa, they asked we be given a copy before the paper comes out. We were asked to share the statement with you." Suzie reached into her shirt pocket and brought out a folded piece of paper and handed it to Terrance. No one said a word as Terrance took the paper, unfolded it and read the announcement.

> *It is with much sadness the Waters family announces Medaron Waters was killed in an automobile accident Tuesday afternoon on her drive home from town. The cause of the accident is unknown and currently under investigation by the police. A private family ceremony was held on Wednesday at which time Mrs. Waters was laid to rest next to her husband in the family cemetery. She is survived by her daughter, Europa and her brother, Jeanip Smith. Her husband, Enok Waters, preceded her in death.*
>
> *To allow the family sufficient time to grieve, the family will remain cloistered at the estate. The family thanks you for any condolences but requests you refrain from flowers or visits.*

"Poor, Europa," Terrance said, unable to think of anything else to say.

"I can't believe they've already buried Mrs. Waters," Rannie stated. "She was loved by everyone in town. I wonder why the quick funeral."

"Terrance, didn't you say the truck was badly burned and smashed?" Suzie asked Terrance.

"Yes. There wasn't much left of it except for a smashed, burned out shell," Terrance replied, remembering what the truck looked like.

Suzie gazed at the three. "That's probably why they buried her so fast. Her body was probably badly burned."

"I guess there is nothing we can do then until Jeanip opens those damn gates" Terrance replied. "Thanks for sharing this with me." Terrance folded the announcement and handed it back to Suzie.

"No, you keep it," Suzie said as she stood. "We should get back to the house in case Europa calls. Call if you need anything, Terrance."

"I will," he replied. After giving each a hug, he watched them leave then returned to his room. He began to examine his father's belongings again, trying to make some sense out of it all. Then he remembered the fact Mrs. Waters was royal and his father had been searching for a lost royal family for years, traveling all over the world investigating stories and leads, determined to discover where they had gone. What if he thought the Waters were part of that royal family? It would definitely explain a lot. Then a terrifying thought entered his mind: What if in some way his father was responsible for Mrs. Waters' death? Could it be possible? Somehow, someway he had to get inside Minnos and find out more about the accident. He had to know the truth. He wished he had told Europa that day they found the blind something strange was going on. Perhaps if he had Mrs. Waters would still be alive. Why didn't he tell her?

Terrance began to pace the floor, consumed with regret and worry. As he passed the dresser mirror he happened to look at his reflection and stopped. "Terrance Landers, what are you doing? Look at yourself – you're making yourself crazy. Forget about what your father may or may not have done and concentrate on what you know, what you have before you on the bed. Making yourself crazy by imagining all kind of scenarios is not going to help Europa or get you inside of Minnos. PULL YOURSELF TOGETHER!" Taking a deep breath, he sat down on the bed and put any thought of his father's connection to Medaron's death out of his mind. He spent the remainder of the day studying the pictures and papers, matching several pictures to references in his father's journal.

One referenced picture in particular he found very intriguing. It was a photograph of an old painting from 1628 of a man and a woman. The journal reference stated his father had discovered it in a little art museum in Ann Arbor, Michigan. The reference stated the portrait was of an E. and M. Waters who were the original settlers of Minnos. Terrance shuffled through the pictures remembering he had seen a similar photograph. When he found it he turned it over and read the notation on the back: Mr. & Mrs. E. Waters, painted in 1682. He placed the two pictures side by side and was shocked to see it not only appeared to be of the same two people in both pictures, but they were also the same age in each. But he knew that was impossible. The two paintings were done fifty-four years apart. Terrance did not know what Mr. Waters looked like, but these two women definitely resembled Mrs. Waters. He quickly looked through the journal to see if his dad possibly referenced the ladies' first names, but could find none. Suddenly a folded piece of paper fell out of the journal and dropped to the floor. He bent down, picked it up and saw a rubbing of a headstone of another woman looking exactly like Mrs. Waters dated 1783 with a name written at the bottom – Medaron Waters, wife of Enok Waters. Could Enok Waters be the name of Europa's father also? Suddenly, he remembered the announcement Suzie had given him contained Mr. Waters' name. He quickly pulled it from his pocket and read it twice, making sure he was reading it correctly. It stated *"Her husband, Enok Waters, preceded her in death"*. This was impossible. Either these were the same two people who had been alive for hundreds of years or the Waters' brothers and sisters were all named the same and were marrying each other. Both possibilities were improbable.

No longer able to contain his curiosity of what the other journal contained, Terrance finally decided to look inside the second journal. Holding his breath in an attempt to control his anxiety, he opened the book and saw it was a detailed journal in which was recorded the daily activities of Minnos beginning twelve days prior to his arrival. Recorded were the times each person rose in the morning and went to bed at night, when they ate their meals, what chores were done and when, what Medaron and Europa did, the times people left the estate and returned, when security grids were turned on, when the front gate was locked and more. Terrance was astonished at the great detail of each event. As he continued to scan the entries he noticed a number-letter code next to many of the entries and remembered seeing the same code marked on the pictures. Taking each picture one by one, he began to match them to the daily entries and was given a complete picture of the happenings at Minnos. He was astonished to see there were even several references and pictures of him, although his father had not known who he was and recorded him as a new young stranger. He continued matching the pictures to the entries until he reached the picture of Europa's red truck. Closing his eyes for a moment to summon his courage, he read the marked code - 'E's EXT'. Frantically he scanned down the page to the last entry and froze, a sick feeling beginning to grow in his stomach. There in his father's handwriting was written the words 'Europa's Extinction'. A wave of nausea swept over him. With his hand over his mouth, Terrance ran into the bathroom and vomited up the little food he had consumed that day as he realized his father WAS responsible for the accident. And more than likely he had thought it was Europa in the truck and not Mrs. Waters. He vomited again as he realized if his father knew he had killed the wrong person he was probably still out there waiting for his next chance to kill Europa. He slumped to the floor, unsure of what to do, where to go. The one thought that kept repeating over and over in his mind was "Somehow I have to get inside that gate before my father finds a way in. I have to get inside Minnos and save Europa before my father tries to kill her again."

JEANIP RETURNS

Jeanip returned to Minnos with Enok's instructions on how to proceed with the protection of Europa and Earon and the capture of JeffRa. As before, to conceal his arrival, he swam into the hidden cave, then entered the cottage through the secret underground passage. As he entered the kitchen Misso was coming down the stairs carrying a tray of food she had taken up to Earon. Evonic was sitting at the table, anticipating his return.

"How is he?" Evonic asked.

"As best as one could expect," Jeanip replied. "How is Europa doing?"

"She's come a long way since you left. I thank the Guardian of the Waters she has a strong, healthy body. From what I can determine, her body was able to absorb the transfer, distribute the energy throughout her body and repair any damage the transfer caused. It's almost as if she healed herself. I have found no damage to her organs and no indication of side effects. But I will not know for sure until she awakens and I see how her body behaves."

"She is still asleep?"

"Yes, I kept her sedated until you returned, as you requested."

"And Earon?"

"Earon has not left her side. He's still trying to deal with the death of his mother, the truth his father is alive and the probability JeffRa is somewhere outside the fence plotting his and his sister's death."

"Evonic, if you would go tell Earon I am back and I need to see him right away. Remain with Europa until someone comes up to relieve you."

Without saying a word, Evonic rose and ascended the stairs to Europa's room. Several minutes later Earon descended and walked into the kitchen. Jeanip gestured for him to have a seat at the table. He asked Misso to give them privacy, and then sat down across from Earon.

"Did you see My Father?" Earon asked, his voice echoing the anger and resentment he was still feeling.

"Yes. He sends you his love and his deepest sorrow for the loss of your mother."

"His sorrow? He sends his sorrow?" Earon screame, as he jumped up, outraged that his "now living" father would have the audacity to send such a greeting. "And his love? If he loved us so much why did he lie to me, to her? I'm sure you're going to tell me again he had good reason, but no reason in the universe is worth the pain and suffering his decision cost her. She would have outlived Europa by hundreds, possibly thousands of years. After Europa died, she could have returned to the Complex and together they could have lived many years together. HE ROBBED HER OF THAT HAPPINESS!" Tears filling his eye and flowing down his cheeks, Earon slumped back into his chair, too emotionally drained to continue with his outburst, his heart still seething with rage and resentment. Almost as an after-thought, he softly said, "Perhaps if she had known Father was alive she might have been more careful, might not have gone into town by herself."

Jeanip looked directly at Earon. "Earon, look at me." Jeanip waited until Earon raised his head to look at him. "We can 'if' and 'perhaps' ourselves into madness. We can't undo the past. Be it right or wrong, it was a decision your father made as our leader for the benefit of someone he loved. And as our leader, his decisions cannot be questioned. Believe me, Earon, you cannot begin to feel the regret or sorrow he does." Jeanip saw the anger in Earon was not easing. "You must realize, Earon, it was JeffRa that ended your mother's life, not your father's decision. And even though you do not want to admit this, Medaron's sacrifice saved you and Europa. We never would have known JeffRa still lived and was so close to fulfilling his oath of revenge if she had not given her life to save yours and Europa's."

"I'm supposed to be glad she exposed him by dying?"

"No, Earon. There is no joy in Medaron's ending. I am just trying to show you some good that came from it. JeffRa pledged to destroy any children your parents had, to bring down the house of Waters. Your mother sacrificed her life to stop both." Jeanip could see his words brought Earon no comfort, no relief from his loss. "Your mother's death is a great tragedy, one we can never totally recover from.

And if anyone deserves blame besides JeffRa, it is me. I was in charge of her protection. I failed at my duty. And that failure warrants only one outcome; that I be relieved of my commander's status and my life be forfeited. But your father would not hear of it. Yes, life without Medaron will be almost unbearable but we owe it to her to ensure you and your sister live a long life. While it would be easier to hide away in some dark corner consumed with grief and self-pity, the reality is we still have you and Europa to protect, an assignment I will not fail in."

Earon looked at Jeanip, somehow not surprised he would have forfeited his life. He was a soldier, a loyal servant who loved Enok and Medaron. He had devoted his life to serving them, protecting them, doing their bidding. Earon had to remind himself his mother was Jeanip's sister and what her death must have meant to him. A bit of the anger Earon had been feeling was replaced with love for this man who sat across from him, this pillar of strength who sacrificed everything he had for them, this soldier whose sole purpose was to ensure he and his sister were alive and remained so.

"Before Medaron died she asked that you two be moved to FarCore for safety. To do that Europa must be told the truth of who she is. And who YOU are. Enok felt to do this would nullify the sacrifices Medaron and you have made. Instead of FarCore, he wants you two taken to Saint's Isle. I can no longer protect you here, but at Saint's Isle I can be sure no harm will come to either of you. Once you are there we can find JeffRa and any remaining Terrians and destroy them."

"Saint's Isle. I forgot about that place. I remember Mother talking about it when we first arrived here. She once told me after Father died," Earon paused for a moment, realizing the falseness of his words. "She said if anything ever happened to her we should go there."

"I remember."

Earon took a deep breath and asked the question that had been plaguing his mind since Jeanip had left. "Jeanip, did my father mention the possibility of us returning to the Complex, of bringing Europa there for protection?"

"No, he did not because he knows that is impossible for two reasons. Firstly, he is not ready for Europa to know all of the truth about her people and who she is, to completely undo the past twenty years. She will be told only those parts essential to her movement to Saint's Isle. And secondly, since Europa was born human she will never be able to have a life at the Complex. Even if by some miracle she was able to transform into a water creature. her lungs would never be able to breathe water instead of air."

"What about the special pressurized capsule?" Earon asked, remembering his last journey up from the Complex. "Could she not be brought down like my mother and I were brought up?"

"She might be able to survive the trip in the transporter, but it would be very dangerous. Human bodies do not do well under high water pressures. She would have to remain in a special pressurized, oxygenated air atmosphere isolated as your mother was. A prolonged stay in such an environment would possibly cause her irreparable cell damage and bring on pressure psychosis. Enok is not willing to subject her to such a lonely life or take the chance the conditions could kill her. Even if there are still a few Terrians alive, her chances of survival here are still greater than down there."

"I thought you would say that. It was a question I needed an answer to."

"I would want to know the same if I were you," Jeanip answered. "I know you would have enjoyed spending time with EeRee also. I know it was very hard to leave her behind."

"Since Mother's death I have been thinking a lot about EeRee and how short life can be. We would have been joined as life-mates by now, had I remained behind," Earon said, remembering with sadness the day he had released the female he loved from her pledge to join with him and said his goodbyes.

"Earon, once Europa is safe on Saint's Isle you can return to the Complex if you would like," Jeanip stated. "You will be safe there and I can watch over Europa. She will not need a canine guard dog on the island. Perhaps EeRee has not taken another."

Without hesitation Earon answered, "No, Jeanip. My duty lies with protecting Europa, wherever she is. I promised Mother I would always be there to watch over her, and that is what I am going to do."

"If that is your decision, Your Majesty," Jeanip replied. "Your father did ask me to give you one other message. Since your sister may now need a brother more than a guard dog, Enok said it is your decision which form you wish to take once you're at Saint's Isle. If you want to be a brother to your sister, Enok has no objections to you transforming permanently to human form."

"And how do we explain my sudden appearance?"

"Thought to be lost at sea with your father," Jeanip replied trying to think of a plausible explanation.

"She would never believe that," Earon replied. "Unless I have been suffering from amnesia somewhere and just regained my memory."

"Stranger things have happened," Jeanip replied, as he rose from the table. "But for now, Europa needs Triton. I am going to have Evonic begin to wake her. When she awakes she will need to see her trusty guard dog, Triton, lying next to her on her bed. So, Your Highness, it is time for you to transform back into your protective role."

Earon knew he was right. Without another word, he transformed back into the Rottweiler Europa would expect to see at her side. Trotting behind Jeanip, he climbed the stairs to Europa's room.

"Evonic, it is time for Europa to wake," Jeanip instructed Evonic as he entered Europa's room. Earon, now Triton, hopped onto the bed and laid by his sister's side.

"How do you want this done?" Evonic asked. "I can remove the IV and let her wake up naturally, or I can give her an injection to bring her around in a few minutes."

"How long will it take if we let her wake up naturally?"

"Probably about an hour or two."

"How long with the injection? And is there any danger waking her that way?"

"It shouldn't take more than five or six minutes. Either way is safe. It just depends on how soon you want her to wake up."

"I believe it would be best to waken her sooner than later. I don't want to take the chance of her waking up and me not being present. Give her the injection."

Evonic detached the IV lines from Europa's arm, then injected her with the serum to awaken her. After several minutes her eye lids began to flutter as she neared consciousness.

"Europa, can you hear me? It's Evonic. Can you open your eyes? Can you wake up for me?"

Europa slowly opened her eyes. She tried to focus on the blurred silhouettes around her room. She could feel Triton next to her arm. "Where am I?" she asked, still groggy from the medications. She blinked her eyes trying to get them to focus.

"You're in your bedroom, Europa." Jeanip answered. "We need for you to wake up. Can you do that?"

"I cannot see," she whispered.

"Your vision will clear in a few minutes," Evonic answered. "Here, take a sip of water." Evonic held a glass of water up to her lips and she took several sips of water. "Just lay there for a few minutes until you get orientated. Then we'll help you sit up."

Triton gently nudged her arm. With effort, Europa lifted her arm and laid it on Triton's back, too weak yet to pet her companion. "Triton" she said, smiling to know her faithful friend was at her side.

After ten minutes, Jeanip and Evonic assisted Europa into a sitting position, stuffing numerous pillows behind her back for support. Her eyes now able to focus, she could make out the faces of Jeanip, Evonic and Misso, who stood by the hallway door.

"Misso, if you would be so kind as to bring Europa some soup and perhaps a cup of tea," Evonic said. Misso immediately turned and headed to the kitchen to prepare her mistress's light lunch.

"What happened?" Europa asked. "I feel like I have been asleep forever." Suddenly, she realized there was someone not in the room, someone who should have been. "Where is my mother?" Panic began to fill her as her memory began to return to the scenario at the bend in the road. "Jeanip," she screamed, grabbing Jeanip's hand and looking directly into his eyes. "Where is my mother? Where is Medaron?" Tears began to fill her eyes and flow down her cheeks.

Not letting go of her hand, Jeanip sat down beside her. "Europa, there is no easy way to tell you this. Your mother was in an accident several days ago . . ."

"Do not say she is dead!" Europa begged.

"Your mother used your truck and went into town alone. On her way back that deer that's been hanging around evidently stepped onto the road in front of the truck. When your mother tried to miss hitting it she lost control of your truck. It flipped several times and she was thrown from the cab just before it plunged over the bluff. I arrived minutes after it happened, but her injuries were severe. She died shortly after my arrival."

Triton jerked his head up, staring at Jeanip. He knew Jeanip was lying about the events of that tragic day. Their mother had been alive when Europa arrived. What was Jeanip going to do if Europa remembered talking to their mother?

Europa's eyes widen in disbelief. "Mother is gone?"

110

"Yes, Europa."

Just as her vision had cleared, so did the fogginess in her mind. She began to remember clearly the events of that day. "I remember being with Terrance and feeling something was wrong. I took his car and came back here. But then I saw you in the road." Then she stopped and turned and looked directly into Jeanip's face. "No, Jeanip, Mother was alive when I arrived. I talked to her."

Giving her the most honest look he could summon, Jeanip replied, "No Europa, she wasn't. She had already died in my arms."

"No, "she insisted. "She took my hand. I remember seeing a bright light and feeling like I was being pricked by thousands of pins. And she said some strange words. I REMEMBER." She peered into Jeanip's face, pleading with her eyes for him to tell her she was correct.

"Europa, the sight of your mother's condition sent you into shock. You passed out and fell, hitting your head on the pavement. You suffered a severe concussion. What you remember did not happen."

"But I remember the touch of her hand" Europa pleaded, still sensing the touch of her hand in her mother's.

Jeanip looked at Evonic for assistance. "Europa," Evonic said "It is not uncommon for people who have had concussions to remember events that did not happen. The mind creates scenarios that are false. Your mother's injuries were extensive. She only lived a few minutes."

"No, it cannot be," Europa sobbed. "She cannot be dead." Waves of uncontrollable grief surged over her. Her body shook as she realized her mother was gone. Jeanip pulled her into his arms and held her, holding back his own tears.

"Jeanip, I'll be downstairs if you need me," Evonic quietly whispered, as he left the room to give Europa some privacy.

After ten minutes Europa was able to quiet down her sobs, stop her body from shaking. "I want to see her body," she softly said.

Jeanip took a deep breath. Telling Europa her mother was dead was painful enough. He now had to lie to her again and tell her that her mother had already been buried.

"Europa, your mother's accident happened five days ago. You've been unconscious that long. Your mother was laid to rest beside your father four days ago."

Jeanip heard Europa's crying subside while her body began to stiffen. With all the strength she could find she pushed Jeanip away from her. "Already buried?" What do you mean already buried?" Anger filled her eyes. "You already had a funeral without me being present, without giving me a chance to say goodbye? How dare you bury my mother without me! How dare you take it upon yourself to make such a decision!"

"Europa, we did what we felt was necessary. We had no way of knowing how long you would remain unconscious."

"You had no right."

"Europa, I . . ."

"GET OUT!" she screamed. "GET OUT OF MY ROOM."

Jeanip stood up and, without a word, left the room. He closed the door behind him, hearing Europa sobbing into her pillow.

Emotionally exhausted, Europa soon fell asleep with Triton curled up along her side. Once he was certain she was sound asleep, Triton silently slipped out of her room and went downstairs. As he entered the kitchen he saw Jeanip sitting at the table with a fresh cup of coffee, his head hung low in despair. He didn't even look up when Triton trotted past him and went into the bathroom. Triton transformed back into Earon and slipped on the robe he now kept behind the door.

"That did not go very well," he softly said, as he sat down in the chair across the table from Jeanip.

"I broke that child's heart" Jeanip wearily said. He turned to face Earon. Earon thought Jeanip looked even more tired, more mentally and emotionally drained, more vulnerable than he did the day Medaron died. Earon knew that was the worst day of Jeanip's life. Was it possible this day was even worse for this dedicated soldier? "She will hate me to the day she dies for not allowing her to see her mother before she was buried. How do I tell her the truth? How do I tell her Medaron's body is not in that fake grave out there? How do I explain to her the fact her mother was a beautiful creature of the water who has dissipated back into its vastness. It would be so much easier if she knew the truth of who she really is, who her mother was. And who you are."

"Then tell her. We can tell her together and see what happens. It cannot be worse than the situation we have now. She certainly cannot hate you anymore than she currently does."

"That is not our decision to make. Medaron left specific orders of what was to transpire if she passed. Your father reconfirmed those orders just yesterday, plus added a few more. As Enok's commander, I am obliged to carry out those orders."

For the first time in his life Earon felt sorry for Jeanip. He knew no one was more loyal than Jeanip and he had laid down his life numerous times to save the family and keep them safe. And for all of this his reward was that Europa hated him; no, hate was too mild a word. Europa loathed him with every fiber of her being because he was bound by a vow to her parents to keep the truth hidden from her. Jeanip might be right – Europa might NEVER forgive him. Earon wanted to relieve some of the pain his parents were responsible for. He quickly thought of what he could say to alleviate some of Jeanip's despair.

"Jeanip, she just received the news her mother is dead. On top of that, her mother has already been buried and she will never see her again. Give her time to absorb everything she has just learned." Earon paused for a moment, then continued. "Jeanip, I know Europa loves you dearly; she just needs time to remember that. You are the only father figure she has ever known. You have been the dominant male figure in her life since she was born. She will not hate you forever, even if it feels like she will. One day she WILL realize you did what you had to do. Time does heal all wounds." He worried about Jeanip. He had just lost his sister, his most cherished thing in the universe. If he lost Europa too, his second most cherished thing, he did not believe Jeanip could bear the loss. Earon knew he personally could not bear everything Jeanip was now bearing. How did Enok think Jeanip would be able to?

"Things will get even worse if she wakes up to discover Triton is not lying by her side," he said to Earon, meaning he needed to transform back and return upstairs. Following Jeanip's advice, Earon transformed into Triton and trotted up the stairs. He knew his words had brought some comfort to Jeanip but he also knew Jeanip was too much a soldier, too disciplined to acknowledge that comfort.

Misso softly knocked on Europa's door before entering. She carried a tray into the room of vegetable soup, a cup of sweet tea and two shortbread cookies, the ones Europa loved. Not knowing if Europa was awake, and not wanting to wake her if she was sleeping, Misso silently walked over to the night stand next to the bed and placed the tray quietly upon it.

"I am not hungry, Misso," she heard a faint voice say. "Please take it away."

"I understand, Your Majesty, but you should try to eat a little something. You need to get your strength back," Misso answered, hoping Europa would have a bite of something. "I brought you your favorite cookies".

"Thanks, Misso," Europa answered. "And until I tell you differently, I will take all my meals here. Tell Jeanip I will not come down as long as he is in this house."

"Yes, Miss", Misso said, as she left the room. She too felt sorry for her commander. He was only doing as commanded and for that he was being shunned by the person he loved the most.

Triton looked up at Europa and gave a low growl. "What, you do not agree with my decision? Are you taking his side? He had no right to bury her without my knowledge. I never want to see his face again."

Triton laid his head on the bed. "That's going to be hard to do once we get to Saint's Isle," Triton thought. "Jeanip's face will be about the ONLY one you will see."

"But Misso is right, I need to get my strength back," Europa said to Triton. "If I am going to leave next week and get away from this place, I need to be able to walk out on my own two feet."

"College?" thought Triton. "Wait until Jeanip tells you your college trip is cancelled indefinitely."

Swinging her feet over the side of the bed, Europa reached for the tea and drank half the cup. She devoured the soup, suddenly realizing how hungry she was. She washed the two shortbread cookies down with the remainder of the tea, wishing Misso had brought more cookies. Holding onto the night stand, and then the dresser, she took a few steps around the room. Her legs were weak, but they were supporting her. Holding onto the furniture and, she managed to shuffle her way to the bathroom. She longed for a shower but was afraid she was too weak to be able to stand up for one. She washed up the best she could, combed her hair and brushed her teeth. After changing into new pajamas, she crawled back into the bed, exhausted. In minutes she was sound asleep with Triton once again curled up along her side.

THE SECRET ROOM

True to her word, Europa remained upstairs when she awoke the following morning. Misso brought her breakfast, lunch and dinner, enabling her to enjoy her meal without the sight of Jeanip's face. Throughout the day she heard Jeanip's voice below in the house and reaffirmed her commitment to avoid him. Triton sat next to her and wondered how long she was going to remain upstairs, although her self-confinement made it easier on him to become Earon and help Jeanip plan for their move.

Evonic paid her a visit early in the morning to check on how she was doing. He gave her a clean bill of health and advised her to take some vitamin supplements for the next two weeks to help her body regain its strength. If she started to get headaches or became ill, he asked her to have someone notify him right away. He thought best not to tell her he was confined to the estate and would be staying at Minnos for a while.

Europa spent the morning reading a book, making a list of items to bring with her to college, another list for items she needed to buy and, finally sitting at her window overlooking the ocean, listening to the music on the MP3 player. She could see the dolphins not far from shore playing in the surf and wondered if Jack and Jill were amongst them. How she wished she could go swim with them now, but that would mean going downstairs and possibly seeing Jeanip.

Still believing her mother was alive when she arrived at the accident, she began to go over the events as she remembered them. She was sure her mother had spoken to her, had taken her hand. But both Jeanip and Evonic swore her recollection was false, that her mother was already dead when she arrived. She had always trusted Jeanip, yet something inside her said he was lying. And for some reason Evonic was backing him. She reached her hand up to her head and felt around for soreness. She found nothing; no tender spots, not scabbed over cuts, no nothing. If she had hit her head hard enough on the pavement to knock her out and cause a concussion, wouldn't there be a wound or some bruising? Somehow she had to find out the truth. But how?

Before she knew it the afternoon sun was starting to send its warmth through the window, making it too warm to continue to sit before it. She stood up and walked over to the bed. She picked up the book from her night stand she had started to read before Terrance occupied her free time, but she could not get re-interested in the subject matter. Terrance! With all that had happened since waking up she had forgotten about Terrance. She knew he must be going out of his mind with worry. Perhaps Jeanip or someone else from the estate had told him what had happened. But if that was true, why wasn't he there at her bedside? She knew nothing would keep Terrance away from her if he knew she had been injured. Had Jeanip banished him from the estate because she disobeyed her mother and went with him? She needed to call him, to let him know she was alright and to see if he was okay and still at the inn. The accident had happened almost a week ago – perhaps he wasn't even in town anymore. Perhaps he had gone to Michigan with his father, or worst yet, back home to Australia. She desperately needed to call him, but the only phones were downstairs and downstairs was where Jeanip was. She would have to think of another way to contact Terrance that did not involve going downstairs. Finding no solution to her problem, she thought it might be helpful to relax for a while. Picking up Triton's ball she stepped into the hallway to see if he had returned from his trip downstairs. As she looked down the empty hall, her breathing stopped for a moment when she saw her mother's bedroom door. Instantly, she felt it calling to her, beckoning her to come and hear the secrets it had to tell her. Without hesitation or thought, she walked the few steps down the hallway to the room. Standing before the ornate door she reached out her hand and entwined her fingers around its door knob and quietly opened the door. As the door opened the smell of her mother's perfume washed over her, making her grab onto the door frame to keep from collapsing. Waves of grief cascaded over her as she flipped on the double light switch just inside the door and staggered over to the bed, reaching it just before she collapsed.

"Mother," was all she could say as she fell onto the bed, torrents of tears and sobbing making it impossible for her to speak. She crawled up to the head of the bed and grabbed her mother's pillows, pulling them tightly to her as she breathed in her smell. Burying her face into their sweetness, she allowed her tears to freely flow until there were no more tears to be shed. Still holding on to the pillows, she sat up and wiped her eyes and face with her pajama sleeve, looking around the room at her mother's belongings. Each object held a vivid and cherished memory of the times she and Medaron spent together in that room discussing the exciting news about what happened in school that day or why some boy was not worth her tears when he broke her heart. Who was going to be there for her now? She had no relatives except for Jeanip and she certainly had no intention of confiding in him. Perhaps this was all a dream, and she was going to wake up any minute to discover her mother was still alive, was still there for her. It was hard for her to accept her mother's death since she never got to see her body, never got to kiss her goodbye, but the emptiness of the room confirmed she was awake and her mother was truly gone.

Europa sat on her mother's bed too emotionally drained to leave, too numb to be aware of time passing or of happenings outside of the room. It was not until the sound of a soft whine bringing her back to reality did she see Triton sitting just outside the room in the hallway staring at her. She had been in such a state of detachment she did not hear him come up the stairs or walk down the hall looking for her when she wasn't in her room. Not wanting to leave the room, or the smell of her mother, she patted the bed signaling for Triton to join her, but instead he gave her a confused look and barked, evidently not wanting her to be inside the room.

"Silent, Triton" she softly said. She knew if Triton started barking again Jeanip would surely come upstairs to investigate the cause. She rose and slowly walked across the floor toward the door, breathing in her mother's smell deeply as she prepared to exit. She flipped off the light switch as she left, not realizing there were two switches needing to be turned off. As she closed the door she saw a light shining through the wall. Where was it coming from? She turned to look at the light switch and realized she had not turned one of the switches off. She reached up and turned the second switch off and watched as the light behind the wall vanished. Wanting to make sure she really saw the light, she turned it on again and the light reappeared. Intrigued by this mysterious, unknown light she began to step back in the room to investigate when she heard Misso coming up the stairs with her dinner. She turned off the second switch and closed the door, reaching her bedroom just as Misso arrived at the top of the stairs.

"Your Majesty, I'm glad to see you are up and walking. Are you feeling better?"

"Yes, thank you, Misso. My legs are still a little unsteady, so I thought I would do some walking in the hallway for some exercise."

"I'm glad to hear that," Misso said. "Since you seem to be getting around better, would you like to eat downstairs this evening? I can help you down the stairs if you would like."

"No, Misso, I will eat it up here. I still have no desire to go downstairs."

Misso sat the tray on the small table in Europa's room and left. Europa sat down, suddenly realizing she was very hungry. As she ate she thought about that strange light in her mother's bedroom. Perhaps there was another room that branched off from her mother's bedroom she was not aware of. But if that were true, why had her mother never shown it to her? The house had many secrets and she believed she may have stumbled upon one of them. Now, with a new sense of purpose, she spent the remainder of the evening formulating a plan of investigation to learn where the light was originating. She allowed her imagination to run wild as she conjured up what secrets an undisclosed room might hold. Perhaps that was why Triton had not wanted her in Medaron's room; he was protecting whatever was behind the wall. She needed to time her next visit just right; a time when Triton would be outside for at least an hour and Birea nor Misso would not be coming upstairs. Emotionally drained from the ordeal in her mother's room, her plans of adventure soon turned into dreams of her mother as sleep overcame her.

Europa awoke early the next morning, showered and got dressed while going over her plan in her mind. She knew Misso brought her breakfast at eight each morning and impatiently watched the minutes tick by. Finally she heard Misso's footsteps upon the stairs and hurried to the door and opened it.

"Good morning. I am glad to see you are up and prepared for the day," Misso commented, as she walked through the doorway, surprised by Europa's sudden appearance. "I hope you slept well."

"Yes, thank you," Europa replied. "It looked like such a beautiful day I thought I would rise early and get some reading done." Thinking her opening of the door might have caused undue attention to herself she quickly added, "I hope I did not startle you by opening my door. It is just that I woke up starved this morning and could not wait until you brought up breakfast."

"You should have rung for me, Miss," Misso replied. "I would have brought your meal up earlier if I would have known."

"Actually, I had just finished getting dressed when I heard you," Europa stated, as she followed Misso over to the small table and sat down, ready to eat. She watched as Misso poured her a cup of coffee and uncovered her plate of scrambled eggs, bacon, hash browns, toasts and grits. She began to eat her breakfast to confirm her story of being extremely hungry.

"My, you are very hungry," Misso said, smiling at Europa's returned appetite. "It is so good to see you have your appetite back. If you are still hungry after you finish that I can bring you up some more."

"You are going to make me fat," Europa teased. "I am sure this will be more than sufficient."

"Very well. If you have no further need of me, I will take my leave," Misso stated. "Come, Triton, it's time for you to go outside." Misso swung her hand through the doorway, motioning for Triton to go downstairs.

With the sweetest look she could muster she looked at Misso and said, "Misso, I am sure Triton is getting tired of staying up here with me. I believe he would enjoy a few hours outside chasing a rabbit or two. He certainly can use the fresh air and exercise."

Triton hesitated, wondering if Europa was trying to get rid of him for a while, then decided it was a ludicrous idea. What trouble could she get into up here? Besides, fresh air sounded a lot better than another boring day watching Europa read or sleep. Plus, a couple of hours outside would give him a chance to talk with Jeanip about their move to Saint's Isle. Not waiting for a second invitation, he eagerly ran down the stairs.

Europa continued eating her breakfast until she heard the side door open and close. Grabbing her breakfast food, she carried it into the bathroom and flushed it down the toilet. After returning the dishes to their tray, she ran over to her bed and stuffed pillows under her covers, giving her bed the appearance she was beneath them. She knew if Misso came back before she returned she would think Europa had fallen back asleep and would not disturb her.

Looking around the room to assure everything was in order, Europa closed her door, then hurried down the hallway to her mother's room. As she entered, the smell of her mother once again overpowered her, bringing tears to her eyes. Knowing she had no time for nostalgia, she shook her head to clear it and quickly switched on the second light switch. As before, a light appeared behind the wall shining through several small cracks. She ran over and began searching for some type of opening or a door, but there was only a wall. Knowing there had to be an entrance somewhere, she followed the wall to her left until she reached the other wall: dead end. Retracing her steps, she followed the wall to the right until it ended at her mother's walk-in closet. She opened the closet door and saw a dim light visible behind her mother's clothes. Quickly she pushed the clothes aside and stared at a secret door now visible in the wall. Excitedly, she reached out and grabbed the door latch and pushed down on its tongue, but it was locked. Remembering her mother always kept a set of keys in her top dresser drawer, she rushed over to the dresser and retrieved them. Holding her breathe, she began trying the keys until she heard the lock open. Once more she pushed down on the latch and pulled the door, rejoicing as she felt it open to reveal a small stairway leading upwards. Dropping the keys into her pajama pants' pocket, she carefully climbed the stairs, cringing as they creaked under her weight.

When she reached the top step she stopped and stared in disbelief. Before her was a large, unfinished attic with pairs of wooden beams above forming 'V's as they held up the roof. The walls contained no boarding, only bare wooden posts spaced equally apart. The floor consisted of wooden planks nailed together in various directions. There was no window to let in light, only a bare light bulb hanging from the ceiling. How different this room was from the rest of the house, she thought. It was primitive, unfinished, resembling a room that had hastily been constructed. As she continued to look around she was amazed to see a treasure of priceless belongings; the attic was filled with countless antique furnishings, golden statues of Egyptian gods, ornate crystal vases, something resembling a pirate's chest filled with gold coins, paintings, sculptures, jewel-filled crowns and shelves filled with books and old clothes. She stepped forward and another light automatically turned on at the far end of the room to reveal a round antique oak table on which an Orb, similar to the amulet she wore around her neck, rested suspended several inches above the table. Forgetting the other treasures filling the room, she walked toward the Orb, feeling almost as if it was calling to her. She stared at the Orb and watched the threads of color swirl within it as it floated above the table. She reached out her hands and, without thinking or hesitation, placed them upon the Orb. Sensing her touch, the Orb began to glow and hum softly while strings of lavender, purple, blue and yellow light flared out and began to entwine over her hands and up her arms. Startled, she yanked her hands away and the Orb became quiet once more. Fearing it was one of Jeanip's security devices, she turned and walked over to a stack of oil paintings and began to look through them, leaving the Orb for future investigations. She shuffled through the paintings noting some were hundreds of years old according to the signature dates, yet all were of the same two people – either together or alone, a man and a woman. She cupped her hand over her mouth as she realized the woman in every painting was her mother.

"But that is not possible," she whispered. "That would make my mother hundreds of years old."

She now turned her attention to the man in the picture, wondering if he too was familiar. At first she didn't recognize him but, as she scrutinized his face further, she thought he resembled the picture of her father her mother kept in the small locket she wore. She discovered a painting with a golden engraved plate attached to the lower frame. Unable to read the plate she lifted the painting from between the others. Now able to read the inscription she read "1702 - Enok and Medaron Waters." Enok - that was her father's name. This man in the painting and the man in her mother's locket were the same person? Her father? How could her parents be in a painting from 1702?

Now intrigued by her discoveries, she turned her attention to a nearby box containing three papyrus scrolls. Carefully lifting one out, she began to open it but stopped as it began to crumble in her hand. Realizing it was very old she carried it to a nearby table and delicately laid it down. With as much gentleness as possible she began to unroll the scroll but halted when it began to reveal another picture of her mother dressed in a purple tunic with a pyramid in the background.

"What is going on?" she said. "This has to be hundreds of years old." She rerolled the scroll and carefully replaced it in the box.

Feeling she could not handle seeing any more ancient pictures of her mother, she crossed the room to a pine wood shelf containing papers and books. She removed one of the papers, unfolded it and saw a detailed map of Minnos showing the cottage and the out buildings along with a secret tunnel leading to a cave beside the ocean. She had lived at Minnos all her life and had never seen or heard of a cave or a secret tunnel. She noticed some strange markings on the map and squinted her eyes in an attempt to determine what they were. They appeared to be some form of writing but in a language she had never seen before.

Feeling the map offered little information, she sat it aside and reached for the next one. It was the deed to Minnos from 1658 with the signatures of the original owners, which read "Enok and Medaron Waters". Below their signatures was the signature of a witness – Jeanip Smith. She knew Medaron's and Jeanip's signatures and there was no doubt the signatures on the deed were theirs. Was Jeanip part of this too?

Almost afraid to open the third paper, she breathed a sigh of relief when she saw a diagram of a large Complex containing many houses and buildings, as well as gardens and walkways. And something called an Exit Chamber. She noticed the diagram was very detailed, indicating everything in the Complex, no matter how minute, yet there were no trees or streets indicated. She also noticed it contained the same strange writing she had found on the Minnos map. Suddenly her eyes caught sight of an old worn diary which had been buried beneath the papers. She sat the Complex diagram aside as she stared at the name inscribed on the cover – Medaron. Her hand began to tremble as she removed the diary from its hiding place. Of all the items she found so far, this item filled her with the most anxiety. She feared what secrets her mother had recorded in this diary, what unknown information would be revealed. Taking a deep breath, she opened the book and recognized her mother's handwriting, but it too was in the same weird language. She sighed and allowed her shoulders to drop as disappointment displaced her sense of foreboding as she gazed at the strange writings. Whatever secrets were contained in the diary would remain so unless she could discover a way to decipher the words. She began to thumb through the pages seeing each contained the same strange writing; then suddenly the writings turned into English. She stopped and read:

February 27, 4051-3 Arrived at Minnos. Enok remains at the Complex. Believed to be safe here – no Terrians seen for 500 years. Europa to be born human in 6 months. My son will be her guard."

Born human? What did that mean? How else would she be born? Her son? What son? Did she have a brother?

Europa felt faint. She was still weak from her extended sleep and the discoveries she had just stumbled upon were making her head spin. She needed to sit down but was now suddenly afraid of being found in the attic, afraid someone would see her with the diary. Quickly, she grabbed the maps and the land deed, along with her mother's diary, and hid them underneath her pajama top. She rushed down the stairs, not worrying if they creaked or not. She closed the door, returned her mother's clothes to their original position, closed the walk-in closet door and exited her mother's bedroom as swiftly as possible, being sure to switch off the second light. She quietly closed her mother's door and turned to return to her room. As she turned she almost dropped her hidden belongings when she saw Triton lying outside her closed bedroom door. When he saw Europa exit from Medaron's room he stood and stared at her, then approached her and began to sniff around her pajamas, as if he suspected she had something hidden under them.

Europa thought she heard a voice inside her head ask, "What were you doing in Mother's room?" Afraid to look into Triton's eyes, she walked down the hall past Triton acting as if nothing was out of the ordinary. She entered her room and closed her bedroom door, barring Triton from entering. Knowing she would have only minutes before she would have to let Triton in, she quickly ran to the bathroom, searching for a secure place to hide her treasures. Seeing nothing sufficient for hiding things, she reached down and pulled out the bottom vanity drawer. As she hoped, there was just enough space between the drawer guide and the floor to hold the items. She carefully placed her attic treasures inside and then replaced the drawer, feeling confident they were safely hidden. She then scurried to her bed and pulled out the pillows and blankets that had served as her sleeping body while she was gone. Looking around to make sure everything looked normal, she walked to the door to let Triton in. To her surprise he was gone. Several minutes later Misso brought Europa her lunch.

"Misso, have you seen Triton?"

"I believe he went outside with Jeanip a few minutes ago."

Triton returned an hour later and hopped onto the bed while staring at Europa, as if he knew something. She wanted to read more of her mother's diary but she couldn't take the chance of someone seeing it. Plus, for some reason unknown to her, she felt uncomfortable with Triton in the room watching. It was almost as if he was spying on her, which she knew was impossible. She tried to find things to occupy her time, but her thoughts kept returning to the diary and the passage she had read. She thought of sending Triton outside again or barring him from her room, but she feared such actions might arouse suspicion or, even worse, bring Jeanip upstairs to investigate her actions. Grabbing her book, she sat on the bed and pretended to read while trying to think of a way to get time alone to do more reading of the diary. After several minutes she realized the solution was very simple - all she needed to do was indulge in a leisurely bath. That would give her time alone to scan through the diary's pages and no one, not even Triton, would think it odd after what she had been through lately. She waited until Misso returned to retrieve the dirty luncheon dishes and told her she thought she would soak in a luxury bath for a while. Misso thought it was an excellent idea and went to run a warm bath for her. While Misso was busy in the bathroom Europa quickly grabbed a pen and secretly slid it inside her pajama pocket.

"Your bath is ready, Your Highness," Misso stated. "Would you like me to bring you a cup of warm tea to enjoy while you soak in the tub? Or perhaps a warm glass of milk?"

"No, thank you. I think I am just going to lay in the water and enjoy its warmth," she replied, as she stepped inside the bathroom, Triton following right behind her. "Where do you think you are going?" she asked. "You know this is the one place you are not allowed. Now go wait for me on the bed." She held out her hand, pointing toward the bed. Giving a snort with his nose, Triton turned and left the bathroom, hearing the door close and lock behind him. He had never known Europa to lock the bathroom door before. She definitely was acting peculiar and he was sure she was up to something.

Europa retrieved the diary from its hiding place and carefully slipped into the water, being sure not to get the diary wet. She skimmed past the pages written in the strange language, stopping once again when she reached the first English written page. She bypassed the pages she had read earlier regarding her mother's arrival at Minnos and skimmed past the passages describing the daily activities of Minnos. She stopped on August 19th and read:

> *August 19, 4051-3   Europa to be born soon.*
> *Earon remains in human form until she is born, then he*
> *will transform. I will miss having my son to talk to. He*
> *has been such a comfort.*

Remains in human form? What form would he be in? What did 'he will transform' mean? Transform into what? She read on.

> *August 23, 4051-3   Europa born.   Beautiful*
> *human girl. No complications, no breathing problems*
> *or side effects that can be detected. I pray JeffRa's*
> *curse has been avoided. Jeanip travels to inform Enok.*
> *Wish he was here.*

So her father was not present for her birth. Was he at sea? Why did her mother mention her being human again? What was this curse? Had one followed them from their homeland that caused birth defects?

She bypassed the entries regarding her childhood and how much her mother missed her father.

> *January 15, 4053-3   Jeanip returns from the*
> *CComplex. Enok sends his love. Breathing problem*
> *still not corrected so he is unable to join us but hopes to*
> *do so soon.*

September 8, 4054 3   Jeanip summoned urgently to Complex.   Returns with devastating news. Complication in treatment for Enok's breathing problem resulting in his passing.   How do I continue for years on this planet without him?   Europa and Earon are now my only source of joy.

Complications in treatment? Her mother told her that her father died at sea searching for treasure. What does she mean by 'this planet'? What planet should she be on? And why does she keep mentioning this Earon? Did he die also?

After her father's death there were several entries over the years, mostly about the daily activities of Minnos and a couple references to how much she missed Enok. Then it appeared as if her mother started writing again several weeks ago.

August 1, 4112-3 Europa soon to be 20.   The leadership of our people should revert to her as I step down.   It cannot.   How can she govern a people she does not even know exists?   She has no idea of who she really is.

"Who I really am? Who am I?" Europa wondered. "And what people? I thought most were wiped out during the war." She continued to read.

August 9, 4112-3 Should be planning a gala event for Europa's birthday with dignitaries and state officials, not a small family gathering.

Dignitaries and State Officials? Why would they be invited to her birthday celebration? She thought perhaps in her mother's country birthdays were a much bigger deal than they were in the United States.

August 21, 4112-3   Woke with uneasiness. Something is wrong but I cannot tell what.   Jeanip has us on high alert.

August 23, 4112-3 Europa's friends report a deer with strange eyes being seen in vicinity.   Europa also saw it and thought its eyes glowed red.   Glowing red eyes mean only one thing – a shape shifter.   I know of no Waters who would be in transformation without mine or Jeanip's knowledge.   I fear somehow one Terrian still survives. Are my children in danger?

Shape shifter? Why would her mother think that? Such creatures do not exist. What children? There is only she and no one else!

August 24, 4112-3 Jeanip and males have gone to discover if the deer is Terrian. I am afraid.

Afraid? Her mother was never afraid one day in her life. Why was she so spooked by this deer down from the mountains?

Europa turned the remaining pages only to find they were blank. Then she realized the last entry was the day her mother was killed and there would be no more entries. Suddenly stricken once more with grief, she dropped the diary. It landed with a plop on the floor and fell open to a page containing numerous numerical entries. She reached down and picked up the diary carefully reviewing the page. She gasped as she realized the entries were the names of banks, account numbers, passwords and dollar amounts all written in her mother's handwriting,

"This cannot be" she said, as she looked over the dollar amounts. "There must be several billion dollars listed here."

She closed the diary and placed it on the floor. Closing her eyes, she slipped down into the warm water. The diary did not give her answers, only more questions; questions having impossible answers. She needed answers, but whom could she go to. She thought of contacting Anna, Suzie or Rannie, but she was becoming paranoid and unsure if she could even trust them. The only person who could help her would be someone who was impartial, someone who didn't know her past, someone like Terrance. Sitting straight up in the bathtub she said out loud, "Somehow I must see Terrance. He is the only one I can trust to help me find out what this diary means."

Europa stepped out of the bathtub and quickly dressed. She knew the only way she would be able to see Terrance was to go into town. She would go under the pretense of buying things she needed for college. She had already written a list earlier so it was a plausible reason. She knew Triton would have to accompany her so she would have to find a way to talk to Terrance without Triton realizing what she was saying. She still did not believe it wise to trust the canine.

As she exited the bathroom, Europa heard footsteps in the hallway. She looked out and saw Birea returning from her mother's room, a key in her hand. Had she locked the door? Her mother's room had never been locked in twenty years. Had Jeanip somehow discovered she had been in there? But how? No one saw her in her mother's room except . . . Triton!

"Birea, could you come here for a moment?"

"Did you need something, Your Majesty?"

"Do you know where my mother's car keys are?

"Probably downstairs on the key hook where they normally are. Why do you ask?"

"I thought I would drive into town and purchase some of the items I need for college. I only have a few weeks to get everything packed and ready to take with me."

"We still have plenty of time for all that," Birea stated, looking a little nervous. "I am not sure you should overexert yourself. You've only been up for a few days."

"Oh, I am feeling so much better," Europa responded, while wondering why Birea was resistant to her going into town. "I thought the fresh air and change of scenery would do Triton and me some good."

Seeing no way to avoid telling her the truth, Birea said, "I'm sorry, Europa, but you cannot go into town. No one is allowed to leave the estate, or enter it."

"What do you mean no one can leave or enter?" Europa demanded, shocked at what Birea had said. "Are you telling me I am stuck here?"

"That is correct. All the gates have been locked and the fences have been electrified."

"By whose orders?" Europa yelled, already knowing the answer.

"Jeanip issued the order immediately after your mother died."

Europa froze for a minute. Birea said "died" not "killed". Granted, Birea was not from this country and sometimes had trouble with the English language, but she didn't believe that was the case here. "Died" indicated that her mother HAD been alive for an unknown time period after the accident. And that meant she remembered correctly - her mother was alive when she arrived at the accident scene.

"Where is Jeanip?" Europa demanded, a tone of authority Birea had never heard in the young woman's voice before.

"I believe he is in the kitchen. Would you like me to ask him to come up to see you?"

127

"No," Europa stated, marching past Birea heading downstairs to confront Jeanip.

"Wait, Europa. I'll tell him you need to speak to him," Birea said, trying to avert Europa from going down to the kitchen.

Europa said nothing, just continued down the stairs and stomped straight into the kitchen. As she entered she saw Jeanip sitting at the kitchen table, but he was not alone. Sitting with him was a young man, probably in his late twenties, with dark curly hair and green eyes. Startled for the moment, Europa stood there saying nothing, staring at the young man. Strangers never came to the cottage, even in good times. Who was this man? As she continued to look at him she was shocked to realize he had her mother's features, especially her eyes. If she had not known better she would have thought it was her mother's eyes she stared into, not a stranger's.

"Europa," Jeanip stuttered, standing up from the table, clearly startled by her sudden appearance. He saw her looking at Earon. Thinking hastily, Jeanip said, "Europa, I'd like you to meet your cousin, Earon Waters."

Earon stood up also, extending his hand to Europa. "Nice to see you again, Your Majesty. It has been many years."

Earon Waters? My Cousin? She had always been told they had no living relatives. And wasn't the name Earon supposed to be the name of her unknown brother? But she had no time for this nonsense now.

Ignoring Earon's outstretched hand, Europa turned her gaze to Jeanip. "Jeanip, I need the keys to my mother's car. I want to go into town to purchase some items I need for college. Birea tells me no one is allowed to leave the estate. Is this true?"

"Yes, Europa, that is true," Jeanip answered, the look of a Commander on his face. "You cannot leave the estate."

"Are you telling me I am a prisoner here?"

"No, not at all," Jeanip replied. He could see the anger in her eyes and knew he needed to carefully pick his words. "You are behind a wall of protection to ensure you remain safe."

"Safe? From who? Or what? "Europa screamed at Jeanip, as she glared at him. "Are there more deer running around waiting to jump in front of my car?"

"I'm sorry, Europa. It is for your protection and nonnegotiable. You must remain behind these walls."

128

"We will see about that," Europa said, as she walked to the telephone to call someone, anyone to help her. When she lifted the phone to her ear she was met only with silence. The telephone was dead. "What's wrong with the phone?" she asked, staring directly at Jeanip.

"So the family may have time to grieve properly, the telephone has temporarily been disconnected." Jeanip answered, his voice totally without a hint of emotion.

Europa threw the phone down. She turned and headed for the front door. She was leaving even if she had to jump off the cliff and swim to town. She turned the door knob, but it did not budge. It was locked.

"As your queen I order you, Jeanip, to open this door," she insisted with as much authority in her voice as she could manage. She remained standing at the door, her back facing Jeanip.

"Once again, I'm sorry Your Majesty. Security protocols already in place as decreed by both your parents takes priority over and supersedes your orders. Therefore the door remains locked and I cannot permit you to leave the protection of the cottage. You must remain inside until I determine it is safe for you to go outside."

"You cannot do this," Europa screamed, turning her head toward Jeanip, her eyes on fire with rage. "You would never do this if my mother was here."

"But she's not," Jeanip softly answered. "And I have to assure you will be."

His statement sent a wave of grief shivering through Europa's body. She turned and ran upstairs, sobbing as she went.

"And Europa, your mother's room is off limits for the time being." Jeanip heard her run up the stairs and slam the bedroom door behind her.

"Jeanip, you need to tell her something," Earon said, as he looked at Jeanip. He could see the hurt starting to show on Jeanip's face. Unlike Europa, Earon knew Jeanip was only following Medaron's and Enok's orders, orders that were making Europa hate Jeanip even more. He also knew the sorrow Jeanip was feeling for causing Europa so much pain and anguish. "Jeanip, you cannot keep silent any longer. You have to tell her the truth."

Jeanip turned to face Earon. "That is not my decision to make. I have been given a set of instructions to follow which will assure her safety. I cannot deviate from them."

"Then at least tell her why she is being kept behind locked doors, why she cannot go outside," Earon instructed. "I give you permission to tell her that. Tell her about the possibility her mother was deliberately killed. Perhaps even tell her the assassin was really after her, not her mother. Give her something to hold on to, or I can assure you, you will lose her forever. And even worse, I fear, Jeanip, she will find some way out of this house and she will run. And if she runs we may never find her before the Terrians do. At this point the only way to keep her safe is to tell her a little bit of the truth."

"You sound like your father," Jeanip replied. "I can see Enok's teachings in you. He always said in a difficult situation someone is more apt to follow your instructions if they understand the reason behind them. And I believe your assumption of her running is correct. And I cannot protect her if she goes outside these gates. Therefore I will take your advice and accept your authority to give me permission to tell her why she must remain here and something of who she really is." As he stood up he added, "You are going to make a great leader someday, Earon. As great as your father."

A sense of pride swelled in Earon upon hearing Jeanip's words. It was a great compliment to be compared to Enok. As Jeanip turned to go speak to Europa upstairs, Earon added, "And while you are at it, you might want to tell her college has been cancelled for at least this year."

Without slowing his step as he went upstairs, Jeanip responded, "Aren't you supposed to be a canine?" When he reached her bedroom, he knocked, then entered. He was actually surprised the door had not been locked barring his entrance. Upon entering he saw her laying on her bed, crying. "Europa, I need to speak with you."

"Get out," Europa whispered, too drained by emotions to say more.

Jeanip sat down on the bed. "Europa, I know this has not been easy for you. And I know you do not understand why I insist you remain inside. I am not doing this out of meanness, or any desire to hurt you. I am doing it because I love you and want to protect you the only way I know how. But I do understand you deserve an explanation, so please hear me out."

Jeanip took a deep breath, then said "Do you remember when you were little your mother always called you her little princess? She told you that you were the daughter of a king and queen from a land where a great war had been fought for centuries which resulted in your great-great-grandparents having to settle here at Minnos. And, even though it was believed it was safe here, there was the possibility their enemy still existed and would find them one day. To keep their little princess safe, your parents enacted strict security protocols and rules, along with the stipulation someone would be with you every moment to protect you. That someone was Birea and your guard dog, Triton. Do you remember your mother telling you these things?"

Europa's sobbing lessened. Jeanip heard her utter a faint, "Yes, I remember."

"What your mother told you is true, but not the entire story." Taking another deep breath, Jeanip continued. "I am going to tell you the complete story so you can understand your past and realize why we have such severe security rules."

"Many, many years ago there were two royal brothers who were the best of friends. But the younger brother began to feel left out, unappreciated and became very jealous. He plotted to destroy his older brother and take the crown for his own. The younger brother's plot was discovered by their father and the younger brother was exiled to a hostile place to live out his days. His life was hard and each day he lived it made him hate his brother and father more, blaming them for his misfortune. Those two brothers were your great-great-grandfather and your great-great-uncle. Your great-great-uncle retaliated by raising an army and declaring war on your family, promising to annihilate every Waters alive or born. He waged war on us for many years until our homeland was destroyed and uninhabitable. Your great-great-grandparents were forced to flee with the survivors who remained, but our enemy pursued them, vowing to never stop until every last Waters was dead. For years our people fled from country to country, fighting off each attack until it was believed our enemy had all been eradicated. Feeling it now safe to settle somewhere, your great-great-grandparents moved here and began a new life. Several generations later, that new life produced you. But always hanging over us was the possibility that somewhere out there the enemy still hunted us, still endeavored to keep their leader's promise of the complete annihilation of our race. To assure this never happened, severe security measures were put in place to protect the monarchs, as you've seen on this estate. Your parents knew, as did your former grandparents, that the one person they would most want to assassinate would be the next leader of our people, which in this case is you, Europa. You are the next monarch."

"Me?" Europa said, sitting up and looking at Jeanip in disbelief.

131

"Perhaps we became too complacent in believing our enemy no longer existed, that we were safe, that you were safe. But our belief was in error. I was in error. We did not know at least one of the descendants of our enemy, your great-great-uncle, was still alive. Even though your great-great-grandparents had covered their travels, he somehow managed to trace your family here to Minnos. He set out to fulfill his great-great-grandfather's vow of ending your family's dynasty by ending your life." Europa held her breath, hoping what she was starting to fear would not be confirmed by Jeanip's words. "We did not know he was here, watching you, waiting for his chance. His chance came the day your mother took your truck to town. On her return she encountered him on the road where the bend is. He believed it was you in the truck. He attacked, causing your mother's accident and her death."

"No," Europa whispered. "He killed her thinking it was me?"

"Yes, I'm afraid so, Europa. I know this is not an easy thing to hear." Jeanip watched Europa, seeing she now realized what had happened, that she had been the assassin's target, not her mother. "Our sworn enemy was also killed in the accident. Unfortunately, with his death ended the possibility of finding out if more of his kind still exists. They may still be out there waiting to finish what he started out to do – to end your life. Until I can confirm if our enemy still hunts us, still hunts you, the only way I can assure your safety is to keep you here inside this house, to keep the estate on lockdown. I am working on a plan to take you somewhere where I know you will be safe. It is another estate your parents built called Saint's Isle."

"Saint's Isle?"

"Yes, Saint's Isle. Your parents built it when your mother discovered she was pregnant with you. They built it as a safety precaution, a place to go in case our enemy ever reappeared." Europa sat up in bed, looking at Jeanip for the first time since she had awoken to learn of her mother's burial. "Europa, remember you are no longer a princess but the Head Monarch of your people. As the only living female child of your parents, you became Supreme Monarch the day your mother died. And I am bound by my duty to protect you and keep you safe, no matter what it takes. I failed your mother. I will not fail you too."

"My mother died because of me," Europa said in a monotone voice that sent a shiver down Jeanip's spine. She lowered her eyes once more as the feeling of responsibility swept over her. "If only I had not disobeyed her and gone into town."

"No, not because of you. Never think that, Your Majesty," Jeanip reached out and gently held her chin in his right hand, raising her head so he could look directly into her eyes. "Europa, do you hear what I am saying? You were not responsible for your mother's death in any way. Because you were his target and he got you and your mother mixed up does not make her death your fault. Europa, do you understand that?"

"Yes," Europa answered, as she removed Jeanip's hand from underneath her chin. Keeping her gaze on him, she asked, "How long will I have to remain under security? Is there any chance I will still be able to attend college this year?"

"No, not this year. But hopefully you will be able to attend next year. But if our enemy still lives, trust me, they will be hunted down and destroyed. You will be able to return to a normal life, I promise you. But for now, I need you to abide by my decisions, to do as I ask. Will you do that? Will you remain inside where you are safe? Will you be the monarch I know you can be and put your people's needs above your own?"

Europa looked at Jeanip, still angry with him for her mother's burial, but she could not dispute his reasoning. He was right – as Supreme Monarch she needed to survive. She stared at Jeanip, a part of her beginning to remember how much she loved this man, this soldier who was trying so hard to protect her. No matter what he had felt compelled to do, she had no doubt he loved her as much as he had loved her mother.

"Thank you for telling me the truth, Jeanip," Europa stated. "Knowing the reason for my confinement does not make it easier, but it does make it tolerable. Why didn't Mother ever tell me more about our past and the fact that someone might be out there wanting us dead?"

"She didn't want you burdened with the knowledge these people may be out there hunting you, especially since we believed they were all dead. Your mother wanted you to have as normal a life as possible, a life free of war, free of worry, free of being afraid. She hoped you would never have to know the horrible truth of our past."

"Since I am the last living monarch of our people, I will do as you ask and remain inside. Now, if you would, please leave my room. I still have no desire to be in your company."

"As you wish," Jeanip stated, standing up and giving the customary salute to his monarch by placing his hand to his forehead. "I take my leave of you, Your Majesty." Jeanip walked toward the door noticing Triton had been sitting in the hallway observing the conversation. "Looks like Triton is waiting to resume his mission of protecting you."

Triton entered the room and jumped onto the bed to sit next to Europa. As Jeanip began to close the door behind him, Europa thought of a question she needed an answer to.

"Jeanip, one moment please."

"Yes, Your Majesty?" Jeanip said, reopening the door.

"I was wondering if you could tell me what any of my grandparents' names were."

"Yes, of course. Your great grandparent's names were Tyrigg and Meeleena Waters. And your grandparent's names were Enoquin and Messor Waters."

"Do you know the name of my great grandparents that settled on Minnos?"

"I believe their names were Treenok and Medaron," Jeanip replied. "But your great grandfather became known as Enok. Your father was named after him."

"And what country were my great-great grandparents from?"

"From a country that no longer exists." With that said, Jeanip closed the door and left.

Europa smiled, reached down and scratched Triton on the head. "So, you really are for my protection, you silly dog." Triton licked her hand and wagged his tail. It was good to see Europa smiling again.

Jeanip gave Europa a lot to ponder. She tried to mentally match up the information Jeanip gave her to the items she had found in her mother's attic, especially the entries in her diary. Still fearing Jeanip would take the items away if it was discovered she had them, she decided not to bring them out into her room. Nor could she use the excuse again of taking a bath in order to spend a lengthy amount of time in her bathroom to study them. Wanting to be sure she would not forget her grandparents' names and the history of her family, she quickly retrieved a notebook from her desk and entered the facts Jeanip just told her. Jeanip's information at least gave her the answer to one part of the puzzle. Her grandparents who had settled Minnos had the same names as her parents. It was their names on the land deed, not her parents. At least that was what she made herself believe.

SHAPE SHIFTERS

Terrance continued to search through the items he found in his father's room. In one of the journals he came across a reference he had not noticed previously, regarding a book written by a local Native American about a race of shape shifters his ancestors had known. Next to the reference his father had written "shape shifters –Waters?" Why would his father think the Waters would have something to do with shape shifters? He scanned the next few pages but could find no other reference of the book. Grabbing a slip of paper, he quickly scribbled the author's name and book title and headed to the local library.

To his delight and amazement, the library had a copy of the book in their reference section. He quickly retrieved the book, sat down at one of the library tables and began to skim through the pages. The book was a collection of tribal stories passed down through the generations. One short chapter relayed a story passed down from over three hundred years ago about six fair skinned, very tall foreigners who appeared at the edge of the ocean one day. Having never seen white men before, the natives believed them to be Spirits of the Water and invited them into their camp. Several days after the strangers' arrival, the chief's only daughter was taken by a neighboring warring tribe. Fearing for his daughter's life, the chief asked the six Water Spirits to use their powers to defeat their enemy and save his daughter. Valuing the tribe's friendship, the strangers agreed to help and left the camp. The next day the chief's daughter came riding into camp on the back of a large white stallion, accompanied by five other horses. As the daughter dismounted, all six horses transformed into the strangers and confirmed the tribe's belief they were Water Spirits, shape shifters. The daughter recounted the story of her rescue, how the strangers transformed into beings of light that swam through the air to attack the village and how with a mighty blast of their hand, slew their enemy. As reward for saving the chief's daughter, the Water Spirits' leader asked they be allowed to settle on the vanquished enemy's land, a meadow set high on a cliff by the ocean. The chief and elders agreed, but with the stipulation one of the spirits would marry his daughter and remain with the tribe to protect them for all time. The strangers became known as the Light Walkers, since it was believed they were born of the sky and water. There was no mention of their names or where the land was they settled on.

Terrance knew many native cultures had stories regarding shape shifting so he wasn't sure why this particular story interested his father or how he could have made a connection to the Waters. He looked at the publication date to see if the author might still be alive. It was published in 1972, which meant the author could be alive and hopefully living in the area. Carrying the book, he proceeded to the front desk.

"Excuse me," he said, trying to get the librarian's attention.

"Can I help you, sir?"

"Yes, I was wondering if you knew anything about the author of this book." Terrance laid the book on the counter so the librarian could see it. "A Mr. Thomas Dark Feather. The jacket states he lived in this area when the book was published. Do you know if he still resides here?"

"Yes, he lives out on the reservation."

Terrance's heart began to beat faster. Perhaps this Mr. Dark Feather could give him some answers about what his father was doing, why he was interested in the Waters family. "Do you know how I can get in touch with him? I really would like to meet with him and discuss one of his stories."

"My uncle seldom leaves the reservation," the librarian said, as she smiled when she saw the surprised look on Terrance's face.

"It's very important," Terrance said, trying to quickly figure out what he could say to get her to ask her uncle. "I think one of the stories in his book may have a connection to the Waters family." Terrance thought of telling the librarian it concerned Mrs. Waters' death but decided against it, thinking she might think he was crazy or something.

"You know the Waters?"

"Yes, I'm a close personnel friend of Europa's. I met Mrs. Waters at Europa's birthday party the other night."

"I am seeing my uncle tonight," the librarian said, her curiosity peaked by Terrance's mention of the Waters family. "I will pass on your request. What is your name?"

"I'm sorry, I forgot to introduce myself. My name is Terrance Landers."

"If my uncle agrees to meet you I will call you and advise you where and when. But I must warn you, Mr. Landers, my uncle seldom talks to outsiders. But since you are a friend of the Waters he may make an exception. How may I get in touch with you?"

"I'm staying at the inn. Here's my phone number." Terrance scribbled his phone number on a piece of paper and handed it to the librarian. "Please tell your uncle I REALLY need to talk with him."

"As I said, Mr. Landers, I will pass on your request."

"Thank you so much. I really appreciate it," Terrance said, as he held out his hand and shook hers. Terrance returned the book to the reference shelf then left the library to return to his room. He hoped the author would agree to see him and shed some light on the ever bigger mystery Terrance had stumbled upon.

That night, as Europa slept, the Orb in Medaron's attic began to glow and hum softly. As it grew in brightness, the amulet around Europa's neck also began to glow a lavender light. Europa began to dream of beautiful luminous beings floating through a sea of lilac waters filled with strands of different colors. The beings were long and slender, with three sets of large translucent wings overlapping each other. The upper section of the body consisted of an oval shaped head containing two large lilac eyes and a smiling mouth. In lieu of hair, strings of white light pearls cascaded down from the top of the head and framed their face. She noticed two of the creatures wore amulets like the one she wore around her neck. Although she did not see their lips move, she could hear them speaking to each other in an unknown language. Abruptly the beings vanished and were replaced with a hideous brown face with two red glowing eyes. Startled, Europa woke up; frightened, but not sure why. The Orb in the attic went silent and stopped glowing, as did the amulet around her neck.

Terrance was awakened by a phone call the next morning from the librarian informing him her uncle was willing to meet with him that morning at ten in the inn's dining room, if he was available. Terrance looked at his watch – nine-fifteen. He told her he would be there. He quickly showered and dressed, grabbed some inn stationery to write on and dashed down to the dining room. When he arrived he saw the librarian already seated at a table by the window with a gray haired older gentleman. He assumed the man with her was her uncle and the author of the book.

As Terrance approached the table, the librarian saw him and gestured for him to join them. "I'd like you to meet my uncle, Thomas Dark Feather."

Terrance held out his hand to shake the older gentleman's. "It is a pleasure to meet you, Mr. Dark Feather. My name is Terrance, Terrance Landers."

At the mention of his last name, Terrance saw Mr. Dark Feather's eyes narrow as he scrutinized the young man. "Yes, my niece told me your name. By any chance, are you related to Jeffrey Landers?"

"Why, yes," Terrance answered, astonished Mr. Landers would know his father. "He's my father."

"Come, Trina, we are done here," Mr. Dark Feather announced to his niece, as he stood up and began to walk away from the table.

Not knowing why he was leaving, Terrance quickly ran after the author. "Please, Mr. Dark Feather, did I say something wrong?" Terrance looked at the librarian, his eyes pleading to her for an explanation. She looked at him and shrugged her shoulders, indicating she did not know either why her uncle had decided to leave. "Mr. Dark Feather, if I could just have a moment of your time," Terrance stated in the most polite voice he could summon. "I would like to talk to you regarding the Waters' family and one of your stories."

Mr. Dark Feather stopped, turned and looked at Terrance. "Since you are a friend of the Waters I will give you a moment." He walked up to Terrance, put his hand over Terrance's heart and closed his eyes. As had happened previously when Mrs. Waters held his hand at Minnos, a wave of warmth quickly raced through Terrance's body then retreated. After a few moments Mr. Dark Feather opened his eyes and smiled. "I can see your heart is pure, that you are on a quest of knowledge." His smile turned into a frown as he said, "Your father's heart was dark and angry. I would not tell him what he wanted to know. Has he sent you here to trick me into telling you?"

"No, Sir," Terrance stammered. "I swear this to be true. I haven't spoken to my father in months. He has no idea I asked to meet with you or that I even know of your book."

"Why did you ask to meet me, Mr. Landers?" Thomas Dark Feather asked, his face expressionless as he studied the young man before him. Unexpectedly, a feeling of importance coursed through Thomas's body, a feeling that this man had an extremely important part to play in the scenario soon to unfold. He needed to proceed cautiously and try to grasp the meaning of this feeling and determine the importance of this young man.

"I have been trying to connect with my father, but we keep missing each other. Could you tell me when you saw him last?" Terrance asked, picking his words carefully so as not to upset Mr. Dark Feather.

"I never met him in person," Mr. Dark Feather replied. "We talked briefly on the telephone. VERY briefly."

"I see."

"What question do you seek an answer to, Mr. Landers?" Mr. Dark Father asked, the feeling of Terrance's importance growing stronger.

"I came across a reference to your book in one of my father's journals. One chapter in particular intrigued him, as it did me." Terrance explained, hoping he would return to the table. "Won't you please sit back down, Mr. Dark Feather? I would really like to discuss this with you." Terrance waved his arm toward the table. To his great relief, Mr. Dark Feather walked back to the table and sat down.

"You want to know about the shape shifters my ancestors spoke of, do you not?" Mr. Dark Feather asked, looking directly into Terrance's eyes to detect any sign of deceit or nervousness.

"Yes, how did you know?" Terrance asked, amazed Mr. Dark Feather already knew the reason for his visit.

"That is what your father asked about," Mr. Dark Feather answered. "He wanted to know about the shape shifters and the luminous beings in my story. And he especially wanted to know where the land they settled on was and about the people who live there now. I would not answer his questions. He became very angry and threatened to drag the truth from my broken body."

139

"Way to go, Dad. Thanks for possibly ruining my chances," Terrance thought to himself. "I truly apologize for my father's behavior," Terrance said sincerely. "He sometimes becomes overzealous in his search for information. But that is no excuse for his behavior. It was wrong of him to treat you that way."

Terrance thought for a moment he saw a smile start to appear on Mr. Dark Feather's face, but if it had been there it disappeared swiftly. "I understand you think my story is related to the Waters family. I can assure you that is not a possibility. I do not understand why you think my story about a legend of shape shifters would have anything to do with that family." Mr. Dark Feather looked again at Terrance, trying to determine what part he would play in Europa's protection. "But I see you search for truth. What is it you wish to know, My Son?"

"In your story you spoke of foreigners who came to your ancestor's lands. Do you know when that was or where they were from?"

"It was hundreds of years ago, before any white man had entered our lands. I do not know where exactly they came from, but the story my grandfather told me said they came from the sky and water. They had fought a great war with an evil one who had pursued them across the skies. The war was over and they sought peace in our land."

"By any chance do you know their names?" Terrance asked, hoping it was not Waters.

"They were known as Light Walkers. That is the only name I ever heard my grandfather call them."

"By any chance, do you happen to know where the land is?"

Mr. Dark Feather did not answer. The tribe had always protected the shape shifters and he was not willing to say anything which might bring them harm. He was preparing to end the conversation when he was suddenly seized once again by the knowledge this man was necessary if the monarch siblings were to survive. "Why would you want to know where the land was?" Mr. Dark Feather asked, still trying to determine what Terrance's part in the future was going to be.

"Mr. Dark Feather, I have told no one what I am about to tell you and I ask that it remain between us. My father studies ancient civilizations and their descendants. His passion for years has been the search of some lost royal family from Egypt. I found several written notes in that same journal that mentioned your book which led me to surmise he may have believed the Waters were descendants of that ancient family." Terrance saw the suspicious look on Mr. Dark Feather's face. "I know it sounds preposterous, but once he gets an idea in his head he can become obsessed with it and will go to any ends to discover the truth. I fear that in his overzealousness he may have inadvertently caused Mrs. Waters' accident."

"Her accident?" Mr. Dark Feather asked, now totally intrigued by this young man. Keeping his face expressionless he asked, "Why don't you find your father and ask him if he is responsible?"

"I wish it were that simple, Mr. Dark Feather. As I mentioned, we keep missing each other. The day he returned to the inn was the day I was out at his camp." Terrance stated, debating if he should tell this man his father was missing. If he was a friend of the Waters he certainly did not want Jeanip to know his father's whereabouts were unknown. He also feared Mr. Dark Feathers would know if he was lying and end their meeting; thus he faced a dilemma – how not to tell the truth without lying. "We were supposed to meet the other day but he evidently got delayed in the field. When he did return from the field I was sitting out at the gate to Minnos hoping to get inside, so I missed him again. I spent two days at the gate waiting for someone to let me in and when I returned to the inn I discovered my father was gone. I should have already left to join him, but I can't go until I make sure he didn't have anything to do with Mrs. Waters' death. Plus, I must see Europa and make sure she's okay. I was hoping if I knew where the original settlers lived, I might be able to determine what my father's part was in all of this, if any."

Terrance watched Mr. Dark Feather contemplating the words he had spoken. After what seemed like forever, he said, "A deer stepped into the road and caused Mrs. Waters' accident. So unless your father can turn himself into a deer, I do not believe he was responsible. As for the location of the property, I am afraid I cannot tell you where it is. It is tribal ground and the people who now live there have it protected by security fences."

"I could ask for permission," Terrance added. "I feel I could find the answers to my questions if I just knew where the property was."

"Permission would not be given. Now, if you have no more questions, I have somewhere I need to be." With that said, Mr. Dark Feather rose and signaled to his niece it was time to leave.

"Thank you, Mr. Dark Feather, for taking the time to speak with me. Might I ask you one more question, please? Do you have any information about Europa? I'm very worried about her."

Mr. Dark Feather could see Terrance was genuinely worried and cared deeply for Europa. He would have to tell Jeanip to allow this young man access to Minnos, that Europa's future depended upon it. "I assure you she is unharmed. If you are truly the friend you say you are, someone from Minnos will be in contact with you no later than tomorrow afternoon and advise you when you may see her."

Terrance breathed a sigh of relief when he knew Europa was okay. Plus, Mr. Dark Feather indicated there was a possibility he would be able to see her soon. Hoping to dispel any doubts the author might have about him, he give Mr. Dark Feather a Waters' greeting. "May the Waters bring you long life and good health."

Mr. Dark Feathers stared at Terrance, astonished he knew the greeting. Now, more than ever, he knew it was imperative for this human to be allowed onto Minnos and be at his sovereign's side. "May the Waters guide you on the path they have put your feet upon." He turned to leave, then stopped and turned to look Terrance in the eyes. "Trust in your heart, Young Terrance, for it will save you all." Without another word he walked out of the hotel, his niece rushing after him, leaving a very confused human pondering his words.

———————

Thomas Dark Feather thanked his niece for the ride and walked into his house. As soon as she was out of visual range he walked out the back door and down to the ocean's edge carrying a small bucket of herring. He casually strolled out to the dock and down the eight feet to its end. Sitting down, he dangled his feet in the water, placing the bucket of fish a few inches away from his side. After looking around to be sure no one was watching, he reached under the dock and pressed a button that sent a specific high-pitched sound out into the ocean. He did not have to wait long before Jack and Jill came swimming up to the dock.

The two bottle nosed dolphins raised their heads above the water and looked at Thomas. "You have need of our services, Chancee?" Jack silently asked, as he chattered, encouraging Chancee to throw him one of the herring.

"Yes. I need to get a message to Jeanip right away," Thomas silently replied, as he threw several herring into the water for the dolphins. The feeding of the dolphins was a deception Thomas had been doing several times a month for many years. It enabled him to keep in touch with other Oonocks via the two dolphins. Plus, at times like this, it allowed him to send emergency messages out without attracting any attention to himself or the dolphins.

"We can do that What is the message?" Jack gave several squeaks and whistles to show his excitement over the herring, copying the behavior of real dolphins to maintain the deception.

"Tell Jeanip I talked to a Terrance Landers who says he is a good friend of Europa's. It is important this young man be allowed access to Minnos and Europa immediately. I don't know how, but this man is important to Europa's future and her existence and has a key part to play in her surviving. He is her quanish, her love protector. The love his heart holds for our young monarch is strong, strong enough to defend her against any danger, even against JeffRa himself. His love and presence is needed if Jeanip hopes to defeat JeffRa. Without it, I'm afraid she will not survive the journey to Saint's Isle."

Jack and Jill saw the seriousness in Thomas' face. Amongst the natives he was known as a spiritual man; but amongst the Oonocks he was known as a keetont, one who could foretell events.

"Tell Jeanip this young man says his father is searching for a lost Egyptian royal family and, in his eagerness to discover them, may have done something that contributed to Medaron's death. It deserves investigation. His father may know something about the Terrians or their plans. Tell him also the Hunting Lodge is ready."

"Do you really think he's back?" Jill asked. "Could he really be alive after all these years?"

"I am sorry to say I do," Thomas replied. "Medaron said it was him on the road and I have no reason to distrust her recognition. She, above anyone else except Enok, would recognize him even after this many years."

"So he's returned to complete his vow of revenge," Jack stated, remembering the toll his revenge took the last time they warred. "Do you think it will come to another war?"

"I hope not," Thomas answered. "A war now would certainly expose both of our existences to the world, something not in either of our best interests. I fear the humans would pay a heavy price in casualties and losses as they are caught in the middle of our war. Plus, there is the possibility that, in their ignorance, they would believe us hostile and assume a defensive profile. Mankind has always had a history of annihilating anything they fear and that fear would destroy them this time. If they attempt to attack us, or especially the Terrians, I am afraid their kind would be eliminated from the universe; the Terrians would have no qualms about annihilating their race and taking Earth for their own planet. Hopefully JeffRa has only a few followers who have survived over the millennia and he is unable to wage a large campaign against us. If that is true, we should be able to eliminate them without any humans knowing."

"I pray you are right," Jill added.

"Here now, finish this fish," Thomas said, as he threw the last few pieces of herring in the water. "Hurry and deliver my message. Time is critical."

Jack and Jill quickly swallowed the herring and raced off to the cave to deliver Thomas' message. When they neared the entrance, they submerged under the water and covertly swam into the outlet, transforming into human form when it was safe. Jack lifted himself onto the walkway and walked over to the silent alarm. He pushed the purple button mounted on the wall which produced a silent, high-pitched alarm throughout the cottage and turned on a light panel in the kitchen.

Misso was preparing lunch in the kitchen when she heard the special alarm. She quickly looked over at the wall and saw the light panel flashing, indicating Jeanip was needed in the cave. To her relief, Triton trotted into the kitchen to investigate the reason for the alarm.

"Triton, go get Jeanip. Tell him he's needed in the cave," Misso silently said. She opened the back door and Triton ran outside to the barn to retrieve Jeanip. Earon quickly returned with him, wearing a dirty overcoat. When they entered the kitchen Jeanip walked over to the light panel and entered his code to cancel the alarm. Then, without a word, he walked into his quarters, closing the door behind him.

"I am going to go get some decent clothes on," Earon said looking down at the filthy, torn overcoat he had grabbed in the barn to put on. "Remind me, Misso, to put a change of clothing in the barn for occasions such as this." Misso laughed as she watched Earon follow Jeanip into his room, already scratching as a result of the overcoat. He quickly changed, then followed Jeanip through the secret door. He hurried down the stairs to the secret cave where he saw Jeanip talking with Jack and Jill. "What's wrong?" Earon asked.

"Good day, Your Majesty," both Jack and Jill said, as they slightly bowed their head and raised their right hand to their forehead.

"Chancee asked us to bring Jeanip an urgent message. He said he talked with a Terrance Landers who says he is a friend of Europa's."

"Yes, that is true. They've actually been an item for several days," Earon said.

"Chancee said this Terrance must be allowed access to Minnos immediately, that he is her quanish. He is important to Europa's future and her existence and will play an important part in her surviving the next few days. Without his help she will not live to see Saint's Isle."

"What's a 'quanish'?" Earon asked.

"A 'quanish' is someone whose love is so strong they can defend the person they love against anything," Jeanip stated, thinking Chancee must be mistaken yet knowing he is never wrong.

"Chancee said if she is to survive her trip to Saint's Isle he must be with her. He said Mr. Lander's love is strong enough to defend Europa against any danger, even JeffRa himself."

"He's certain?"

"Yes."

"Is that the entire message?"

"He also said young Mr. Landers' father is searching for a lost royal family from Egypt. He believes his father may have inadvertently done something that contributed to Medaron's accident. Chancee said it warrants checking into it, that perhaps his father knows Terrians."

"If he is connected to the Terrians or JeffRa, knowingly or not, should we allow him on the estate?" Earon asked, concerned over the possibility of Terrian involvement.

"Chancee said he MUST be brought here," Jill replied. "Immediately."

"Chancee would do nothing to endanger Europa. He must have good reason to insist Terrance be brought here even if there is the possibility of Terrian involvement. But you are right, Earon. Possible Terrian involvement does complicate this situation. I will have to think this through before allowing Terrance access to Minnos. Did he say anything else?" Jeanip asked.

"That the Hunting Lodge is ready for you."

"Thank you. I need to get back inside." Jeanip turned and climbed back up the stairs. Jack and Jill slipped back into the ocean and swam out to continue their protective watch.

145

Europa woke the next morning a little unsettled by the previous night's dream of luminous beings and the thing with the red eyes. But she did not have time this morning to dwell on its meaning. She remembered something her mother and Jeanip had both said – she was now the leader of their people, she was a queen. That meant Jeanip had to obey the orders she gave him. And she knew exactly what her first order would be.

She quickly showered and dressed, then walked down the hallway to her mother's room, trailed by Triton. She tried the door knob. It was locked, as she feared. Jeanip had told her to stay out of her mother's room. Again she wondered how he know she had been in there. No one had seen her leaving the room except Triton. But how could he have told on her? Europa looked down at the canine waiting at her feet, the feeling Triton could not be trusted again materializing inside her head. Frustrated her mother's room was now locked, she turned and headed down to the kitchen to confront Jeanip and present her demand.

As she entered the kitchen Jeanip stood at the table but did not say a word. This was her first time to come downstairs since their confrontation over her confinement to the cottage and he did not want to say anything which might upset her and send her back to her bedroom.

"Europa, I am glad you decided to come downstairs for breakfast," Misso stated upon seeing her. "What would you like for breakfast?"

"Nothing right now, Misso. I am here to see Jeanip," Europa replied. She walked straight to Jeanip and stood before him, looking at him with glaring eyes. "Jeanip, why is my mother's room locked?"

"Your mother has a lot of important documents in her room. Until I can go up and secure them, her room is off limits."

Europa wanted to argue the point that since she was now the sole owner of Minnos she had a right to be in that room. But she had more important issues to discuss with him.

"Jeanip, as I understand it, my mother's passing made me the Supreme Monarch. Is this correct?"

"Yes, "Jeanip replied.

"And, as your monarch, you are subject to my rules and orders, is that not correct?" Europa watched his expression, expecting to see nervousness or stress, but there was none.

"To a certain extent," Jeanip said "There are certain security procedures in place your parents made. They are unretractable and cannot be overridden."

Europa thought for a moment. She had to word her orders correctly if she wanted to bypass her parents' procedures and obtain her goal. "As I told you last night, I am willing to remain for the time being in the house where I am protected. But I want the front gate unlocked and the security fences turned off. If you feel it necessary, you can post someone at the gate to question anyone wishing to enter – this will still keep the estate safe, plus, the other gates will still be locked to keep someone from entering without your knowledge. I want someone to drive into town and bring back Anna, Suzie, Rannie and Terrance out to see me."

"Not four at once. You can start with one, and then we can try two," Jeanip answered. He had already contemplated Chancee's message and had agreed to allow Terrance access to Minnos. Jeanip knew the tremendous power a quanish possessed, as well as the rarity and importance of such a bond. He had seen few quanish relationships in his lifetime but the ones he had seen were unstoppable, beyond explanation and totally undefeatable. The strongest had been Enok and Medaron's. If Terrance's love for Europa and hers for him was even half as strong as Europa's parents, then he could ask for no stronger protection. He knew it was imperative for Terrance to come out to Minnos immediately and had been trying to determine the best way to approach the subject when Europa's request for company gave him the perfect opportunity. She would believe it was her decision for Terrance to be brought out and Jeanip was simply following her orders.

Europa almost smiled. She was hoping Jeanip would not agree to four people coming onto the estate the first time but that he would compromise and agree to one or two. Since Jeanip did not specify the gender, she knew he left the door open for Terrance to be the one.

"Then I want Terrance brought here," Europa stated, looking Jeanip directly in the eyes.

"I'd prefer if it were one of the ladies," Jeanip said, not wanting Europa to know she was doing exactly what he wanted her to do.

"No, they can come out later. Terrance will be the first to come."

"I will obey your order on one condition, Europa." Seeing an opportunity to begin to rectify some of the past, Jeanip hurriedly created a condition to Terrance's arrival that he knew Europa would agree to. "I would like for you to come downstairs and join your family as their monarch. If you agree to eat your meals here at the head of the table, then I will send someone to bring Terrance here this very morning."

"Misso, I'm ready for breakfast now," Europa said, sitting down in her usual seat. "Oatmeal and coffee, please." She looked at Jeanip as she said, "I am willing to be your monarch and sit at my rightful place at the head of this table. But I cannot sit in her place quite yet. I ask, Jeanip, that you allow me more time to adjust to her being gone."

"Agreed," Jeanip stated. He understood how hard it would be for Europa to sit in her mother's chair, to completely accept the fact she was gone. He knew with time she would heal and accept her rightful place as monarch. Without another word he turned, walked to the back door and rang the bell for Sunam. When Sunam came to the porch Europa heard him instruct Sunam to unlock the front gate and go into town and bring Terrance back.

"I have one more request, Your Majesty," Jeanip stated, as he returned to the table. "I would like to leave the fences electrified. Turning them off would allow someone or something to go over them and have access to the property. Even though we have motion and security detectors throughout the estate, I no longer trust their accuracy. We have recently discovered a number of devices purposely deactivated to prevent us from seeing activities being conducted in that section of the property. We have repaired the devices and the grid shows everything is working as it should but, until I can run a complete diagnosis of the system and develop a more sophisticated grid, I believe we should not trust what the grid is telling us. Therefore, we need to leave the fences electrified to keep out anyone trying to get in. Leaving the fences on will not interfere with the front gate being unlocked during the day."

"Make it so," Europa replied, as Misso sat before her a bowl of oatmeal and a cup of coffee.

TERRANCE VISITS

The next morning Terrance rose early, showered, dressed, then decided to go downstairs to the dining room for breakfast. He had been skimping on his meals lately and realized he needed a good meal to boost his stamina. He chose a table by the window which gave him a good view of the street so he would be able to see the girls if they came with more news.

After ordering he began to go over in his mind his conversation with Mr. Dark Feather the day before. Although he did not directly say it, it was evident the land the foreigners had purchased was Minnos. That also meant the original Waters who settled there were the shape shifters in the story. It seemed the more information he collected, the more mysterious and unbelievable his father's actions and the Waters' history was becoming. Once again he wished he could talk with Europa. Perhaps she could shed some light on the subject.

Suddenly, he realized there was a person walking toward him calling his name. He was shocked to see the person was Sunam. He quickly rose and walked as fast as he could without breaking into a run to Sunam, relieved to see a face from Minnos. Perhaps he was finally going to find out how Europa was doing.

"Sunam, what are you doing here?" Terrance asked.

"Jeanip sent me to bring you back to Minnos at Ms. Europa's request," Sunam replied, as if it were an everyday occurrence to be invited out to Minnos while it was on lock down. "If you are available, I will drive you out to the estate right now. Or, if you have business to attend to first, I can wait for a short time."

"No, I can leave now," Terrance replied. "Is Europa okay?"

"She is as well as can be expected," Sunam responded. "If you would come with me, please."

"Are the girls coming also?" Terrance asked, delighted and amazed Sunam was going to take him to Europa.

"No, just you."

After tossing a ten dollar bill at the greeter to cover the expense of his undelivered breakfast, Terrance ran out of the inn to the car. He was finally going to see Europa after so many days and he was getting to go by himself. He had so much to tell her and her friends would definitely have compromised their discussion of what he found in his father's room. But most of all, he was finally going to see for himself that she was truly alright. It was a thirty-minute ride to the estate, all of which was driven in silence. When they neared the bend in the road where the accident had occurred, Terrance began to see countless bouquets of flowers lining the road, tributes brought by the town's people to display their love for Mrs. Waters. Sunam slowed the vehicle to a crawl as they passed the scene of the accident, raising his hand to his forehead and bowing his head in respect for his fallen sovereign until they were past the scene. Terrance wondered if he did this every time he drove through.

As they neared the gate Terrance saw more flowers and cards lining both sides of the roads a few inches from the fence. Mrs. Waters was truly loved by the town people.

"Go right in. You are expected," Sunam said, as he parked the car in front of the cottage.

Terrance bounded up the steps, having a hard time believing he was about to see Europa. As he came through the door he saw her standing there waiting for him. She ran to him and threw her arms around him, holding him tight.

"I have missed you so much," Europa said.

"I've been crazy with worry about you," Terrance replied. "I'm so sorry to hear about your mother's accident."

Terrance noticed Jeanip standing behind Europa. Holding Europa in one arm, he extended his other hand to Jeanip. "Glad to see you again, Sir. Thank you for allowing me to come out and visit with Europa. If I can be of any help in any way, please do not hesitate to let me know."

"Thank you, Terrance. I may have need of your help in the future. For now I am just glad you were able to come for a visit. Europa has been becoming a little tense being confined to the house." Jeanip shook Terrance's hand. "It will be good for her to have someone besides Triton to talk to. By the way, did your father ever return?"

"Yes, he returned the next day. He has already returned to Michigan with some fantastic findings about the Red Rock Sparrows," Terrance lied. He did not want Jeanip to start investigating why his father had never appeared. Until he could determine if his father's actions had anything to do with Mrs. Waters' death he needed Jeanip to believe his father was back in Michigan.

"I'm glad to hear that. And you are staying on longer?"

"Yes, I couldn't leave until I was sure Europa was okay," Terrance said, smiling at her. Looking directly into her eyes he added, "I was going to wait as long as it took for that damn gate to open."

Jeanip could see the young man truly did love Europa. He began to think Chancee knew what he was talking about when he referred to Terrance as her quanish. "Now, if you will excuse me, I have some work out back that needs attending to. Your Highness, I take my leave of you." With that said, Jeanip turned and walked out the back door toward the barn.

"Mr. Landers, so glad to see you again," Misso greeted. "Would you like some breakfast and coffee?"

"Just coffee, please. I'm too excited to eat."

The two sat at the kitchen table drinking their coffee, holding each other's hand and saying very little. Neither could take their eyes off of the other, fearful if they looked away they would discover this was a dream. When they finished their coffee Europa led Terrance to a small sitting room off the front living room, Triton following close behind. Fearing Terrance might say something in front of Triton, Europa hugged him saying, "It is so good to see you," then quickly whispered in his ear, "I have much to tell you, but we cannot speak in front of Triton. Do not say anything of importance in front of him."

Terrance gave her a confused look. Why couldn't they speak in front of the dog? Who was he going to tell? Then he remembered Mr. Dark Feather's account of the shape shifters' legend. Was it possible Triton was a shape shifter? He quickly dismissed the idea, realizing it was too preposterous to even consider.

"I will explain later," Europa added, as she and Terrance sat down on the settee.

Europa told Terrance what she knew of the accident, her anger at Jeanip for burying her mother without her and the fact she would not be starting college as planned. She told him she was glad his father finally arrived and very glad he had chosen to stay behind. Terrance told her about the few times he had seen Anna, Suzie and Rannie, how worried they all had been when they could not contact her and the countless bouquets of flowers and cards he saw at the road's bend and in front of the fence.

Misso brought in a tray with cookies, coffee, tea and orange juice in case Europa and Terrance were hungry. Europa thanked her and asked her to let Triton outside for a while. Triton looked at Europa and did not move. He did not want to leave the couple alone. But Europa insisted he go outside for some exercise. Reluctantly, Triton followed Misso out of the room and headed for the side door.

As soon as Europa heard the side door open and close, she moved very close to Terrance. "We don't have much time. Triton will not remain outside for long."

"Why can't we speak in front of the dog?" Terrance asked, bewildered.

"I know this sounds very strange, but I don't trust him. Jeanip has known things about me only Triton could have told him. Since dogs don't talk, he must have a transmitter on him or some type of listening device so Jeanip can track my movements."

"Europa, I lied to Jeanip," Terrance said, barely hearing a word of what Europa said as a look close to terror spread across his face. He knew if Jeanip discovered his father was still missing there would be hell to be paid. "My father never returned from his field work. I haven't seen him. When I cleaned out his belongings in his room I found some strange things – pictures, a journal, a copy of this property's deed and more, all relating to you and your family."

"My family?" Europa asked in surprise. "Why would your father have things related to my family?"

"I don't know. The only plausible explanation I've been able to come up with is he thought your family was somehow associated with a lost race he has been searching for since before I was born. He came across a reference to this mysterious race years ago while doing research in Egypt and became obsessed with finding them."

"But how would my family be connected to a race from Egypt?"

"I have no idea." Terrance knew Triton could return at any moment and he wanted to hear what Europa had to say. "But we can talk about my father later. You said you had something important to tell me."

"Terrance, something is going on in this house, some kind of secret is being kept. I was in my mother's room the other day and discovered a secret staircase that led to an attic above her room, an attic I never knew existed. There are all kinds of stuff up there, stuff that's hundreds, maybe even thousands of years old. And, now that I think of it, there were a number of Egyptian golden statues."

"Egyptian?" Terrance asked in disbelief. "You're kidding!"

"That is really strange. Your father is searching for an Egyptian family and my mother has Egyptian statues," Europa said, taking Terrance's hand in hers. "Terrance, I found other things too: pictures of my parents that are hundreds of years old, a map of Minnos and a huge diagram of a habitat with really strange writing on it."

"Europa, my father had pictures of people from hundreds of years ago also. One of them looks just like your mother." They both sat there staring at each other, both realizing they had found similar items in the parent's rooms, both wondering what it all meant, wondering if their parents were connected and how.

"Terrance, I found something else, something really strange," Europa stated, drawing even closer to Terrance to whisper in his ear. "I found my mother's diary. On the day I was born she wrote that I was born human."

"Human?" asked Terrance, perplexed. "Are you sure she wrote human? You didn't read it wrong?"

"Yes, she wrote human. I read it several times to make sure I read it correctly. What else would I be? There is also an entry regarding my brother and that he will remain human until I am born."

"I didn't know you had a brother," Terrance stated, astonished at this bit of information, wondering why Europa had never mentioned him. "Does he live around here?"

"No, he does not because I do not have a brother, at least not that I know of. But you are missing the point – why would he not be human AFTER I was born? What difference does my birth make?"

"Europa, this is really weird."

153

"Tell me about it. And it gets weirder. My mother made an entry a few days before my birthday. She said I did not know who I really was. It scared me because that would mean my whole life has been a lie."

"Did you ask Jeanip about it?"

"No, I do not feel I can trust him or anyone except you, Terrance. Everyone here was loyal to my mother, and still are. They will never break her confidence even though she is gone. They will take her secrets to their graves. "

"What are you going to do?" Terrance asked, concerned for Europa. "Do you think Annie, Suzie or Rannie might know anything or be able to help?"

"I do not believe they know anything, but even if they do not, I feel I cannot trust them either," Europa said to Terrance's surprise. "If Jeanip was to question any of them about things I told them, I do not believe they could keep my secrets. Jeanip has a way of getting people to tell him things just by looking at them. No, you, Terrance, are my only ally in this." Europa took a sip of coffee before she continued, "I was able to smuggle some of the smaller items from my mother's attic into my bedroom and I have them hidden in my bathroom. But I can only look at them once a day when I am supposedly taking a bath because Triton is always at my side. Plus, I have to get back into that attic somehow so I can explore more. There are more secrets up there. I just don't know how to get away from Triton long enough."

"Drug him," Terrance said nonchalantly.

"What?" Europa said, removing her hand from Terrance's, startled at the suggestion.

"Drug him. Put him to sleep. Haven't you ever heard of dog tranquilizers? You can knock him out for several hours. Trust me," Terrance said, taking Europa's hand back. "They won't hurt him. He'll just get a good sleep."

"Are you sure?"

"Yes, I'm positive. My dog back home gets car sick whenever we travel. Our vet gave us tranquilizers for him and believe me it has made a world of difference. I give him two pills and he sleeps until we arrive at our destination; he's happy and I don't have a mess to clean up in the car."

"But I do not believe we have anything like that here. And if we did, it would be under Jeanip's control." Europa looked at Terrance knowing once again he would have to be her salvation. "Terrance, could you buy some in town and bring them to me tomorrow? I will make sure Jeanip allows you to return. In fact, I am going to make sure you come back every day."

Still having much to tell each other, their conversation was interrupted by the sound of a loud yelp outside. Europa ran to the side door recognizing Triton's cry. She saw Tinderoon carrying Triton up the stairs, blood dripping from one of his paws. She saw Jeanip running toward them from the barn.

"What happened?" Europa asked, as Terrance opened the door so Tinderoon could carry Triton inside.

"He'll be okay, Miss," Tinderoon answered. "Just a little cut. It looks worse than it is. It appears he stepped on a piece of glass out in the yard."

Jeanip came bursting through the door, worried there had been another attempted attack. "What happened?" he asked, worry clearly sketched across his face. "Is everyone okay in here?"

"Triton stepped on some glass out in the yard and cut his foot," Tinderoon answered. "That's all. Everything is secure."

"Take him into the kitchen so I can have a look," Jeanip ordered, the worried look diminishing. "Put him on the flower arranging table. It has the best lightening. Misso, bring me a pan of warm water and a cloth. Tinderoon, there's some peroxide and bandage wrap under the sink in my room. Would you get them after you put Triton down?"

Tinderoon placed Triton gently on the table then went to retrieve the peroxide and bandage wrap from Jeanip's room. Jeanip switched on the overhead light and carefully lifted Triton's paw. He washed away the blood and examined the paw, seeing a shard of glass imbedded in one of the foot pads. He carefully grabbed the shard and pulled it free. Triton yelped in pain.

"Is he going to be alright?" Europa asked.

"I believe so," Jeanip replied. "This might sting a little, boy," he said to Triton, as he poured peroxide over the wound. Triton flinched but did not cry out loud. Jeanip reexamined the wound to determine if stitches were needed. Luckily the glass shard had not penetrated too deep. Jeanip wrapped the paw and lifted Triton down to the floor. "There you go, boy. That foot's going to be sore for a while." Jeanip

155

turned to face the worried Europa. "Don't worry, Your Highness, he'll be running around the yard again in a few days. He just needs some extra rest and should avoid the stairs. He will need to remain downstairs for the next few days to give the cut a chance to heal. I'll keep an eye on his paw to be sure it doesn't get infected."

"Thank you, Jeanip," Europa stated. "As always, your service is very much appreciated." She reached down and petted Triton's head. "You need to be more careful out there in the yard." She turned, took Terrance's hand and walked back toward the sitting room. As they passed the door Terrance suggested they go outside for a breath of fresh air. After her fright over Triton Terrance thought it would do her good.

"I am sorry, but for now I am not allowed outside," Europa said. "I must remain behind these walls."

"What do you mean you're not allowed outside?" Terrance asked, suddenly very concerned Europa was being kept a prisoner in her own home.

"It is for my own protection," Europa said, seeing the concern on Terrance's face. She realized he couldn't comprehend why she was confined to the house. "It is okay, I have agreed to it."

"Your protection? I don't understand, Europa," Terrance confessed. "You're telling me you're a prisoner in your own home and you're okay with it? Europa, that's not right. I need to get you out of here right now." He took her hand and began to walk her toward the front door. He didn't know how, but somehow they were leaving even if they had to walk all the way to town.

"Stop, Terrance," Jeanip ordered, as he and Tinderoon rushed forward to prevent Europa from leaving. Both immediately took positions in front of the door preventing the two from exiting. "If you choose you may go outside, but Europa must remain inside."

"So she has told me" shouted Terrance, now more determined than ever to get Europa out of there. "You can't keep her prisoner. I won't allow it. "I'll . . .""

Europa placed her hand on Terrance's shoulder. She smiled at him and relished in his desire to protect her. "Come back to the sitting room with me, Mr. Landers. I will explain what is going on." She turned to face Jeanip and Tinderoon. "It is okay, Jeanip. I will explain to him why I cannot go outside. I am in no danger. You may return to your duties."

Jeanip looked at Europa, then at Terrance, then back at Europa. "As you wish, Your Majesty," Jeanip said. "We will return to the barn and finish our work." He looked directly at Terrance. "If you wish to remain visiting, Terrance, do NOT try anything like that again." Having said that, he and Tinderoon walked into the kitchen and out the side door.

Europa took Terrance's hand and started to walk toward the sitting room. "I have a short tale to tell you about whom I am, or at least who I think I am. I believe after you hear it you will understand why I have agreed to remain inside the cottage."

"I doubt that!" Terrance replied, as he followed, thinking there was no reason acceptable for keeping her sequestered.

Once they were seated Europa began to tell Terrance the remainder of the story she had begun when they first met. She reminded him about her being of royal blood, then proceeded to tell him about the years of war her family fought, their enemy's oath to annihilate every member of her family and lastly, the possibility her mother had been assassinated when mistaken for Europa. "This assassin may still be out there waiting for another chance to end my life. So you see, Terrance, I must remain behind these walls. Here I am safe. No harm can come to me as long as I am protected behind Minnos' walls."

Terrance just sat there not saying a word. He knew the assassin might be his father and he debated about telling Europa his assumptions. He wanted to tell her the truth but, at the same time, he did not want to be barred from Minnos again. He knew Jeanip would not hesitate to throw him off the property if he knew what Terrance suspected. Terrance reminded himself he had no positive proof it was his father, just the journal and the picture of Europa's truck.

When Terrance remained quiet Europa took his silence as him having trouble believing her again. She wondered why he could believe everything they had both found but he couldn't believe this simple truth. "Terrance, I know it sounds like I'm making this up, that I am fantasizing, but it is the truth. Luckily, I can prove it." Before Terrance could reply that he did not doubt her story, Europa rang for Misso. Misso immediately came to see what she needed.

"Yes, Your Majesty, did you need something?" Misso asked. "Something to eat or drink?"

"Nothing to eat or drink right now, Misso. I need for you tell Terrance whom I am the daughter of."

"You are the daughter of Enok and Medaron Waters."

"And who were my parents to you, Misso?" Misso looked nervously at Europa. She wasn't sure how she should answer. "It is okay, Misso. I give you permission to tell Terrance who my parents were and who I really am."

"Your parents were the leaders of our people, the sovereigns of our nation. You are the daughter of the Head Monarchs of the royal family."

"And why am I not allowed to go outside of the cottage?" Again, Misso looked at Europa, obviously very nervous about telling Terrance some of the family's secrets. Misso wondered where Europa was going with this line of questions. "It is okay, Misso. Tell Terrance why I cannot go outside."

"Your great-great-grandparents fought against an enemy who swore an oath to eradicate your family – both current and future generations. It is now believed some of their descendants have discovered your family's location and are trying to fulfill their ancestor's oath. They killed your mother, believing it was you in your truck and are probably out there planning another attempt to end your life." Tears started to fill Misso's eyes as she recanted the story, reliving Medaron's death. "Is there more you wish me to tell him?"

"No, Misso, that is all," Europa said, suddenly realizing the sadness she caused Misso in reliving the past weeks. "I did not mean to bring you such sadness. I apologize for that." Misso did not say a word, but simply turned and left the room. Europa and Terrance could hear her crying in the kitchen.

"I did not mean to make her so sad," Europa softly said. "Had I known, I never would have asked her those questions."

"It's my fault," Terrance replied. "I should have stopped you and told you I believed what you told me and there was no reason to question Misso. I can see Misso loved your mother dearly and has been traumatized by her death." Terrance pulled Europa into his arms and held her tightly. "I am truly sorry, Europa. I'm sorry you didn't think I believed you again." Europa laid in his arms, warm and secure, the horrors of the recent past gone, at least for a few moments. She felt Terrance's hand lift her head and then felt his soft lips on hers, kissing her so tenderly. She kissed him back, not wanting this moment to end – it was the first moment of happiness she had experienced since leaving Terrance in the Inn's dining room. When the kiss ended she put her head back on Terrance's chest, feeling his heart beating as he said, "So you're really a princess just like you told me the day we went to the rookeries?"

"Well, I was a princess," Europa answered, wondering how Terrance would react to the next part of her statement. "When my mother died I actually became the queen."

"Oh great, like that makes it better. I was in love with a princess; now I am in love with a queen!" Europa's heart skipped a beat when she heard Terrance say he was in love with her. Had he realized he had said it? Should she say she loved him back? Before she could determine what to do she heard Terrance say, "And someone might really be out there trying to assassinate you?"

"That is what Jeanip believes. And that is why I remain behind these cottage walls; here I am safe, completely shielded from anything outside which may which to harm me."

"Is there the possibility the accident was just that – an accident? Could someone have unintentionally caused her death by accidentally scaring that deer and causing it to go into the road?" Terrance asked, still hoping his father had not purposely killed Mrs. Waters.

"All evidence points to the fact my mother was purposely killed; assassinated. And because of that our time to discover what is going on is very limited, Terrance. Jeanip feels I am no longer safe here and is preparing to move me to a location where he can assure my safety. He said my parents built it before I was born just in case our enemy reappeared and my life was in jeopardy. Once I am there I may never be able to discover the truth."

"Leave? To where? When?" Terrance was frantic. He had finally been able to enter Minnos to see Europa and now she was telling him she would be leaving soon for an unknown location. He could not lose her again. Plus, if someone was trying to kill her, he needed to stay with her, to protect her.

"I believe just as soon as he can make the arrangements, probably in less than a week."

"Less than a week! Terrance repeated, dumbfounded by the possibility he only had a few days with Europa remaining. "Did he say for how long?"

"No, only that I would have to remain there until he could be sure there was no longer a threat on my life. I imagine we are talking at least several months."

"Or YEARS!" Terrance screamed, as he jumped up, realizing the possibility of their separation. They might only have days to discover the truth about what each had found, to uncover the truth about who their parents were, who they themselves were. He hadn't even had a chance to tell her about his meeting with Mr. Dark Feather and the tale of the shape shifters. "This is totally unacceptable, Europa. I cannot allow it. I . . .". Terrance stopped when he saw Triton limp into the room and stare at him. Terrance realized he had once again raised his voice and may have caused some apprehension on Triton's part. Seeing there was no trouble, Triton walked over to Europa and laid down at her feet. Realizing Triton was there to stay and remembering Europa's warning about the possibility Triton was wearing a listening device, Terrance was upset with himself for becoming so emotional and raising his voice. Now he and Europa would not be able to continue their discussion and they had much more to talk about.

Unable to discuss anything of importance, Europa and Terrance spent the afternoon talking about the accident, the concussion Europa suffered and her lying unconscious for five days and other known facts. Just as they were running out of general conversation, Triton stood up and hobbled into the other room heading toward the kitchen. Europa heard the side door open and close, making her believe Triton had gone outside. She scooted closer to Terrance so she could tell him more of what she found in the attic.

"Terrance, I need to tell you what else I found in the attic before Triton comes back. There is a larger version of the amulet I wear suspended in the air. I put my hands on it and it began to hum and glow, sending out strands of light. It . . .". Just then Misso appeared at the doorway to announce dinner was ready. Europa sighed, knowing her story would have to wait until later.

They entered the kitchen to see Jeanip and Earon already seated at the table. Both stood up as Europa entered. Earon raised his hand to his forehead and bowed. As he bowed Europa was stunned to see an amulet identical to hers hidden beneath his shirt. Only the royal family supposedly wore the amulets, so why did Earon wear one? She quickly moved her eyes up to Earon's face so no one would notice she had seen the amulet.

"Earon, I am glad to see you again. I thought perhaps you had left without saying goodbye."

"It is nice to see you again also, Europa. I told Jeanip I would stay for a while to help around the estate." Earon diverted his gaze from

Europa to Terrance. "This must be Terrance," he said holding out his hand.

"Terrance, this is my cousin, Earon," Europa said, as Terrance shook his hand. "Earon, this if my friend, Terrance."

"It is nice to finally meet you, Terrance," Earon said. "I have heard so much about you."

"You have?" asked Europa, wondering how Earon heard about him if Earon had just arrived a few days before.

"Yes, Jeanip has been telling me about him," Earon said, looking directly at Europa. Turning his gaze back to Terrance he added, "You evidently have made a good impression on Jeanip. If you knew Jeanip better you would know, Terrance, that is some accomplishment." Out of the corner of his eye he saw Jeanip give him a scowl.

"Earon, did you get hurt? I see your hand is bandaged." Europa asked, noticing Earon's left hand was wrapped in a bandage. She immediately looked around for Triton but did not see him anywhere. At that moment it occurred to her that whenever Earon was around Triton was not, and vice versa. She also thought it strange Earon's left hand was bandaged just like Triton's left paw was. Could there be a connection between the two? Was it possible that Earon and Triton were the same person and he was the brother her mother spoke of in her journal? Could he be her lost brother?

"Little accident; nothing to fret about. Seems like I cannot cut an apple without stabbing myself," Earon chuckled. "I should have left the slicing to Misso as she suggested."

Jeanip shifted slightly in his chair, cleared his throat and looked at Terrance. "Terrance, Europa explained to you why she is required to remain within these walls?"

"Yes, Sir, she did." Terrance replied. "And I totally agree, Jeanip. If her life is in danger she needs to stay behind these walls where nothing can harm her."

"I am glad to hear that. Did she also tell you her mother's death may have not been an accident?"

"Yes, Sir, she told me that too." Terrance replied, concentrating as hard as he could not to show any sign of emotion. He knew Jeanip would be watching for any change in his expression or demeanor to signal he knew something or was withholding information. He quickly hid his thoughts that his father may have caused the accident.

"Did she also tell you she may have been the true target, that her mother was killed in error?" Jeanip asked, as he fought to keep a tear from sliding down his cheek.

"Yes, Sir." Terrance prayed Jeanip would stop this line of questioning. He knew he could not hold his composure for much longer. And if he broke it would be all over – Jeanip would never allow him to see Europa again.

Chancee had suggested Terrance was her quanish. If so, this was the perfect opportunity to solicit his help. Jeanip asked, "As her friend, Terrance, are you willing to help us keep her protected?"

"Yes, Sir. There is nothing more important to me than her safety." Terrance turned and looked at Europa, taking her hand in his. "Just let me know what I need to do and I will do it." Turning back to face Jeanip he added, "I am licensed to carry a weapon so, if you'd like, I can purchase one in town and start carrying it."

"That won't be necessary, Terrance, but thank you for the offer. There are currently enough armed guards on the estate, but I will keep your offer in mind if things ever change and necessitate another armed guardian. The biggest help you can give me is to stay with her and keep her company, keep her entertained throughout the day and, most importantly be sure she does not go outside."

"I can do that, Jeanip," Terrance replied, delighted to know Jeanip trusted him enough to solicit his help.

"You are a man of honor, Terrance. I welcome your help'" Jeanip said, giving Terrance a smile. He did not look at Europa to see the smile on her face, but he felt it. "I do have one more favor to ask of you, if I may. I was wondering if you would mind staying out here for a few days. You could bring your things with you tomorrow morning. Or if that's not convenient, I can have Sunam drive in and bring you back each morning and take you back to the inn each night. It's up to you."

Terrance and Europa looked at each other. Neither could believe Jeanip was asking Terrance to come and stay on Minnos. It was more than Europa dreamed of. Perhaps Jeanip was trying to make up for burying her mother while she was unconscious.

"It's no inconvenience at all, Sir," Terrance quickly said, barely able to remain in his seat. "I would love to spend a few days on the estate. In fact, I have been trying to figure out a way to bring that very subject up. I was going to ask if I might be allowed to stay out here and help protect her. If there is someone out there trying to hurt her then my place is at her side."

"Then it's settled," Jeanip replied. "I'll have Sunam and Birea prepare the guest room in the bunk house. Now, let us enjoy this meal. Earon, would you please give the thanks."

Everyone bowed their heads as Earon gave thanks. "May the Waters bless this food we are about to eat and guide us on our journeys. May they keep our dearest Europa safe and guide us in our endeavors to accomplish this task." He wanted to add "And for Jeanip allowing Terrance to stay at Minnos and keep my little sister happy and content" but knew that was not possible.

Once Europa had taken the first bite, the four enjoyed the wonderful meal Misso had fixed. Jeanip thought Europa seemed much happier. He was glad he had agreed to let Terrance visit and he would be a part of her protection. Plus, if Terrance's father did have a part in Medaron's accident, be it intentional or not, having Terrance on Minnos gave Jeanip the opportunity to keep an eye on him and, if involved, bring any possible Terrians out of hiding. He hoped to find time to talk to Terrance about his father.

After dinner they moved to the living room for coffee and berry cake, one of Misso's specialties. All too soon for the young couple, Jeanip announced it was time for the front gate to be locked for the night. It was necessary for Terrance to return to town. Terrance and Jeanip agreed upon a time when Sunam would pick him up the following day to return to the estate. Europa walked Terrance to the front door, then turned to see if Jeanip and Earon were watching. To her relief, they had stood up with their backs to the young couple, giving them what privacy they could. The two said their goodbyes, sealing their blossoming love with a goodnight kiss. Scurrying to the window she watched Terrance walk down the stairs and over to the car where Sunam waited. Just as he disappeared inside he turned and waved to her. She waved back then watched the car back up and head toward town.

When she could no longer see the tail lights, Europa bounded up the stairs, feeling as if she were floating on clouds rather than walking on wooden floors. Who knew a kiss could lighten one's heart so much? Adding in the fact that, starting tomorrow, Terrance would be staying at Minnos instead of in town, she couldn't be happier. As she reached her bedroom she looked around for Triton to assure he entered the room before she closed the door. Then she remembered he had hurt his front paw and was confined downstairs. This day was just getting better, she thought. She would be able to really study the articles she brought back from her mother's bedroom, possibly even sneaking back inside and visiting the Orb again.

Just as she went to close her door she heard a creak on the top stair and Jeanip's voice. "Europa, one moment please."

"Yes, Jeanip?" Fear suddenly seized her as she thought Jeanip might have changed his mind about Terrance staying on the estate. Or he objected to Terrance kissing her in front of him and Earon. Open displays of affection were not common in the family. To her delight she was pleasantly surprised by his reply.

"Since Triton is confined downstairs you do not have any one to guard you in your room tonight. I know Birea sleeps in the room next to you, but I was wondering if you would like her or Misso to sleep on a cot in your room? Or, if you would prefer, I could post a guard outside your door for the night? I can even be the one to stand guard, if that makes you feel safer."

Europa knew for Jeanip to offer such a lowly task as to stand guard outside her room was a great honor and a show of how much she meant to him. She could recall no memory of him ever standing outside her mother's door. He must truly be worried about her safety.

"I do not think that will be necessary, Jeanip" Europa answered. "As you said, Birea sleeps right next door to this room. I will make sure my door is left open and she will be able to hear me if I need anything. Besides, with the upgrades you made in the security system I do not believe anyone could get into this house, let alone my room."

"As you wish," Jeanip stated, turning to leave. As he saw Europa close her door he said, "Europa, remember, your door needs to be open."

"I will make sure it is, Jeanip. I planned on staying up and reading for a while. I did not want the light from my room to disturb Birea. Once I am done reading I will reopen the door. I promise." Europa looked at Jeanip, trying to give him her best confident and honest look. She needed to keep the door closed in order to explore the attic items. "Say okay, say okay, say okay," she kept repeating over in her mind.

"Don't forget," Jeanip said, as he began to descend the stairs.

With a smile on her face, Europa watched Jeanip walk downstairs. Thinking she should say something about him allowing Terrance to stay on the estate she quickly said, "Jeanip, thank you for allowing Terrance to visit today and for the invitation that he stay out here. It means a lot to me."

Jeanip stopped on the third step down and turned to face her. "I like your young man, Europa. I am glad you are friends. If you have no further need of me I will take my leave of you, Your Highness. Sleep well."

"You try to sleep well also," Europa said, knowing Jeanip would be up most of the night planning for her departure and her continued safety. As she closed the door her smile grew until it stretched across her face. She felt like jumping and bouncing around the room she was so excited. "Jeanip accepts him. He approves. Hurray!" Europa shouted, and then realized she might wake Birea. To avoid Birea rushing in to see what was wrong and staying forever to chat, Europa silenced her words and did a merry jig around the room instead.

As Jeanip descended the stairs he heard Europa's shouts of joy. For a brief moment he allowed himself to feel the warmth her words brought to his heart. He relished in their joy and comfort, the first he had felt since Medaron's death.

"Looks like our girl might be in love, Triton." Jeanip said, as he passed Triton at the bottom of the stairs.

Triton looked up at him. "I believe you are correct," he silently said. "You made her very happy tonight. I believe she has remembered how much she loves you and has forgiven you for burying Mother without her." He laid his head on the rug in preparation for a night of sleep.

Jeanip smiled and tucked the joy of Europa's happiness and Earon's words behind his heart. Straightening his shoulders, he returned to being the Commander in charge of keeping his people's two monarchs safe.

THE ORB

Once Europa was sure Jeanip had gone into his room, she quickly retrieved her hidden treasures and laid them on the bed. She retrieved a notebook and pen from her desk and recorded the items on the pad. She wanted to compare her list with Terrance's when he returned to see if they could find a connection.

The map to the Complex did not interest her since she had no idea what or where it was, nor could she read the writing on it. The deed was straightforward, showing the people who originally purchased the land were an Enok and Medaron Waters in 1658. Jeanip had confirmed her grandparents that settled there bore the same name as her parents. Setting the deed aside, she picked up the map of Minnos and concentrated on it. Remembering seeing a secret tunnel, she scanned the map looking specifically for it and its entrance to the ocean. At first its location eluded her, but then she saw it clearly indicated on the map. Europa traced the tunnel back from the cave into the house and was not surprised to discover it ended in the room next to the kitchen on the main floor - Jeanip's room. She knew it was the perfect place for a hidden entrance because no one was allowed inside that room without a special invitation from Jeanip himself due to all the hi-tech security devices and grids the room contained. She wondered why Jeanip had felt the necessity to construct such a tunnel. Then she thought perhaps Jeanip had nothing to do with its construction; perhaps it was built when the original settlers built the cottage to give them a safe escape route in case of attack or other unforeseen danger. Her ancestors were the only Caucasians at the time within hundreds of miles and perhaps they feared for their safety.

She began to scrutinize the map further trying to determine where the cave was located. If she was reading it correctly, the cave appeared to be right under Water's Rock, a large bluff with a sheer drop to the ocean. Several of the streams on the property emptied into a larger stream several miles before the edge of the bluff before cascading over the edge as a waterfall. She made a mental note to search the area once she was able to leave Minnos and to investigate if the cave still existed, and if so, what purpose it served.

Europa jumped, startled by the sound of her watch's alarm announcing the hour of midnight. She had become so engrossed in her treasures she forgot it was set to tell her when it was time to return to the attic. Ever since her dreams the previous night, she felt an ever increasing desire to see and possibly touch the Orb again. It was almost as if it was calling to her, beckoning her to return and connect with it once more. She knew this was an absurd idea, but she had to admit she and the Orb had somehow interacted together, forming some strange bond. Having no previous experience with such a device she had no idea what it was capable of or what her touch might have triggered – or awakened. The thought she might have activated the Orb scared her yet intrigued her at the same time.

Europa quietly crossed the room to her dresser, opened her sweater drawer and felt around underneath them until her hand hit cold metal. She grabbed the metal and pulled it out, revealing her mother's ring of keys. She had slipped them into her pajama pants' pocket the last time she was in her mother's room and had left in such a hurry she had forgotten to put them back. She was now glad she hadn't. These keys were going to unlock her mother's door and grant her access to the attic and the Orb. She slipped the keys into her pocket where they would remain safely hidden in the event she was discovered out in the hallway.

However, before she could leave her room she needed to devise a plan to make anyone who might check on her think she was in her room. Since she had promised Jeanip she would leave her door open when she went to bed she opted not to stuff her bed to give the illusion she was sleeping. As she looked around trying to determine a good disguise, she saw her shower. She knew instantly that was her cover. She quickly turned the bathroom lights on, turned the shower on low and closed the bathroom door. The masquerade of a shower would also allow her to leave her bedroom door closed, thus giving her an added concealment. Taking a deep breath, she silently opened her door and stepped into the hallway. Motionless, she listened for the sound of any one up. She could hear Birea snoring lightly in the next room signaling she was still asleep. She peered carefully down the staircase to see the almost indiscernible figure of Triton asleep on the rug to the right of the

167

stairs. Assured the silence meant it was okay to proceed, Europa carefully tiptoed down the hallway toward her mother's room, being careful to avoid the wooden boards known to creak. At last she made it to the door, carefully removed the key ring taking care they did not clank together, inserted one of the keys and turned the lock. Silently stepping inside, she closed and relocked the door behind her. She flipped on the second light and scurried across the floor to her mother's closet, pushing the clothes aside and almost running up the small flight of stars. As she stepped off the top step the Orb began to glow and softly hum as it had when she touched it. But she was still several feet away. Was it glowing and humming in response to her presence? Had she been right, had the Orb been waiting for her to return?

As she tried to determine what was happening with the Orb, she suddenly realized another light was illuminating the room. Alarmed, she looked around expecting to see Jeanip or Birea, but there was no one. She looked down and realized the newly introduced light was coming from the amulet around her neck. It too was now glowing and omitting a low hum in unison with the Orb. Without hesitation, Europa walked to the Orb and placed her hands upon it. Just as before, threads of lavender, purple, blue and yellow began to emanate from the Orb, entwining around her hands and circling up her arms. This time she did not remove her hands but kept them firmly upon the Orb, no longer fearing it was some type of security device. The threads of light continued up her arms, then progressed to her shoulders, her neck, her chest, her head, until her entire body was entwined in glowing light. Although she knew she should be scared, Europa felt relaxed and unafraid, somehow knowing the Orb meant her no harm. Europa closed her eyes and images began to appear in her mind of the luminous beings she had seen in her dreams. There were thousands of the beings swimming through the waters, so graceful and beautiful that the image almost brought tears to her eyes. As she continued to watch them she suddenly realized she could hear them talking, but not verbally as humans do. These beings spoke telepathically; she was hearing their thoughts. Suddenly the water churned a bright purple as many of the beings vanished amidst screams of terror and pain. The scene shifted and before her appeared the male and a female who wore the amulets identical to hers. She watched as another being approach them, raised one of his wings to his forehead and addressed the two.

"Enok, Medaron, it is time for us to leave. The time Enoquin stipulated came and passed several days ago. We can delay the evacuation no longer, Your Majesties. If we see we are in error we can always return. But for now, it is important that we get our people and you to safety, away from our home world."

"But we do not have enough transports to take everyone. And what about the Orbs? We cannot allow them to be destroyed," the female sadly said.

"Many Oonocks had already stated they will not leave their homeland, Your Majesty. For those who do wish to leave, we will take as many as we can. As for the Orbs, you are right – they cannot be destroyed. Our history, our culture, our very heritage is contained within them. But remember, FarCore is not of this world; only its entrance is. The Orbs are safe inside FarCore. As for the empty Orbs, they have already been gathered and taken to the ships. Each group will take several Orbs with them to record their travels so that future generations may know of our struggles to live, where we came from and why we left our home world," the male being replied.

"Jeanip is right, Medaron," the first male stated, taking his mate's hand into his own and looking into her eyes. "This was the decision we made when my parents left. We must get as many of our people as possible to safety and help them build a new life, a new world. You carry with you the entrance to FarCore. I promise you that, when we reach our new home, I will build you a sanctuary where you can place the entrance to FarCore. Together, we will place the Orbs that travel with us inside FarCore where they will be safe for all eternity."

"As always, you are right, My Dearest Love," the female said as she softly placed her hand beside his cheek. "Together, with the aid of the Quanundocii, we will save our people."

"Yes we will, My Only Love." The first male turned to address the second male. "Alright, Jeanip, we are ready to leave. Are Misso, Tiree and Reemee on board?"

"Yes, Sire."

Europa watched as the scene changed to a landscape of ice with a large brownish-red planet floating in space in the distance. Suddenly the ice burst open and through the opening emerged a number of spaceships. They hovered for a moment above the ice then broke into groups of two and three before sailing off in different directions. As she watched the ships sail away, she was startled when a huge flash of light erupted behind them. A plume of red liquid fire shot out into space to the right of the ships, destroying several. She watched as the planet became a large ball of fire as the fire plume ignited the volatile gases encircling the planet, consuming everything in its path. Soon it began to fold into itself as huge windstorms were created, ripping the very planet apart. She gasped as the planet turned into a reddish-orange and white sphere of swirling gases with an enormous red wind storm clearly visible

169

in its lower quadrant. Europa realized she had just witnessed the birth of the great gaseous planet Jupiter and the spaceships had emerged from beneath the ice barrier of their moon. Their home world was Europa!

Terrance hurried and got dressed the next morning, quickly packing his suitcases. In his backpack he placed the articles from his father's room, burying them safely under a jacket and hoodie. He grabbed the envelope of dog tranquilizers he had purchased and slipped it into his pocket. As he heard the bellboy knock, he looked around the room to be sure he had not left anything behind. He opened the door and handed the bellboy his father's luggage. Picking up his two suitcases plus his backpack, he followed the bellboy downstairs, closing his door behind him. He walked to the front desk and checked out, still having trouble believing he was really going to stay at Minnos. Handing the desk clerk his father's two suitcases and his address, he asked her to ship the baggage to his father's residence in Michigan.

Knowing Misso would have breakfast for him, he bypassed the dining room and walked briskly out the door. Anxiety racing through his body, he waited for Sunam on the porch, his backpack containing his treasures securely on his back, a suitcase in each hand. As he waited he noticed the sheriff crossing the street heading toward him.

"Hi, Mr. Landers, I was wondering if you had a minute?" the sheriff asked, as he walked up to Terrance.

"Actually, I'm waiting for a ride," Terrance replied. "He should be here any minute."

"Since it seems he has not arrived yet I'd like to ask you about your father."

"My father?" Terrance repeated, suddenly alarmed his father's disappearance had become known to the police. Or even worse, they also thought he had something to do with Mrs. Waters' death.

"We received a call from the University of Michigan saying he had not returned and they were wondering if we knew if he was still in town," the sheriff stated. "The inn's manager said he never returned to claim his belongings in his room. Do you know where your father is?"

"He left me a note stating something important had come up and he had to return immediately to the university. He said he didn't have time to collect his belongings and asked if I would bring them with me when I returned to Michigan," Terrance lied, commanding his eyes to look directly into the sheriff's. "I haven't heard from him since then."

"Did he tell you what prompted his return?" the sheriff asked, doubt clearly visible on his face.

"No, just that it was something important. If he didn't go back to the university, perhaps he's out on another field study."

""Could you please get the note for me, Mr. Landers?"

"Excuse me?" Terrance asked, hoping he had not heard the sheriff's request correctly.

"The note your father left you telling you he was returning to Michigan. Would you please get it so I can verify your story and inform the university," the sheriff stated, apparently having no intention of leaving until he saw the note.

Terrance froze, panic starting to seep into his being. How could he get the note when he had made it up? Trying to quickly think of his next move, he was relieved to see Sunam pull into the parking lot. "Sorry, Sheriff, but my ride is here. I remember throwing the note into one of my suitcases. I'll dig it out and send it to your office tomorrow morning, if that's okay."

"No, that is not okay," the sheriff replied. "I need to see it now."

"I'm sorry, Sheriff, but my ride is on a tight schedule," Terrance stated. "So unless you have a warrant or plan to arrest me, you will have to wait until tomorrow."

Terrance could see the sheriff was annoyed by the thought of having to wait until the following day to see the note, but, upon seeing it was Sunam in the truck, he did not press the matter.

"Is there a problem here?" Sunam asked, as he exited the truck and took Terrance's suitcases, putting them in the back of the truck and securing them. He turned to stare at the sheriff. "We are on a very tight schedule, Sheriff."

"No, no problem, Sunam," the sheriff answered. Looking at Terrance he added, "I will expect that note first thing tomorrow, Mr. Landers. Or I will come looking for it." He then turned and left.

Without saying a word Terrance quickly hopped in the truck hoping they would leave before the sheriff changed his mind and took him in for questioning. Sunam nodded to the sheriff, then slid into the driver's seat, started the engine and drove away. Terrance saw the smirk on Sunam's face and realized how much power the Waters commanded in town. Not even the sheriff would go up against Jeanip or one of his men, a fact for which he was truly grateful at the moment.

171

As the day before, the ride to Minnos was quiet. Sunam did not speak, not even to ask Terrance what the sheriff wanted. Terrance was thankful for Sunam's silence but was also curious as to the reason; was he simply respecting Terrance's privacy or did he plan on informing Jeanip and leaving it up to him to deal with Terrance and the sheriff. Whatever the reason, he could not allow himself the luxury of worrying about it at the moment. He had bigger problems – mainly the nonexistent note. He used the time in the car to devise a plan to cover his father's disappearance. His father often disappeared so he really was not concerned about him, but he was alarmed about what would happen if Jeanip and the sheriff found out he lied to both of them.

Europa sat at the kitchen table waiting for Terrance, holding a cup of coffee in her hand, occasionally taking a sip. She had informed Misso she would wait for Terrance so they could eat breakfast together. She had so much to tell him, things she could barely believe herself. Glancing at the clock for the tenth time, she wondered what was taking them so long; it was less than a thirty minute drive. Finally she heard the sound of the truck as it pulled up in front of the house. She bounded from the table and ran to the door. Just as she was about to go through the door and run down the stairs into his arms, she heard Birea remind her she was not to go outside. Remembering her promise to Jeanip Europa stopped, almost falling over from the suddenness of her halt. She took several steps back and waiting for Terrance a few feet in front of the doorway.

"Royals do not run to people," Jeanip said from the stairs. "Even if they are one's boyfriend. A royal waits for people to come to them."

Europa had not seen Jeanip sitting on the stairs examining Triton's injured paw. She was very thankful for Birea's reminder. Jeanip had been so accommodating about Terrance's visits she did not want to do anything to jeopardize them. Her face red with embarrassment, she looked at Jeanip and nodded her head.

"You are correct, Jeanip. I forgot for a moment who I was."

"Understandable," he replied. "If I was a young woman and had such a handsome man coming to see me, I'd probably want to run down the stairs too. Thank you for abiding by your word not to leave the cottage." He rewrapped Triton's paw, patted him on the head and said, "That paw still has some mending to do. Remember, Triton, no stairs."

Triton gave a huff through his nose, as if he disagreed. He limped over to his rug and plopped down on it, clearly not happy.

"See, Europa, even the dog doesn't like my decisions," Jeanip chuckled, then left the room.

Hearing the sound of the front door opening, Europa acted the part of her position and walked to Terrance. He grabbed her in his arms and pulled her close to him.

"We've got problems. We need somewhere private to talk," he whispered as quietly as possible in her ear. Then he gave her a small 'good morning' kiss.

"It will have to wait. Misso is waiting for us to serve breakfast," she whispered back as he released her. Taking Terrance's hand, Europa led the way to the kitchen where Jeanip was also waiting. Both men waited until Europa sat, then seated themselves. Misso brought coffee, orange juice, platters of pancakes and scrambled eggs, bacon and sausage, a bowl of hash browns and freshly made cinnamon rolls.

"Are you expecting more company?" Terrance asked, amazed at all the food.

"No, Misso just got a little carried away," Europa answered, sending Misso a warm smile. "This is the first big breakfast she's cooked since . . ." Europa stopped in midsentence, then added "for a few days." Quickly changing the subject she added "Jeanip, is Earon joining us this morning?"

"No, I believe he ate with the men earlier," Jeanip said. "He went with them to do some surveillance. Perhaps he'll be back in time to join us for dinner."

The three ate their breakfast, chitchatting about nothing of great importance. Jeanip never mentioned Terrance's incident with the sheriff so Terrance assumed Sunam had not told him about the confrontation. Evidently, Sunam had felt the matter was something between Terrance and the sheriff and was not his concern. Terrance made a mental note he owed Sunam big time. When they had finished eating, Jeanip took his leave and headed to his room to work on the plans for the move to Saint's Isle. Europa informed Misso she and Terrance would be upstairs in her room if anyone was looking for them.

"Very well, Ma'am," Misso replied. "Would you like me to bring you some coffee or tea?"

"Not right now," Europa answered. "If we decide we want some before lunch I can always ring for you."

Taking Terrance's hand once again, Europa led him upstairs to her room, passing an unhappy Triton still lying on the rug. She led him to the sitting area and gestured for him to have a seat. Sitting beside him, she snuggled into his arms, content and feeling secure. He leaned in and gave her a long, warm kiss – the one he had wanted to give her when he first walked through the door.

"Before I forget, here are those tranquilizers," Terrance said, as he removed the small packet from his pocket. "Just slip one in a treat and he'll be asleep for hours." Seeing Europa's concerned look, he added, "And I promise it will not hurt him at all. They are perfectly safe."

Europa took the packet and stuffed it underneath the settee cushion. She had more important things to discuss than drugging Triton so she could snoop around the house.

"Terrance, you are not going to believe what happened last night!" Europa began.

"Wait, Europa, before you tell me I need to tell you we have a big problem, a problem that could end my visits here to see you," Terrance interrupted.

A deep look of concern came over Europa's face. "What do you mean? What problem?"

"Remember I told you I lied to Jeanip about my father leaving without me?"

"Yes, I remember."

"This morning, while waiting for Sunam, the sheriff approached me and asked if I knew where my father was. He said the university had contacted him because he had not returned to school. And he knew my father never picked up his belongings from his room."

"What did you tell him?" Europa asked, a feeling of fear starting to invade her mind.

"I told him I hadn't seen him but he had left me a note stating he had to return to the university immediately and for me to bring his belongings when I went to Michigan. He asked to see the note."

"Then show him the note," Europa stated, not seeing why there was a problem.

"Europa, there IS no note. I made it up. I had to think of something quick to say and that's the story I came up with. Luckily, Sunam arrived just then so I told the sheriff I'd send it to his office."

"Oh, Terrance," Europa said, standing up from the couch and beginning to pace. "When you cannot produce the note the sheriff will know you lied. And if Jeanip finds out, he will not trust you anymore."

"And I'll be barred from the estate. I know," Terrance added, a look of regret and worry clearly visible on his face.

"And once I leave we will never see each other again. What are we going to do?" Europa asked, her pacing increasing.

Terrance grabbed her by the shoulder and held her firmly, stopping her pacing. "On the drive here I came up with an idea that might work."

"What?" Europa asked, hoping his idea could correct this pending disaster.

"When I was in school I used to forge notes from my father all the time. He was gone a lot and, well, it was easier for me to write the note than to tell my father what trouble I had gotten in to. I became so good at forging his writing even he didn't know the difference. I thought I would write a note in his handwriting stating he had to leave."

"Do you think it will work?"

"I think so. My father is known for disappearing for weeks, even months at a time, as he goes off on one of his field studies. That's the reason my mother divorced him. He'd disappear, then show back up, never telling us where he'd been. His trips were always so secretive. Finally one time when he disappeared my mother took me and we moved to her hometown in Australia. He's been in trouble several times over the past few years with the University for disappearing for weeks. I think they would be surprised he would do it again after he almost was suspended last time, but they would definitely believe it. I think it is our only way out of this mess."

"I do not think we have any other choice, Terrance," Europa stated. "We are going to have to chance it. What do you need to write the note?"

"Do you have any notebook paper? I thought I'd write it here and drop it in today's mail. That way the sheriff will get it tomorrow as promised and I won't have to go back to town to personally deliver it."

175

"I have regular printer paper or stationery. Will either of these do?" Europa asked, as she held up a piece of each

"No, it has to be notebook paper. My father would only have notebook paper with him in the field."

Europa rummaged through her desk, assured that somewhere inside was an old notebook. "Found one," she announced. "Do you need something to write with too?"

"I need a pencil. He only takes a pencil with him into the field."

Europa quickly brought the notebook and pencil to Terrance. He tore out a sheet of paper and carefully wrote the note in his father's handwriting. He then folded it in half, then in half again.

"Do you have an envelope for it?" Terrance asked. 'It needs to be a plain, white one."

"Yes, I believe there is one in my desk." Europa walked back to her desk and searched through the drawers, finally finding an envelope. "Will this do?" she asked, as she held it up for Terrance to see.

"Yes, that's perfect. Would you happen to have a stamp too?"

"I know I do not have one of those up here. I usually get them from Misso. We can ask her for one when she brings us coffee later."

Terrance addressed the envelope to the sheriff. He then took the folded letter and wrote a short note to the sheriff on the back, saying he was unable to return to town but here was the note his father had left him. Then he placed it in the envelope and sealed it.

"Why did you fold it so many times?"

"My father would have folded it in fourths so it would fit in his pocket, then unfold one fold so it would slip under the door. I watched my father's habits over the years. If you're going to try to fool someone that something is from my father, you have to do things the way he would have." Terrance clarified.

"Sounds like you have had plenty of practice," Europa teased.

"Yes, I'm ashamed to say. I was not the best behaved kid when I was young," Terrance admitted. "Do you have a mailbox here?"

"Our mailbox is out at the main gate. I am sure one of the helpers would mail it for us."

"What time is your mail run?

"Gee, that is a good question. Again, we will have to ask Misso. I always just give her my letters and she makes sure they are mailed."

"Then perhaps we should ask for coffee now so we can be sure it gets mailed today. Otherwise, the sheriff will be at the front gate tomorrow shouting out my name and demanding to see the letter."

"I truly believe that is something we want to avoid." Europa quickly commented. The thought of the sheriff standing at the front gate shouting out Terrance's name and Terrance having to explain to Jeanip what the sheriff was doing there sent shivers down her spine. Europa rang the bell for Misso. When she appeared in the doorway Europa said they were ready for coffee and asked if she might have a stamp for a letter Terrance needed mailed today.

"Yes," Misso replied, "I have some downstairs. If you'd like, I can have one of the men run it down to the mailbox for you."

"Can we still make today's mail run?" Terrance asked. "It's important it goes out today."

"The mail man comes around one o'clock," Misso replied. "I can have Ebar take your letter to the mail box immediately."

"Thank you, Misso," Terrance said, as he handed Misso the letter. Misso went to the kitchen and returned five minutes later with a refreshment tray, stating Ebar had already left with Terrance's letter. Taking her leave, she left Terrance and Europa to discuss their findings.

"Now that that disaster is diverted, what did you want to tell me about last night? I interrupted you earlier." Terrance asked, as he reached for his cup of coffee and several cookies Misso had brought on the tray.

Europa took a sip of coffee and began to tell him more of her findings. "Terrance, I did not get to tell you everything earlier. There is an Orb up there suspended above a table. It seems to be a larger version of the amulet my mother gave me to wear on my birthday."

"An Orb? Like they have in fairy tales?" Terrance asked

"I guess you could say that, except this is not a fairy tale. This is reality." Europa stated, a tinge of annoyance in her voice. "The first time I touched the Orb it began to glow and hum very quietly. Strings of light encircled my hands and entwined up my arms. I feared it might be one of Jeanip's security devices, so I let go and avoided it the rest of the time I was up there. Later that night, while I was asleep, I dreamt about the Orb and some luminous beings floating in lilac water."

"Luminous beings? You mean like aliens?" Terrance asked, regretting his words as he saw a look of anger cross Europa's face.

"Do you want to hear this or not?" Europa demanded.

"I'm sorry, Europa. It's just that things are really getting weird. Wait till I tell you about the shape shifters."

"Shape shifters?" Europa asked in surprise. "What do shape shifters have to do with all this?"

"I'll tell you in a moment. You finish your story first."

"Are you sure?" Europa asked.

"Yes, you finish," Terrance replied, as he smiled warmly. "We have so much information, I think it best we exhaust one subject before going on to another."

"Very well then," Europa began. "Last night I returned to the attic. I felt as if the Orb was calling to me, beckoning me to come touch it again. But this time when I put my hands on it I did not remove them. Just like before it began to glow and hum, strings of light emerged and began to entwine up my arm. Then I realized the amulet around my neck was starting to glow also and it was humming in unison with the large Orb. As the strings encased my entire body the humming changed to voices and images appeared before me, images of the same luminous beings I saw in my dreams. There were hundreds of them floating in lilac water, then the water turned purple and there were only three of them before me. From what they were saying it sounded like someone named JeffRa was planning to destroy their world and they had to flee. From what I could tell there were hundreds of these Orbs and one of the beings said they contained records of their past and would record their journey to this world."

"You mean there are more of them? That's weird."

"Wait, Terrance, it gets weirder. Two of the beings I saw wore amulets like the one I have. The third person with them addressed them as Enok and Medaron. They called him Jeanip. Terrance," Europa said, as she reached for Terrance's hand, squeezing it hard. "The last thing I saw were spaceships emerging from underneath a barrier of ice and rising into space. The space ships broke off into groups of two or three and headed in different directions. As they flew away I saw behind them a large planet with this large swirling red storm Terrance, it was Jupiter!"

Terrance did not say a word when Europa finished. He pulled his hand away from hers, stood up abruptly and stared down at Europa. Then he began to pace in front of her, trying to absorb the things Europa had just told him. She watched him, waiting for him to say something. She couldn't tell if he was angry, or upset, or thought she was insane. Finally, unable to withstand the silence anymore, she shouted at him, "Say something, Terrance."

Terrance stopped directly in front of her, his eyes meeting hers. "What do you want me to say, Europa? You just basically told me your parents and Jeanip are aliens who fled their world because someone named JeffRa was going to destroy it, a world covered in ice circling Jupiter. Europa, don't you see? You are talking about Jupiter's ice moon Europa, the very celestial being your father named you after! Don't you think that's a little strange? Plus, we know Europa still exists today; it wasn't destroyed."

"You think I am making this up?"

"No, not making it up. But I do think you're imagining things. You yourself told me you suffered a concussion and was unconscious for days. It's not unheard of for people to have hallucinations when they get a serious concussion. Plus, you just lost your mother and woke up to find out she had already been buried. How do you know your mind is not making this all up as a way for you to deal with your mother's death?"

"Because I am not!" Europa yelled. She ran and brought back her mother's diary and the maps. She threw them at Terrance. "Here's proof. Did I make these things up too? Did I write the diary and draw the maps in my state of fantasy? Did I hide those pictures in your father's room while I was delusional, forge his journals? Did I?"

Europa heard loud steps running up the stairs, probably frightened by Terrance and her shouting. She quickly grabbed the diary and maps and hurriedly threw them beneath the couch. Seconds later her door burst open, a clearly worried Jeanip in the doorway holding a rifle in his hand.

"Jeanip, there is no need for the weapon. We just got into an argument and we got a little bit loud," Europa promptly stated when she saw Jeanip's rifle in his hand. Terrance did not say a word but slowly stepped away from Europa.

"That you did," Jeanip said. He looked at Terrance, then back at Europa. "You're sure you're okay?"

"Yes, Jeanip, I swear I am okay," Europa replied.

Looking at Terrance once again, Jeanip asked, "Terrance, this is the second time your actions have not been favorable. Was it a mistake asking you to stay out here? Should I have Sunam take you back to town?"

Terrance did not answer. Jeanip turned to look at Europa. "Europa, should Sunam take him to town?"

"That is totally up to him," Terrance heard Europa say. He looked at Jeanip then back at Europa. The last thing he wanted was to leave and return to the inn now that he had finally gotten to enter the property.

"Terrance?"

"I would like to stay," Terrance replied nervously. "If Europa has no objections."

"Europa, is that agreeable with you?"

Europa looked at Terrance "Yes, that is agreeable with me."

"Then I'll take my leave. And I suggest you two either discuss whatever it is you're discussing in a more genteel voice or change the subject. This house is already on high security alert – loud arguing voices do not go well with high security alerts. Keep it down. And keep the door open. Understand, Terrance?"

"Yes, Sir." Terrance answered. "I promise it will not happen again."

Terrance heard Jeanip say as he left, "Well, you now know she comes with a temper. At least it's not me she's mad at for a change."

"I'm sorry, Europa," Terrance said as soon as Jeanip was out of sight. "This is just so unbelievable. Put yourself in my place. Wouldn't you have a hard time accepting these things?"

"No, not if I had found what you did in my father's room," Europa stated, still annoyed at Terrance's disbelief. "I believed what you said. Why can't you believe what I am telling you?"

"It's not a matter of believing or not. It's about what's possible and what isn't. Just give me a few minutes to try to digest all that you're telling me."

"But this is not about you, Terrance. It's about me. Do you not think I am having a hard time believing it too?"

"I really am sorry," Terrance said, as he sat down. "If you say this is all real than I will believe you. All I ask is that you allow me to reserve some things as plausible until we can make sense out of all this." Europa returned to her seat next to Terrance. To show her he was truly sorry, he leaned over and gently kissed her. She kissed him back, forgiving all that was said. The kiss lasted a long time, then she curled up inside his arms once again, feeling safe and warm.

"But just think, Terrance," Europa said, as she felt his arms around her. "It would answer some of our questions, like why my mother wrote I was born human and why people in paintings hundreds of year's old look like my parents. The Orb is real, Terrance. And there are more of them somewhere. I think the answers I am looking for are contained in those other Orbs."

"But you said there was only one in the attic?" Terrance stated, wondering where the others could possibly be.

"Yes, but the beings in my vision said something about a place called FarCore. They said they were safe in FarCore."

"FarCore? But where is FarCore? Did your mother's diary give you any hint on where it could be located?"

"No, not that I remember. But I was not looking for anything called FarCore when I skimmed through it. We need to go through it again." Terrance released his hug as Europa sat up and reached under the couch to bring out the diary. She opened it in hopes of finding the word "FarCore". And she turned the first few pages her eyes suddenly widened, her mouth dropped open and a strange look came over her face.

"Europa, what's wrong?" Terrance asked, concerned by her look. He feared something was happening to her, perhaps a relapse from the concussion. "Are you okay?"

Europa raised her head and looked directly into Terrance's eyes. It took her a moment to speak due to the astonishment she was feeling. "Terrance, you are not going to believe this, but I can read some of this writing." Terrance quickly looked at the opened page of Medaron's diary and saw only a strange scribbling.

"What do you mean you can read it?"

"I can READ it; I can understand what it says. Not all of it, but I can decipher some of the words."

"But how?"

"I do not know. I could not read it yesterday, but I can now. Perhaps the Orb did something to me when I held it last night. Do you think it somehow gave me the ability to read this writing, transferred some kind of deciphering technique?"

"After what you told me I'm beginning to think anything is possible. What does it say?" Terrance asked eagerly, yet unsure if he should be worried or not.

"I cannot make all of it out." Europa scanned the pages and read:

"11913 – JeffRa found and exiled for his treachery. Vows to eradicate all members of the royal family alive and to be born."

"11958 – Disaster. Creeno has imploded. Twenty ships left, only seventeen made it. Many had to be left behind. Enok and I decided to resettle on the first blue planet. JeffRa's vow of revenge has begun."

"11970 – Arrived on blue planet with three ships. Something about shape shifting here."

"12020 - Received word from colony on Fenoll. Ah, JeffRa found them. Cannot make out this part. Presume they are all dead. To hide ourselves we are sinking the city immediately."

"12052 – JeffRa found us at New City. City destroyed, JeffRa killed. Something about him killing her son. *Enok seriously injured. We must return to the deep. I am responsible for Tiree's death."*

"12053 – Enok recovering. She is consumed with guilt and grief for Tiree."

"12058 – Complex finally completed. I am lost in despair."

Europa stopped reading when she heard footsteps on the stairs. She slid the diary under the pillow as Misso appeared in the doorway.

"Lunch is ready, Your Majesty," Misso said.

"Thank you, Misso. We will be right down. Did Terrance's letter make today's mail?"

"Yes, the postman picked it up."

As soon as Misso left, Europa hurriedly grabbed the diary and maps and returned them to their hiding place in the bathroom. She hoped they would find time to read more later.

"Just a minute, Europa" Terrance said, stopping Europa from leaving. "When you were reading you said something about shape shifting. That's what I've wanted to tell you. My father had a reference in his journal about a book talking about shape shifters. I found a copy of the book at the library. It was a collection of native folk tales and one was about a group of shape shifters. The author was a Mr. Dark Feather, who is a resident of these parts."

"Thomas Dark Feather?" Europa asked, intrigued by this new information.

"Yes, you don't happen to know him, do you?"

"Yes. He is a good friend of Mother's and Jeanip's."

"You've got to be kidding me," Terrance said in astonishment.

"What did he say?"

"He said legend tells of a band of strangers who settled here hundreds of years ago on a high bluff overlooking the ocean. He said they were shape shifters, born of the sky and water. They saved the chief's daughter and were given a parcel of land to live on."

"Did he say where the land was?"

"No, he wouldn't tell me. But from a few statements he made, I think it's Minnos."

"Of course. Where else would it be?" Europa said sarcastically. She walked over to her desk and brought out a jar of permanent ink. She dipped one of her fingers in the ink, and then headed downstairs.

"What are you up to?" Terrance asked her.

"You will see." As they reached the bottom of the stairs, Triton was waiting on his rug, wagging his tail to show his eagerness to see her. Europa walked over to Triton and rubbed his ears, secretly marking the right ear inside with the ink. Terrance gave her a confused look. "A little test," she whispered.

THE TEST

After lunch Europa and Terrance returned to Europa's bedroom to discuss more of their findings and their suspicions. Since they had to leave the door open, both felt it unsafe to bring out the attic articles where they might be seen. They were glad of that decision when, ten minutes later, they heard footsteps coming up the stairs. Suddenly, Jeanip appeared in the doorway.

"Europa, I will be working in your mother's room with Earon, Birea and Sunam. We will be boxing up some of her more valuable belongings for storage. Is there anything in particular you wanted to keep for yourself?"

Europa thought for a minute. "My mother had a box of some of my baby things. Could you have someone bring them to me so I can look through them? I know my baby blanket is amongst them, and I would like to have that for sure. Anything I do not want to keep I will leave in the box and place it in the hallway for someone to take to storage. I would also like the locket with my father's picture in it. And the two paintings my mother has on her wall of the Dumbo Octopus." In her mind she added "I would like the Orb in the attic too. Would you not have a heart attack if I said that?"

"I'll have someone bring those to you shortly," Jeanip said. He followed after the others, who were now waiting at Medaron's door. Europa heard the clatter of keys, then the sound of a door unlocking.

"Dumbo Octopus?" Terrance asked. "I have never heard of such a thing. What are Dumbo Octopus?"

"They are a form of octopus which live in the deep depths of the ocean. They are called Dumbo because of the way their large fins protrude from their sides right behind their head. They look just like Dumbo the elephant. My father surprised my mother with paintings of two Dumbos when she first arrived here. They were one of her most cherished possessions."

Several minutes later Birea appeared at the door carrying a box with two picture frames on top. She placed them on the floor next to Europa. "Jeanip said if you think of anything else you would like to let one of us know."

"Thanks, Birea, I will." Europa carefully lifted the two pictures frames and showed Terrance the paintings of the Dumbo Octopus.

"These were your mother's cherished possessions? I hate to say it, Europa, but they are really ugly – and weird." Terrance stated, as he stared at the pictures, laughing.

"They are not ugly," Europa chuckled. "They are cute, in a very unique way."

"If you say so," Terrance teased, smiling broadly. "But I think if you sold them at a garage sale you'd be lucky to get a dime for the pair."

"Ha, ha," Europa mocked laughed. "I asked my mother once about them when I was little. She said she had seen a picture of them once and fell in love with them. She said they were one of nature's wonders, surviving in a hostile world while maintaining their beauty and dignity. Because they live at such depths in the ocean, they cannot be brought up here." Terrance looked at the octopus again, seeing nothing cute about them. "My father was not able to come with my mother when she first came to Minnos. He wanted her to have something special to welcome her to her new home, plus something that would remind her of how much he loved her. He painted these two paintings for her as a symbol of his love and a representation that, although they were separated like the two octopuses in the paintings, they were eternally united as one pair. Occasionally, I would see her run her fingers over them so gently. And there would be tears in her eyes. I think she did it when she missed my father the most. They always seemed to give her strength."

"Now I feel really bad about teasing you about them," Terrance said, embarrassed to learn the truth behind the paintings. "I can't believe your father did such a beautiful thing. He must have loved your mother very, very much."

"Yes, and she loved him just as much." Europa sat the paintings down on the floor and reached into the box, bringing out a silver locket. "I never remember a day when my mother did not wear this locket around her neck along with her amulet." She gently opened the locket and showed the picture inside to Terrance. He looked down to see a very distinguished man, very muscular, with brown hair and blue eyes that almost looked lilac. "Terrance, this is my father."

Terrance slipped the locket into his hand and stared at the picture, totally in disbelief. "Europa, this is the same man in those paintings my father had pictures of."

"Oddly enough, Terrance, he is also the same man in the paintings in the attic," Europa added. "Yet how can that be? How could my parents have been alive hundreds of years ago?"

"I don't' know" Terrance stated. "It seems the more we discover, the further we get from the truth."

Due to the constant stream of people parading up and down the stairs with boxes for storage, Terrance and Europa decided to go downstairs to the front sitting room in hopes it might offer them more privacy. Upon reaching the main level Europa noticed Triton was nowhere to be seen. She peered through the window to determine if he was outside, but there was no sign of him. She saw Misso in the formal living room dusting the furniture and went to inquire about Triton's where about.

"Misso, do you know where Triton is?"

"Yes, Miss, Jeanip put him in his room after he caught Triton trying to sneak upstairs when you and Terrance had your loud discussion earlier. Since he would be working in your mother's room he thought Triton might try to go upstairs again and possibly reinjure his paw."

"Poor Triton. He is not use to such confinement," Europa said, as she and Terrance headed for the kitchen. Europa suddenly stopped upon seeing the door to Jeanip's room and whispered to Terrance, "Go keep Misso busy. I want to see if Triton is really in Jeanip's room."

"How am I supposed to do that?" Terrance whispered back.

"Be your charming self and ask her about some of the antiques in there," Europa said softly, as she quickly kissed him. "You have a wealth of knowledge about the subject. I am sure you can think of something to ask her." Quickly formulating a few questions in his head, Terrance went off to engage Misso while Europa hurried over to Jeanip's room. Waiting until she heard the two discussing her mother's prized display case of antique vases, she scurried over to the door. Holding her breath and hoping the door was not locked, she turned the knob. To her surprise it opened. In all the years she had lived there, she had never been inside and she was surprised to see the expanse of his domicile. There were several rooms, the first of which was a small sitting room from which a hallway extended back into the house. At the end of the hallway she could see blinking lights and gadgets; probably the main security room. There were two closed doors on the left hand side of the hallway and one on the right. She assumed the two on the left were probably a bathroom and bedroom. As for the third door, she wondered if it was the entrance to the secret passage leading to the cave below. She desperately wanted to open the three doors and see if there was indeed a secret passage, but she feared she might get caught inside the room. She knew Jeanip would be very upset if he knew she was being nosey. Remembering the reason for being there, she quietly called for Triton. He did not respond – he was not in the room. She peeked out into the kitchen to assure no one was around, then quickly stepped out, closing the door behind her. She walked to where Terrance could see her and signaled she was finished. Terrance thanked Misso for her informative speech, excused himself and returned to where Europa was.

"Well, was he in there?" Terrance asked, looking around for the canine.

"No! I did not think he would be but I had to be sure. Have you ever noticed when Earon is around, Triton is not, and vice versa?"

"What are you suggesting, that Earon and Triton are the same person? That Earon's a shape shifter?"

"No, I am not suggesting that. Well, yes, maybe I am. You said yourself Mr. Dark Feather wrote about shape shifters and chances are the property they settled on is Minnos. It certainly would explain how Jeanip knew of my activities. I have searched Triton's collar and coat several times for some sort of hidden radio transmitter, but I have never been able to find one. So, if Jeanip is not eavesdropping on my activities, the only other explanation is Triton is telling him what I am doing. How does that saying go; something like if you eliminate all the impossible reasons usually the remaining simplest reason is the truth. It goes something like that." Europa paused for a moment in thought. "Plus, how did Earon get on Minnos? You said the front gate was padlocked and all the fences electrified immediately after the accident. And Jeanip would never have unlocked the gate to let him in, royalty or not. He wasn't here, Terrance, before the accident, so how did he get here right after? I'll tell you how – he didn't. He was already here inside this house, disguised as Triton!"

"Ackman's razor," Terrance whispered, seeing the truth in her statements. "This time I think you are right, Europa. I've noticed Earon speaks a lot like you do. I don't know if you realize it or not, but you seldom use contractions. You say 'cannot' instead of 'can't' and 'will not' instead of 'won't'."

"That is my mother's upbringing," Europa stated, smiling. "She said royals have to speak correctly."

"See, you just did it again. You said 'that is' and not 'that's'. Earon does the exact same thing. So someone had to have instructed him in proper speaking also." Terrance paused for a minute trying to determine how they could test his hypothesis. "But how can we prove Triton is Earon?"

"Already covered," Europa smiled. "That was what the ink smug in Triton's ear was all about. If by some weird, unbelievable circumstance Triton and Earon are the same person, Earon will have a black mark inside his left ear too. If Earon has dinner with us this evening, like he usually does, we will be able to check his ear. If it is there, we will know he is Triton."

"And if he doesn't?"

"Then we are back to square one."

Misso announced dinner was ready. Terrance and Europa hurried to the kitchen to look at Earon's ear. As they entered the kitchen both were disappointed to see only Jeanip waiting at the table. Europa quickly looked around for Earon. Not seeing him, she checked to see if Triton was there. He too was missing. She hid her disappointment and smiled at Jeanip.

"Were you able to box up all of Mother's valuables?" she asked, as she approached the table.

"I sure hope so because I do not believe I could carry another box out to the barn," came a voice from behind Europa. She turned to see Earon entering the kitchen. She gave him a big smile, almost leaping for joy when she saw a black mark inside his left ear as he passed. She poked Terrance in his side to get his attention, then tugged on her left ear. Terrance turned just as Earon walked by. He had to turn his head to hide his smile when he noticed the black mark inside Earon's ear. When he locked eyes with Europa, the two could not help themselves and began to giggle.

"What are you two laughing about?" Earon asked, looking over his clothing. "Do I have paint on my face or are my clothes on wrong?"

Laughing, Europa answered, "Not paint, Earon, but you do have something black inside your ear?"

"Pardon me, Your Majesty?" Earon asked, surprised by Europa's announcement.

"Yes, you seem to have gotten paint or ink on your ear," Jeanip stated, as he too now saw the mark. "It is an amusing addition to your attire. A little one sided, though." Everyone could see Jeanip was trying not to join in the laughter.

Excusing himself, Earon left for the washroom. He returned several minutes later still with a blacked ear. "Looks like it will not come off," Earon stated. "I must have gotten marker on my hands while boxing up Medaron's items and touched my ear. Looks to be permanent for a while. Maybe I should put a mark in the other ear so they match."

Everyone laughed, especially Europa. She felt bad about playing such a trick on Earon, but it did confirm one of their suspicions – Earon and Triton were somehow the same being.

As soon as Europa was seated, the men sat down at the dining table. They enjoyed a delicious meal of fresh vegetables from the garden, broiled chicken, rice pilaf and a cucumber and tomato salad.

"Terrance, I do apologize for not being much of a host today," Jeanip announced, as he looked up from his plate at Terrance. "The job of packing up Medaron's valuables took longer than I had hoped."

"That's okay, Jeanip," Terrance replied. "I understand you have a lot to do. Besides, Europa has been an excellent hostess."

"And I am sure he did not come out here to see you, Jeanip," Earon teased.

Ignoring Earon's remark Jeanip announced, "Europa, I thought it would be nice if your girl friends came to visit tomorrow. I'm sure they have been worried about you. And since you will be leaving soon, I thought perhaps you would like the opportunity to say goodbye."

"Leaving?" asked Terrance, hoping Jeanip would reveal more information about when he planned on moving Europa.

"For college," Jeanip lied.

"Yes, I would very much like to see them before I leave," Europa said, Both Terrance and Europa knew she was not leaving for college but to a safer location, but they played along with Jeanip's explanation.

"I had Misso write up three invitations inviting them to come out tomorrow morning. I'll have one of the men take them into town and deliver them," Jeanip replied.

After having coffee and dessert in the front living room, Terrance entertained everyone with stories of Australia and what it was like to live in the outback. He told several stories of friends or acquaintances who had close encounters with the notorious saltwater crocodiles. But even with the tales of crocodile and wildlife encounters, Europa thought it sounded like a beautiful and wonderful place to visit. She hoped when this was all over she could travel with Terrance to see his country and meet his mother. Misso stepped into the room to see if anyone wanted anything before she retired for the evening. No one did. Jeanip took leave of the royals to retire to his room, stating he would be back when it was time to secure the estate for the night and escort Terrance to the bunkhouse. After Jeanip left, the three decided to go into the kitchen and play a game of monopoly. They played for several hours laughing and having a good time, the concerns of Terrian stalkers momentarily forgotten. All too soon Jeanip re-emerged from his room, announcing it was time to lock the cottage, which meant it was necessary for Terrance to retire to the bunk house for the night. Earon said his goodnights and retired to Jeanip's room to give the young couple some privacy. He needed to transfer into Triton for the evening, but wasn't sure how he could without raising Europa's and Terrance's suspicions of where he went. Then an idea came to him. He undressed and stood behind the door, opened it slightly and poked his head out.

"Hey, do you guys know poor ol' Triton is in here?"

"I was wondering where he went," Europa responded, forcing herself not to laugh.

"I'm sorry, Your Highness, I had placed him in the room when I caught him trying to sneak up the stairs earlier today," Jeanip stated. "He was sleeping when I entered my room earlier and forgot to bring him out with me."

Europa knew Jeanip never forget where Triton was. He never forgot anything. But she played along with the masquerade. "Can you let him out, Earon? I am sure he needs to go outside."

"Yes, Ma'am," Earon said. As soon as his sentence was completed he swiftly transformed into Triton and trotted out of the room. He walked over to the back door and waited, wagging his tail, indicating he needed to go outside. Jeanip opened the door and Triton ran down the steps believing his deception had been believable.

"Terrance, if you would please take your leave now I'll walk you out to the bunk house," Jeanip said, as he let Triton back inside. "Remember, once you are in the bunk house you cannot leave until one of the men turn off the security grid tomorrow morning."

"Good night, Europa. I will see you early in the morning." Hesitating for just a moment to determine if it was acceptable or not, Terrance leaned toward Europa and gave her a quick kiss goodnight. Triton barked, but did not advance toward the couple. He laughed to himself when he saw their expressions; he thought it funny to give the young ones a little scare.

"Good night, Terrance," Europa said, as their kiss ended. She looked over at Jeanip who was pretending not to have noticed, but she could see he definitely had a smile on his face. She walked Terrance to the back door and watched as Jeanip led Terrance to his room in the bunk house.

When Jeanip returned, he secured the cottage for the night. He informed Europa Triton's foot had healed and he could now go upstairs again. As soon as Europa gestured to Triton to come up, he bounded up the stairs, ran straight into Europa's room and hopped on the bed. He began to roll around on the covers, thrilled he wouldn't have to sleep on a floor rug any longer.

"Well, I guess you definitely missed my bed, didn't you?" Europa said. Triton just rolled over on his back and looked at her.

She had planned on visiting the attic after everyone had gone to bed, but with Triton back in her room she wouldn't be able to chance it. Then she remembered the packet of tranquilizers Terrance had brought her. They were still under the cushion where she had stuffed them earlier in the day. She walked over to the settee and pretended to rearrange the pillows while retrieving the packet and quickly slipped it into her pocket.

"You know, Triton," Europa said looking at the relaxed canine, "I think I am going to go get some of those cookies Misso made and a glass of milk. Would you like anything?" Triton gave a soft bark.

Europa quietly walked down to the kitchen. She poured herself a glass of milk and placed several cookies on a napkin. She then went to the refrigerator to see if there was some treat she could hide the tranquilizer in. Europa smiled when she saw a package of hotdogs. Jeanip frowned on having them in the house, but Misso always keep some around for Europa. She removed two hotdogs and brought them with her upstairs. As soon as she returned to her room, Triton smelled the hotdogs. He jumped off the bed and came to her, wagging his tale.

"You are going to have to wait, Triton," Europa said, smiling at the salivating canine. "I have to visit the little girl's room first. I think I will take our goodies with me or they may end up in your mouth before I return." Walking into the bathroom, she sat the food down on the counter. She broke one of the hotdogs in half and stuffed a pill inside. After flushing the toilet and running the faucets to add belief to her story, Europa walked back into the bedroom, dressed for bed.

"Okay, here you go Triton," she said, throwing Triton the half hotdog with the pill, then the other half. The extra hotdog she ate with her cookies and milk. Grabbing her book from the night stand, Europa crawled into bed and pretended to prepare to have a good read. Triton hopped back up on the bed and curled up beside her. A few minutes later, when Europa looked, he was fast asleep.

After listening for movement in the house, Europa tiptoed down to her mother's room. With the valuables removed, there was no need for the door to be locked now. Europa turned the knob and walked in. As she stepped into the room the smell of her mother's perfume once again engulfed her, stirring up emotions she fought daily with. She wanted to just stand there, drinking in her mother's smell but she knew time was short. She hurried to the closet and up the stairs. When she reached the top step she froze in disbelief. The place where the Orb had been was now empty. She looked around the attic for it, searching in boxes that had been left behind, but it was not to be found. She had to accept the fact it was gone – Jeanip had packed it up and put it in storage. And she had no idea where the storage was.

Disappointed, she left the attic and returned to her room. Having no interest in tackling a book, she crawled into bed beside Triton and drifted off to sleep.

ANNA

As usual, Terrance awoke early the following morning. He listened to hear if any of the men were up and was relieved to hear them talking in the next room. That meant the security grid would be off and he could go up to the cottage as soon as he dressed. Every minute he was able to spend with Europa was precious, because he knew his days with her were numbered; soon Jeanip would be moving her to a more secured location. He was still pondering the idea of asking Jeanip if it was possible for him to go along, but he was pretty sure Jeanip would not allow it. The very concept of a secured site was no one knew of its location. And he was sure the sheriff would not appreciate having another Landers disappear on him.

As Terrance showered and dressed, he felt a little apprehensive. He didn't know why, but he felt that something wasn't right. He attributed the feeling to the fact that this could be the last day he would see Europa. If that was the case, he needed to show her the other articles he had taken from his father's room, especially the weapon. He hoped Europa would be able to decipher the markings on it, just as she had the symbols in her mother's diary. He walked over to his backpack and felt inside for the weapon. It was still securely hidden in the bottom of the pack. With the girls coming to visit today it would be difficult to find time to talk to Europa alone, but he'd figure something out.

Terrance walked into the other room to check with Sunam that it was okay to go outside. He did not want to set off any alarms by going to the house too early. Sunam assured him it was safe. Terrance noticed Sunam hesitated for a moment, perceiving he had more to say.

"Did you need something, Sunam?"

193

"I hate to ask this of you, Mr. Landers, but might I impose on you to accompany me this morning to pick up Miss Europa's friends?" Terrance could see Sunam definitely was uncomfortable about the idea of being the only person in a car with three young chattering women. "As I am sure you have noticed, I am not the most loquacious person and the three young ladies will have all kinds of questions to ask during the drive back to Minnos. I thought perhaps you could ride along and help with their questions."

Terrance smiled, not only because he felt sorry for Sunam, but because Sunam trusted him enough to ask for his help. Plus, he owed Sunam a favor for not saying anything about his confrontation with the Sheriff the day he picked him up from the inn. "I would be delighted to tag along. Just let me check with Europa to be sure she has no objections. And I assume I also need to get Jeanip's approval?"

"No, it is not necessary to ask Jeanip. Jeanip's approval is implied with my asking you. However, regarding Miss Europa, you will definitely need to ask her for HER approval. Not even Jeanip can speak for her." Sunam smiled, amused his monarch was already training her suitor on what was expected of him. "I'm glad to see you're learning the idiosyncrasies of dealing with a young female monarch. They can be quite exasperating at times."

"So I'm learning! What time are you leaving?"

Sunam looked down at his watch. "The girls were told to expect me outside the inn at nine-thirty. It is now eight-fifty. I will need to leave by nine o'clock."

"I'll meet you out front in eight minutes," Terrance said, as he grabbed his backpack and headed toward the cottage. He ran up the stairs and entered the kitchen, delighted to see Europa already sitting at the table with a cup of coffee waiting for him. She gave him a big smile as he walked over to her and gave her a kiss. "Good morning," he said.

"Good morning, Terrance," Europa said, visibly pleased to see him. "Is it not a lovely morning? Would you like some coffee? We are going to wait for my friends to have breakfast. I hope that is okay."

"Yes, that would be fine," Terrance answered. "And it is a beautiful morning and no, I'll pass on the coffee at the moment. Sunam has asked me to ride along with him to pick up your friends. Would you object if I accompany him? I think he's afraid to be the only male in the car."

Europa laughed, for she knew Terrance was absolutely right. Sunam was often shy and awkward the few times he had been around her friends. She knew he would be very nervous driving them by himself. "I think that is an excellent idea. Poor Sunam would probably have a nervous breakdown before he got back if he had to go by himself. I think he would prefer desertion over that."

"Desertion?" asked Terrance, wondering why Europa used that particular word.

"It seems like I have known you forever, so I forget you do not know a lot of our backgrounds. Sunam was a soldier under Jeanip. In fact, he was his Second in Command."

"That's why they're both so disciplined. They're former soldiers."

"Actually, Terrance, they are not former soldiers. They ARE soldiers." Europa could see the perplexed look on Terrance's face. She thought more explanation was warranted. "They are members of a very small, elite group of soldiers my father created to protect my mother and me. Even though they appear to be civilians, to them they are still under a strict military code and discipline. Their one assignment is my security and happiness."

"I don't know why that even surprises me," Terrance said. He looked at his watch, gave her a small kiss goodbye and ran out the door. It was eight-fifty-seven. "Be back soon," he yelled back as he raced to the car where Sunam waited.

Sunam and Terrance pulled in front of the inn at nine-twenty-six to see Anna and Suzie sitting on the porch swing outside the inn. When they saw Terrance step out of the car, they immediately ran up to him, each giving him a big hug while thanking him for getting them access to Minnos.

"Is Rannie coming?" Terrance asked, as he looked around to see if Rannie was running late.

"We haven't heard from her," Anna replied. "She had mentioned something last week about her family going on vacation, so she may be out of town."

"It's just the two of us," Suzie replied.

Terrance opened the door for Anna while Sunam did the same on the driver's side for Suzie. "Good morning, Sunam. Thanks for picking us up this morning," Suzie said, sliding onto the back car seat.

"Good morning, Miss Suzie, Miss Anna," Sunam replied, as he nodded to both women. "It was no trouble to come and get you. Miss Europa is very excited about your visit."

Terrance closed Anna's door and turned to take a seat in the front when he noticed Mr. Dark Feather's niece, the librarian, walking toward him, calling his name. Leaving his door open to ensure Sunam did not leave without him, he walked to meet the librarian.

"Oh, Mr. Landers, I'm so glad I caught you," she began. "My uncle asked me to give this to you. He said it might help you on your journey to knowledge." The librarian opened her hand to reveal a small leather pouch tied with a purple cord. Terrance opened the pouch to find a smooth oval purple rock. On one side were markings similar to those on the strange weapon and on the other side was an etching of the woman resembling Europa's mother.

"This looks very old," Terrance said.

"It is," the librarian confirmed. "I believe over three hundred years. My uncle said to tell you this stone was given to our people by the strangers who settled on the bluff. Mr. Landers, this is a great honor my uncle has bestowed upon you. This is a cherished relic of our people. I've never know him to give something this important, this valuable to anyone, especially a stranger. I asked him why he was doing this and he said your future demanded you have the stone."

"Do you know what he meant by that?

"No, I'm sorry."

"I don't know what to say," Terrance stammered. "Please thank your uncle for me. Tell him I will take good care of this. Now, if you will excuse me, Sunam wants to return to the estate."

"One more moment, please, Mr. Landers," the librarian stated, reaching out to hold Terrance's arm so he didn't leave. "My uncle also gave me a message for Jeanip. He stated you needed to tell Jeanip immediately upon your return to Minnos that a large herd of deer have been seen coming down from the mountains following the canyon trail to the ocean. There have also been numerous signs of bear and cougar. Hunting will be possible in two days. If he wishes to join the hunt he must come to the hunting lodge no later than noon tomorrow. He cannot ensure success past noon. "

196

Terrance gave a perplexed look. "I didn't realize Jeanip was a hunter."

"Often one does not know what another is capable of," the librarian said. "This hunt is special because the trail they are following takes them right behind Minnos."

"I will tell him immediately. Thank you."

"Good luck, Mr. Landers." The librarian turned and walked away. Terrance thought her last words were very usual. Why did he need luck? Sunam tooted the horn, bringing him back to reality. Hurrying back to the car, he slid in to see an overwhelmed Sunam trying to answer the barrage of questions Anna and Suzie were directing at him. This was going to be a long ride.

Terrance wanted to ponder over what the librarian had said, but Anna and Suzie were nonstop chatterboxes. They kept asking him all kinds of questions, then speculating amongst themselves, then more questions. Terrance thought he should leave the answers to Europa so most of their questions were answered with "You'll have to ask Europa." His one wish was they'd understand he had no information to give them and they would stop asking questions thus allowing him time to think. But this ride to the estate was not going to be the usual quiet one. He looked over at Sunam to see how he was doing. Sunam had his eyes on the road and drove, allowing Terrance to do all the talking for the two of them.

Europa paced across the living room, too excited to have a seat as she waited for her friends to arrive. Finally, she saw the car pull up out front and two of her friends jump from the car. Leaving Sunam and Terrance behind, they ran up the steps and through the front door. As they saw Europa and she saw them, each ran to the other and almost fell over as they collided. Anna and Suzie both began to talk at once as they hugged Europa, saying how sorry they were about her mother, how they had wanted to come before this but were unable to, asked how she was doing and stated how well she looked. After several minutes of hugging, Europa noticed Terrance too had walked inside. She let go of Anna and Suzie and walked over to Terrance, giving him a kiss on the cheek. "Thank you for going to get them."

"Any time," Terrance replied.

Leaving Terrance's side, Europa returned to her friends and took one of their hands in each of hers. "Come into the kitchen. Misso has made breakfast for us all." As they walked toward the kitchen Europa turned to make sure Terrance was following them. She gave him a big smile, then returned her attention to her friends.

Terrance searched the kitchen for Jeanip as soon as he entered but did not see him. "Misso, do you know where Jeanip is?"

"Jeanip had breakfast several hours ago and went out with the men to do some work on the back property," Misso said, as she began to carry platters of food to the table.

Remembering the librarian's statement that Jeanip needed Mr. Dark Feather's message immediately upon his arrival, he asked, "Misso, is there any way to get in touch with Jeanip while he's out there?"

"I'm afraid not, Terrance," Misso stated, as she carried more food to the hungry guests. "If you would like I can try to catch Sunam before he rides out to join him. He can take a message to Jeanip for you."

"No, that's okay. It can wait until Jeanip returns. Besides, you are much too busy taking care of Europa's guest. But would you please let me know as soon as he returns? It's very important I see him."

"Yes, I will let you know," Misso stated, turning her attention back to kitchen matters.

Europa gave him a perplexed look. "What's that about? Why do you need to see Jeanip?"

Terrance looked at her, "I ran into Mr. Dark Feather's niece outside the inn this morning when we went to pick up the girls. She had a message from her uncle for Jeanip. Something about a hunting trip and a herd of deer that will be passing Minnos in two days." When Triton heard what Terrance said he left Europa's side and went and laid at the back door, staring into the wooded area behind the big barn. Terrance looked at Triton, then back at Europa. "That's weird."

"I have never seen him do that before," Europa said. "He occasionally leaves my side, but he never lies in front of the door staring. It is almost as if he expects some sort of trouble."

"Or he simply likes the idea of a good hunt," Misso said, as she placed a pitcher of orange juice on the table. She now wished she had gone out to stop Sunam from leaving as she had suggested. Fear now starting to grip her heart, she quickly glanced at Triton, sending him a message, "Yes, I heard what Terrance said too. This can mean only one thing - there is an army of Terrians headed for us. If Jeanip is not back in an hour I will ride out and find him and the males."

"I do not think we can wait that long, Misso," Triton answered her back. "And I do not feel it is safe for you to ride out alone, plus that will take too much time. We need him here NOW. Go into Jeanip's room and send out a silent alarm through the security grid. Jeanip will be able to hear it and he will return immediately."

"Your Majesty, the front gate is wide open and Jeanip turned off the front fences right before Europa's friends arrived. The front border is unprotected. The Terrians, and possibly JeffRa himself, can walk right up to the front door. Would you like me to activate the fences while I am at the control panel?"

"Yes, I believe we need to secure the estate immediately even though Mr. Dark Feather's message said two days. Close the front gates and re-electrify the fences. Also activate the cottage's circular defense for remote activation. I will keep watch here at the door and, if I see or hear anything, I will have you remotely activate them."

Misso looked at Triton, a look of alarm and concern briefly appeared on her face. "But, Earon, if we activate the cottage's circular defenses Jeanip and the males will not be able to enter. They will be trapped outside."

"I know, Misso, but if we are attacked before Jeanip arrives our only defense will be to activate the high security fields. The two of us cannot defend Europa from an entire army. Besides, if Jeanip sees we are under attack he will know he cannot enter through the door and will come up from the cave."

"Very well, Your Majesty."

"Are there still weapons concealed under the kitchen table?" Earon asked, formulating a defense plan.

"Yes, they are still securely hidden there. And there are more in the secret side panel on the wall. There is plenty of ammunition and weapons to mount a good defense." Misso paused for a moment. "Your Majesty, might I suggest we take Europa and the young women down to the cave in the event of an attack."

"I concur, Misso. I see no other alternative but to take them below if an attack comes. We will figure out how to explain everything to Europa's friends and Europa later. Let us hope it just does not come to that."

Confident their defense plan was sound, Misso quickly snuck into Jeanip's room while the young women chatted away at the table. She raced to the security panel and sent out a silent alarm through the security system, informing Jeanip he needed to return to the cottage while Triton kept watch at the door. Feeling eyes upon him, Triton looked back at the group seated at the table and realized he was drawing attention to himself. While still keeping an eye on the woods, he rested his head on his paws to give the appearance he was going to sleep. With his back to the table, the four could not tell he never averted his eyes from the possible danger in the woods Mr. Dark Feather had just warned them about. He hoped Jeanip would return soon. Earon feared things were about to get bad.

———————

"Tinderoon, check that relay over by the apple tree," Jeanip ordered, as he surveyed the schematic displayed on his remote security grid. "I'm not getting a reading from that one either."

"Jeanip, this appears to be a deliberate breakage of specific alarms like last time," Sunam said, looking at the display. "Someone certainly does not want us to know he's out here."

"I agree, Sunam," Jeanip replied. "I think we should . . ." Jeanip stopped in midsentence as he heard a low toned beeping in his ears. As he looked down at the grid, he saw the locations of the motion detectors blinking red. "Soldiers, back to Minnos, NOW!" he said, as he threw Sunam the remote security grid, ran to his horse, jumped into the saddle and took off at a full gallop toward Minnos. The males dropped what they were doing and ran to their horses while Sunam secured the grid display in his backpack. Together, they galloped after Jeanip, all wishing they had been able to use one of the small flying ships to conduct their work in the back fields, thus cutting their arrival time to Minnos to minutes.

———————

Unaware of any potential danger Europa, Anna and Suzie chatted all through breakfast. When they decided to retire upstairs to Europa's room, Terrance elected to remain in the kitchen with Misso. He certainly did not want to listen to three girls chattering nonstop; besides, he thought he could help Misso with kitchen cleanup. After the table was cleared and the dishes washed and put away, Terrance retired to the small sitting room in the front of the house. He grabbed a book off the shelf and pretended to read it. He put his hand in his pocket and felt the purple stone, mostly to assure himself it was real. The sketching of the woman did not surprise him because Europa and he had been seeing that face on so many items. But what did surprise him was the odd letters similar to the ones on the strange weapon. As he thought about the stone and what the librarian had said, his eye lids began to grow heavy. Within minutes he was asleep.

Terrance's head tilted forward, jerking him awake. He immediately looked at his watch and saw twenty minutes had passed. Rising from the sofa and stretching, he walked toward the kitchen to ask Misso if Jeanip had returned yet. She said he had not. Terrance noted Misso was preparing a tray of tea and cookies and asked if she was taking it upstairs. She said she was. Deciding it was better to listen to three chattering women than to be bored alone, Terrance offered to help carry the tray for her.

"So, Anna, tell me about this new beau of yours," Europa said. "Where is he from?"

"I wouldn't call him my beau," replied Anna, as she looked through the clothes in Europa's closet. "We've only gone out a couple of times. He's here on vacation from Boston with his family. We're all supposed to go tomorrow night to that new Chinese restaurant off Highway One." Anna removed a sweater from the closet and held it up in front of her. "Do you think I could borrow this to wear tomorrow night? I'd like to make a good impression on his family."

"Sure," Europa said. "But do you think it will fit you? You are a bit bustier than I am."

"I am not!"

"Yes you are," Suzie said. "Perhaps you should try it on in the bathroom and see how it looks."

"Great idea!" Anna answered, scurrying off to the bathroom. Removing her scrunchie from her hair, she slipped the sweater over her head and looked at herself in the mirror. She was pleased at how the sweater accented her figure. "Talk about being good looking, do you two remember that drop-over-dead gorgeous man at Europa's tenth birthday?" she yelled from the bathroom.

"The one with those lovely eyes?" Suzie answered. "They almost appeared to be lilac in color."

"That's the one," Anna confirmed. "What ever became of him? Did you ever get to see him again, Europa?"

"No, he was only here that one time on my birthday. He had come to see Mother and Jeanip regarding some special business," Europa replied, remembering back to that day he escorted her and kissed her hand. "I asked Mother about him several days later, who he was and if he would return, but she said very little; just that he was someone they did business with." Europa paused for a moment, her cheeks turning a slight shade of pink. "Although to tell you the truth, I use to dream about him for years afterwards. I can still visualize his eyes today." Coming back to the present Europa shouted, "How does the sweater look?"

"See for yourself," Anna answered, as she emerged from the bathroom. Both Suzie and Europa gave a cat whistle to signify how well Anna looked in the sweater.

"You know, Anna, with your hair down like that and in her sweater, you and Europa could almost pass as sisters," Suzie said.

"Think so?" Anna asked, as Misso and Terrance arrived with the trays of tea and cookies. Distracted by their arrival, Europa did see Anna open the French doors and step out onto the balcony. "It is so beautiful today we should have our tea and cookies on the balcony," Anna stated.

"Anna, you're not allowed outside the walls of the cottage," Misso stated, hurrying toward Anna, still holding the tray of tea. Suddenly there was a "ping" sound. The pane of glass on the side of the French door shattered. Misso dropped the tray and looked down at her abdomen. A purple blood stain began to grow across her shirt as she collapsed. "Anna," Europa shouted, as another ping sound was heard seconds after the first. Anna turned to face Europa, a bewildered look upon her face. Europa watched as Anna took a step toward her, blood streaming down her neck, staining the sweater a deep crimson red. Anna collapsed before she could take her second step. Immediately the sounds of alarms went off everywhere in the house and outside. Birea came running from her room next door. As she ran through the door to protect her sovereign, another ping was heard. Birea fell backwards to the floor with a shot to her forehead.

"Anna," Europa shouted again, as she rushed forward to help. Seeing what she was about to do, Terrance dropped the tray of cookies and tackled Europa to the floor.

"Stay down, Europa. It's you they're after," Terrance yelled above the alarms ringing.

Upon hearing the alarms Triton ran up the stairs He quickly surveyed the scene In the bedroom and located Europa on the floor next to Terrance. He could not tell if she was hurt or not, but he could tell Birea, Misso and Anna were injured. Shocked to realize the shield was down and anyone entering the room was an easy target, Triton crouched down and crawled to where Europa laid. Upon reaching her, he placed his body across hers, shielding her from any new bullets. Whimpering, he nudged her gently to determine if she was injured. To his relief he saw her look at him and heard her say she was alright. He turned his attention to Misso lying on the floor to ascertain if she had activated the circular defense; but when he saw the large pool of purple blood on the floor beneath her he surmised she had not had time to secure the cottage. He knew their only hope was Jeanip. He prayed Jeanip had gotten Misso message to return and would arrive soon.

Terrance had seen Birea, Misso and Anna get shot, but he didn't know Suzie's fate. He had seen her drop to the floor when Misso was hit, but he didn't know if it was out of fear or the fact that she had also been struck. Terrance looked across the room and saw her crying. "Are you hurt, Suzie?" he asked her. She did not answer. "Suzie, answer me. Are you hurt?"

"No," Suzie said, shaking with fear. "I'm not hurt. What in the world is happening?"

"I'm not sure, Suzie, but don't move. Stay right where you are. You are out of their line of sight as long as you remain on the floor," Terrance said, trying to sound confident. "I'm sure help will be here any second."

"But what about Anna?" Suzie asked, looking at her friend lying in her own blood. "We can't just leave her there." Several more bullets sped into the room, shattering the dresser mirror and pulverizing the wall. Suzie covered her ears and screamed.

"Anna, if you can hear us move your hand, or a finger," Europa yelled to Anna, hoping for some sign of life. As the seconds ticked by into seemingly minutes, Europa watched for some movement. Finally, she was relieved to see Anna lift her index finger on her right hand. Anna always had a warped sense of humor, Europa thought. As she watched Anna's finger her attention was drawn to something moving rapidly on the ocean about a mile offshore. She stared at the object, narrowing her eyes in an attempt to see what the object was. At last she realized the object was a speed boat containing two, perhaps three men standing on the deck with what looked like high powered assault weapons. As she stared at the boat, trying to commit every detail to

203

memory for Jeanip, something very big suddenly emerged from beneath the boat and flung it into the air. The boat flew up, flipped over and threw its passengers into the water. As the boat came down and made contact with the ocean's surface, it exploded into pieces. Mesmerized by the scene playing out before her eyes, Europa watched as what appeared to be a pod of dolphins descended upon the men, leaping upon them, pushing them beneath the water. She could not identify what it was, but in the midst of the commotion was the large object that had risen beneath the boat and destroyed it. Then, to her amazement and disbelieve, the water erupted into the form of a giant sperm whale breaching almost its entire body from the water, flipping on its side and purposely landing on the struggling men, crushing them. After the breach the ocean became quiet, devoid of dolphins, empty of men, empty except for the large whale's fluke rising above the water once again as it dove down into the depths of the ocean.

After what seemed like an eternity, Jeanip could at last see the cottage ahead. His mount was covered in froth and breathing hard, yet he spurred him on, demanding even more speed. He had to get to her. When he reached the back porch he reined in his horse and jumped from its back, running up the stairs two at a time, his men seconds behind him. As he opened the porch door he heard the house alarms began to sound throughout Minnos as a horrifying scream emanated from upstairs, sending a cold chill of terror down his spine.

"Europa, where are you?" he screamed in terror as he ran through the house and up the stairs, trying to make himself heard over the deafening sound of the alarms. "Europa, answer me!"

Europa was startled back to reality when she heard loud shouting and footsteps running up the stairs. With all the alarms ringing, she was unable to make out the voices, unable to determine if it was friend or foe advancing toward her and the others. She held her breath as she waited to see if help was coming to their aide or Terrians to end her life. She was overjoyed when it was Jeanip's face that burst into the room, a look of pure horror on it as he surveyed the scene before him. The floor was covered with shattered glass, splintered wood and pulverized plaster. He immediately searched for Europa and saw Triton lying on top of her as her shield, Terrance beside them.

"Jeanip, thank goodness you are here," Jeanip heard Triton say. Earon knew Jeanip's first priority would be to ascertain Europa's and his condition, so he immediately advised him they were both okay.

"Europa, Terrance and I are safe. I believe Suzie is too. But Birea, Misso and Annie have all been injured. The attack came from the direction of the French doors."

Assured his monarchs were safe, Jeanip turned his attention to the scene before him and the best way to secure the cottage. He scanned the room seeing pools of red and purple blood mixing together under the bodies of Anna, Misso and Birea. He could not tell if any were alive. And worst of all, he did not know if the assassins were still out there, waiting for someone else to step into their view. As Sunam, Ebar, Mintoo and Tinderoon reached the doorway, Jeanip put out his arm to stop them from entering and possibly becoming the next victims.

"Wait, we cannot enter yet. With the screen down we are easy targets." Jeanip said to his men.

"But our sovereigns," Tinderoon stated, realizing only the fact that Europa and Earon were in grave danger and he needed to save them.

"They are safe at the moment," Jeanip responded. "And you are no good to them dead."

"Yes, Sir," Tinderoon replied, taking a step back into the hall.

"Everyone listen. I know you're all scared and confused, but before we can help I have to reset the security grids and reactivate the screen. Everyone remain on the floor," Jeanip shouted above the sound of alarms, trying to keep his voice from shaking in rage and fear.

Jeanip yelled, "Security alarms silent, authorization code CJ1-1." Nothing happened. The alarms continued to sound.

"Security alarms silent, authorization code CJ1-1." Jeanip said loudly, fearing that perhaps the pitch of his yelling voice was not recognized by the security grid. Again nothing happened.

"Security grid comply."

"Authorization required," the grid answered.

"Authorization CJ1-1," Jeanip repeated.

"Pure authorization required, article SC-E-J-2a," the grid responded.

"Damn" Jeanip said under his breath. He would have to perform a pure identification before the humans in order to reset the security grid and get it back up. Facing the wall opposite Europa's room, Jeanip lifted his hand and placed his palm on the wall, giving a verbal command. As

Europa watched, Jeanip's hand began to glow in a soft light. The wall where his hand rested disappeared, revealing a panel filled with numbers, lights and knobs. The panel's lights flickered off then returned. Jeanip quickly removed his hand from the wall hoping none of the humans had noticed his hand's transformation. With his palm no longer there, the panel disappeared and the space became the wall once more.

"Pure authorization completed, article SC-E-J-2b," Jeanip spoke loudly. "Security alarms silent, authorization code CJ1-1." The alarms immediately stopped, leaving only Suzie's crying and Anna's labored breathing audible. For a second Jeanip allowed himself a sigh of relief, for at least the child was still alive. "Security grid reset with a five feet forward extension on grid UB2. Authorization CJ1-11b." There were several sparks in the air on the balcony, five feet past the space where the French doors use to stand, signifying the grid was up and operational. The men rushed into the room to help the injured and secure Europa.

"Ebar, at the end of the hall in the closet is a large first aid kit. Get it. Sunam, check on Misso. Tinderoon, check on Birea. See if they are alive, and if so, can they be moved. I'll check on Anna. Mintoo, help Terrance get Suzie and Europa into the hallway." Jeanip began shouting orders. Looking over at Triton he ordered, "Triton, go get Earon. We need him." Without hesitation, Triton ran from the room and down the stairs.

Terrance helped Europa up from the floor and ushered her into the hallway to sit on the floor. Europa desperately held on to his hand, not wanting him to leave her, afraid the bullets would start again. Mintoo tried to get Suzie to her feet but she was too traumatized to move. He called her name repeatedly trying to bring her back to the present. In desperation, he shook her lightly and was relieved to see her make eye contact. Finally able to get her to stand, he wrapped his arm around her shoulder and walked her out in to the hallway. He brought her next to Europa and helped her sit down beside her. Europa immediately placed her arms around her and drew her close to her body for comfort and protection. Mintoo then asked Terrance to sit down next to Europa and to stay with them. Doing as asked, Terrance took Europa's free hand in his and tried his best to assure both frightened females everything would be okay now that Jeanip was there.

"Terrance, what just happened?" Suzie asked between sobs, still shaking from the experience.

"Some kind of attack," Terrance answered. He didn't know how much he should say about what had happened. He didn't know what Jeanip would want her to know or what she already knew.

"But why?" Suzie asked. "It doesn't make any sense."

"I don't know, Suzie," Terrance lied.

AFTERMATH

Jeanip knelt at Anna's side and inspected her wounds. She had taken a bullet in the right shoulder, shattering her shoulder bone. The bullet had also nicked her neck, just missing her carotid artery, evidently the real target of the shooter. Luckily for Anna, she had either moved at the last second or the shooter was a poor marksman. She should be dead. Jeanip reached over and picked up some of the cloth napkins that had been on the tea tray Misso had been carrying. He stuffed the napkins into Anna's shoulder to try to stop the bleeding. Anna screamed in pain, and then slipped into unconsciousness.

"Tinderoon, how is Birea?" Jeanip asked.

Tinderoon looked up from Birea and shook his head no at Jeanip. He pulled the cover from Europa's bed and laid it over Birea's body to hide her passing from the humans. As he watched the form underneath the blanket changed as Birea's brain stopped sending signals to her body to maintain her transformation into a human. Once she returned to her true form the air pressure was too low for her membranes to maintain their shape and consistency. Her fluids flowed out onto the floor beneath the blanket as the membranes disintegrated into nothing.

"She was a good soldier. There is nothing we can do for her now except take down the ones who took her life and try to save these other two. Tinderoon, I could use your help over here" Jeanip said. He then turned his attention to Misso.

"She got hit in the abdomen, but it looks like the bullet went straight through. I don't think any major organs were hit, but she's still in bad shape," Sunam said, as he looked up at his commander.

"Hold on, Misso. We'll get you fixed right up." Jeanip said, smiling at her as he squeezed her hand.

Ebar came back into the room with a large suitcase. He opened it after placing it on the floor, revealing a huge assortment of medical supplies. Mintoo entered right behind him.

"Mintoo, is Europa safe?" Jeanip demanded to know.

"Yes, Sir," Mintoo responded. "Terrance is with her and Suzie".

"Good. Go into my room and re-activate the front gates and fences. I don't want Terrians strolling up the driveway."

"No need to re-activate them, Mintoo," Earon stated, as he walked into the room. "I sealed the estate as soon as I heard Mr. Dark Feather's message."

"Message?" asked Jeanip. "What message?"

"Terrance has a message for you," Earon replied. "Mr. Dark Feather's niece gave it to him this morning when he went with Sunam to pick up Europa's friends."

"That will have to wait," commented Jeanip as he gathered items from the medical case. "Mintoo, go downstairs and call Evonic and tell him we need him out here NOW. Tell him make it in five minutes, that Misso has been shot. Then call the sheriff and tell him we've had a shooting and have casualties. Tell him to have an ambulance waiting for us at the gate. Tell him under NO circumstances is ANYONE to enter Minnos. Tell him the fences are electrified again. Ebar, take over for Tinderoon. Tinderoon, go downstairs into my room and bring up two stretchers. Sunam, give Misso a shot of AC13, 5 ml. Then hook up an IV with the home water," Jeanip continued, giving orders as he had during the years at war with the Terrians.

With bandage pads, surgical tape and a syringe filled with a purple liquid in hand, Jeanip returned to Anna. He injected her with the serum, hoping it would help stabilize her enough to give her a chance to make it to the hospital. He then began to prepare her for transport as Tinderoon returned with the two stretchers. He placed one next to Misso and one next to Anna.

"Tinderoon, bring the station wagon around to the side door. Be sure the middle and back seats are down. Ebar and I will bring Anna right down. Then I need for you to drive her to the front gate to meet the ambulance," Jeanip stated. Stepping in to the hallway, he said, "Suzie, I need you to accompany Anna. Please go downstairs now and wait at the side door for us." Suzie just sat there, curled up in Europa's arm. She was still too frightened to move. "Suzie, I need you up on your feet and heading downstairs, NOW," Jeanip yelled, but he could see it had no effect. Suzie was not one of his soldiers and screaming at her would do no good. She was a young human too traumatized to move. Jeanip turned to Terrance and in a surprisingly soft and tender voice said, "Terrance, it is very important for Suzie to go downstairs now. Every second she delays brings Anna closer to death. Can you please try to get her downstairs? Perhaps Europa can help you."

"I will get her downstairs even if I have to carry her over my shoulder," Terrance said, as he got to his feet. He pulled Suzie away from Europa and leaned her against the wall. Then he got Europa to her feet. Next he pulled until Suzie stood up and he leaned her back into Europa's arms. "Europa, it's important for Suzie to go downstairs. She's too traumatized to go on her own. Can you help me?"

"Yes, I can do that," Europa said, as her mind began to come back to the reality about her. She realized Suzie's delay in going downstairs was endangering Anna's life. "Suzie, I know you are frightened. I am too. But it's very important for us to go downstairs now so Anna can be taken to the hospital. I am going to hold on to you real tight so you will know you are safe and together we are going to walk over to the stairway. Terrance is going with us too." Terrance stood on the opposite side of Suzie and stretched his arm around the two young women. "Okay, Suzie? I know you can do this. You can do this for Anna."

Europa heard a very faint, "Okay" from Suzie as she hid her face in Europa's arm.

"When I say 'walk' we are going to start walking together. Remember, Terrance is on one side of you and I'm on the other. If you need to you can lean on one of us. Okay, get ready. Now walk." To Europa's relief, Suzie took a step toward the stairway, then another. Soon they stood at the top. "Suzie, you are doing great. We are at the top of the stairs. We are now going to walk down them and then straight to the back door. When I say 'step' I want you to move down one step. We will take them one at a time. Here we go. Now, step." Suzie stepped down onto the top step, then down to the next and so forth as Europa repeated the word 'step' for each stair rung until they reached the bottom. Still huddled together, they continued walking Suzie to the back door where they waited for Jeanip.

With Ebar's assistance, Jeanip was able to lift the badly injured Anna carefully onto the stretcher. They waited until Suzie was at the bottom of the stairs before they picked her up and carried her down the stairs to the side door. Once at the door Tinderoon stepped in and took Jeanip's position on the stretcher. He knew like Europa and Earon,

Jeanip needed to remain inside where it was safe, secure from any assassin's bullet so he could coordinate Europa's protection and get away if needed. All Jeanip's men realized Jeanip's survival was a top priority, even though Jeanip himself did not realize it, for without his command decisions none of them stood a chance, especially Europa and Earon.

"What about Birea and Misso? Aren't they going to the hospital too?" Europa asked as they carried Anna past her. She didn't understand why they were being left behind.

"Evonic will be here shortly to treat Misso's wounds. There's nothing we can do for Birea," Jeanip said.

Europa was shocked to hear Evonic's voice say, "Already here" as he walked through Jeanip's bedroom door. She noticed his hair was dripping wet and he had no shoes or shirt on, only a wet pair of paints. It almost appeared he had swum there from town, but she knew that was impossible. Only a dolphin could swim that fast.

"Misso's upstairs with Sunam and Earon," Jeanip said, tilting his head toward the staircase. "She's in pretty bad shape."

Without a word Evonic took off running across the room and up the stairs into Europa's bedroom. He saw Sunam holding Misso in his arms, gently rocking her back and forth as he very quietly sang her favorite Waters' song. Evonic knelt down beside them and began to examine Misso, trying to determine the extent of the bullet's damage. He retrieved from inside Jeanip's medical bag several medications and injected them in Misso's IV to help ease her pain and to help her purple blood clot inside the human body.

"Sunam, I need you to lay her on the stretcher so I can dress her wounds," Evonic said, as he reached out and touched Sunam's shoulder. Sunam turned and looked at him, not realizing at first what Evonic was asking. "Sunam, lay her down on the stretcher," Evonic said again.

"Here, let me help you," Earon stated, as he saw Sunam's bewilderment. "We are going to gently lay Misso down on the stretcher so Evonic can help her. Then we are going to take her downstairs." Sunam looked into Earon's eyes and this time he understood. With Earon's help he lowered Misso gently onto the stretcher where Evonic began to address the bullet wounds. After washing them out with a special mixture of their home world's lilac water and peroxide, he bandaged them with a medical cloth they had invented during the war to help with infections and bleeding. "Misso, this is the best I can do up here. I need to take you downstairs. Earon is going to help me. Okay?"

Evonic saw Misso look up at him and tried to give him a smile. Together, he and Earon carefully lifted the stretcher and carried it downstairs to the kitchen, Sunam following close behind.

Suzie waited at the back door along with Europa and Terrance. Seeing she was still in a state of shock, Mintoo walked over to her and placed his arm around her shoulder. "Miss Suzie, we need to go out to the car now so we can take Annie to get medical help. I need for you to walk with me. Okay?" Suzie did not say a word, but nodded her head affirmatively. Mintoo gently led her to the car, helping her in the front seat. Tinderoon and Ebar followed, carrying Anna's stretcher to the back of the vehicle and carefully slid the stretcher inside. Jeanip noticed as Anna was carried past him she was still unconscious and he hoped she would remain so until she arrived at the ambulance.

Europa and Terrance watched her friends' departure from the safety of the kitchen. Terrance turned to Europa and asked, "Are you sure you're not hurt at all?"

"No, I am fine. Just really scared. Did you see all that blood? And Terrance, did I imagine it or was Misso's and Birea's blood purple?" Europa asked.

"You saw it too," Terrance answered softly so no one else could hear. "Maybe it had something to do with the tea Misso was carrying. Maybe it reacted with her blood to make it look purple."

"Maybe. But Birea wasn't anywhere near the tea. And why didn't Jeanip have Misso taken to the hospital too? Evonic seems to be the only medical person who can treat this family. And come to think of it, how did he get here so fast? He lives on the other side of town. It should have taken him at top speed forty minutes to get here. Plus, Jeanip said the fences were electrified again. How could he get in?"

The sound of Tinderoon starting the car's engine brought their attention back to the scene outside. They watched as Mintoo closed the back hatch while Ebar crawled in next to Anna through the side middle door. Slowly the car pulled away from the cottage in route to the front gate, two of Europa's best friends inside, one now fighting for her life. Mintoo walked over to the horses; each remained where their riders had dismounted them. He gathered up their reins and walked them to the barn where he would unsaddle them and give each a good rub down. After all the galloping they had been forced to do he thought each also deserved a few extra carrots for a job well done.

Jeanip closed the back door then turned his attention to Misso. "How's she doing, Evonic?" Jeanip asked as he looked at the very pale, sleeping Misso. Sunam was at her side as Jeanip expected, holding her hand in his. He didn't think Sunam even knew he was standing there.

"I'm not going to lie to you, Jeanip, she's hurt pretty bad. If she can make it through the next thirty-six hours she has a good chance of making it. That was quick thinking on your part giving her that shot of AC13. It probably saved her life."

"An old trick I learned during the Terrian war. It saved many an Oonocks' lives. I never thought I would have to use it again – not here, not at Minnos."

"How's Europa's friend?"

"I think she'll pull through, but she took a bad hit to the upper shoulder and throat. She'll probably lose the shoulder and arm. I don't know if she'll ever be able to talk again."

"Poor kid," Evonic said. "What happened, Jeanip?"

"If Misso can do without you for a few minutes, we'll debrief over by the fireplace," Jeanip announced, as he motioned for Europa to come to the table. "Europa, would you stay with Misso for a minute while I talk to the men. Sunam, Terrance and Earon, if you three would join Evonic and me by the fireplace."

Everyone except Sunam walked over to the fireplace. Jeanip waited a moment then walked over to Sunam. "Soldier, you have been ordered to the fireplace for a debriefing. Comply," Jeanip ordered in an unusually soft voice, Europa thought. Normally, Jeanip would be screaming at one of his men if they had not obeyed an order.

Sunam's preoccupation with Misso was broken. Realizing his commander was standing at his side he immediately stood at attention. "Yes, Sir. What do you need, Sir?"

Jeanip looked at Sunam and placed his hand on Sunam's shoulder. "Sunam, Europa is going to stay with Misso. I need for you to join us at the fireplace for a few minutes. Then you can return to Misso." Without a word, Sunam bent down and kissed Misso's forehead, then walked over to where the others waited.

"Are you sure you two are okay? There was a lot of glass up there?" Jeanip asked, as he returned to the fireplace, scanning Terrance and Earon for signs of blood or cuts. "Terrance, you're positive Europa is not hurt in any way?"

213

'Yes, Sir, she's fine, as am I. What happened?" Terrance asked. "Were those men after Europa?"

"Jeanip, why did the security grid fail? Those bullets should have never gotten past the screen," Earon inquired.

"I'll answer all your questions the best I can in a minute. But what I am more concerned about at the moment is where they were hiding that allowed them to get a shot off," Jeanip stated, worried the Terrians had found a weakness in his defenses. "And how did they know which room was Europa's?"

"They were in a boat," Europa said, as she reached down and took Misso's hand in hers. Even though the men were talking low she had been able to overhear Jeanip's conversation.

"What did you say?" Jeanip asked Europa, taking a few steps closer to her.

"They were on the ocean in a boat. When I was lying on the floor and I looked to see how Anna was, I saw them through the balcony bars. It looked like a nineteen feet Craftsman."

"A boat? I didn't see any boat," Jeanip replied. "The security sensors didn't pick up a boat close to shore."

"Could the grid have malfunctioned? Or could they have found a way to beat it?" asked Sunam.

"I am sure it didn't malfunction. As for them finally developing a way to hide from the grid, anything is plausible," Jeanip replied.

"It wasn't close to shore, Jeanip," Europa continued. "It was quite a ways out there, definitely past our sensors."

"That's great. If they were in a boat that means they could be anywhere by now. And can return again when they want," Earon said, anger now replacing his concern. "They just won't leave us alone, will they?"

"No, their boat exploded," Europa said, looking straight at Jeanip, her voice almost monotone. "I was watching it, trying to memorize every detail about the boat for you when something came up from underneath it and threw it into the air. The men were thrown into the water and the boat exploded. I think they were still alive until a huge whale breached and crushed them."

"A whale? Are you sure, Europa?" Jeanip asked, a smirk beginning to show on his face.

"Yes, I am sure of it. It came almost entirely out of the water. I have never seen one so big. The last thing I saw was its fluke as it dove beneath the waves," Europa answered.

"But a boat on the ocean should have posed no threat. We anticipated that area of attack and made sure a bullet fired from a boat could not penetrate the security screen, no matter how powerful the weapon. The screen should have held," Sunam stated.

"It should not have been possible, but we saw that it was. There are only two reasons that could explain how their bullets penetrated our shield. One, their technology has advanced over the decades to produce a bullet which can go through our shields or two, someone broke the connection." Jeanip looked directly at Europa. "Europa, did anyone try to go out on to the balcony?" he asked.

Europa looked at Jeanip, tears beginning to form in her eyes and roll down her face. "Yes, Anna did," she answered. "She opened the doors and stepped outside suggesting we have tea on the balcony. She moved so fast I did not have time to stop her. Misso tried to warn her and that is how she was hit. Anna did not mean to break the connection. She had no knowledge the balcony was off limits. I should have remembered to tell her and Suzie about the security screen. They were my guests, they were my responsibility. It is my fault. I should have told them." Europa crumbled to the floor and began to sob, finally releasing the emotions she had been holding inside since the shooting began. "It was me they meant to kill. Anna had my sweater on and with her hair down she easily could have been mistaken for me. It is just like what happened with Mother. The assassin attacked someone else because he thought it was me." Europa looked over to the group of men. "My friend may die just like Mother because they were trying to kill me." Terrance rushed over to her, knelt down beside her and lifted her into his arms, holding her securely as she wept.

"No, Europa, it was not your fault Anna broke the connection. It was my fault," Jeanip said, his voice echoing the tone of guilt he felt. "As Commander in charge of security, it is my responsibility to tell visitors what they can and cannot do. I was not here to greet your friends when they arrived. The error was mine."

Tinderoon stopped the vehicle just before the electrified fence. As he exited the station wagon he could hear the ambulance and police sirens as they sped toward the estate. Knowing time was short, he hurriedly walked around to the passenger's side of the car and opened the door for Suzie to get out. He helped her exit the car while instructing

215

her to wait there and follow them when they came back with Anna. Hoping Suzie was coherent enough to follow his instructions, he ran to the rear to help Ebar with the stretcher. Keeping their weapons over their shoulders, the two males lifted Anna out of the vehicle. They carefully carried her toward the gate, stopping just long enough for Suzie to step next to the stretcher and followed alongside. Several steps before the gate Tinderoon said the password that opened the gate while leaving the surrounding fences still electrified. A few feet past the gate, Ebar and Tinderoon gently laid the stretcher on the ground. Ebar helped Suzie sit down beside Anna and told her to wait beside her until the ambulance arrived, assuring her it would be there in seconds. While Ebar was helping Suzie, Tinderoon ran back to the car and remained there on guard, ready to shoot anything or anyone who tried to walk through the gate other than Ebar. Seeing the emergency vehicles, Ebar ran back inside the estate, closing and locking the gate just as the sheriff's car pulled up.

"Just a minute, Ebar," the sheriff yelled, jumping out of his car. "Don't you dare turn that gate back on. This is a crime scene. I have an investigation to do."

"Sorry, Sheriff, Jeanip's orders are no one comes in. He needs you to take the injured girl to the hospital and return the other to her home," Tinderoon replied.

The two watched as the Sheriff drew his gun and aimed it at them. "Listen you two; I have people missing, Medaron's accident a few weeks ago and now an attempted murder. What in the hell is going on in there? I need answers. I demand you let me on that damn property so I can do a proper investigation. I cannot allow you to reactivate that gate."

"So you're going to stop me by shooting me?" Ebar asked, almost chuckling.

"If I have to," the Sheriff replied. "This is your only warning. If you try to reactivate the gate, I will shoot you."

"I am sorry to hear that, Sheriff, for you will be dead before you can complete the shot. Tinderoon never misses," Ebar said, tilting his head toward the station wagon where Tinderoon stood with his weapon aimed at the Sheriff. "And if you are lucky enough to kill me, Tinderoon will simply activate the gate after you and I are both dead. So you see, Sheriff, either way you are not setting a foot on this land. At least not today."

216

Seeing the futility of his endeavor and furious at failing once again to enter Minnos, the sheriff lowered his gun. He hated the fact Jeanip was still calling all the shots, especially since Jeanip wasn't even there but probably back at Minnos. Once he saw the Sheriff lower his gun, Ebar repeated the code reactivating the gate. Not wanting to turn his back to a potential enemy, he walked backwards to the car.

"Tinderoon, you tell Jeanip this isn't over. I'll get a court order and be back," the Sheriff shouted, his face flushed red.

"Then let me remind you of what you already know. You have no authority here – this is tribal land. If you want a court order you have to go through their courts, and I can assure you they will not grant you access. Plus, as a foreign monarch seeking sanctuary, we have diplomatic immunity."

"Yeah, well, we'll see what the State Department has to say about that," the Sheriff screamed.

"Have a good day, Sheriff," Tinderoon said with a smile as he lowered his weapon and slid back into the driver's seat. Once the car was started Ebar slid into the passenger's seat still keeping his weapon aimed at the Sheriff. Tinderoon backed the car half way down the driveway before turning it around and returning to Minnos. "That man has no idea the only way he will ever step foot on Minnos is if we are all dead."

"Sometimes you have to feel sorry for him," Ebar stated, shaking his head as he laughed.

"Jeanip, I have a message for you from Mr. Dark Feather," Terrance said, still kneeling on the floor with Europa in his arms. "I was supposed to give it to you as soon as I arrived but you weren't here. Then the shooting happened."

"So I have been told," Jeanip said, as he walked over to Terrance and lifted Europa into his arms. "Follow me." He carried Europa over to one of the couches. "Please have a seat, Terrance." Once Terrance was seated he placed Europa back into his arms. "This should be more comfortable for the two of you than the floor." Even in this aftermath Jeanip's first concern was for Europa's safety and comfort. Terrance cradled her in his arms again, thankful Jeanip realized Europa needed the security of his embrace. Once they were settled Jeanip asked, "What is the message?"

"Mr. Dark Feather said to tell you a large herd of deer have been seen coming down from the mountains and they will pass close to Minnos. He said there are also bear and cougar sign. They should be ready for hunting in two days. If you wish to join them on the hunt you must come to the hunting lodge by noon tomorrow." A grave look overshadowed Jeanip's face at hearing the message.

"Thank you, Terrance," Jeanip said, giving no explanation of what the message meant. "If you will excuse me, I have some adjustments to do on the security grid. Earon, stay with Europa and Terrance. Evonic, I leave you in charge of Misso. Sunam, if you would join me in the security grid room." Saying no more, Jeanip turned and walked into his room, Sunam close behind him.

Tinderoon pulled the station wagon up by the side door. After checking to be sure the area was secure, he and Ebar exited the car and entered the kitchen, bolting the side door behind them.

"Tinderoon, how was Anna?" Europa asked.

"She was stable, Your Majesty. The ambulance arrived several minutes after we did."

"What did the Sheriff have to say?" Earon asked, an awkward smile on his face.

"Besides screaming this was a crime scene and he had every right to enter our property, not much," Ebar replied, snickering at the remembrance of the Sheriff in a rage. "Excuse us now, Your Highnesses. We need to brief Jeanip and Sunam on the transfer of your friends. We take our leave of you." Both bowed their heads and raised their right hand to their forehead, turned and entered Jeanip's room.

Europa lightly kicked Terrance's leg. Ebar said "Your Highnesses" not "Your Highness", meaning he considered Earon royalty. Europa looked at Earon wondering once more if he was the brother her mother spoke of in her diary. Medaron had said he would transform into her guardian when she was born. And Triton had been her guardian for twelve years. Before that Sattinii had been her guardian dog. Was it possible Sattinii, Triton and Earon were all the same being? Wanting to expose the truth, Europa pretended to look around the kitchen and asked, "Where is Triton? I hope he did not get hurt too."

"I'm sure he's okay. He's probably down here somewhere," Evonic said. Europa looked at Evonic and Earon, wondering why everyone was still keeping up the charade of Triton being a canine.

218

After all that had happened, why didn't they just tell her Earon and Triton were the same person, being? She was just about to be bold enough to say that when she heard Earon speak up.

"He is fine," Earon said. "I was afraid he might go back upstairs to Europa's room and get hurt on all that broken glass up there. To ensure his safety I locked him inside Jeanip's room. I will go get him for you."

"I can go get him," Europa said, again trying to force them to admit their deception. "I need to walk a bit anyways."

"Do not bother yourself, Your Highness. I was going to go help Jeanip and Sunam in the security room any way. I will let Triton out," Earon said, quickly stopping Europa from her search for Triton. "Just have a seat, Missy. Or better yet, perhaps you could make some coffee for all of us since Misso is unable to." As Earon walked toward the door he added, "One Triton on his way,"

Europa just sat on the couch, secure in Terrance's arms. She had heard Earon's suggestion about the coffee but she had no idea how to make it. Misso had always taken care of that. And during the few times Misso wasn't around Birea or Jeanip did. How did Earon think she was going to make coffee?

Earon whistled for Triton as he opened Jeanip's door, keeping up the pretense the canine was inside. "There you are," he said. "Come on and get up." Earon turned to face Europa who was still sitting on the couch. "Looks like I woke him from his nap. He will be there in a minute. Oh, by the way, you probably surmised you will not be sleeping in your room for a while. Have one of the men go upstairs to your room and get anything you will need for a couple of days. And, Europa, under no circumstances are you to go upstairs. Do you understand?"

"Yes, I understand." Europa answered.

"Promise me you will not go or attempt to go upstairs."

"I will make sure she doesn't attempt it, Earon," Terrance stated, giving Europa a serious look.

"Europa, your word," Earon repeated again. He was not going anywhere until Europa gave her word.

"I promise, Earon"

"You promise what?"

219

"I promise I will not go or attempt to go upstairs," Europa said, staring back at Earon. Besides, she was too afraid to go upstairs and witness the destruction and blood in her room.

Satisfied Europa would remain downstairs where she was safe, Earon entered Jeanip's room. Slipping behind the door he quickly undressed and transformed into Triton. He trotted over to Europa and laid at her feet, assured his secret identity and his sister were both safe. He was also delighted Europa had not gotten up to try to make coffee. Earon knew if she had it would have been a disaster. But the suggestion had kept her mind distracted long enough for him to transform into Triton without detection.

CONFIRMATION

As soon as Jeanip entered his room, he slipped through the secret door and down the stone steps leading to the cave. Europa had said a whale had destroyed the boat. That could mean only one thing – Enok. And if it was Enok the bodies would have been taken down into the deep to ascertain if they were Terrian or not. Hopefully someone would be waiting in the cave to tell him their origin. As he neared the entrance to the ocean he heard voices chattering. Since no alarms were going off he assumed they must be Oonocks, but he no longer fully trusted the security grid. He grabbed a rifle from the gun locker inside the sleeping quarters ready to shoot if the occasion called for it. As he drew closer to the ocean entrance he saw two naked humans sitting on the edge of the water; one man and one woman.

"You know, you two, we keep clothes down here so when you transform into human form you can put them on," Jeanip said lowering the rifle.

"Why is that?" asked Runbee, the male. "Except for humans, all living things on this planet are very content to exist in their skin, feathers, scales and hair their creator gave them. Only humans seem obsessed with covering their bodies with some kind of cloth. Why do you think they do that?"

"I don't know, Runbee," Jeanip replied. "If the day ever comes when I don't have to be concerned with security and a maniac trying to destroy my sovereigns, I will devote my new time to answering your question."

"I'll hold you to that, Jeanip," Runbee replied.

Returning to serious matters at hand, Jeanip asked, "It was Enok whom Europa saw out in the ocean, wasn't it? He destroyed the boat."

"Yes," Graybin replied. "It was Enok. Ever since you advised him of Medaron's death, he's been transforming more and patrolling the waters searching for any signs of Terrians."

"Mostly he searches for JeffRa," Runbee added.

"True. With the return of his arch enemy, Enok has returned to the role of protector and warrior. He is determined to rid the universe of JeffRa's existence once and for all. He is consumed with making JeffRa pay for robbing him of his life's mate," Graybin continued.

"He didn't tell me he was able to come to the surface for extended periods of time. Have the medical assistants been able to correct the problem of him breathing air?" Jeanip asked, a ray of hope materializing that his leader might be able to join him again in this battle with the Terrians.

"Partially. When transformed into a Moby he possesses enormous lungs which are able to process oxygen more efficiently. For the moment he can remain above for three or four hours before he must descend back into the oceans depths and return to his true self. Each day he can stay above a little longer as a Moby, but he still cannot breathe for long in a human form." Graybin explained. "Luckily he was up here when the Terrians attacked Minnos."

"So they were as I feared," Jeanip stated. "They WERE Terrian."

"Yes," Runbee replied. "Enok tore them to pieces to see if they had a double-quad chambered heart and the purification organ that only Terrians possess. After his erroneous attack on Medaron, we were pretty sure JeffRa would try again to assassinate Europa and Earon. Enok did not even hesitate to attack the boat or kill its occupants. Unfortunately, neither one was JeffRa. "

"Was anyone hurt up at Minnos?" Graybin asked.

A somber look came over Jeanip's face. "Birea was killed. One of Europa's friends, a young female human, was badly hurt." Hesitating for a moment, he added, "Graybin, Misso was gravely injured. Evonic doesn't know if she'll pull through or not." Jeanip watched as Graybin's face showed her grave concern about the injured Misso. He wished he was able to give her better news.

"We're so sorry to hear about Birea and Europa's friend. As for Misso, she is a soldier assigned to protect our sovereigns. If her life must be forfeited to accomplish her mission, then so be it," Graybin said, bowing her head. She reached over and took Runbee's hand in hers, tears clearly visible in her eyes. "Perhaps we could visit her, Jeanip? If we are to lose her we would like the chance to say goodbye."

"Jeanip, someone is coming down the stairs," Runbee announced silently before Jeanip could reply to Graybin's request.

"That's probably Sunam. I told him to meet me here after Ebar and Tinderoon gave him their report. But with everything that has happened in the past hour we can't assume anything anymore. You two, slip back into the water and wait until we're sure there is no danger," Jeanip stated. Graybin and Runbee silently slipped over the edge and underneath the water, waiting to see who or what came down the tunnel. Jeanip hid behind a stack of crates, his rifle posed to be fired if the approaching sound was not Sunam or another one of his soldiers. He lowered his rifle as Sunam appeared seconds later.

"How did it go?" Jeanip asked.

"Tinderoon and Ebar were able to deliver the women with no problems," Sunam reported. "They followed proper security protocol. The vehicle remained behind the protection of the fence to assure no one could place any type of device on it that would pose a threat to Minnos or its occupants. The front gate is locked and reactivated as is the entire fence. No one will be entering that way."

"Did either of them say how the Sheriff took the news that he could not enter?" Jeanip asked, knowing ahead of time what Sunam's answer would be.

"Just about how you said he would – a lot of empty threats about getting court orders and contacting the State Department," Sunam answered. "He even threatened to shoot Tinderoon and Ebar." Sunam chuckled. "Sounds like the man does not like you."

"I guess I have given him reason not to over the years. I would not like it either if some foreigner was keeping me from doing my job, telling me where I could or could not go, denying me access to security breach scenes," Jeanip answered. He did admire the Sheriff for always trying to do his job of keeping his citizens safe. The Sheriff just did not realize the safety of those on Minnos was his responsibility and no one else's.

Sunam turned and looked at the water when he heard splashing as Graybin and Runbee jumped back up out of the water. "Hi, you two. By the way, you two do remember we have clothes for you in the sleeping area?" Sunam asked upon seeing the two naked humans.

"Already reminded them," Jeanip said.

"Jeanip has promised to discover for us why humans insist on wearing those things once all the Terrians are gone," Runbee said, seeing the smirk on Jeanip's face and the smile on Sunam's.

"We are very sorry to hear about Misso, Sunam," Graybin stated. "Jeanip tells us her injuries are grave and she might not survive?"

"Yes, Evonic says if she can survive the next thirty-six hours she has a chance," Sunam said somberly, as he was brought back to the reality of the present. "But I must be honest with you. I don't think she'll last over a few hours. She's lost a lot of blood and I believe her injuries are more severe than Evonic is telling me."

"Jeanip, have you thought of returning Misso to the Complex? She would have a much better chance of surviving down there," Graybin asked, a tinge of hope in her voice.

"Yes, I thought of that option as soon as I saw her," Jeanip replied. "But my priority; no, make that OUR priority, is Europa and Earon. We must be sure they are safe before we can worry about our wounded." Jeanip saw the sorrowful look of worry on both Graybin's and Runbee's faces as they heard his words. "As soon as I can get the sovereigns on their way to safety you two have my permission to take Misso down to the Complex so she can recover. Surely you must know that even though Misso is a soldier under my command, she is like a sister to me, and very dear. I will do whatever is necessary to help her survive – but it must come AFTER we get Europa and Earon to safety. You three know as well as I do that above all Misso is a soldier and she will fulfill her duty even if it means her death. She would not even consider a trip to the Complex if she thought it would jeopardize the monarchs' safety."

"Jeanip is right," Sunam added. "Misso will not go until Europa and Earon are safe."

"Then let's get them to safety," Runbee stated. "What do you need us to do?"

"Start carrying out some of the supplies from the storage chamber. We need to get them loaded onto the boat," Jeanip answered.

As they walked toward the chamber, Sunam turned toward Jeanip. "So you told Runbee you are going to discover the reason for human clothes?" Sunam said, smiling at Jeanip. "I sure hope I'm around to see that."

"Ha ha, very funny," Jeanip said, not at all amused. "Why don't you put some of that energy you use to ask ridiculous questions into carrying out these crates for Runbee and Graybin so you can get Misso to the Complex for medical treatment?"

"Jeanip, why didn't the security screen work?" Graybin asked as she lifted a crate of food.

"It was Europa's young friend, Anna. Unaware of the danger, she opened the French doors and stepped out on to the balcony. That broke the grid's connection and the screen went down. The Terrians must have been waiting for such an event."

"They probably saw me pick up the young humans in town and bring them out to the cottage. Hoping one of them might make a mistake and break the grid, they must have planted themselves in key locations and waited for the opportunity to strike," Sunam said.

"Anna was wearing one of Europa's sweaters. I believe the Terrians thought it was Europa standing on the balcony and fired," Jeanip stated, thankful it had not been Europa who had been shot but also wishing it had not been one of her friends either. "Otherwise, I don't believe they would have given away their existence. They not only failed at their assassination attempts, but basically told us we still have a Terrian problem."

"I bet that really ticked JeffRa off," Graybin said. "I am sure his whole plan relied on the element of surprise."

"Must have sent some flunkies," Runbee stated with a hint of laughter. "Anyone who knows our Europa would know she would never break security. If Medaron taught her one thing, it was the importance of following security protocol to the letter."

"That she did," Sunam agreed

Ebar and Tinderoon returned from Jeanip's room. Tinderoon walked over to the kitchen counter and removed the coffee canister from the cupboard. Europa was relieved to see he knew how to make coffee and was preparing to do so. Ebar pulled up a chair beside Misso and sat down beside her. He looked down at her face and silently said a prayer for her. He then looked over to Europa. "Your Majesty, if you wish I can go upstairs and retrieve any items you may need for your stay down here. If you make me a list, I'll go right away."

"Thank you, Ebar. I do not need much," Europa answered. She rose and walked over to the desk and retrieved a piece of paper on which she quickly wrote down a few items she wanted from her room.

"Evonic, perhaps you could help me bring in some boards from the barn to board up Europa's broken doors. Even though the security screen has resealed the area, I'm sure Jeanip will not want to leave a gaping hole in the wall." Tinderoon said to Evonic.

"I'm not sure I should leave Misso," Evonic answered.

"Perhaps Europa would be willing to sit beside her while we retrieve the boards. It will only take a few minutes," Tinderoon replied.

Terrance walked over to Europa and whispered, "Europa, I need to get my backpack. I brought some items I found in my father's room and I don't think it's a good idea to have Ebar bring the pack down. Plus, you need to get your mother's diary and anything else you don't want to leave behind."

"Leave behind?" Europa whispered, curious at Terrance's statement.

"After what just happened, I think we should be prepared to leave at an instant's notice. We need to keep anything important with us at all times," Terrance replied.

"You are right, Terrance," Europa whispered. She looked up and announced, "Evonic, I would be pleased to sit by Misso while you help Tinderoon. And Ebar, now that I think of it there are a few special items I would like from my room. I will have Terrance go upstairs and get them for me. You go with Tinderoon and Evonic and help carry in the boards. Three can carry more than two can." Europa knew that as their monarch, the males would not question her instructions as long as it did not put her in harm's way.

She handed Terrance the list she had been preparing for Ebar and said, "There's also a book (silently mouthing the word "diary" for only Terrance to see) in my bathroom I would like. It is under the towels on the second shelf in the linen closet. There is a red backpack hanging on a hook in my closet you can use to put these things in. Oh, and would you please bring down the two paintings my father painted for my mother?"

"You really want me to bring down the Dumbo's?" Terrance asked, not sure if Europa was kidding or not. When he saw the serious look on her face he knew she was indeed serious. Those two pictures really did mean a lot to her. "I'll grab a change of clothing for you too," Terrance added, looking over the list and noting Europa had forgotten to include any type of clothing.

As Terrance went up the stairs, Europa walked over to Misso and sat in the chair Ebar had just vacated. Triton followed and laid at her feet. Europa gently picked up Misso's hand and held it in hers. She was surprised at how cold it was. Looking down at her sleeping face, Europa realized she had never seen Misso look so pale, so vulnerable. "Is she going to make it?" she softly whispered.

"We hope so," Evonic answered.

"What do I need to do?" Europa asked, not taking her eyes off Misso's face.

"Just sit there and keep an eye on her. If you need me, or any of us, for any reason, have Terrance ring the back porch bell and I'll come running. Remember, Europa, do NOT ring it yourself. You are not to go outside these walls." Evonic stated. He was sure Europa did not need another reminder, but he decided to play it safe and tell her once more about her confinement.

"Believe me, Evonic, after the shooting today the last thing I will attempt is to step foot outside this cottage," Europa stated. Today's events had shaken her to her core. For the first time in her life she really believed she was royalty, and with that title came the reality someone out there was determined to end her life.

"We will take our leave of you then," Tinderoon said, bowing slightly, raising his hand to his forehead in the proper royal salute. "We will return shortly." Europa bowed her head slightly as she had seen her mother do in response hundreds of times in the past. This was the second time any of the help had saluted her so and she wanted to do her return actions properly.

The three males exited the cottage through the side door, locking it behind themselves. Once off the porch, they broke into a run to the barn to obtain the lumber for Europa's room. Not wanting to leave the monarchs alone for long, they hurriedly gathered some lumber and prepared to return to the cottage. Just as they were ready to leave, their arms laden with strips of wood, the door at the other end of the barn swung open to reveal red, glowing eyes.

Terrance stopped at the top of the stairs and took a deep breath. He knew he had to hurry, but he also knew he needed to prepare himself for what was inside Europa's room. Birea's body still laid inside because the caring for the wounded took precedence over the deceased. And the blood of the three women would cover a good portion of the floor. Taking another deep breath, Terrance stepped inside and stared in disbelief. Birea's body was gone. All that remained where she had fallen were her clothes and the blanket that had covered her body, both now devoid of any substance to give them shape. The purple blood that had surrounded Birea and Misso was also gone, replaced by a dark tinge in the wooded floor. Terrance shifted his eyes to where Anna had fallen to see if her blood too had disappeared. As he thought, Anna's blood was still clearly visible on the floor. No one had returned upstairs, so what happened to Birea's body and the purple blood? Had Jeanip somehow snuck back upstairs to remove Birea's body and clean up the purple blood so Europa and he would not see it or ask questions? This house had so many secret tunnels and rooms, was there a secret passageway upstairs? Then a spark of panic struck him. If someone had been in the room, had they seen his backpack and looked inside? What if they found the strange weapon? Even worse, what if the weapon was gone? Now afraid of the possibility someone had been in the room, Terrance picked his way through the debris to the settee where his backpack laid. Grabbing it by its straps, he pulled open the zipper and looked inside, hoping everything was still there. He closed his eyes as he breathed a sigh of relief – everything was where it should be.

Crunching his way over the glass, Terrance proceeded to the bathroom. Placing his hand beneath the towels on the second linen closet shelf, he located the diary and maps. He stuffed them into the front part of his backpack. At the sink he grabbed Europa's toothbrush, toothpaste, hairbrush and something he thought was her face cleanser and put them in the back section of his backpack. Upon exiting the bathroom he crossed to the closet and retrieved Europa's backpack and quickly stuffed inside a pair of jeans, two shirts and two sweatshirts. He next crunched his way to her dresser where he grabbed a bra, some panties and several pair of socks,placing them in the pack beside the other clothes. Leaving only the two Dumbo Octopus paintings to obtain, Terrance looked around the room and saw them hanging on the wall by the side of the bed. He ran over, removed them from their hanging spot, swung the two backpacks over his right shoulder and placed the paintings under his left arm. Satisfied he had gotten everything Europa wanted or would need, Terrance ran downstairs to tell her about Birea and the blood.

ESCAPE

Jeanip helped Sunam lift a box into the water for Graybin and Runbee to take to the boat docked a few hundred feet away. With their help the past few days, Jeanip had been stocking the vessel with supplies and some of the more valuable objects from Medaron's attic in case a hasty retreat became necessary. Sunam, with Tinderoon's help, had been busy upgrading the weapons system and installing a new security screen. Both still needed several more days to complete.

"Chancee has sent a message that a large group of possible Terrians is moving down from the mountains and up the canyon. He estimates they will be here within two days. He wants us under his protection by noon tomorrow, which means we have to leave tonight under night's cloak for Saint's Isle," Jeanip explained. "So we need to get everything possible out to the boat."

"Jeanip, I can't get the new screen up by then," Sunam stated, worried about trying to move the monarchs without its completion.

"We'll have to chance it, Sunam. Right now it's more important to get Europa and Earon off of Minnos and to somewhere protected. Plus, I don't believe there will be an attempt to attack us by sea," Jeanip surmised.

"I agree. They know we'd be waiting for them and our troops would cut them down," Runbee stated.

"And since we know they can't transform into any flying creature, we should be okay without the screen. Once we get to the Hunting Lodge you can try to get it up and running." Jeanip addressed Sunam.

Turning to Runbee, Jeanip said, "Once it gets dark I need you to move the boat to the cave's entrance. I don't think it's safe to try to move it until dark. Hopefully no one will see it has been moved and try to investigate the reason for its new location."

"I will get my troops to help me pull it over here. A silent move would be less noticeable than a noisy one." Runbee said.

"Make it so," Jeanip said. Turing to Graybin he said, "I need you to find Enok and let him know we will need help. Tell him I believe the time has come to deploy those who are left and engage the enemy." Graybin looked at him in surprise. "Tell Enok that is my commanding suggestion. The decision, as always, is his."

"So you think war has returned after all these centuries?" Graybin asked.

"That is Enok's decision," Jeanip stated without hesitation. "Tell Enok if we have to evacuate Minnos I will implement security order EW1. Every Waters must be clear. Minnos will be destroyed fifteen minutes after the front or side door is breached by Terrians."

"Yes, Jeanip," Graybin said, as she transformed once again into a bottle noised dolphin.

"Graybin, wait just a moment." Graybin stopped and turned to look at Jeanip. "Once we have the monarchs aboard the boat I want you and Runbee to take Misso down to the Complex. I will need Sunam to stay with me until we reach the Hunting Lodge and he can finish the modifications to the new security screen. Once he has completed that I will send him down to join you."

"Thank you, Jeanip," he heard her say. Then she quickly swam out to the ocean to inform Enok.

"Jeanip, last time we engaged the Terrians the humans were few and scattered across this world. If war begins once again between us, what will happen to the humans?" Sunam asked.

Jeanip stopped and looked at Sunam. He couldn't decide if Sunam had grown fond of these two-legged creatures after all these years or if he was simply curious. "If we can contain the fighting to these lands I believe the threat to the humans will be minimal. But if it goes beyond these lands then many humans may die. And if the humans are ignorant enough to try to engage JeffRa in an attempt to protect themselves and their planet, then I fear they will meet the same fate as other worlds have, such as the planet they call Mars. Their race will exist no more and the majority of their planet will be devoid of life."

"Then I guess for everyone's sake we can't let it go beyond these lands," Sunam stated, as he lowered a box of ammunition down to Runbee.

After running down the stairs, Terrance went directly into the kitchen. He placed the paintings side by side, painted side up on the kitchen table above where Misso laid and Europa's backpack on the chair in front of them. Keeping his backpack hanging over his shoulder for safe keeping, he then walked over to the coffee pot and poured Europa and himself a cup of coffee. He smiled as he thought of Misso – she never let the coffee pot get empty.

"How is she doing?" he asked, as he handed Europa her coffee.

"She's still sleeping. Did you get my book?" Europa asked, taking a sip of her coffee, savoring the familiar flavor.

"All the important things are in my pack here," Terrance said, laying his pack at Europa's feet. "There are a couple of things from my father's room in there too. I was hoping we'd have a chance to look them over together today, but looks like it's going to have to wait. I put your paintings on the table along with your backpack that I put some clothes in."

"Thanks, Terrance. I am grateful you remembered to add clothes to the list," Europa said, a little embarrassed by the omission of such a necessity. "I was so worried about the book that I did not think of anything else." Europa looked at Terrance, trying to determine if the scene upstairs was as bad as she imagined it would be. Not able to contain her curiosity, she asked, "Was it really bad up there, in my room, with Birea's body still up there and all that blood?"

Terrance looked around the kitchen. It was so quiet. He had never known it to be this silent. Seeing the males had not returned yet, nor had Jeanip, he leaned toward Europa and said, "Europa, Birea's body was gone. All that was left where her body had fallen was an empty blanket and her clothes. And all the purple blood was gone too. The only blood up there now is Anna's."

Europa's eyes widen in disbelief. "What do you mean her body is gone?" she whispered. "No one has been up there."

"I know. Do you think Jeanip could have a secret passageway and snuck up there?" asked Terrance.

"It seems like anything is possible in this house," Europa answered, "but I don't think so. Are you sure it . . ." Europa did not finish her sentence. Triton had risen from where he laid at her feet. He turned and faced the side door, his hair beginning to rise on his back, a deep menacing growl starting to grow in his throat. As Europa uneasiness rose as Triton's growl grew, the amulet around her neck began to hum and emit a soft red light. At the same time a red light began to turn off and on throughout the house.

Realizing Jeanip's new silent alarm had been activated and considering the gravity of the situation, Earon transformed from Triton the canine into Earon the human before Europa and Terrance. "Sorry, Sis, but I do not have time to hide the transformation or run and grab some clothes," Earon said to an astonished Europa and Terrance. "You are going to have to deal with a naked brother until I get you down to safety."

"Something really bad is coming," Europa announced, rising to a standing position, staring at her brother and the glowing amulet also around his neck.

Europa screamed as the side door suddenly flew open and reclosed. To her relief she realized it was Tinderoon, but that relief left when he turned around and she saw he was covered in blood, purple blood.

"Tinderoon, what happened? Where are Evonic, Mintoo and Ebar?" Terrance asked, fear mounting inside him also.

Tinderoon looked at the three, shaking his head negatively. "They didn't make it," he said. "They were waiting for us in the barn. They got Mintoo as soon as he took the horses back to their stalls after the ride here. They killed the horses too. They must have been waiting for some of us to come out to the barn. As soon as we had our arms full of boards they struck. We didn't have a chance."

Earon ran to Misso and scooped her up in his arms. Looking directly at Europa and Terrance, he began to give orders. "You two follow me. Stay as close as you can. I will get you to safety."

Europa reached down and picked up Terrance's backpack, then followed Earon. As they passed the kitchen table, Terrance quickly grabbed the two paintings and Europa's backpack while not missing a step in following Europa and Earon toward Jeanip's room.

Looking at Tinderoon, Earon directed, "Tinderoon, I need you to protect our back and keep them from trying to follow as long as possible."

"Yes, My Lord," Tinderoon answered, as he opened a side wall panel to reveal numerous weapons. He removed as many weapons and ammunition as he could carry and took them over by the kitchen table. Tinderoon turned to face the three. "Hurry, Your Majesties, get to safety. They will be here shortly. May the Waters protect you and get you to Saint's Isle safely."

Fearing this might be her last time to see Tinderoon, Europa quickly replied, "Thank you, Tinderoon, for always watching over me." Tinderoon smiled at her and winked, then turned his attention back to his arsenal, forming a plan of defense.

"Remember, Tinderoon, you have fifteen minutes after the alarm sounds," was the last thing he heard Earon say as he disappeared with Misso, Europa and Terrance into Jeanip's room. Grabbing the table, Tinderoon flipped it on its side, positioning it in front of the weapons thus creating a barricade for himself. He loaded the weapons, and then stacked them against the table for easy access. He reached under the kitchen table lip and flipped a switch. A secret panel opened revealing a blaster that turned his army of one into an army of twenty. Weapons in hand, he braced himself for the assault to come, determined their enemy would never reach his monarchs or the others below.

Graybin returned to the cave to offer any assistance Jeanip might need and deliver Enok's reply. She had found Enok still patrolling the ocean, thus making her trip a short one. When Jeanip asked if Enok had a response, she looked at her life's mate, Runbee, then back to Jeanip. "Enok says war has begun," Graybin said softly, a tear emerging from her eye. Jeanip pretended he did not see her tear. He knew Graybin did not fear war, or even death. But all of them, including Jeanip himself, had believed the Terrians to be destroyed and the possibility of war nonexistent. Now here they were again, after so many centuries, fighting an enemy whose sole purpose in life was to eradicate their race. Graybin had already lost her two sons in the war. The possibility of losing her daughter along with this new world she now called home was too devastating a thought to even contemplate.

"Help me carry this box out to the vessel," Runbee said to Graybin. "I'll fill you in on what you missed on the way." As Graybin took ahold of the box, a red blinking light began to flicker on and off, filling the cavern with its flickering light. Jeanip and Sunam knew it was the new silent alarm they had installed, an alarm that would warn them of a Terrian attack without the Terrians knowing they had been detected.

"Runbee, get that vessel over here NOW," Jeanip yelled, as he raced down the tunnel toward the stairs and Europa. Feared gripped him as it never had before. His charges, his sovereigns were up there without him there to protect them. Were they safe? More importantly, were they alive? Had he failed in his duty again? The only thing that gave him hope was the fact the sound alarm had not yet sounded meaning the structure of the cottage had not been breached. His heart pounding so loud he could barely hear any sounds outside his head, his lungs burning with the need for more air, Jeanip pushed himself to run up the stairs leading to his room. Keeping his eyes on the steps to avoid tripping, he did not see the figures descending the stairs above him.

"Jeanip, stop," Earon called out, turning around in an attempt to shield Misso from a possible collision with Jeanip.

Even before he looked up Jeanip knew it was Earon by the sweet sound of his voice. At that moment he believed nothing had ever sounded sweeter than the two words he spoke. Stopping abruptly, he was able to avoid colliding with Earon by hitting the stone wall and falling to the steps. Sunam, who had been running close behind Jeanip, threw out his hands and braced them against the stone wall to stop, breaking his left hand in several places. As Jeanip picked himself up from the steps, Earon noticed a long cut along his cheek bone and another above his right eye, blood flowing from each wound.

"Earon, thank God," Jeanip said, as he hugged Earon around Misso, being very careful not to injure her. "I feared the worst." Seeing Europa behind him, Jeanip stepped over to her and pulled her into his arms. "Forgive me, Your Highness, for not being there to protect you. Until we arrive at Saint's Isle, I will not leave your side again."

"It is okay, Jeanip," Europa said, as she took a handkerchief from her pocket and wiped away the blood on Jeanip's face. "You had no way of knowing they would attack again so soon."

"That is irrelevant, Your Highness. Once an attempt was made on your life I should not have left you for any reason. That error will NOT be made again." Jeanip looked around to see who else was with them. When he saw only Terrance he wondered where his soldiers were. "Earon, where are my men? Why didn't they accompany you down here?"

Continuing to walk down the stairs, Earon said, "Evonic, Tinderoon and Ebar went out to the barn to get some wood to board up the hole in Europa's room. The Terrians were waiting for them. Somehow Tinderoon managed to make it back inside, but he looked badly wounded. He has barricaded himself in the kitchen with a stockpile of weapons to cover our escape."

"And Mintoo?"

"The Terrians ambushed him when he took the horses to the barn. None of them had a chance."

"Sunam, go help Tinderoon." Jeanip stopped as the alarms began to sound throughout the estate, followed by weapon firing from above. "Never mind, Sunam. They've breached the walls. May the Waters give Tinderoon a warrior's death." Turning around to face Terrance, Jeanip added, "Terrance, I'm afraid you'll have to go with us."

"Where Europa goes, I go, Sir," Terrance said with determination to keep her safe from whomever was trying to end her life – and Earon's.

Jeanip led the small group down the tunnel to the ocean entrance. Runbee had moved the vessel to thirty feet from the entrance, unable to bring it closer due to the rocky shelf that had been built to prevent boats from entering the cave.

"Everyone in the water. We'll have to swim out to the boat. Time is short, so hurry." Jeanip announced. "Sunam, carry Misso out. Earon, you help Europa."

"Jeanip, I don't think I can carry Misso," Sunam said. "I broke my hand when I hit that wall on the stairs and I wouldn't be able to hold her plus swim."

"Earon, you take Misso. Sunam, you help Europa if she needs it." Jeanip knew that, like all Waters, Europa was an excellent swimmer and probably wouldn't need much assistance. He then turned and disappeared into the treasure room Europa had seen.

As Sunam stepped into the water, he looked up at Terrance and Europa. "You'll need to leave those backpacks and paintings here."

"We can't leave the backpack," Terrance said, knowing he could not leave the items it contained behind.

"Then you'll have to swim with it," Sunam announced.

"There are valuable, irreplaceable items in here. They can't get wet. Isn't there another way to get to the boat?"

"No, the vessel cannot come any closer. If you want your things you'll have to swim with them," Sunam said again, getting annoyed as the time ticked by.

"The valuables he speaks of are mine, Sunam. I need them to go with me, along with the two paintings. They cannot get wet," Europa interjected.

"Sunam, put the backpacks containing her majesty's and Terrance's items in a waterproof container along with the two paintings and this," Jeanip ordered as he threw Sunam the missing Orb.

"And I would appreciate it if someone would throw some clothes in there for me too," Earon said, as he began swimming with Misso toward the vessel.

Without speaking a word, Sunam jumped up out of the water, grabbed a nearby container and placed the backpacks, paintings and Orb inside. He quickly ran to a nearby trunk and grabbed some clothes, throwing them also in the container. Holding on to the container with his uninjured hand, he jumped into the water and began to swim alongside Europa as she followed Earon to the vessel.

"Terrance, if you're coming I need for you to get into the water," Jeanip said as he jumped in. "We are running out of time. If we don't leave within the next few minutes we won't have to worry about the Terrians ending our lives. We will blow ourselves up."

A look of horror covered Terrance's face. "I can't swim," he said.

"What did you say?" Jeanip asked in astonishment.

"I said I can't swim. I don't like the water. In fact, I avoid it. I don't even like being on a boat," Terrance admitted. "Leave me here. Maybe I'll be okay down here."

"You'll be dead down here," Jeanip said. "Now get in the water now or I'll drag you in myself."

Graybin swam up alongside Jeanip, "It's okay Jeanip, we'll take him. You go ahead." As Jeanip began to swim toward the vessel, Graybin looked up at Terrance. "Young man, Runbee and I will swim you out to the vessel. You just have to hold on to us. We promise we will not let you drown. Now get into the water and grab our dorsal fins. Europa needs you."

They were right   Europa did need him. He stepped into the water as Graybin and Runbee transformed into bottlenose dolphins. Positioning themselves on each sign of Terrance, they carefully swam him to the boat as he tightly held on to their dorsal fins. He saw Sunam and Earon waiting for him on the swim deck to help him on board, Europa standing behind them. Terrance focused his attention on her face while remembering his promise to Jeanip to help protect her. He could do this; if he just concentrated on Europa he could reach the boat. Finally he heard Earon's voice telling him to give him his hand. He looked away from Europa and discovered he was within arms' length of the boat and both men were reaching for him to help him up. Taking a deep breathe, he let go of Runbee's dorsal fin first and grabbed Earon's hand. Once he was sure Earon had him, he let go of Graybin and reached for Sunam's good arm. He scrambled aboard the swim deck and stepped on to the vessel. Not knowing if he was shaking from the cold water or fear, Europa quickly brought him a towel she found on deck and threw it around his shoulders. As she escorted Terrance away from the bow, Europa heard a familiar clicking sound and glanced over the side to see the two dolphins who had helped Terrance. In amazement she noticed lilac stars on their side and instantaneously realized the two unfamiliar humans inside the cave were actually her play pals, Jack and Jill. They too were shape shifters.

"Is no one who or what they seem?" she asked, looking at a shivering bewildered Terrance. "Do you not see, Terrance? The two humans from the cave who shifted into dolphins; they are Jack and Jill, the two dolphins I have been playing with all my life." As they entered the wheel house she turned and yelled back, "And brother, I would appreciate you putting those clothes on. I am delighted to know I have a brother, but meeting him for the first time as he walks around naked is a bit disturbing."

"Okay, Sis," Earon laughed, giving her a big smile. "I am glad we finally get to meet," he said, as he opened the container Sunam had brought aboard and pulled out the clothes to put on.

"Sunam, man the guns," Jeanip ordered, cradling Misso in his arms. Sunam reached down and tore off the bottom of his shirt. Holding on to the rag, he pulled his hunting knife from his boot and laid it across the palm of his broken hand, being sure the blade pointed outward, the edge of the torn cloth secured under the knife. Using his good hand, Sunam wrapped the strip of cloth around his hand, binding the knife to it. The knife would act as a splint as well as a weapon. Although unlikely, he knew the Terrians might try to disable their vessel and board it. If that happened he was now equipped to protect his royals, ready to defend them in hand-to-hand combat.

"Europa and Terrance, I need you to have a seat in here," Jeanip yelled, as he entered the wheel house and laid Misso on the bench. "Sit here next to Misso. Europa, if you would be so kind as to keep an eye on her for me. If she wakes or seems in pain, let me know. Earon, I need you to drive the boat so I can help Sunam."

Now dressed, Earon entered the wheel house. "I can help Sunam. You know these waters better than I. You should pilot the ship."

"Just keep her on this heading," Jeanip answered, placing his hand on Earon's shoulder. "Earon, I need you to be safe. I need Europa, Misso and Terrance to be safe. That means you need to stay here inside the wheel house, the safest place on the ship. And you need to make sure they stay here. My place, Sire, is out there defending you alongside Sunam." He removed his hand from Earon's shoulder and exited the wheel house.

"Are we not going a bit slow?" Earon yelled after Jeanip. "Can I give it some more gas?"

"No, keep it at this speed. A speeding boat racing away from Minnos may draw attention. We want to look like a normal vessel out for a tour on the ocean. Once you pass the lighthouse give her all she's got and get us the hell out of the area. Head out into the open ocean as fast as you can," Jeanip ordered.

"Is that not cutting it pretty close, Jeanip?" Earon asked, remembering the blast range of the upcoming explosion.

"With about five seconds to spare," Jeanip answered, giving Earon a wink.

As soon as they reached the lighthouse, Earon pushed the throttle forward. Within seconds of the vessel picking up speed, the sound of several huge explosions filled the air. The five comrades turned toward the sound and watched as debris rained down from the sky, debris that had been the cottage. Europa raised her hand to her mouth to stop herself from crying out. Her home, everything she loved, everything she owned was gone. Ten seconds later three more explosions sounded. Rock and water burst from the cave as the blasts destroyed the stairway and the secret tunnel to the cottage, destroyed all the treasures held in its chambers, wiped away any existence of their secret world. The complete destruction of the cottage and the cave gave assurance nothing would be left for the Terrians or the humans to find. As Earon, Terrance and Europa watched the destruction of Minno,s they knew Tinderoon had sacrificed his life to keep the advancing Terrians occupied during the fifteen minute countdown.

Jeanip looked over and saw the look on Europa's face. He wished he had had time to prepare her for what just happened, but everything had happened so swiftly there had not been time to warn her. He saw Terrance take her in his arms as she began to cry for all she had just lost; he was glad Terrance was there to comfort her for he had a job to do. "Earon, keep this course," Jeanip ordered, as he opened the weapons locker and removed several assault rifles. He walked to the opposite side of the deck from Sunam and knelt, placing the weapons next to himself. He then began to load each and stack them against the ship's side in preparation.

"Jeanip, I think Misso is coming around. She is starting to moan," Europa called to Jeanip, her tears stopped for the moment.

"Damn, I hoped she'd stay asleep until we made it to the Hunting Lodge," Jeanip said under his breath. Turning to face Sunam he said, "All I can do is give her a shot for the pain. I'll be right back."

Jeanip returned to the wheel room and injected Misso with pain medication. "This should take away her pain," Jeanip said to Europa. "Unfortunately, without Evonic that's all we can do for now."

"What is the plan?" Earon asked.

"I had hoped once you and your sister were aboard I could allow Runbee and Graybin to take Misso below for treatment."

"No, Jeanip, I will not leave as long as my sovereigns are in danger," they heard a faint voice say before Jeanip could complete his statement. "My place is here with them."

"So it is, Misso," Jeanip softly said, as he gently placed his hand on her head. Turning back to the three youths he stated, "We'll have to remain out in the ocean until night falls to assure no one can follow us to our next destination. It will be tricky; we'll have to travel without the aid of lights."

"We have to navigate back to land without using lights?" Terrance asked, concerned about the vessel running aground. "Isn't that going to be impossible?"

"Don't worry, novice sailor," Jeanip said. "The jumpers will be our eyes. They will lead us up the coast through the fog and into Medaron's Cove.

"Jumpers?" Terrance asked.

"Dolphins, Terrance," Europa said. "Jack and Jill will lead us to where we have to go."

239

"Oh," Terrance said, acting as if this was a normal occurrence. "But what's to keep them from coming after us out here in the ocean?" Terrance asked.

"They could, but Terrians are like you Terrance," Earon stated, smiling down at Terrance. "They don't like the water. They avoid it whenever possible. Plus, they know the ocean will be guarded by the jumpers, our Shooniffs, a special elite Oonocks' army sworn to protect their monarchs. They will never allow a Terrian to get within several miles of us."

"What about an attack from the sky?" Terrance asked, as he tried to imagine every angle an attack could come from.

"True Terrians do not have the capability of transforming. Only Oonocks who have become Terrians do. Plus, there's the law of physics. We cannot transform into creatures much smaller than ourselves and then we need the animal's DNA to transform into them. So you see, we can't transform into birds, or insects, or into mythical creatures such as fire-breathing dragons," Jeanip replied. "So, unless they've figured out how to fly as ostriches, we should be safe."

Terrance dropped his head onto his chest. "This is just too weird."

"Welcome to my world," Earon teased.

Europa reached over and took his hand in hers. "I am so sorry, Terrance, I got you involved in all of this. If I had had any idea about whom, or should I say what I was, I never would have allowed us to become friends."

Terrance raised his head and looked at Europa. "Don't ever say that, Europa. Please don't ever regret meeting me. I don't. If my being here means you will live for years to come, then I welcome all that has happened and is yet to happen. Besides, I said it was weird, not that I was sorry I was here."

"Weird is an understatement," Europa replied in a low voice, smiling back. "And to tell you the truth, I cannot imagine making this journey without you being with me."

Jeanip looked up at the sun. From its position he estimated it was about four hours before night fall. He turned to scan the ocean's surface. No other vessels were in sight. Just as he was beginning to feel they were going to make it, he heard Sunam cry out. "Jeanip, Sir, you need to come out here right away. I believe we may have a problem."

Jeanip ran outside after ordering the three to remain inside the wheel house. "What's the problem?" Jeanip asked, dropping down beside Sunam. He resurveyed the ocean for ships thinking perhaps he had missed one, but again he saw nothing.

"I believe THAT is going to be," Sunam said, as he pointed toward the sky. Jeanip lifted his vision upward. There, in the distance, was a dark speck against the blue sky which was growing larger. As he continued to watch, Jeanip recognized the dot as a sea plane and it was flying straight toward them.

"Terrance, I stand corrected," Jeanip shouted. "They might not be able to turn into flying creatures, but evidently the Terrians have learned how to fly machines." He turned to face Sunam. "I don't suppose you and Tinderoon were able to install that blaster?"

"No, Sir. That was on our list for this evening. We have some good weapons, but nothing that can knock that out of the sky unless they get really close to us."

"Well, then, Sunam, without that blaster that plane could definitely be a major problem." Jeanip surveyed the horizon in hope the nightly fog bank would be moving in early tonight. As he strained his eyes to search, he thought he saw a darkening on the horizon. Could they be that lucky? Could the fog be coming in early? He continued to watch, but could not be sure if it was the fog.

"Sunam, look north-west. Tell me what you see," Jeanip ordered, knowing Sunam's eyesight was much sharper than his.

Sunam placed his good palm over his eyes to cut down on the sun's glare and stared in the north-west direction. A hint of hope flittered in his eyes as he said, "Sir, I believe that is the fog coming to our defense, but it's a long ways out there. I'm not sure we can make it there before that plane reaches us."

"Maybe we can combine a couple of these assault rifles and create something we can use to slow them down. We only need to buy ourselves about twenty minutes," Jeanip replied.

Sunam immediately began to dissemble some of his weaponry, as did Jeanip. Brainstorming together, they began building a new weapon that would hopefully stop the advancement of the aircraft. With a lot of luck it would bring the craft down.

"Earon, head north-north west. There's a fog bank out there," Jeanip yelled, pointing toward the fog. "And see if you can get some more speed out of her by changing the mixture flow to a minus two."

"How do I tell where north-north west is? And what the hell is a minus two mixture?" Earon yelled back, staring down at the numerous dials and switches in front of him.

Needing to stay working with Sunam, but not wanting Earon to do anything that might jeopardize their mission such as changing the flow wrong and stalling the engines, Jeanip stood up to return to the wheel house. Before he could take a step he saw Europa jump up and immediately go to the controls and Earon. "I will show him, Jeanip," she shouted. Knowing she was an experienced sailor Jeanip returned to building the new weapon with Sunam, leaving the corrections in Europa's capable hands. "Here, let me do it," Europa said as she lovingly nudged Earon aside. "After all the years you have lived up here, I cannot believe you do not know the first thing about navigating a ship."

"Hey, it is not my fault they never taught the canine the mechanics of ocean vessels," Earon answered, as he nudged his sister aside in return. He was disappointed his funny remark did not bring a smile to his sister's face but he realized things were probably too serious for her to appreciate his humor.

"Give me the wheel for a minute!" Europa said, as she placed one hand on the wheel and pointed to the direction dial with the other. "See this dial? It tells you your direction. Turn the wheel until the needle is lined up with the direction you want to go." She turned the wheel until the needle read NNW. She then pointed to a black knob with a white arrow on it. Under the knob printed in an Orbital array were numbers descending from "nine" to "minus nine", each number having a white notch line to indicate its position. Europa turned the knob until the white arrow rested on the notch marked minus two. "Now listen for the engine valves to open." Within seconds Earon could hear the clicking of valves opening. "Flip the switch and count to ten: one, two, three, four, five, six, seven, eight, nine, ten. Now push the throttle forward." Earon pushed the throttle forward and was surprised to feel the vessel pick up speed. Changing the mixture had worked.

Jeanip and Sunam completed the new weapon. It looked like a piece of junk with different weapon pieces tied or taped together, but they both felt it had a chance. They only had to slow the sea plane down to give them the time they needed to reach the fog bank.

"Terrance, you and Europa go lay on the floor between the Captain's chair and the side now. Earon, if firing starts tie off the wheel and lie down next to your sister. There is a rope hanging on each side of the wheel for tying it off. Do not, I repeat, DO NOT try to remain at the

242

wheel to steer the vessel. Do you understand?" Jeanip handed Sunam the new weapon, then returned to his original spot with his remaining stockpile of weapons. Even with a broken hand Jeanip knew Sunam was the better shot, and therefore the one to fire the new weapon.

"What about Misso?" Europa asked. "Should we put her on the floor also?"

"No, there is no time and I don't believe she should be moved. Plus, they shouldn't fire into the wheel house for fear of hitting you or Earon. If I'm wrong, we just have to hope she'll be safe laying on the bench."

Earon scanned the horizon searching for the fog bank Jeanip said was out there. While wondering if the fog was just a dream, it suddenly came into Earon's view. As he watched, the bank grew in size. It was huge, the kind they could easily get lost in if they could just reach it. He kept the vessel on course straight toward the fog.

Jeanip and Sunam watched the image of the sea plane grow larger as it came nearer. There was always the possibility it was not Terrian, but the probability was slim. The plane's purpose was confirmed when it altered its course to intercept their ship before it could reach the fog bank. They could hear the engine's sputter as the pilot pushed the throttle forward to go faster, perhaps fearing they would reach the fog bank before they reached them. As the plane continued to advance toward them, Sunam could make out the weaponry mounted on its wings.

"They're carrying some heavy artillery," Sunam announced.

"Definitely an aggressor," Jeanip stated, as the now familiar sound of a "ping" was heard as a bullet hit the boat. "Earon, get down," Jeanip yelled as a barrage of bullets hit the boat. Jeanip and Sunam both opened fired, but their weapons did not have the capability of reaching the plane. Sunam knew he would probably only have one, possibly two shots with the new weapon to either stop or bring the plane down. He had to wait until the plan came closer. Another round of bullets hit the vessel, shattering the windshield, punching holes through the sides. Jeanip winced in pain as a bullet ricocheted and entered his leg.

"Sir, fall back to the wheel house," Sunam said.

"No, I'm okay." Jeanip yelled, firing at the untouchable target.

"Sir, our weapons are not inflicting any damage. The only hope we have is this new weapon we built, but I have to wait until they're closer before firing it. Our monarchs need you with them," Sunam said,

243

looking directly at Jeanip. "The Terrians will try to kill you and me and disable our engine. That will leave them with only Earon for protection. Sir, the Terrians will not hesitate to kill Earon– it's Europa JeffRa wants. If it looks like you'll be boarded you can put the three in the water while I keep them pinned down. Once in the water you and Earon can transform into jumpers and take Europa away from the boat to the pod's protection. If Enok is in the area he might even be able to take her underwater for a short period of time." Sunam paused and stared at Jeanip. "Sir, you know I'm right."

"And what about Terrance? He can't swim. And Misso can't be put in the water." Jeanip stated. "I can't leave them behind."

"I know, Sir. Hopefully a life preserver will help Terrance. And I'm sure Graybin and Runbee will be glad to assist him like before. As for Misso, she is a soldier ready to give her life for her sovereigns," Sunam answered, knowing it might not be possible to save Terrance and Misso. Jeanip saluted Sunam, saluted the best soldier he had ever known, saluted him with all the homage deserving of a king. He then turned and scurried across the deck to the wheel house. Sunam looked ahead at the fog bank. It was still too far off to offer assistance.

"Jeanip, you're wounded," Europa said, as she saw the purple blood stain on Jeanip's leg.

"I'm fine, Europa," he said, trying to reassure her. The seriousness of their situation on his face, he stated, "If the re-engineered weapon does not at least slow the plane down, we are going to have to go into the water. It's our only chance." He saw a look of terror come across Terrance's face. "Europa and Terrance, grab one of those life jackets next to you and put it on. And I would suggest you all cover your ears. This new weapon is going to be pretty loud."

Terrance quickly handed Europa her life jacket, then put his own on while praying they would not have to go into the water again. Then all placed their hands over their ears while Jeanip placed his hands over Misso's. As the plane came closer, Sunam pulled the trigger. A large boom signaled the firing of the weapon as the barrel blew apart, sending fragments into Sunam's chest.

"Did it work?" Earon yelled, unable to see through a cloud of black smoke.

Jeanip waved his hands trying to dissipate the smoke so he could see if the sea plane was still in the sky. As the smoke cleared Jeanip saw the plane was still air born, but definitely damaged. It retreated some and began to circle the ship, apparently afraid of being hit again.

244

"Damn, it didn't go down. And it looks like we only get one shot at it," Jeanip said, a note of defeat in his voice. "Get ready to get wet. Without a blaster I can't stop that plane."

"Wait," Terrance yelled, terrified of having to go back into the water. He had suddenly remembered the strange weapon he had brought in his backpack. Perhaps Jeanip could use it. Frantically looking for the container it came aboard in, he spotted it behind the captain's seat. Keeping as low to the floor as he could, he scrambled over to the container, yanked open its lid and retrieved his pack. Dragging it behind him, he crawled up next to Jeanip.

"Sir, I have something here. I don't know if it will help or not," Terrance said, as he removed the weapon from his backpack.

In disbelief, Jeanip stared at the weapon. "Where in the hell did you get a Terrian blaster?" he asked, as he took the weapon from Terrance's hand. "It's exactly what I need!" As Jeanip turned it over he saw the power source was missing. "Well, it almost was what we needed. The power source is missing."

"What does it look like?" Terrance asked, hoping somehow he might have accidentally brought it with him.

"It's an oval stone, purple in color, about the size of a half dollar. It usually has some form of etching on it. So unless you have something like that in your pocket, you can use that weapon to float on."

Terrance reached inside his pocket and brought out the leather pouch. As he removed the stone from inside, he looked at Jeanip and said, "Does it look something like this?"

"Kid, I don't know if I should tear your heart out and feed it to the sharks or give you a big kiss," Jeanip somberly said, as he grabbed the stone and placed it in the power chamber. "We'll discuss which choice I choose after we stop this plane."

Terrance watched as the weapon seemed to come to life when Jeanip put the stone in the power chamber. Lights, which had been dormant seconds before, now shined brightly, displaying an array of colors under foreign symbols. Dials began to twirl and rotate. On the side Terrance noticed a group of lights beginning to blink on one at a time, progressing up the panel. He hoped that meant the weapon was charging and would be ready to fire when all the lights were lit to the top. As the last light lit, Terrance detected a low hum emanating from the weapon as what appeared to be the barrel began to glow red.

"It's charged," Jeanip announced. "Now let's hope I remember how this damn thing works. I haven't had to read Terrian in" stopping himself from saying eight hundred years he quickly added "a very long time."

"Soo Na-Je Ree," came a voice from Misso. "Press the lightening large S, the n inside the j then the single l with a 3 attached on the lower right. When the humming stops, pull the trigger."

Jeanip took aim and pressed the three buttons to correspond to Misso's description - ꕫꕩꕬ. As the humming stopped he pulled the trigger. A pulse of invisible energy erupted from the end of the weapon and soared toward the sea plane. Seconds ticked by as everyone waited and hoped the blaster would come to their rescue. As they watched, the sea plane was enveloped in a misty cloud that began as a pinkish light, then grew to a golden fog and finally to a blinding white light. The white light appeared to expand three fold, then, having reached its maximum expansion, began to quickly fade away. Bits and pieces of metal began to rain down from the now disseminating cloud. Terrance and Europa turned and looked at each other, each astonished the sea plane had been destroyed without a sound – no blast, no boom, and no explosion. Then as they realized the plane had truly been destroyed, they all began to cheer.

"You have to love those Terrian weapons," Jeanip said, as he limped over to Misso. Bending over her wounded body, Jeanip softly said, "Thank you, Misso. Today you saved the lives of everyone on this ship."

"As is my duty," Misso said, trying to put a smile on her face. "I told you, Sir, I was needed here." Jeanip reached down and brushed a piece of hair from Misso's face, returning her smile. He wished Evonic was here to give her the medical attention she needed. He knew Chancee could help her once they reached the Hunting Lodge, but Jeanip doubted Misso would be able to hold on until then.

Jeanip stood up and looked over his charges. "Is everyone okay? Any one hurt?" Europa, Terrance and Earon all answered they were fine. Not a sound came from the back of the ship. "Sunam, you okay back there?" Jeanip called, beginning to become concerned Sunam did not respond. "Soldier, are you okay?" he repeated as he limped to where Sunam sat.

As Jeanip reached Sunam's location, Sunam leaned back against the side of the vessel. Purple blood poured from the wounds the scrap metal had ripped into Sunam's chest. "I'm sorry, Sir," Sunam said. "I may have put a little too much power in that weapon. ."

"Don't move, Sunam. I'll get the medical kit and patch you up. As soon as we reach the fog I will have Runbee and Graybin take Misso and you down to the Complex. The fog's not far off."

"I think it's too late to take me below, Sir," Sunam said, grabbing Jeanip's arm to keep him from leaving. "Please, Jeanip, take me to the water so I can return home."

"Are you sure?"

"Yes, there is nothing that can save me now. I'm torn up pretty bad inside," Sunam silently said so Europa could not hear. He closed his eyes until the pain ravaging his body passed. He opened his eyes and looked at Jeanip. "Sir, would you do me one favor first?"

"Anything, Sunam."

"Take me to say goodbye to Misso."

"Of course," Jeanip answered. He bent down and picked Sunam up in his arms. As he stepped forward, pain shot through his wounded leg and he faltered, going down on one knee. Earon told Europa to take the wheel and ran to help. As he approached the two men Earon could see the seriousness of Sunam's injuries.

"Sorry, Your Highness," Sunam whispered. "I am afraid I cannot continue with you on this journey. It is necessary for me to take my leave of you."

"He wants to say farewell to Misso," Jeanip stated, fighting to keep the emotion he was feeling out of his voice.

"I'll take him," Earon said. Earon reached down and gently took Sunam into his arms. Trying to walk as smoothly as possible so as not to cause him more pain, Earon walked directly to Misso. He positioned himself so Sunam was just above her, facing her. With difficulty, Jeanip stood and followed behind. As they entered the wheel house Jeanip saw they had at last reached the fog bank.

"Europa, back her up and stay just outside that fog bank. Put her in neutral and let the engine idle," Jeanip said, seeing a bewildered look come across Europa's face. "It will be okay. We're out of danger. Before we do anything else there is an important matter we need to take care of without delay."

"Misso, it's Sunam," Sunam softly spoke. Misso opened her eyes and looked at Sunam. As she saw the bleeding holes in his chest, she knew immediately his time had come to go home. "Misso, my time here has come to an end. I wanted to tell you that it has been my honor to be your life's mate and to fight by your side once again. I've loved no other but you and will continue to love you as I float upon the waters."

"Sunam, my love I promise to you for all time. You have brought me nothing but happiness and fulfillment as your life's mate. But know that my time here is also at an end. We will go together, forever one in the Waters of Life." Misso looked up at Jeanip and said, "Grant me this, Sir."

"As you wish," Jeanip replied, a lilac tear escaping his eye.

Jeanip limped over to the side of the ship and knocked on its side. Runbee and Graybin appeared in the water. He leaned down and spoke to them, then returned. "Earon, would you please take Sunam to the swim deck. And, Terrance, would you carry Misso?"

Without saying a word, Terrance walked over and picked Misso up into his arms. He was amazed at how light she was, how fragile. He walked beside Earon to allow Misso and Sunam to keep eye contact as long as possible. Europa walked over to Jeanip and slipped her arm around his waist, helping him to the back of the ship. Graybin and Runbee were waiting on the swim deck with several other people Europa did not know but suspected were part of the dolphin pod she had often played with. They took Sunam and Misso from Earon and Terrance and lowered them to waiting hands in the water. Once Sunam and Misso were in the water, those on the swim deck dove back into the ocean. Holding onto Sunam and Misso, they swam a few feet from the ship. Europa watched as Graybin placed Misso's hand in Sunam's. Then, to her amazement, she watched as their arms and legs transform into delicate floating wings, their hair into droplets of lilac pearls cascading down from the top of their heads, their eyes into large circles of lilac; Sunam and Misso had transformed into their true selves, into the beautiful luminous beings of Europa's dreams. Tears began to flow from her eyes as she witnessed two of the most beautiful creatures she had ever beheld. As their eyes closed, Sunam's and Misso's bodies began to glow in a lilac light. As the glow grew stronger, their skin become transparent until only the glow remained. Their brightness spread itself thinner and thinner upon the water until it too was gone.

"May the Waters welcome you home and honor you as the true soldiers you are," Jeanip said, letting a salty tear for each drop into the ocean to accompany them on their journey.

CONFESSION

After moving the ship into the safety of the fog bank, Jeanip sat down on the bench in the wheel house, allowing the boat to drift aimlessly in the ocean for the moment. It was still too light to risk traveling to the Hunting Lodge. He looked over at Europa and Earon and could see they were deeply saddened by Sunam and Misso's passing. He glanced at Terrance, who was trying his best to console Europa on the loss, but Jeanip could see he too was affected by their deaths. Realizing he was the only one still alive to assure the two monarchs made it to safety, he reached down and pulled his hunting knife from his boot. Knowing there was no longer the need to hide the fact his blood was purple, he placed the knife's tip inside the bullet hole in his pant leg and slid the blade down the material to expose the wound. There was a large amount of purple blood, but at least it had missed the artery. He tried to turn the leg to see if perhaps the bullet had gone clean threw but was unable to turn it due to the amount of pain he experienced. Seeing his attempt, Earon walked over and began to inspect the leg to ascertain the extent of the injury.

"Looks like it didn't go through, which means the bullet is still inside your leg," Earon stated, as he lifted the cut pant leg to reveal the back of Jeanip's leg. "Jeanip, that bullet needs to come out, but I do not know if I can dig it out."

Jeanip lifted his eyes from the wound to face Earon. "No, I don't expect you to. You're a top notch field dresser, but I'm not sure I'm ready to trust my leg to you as you dig around inside it for the bullet. Wash out the wound and dress it. The bullet can be removed once we reach the Hunting Lodge." Jeanip looked over at Europa, who was sitting with Terrance on the opposite bench. "Europa, might I impose upon you to bring the medical bag from the galley? It's under the sink." Europa stepped down into the galley, retrieved the medical bag and then walked back to the wheel house. When she reached Jeanip and Earon, she sat the bag down and knelt at Jeanip's feet. "Your Highness, you cannot kneel at my feet. I cannot allow it. You can sit at my side, but you cannot be below me," Jeanip stated, clearly shaken at the sight of Europa kneeling.

"I cannot tend to your wounds at your side, Jeanip," Europa answered, as she opened the bag and brought out the peroxide. "I need to be down here to satisfactorily cleanse and dress it."

"You cannot kneel to me, Europa," Jeanip repeated, this time even more agitated, more flustered. "I will sit on the floor next to you."

As Jeanip lifted his body in preparation to sit on the deck next to Europa, Earon held out his hand. "Jeanip, sit your keester down and let Europa take care of that leg. That is an order," he said with the authority of a monarch. Without hesitation Jeanip sat back down, obeying the order of his leader. Earon bent his legs and knelt beside Europa to assist her.

Jeanip fought to keep the tears that were filling up his eyes from escaping, but he was having little success as they streamed down his face. No honor was greater than the honor of having a royal kneel to someone of such unimportance as he. He had never heard of this being done before. And here was not one, but two monarchs kneeling at his feet.

After removing the cap Europa positioned the peroxide over Jeanip's wound, then hesitated for a moment. "I know," Jeanip said in anticipation of what she was thinking. "This might hurt a bit." Europa slowly began to pour the peroxide into the wound. Jeanip clenched his teeth in an attempt not to show any pain as the peroxide bubbled green in the wound and washed down his blood soaked leg. "A Commander shows no pain," he repeated to himself over and over again in an attempt to ignore the pain. Even with his eyes squeezed tight, he could feel the room start to spin around him. A cold sweat drenched his body. Finally, the pain began to subside and he was able to open his eyes, only to discover all three passengers were staring at him. Feeling a little embarrassed, Jeanip's cheeks flushed red for just a second before he regained his composure. "There should be a bottle of lilac water in the bag. That needs to be poured into the wound, then a dressing can be put on," he said, as he looked down at Europa.

"I saw Evonio pour this water on Misso," Europa stated, as she opened the bottle of lilac water and poured it into the wound as Jeanip had said. "May I ask what it is?"

"It's water from our homeland. It helps us heal," Jeanip said.

Earon reached inside the medical bag and retrieved the ball of gauze and handed it to Europa when she had finished with the lilac water. "Are you sure you know how to do this?" he asked his sister. "I am pretty good at this."

"Believe it or not, Earon, your sister is a better field dresser than you are," Jeanip replied.

"I had a wonderful teacher," Europa stated, as she looked into Jeanip's eyes. "You made me practice over and over again when I was young until it became second nature. You always said I needed to know how to do this because I might need it someday to save someone's life."

"That is the same line he gave me," Earon stated. "Made me practice for hours."

"Aren't you glad I did? Who knew it would be my life you two would be saving?" Jeanip whispered, trying to ignore the pain and lighten the mood at the same time.

Earon held two thick bandage pads over the cleaned out wound while Europa began to wrap gauze around the leg. Without removing her eyes from her task, she asked, "Jeanip, is that what happened to my mother when she died? Did she disappear like Sunam and Misso did? Did she turn into light and then vanish? Or was her body really in that grave in the family graveyard?"

Jeanip looked at Earon, who gave a nod of approval. "Yes, that is what happened to your mother when she died; there was no body in her grave. When we die, and our brains stop sending out the signal for transformation, we return to our true selves, the beings of light you saw Sunam and Misso turn in to. In our true state, we cannot exist up here because our bodies are designed to exist in high pressure. The lack of pressure makes our body's molecules disintegrate and lose their cohesiveness. The result is we 'flow out', which means our outer skin cannot hold our insides in and they spill out. Hopefully, when this happens our body is in water so we can return home. We are beings of the water; created in water, born in water and exist in water. If one flows out in water, the essence of who we were combines with the particles of water and we literally become part of the ocean. Although we can never take a form again, who we were continues to exist."

251

"And what happens if you die away from water?" Europa asked.

"Then the essence of who we are is lost forever as it flows out into dirt, or rock, or whatever substance we are on," Jeanip answered. "Who we were exists no more."

"Is that what happened to Birea? Why her body disappeared?" Terrance asked, remembering the absence of Birea's body.

"Yes, that is what happened to her. There was no water for her essence to adhere to. No matter where we die, be it on land or in the water, we leave no body behind to show we ever existed. That is one of the ways we have been able to hide our existence from humans."

"But my mother was on land when she died," Europa said sadly. "Does that mean she flowed out onto dirt and her essence is lost forever?"

"No, Europa, your mother did not die on land," Jeanip answered. Europa stopped her wrapping and jerked her head up to see Jeanip. "I carried your mother out into the ocean as she was dying. She was able to flow out into the water and she now exists out there as part of everything the ocean is and will be."

"So you lied to me. She was not buried while I slept. If that was a lie, did you lie about her being dead when I arrived too? Was my mother alive when I arrived?".

"Yes, your mother was alive," Jeanip stated. "And I am sorry, Your Majesty, that I lied to you. You had no knowledge of your mother's true form and I had no way to explain to you why there was no body except to fabricate an explanation. So I told you she had already died before you arrived and had been buried in the family cemetery. But we will go over the events of that night and I will tell you the true story when we reach the Hunting Lodge. For now, know I would never have allowed your mother, my sovereign and most beloved sister, to be so dishonored as to flow out onto dirt. Dirt is the filth Terrians come from. The dirt of many lands has claimed the essences of many Oonocks – I would not allow them to have your mother's too."

Jeanip could see the anger Europa had started to feel start to recede as she understood why he could not tell her the truth about her mother. "Now, I believe Mr. Landers and I have some unfinished business." Jeanip looked directly at Terrance. "I have to determine if I'm going to cut your heart out or kiss you."

Trying not to show his nervousness, Terrance replied, "Yes, Sir, I believe that is what you said your two choices were going to be."

"Earon, would you kindly bring me that blaster" Jeanip asked Earon, pointing to the blaster that lay on the floor a few feet away.

Earon picked up the blaster and handed it to Jeanip. Jeanip held it up so Terrance could have a good view of it. "Do you know what this is, Terrance?"

"I believe it's what just saved Europa's and Earon's lives," Terrance said, hoping Jeanip would remember that fact and not decide to cut out his heart.

"You are correct about that. Had that not been the case I would have already killed you," Jeanip stated, watching Terrance for any sign of faltering. He did not falter, but kept his ground, ready to answer the next question. Europa suddenly realized the seriousness of this questioning and began to stand up to intercede. Earon grabbed her arm, pulling her back down to the deck. He shook his head negatively, telling her not to interfere.

"But do you know what KIND of weapon this is? Where it comes from?" Jeanip asked, maintaining his sight on Terrance while gripping the knife in his hand tighter.

"No, Sir.

"Let me enlighten you, then. This is a Terrian blaster, top of the line. The primary assault weapon of our sworn enemy. This particular type of weapon has been responsible for annihilating most of my race. Would you mind telling me how you came about having it in your possession? And, Terrance, please don't insult me by lying."

Europa held her breath. She knew Terrance had to tell Jeanip the truth, but what would Jeanip do? She feared if his answer did not meet with Jeanip's approval, he would not hesitate to kill Terrance.

"I'm waiting, Terrance," Jeanip said, as he handed the weapon back to Earon. He wanted both of his hands free in case Terrance's answer mandated his life be extinguished.

"Yes, Sir," Terrance said with as much bravery as possible. "It's my father's. I found it in his room."

"Your father's?" Jeanip repeated.

"Yes, Sir. Sir, I lied to you. My father never returned from his field study. I haven't seen him since I arrived here. When he failed to return to his room the inn manager asked me to gather his belongings. While packing up his things I began to discover some really odd things – and the weapon."

"Odd things? What kind of odd things?" Earon asked, his curiosity peaked.

Terrance turned to face Earon. "Things related to Minnos. There were photos of Europa, and her mother, and of you, Jeanip," Terrance said, turning his gaze back to Jeanip. "He had hand-drawn maps of Minnos and of security devices. There was a copy of the original land deed and copies of old paintings of a woman who looked like Mrs. Waters."

Jeanip raised his hunting knife and said, "Before I make my decision, Terrance, can you give me a reason why your father would have these things? What was his interest in Minnos?"

"I've been asking myself that same question for days. The only reasonable explanation I can come up with is he thought he had found this lost royal race from Egypt he has been searching for for years. He's practically become obsessed with the idea. He believes they were a race of shape shifters that migrated here to the United States centuries ago."

"Well, he got the shape shifting part right," Earon stated, trying to lighten the mood, which was way too serious.

Not taking his eyes off of Jeanip and the knife he held, Terrance added. "He never talked about his search for them. It was always very secretive, but I had my ways over the years of finding out what he was looking for. In my backpack is a journal he kept. I can't make out a lot of the writing – it's in some weird language. I brought it to the cottage today hoping perhaps Europa could read some of it."

"Europa?" asked Earon. "Why Europa?"

"She was able to decipher some of her mother's weird writing in her diary after she touched that Orb in the attic. I was hoping maybe she could decipher some of my father's writings too," Terrance answered, still staying focused on Jeanip.

"The Orb?" Jeanip asked, turning his attention to Europa. "So you were in the attic above your mother's room. And you found your mother's diary? And Terrance has just told me you touched the Orb." Terrance quickly looked at Europa, realizing he had just told Jeanip her secret. But he could see she was too scared to be mad at him, too scared of what Jeanip might do. "And if you were able to read some of your mother's Waters' writings you must have received energy and power from it when you touched it. Am I correct, Europa?"

"Yes, you are correct," Europa answered, not sure if Jeanip was upset with her or not. "I could only read Mother's strange writing after I touched the Orb."

"We will discuss the attic, the Orb and your mother's diary at a later date. For now please tell me, were you able to decipher any of his father's writings?" Jeanip asked.

"No, Jeanip, we never got a chance to look at the journal," Europa answered.

Earon had absent mindedly been rubbing his thumb across the handle of the blaster. He suddenly became conscious that the surface had become rough. As he looked down at the handle he saw the emergence of some type of symbol. Licking his thumb, he rubbed off more of the symbol's covering. "Jeanip, there is some type of symbol or lettering on the handle of this blaster," Earon reported to Jeanip.

Returning his focus back to Terrance, Jeanip asked, "What does it look like?"

"It is a round circle outlined in white with a large red letter 'J' inside the circle with two parallel lines crossing the J," Earon responded.

Without anyone noticing, Jeanip tightened his grip harder on his hunting knife as he asked, "Earon, underneath the circle, is there a large red oval?"

"I do not see one, but it might me hidden like the symbol was. Let me see if I can wipe some more of the dirt off." Earon begin to rub the handle underneath the discovered symbol.

"No, I do not see anything," Europa heard Earon say. She breathed a sigh of relief. Whatever Jeanip was looking for was not there. But then she heard, "What, there is something here," Earon said, as a red oval began to appear. He looked up into Jeanip's face. "It is a large red oval."

Jeanip leaped to his feet before anyone could react, knocking Europa and Earon over. He grabbed Terrance and threw him to the floor, pinning him under the neck with his one arm as he brought down the other arm holding his knife to cut out Terrance's heart. "You filthy Terrian scum!" Jeanip yelled. As he pushed the knife into Terrance's chest he realized only the tip had penetrated the skin and he could not push it in any further. Looking to see the cause of his arm's failure, he saw Earon holding back his arm with all his strength. Europa had regained her feet and was also pulling on Jeanip's arm, shouting to Jeanip to stop.

"Europa, give Jeanip an order to stop!"

"What do you think I am doing?"

"No, tell him it is a direct order. Do it now before he kills Terrance!"

"Jeanip, as your sovereign, I order you to release Terrance immediately." Jeanip turned to look at Europa. She had never seen such hate on his face before. "Comply. NOW!"

Jeanip removed his arm from under Terrance's neck and withdrew his knife. "Europa, he's Terrian. He said he got that weapon from his father's room. That symbol on the handle has only one meaning – that is the personal weapon of JeffRa that he made specifically to kill any children Enok and Medaron would have. He's JeffRa's son. He even had the power stone to power the damn thing."

Terrance scooted away backwards as best he could, coughing, trying to regain his breath after Jeanip's death hold. Blood trickled from the puncture wound the knife's blade had made in his chest. He looked at Europa and could see fear and hatred swell in her eyes as she stared at him. "JeffRa's son?"

Terrance coughed, desperately trying to regain his voice so he could explain. Finally he was able to mutter, "He's my stepfather."

"What?" Earon asked, having barely heard Terrance.

"He's my stepfather, not my real father. He married my mother when I was four. I'm not his biological son." He looked at Jeanip, coughing and trying to get his breath. "I had no idea who, or what, my father was until just now. Had I known I would have told you, for you see I am in love with Europa, Sir. I would never allow anything to happen to her. And if my stepfather is this JeffRa person you speak of, then he just became my enemy too. As for the stone, Mr. Dark Feather gave it to me two days ago. He said I would need it on my journey."

Jeanip pushed Europa's and Earon's hands off his body. He walked over to Terrance and yanked him up from the floor. Terrance closed his eyes, prepared for the worst. Earon quickly grabbed Europa as she went to Terrance's aid, afraid if there was a struggle Europa could be hurt. To their amazement, and relief, Jeanip leaned forward and kissed Terrance on the cheek.

CUTTING OUT OF THE HEART

"Take your shirt off so I can dress that wound," Europa instructed Terrance. She knew Terrance was still really shaken by the incident with Jeanip, but he was putting up a good front of confidence and assurance. She admired him for his bravery to stand up to Jeanip. Few people had done that. No, come to think of it, she couldn't remember anyone who had every faced Jeanip and admitted to him they had lied. And combined with the fact the lie concerned her safety, she knew Terrance was very lucky to be alive.

"I thought for a minute there Jeanip was really going to cut my heart out and feed it to the sharks," Terrance said, as he pulled his shirt over his head, revealing a small wound over his heart where Jeanip's knife's tip had penetrated the skin.

"I thought he was too," Europa added. "If Earon had not thought quickly enough to tell me to give Jeanip a direct order I am afraid he would have."

Looking up at Europa, Terrance added, "When Jeanip announced who my father really was, I thought you were going to LET him kill me."

"For a second, I was," Europa answered, keeping her focus on Terrance's wound so she could not see the expression on his face. "But only for a second. I remembered our times together and how much you have supported me these past few days. I knew you were not capable of such horrors, even if you were JeffRa's son. You could not be a cold-hearted assassin like he is. Plus, I remembered how very much I loved you."

"You love me?" Terrance asked, not sure his ears heard the words he had been longing to here.

"Yes," she softly replied, keeping her eyes on his chest as she poured peroxide on the wound and placed a large bandage over it. "Luckily the blade's tip did not go in very far. It is mostly a superficial cut and should heal quickly."

After a few seconds of silence, Europa finally looked up in to Terrance's eyes and saw the warm smile on his face, the twinkle in his eyes. Placing his hand underneath her chin, Terrance looked directly into her eyes and asked, "So you really love me?"

"After all we have been through, after all the weird stuff we have seen in the past few hours, you doubt something as simple as I love you?" Europa inquired, giving him a huge smile. "Yes, Terrance, I love you."

"As I do you," Terrance said, as he kissed her with all the love he felt. Europa kissed him back, allowing the deep love she felt materialize in her kiss. When the kiss was over Europa curled into his arms, being careful not to put pressure on his wound. Suddenly, both remembered where they were and turned their gaze to see if Jeanip or Earon had seen the kiss. They realized both had witnessed it since each had his eyes averted and a huge grin on their faces. Slightly embarrassed, Europa quickly said the first thing that popped into her mind, "So, your father might be JeffRa! That complicates things a little."

"Just a little bit," Terrance replied, laughing.

"What was he like? Your father, I mean."

"You mean my stepfather? I never knew my real father. He died in the war shortly after I was born."

"Yes, your stepfather. What was he like?" Europa asked. "Did he seem to be someone who could be this JeffRa?"

"A cold man, got close to no one, pretty much stayed to himself. He was never mean to my mother or me, but I remember at a young age wondering why he never showed much affection toward us. As I mentioned before, he used to disappear on his field studies a lot. I do remember once, though, I was on a baseball team. I hit a home run and was coming into home plate when this big kid on the other team tripped me and caused me to be out. I confronted the kid and got kicked out of the game. As we were leaving, the kid's father made some derogatory remark about me. My father walked over to him, lifted him off his feet and slammed him into the wall. He never said a word to the man, but I'd never seen someone so scared as that man was, So I guess you could say he was protective of us."

"If he was so unloving, why did your mother marry him, if you do not mind me asking?"

"Not at all. I don't know if she ever really truly loved him. She was fond of him. Plus she was a single mom trying to raise a son on her own and hold down a low-paying job. I think she married him for financial security and so we could remain in this country."

"It does not sound as if he was capable of the atrocities this JeffRa has done," Europa stated. "Perhaps your stepfather is not JeffRa. Perhaps he found the weapon and was really conducting research on this lost royal family."

"I hope that's true," Terrance said. "It's hard for me to believe he could be this JeffRa person. As I said, he was not a loving man but he never struck me as a cold hearted killer, certainly not the annihilator of an entire race. He is persistent when he is investigating something, but I don't believe he could carry a grudge for thousands of years. Let's hope you are right and he found that weapon. And that my stepfather is really Jeffrey Landers and not some psycho."

Concentrating on talking to Terrance, Europa did not see Runbee come aboard. She was startled when she heard his voice as he spoke with Jeanip. "Jeanip, it's been two hours since you entered the fog. We've searched along the shoreline and fifty miles out to sea. We've seen nothing to indicate anyone is following you or even looking for you at the moment. You are my commander; I follow your orders. Hoping I do not offend you, I suggest we start toward the Hunting Lodge. You are in need of medical attention and your charges need rest and food. There are a few hours of light left and it will be easier to follow the jumpers now than when it is totally dark." Runbee waited to see if his recommendation would be met with retribution or acceptance.

"A sound recommendation," Jeanip said. "Tell the jumpers to begin their departure." Runbee left to inform the dolphins to start the journey to the Hunting Lodge. Jeanip looked at Earon, saying, "Earon, can you follow the jumpers in this fog? Or do you want Runbee to navigate the ship? You'll need to keep it at a low speed so our movement is not detected."

"I can navigate for now," Earon answered. "Maybe Runbee can take over when we lose the light. It is going to get a bit tricky trying to navigate in the dark without lights AND through the fog."

"That it is," Jeanip agreed.

"Jeanip, why not get some rest while we travel to the Hunting Lodge?" Europa suggested, seeing how drained Jeanip was. She could see that, beside sheer exhaustion, his leg was causing him considerable pain. "We will wake you if anything happens."

"No, I am fine. I can rest once I get you two to safety," Jeanip stated, afraid if he closed his eyes even for a minute he would never open them again. He could feel his strength escaping through the undisclosed wound in his side and, with that knowledge, the realization his time on this planet was drawing to a close.

"Would you like something for pain?"

"No, I cannot chance taking anything that could cloud my decision making. But if I may impose upon you, I could use two of those syringes marked AC-13 in the medical bag. It will be a dark purple and gold liquid."

"I'll get it," Terrance said, quickly retrieving the syringes from the medical bag and bringing it to Jeanip

"Thank you, Terrance," Jeanip said. Removing the cap from the two needles, he pushed the liquid to the top of each and injected the serum into his leg. He prayed his miracle water would keep him alive long enough to get his monarchs to the Hunting Lodge where protection awaited them, but he also knew it would not keep him alive long enough to reach Saint's Isle. He accepted the fact the wound in his side was a killer and this would be his last voyage with his monarchs. Delaying their arrival at the Hunting Lodge had sealed his fate, but he was the only one still alive to carry out his team's mission to protect Europa and Earon. He would not fail them by diverting from the plan in order to save his own life. The situation demanded they travel quietly and slowly in order not to attract any type of attention, and that is exactly what they were going to do. His monarchs' survival was what was important and the only priority, not his survival. He sat on the bench observing his three charges, afraid to move too much for fear one of them might notice his second wound. If they discovered he had taken a shot to the side they would insist on going faster and jeopardize their own lives. Better to keep it a secret so they would think clearly and concentrate on the matter at hand. His vision was beginning to become blurry and he could feel his life force draining away. He only had to hold on for a little while longer; they were almost there. To keep his mind alert and active, he decided to question Terrance about his real father.

"Terrance, you said JeffRa was your stepfather. Do you know who your biological father was?" Jeanip asked.

"I never knew him, Sir. He was killed in the Middle East shortly after I was born."

"Your father was a soldier?"

"Yes, Sir. He was a commander in the army, in the unit known as the Big Red One."

"I have heard of that unit. History speaks of them as a very important part of the U.S. Army during scrimmages in the Middle East and many others in that country's past, especially the Viet Nam war. You should be very proud your father commanded such a fine unit of soldiers."

"I am, Sir. I always have been."

"I can see the soldier in you. Very few have had the courage and audacity to stand before me and tell me they lied to my face," Jeanip said, then thought for a moment. "No, that is incorrect. Only two have had the courage; one was Sunam and the other I killed for his lie." Jeanip searched Terrance's face once more for some type of falter, some sign of weakness. There was none. "You have the heart of a warrior, young Terrance, the resolution of a great man. I am glad Europa has chosen you and very much approve of this relationship. Having said that, know this: If you ever lie to me again about anything, I will not hesitate to end your life. Do you understand? I will not tolerate falsehoods when they jeopardize my monarchs' safety. Nothing is more important to me than they are."

"Nor to me," Terrance answered, looking at Europa. He saw a slight blush rise in her cheeks.

"This incident is behind us and will not be spoken of again. Terrance, I believe you said you had one of your father's journals with you. Might I be allowed to see it?"

"Yes, Sir, I'll get it right away," Terrance rumbled through his backpack happy Jeanip needed something from him. He found the journal and brought it back, handing it to him without hesitation. "This is it, Jeanip. I can't make out most of what he wrote."

Jeanip opened the cover and began to leaf through the pages. When he arrived at the section where the writings were done in English, he closed the book. "Yes, it definitely is written in Terrian. More than likely in a secret code."

261

"Are you able to read any of it?" Europa asked, hoping Jeanip could decipher it.

"Unfortunately, no. Misso was the expert on the Terrian language. She could break down just about anything. Sunam was a good decoder too, so the two of them together created a dynamic team." Jeanip saw an odd look come across Europa's face. "Do you doubt my words, Your Majesty?" Jeanip asked her.

"Not at all, Jeanip. It is just that I only knew Misso as the kitchen maid and Sunam as a farm hand. It is just hard to imagine them as this dynamic team you speak of. I lived with them my entire life and I never knew who they were. I did not even know they were husband and wife. How sad does that make me?"

"You were never supposed to know they were anything other than what you knew them as," Jeanip replied, wanting Europa to realize her lack of knowledge was not of her doing. "That was their role, a role they played well. They were soldiers who were assigned one order - to ensure you lived a long, happy life as a human, unaware of your true Waters' identity."

"And never know who any of you really were? Not even to know my own brother?" she stated coldly, turning to look at Earon who still sat in the Captain's chair steering the vessel toward safety.

"You cannot know what is hidden from you, Europa," Jeanip replied.

Knowing Jeanip spoke the truth she saw no point in pursuing this line of thought. "Would you like me to see if I can decipher any of the writing in the journal?" she asked.

"If you feel up to it," Jeanip responded.

Europa held out her hand and saw Jeanip was having trouble handing her the journal. Concerned, she reached for it and began to slowly turn the pages while keeping an eye on Jeanip's face. Was he hiding something from her? Were his wounds more serious than she knew? She dismissed his trouble of handing her the journal to being overly exhausted and concentrated on deciphering the journal. After reading the first fifteen pages and having no luck, she handed Terrance back the journal. "No, I am sorry, Jeanip, but I cannot make out any of the words."

A little disappointed, Jeanip said, "Terrian is a very hard language to read. And add the fact that it is written in a secret code and it is just about impossible. Perhaps Mr. Dark Feather will have someone at the Hunting Lodge who has some experience in deciphering Terrian."

As the sun began to dip below the horizon and the darkness descended upon the vessel, Runbee returned to the wheel house to take over the ship's navigation. Soon it would be impossible to see an inch in front of oneself due to the thick fog and the darkness of night. Runbee's talents were needed to safely bring the monarchs to safety. To minimize the possibility of injury in such total blackness, Jeanip suggested Europa, Terrance and Earon wait below in the galley. As they entered, Earon gestured toward the small table with a bench on each side. Terrance slid in on one side along with Europa sliding in next to him, snuggling her back against his chest. Terrance wrapped his arms around her and kissed her on the back of her head.

"Oh, Earon, why is this happening?" Europa asked, as Earon sat down across from her. "Why is this JeffRa so intent on my destruction? He has killed everyone: Misso, Sunam, Birea, Tinderoon, Evonic, Ebar, Mintoo and Mother. All we have left is Jeanip, and no matter what he says, I think we may lose him too. Earon, I cannot shake this feeling he is hurt worse than he said he is. He was not even able to hand me that journal earlier. I fear something is wrong."

"I know, Sis. I feel Tinderoon, Misso and Sunam's loss deeply also. I cannot remember a time when they were not part of our family. The others joined us when we came up to the surface to live at Minnos, so I did not know them as well. As for an explanation of why this is happening, why this JeffRa hunts us, it is not my place to explain it to you. Plus, I am not even sure I could explain it all; I do not know how much of what I have been told is the complete story, what might be fabricated and what is pure omission. But Jeanip promised to reveal all once we arrive at the Hunting Lodge. Regarding his injuries, I think you are right. He is hurt worse than he is letting us know. But he is a strong old soldier – he will stay alive just out of principle. He would consider it undignified if he died before he got us to safety." More out of nervousness than comedy, the three of them chuckled lightly, knowing that was exactly what Jeanip would think. "He gave himself several shots of that special serum he has. I remember hearing about it when I lived at the Complex. They called it a miracle drug. He just has to hold on until we reach the Hunting Lodge, until we get him to Mr. Dark Feather."

"When you lived in the Complex? What Complex? The Complex I found a map of in Mother's attic?" Europa asked, instantaneously invigorated by a new piece of the puzzle.

"Is the Complex on another planet? Were you born in outer space?" Terrance asked simultaneously with Europa, enthralled Earon might be willing to talk about his life as a shape shifter.

"I do not know what map you are talking about, Europa, so I cannot say if it is a representation of the Complex. No, it is not on another planet but right here on earth, not far from this location at the bottom of the ocean. And I was born on Earth, just like you two were." Earon smiled, as he imagined the disappointed looks on Terrance and Europa's faces when he said he was born on Earth. "And that is all I have to say on that subject."

"That is not fair," Europa stated, as the three felt the boat tip slightly to the left as it made its turn into the channel that lead to the Hunting Lodge. "You know everything, Earon, and I do not know anything."

"You know some things," Earon replied. "In fact, you know more now than you were ever supposed to know, Sis. And Jeanip will tell you about our parents' past when we arrive at the Hunter's Lodge and the truth about our people."

"If he makes it," Europa stated. Beginning to understand the true severity of their situation, she asked, "Earon, what if he does not? What if Jeanip dies on us? Then what do we do? Who will help us reach Saint's Isle? Who will tell me about our past and my true family history?"

"If the worst happens and we lose Jeanip, Sis, our protection and the truth of who we are will fall to Mr. Dark Feather. From what I have observed over the decades, Mr. Dark Feather knows as much about our past as Jeanip and Mother. And as a Commanding Leader, he will not hesitate to step into the position of our chief protector if need be. He is bound by the same vows as Jeanip and will fulfill his duty."

All three travelers sat quiet for a moment pondering Earon's words about the future. After several minutes Terrance broke the silence. "Earon, how does Runbee know in which direction to steer the ship if he can't see where he's going?"

"Dolphins do not need to see at night. They are able to navigate very well by using their sonar. The dolphins have positioned themselves on all sides of the boat – stern, bow, starboard and port. If a course change is needed, the dolphins on the side of the vessel needing the adjustment will let Runbee know by whistling and clicking. These Waters have lived as dolphins for so long they are able to communicate with each other no matter what form they take."

"That's amazing," Terrance said.

"Yeah, I guess it is," Earon said. "For me it is just a part of normal life. It would be like a caterpillar transforming into a butterfly, or a tadpole becoming a frog. Those are amazing things if it is the first time you saw them transform. But if you saw it all the time, you would accept their transformation as a normal part of life."

"Have you ever transformed into a dolphin?" Terrance asked, curious as to what Earon was capable of.

"I used to quite regularly before Europa was born," Earon replied. "I use to go out on patrols with Graybin and Runbee while we waited for her arrival. Before that I did it just for fun. And yes, in case you were wondering, I have also been a whale numerous times. Talk about some powerful muscles!"

"Can I transform into something?" Europa asked, a tone of hopefulness in her voice. She thought how wonderful it would be to transform into another animal and travel the oceans and explore its depths. She closed her eyes hoping Earon's answer would either be 'yes', or at least 'possibly'.

"No, Sis, I am afraid you were born as a human. In order to transform you would have had to be born as an Oonock," Earon answered truthfully, regretting he was the one to deliver even more bad news to his sister. As he looked in Europa's direction he realized he was able to see a few disappointed features on her face. Then more and more of her features became visible. Realizing the cabin was becoming lighter, he turned toward the bow and saw the fog was dissipating and there were lights ahead. "Hey, I can see lights. I think we have finally made it to the Hunting Lodge."

Hearing voices downstairs, Jeanip yelled, "Europa and Terrance, you two stay seated until we have docked and I tell you it is okay to move. Earon, I need you on top. Bring that rifle under the seat."

"Why does he want you to bring the rifle? Does he think this place has been compromised?" Terrance asked, beginning to worry.

"No, I am sure it is just normal security protocol. There is a huge set of rules and regulations regarding security, especially when it comes to Europa and me," Earon answered.

"Jeanip's rules and regulations," Europa said, quiet enough that Jeanip would not be able to hear her.

"Actually they are not Jeanip's, Sis. He just enforces them – to the letter. I have never seen him deviate from them; not even once," Earon replied.

"Then whose rules and regulations are they?" Europa asked

"Our father and mother's. It is their law, their rules, their regulations. Many were devised when the war with the Terrians broke out in their homeland, but more restricted ones were added the day Mother found out she was pregnant with the next ruler of our people. Jeanip is bound by the Security Protocol Laws until the day he dies. All Oonocks are who live under Father's rule. And they will follow them to their death, especially in matters concerning you, Sis." Earon clarified. "I need to go top side. I will see you two when we dock."

"Especially in matters concerning me," Europa repeated after Earon left, snuggling deeper into Terrance's embrace. "How many more beings are going to have to die for my protection? I have already lost almost everyone I have known. People I took for granted and, now that they are gone, I am learning they were so much more than I ever knew." Tears began to fill her eyes again as she thought back on Misso, Sunam, Ebar, Tinderoon, Evonic, Mintoo, Birea and her mother. "If my safety as a monarch means more people are going to die, then I do not want it. Maybe if I just resign as the royal leader JeffRa will leave everyone alone."

Terrance hugged her tighter, realizing the weight of responsibility on her shoulders. "Europa, I don't think it works that way. You are the royal leader by birth, by blood. You just can't stop being who you are because it becomes difficult. And to do so would also make everyone's deaths meaningless." Terrance hoped his words would help Europa somehow accept what was happening. He had no doubt more would die before this journey was over. He just hoped it wouldn't be anyone else Europa loved. "I've only known you for a short time, Europa, but during that time I've seen in you the qualities of leadership, pride, compassion and real heroism. You may not feel it now, but you possess all the qualities of a true monarch, a real royal."

"Do you really believe that, Terrance?" Europa asked, turning around to face him. "Because I certainly do not."

"With all my heart," he answered, as he bent down and gave her a deep kiss.

ARRIVING AT CHANCEE'S DOCK

Terrance and Europa watched out the window as the lights ahead grew brighter. Before long they could make out the inside of a large cave with a modest dock, but both were surprised at how few people were waiting for them. They had assumed, after what they just went through, the dock would be swarming with security personnel holding assault rifles and bazookas. They could see six, maybe seven men. And only one of them had a weapon.

Runbee steered the vessel along the side of the dock. He stepped down into the galley to wish his monarch farewell. "You have arrived safely, Your Majesty," he announced, placing his hand to his forehead and giving a slight bow. "If you have no further use of me, I will take my leave of you and leave you in the capable hands of the commander of this facility."

"Thank you, Runbee, for all your help and the help of your team," Europa said. "Please thank them for me. I owe you and them much, as does my brother,"

"Part of our duty, Your Majesty." Turning toward Terrance, Runbee added, "It was nice to meet you, Terrance. I hope we have the pleasure of meeting again." With that said, Runbee stepped up into the wheel house and said goodbye to Earon, then walked over to Jeanip. After saying a few words to him, he jumped overboard and returned to the ocean. Europa and Terrance watched as he surfaced, transformed back into a dolphin. The other dolphins joined him and together they swam back down the channel to patrol its entrance from the sea.

Europa poked her head through the doorway. "Okay for us to come out now?" she asked Jeanip. Jeanip said nothing, only gave a nod of his head. As she stepped onto the deck Europa noticed Jeanip still sitting on the bench where he had been before they had lost the light. His skin color was pale, he was covered in sweat and it appeared he was having some trouble breathing. Realizing Jeanip had not risen when she entered the wheel house, she knew he was in serious trouble.

"Your Majesties, I am thankful you arrived here safely," came a voice from a man stepping down onto the deck from the dock. Although the cave was well lit, Europa could not see the man's face because he wore a hooded cloak that hid his face from view. "And, Mr. Landers, I see you continue on your quest for knowledge," the man said, seeming to know Terrance.

Terrance took a step closer to the man. Now able to see the face under the hood, he immediately recognized the man. "Mr. Dark Feather, how nice to see you again."

"Mr. Dark Feather," Europa said, "I did not recognize you at first. I do not know if you know my brother," she said.

"Earon, it is so nice to see you without your covering. It has been many years since I got to see the man who protects our treasure."

"Hi, Mr. Dark Feather. It is a pleasure to see you again also," Earon stated.

Europa was not surprised Mr. Dark Feather knew Earon, or that he knew Earon was a shape shifter and had spent the past twenty years in the form of her guardian canine. She now wondered in what other form she knew Mr. Dark Feather as.

"Jeanip, I see the journey has not been kind to you," Mr. Dark Feather said, as he walked over to Jeanip.

"I have had more agreeable journeys," Jeanip softly spoke, trying to force a smile on to his face but not having the strength to accomplish it.

"Let the unkindness of your journey end here. You need rest before you begin a new journey," Dark Feather said, knowing before he even spoke the words Jeanip would object and insist they must continue on their way.

"There is no time for rest, Chancee," Jeanip said, addressing Mr. Dark Feather by his Waters' name. "JeffRa is out there hunting for her. I must get her to safety as I promised Medaron."

"And so you shall, My Old Friend," Mr. Dark Feather said, as he injected Jeanip with a syringe of sedatives.

Realizing he had been tricked into a false sense of security, Jeanip tried to jump to his feet. "Chancee, not you," he shouted, as he stared at the betrayer standing before him. But due to his physical condition, the adrenaline pumping through his system was not enough to keep him standing. As his eyes closed, Jeanip summoned every ounce of energy he could find and yelled one final command to Europa and Earon, "RUN!" Darkness engulfed him as his legs buckled beneath him and he slumped forward, sedatives pulsing through his body. Chancee caught the motionless Jeanip in his arms, motioning to the males on the dock, who immediately came aboard with a stretcher for Jeanip.

Fearing they had been betrayed, Europa screamed out as Jeanip crumbled into Chancee's arms. "NO!" Earon grabbed her arm and pulled her back, positioning her behind Terrance and himself. He raised the rifle he still had in his hands and aimed it toward the oncoming males.

"I'm sorry, Your Highnesses, I did not mean to alarm you," Mr. Dark Feather said, as he firmly held on to the unconscious Jeanip. "I had to surprise Jeanip with the sedatives. He would not have allowed us to treat him until he had you hidden safely away. He is so dedicated to you two he will not consider slowing down. Unfortunately, this time that dedication would have cost him his life. You can lower your weapon, young Earon. You are safe. You all are safe. This I swear is true, and bind the truth with my life and water."

Earon looked at Mr. Dark Feather. The binding of the truth with his life was the most sacred, the highest assurance a Waters could give. To break the truth would mean he would not only forfeit his life, but he would not be allowed to flow out in water. His essence would be condemned to a nonexistence in dirt. Earon lowered his rifle but remained standing in front of Europa.

As the two males with the stretcher came closer, Europa noticed a tall, dark skinned man with long hair tied at his neck in a ponytail accompanying them. He waited until the males lifted Jeanip from Mr. Dark Feather's arms on to the stretcher, and then began to scan Jeanip's body with mechanical devices. He then removed a syringe from his pocket and injected Jeanip with it, followed by instructing the males to take Jeanip to the medical room.

"Forgive me, Your Highnesses, for not introducing myself upon arriving in your presence, but I needed to get Jeanip stabilized," the male said, addressing both Europa and Earon. "My name is Leenow," he said, as he raised his hand to his forehead and gave a small bow. "I am a medical helper. And I too apologize if our tactics gave you worry. We knew the only way Jeanip would allow us to treat him would be if he didn't know about it."

"How is he?" Europa asked, pushing her way past Earon. "He does not look well. Is he going to be okay?"

"I wish I could say he was going to be fine, but the truth is I do not know. The shot he took in the side seems to have done a lot of damage and is extremely serious. I will have a better idea of a prognosis in a few hours, after I've had time to remove the bullets and repair his wounds," Leenow replied. "Now I must take leave of you and tend to my patient while I'm able to. Once he wakes up he probably won't let me within ten feet of him." Leenow hurried off after Jeanip.

"There must be some mistake," Europa said, as she stared at Mr. Dark Feather, confused at Leenow's statement. "Jeanip took a hit to his leg. There is one, possibly two bullets in the leg, but it did not hit his artery. The bleeding was contained."

"That is true, Europa," Mr. Dark Feather confirmed. "But what you did not know is he had also taken injury to his side. He kept that truth from you. And, as Leenow has stated, that wound is very serious, serious enough to end his life. Fortunately for us Runbee saw the wound and had Graybin swim ahead and advise us of his condition."

"Why did he not tell us? He could have died," Europa said, trying to contain the terror growing inside her that she might lose another person whom she loved, another member of her family.

"Because he thought he was," Earon said, shaking his head slowly from side to side, angry with himself that he did not realize the seriousness of Jeanip's condition.

"What do you mean, Earon?" Europa asked, as she looked into her brother's eyes.

"Europa, do you not see? Jeanip never thought he would make it here, at least not alive. After all the Waters we lost today, he did not want us to worry about losing him too. Crazy as it sounds, he would have believed us knowing would somehow jeopardize our safety. Plus, he would not want to be disgraced in front of you?"

"Disgraced in front of me?" Europa asked, still trying to comprehend Jeanip's thinking. "Why in the world would he be disgraced?"

"Because he is a soldier," Earon replied. "If for any reason, including death, prevents him from completing the mission Enok and Medaron gave him – namely our safe arrival at you know where – he failed the pledge he made to the royal family. Failure to him is a disgrace."

"You understand him well, Earon," Mr. Dark Feather softly said, admiring the young monarch standing before him. He was definitely his father's son, possessing the same intuition as Enok. "Failure is not a word in Jeanip's vocabulary. And your safekeeping is ingrained in every part of his being, in every corner of his soul, in every thought and action he thinks and does. He would forego any thoughts not related to your safe journey."

"But if our safety is such a high priority to him, did he not realize we could not go on without him?" Europa asked while still trying to understand. Wiping away a tear she softly added, "Does he not know I need him?"

"No, Sis, all Jeanip knew was he had to get us here," Earon answered. "He did not fail us; it was us who failed him, especially me. As his monarchs it was our responsibility to make sure he was okay, that he was able to fulfill his promise to keep us safe. We became so wrapped up in ourselves, what happened to us, who we lost today that we did not see the pain he was in or recognize that his very life was dwindling away. It was OUR duty to keep HIM safe!"

Mr. Dark Feather looked at Earon, astonished at the wisdom this young monarch processed. "Not only do you understand Jeanip, young Earon, but you truly understand what it is to be a monarch. Yes, the role of a monarch is to ensure his or her people are safe and are able to fulfill the vows they have made. But no one expects that of you two – not yet. Europa has been a true monarch for less than a day and you have not been given the ability to reign over your people yet because your father is still alive." Seeing the seriousness on the faces of Earon and Europa and the weariness on Terrance's, Mr. Dark Feather changed the subject. "For now, let us put such talk aside to be discussed later. Come, I know you are tired and hungry. Jeanip is alive and in the best hands possible. We have a dinner waiting for you, and warm, soft beds for you to rest in." He extended his arm, palm up indicating they move onto the dock and into the cave.

"By any chance, Mr. Dark Feather, might there be coffee?" Europa asked, as she stepped onto the dock. The thought of food and a warm bed sounded like heaven.

"As much as you would like, My Child," Mr. Dark Feather answered with a smile, thinking how much Europa was like her mother. "As much as you would like."

Europa lifted the steaming brew to her lips, slowly sipping it into her mouth, savoring the beloved taste of fresh brewed coffee. As before, her thoughts returned to Misso and she wondered if the day would ever come when she could drink a cup of coffee without thinking of her. She took another sip, then sat the cup down softly on the table, allowing her head to hang down. All the simple, wonderful things Misso had done for her without receiving many thanks. Misso was now gone, as was the kitchen she had made that coffee in. Now she was in danger of losing the only father figure she had ever known – Jeanip. She could survive all that had happened, all she had lost; but she didn't believe she could survive loosing Jeanip and her mother both. She could survive the loss of one, but not both.

"Unless you would like something more to eat, I'll show you to where you can lay down for a while," Mr. Dark Feather said, bringing Europa back to the present.

"Mr. Dark Feather, I would like to see Jeanip before I retire," Europa announced, as she turned to address him. "Would you please take me to his room."

"I'm not sure Leenow would want him disturbed," Mr. Dark Feather answered. "I'll make sure you're taken there first thing tomorrow morning, Your Majesty."

"This is not a request, Mr. Dark Feather," Europa said, putting down her cup of coffee and rising to her feet, taking one step toward her caregiver. "It is a statement, an order. I want to see Jeanip. You are to take me to him now."

"Yes, Your Majesty. This way," Mr. Dark Feather said, gesturing down the corridor to the left. He was delighted to hear Europa using such a commanding voice. She was becoming the leader she was born to me, she needed to be. That leader, along with her quanish and brother, would get her safely to Saint's Isle.

As Europa walked with Mr. Dark Feather, Earon and Terrance quickly rose and followed the two. Europa turned toward them, saying, "You two can go ahead to the sleeping area. I will be okay going by myself."

Earon shook his head negatively. "Europa, I have been your guardian since you were born. I was given this assignment by our father. Unless I am mistaken, he has not been here to tell me my assignment is over. Therefore, I am coming with you. If you would prefer I can accompany you as Triton."

Europa gave him a smile. "The form of Earon is perfectly okay." She reached out and grabbed his hand.

"Well, if he gets to go, I'm going too," Terrance said. "I'm an honorary protector."

"That you are," Europa said, as she slipped her arm inside Terrance's. Together, the three followed behind Mr. Dark Feather as he led them to the medical room.

A few feet down the hallway Mr. Dark Feather turned right and walked down several steps. He continued down this hallway for thirty feet until he stood before a double set of doors with the word "MEDICAL" above the door frame. As they entered they saw a large, semi-lit room that reminded them of an Emergency Room. White drapes hung from the ceiling dividing the room into twelve different sections. In each section was a medical bed, a basin, two chairs, an IV pole, numerous medical machines and a tray of supplies. All of the beds were empty except for the one straight ahead. Europa could see Jeanip laying in the bed and still being attended to by Leenow. In silence and alone, she walked straight across the floor to Jeanip's bed. As Terrance stepped to follow, Earon grabbed him by the arm.

"Give her some time with him by herself," Earon said. "We can wait over here." The two men stepped to the side where they waited while still keeping an eye on Europa.

"How is he doing?" Europa asked Leenow as she neared Jeanip.

Leenow looked up from the pad he was writing on. "He's about the same. So far he hasn't been responding to any of our treatment. We're pumping him full of fluids, vitamins and other elements his body needs, but his organs may be past the capability of utilizing them."

"Is he going to die?" Europa asked, her voice emotionless, the thought of Jeanip's death something she could not fathom at the moment.

"I honestly don't know, Your Majesty. We're doing all we can. If he had gotten here just a few hours sooner he'd have a better chance. If he can make it through the night without any organs failing, then I'd say he has a fighting chance."

Europa looked at the IV tube in Jeanip's arm. With her eyes she followed the tubing back to the bottle of lilac liquid that flowed through the IV tube. "Leenow, is that the same lilac water Jeanip give Misso?"

"Yes, Your Majesty, it is the water from our home world," Leenow replied. "In our transformed shapes we Oonocks take on the healing process of the animal we have transformed into. But in our true state, our healing process is accelerated. A two-week healing would be completed in several hours in our true state. When an Oonock cannot return to the deep ocean to heal, we have found putting some of our water in our blood stream will also accelerate the healing process."

"So, if Jeanip was to return to the deep and transform into his true self, he'd be okay?" Europa asked.

"More than likely. There could be some side effects from his wounds, but for the most part he'd be completely healed."

"Then why doesn't he return to the deep?"

"Probably for the same reason he didn't head for here when he could. Until you reach your security destination, everything else is of no importance, including his own life," Leenow answered.

"Then, as your leader, I command you to take him down to the Complex," Europa ordered. She saw Leenow was not moving, was not carrying out her orders. "Leenow, why are you still standing there? Carry out my orders immediately. HE MUST NOT DIE!"

"Forgive me, Your Highness, but it is too late to transport him below," Leenow replied. "If you so order it again, I will prepare him to return to the Complex. but in his present condition I can assure you he will not survive the journey." Leenow waited, letting Europa comprehend his words. "Do you wish me to transport him?"

"No," whispered Europa.

"I'll give you some time alone with him." Leenow pulled one of the chairs closer to the bed for Europa to sit in. He pulled the white curtain shut as he left the room giving her privacy.

Europa gently lifted Jeanip's hand and held it lightly in her own. She looked down upon his face, seeing the fine lines of crow's feet around his eyes, the dimple in his chin, the gray in his temples, the battle scars on his face. It was the same face she had been looking into all her life. It was a face of strength, of determination, of honor. A face that always showed her love and tenderness, a face that always reassured her she could do anything. A face that believed in her for who she was, especially when she didn't. But for the first time she could remember, this beautiful face also looked pale, fragile, beyond help.

"Jeanip, it is me, Europa. I do not know if you can hear me or not," Europa softly spoke. "You did it. You got us here to Mr. Dark Feather. We are safe. But you were hurt and did not tell me, and now you might leave me. And Jeanip, I cannot go on if you are not there to take me the rest of the way." Tears began to fill her eyes until it was hard to see his face, then they rolled down her cheeks on to his hand. "I cannot lose you, Jeanip. You are the only father figure I have ever known. I never realized it until now how much I love you, how much you mean to me. It was your face I saw above my crib when I would wake up at night and was afraid. You would rock me and hum to me until I would fall asleep. When I learned how to ride my bike, it was your hands that held it steady for me until I gained my balance. You taught me so many things, Jeanip. You may think you have no more to teach me, but you do. I do not know how to lead our people; I do not know how to be a monarch. I need you to help me, to show me how to be a great one like my mother. Do you hear me, Jeanip? I NEED you – now more than ever." The tears continued to drip onto his arm, soaking the sheet beneath it. "Earon needs you too. He will not tell you that, but I can sense he is afraid of losing you also. Neither of us can make it without you. Do you hear me? You have to get better."

Suddenly, an alarm began to sound on the panel above Jeanip's bed, bringing her to her feet. Another alarm followed. Jeanip's body began to shake as a wave of convulsions swept through his body. Europa heard the white curtain pushed open as Leenow rushed in, medical scanner in hand. He began to scan Jeanip's body, giving orders to two other medical personnel who had entered with him.

She felt someone's hands on her shoulder urging her away from Jeanip's bed. "The medical personnel need room to work on him, Sis. Why do we not wait over here?" she heard her brother's voice say.

"No, I am not leaving him," she said, trying to shake Earon's hands off her shoulders as she firmly planted her feet on the ground.

"Europa, you are right, you should stay here," this time is was Terrance's voice she heard from behind her. "But you do not want to get in the medical team's way and prevent them from helping Jeanip. Just take five steps backwards; that's all. Just five steps." Terrance looked at Earon and nodded, indicating for him to walk her back five steps. "Come on, I'll count them with you. One, two, three . . ."

"Four, five," she said, as she allowed Earon to lead her back five steps. There she stood, frozen in time, watching the medical team work frantically on her protector.

For what seemed like hours, Europa, along with Earon and Terrance, watched as the medical team worked to stabilize Jeanip. They injected more medications into his IV and directly into his body. Several medical instruments of unknown design were used to repair internal organ damage and strengthen his heart. Finally, Jeanip's convulsions stopped and his body laid there motionless. Europa strained her eyes to see if Jeanip's chest still rose and fell as he breathed, but she could not see past the medical assistants who were wiping the perspiration off of Jeanip's face and body. After laying a clean sheet across him, all left except Leenow. Leenow turned and walked toward the three.

"Is he still alive? Is he okay?" Europa asked, not taking her eyes off Jeanip.

Leenow met Earon's gaze and shook his head negatively. He then turned his attention to Europa. "Your Majesty, he's not responding to the treatments. There's nothing else we can do. I believe it's time to take him down to the water so he can go home."

Europa jerked her head around to stare at Leenow, her eyes wide open, filled with emotion. "What are you saying?" she yelled.

"He's been a magnificent and noble commander for thousands of years," came a voice from behind them. Europa turned to see Mr. Dark Feather standing there. "He deserves to be allowed to go home and flow back into the water."

"No, you cannot be serious," Europa shouted, wiggling herself free of her brother's grasp. She stood there, at the side of Jeanip's bed, looking at the faces of all who stood before her, her face pleading with them to tell here there was another way.

"Sis, we owe him that," Earon said, knowing not to give this wonderful commander of theirs the honorable death he deserved would be unspeakable. "He has given so much to us and our parents. It is time for us to honor his dedication by giving him the death he deserves."

Standing there, staring at her brother in disbelief, she knew he spoke the truth. "That we do," she quietly whispered, as she sank into the chair beside the bed. "Make it so."

"I'll give you a couple of minutes to say goodbye," Leenow announced. "I'm sorry I can't give you more time, but he won't hold on much longer. We have to get him into the water before he passes."

Everyone but Earon and Europa stepped out of the room, closing the white curtain once again to give the monarchs privacy. Earon leaned down and put his arms around Jeanip, laying his head on Jeanip's chest, tears flowing down his face as he said his goodbyes to his protector. Europa gently took Jeanip's hand and held it one of hers. With her other hand she reached up and enclosed her fingers over the amulet around her neck, saying a prayer. Unexpectedly, Earon heard Jeanip's heart beat begin to beat stronger.

"What did you just do?" Earon asked, as he jerked his head up, staring at his sister, a glimmer of hope in his eyes and his heart.

"I didn't do anything."

"Yes, you did. THINK!"

"I was just holding his hand."

"What else?"

"I reached up and took hold of the amulet Mother gave me in one hand and said a prayer for Jeanip," Europa responded, wondering why Earon was so excited.

"Do it again."

"What?"

"DO IT AGAIN!"

Europa reached up and again took hold of the amulet around her neck. As she and Earon watched, the amulet began to glow as a soft lilac light began to travel into her body, travel down her arm and through her fingertips into Jeanip's body.

"Look at the panel," Earon shouted.

As they both watched in amazement, the instruments on the panel above Jeanip began to move into the green area, indicating he was better. As soon as Europa let go of the amulet the dials recessed back into the red, but not as far back as before.

A look of surprise and knowledge spread over Europa's face. "I know what to do, Earon. I know how to save Jeanip," she shouted, as she jumped up from the chair. Europa ripped the curtain back and began to run as fast as she possibly could toward the exit. "Terrance, whatever you do, DO NOT let them put Jeanip in the water," she yelled behind her at a confused Terrance. "Do you understand? I know how to save Jeanip! He is not going to die on us."

"Where are you going?" Earon asked, as he ran behind her through the doors and down the hallways.

"To the boat," she yelled back. "We need that Orb Jeanip brought from Mother's attic. It's in the box Sunam brought aboard."

"The Orb?" Earon questioned, as he followed her down to the dock. "What do you need the Orb for?" Then the realization of what his sister had realized became apparent to him also. "You can use the Orb to heal him. But what if the box is not still there?"

"It is. I heard Mr. Dark Feather tell his men not to take anything off the ship."

Racing against time, the two siblings raced to the dock and leapt onto the ship. They frantically looked for the box Sunam had carried aboard containing Europa's paintings of the Dumbo Octopus, hers and Terrance's backpacks and the Orb. Unable to locate the box on deck, they ran down into the galley in case it had rolled down the stairs during their journey. Earon reached under the bench and pulled out the box, a huge grin upon his face.

"Found it," he yelled.

"Hurry, get it," Europa replied, watching anxiously as her brother reached inside the box. Earon raised his face to see his sister, his grin turned to disappointment. Europa could see the box was empty, indicating somehow the lid had come loose during their voyage and its contents scattered below.

"It is not in here," he said. "Nothing is. Everything has fallen out."

"Oh, no," Europa said, panic now seizing her. "It could be anywhere then. It could even have rolled overboard."

Just then they heard Terrance yelling for them from the dock. "What are you two doing down there? They've taken Jeanip down to the ocean. I couldn't stop them."

"We are trying to find the Orb we brought with us," yelled Earon, still frantically searching for the lost Orb. "Europa needs it in order to help Jeanip."

"The Orb? I have it here in my backpack. I put it in there before it got dark last night so we wouldn't lose it."

Looking at each other, they leaped off the vessel. Europa grabbed Terrance's backpack as she ran past him. "Which way did they go to the ocean?"

"Straight ahead, over by that flag," Terrance yelled, as he tried to keep up with her and Earon.

"There they are," Earon said, pointing toward a small band of people standing at the water's edge. "They are getting ready to walk into the water."

"Stop," yelled Europa. "As your monarch, I order you to cease what you are doing and put Jeanip down on the sand."

Mr. Dark Feather turned his attention to the three running toward them. He ordered the medical personnel to follow her orders and place Jeanip on the sand. As she reached Jeanip's still body, she dropped to her knees on the sand beside him, trying to catch her breath from all the running.

"Your Majesty, we cannot wait to take Jeanip out into the water," Mr. Dark Feather began. "If he dies over land we will lose his essence forever. It is imperative that we take him out into the water now."

Unable to speak as her human lungs sucked in air, she held out her hand to silence Mr. Dark Feather. Reaching inside Terrance's backpack Europa brought out the silent Orb. Calming her insides so she could concentrate on nothing but the Orb, Europa placed it inside her cupped hands, then laid them upon Jeanip's chest. She closed her eyes and began to hum the song of the Orb. It began to emit a low hum in unison with Europa and it began to glow a faint glow. The glow grew brighter and brighter as threads of lavender, purple, blue and yellow began to emanate from the Orb, entwining around Europa's hands and flowing down from her fingertips into Jeanip's body. In Europa's mind she heard her mother's voice speak the words she had spoken that day on the road before she died. "Ennay Benu Carif," Europa said out loud. The Orb's humming intensified, the threads of light encasing Jeanip's entire body. The amulets around Europa's and Earon's necks began to cast off a soft purple glow. The group watched in awe as color began to return to Jeanip's face, his breathing becoming regular and the blood on his bandages began to disappear. After five minutes the Orb grew dim, the humming ceased. The threads of light that had encased Jeanip and Europa's hands returned to the Orb. As Europa released her grip of the Orb, she fell backwards. Terrance rushed forward to grab her before she hit the ground.

Leenow ran over to the still Jeanip and scanned his medical detector over Jeanip's body. He looked at the readings, then rescanned his patient, unable to believe what he was reading. "This isn't possible," he said, a look of astonishment upon his face as he turned to stare at Chancee. "There's nothing wrong with him; his injuries are gone". Leenow turned to stare at Europa. "There are no bullet wounds and all damage done to his body has been reversed. He's completely healed."

"What have you done, Child?" Mr. Dark Feather asked, trying to make sense out of what just happened as he turned to stare at Europa.

Everyone stared at Europa in disbelief as she laid in Terrance's arms. All knew the miracle they had just witnessed and its impossibility; she had saved their commander, brought him back from the very brink of death. No Oonock had ever been capable of such powers for thousands of years, and then only in the legends of old. One by one, they lowered themselves on one knee, placing their hands on their forehead and bowing before their monarchs paying her their deep respect and honoring her for what she had done. Europa slowly bowed her head in response. Today she saved the life of the man who had saved her life countless times. Today she had become a true monarch, a true leader of her people as Jeanip had always believed she could be.

THE ORB HEALING

Several hours later, Jeanip woke in the medical unit surprised to be alive, yet feeling refreshed and invigorated. He opened his eyes, taking a moment to remember where he should be. Apparently, they had made it safely to the Hunting Lodge and he was being treated for his wounds. He thought he'd have to give the medical staff praise on a job well done; he felt no pain, no exhaustion. In fact, he felt years younger. Jeanip wondered what miracle drug they had given him. Whatever it was, he needed to add it to all the medical kits.

Jeanip tried to turn over to his right but was unable to get assistance from his left arm. He looked above himself and did not see an IV pole or any machines attached to him, so he could not comprehend why he was unable to move his arm. As he shifted the center of his weight to roll to his left, he was surprised to see the reason he could not move his left arm. Lying partially in his medical bed was Europa, with his left hand firmly held in her own. The lower half of her body was lying across another bed that had been pulled up next to his. As he processed the scene before him, he realized Earon was asleep below Europa, the upper half of his body also on Jeanip's bed and the lower part on Europa's bed. Knowing Terrance probably wasn't far away, he raised his head slightly to see Terrance sitting in a chair next to the second bed, his head on Europa's bed, sound asleep.

"Sh-h-h, don't wake them," Chancee silently stated. Jeanip had not seen him sitting at the foot of his bed watching over the four. "Let them sleep a little longer. I believe you'll be able to climb out of bed on your right side."

Jeanip reached down with his right hand and gently removed his hand from Europa's grip. As quietly as possible, he swung his legs over the right side of his bed and stepped down onto the cold stone floor. Not saying a word, Chancee motioned for Jeanip to follow him from the room. As Chancee began to lead him across the hall to a room where Leenow was waiting to do his final exam, Jeanip stopped.

"I can't leave this room as long as she is in here," Jeanip stated.

"What are you talking about?" Chancee asked.

"I was down in the cave when the Terrians attacked Minnos. She was alone and without my protection."

"She wasn't alone. Terrance and Earon were with her, weren't they? And if I am not mistaken, Tinderoon was also there."

"Yes, but I wasn't. I promised her I would never leave her side again until I have her safe at Saint's Isle. I will not break that promise," Jeanip stated, refusing to budge an inch outside the room.

"Jeanip, it's just across the hall. You can keep an eye on her from over there. Besides, she's perfectly safe here at the Hunting Lodge."

"She was perfectly safe at Minnos too and look what almost happened. She came very close to being killed. I will not step outside this room, Chancee."

Shaking his head in both amusement and astonishment, Chancee said, "I see. Because you promised you would never leave her again you will not step foot outside this room, but you were willing to die by saying nothing of the wound in your side so she wouldn't worry." Chancee looked at Jeanip. "Jeanip, that makes no sense."

"Perhaps not. But I didn't die. Therefore I will not leave this room as long as she lies there asleep."

Seeing the futility in trying to change Jeanip's mind, Chancee looked around the room for someplace they could talk without disturbing the sleeping monarchs and Terrance and still allow Leenow to conduct his examination. He saw a portion of the room partitioned off by a glass wall that would suit their needs. Pointing toward the glass wall Chancee asked, "How about over there, Jeanip? Would you be willing to go inside that room? You will still be in the same room so you can keep an eye on her. Leenow's physical will not disturb them and our voices will not carry."

Jeanip looked at the partition. As Chancee stated, he could watch Europa through the glass and ensure she was safe, but he still did not like the idea of being more than a few yards away from her. "It's not perfect, but it will suffice."

Chancee again chuckled to himself. There was just no pleasing this Waters. "I will go get Leenow." Jeanip watched as Chancee crossed the hall and talked with Leenow. The two then came back to the Medical Room and walked straight to the room where Jeanip waited.

"How are you feeling, Jeanip?" Leenow asked, as he entered.

"Great," Jeanip replied, never taking his eyes off the sleeping Europa. "A little surprised that I am still alive. How did you manage to save me? Whatever you did or gave me sure did the trick. I haven't felt this good in years," Jeanip stated as Leenow ran his medical scanner over Jeanip's body. "I'm not even sore." Jeanip lifted his shirt to inspect his side wound. "I thought when I took this hit my days were up." Jeanip averted his eyes away from the monarchs long enough to look at his wound. He stared in disbelief; there was no bandage, no wound, no scar, no indication of a wound ever existed there. "I don't understand. Where is the wound? I should either have a sizeable hole in my side or a lot of stitches, but I see neither. Have you found a miracle cure?"

"No, but you may have," Chancee stated.

"Pardon me?" Jeanip asked, giving Chancee a confused look.

Chancee looked at Leenow. "Is he okay to leave?"

"He's in perfect health," Leenow stated. "But I do recommend he eat something to help build his strength up again."

"Well, since he won't leave this area would you mind asking someone from the kitchen to bring him some food?" Chancee asked.

"I'll have someone bring him something right away," Leenow replied. He turned and looked at Jeanip, who was still staring at his side, trying to comprehend why there was no wound. "Jeanip, I don't think you'll need my services, but, in case you do, don't hesitate to have someone come and get me. Will you do that?"

"Yes," was all Jeanip said.

"Jeanip, I'm serious. Do not wait like you did last time. Send for me immediately. Agreed?"

"Yes, I will send for you right away," Jeanip replied, a little irritated by the question being asked again. He felt so healthy he couldn't imagine needing any more of Leenow's services.

"I'd ask you to walk with me but since you won't leave her I guess we'll talk here," Chancee said to the still confused Jeanip. "Have a seat." Chancee pulled up two chairs in front of the glass plate so they could talk while Jeanip kept his vigil.

"Chancee, what's going on?" Jeanip asked, as he sat down. "What happened to me? Why is there no wound in my side?"

"Not only are the wounds in your leg and side healed, the scars on your face and left arm are also gone," Chancee stated, amused at the surprised look on his old friend's face.

Jeanip quickly lifted up his left shirt sleeve and stared at the place on his arm where a long scar normally could be seen extending from his shoulder down to his elbow, a souvenir from the Terrian wars. He reached up with his hand and felt his face. He could not feel the scar tissue that had been there for centuries. Perplexed, he looked at Jeanip. "Chancee, please don't make me ask you again. Tell me what happened to me!"

"Europa happened to you," Chancee answered.

"What do you mean Europa happened to me? What does Europa have to do with my injuries?"

"She healed you," Chancee said.

Jeanip quickly turned and faced Chancee, his words breaking Jeanip's watch. "What do you mean 'she healed me'? Stop talking in short sentences, Chancee. Tell me what happened!"

Chancee looked directly at Jeanip. "Jeanip, your injuries were too severe. You waited too long to bring the ship in and, as a result, the medical personnel were not able to save you. We didn't even have the option of taking you down to the Complex. When there was no doubt you only had minutes to live, we prepared to bring you down to the ocean so you could return home. Europa ran from your room screaming she knew how to save you. I feared she was having a breakdown. What I did not know was she had run to retrieve the Orb you thankfully brought with you. We were just getting ready to take you into the ocean, so you could return home, when she came running with the Orb in her hands and ordered us to put you down on the ground. Against my better judgment, I did as she ordered; and I am grateful I did." Chancee paused for a moment, as he grabbed Jeanip's hand, the most serious look upon his face that Jeanip had ever seen "Jeanip, what she did was unbelievable. She knelt down beside you and laid the Orb on your chest while cradling it inside her hands. She began to hum an old healing chant our ancestors sang. The Orb began to glow and threads of light began to materialize. Then I heard her say three words in the old ones tongue. Upon her speaking them, the lights began to migrate out from the Orb, into Europa's hands and then flowed from her into you. Your body began to glow and as I watched, I saw life flowing back into you. Your color returned, your breathing was no longer labored and then the blood of your bandages began to disappear. When the Orb stopped glowing and the threads of lights ceased, your injuries were gone. You were totally healed." Jeanip just sat there, trying to comprehend what Chancee had just told him. "Jeanip, has anything happened to Europa lately?" Chancee asked, as he let go of Jeanip's hand.

Chancee's voice snapped Jeanip back into reality. "What did you say?"

"Has anything unusual happened to Europa lately? Did anything happen when Medaron died?"

Jeanip turned his vision back to his sleeping monarch, remembering the events of that fateful day. "Europa had already turned twenty and Medaron had given her the amulet. Europa arrived at the accident scene while her mother was still alive. Medaron knew she had only minutes to live and there was the possibility JeffRa was still out there hunting her children and she would not be there to protect them. In an act of desperation she transferred her powers to Europa. The transfer sent Europa into shock and she collapsed and fell into unconsciousness. The transfer nearly killed her." Jeanip continued to stare at Europa. What Chancee said about Europa healing him was impossible, yet there he was completely healed. Somehow this beautiful sovereign of his had brought him back from the door of death.

"Medaron must have indeed been frightened to try such a transfer," Chancee stated. "She had to have known it could kill the child. But Europa survived it? Her body accepted the transfer?"

"Yes, she survived." Jeanip said, then after thinking for a minute added, "But Chancee, Medaron did not possess the power to heal. Plus, Europa's human and, as such, should possess no powers at all. Again I ask, how was she able to heal me?"

"I do not know for sure. As you said, she's human. Yet there must still be a part of her that is Waters; otherwise she never would have survived the transfer. It is possible Medaron's powers combined with her human genes and produced new powers, but that too seems impossible, for I have never heard of humans having the power to heal using Orbs. Perhaps one day we will discover the reason she was able to heal you. For now, we must be content with the fact that she did and is the first healing monarch in over one hundred and fifty thousand years." Chancee placed his hand on Jeanip's shoulder. "And truth be told, I am thankful she did. I would miss you, Old Friend."

"As am I. There's no one left but me to take them to safety. Plus, my death would have prevented me from fulfilling my duty to Enok."

"You are unbelievable, Jeanip," Chancee said, as he stood up, shaking his head in disbelief. He saw a young male enter the room carrying a tray of food for Jeanip. Stepping into the doorway, he motioned the male toward them. "You can put the tray down on the table next to him," he instructed the food carrier, pointing toward Jeanip. After the male left Chancee finished his statement. "You know it was your damn dedication to your duty that almost got you killed."

"And your point is?"

"My point is, Jeanip, those two kids need you. They can't make it without you. So next time you decide to keep quiet about a killing wound to your body because it's your DUTY to, think about what those kids need."

"Chancee, why were Europa and Earon lying next to me this morning when I woke? That is not acceptable monarch behavior." Jeanip took a bite of the breakfast before him, thinking nothing had ever tasted so good. Whatever Europa did to him it certainly helped his appetite.

"No, it's not acceptable behavioral for a monarch, but it's totally acceptable behavior for two kids who love you. Europa almost lost you. She refused to leave your side even though the medical personnel told her you were out of danger. Hell, Jeanip, she may never let you out of her sight again."

"Don't say that, Chancee," Jeanip responded, as he lowered his head, sitting for a moment in silence, his appetite temporarily gone. Chancee had given him much to think about. Plus, plans needed to be made for their continued journey to Saint's Isle. And he was sure Europa would not have forgotten his promise to tell her where she came from once they reached the Hunting Lodge.

"Where is he?" Europa asked, as she bolted up, realizing Jeanip was no longer in his bed. Fearing she had dreamed the healing with the Orb, she desperately looked around the medical room for any sign of Jeanip.

Earon was sitting on the edge of their bed, having woken up fifteen minutes earlier. "Take it easy, Sis," Earon said, as he stretched his arms. "Leenow already told me he is fine. He is sitting over there behind that glass wall eating something." Earon pointed toward the glassed-in area occupied by Mr. Dark Feather and Jeanip. "They are probably planning our next move."

Europa jumped down from the medical bed. Looking at Terrance she said, "I am starving, Terrance. We will grab Jeanip and Mr. Dark Feather and go eat. And do not forget to bring that wonderful life-saving backpack." Thinking perhaps she should double check on the Orb's location, she added, "The Orb is still safe in there, is it not?"

"Yes, along with the diary and our other important items," Terrance stated.

Europa almost ran across the floor heading toward Jeanip with Earon and Terrance right behind her. Seeing her coming, both men rose from their seats as she entered the room. "Nice to see you this morning, Europa," Chancee said. "I hope you were able to get some rest."

"Yes, thank you, Mr. Dark Feather," Europa said, stopping a few inches in front of the two men. Fearing it could still be a dream, she kept her eyes on Jeanip.

"Good morning, Your Majesty," she heard him say. She was not dreaming. Jeanip was alive and standing in front of her. Then as she watched, Jeanip bent down on one knee and knelt before her, bringing his hand to his forehead and bowing deeply. "To you, My Queen, I pledge forever my allegiance and life."

Forgetting all the protocols her mother and Jeanip ever taught her, Europa rushed forward, knelt and threw her arms around Jeanip. "I thought I lost you," she whispered in his ear, trying to hold back the tears, but having little success. "Never do that to me again."

"Your Majesty, one of the royal family does not show such emotion to one such as me," Jeanip said, as he stood, Europa's arm still wrapped around him.

"You know what, Jeanip?" Europa said. "To hell with protocol. I never realized until yesterday how much I love you, and I almost never got the chance to tell you. I will NEVER allow that to happen again. I

287

may be your sovereign, your queen, but you are the closest thing I have ever had to a father. And I love you." She wrapped her arms around Jeanip even tighter and this time Jeanip wrapped his arms around her, hugging her tightly, for once allowing himself to relish in the sweetness of the moment. She heard him whisper, "I love you too, kiddo."

Before he could say anything else he heard Earon next to him say, "Hey, can I get in on this hugging too?" Jeanip removed one arm from Europa and wrapped it around Earon, pulling him in beside himself and Europa. Looking at Terrance standing alone, Jeanip removed his arm from around Earon and motioned for Terrance to join them. With a big smile on his face, Terrance hugged all three of them, happy to be included in the family.

Letting go of Terrance and his two charges, Jeanip took a step backwards. Several tears were clearly visible on his cheek, but the three gave no indication they had noticed. "Okay you three," Jeanip began, standing up straighter and pushing his shoulders back. "Due to recent events I will allow this one demonstration of emotion on your part. But it is never to be repeated. Europa and Earon, you are both to remember your place and show the proper attitude toward others. And Terrance, well, I don't know what to tell you because you are human and might not know better." Looking as sternly as he could he added, "If anyone ever asks, this display never happened." He reached up and quickly wiped away the tears on his cheek. Not knowing the proper words on how to thank Europa for restoring his life, he said no more on the subject. "Chancee and I were just discussing the best way for us to continue your journey," Jeanip said. "But before we get into that I am sure you three must be hungry. Let's all go down to the meal room and have a wonderful breakfast together."

The three hurried down the hall with Jeanip and Chancee close behind them. Even before they entered the room the three could smell the aroma of fresh brewed coffee, bacon, sausage, toast and eggs. Their mouths began to salivate at the delightful smells; their stomachs started to rumble, having had nothing to eat since last night when they arrived. Even with all the tempting smells Europa waited for Jeanip before entering the room and sitting at a table, still not sure he was really alright. Chancee signaled for one of the helpers to come to their table. "Please bring these three some breakfast."

"And lots of coffee," Europa said.

"And lots of coffee," Chancee repeated, smiling at how much this young monarch was like her mother.

The kitchen helper soon returned with several containers of coffee and five coffee mugs. After pouring everyone a cup of coffee, he took their individual breakfast orders. Europa noticed Jeanip passed when it was his time to order food. Concerned by Jeanip's lack of appetite, she asked, "Jeanip, you are not eating? Are you not feeling well? Should we get Leenow?"

Jeanip turned and smiled at Europa. "Thanks to you I am totally fine, completely healed. I am not hungry because I already ate breakfast while you were sleeping. Chancee can vouch for me."

"He speaks the truth," Chancee confirmed. "He ate a very healthy breakfast."

"So you really are okay? You are totally healed?" she asked.

"Yes, Europa."

"Leenow said so?"

"Leenow said so," Jeanip repeated.

"He told me the same," Earon added, knowing his sister might not totally believe Jeanip after his omission of the wound that almost took him away from her.

Finally satisfied Jeanip was okay, she turned her attention to another matter she had just remembered. "Mr. Dark Feather, we have in our possession a journal which contains coded Terrian writing. I was wondering if anyone here might be able to decipher it for us."

Chancee looked surprised. "Terrian writing? I cannot wait to hear how you came upon that! Unfortunately, there is no one here at the Hunting Lodge who can read Terrian. Misso and Sunam were the experts in that area."

"That is what Jeanip said," Terrance replied.

"There may be an old Oonock of the Cree Clan still living down at the Complex who instructed Misso in the language. Perhaps once you are safe he can come up for a visit and have a look at them."

"Thank you, Mr. Dark Feather. I hope so," Europa replied, then turned her attention back to Jeanip. "Jeanip, I know our journey takes priority and it is imperative we get to Saint's Isle as soon as possible. But you promised me when we reached the Hunting Lodge there would be time to tell me why all of this is happening, who I really am. I need to know why my mother and many of the people I cared about are dead, killed by a man I have never met, who is determined to end my life at any cost. And I need to know how I was able to heal you, what the Orb has done to me. Jeanip, I can never be the monarch you believe I can be unless I know the truth; the WHOLE truth, not just part of it."

"Yes, Your Majesty, you are right. You deserve to know why this being is trying to kill you. And, since you already know part of the truth, you now need to be told all of it, although it is not my place to tell you. But since neither of your parents are here, it falls upon me to try to explain our past and the decision your parents made regarding you." Jeanip suddenly wished Medaron or Enok were here to explain this to their daughter. "As for the Orb's power and what it may have done to you, I think Chancee here is better to address that issue. If you do not mind, Your Majesties, I would like your permission for Chancee to join us. I can assure you his insight and input will be most valuable."

"Yes, certainly," Europa replied, as she turned her gaze to Chancee. "Please join us, Mr. Dark Feather. My mother often spoke of your great wisdom and I agree with Jeanip regarding your insight."

"It would be my pleasure, Your Majesty," he replied. "If you have no objections, Jeanip and I will adjourn to the table next to you three to finalize your traveling plans while you finish breakfast. When you are finished, Jeanip can accompany you to your room to shower and change into clean clothes. Then I will meet you four in the Meeting Room on the second floor in about ninety minutes where Jeanip will tell you the story of our race and how we came to this planet. He will also try to explain to you why your parents decided it was best for you to be born human and whatever else you may wish to know. And I will try to answer the question of how you healed Jeanip. Is that agreeable to you?" Chancee looked at Europa.

"Yes, that would be fine," Europa answered.

"Is that okay with you, Your Majesty?" Chancee asked Earon.

"Yes, that is agreeable," Earon said.

"Jeanip, does this meet with your approval?" Since he knew Jeanip would not leave Europa's side he tried to arrange things so he was always with her.

"Yes, ninety minutes would be fine," Jeanip stated, thankful Chancee remembered his promise.

Not wanting to make Terrance feel left out or not a part of the team, Chancee lastly turned to him and asked, "How about you, Terrance? Is ninety minutes agreeable with you? After all, I believe you have any important role in this saga also."

"Ah, yes, Sir," Terrance stuttered, surprised by the question and glad to be included at the same time.

"Then I will see you in ninety minutes," Chancee said, as he and Jeanip stood up and moved to the table adjacent to the trio. Looking at Europa, he added, "It's going to be a long story, so, if you'd like, I can have someone from the galley set up coffee and other drinks, and perhaps some snacks."

"Yes, thank you, Mr. Dark Feather, I think that would be delightful. Please make it so."

"There is a lot of history to go over and I am sure Europa, and possibly Earon, will have questions. You may want to also advise the galley staff we will have lunch and possibly dinner in the meeting hall," Jeanip suggested. "We should all have a good meal before we embark."

"We will be leaving tonight?" Earon asked.

"Yes, we will leave an hour after it gets dark. We will have one more night of traveling under the cloak of darkness," Jeanip answered. "I will update you on our travel plans once they have been finalized."

"Then we will leave you to your planning," Europa stated, signaling for Terrance and Earon to devote their time to eating and allow Chancee and Jeanip to finalize their travel plans.

Chancee entered the meeting room to discover the three youths and Jeanip already waiting. He was delighted to see the elaborate array of goodies and drinks the galley staff had assembled in the room for their guests' consumption. As he walked over to the table and poured himself a glass of lemonade, he wondered how Europa would react to the story Jeanip was going to tell her. It was one thing thinking you might know what was going on, but an entirely different thing to be told the real truth. He sat down in a seat across from Europa and Terrance, smiling to himself as he saw once again how devoted Terrance was to her. He also chuckled to see Terrance had his backpack secured next to him. He wondered what things were hidden inside.

"I've been trying to think how to start this story," Jeanip began, after taking a sip of coffee. "In order for you to understand why your parents made the decisions they did regarding you and your brother, you need to know back to our very beginning. I'm sure you're going to have a lot of questions through this telling, but I ask you to hold as many as possible until the end to ask them. Many will be answered as I go forward in time. Chancee and Earon," Jeanip said, turning his head toward each and giving them a nod. "If at any time you feel I have forgotten something, please feel free to speak up." Looking over at Terrance, he said, "Terrance, your stepfather's part in this tale is not a kind one. I apologize in advance if I offend you in any way during my telling. If it becomes too painful to hear the truth I will understand if you have to leave the room."

Terrance reached down and took Europa's hand. "No apology is necessary, Jeanip. If my stepfather is indeed this JeffRa, I need to know why he is trying to kill the woman I love so I can better protect her. I need to know who he might be."

"If? You still doubt your stepfather and JeffRa are the same person?" Chancee asked.

Terrance turned and faced Chancee. "Yes, Sir. As I told Europa, my stepfather was not a loving man, but I never saw in him the cold hearted madman this JeffRa is. It is hard for me to accept my stepfather is a mass murderer, someone bent on the annihilation of an entire race. The only connection he has to this JeffRa is the weapon I found in his room, and he may have found that in his search for the lost royal family. Mind you, I am not defending him, but I need more than this circumstantial evidence to convince me he and JeffRa are the same person. Right now the only thing I know for sure is he was overzealous in his search for that family and spied on Minnos. What he did was terribly wrong, but it doesn't make him a murderer."

"You are correct, Terrance," Jeanip commented. "And I do hope you are correct in your suggestion he found the weapon and has no connection to JeffRa. Since we have no way of knowing the truth at this time, I hope you will understand why I must still assume your stepfather and JeffRa are the same person."

"Yes, Sir, for Europa's and Earon's safety I can understand the necessity of assuming that fact," Terrance responded.

"Then if no one has any objections, I will begin to tell you of our people's history."

"Please begin," Europa said, as she snuggled deeper into Terrance's arms, preparing herself to at last hear the truth, a little apprehensive.

"So that everyone understands I will refer to any locations or celestial bodies by their Earth names," Jeanip began. Looking at Europa he added, "I know you found your mother's diary in the secret attic and have read it. And we all know the Orb has joined with you and given

292

you some powers you did not have before. Often with that joining and with the powers your mother gave you, which we will go into later, one is given past memories. Am I correct?"

"Yes, I have seen several things," Europa replied.

"What things have you seen, Child?" Chancee asked, intrigued by what the Orb had shown her.

"I saw these beautiful luminous beings swimming in lilac water, happy and content. Then I saw the water turn a deep purple and a pair of red glowing eyes. In my next vision I saw the same beautiful beings at first. Then they all disappeared except for three. I now realize the three were my parents and Jeanip. Jeanip, you were telling them they had to leave. Something was said about the Orbs and then I saw this layer of ice open up and space ships emerge. The last thing I saw behind their home world was the planet Jupiter."

"Very interesting," Chancee commented, placing his hand under his chin and thinking for a moment. "The Orb has made a deep connection with you and has begun to reveal its memories of our past."

"So from those visions do you know where your people come from?" Jeanip asked.

Europa looked at both adult males. "We are from Jupiter's moon Europa, from which I am named after. Is that correct?"

Chancee smiled. "You visions have served you well. Yes, our home world is Europa."

"So you really are aliens?" Terrance asked. "You really came here in space ships?"

"Yes, young Mr. Landers, I guess we are," Chancee laughed, amused by Terrance's excitement and wonder. He turned his attention back to Europa. "Before Jeanip begins I would like to clarify your visions, Europa. I believe it will help you better understand the things he is about to tell you. The luminous beings you saw are what we – Earon, Jeanip, myself and all Oonocks – look like as our true selves. Since our home world is made of water, our bodies evolved to exist in a liquid world. And since that world contained little natural light, we developed our own light, much like your deep sea creatures here on Earth have."

"But what of the red eyes?" Europa asked, vividly remembering the trepidation she felt at seeing them in her dream. "Do some Oonocks have red eyes?"

"No, the red eyes you saw were Terrian eyes, our enemy," Chancee explained. "More than likely they were JeffRa's eyes. And as you already know, our blood is purple, not red as a human's. So when you saw our lilac waters turn deep purple it was because of the blood being spilled into it, blood spilled because of JeffRa. Your second vision sounds like the day we fled our home world to escape JeffRa's revenge and traveled here to Earth."

"Who is this JeffRa?" Terrance asked.

"JeffRa's identity I will reveal shortly," Jeanip replied. "Europa, since you already know what you are and where you come from, let me tell you the rest of the story." Jeanip took a sip of coffee and settled back into his chair. "Here is the story you were never meant to hear."

BEGINNINGS

"Hundreds of millions of years ago, the universe was a very different place than it is today. As Earth was struggling to create a habitual planet for life, several of Jupiter's moons already had established life forms. It was on the moon you know as Europa our race began. Europa was then, as I hope it is now, a world covered completely in water; no land rose above her oceans. Therefore, without land to crawl out onto, life began and evolved in her warm, nutrient-rich lilac waters. While dinosaurs still walked your earth, our race had already evolved into the top sentient being on Europa."

"Unbeknownst to us, our world was an isolated one. A layer of ice encased and shielded our watery sphere. For tens of millions of years, we had no knowledge anything existed beyond Europa's ocean depths. We never ventured to the surface because it was a dark, cold, a barren stretch of our ocean. For you see, Europa is the upside-down version of Earth. The ocean floor was the most brilliant and warmest part of the ocean, while the surface was the darkest and the coldest. The reason for this was the existence of millions of hot water vents on the ocean floor that shot columns of light particles and heated minerals into the water. Add in the fact that no sunlight reached into our oceans, most of our life on Europa, both plant and animal, developed their own luminosity, making our world as bright as a sunny day here on Earth."

"Possibly because we were so isolated and shielded from outside intervention, our race, known as the Oonocks, grew into a peaceful, yet extremely intelligent race. The words 'greed', 'hate' and 'war' did not exist in our vocabulary. We devoted our lives to the enrichment of our people. We pursued knowledge, philosophy, spiritual growth and intellectual learning. We were expert craftsmen and builders and we excelled in science and medicine. Our lives centered around families."

"Over millions of years, the Oonocks divided into many diversified groups, or clans, each governed by a special royal family. The numerous clans chose different expanses of the ocean to inhabit. Some clans were bottom dwellers and built their abodes on the ocean floor or in caves. Others were top dwellers and built theirs homes floating high above the ocean floor or on top of underwater mountain peaks. Each clan was unique and specialized in one or two expertise, such as medicine, physics, engineering, painting, wood working, metallurgy and so forth. And, just as you humans did here on Earth, occasionally some clans intermarried and established larger, unified clans. A clan's members numbered from less than a hundred to tens of thousands. But no matter the clan's size, each clan held the same importance, the same authority as the next clan, each ruled by its own royal lord and lady."

"One of the larger, top-dwelling clans devoted their talents to building ships. which enabled the trading clans to travel long distances in a short span of time. Because of their ship building and the fact some of the younger clan members tended to drive their ships very fast through the ocean, this clan became known as 'The Waters'. This is the clan we are descended from."

"But none of the clans, including our own, could have excelled had it not been for the wonder mineral called 'bendicor'. Bendicor is a purple stone abundant on our world, a very powerful mineral that even in its smallest form can produce enormous amounts of energy. It was, and still is, the source of our energy, our technology, our very existence. Legend even credits it as the reason we are able to shape shift."

"So the Oonocks have always been able to transform into other beings?" Europa asked.

"Yes, as far back as we have history," Chancee replied.

"One day the world of Europa trembled, as if it had been hit by a massive earthquake. Buildings toppled, mountains fell, but no damage was done to the ocean floor. The oldest son of the Waters' monarch found this very intriguing. This young male was your great-grandfather, Tyrigg. Determined to discover the cause of the shaking, he sailed his ship through the ocean searching for the cause. It did not take him long to realize the higher he went from the ocean floor the more severe the damage was. Therefore, he deduced the cause must have originated from above, not below. With the help of some fellow clansmen, Tyrigg built a special ship that was capable of taking him to the surface. It is important to remember no one had ever ventured to the surface of the ocean, so when Tyrigg ascended he was astounded to find there was a hard surface above the water – the layer of ice. He continued to glide below the ice and soon saw large cracks in the icy shell, cracks which grew to enormous size as he continued forward. To his astonishment the cracks ended at a large gaping hole created by a meteor that had smashed into our moon. It blew apart a large portion of the ice barrier, thus creating a hole miles wide. Through this hole your great-grandfather became the first Oonock to ever see space. He was mesmerized, as he saw the twinkling of thousands of stars and the planet Jupiter. It was then he realized how isolated his world was and how the ice barrier had protected them. Fearing his lilac waters could escape through this enormous hole in the barrier, he rushed back home to solicit the help needed to repair the shield."

"Jeanip, you had told me my great-grandparents' names were Esoquin and Meeleena," Europa suddenly stated. "Now you are saying my great-grandfather's name was Tyrigg. Which is correct?"

"Actually both, Your Highness," Jeanip replied realizing clarification was needed. "Your great-grandparents' real names were Tyrigg and Bytroom. To hide their longevity to the humans, your parents assumed your great-grandparents' identity for a while and changed their names to Esoquin and Meeleena to cover up their own names of Enok and Medaron."

"Were my grandparents' names really Enoquin and Messor?" she asked, now wondering if their names were also a fabrication.

"Yes, those were their real names. Your parents were able to assume their identities using Enok's parents' real names."

"It does get a little confusing," she softly said.

"That it does," Jeanip smiled. "Let's see, where was I? Oh, yes. Upon returning home, Tyrigg informed his father of what he found and requested a special clan leaders' meeting. At the meeting he explained to the clan leaders what he had seen and the danger it posed to their existence. Several of the clan leaders laughed at the possibility of there being other worlds outside of their home world and considered any investigation into the matter foolish and unworthy of their consideration. Luckily, his father and several other clan leaders believed him and understood the implications of the hole. An expedition was launched to determine what danger their home world was in. Tyrigg led a team of top scientists to the surface and they saw for themselves the fact that our isolated world was in mortal danger. They returned with confirmation of the ice barrier breach and the threat that our oceans could be pulled out into space. Tyrigg was able to unite the clans and, together, they designed, engineered and constructed a force field which kept our water from evaporating into space, but also kept it from refreezing, thus allowing us to study the world outside of Europa. Your great-grandfather was hailed as a hero for saving our world and, as his reward, the royal families united and made him the first Ruling Monarch over all the clans. And when he joined with his life's mate, Bytroom, she became our first Supreme Monarch. A new palace was built to house the new monarchs and the clans pledged their loyalties to their rule."

"Several thousand years later, Tyrigg and Bytroom were blessed with their first of four younglings, a son, Enoquin, your grandfather. From the time he was little he was intrigued by what might lie out in space and dreamt of exploration. He was recognized at a very young age to be a gifted ship builder and designer. Putting those talents to use, he and a handful of Waters engineers devoted their time and talents over the next few millennia to constructing space traveling ships capable of holding several hundred inhabitants. It was during this time Enoquin took over the role of Head Monarch and married his life's mate, Messor, the daughter of a rival clan's leader. Messor's clan was known to have some of the best minds in physics, mathematics and aero dynamics; all important areas needed for space travel. But the clan's leader did not support Enoquin's desire for space exploration and contributed little to the development of the space ships. To enlist their aid, Enoquin set out to win Messor's heart and make her his life's mate, thus assuring his access to her peoples' talents. Since Messor was your grandmother you know Enoquin won her heart, but few know the real story of their relationship as life's mates. In our society, the joining of two people is something very sacred, very unique. We do not have a word for 'divorce' because such a thing does not exist in our world. When two people are joined together it is for eternity, thus the term of 'life's mates'. Your parents were good examples of a proper match – they not only loved each other very much, they were part of each other, sensing what the other felt and was thinking, connected in a way that defies reality, that makes one totally incomplete without the other. This was not true for Enoquin and Messor – they were never meant to be joined as life's mates. Mind you, they were fond of each other and, over the years, I suppose a type of love developed, but there was no real connection, no fulfilling the other one, no real love. It did not take Messor long to realize she had been used, that Enoquin had married her for the benefits she brought to his plan for space travel. But since we had no way for two beings to be unjoined, Messor remained Enoquin's mate, unhappy and unfulfilled, resenting him more each day. As our Supreme Monarch she stood beside him, supported him and led her people, hiding from them her unhappiness. She also fulfilled her role as Enoquin's mate and from their union came three younglings, her one main joy in life. Your father was born first, then JeffRa and lastly a female, Quinsong, who died tragically at an early age. Enok, as the first born, was his father's pride and joy. Enoquin denied him almost nothing, spoiled him and doted upon him. He showered him with gifts, praise and rewards as he prepared him to take over the leadership of the kingdom. He treated Quinsong the same because she was his only daughter and, by our tradition, destined to be the next Supreme Monarch. But Enoquin had no love for JeffRa and literally abandoned him to the care of Messor, who probably loved him the most of her three children. It was never known why Enoquin walked away from JeffRa; he was a fine young Oonock and someone who deserved to be honored and loved. Some felt Enoquin saw his own lust for power in his second son and therefore shunned the child. Others speculated JeffRa was not Enoquin's offspring, but adultery is something else which does not exist in our society, so it is hard to imagine JeffRa's father was not Enoquin."

"But whatever the reason was, Enoquin's contempt for JeffRa made your father love him dearly and he did everything in his power to protect JeffRa. The two brothers were inseparable, the best of friends and shared everything together. Like his father, JeffRa was a natural engineer, a genius, and he developed many new ways to increase the ship's energy output, as well as shield it and its passengers from radiation and other dangers of space. He even invented a new power chamber to harness more of our bendicor's energy, thus giving our ships the ability to travel outside our solar system. Working together side by side, Enok and JeffRa incorporated all of JeffRa's ideas into a new ship they planned to use for an exploration to Jupiter. But such a journey was not in JeffRa's destiny, for when the day came to embark on their voyage he was forced to remain behind. Wanting only his oldest son to receive the recognition and glory of exploring Jupiter, Enoquin ordered JeffRa to remain on Europa. Your father tried to persuade your grandfather to allow JeffRa to accompany him, telling him it was JeffRa's ingenuity that made the flight possible, but your grandfather would not hear of it. He said as the first born it was Enok's right to get the credit for the mission but, as the second born, JeffRa had no rights. It broke Enok's heart to go without his brother, but as a proper son he followed his father's orders. I think he always regretted not standing up to Enoquin that day and demanding JeffRa accompany him. How different things might have turned out if he had, for that trip to Jupiter was the beginning of the rift between the two brothers, a rift that would end our world and force our evacuation and eventual settlement here on Earth."

"Enoquin continued to deal degradation after degradation against JeffRa, each one more cruel than the last. Enok did his best to shield his younger brother and include him in his experiences, but Enoquin's favoritism toward Enok soon made JeffRa embittered and jealous of his older brother. Realizing he would never hold a place in Enoquin's heart as long as Enok lived, he began to dream of Enok's demise and moving up to first born, believing that would ensure his father's love and acceptance. So this hatred grew with each passing day and with each new task, homage and adornment given to Enok until it completely consumed JeffRa. The final insult was the day Enok took Medaron as his life's mate; on that day something inside JeffRa snapped and the brother Enok loved was no more. In his place was an evil, vengeful being, determined to not only end Enok's life, but to end his parents' and sister's as well and take over as Head Ruling Monarch. Thus JeffRa devised a plan to destroy us all."

"Knowing there must be others who were unhappy with their positions, JeffRa began to search them out, especially the male children of royal families not first born. Promising them glory and rise to power, he was able to raise a small army. With his army assembled, he waited for his chance to strike. That chance came on the day your father was named Ruling Monarch and your grandfather stepped down. JeffRa knew many of the clan leaders would be attending the celebration and would give his army the opportunity to eradicate many of them in one strike. Plus, he knew Enok and his father would be so distracted with all the festivities they would not notice anything unusual. And JeffRa might have succeeded in Enok's downfall if their younger sister, Quinsong, hadn't stumbled upon her brother's plot. Upon learning of JeffRa's plan, she raced to warn her father and Enok, but JeffRa and several of his followers intercepted her and a struggle ensued. Quinsong was seriously injured in the confrontation; by whose hand it was never known. She managed to get away and make it to her father's side and inform him of JeffRa's plot to kill them all at the ceremony. She died in Enoquin's arms and he literally went insane. He ordered the immediate execution of JeffRa and his followers, refusing to hear anything Enok said regarding JeffRa. Civil war broke out; many Oonocks died. Our utopia was destroyed. For the first time in our millions of years of existence, the words 'hate', 'revenge' and 'war' were added to our vocabulary."

"Enoquin was relentless in hunting down his son and his followers, determined to bring them to justice not only for Quinsong's death, but for the destruction of our way of life. Never in the history of the Oonocks had one Oonock killed another and now that it had, Enoquin was going to ensure it happened again to his youngest son. He devoted every second he was awake to ending JeffRa's life. Finally, after years of civil war, JeffRa was caught and brought before Enoquin. But Enok was now Ruling Monarch and he would not allow his father to kill the brother he loved. Since there was no law, no punishment for a crime such as JeffRa's, it fell upon Enok's shoulders to determine JeffRa's punishment and pronounce sentence. But Enok could not end the life of his brother because he felt partly responsible for JeffRa's demise. Runbee and I pleaded with him, explained to him the brother he knew and loved no longer existed, but our counseling feel upon deaf ears. Since Medaron was Supreme Monarch and her decree superseded Enok's, we took our cause to her. With Chancee's help we pleaded with her to persuade Enok to end JeffRa and his followers' lives. But our pleas fell upon deaf ears, for she sided with Enok, stating only that they had good reason for sparing JeffRa's life."

"A decision that would change our course of history and destroy her happiness," Chancee interjected. "She soon came to regret that decision and, I believe, regretted it to the day she died even though she felt she had sufficient reason to let JeffRa live."

"Sufficient reason?" Earon asked. "JeffRa tried to kill them and all their family. He brought war upon them. What reason could possibly be worth letting him live?"

"So you knew, Chancee?" Jeanip asked.

"Yes, Medaron told me may years later why she had not given the order to execute him," Chancee replied. "Did she tell you too?"

"No, Enok did," Jeanip said. "I asked him after the last major war when he laid in the medical room fighting for his life while Medaron dwelled in a state of deep depression at their abode, fighting for her life also. I asked him why he ever spared JeffRa and was it worth all the destruction he had caused. To this day, I don't believe I had the audacity to speak to him the way I did, but I was so angry, so totally enraged after Tiree's death and the death of so many Oonocks that I had to know if the sparing of JeffRa's life was worth it."

"What did he say?" Earon asked.

"He finally admitted it was not worth it, especially because of the sorrow JeffRa had caused Medaron. He told me he wished he had taken my advice and executed his brother," Jeanip answered. "But he also said, knowing what he knew then, he still could have made no other decision. That's when he told me the reason."

"Can you tell us the reason?" Europa asked, intrigued as to what could have prevented her parents from carrying out the needed sentence.

"It should be your father that tells you the reason, but since he is not here and Jeanip cannot break Enok's confidence, I will give you a very brief account of your parents' reasoning," Chancee stated. "Enoquin's hate was so strong against his middle son he did the ultimate act of betrayal, the one thing that would destroy his son's chance at a future, happiness or a family forever. Enoquin learned Medaron had agreed to join with JeffRa and JeffRa had entered into negotiations with her father to join with her. Upon learning the news, Enoquin immediately forced Medaron's father to abandon his promise to JeffRa and agreed for Enok to join with Medaron. Neither Enok, Medaron nor JeffRa had any knowledge of this agreed-upon union until it was announced to the people. And once it was announced, they were forced to honor the agreement and join. JeffRa was disgraced, considered a fool, someone unworthy of respect and homage."

"Why would he do that?" Terrance asked.

"Which he?" Jeanip asked Terrance. "Enoquin did it out of sheer spite, out of a desire to destroy his son once and for all. He knew JeffRa would never recover from such an insult to his pride. As for my father, it was merely a political decision. Once Medaron joined with Enok her status would be raised to Supreme Monarch, giving our father more power and prestige than he ever thought possible to obtain."

"Even though they could not terminate his life, Enok and Medaron did realize JeffRa and his followers had to be banished somewhere where they would not pose a threat. Both knew the only way to keep Europa safe was to ensure JeffRa and his men could not continue to live as Oonocks," Jeanip continued. "They searched for a location where life was possible but hard enough to keep them busy surviving, somewhere where they had to live as land creatures, a place containing no large bodies of water. Ganymede, one of Jupiter's moons, was chosen. It contained just enough water to sustain life, had sparse vegetation and mostly consisted of dirt and sand."

"Throughout the sentencing of his men and himself, JeffRa remained emotionless, never speaking a word. Some wondered if he even realized what was happening. But, as he was led away, he screamed out to Enok his oath of revenge stating he would personally kill all the Waters' royal family and any future born royals. And he would see our home world of Europa destroyed."

"The next several centuries passed quickly. Several assassination attempts were made against Enok by a handful of JeffRa's followers who were missed when JeffRa's men were gathered and exiled. These attempts served as reminders of JeffRa's promise to eradicate the royal family, a promise Enok now realized his brother would never abandon. It was during this time he, along with Medaron, wrote and decreed the security laws and protocols that would keep not only the royal family, but all Oonocks safe. Together they ruled the Oonocks and oversaw the clans while preparing for the war to come; they knew that somehow JeffRa would find a way to carry out his threats. Craftsmen from all fields designed and built superior weapons. Strategists developed detailed evacuation plans. Astronomers searched the heavens for a location the Oonocks could relocate to if need be. Ship builders incorporated JeffRa's ideas and designs into new larger vessels that could carry thousands of Oonocks and withstand a long space migration to distant planets. Provisions were stored, the Orbs were gathered into traveling storage containers and an army was assembled in preparation for a future war. Enok and Medaron chose me to be the Chief Commander of their army and the Keeper/Enforcer of the security laws and protocols. With the assistance of Enok, I trained an elite army in combat and warfare, as well as a special unit to protect the royal families. Nothing was left to chance; we were ready for whatever JeffRa dealt us. And so we waited."

"Having little knowledge of the living conditions on Ganymede, and still feeling guilty about JeffRa's downfall, Enok at first sent a supply ship each month filled with medicine and food to aid JeffRa in his exile. He hoped the supplies would allow his brother to live a decent life on his exiled world. But the ships did not return from their delivery so Enok was forced to abandon the shipments after three months. He feared Jeanip might be capturing the ships and refurbishing them to launch an attack against Europa."

"We know little of what JeffRa did after his exile. Over the years we've been able to gather bits of information from captured Terrians concerning his activities. The story they told was that sometime after his arrival on Ganymede JeffRa encountered an intelligent race of beings called the Terrians. Although intelligent, they were aggressive, barbaric, fierce warriors with a tremendous thirst for blood, wealth, power and the demise of their enemy, characteristics JeffRa himself possessed. With his superior intellect and ability to shape shift, JeffRa was able to overthrow their leader, finally obtaining one of his life's dreams – to be a Head Ruler. He united several of the clans together and, with their help, began to plot the downfall of Europa."

Jeanip paused for a moment as he rose and poured himself a cup of coffee. After returning to his seat he continued his story. "I don't believe I mentioned the fact our culture is a matriarchal society. Female monarchs are above the male monarchs. When Enok married Medaron, Medaron rose above him in status and her word and decisions were above Enok's. And had Enok's sister, Quinsong, lived she would have become Supreme Monarch when she reached the age of Tiipow and Enok would have been demoted to second monarch."

"Tiipow?" Europa asked, hating to interrupt Jeanip but needing clarification of the term. "What is Tiipow?"

"Tiipow is the age of consent, when an Oonock becomes basically an adult," Chancee answered. "In human terms, I guess it would be the age of twenty; when one is no longer a teenager."

"Is that why Mother gave me the amulet on my twentieth birthday?" Europa asked, as she reached up and touched the present around her neck. "I had reached the age of Tiipow in human age and was now an adult and ready to lead our people?"

"Yes."

Seeing Europa's question had been answered Jeanip continued. "It is important you comprehend this principle of female monarch status in order to understand what happened next. Enok's parents, Enoquin and Messor, were getting close to the time when they would return to the waters from which they came. Although Messor knew of the horrible things her son had done, she still loved him. A mother's love does not die easily, especially for her favorite child. Plus, she had learned of Enoquin's deceit in arranging for Enok and Medaron to be joined. Feeling JeffRa had been unjustly sentenced, in addition to feeling very guilty for not stopping Enoquin's cruelty toward JeffRa, Messor vowed not to leave this world without seeing JeffRa one last time. She decreed a ship take her to Ganymede to see him and say her final goodbyes. Because she was still a Supreme Monarch, her decree was carried out although Enok, Medaron, and I voiced numerous objections. But her mind could not be changed. Finally, a compromise was reached and it was agreed a small band of protectors would accompany her. To everyone's surprise, Enoquin also stated he would make the trip with her, a fact Enok was suspicious of. He knew the hatred Enoquin still had in his heart toward JeffRa and he actually feared Enoquin might have some alterative motive for going. But if there was, Enok was never able to discover it. So, against his better judgment, Enok watched his parents leave. That was the last time he ever saw them. We never discovered what happened to them or if Messor every saw her son before she died. When Enok returned to his abode later that day, he discovered a note from his father stating that if Messor and he did not return within two rotations Enok should abandon Europa and set sail for a new home. He wrote that his failure to return would mean we and our home world were about to be destroyed."

"When your grandparents did not return, Enok and Medaron followed Enoquin's advice and gave the order to evacuate our world, but not all the clans believed evacuation was necessary. Of all the clans, only fifteen chose to leave. The remaining clans remained on Europa, believing her layer of ice would keep them safe. A total of twenty ships were outfitted for the journey into space. Together they emerged from beneath the ice canopy, prepared to carry the Oonock race to begin an existence on a new world. It was decided to give the Oonocks who remained behind not only a chance of escaping JeffRa's revenge, but a chance of survival. The force shield was deactivated and explosives set off to reseal the opening. The world of the Oonocks was once again sealed, protected and isolated from the rest of the universe under miles of ice, safe from outside aggression. Or so we hoped. We had just sealed the opening and were beginning to regroup not far from Europa when JeffRa's revenge hit our home world along with Jupiter and several of her moons. As we watched the magnitude of his revenge, we realized Messor's irrational decree to see JeffRa had saved ours and many other Oonocks' lives."

"This next part again is more speculation than actual known facts. We believe JeffRa's plan consisted of melting off the ice covering on Europa and exposing her ocean to space and solar winds. Europa had almost no atmosphere, so without the protection of her ice her waters would evaporate and eventually leave a dry, waterless world. And without water the Oonocks could not exist. To melt the ice JeffRa created an energy pulse emanating from Jupiter's moon Io and directed that energy into Jupiter's highly volatile atmosphere of methane and helium. The result would be a localized implosion on Jupiter's soil, causing its hot, liquid core to erupt into a tremendous geyser which would cover the surface of Europa and melt all her ice within hours, perhaps minutes. But something went wrong. The implosion occurred too early and Europa was behind Jupiter, just beginning the longest part of its elliptical orbit, not in front of the implosion point, as planned. And JeffRa's calculations for the energy pulse were also incorrect and produced a reaction too strong to remain localized. It rapidly spread across half of Jupiter's surface, creating an unstoppable storm I believe even JeffRa was not prepared for. Fed by the magnetic energy impulse from Io, the implosion grew in intensity and size, ripping the very inner fabric of Jupiter apart. Hot molten liquid burst through Jupiter's crust and spewed into space on all sides, igniting the helium, methane and other released flammable gases. The burning gases spread until the entire globe was consumed in a sphere of fire of unbelievable temperatures, incinerating everything, including the planet itself. Jupiter began to fold into itself, creating huge wind storms of dust and debris. Jupiter, the land planet, ceased to exist and was replaced by a planet of swirling, lethal gases with the originating entry point now visible as a raging red molten wind storm fed by the continuous energy pulse from Io. That storm still exists today. One can see it from Earth with the aid of a telescope. Humans know it as the red eye of Jupiter. JeffRa had released his revenge in a form we never, ever expected. But in his desire to destroy Europa, he inadvertently destroyed all life that existed on Jupiter, Callisto and Ganymede, including his newly formed clan."

"We know that Europa today is still covered by ice," Terrance interjected. "Did those who remained behind survive?"

"That, Terrance, is a question we have asked ourselves millions of times over the past few millennia," Jeanip answered, unconsciously inserting the word 'millennia' in the place he usually said 'centuries', thus giving a hint as to the Oonocks' time on Earth.

"Millennia?" Europa quickly asked, having picked up Jeanip's slip. "How old are you?"

"If I keep stopping to answer questions not related to the current story we will be here for days, Your Highness," Jeanip replied. "I will answer your questions at the end if you so wish, but for now I need to continue with the story. And the answer to Terrance's question is part of this story." Jeanip looked directly at Terrance. "You are correct, Terrance, Europa is still covered by ice today, but we do know a good portion of the ice was melted away during the attack. Whether enough of a layer remained to protect those who remained behind we do not know. To this day we have never heard a sound or received a signal from Europa. Over time the ice barrier did rebuild itself, so it may be the layer of ice is too thick for a signal to get out and those that remained behind survived. Or it may mean too little ice remained to protect them and all life was eradicated from Europa."

Jeanip turned his eyes back to Europa and continued. "Twenty ships left Europa, but only seventeen made it to safety. The last three ships were unable to obtain enough distance before the implosion occurred and were destroyed. Twelve of the ships set courses for worlds outside our solar system; five remained here. Two settled on Mars, which at that time was a lush, green planet full of life. Enok brought the last three here to Earth."

"When we arrived on Earth we thought we would live in Earth's oceans, but we soon realized our bodies could not maintain their cohesiveness in its low pressure. We could, however, live in her depths, but it was pitch black there and we had no way of knowing what creatures might inhabit its depths that would pose a threat to us. Knowing it would take time to explore this world's oceans and determine if a habitat could be built below, we decided to construct a temporary structure on the surface. We transformed into humans and lived as air breathers until the Ocean Complex could be constructed."

"Earth humans were still primitive at this time and their accomplishments were very minimal. Not wanting to contaminate their development and evolutionary growth, Enok and Medaron decided to avoid contact with humans as much as possible. They chose a secluded location in the ocean surrounded by a 'C'-shaped section of land, which hid us from view. Using two of our three ships, we built a city in the circle of the 'C', a city that appeared to be made of gold. We were able to enjoy the wonders of this world's oceans, explore her depths and begin life anew while remaining unknown to the humans who occupied the mainland. Or so we thought. Even with our best efforts to remain concealed and secluded, over time word spread of an advanced race who lived in a city of awesome architect made of gold. We became known for our wealth, our technical superiority, our great palaces and our machines that flew in the sky. The waters surrounding our city soon became a harbor for many trading vessels of various nations. Egypt, the dominant power at the time, became our friend and ally and was instrumental in helping us understand humans and their culture. While history describes us as a conquering people seeking world domination, nothing was farther from the truth. We lived in harmony with the human race, educating them with agricultural advancements, such as irrigation and field maintenance, while acutely restricting their knowledge of our advance technology. Thus we lived for hundreds of years at peace, a center for commerce and education, beings of air and water. Life was so wonderful many began to believe JeffRa had been destroyed in the blast and we had escaped his wrath. But Enok never doubted his brother was somewhere out there feverishly searching for him and Medaron. Both insisted our military be ready for war, our weapons constantly upgraded and the security protocols followed to the letter. Our troops trained daily outside of the city, hidden from human eyes and prepared for any attack we dared to hope would never come. Only a small garrison remained in the city to protect the royal family. It was also during this time a suitable location was discovered in the ocean's depths where the underwater Complex would be built and Enok ordered construction to begin."

"Then one day Enok's beliefs came true. We received a communication from the colony on Mars stating JeffRa had found them and they were under attack. The communication stated he was destroying the planet and there was no hope for their survival. It warned us to prepare for his wrath and wished us luck. Years later we learned to what extent JeffRa's revenge devastated Mars. The lush green planet of blue oceans and wondrous wildlife, Earth's twin, had been reduced to a barren rock devoid of life and atmosphere, devoid of any Oonocks or any sign they had ever lived on that beautiful planet. The only water that remained on the planet now buried in her soil."

"Knowing Earth would be next, and not wishing the same fate for her, we sunk our city that night in a blaze of fire and lightening, hidden by numerous tidal waves and earth shaking as we moved it to the location where we were building the new Complex, deep in the depths of the ocean where no humans and no Terrians could find us. All records we or our city ever existed were erased from existence; all that remained were a few stories the people told each other over the years."

"That is until someone named Plato decided to write a record of it," Chancee commented. "He almost blew our entire cover with his story."

Ignoring Chancee's comment, Jeanip continued. "Our hope was if JeffRa saw no trace of Oonocks or our technology from space he would leave the planet unharmed and believe Mars was the only colony. Our identity now hidden beneath the deep ocean, we kept a constant vigil for JeffRa's ships, keeping our gaze fixed on the heavens, but no attack came. We believed our plan was successful; we were able to hide our existence from JeffRa and therefore spare Earth Mars' fate. We remained in the Ocean Complex for over a thousand years with no contact with humans. And, as before, prepared for JeffRa's revenge while we waited and hoped."

"During this time scouts were sent out to explore the Earth for any sign of Terrians, none of which were found. Feeling enough time had passed, Enok and Medaron announced one day it was safe for anyone who wished to live in the world above. During the time we were gone the human race had evolved and spread further across Africa and Europe, making it necessary to choose a new land location. We decided upon an isolated area close to the ocean in the Orient for our next city. Hoping not to repeat the same mistakes we made with our first city, we did not build elaborate structures of gold. Instead we built a simple city made of wood and stone, designed to appear unimportant. We were able to live in isolation for a while, but soon word of an advanced civilization with superior technology and the ability to fly spread through the humans, just as it had happened at our first city. No matter how we tried to blend in and remain invisible, we failed to remain anonymous. Before long we were the center of trade and commerce once again. As before, we lived In harmony with the local inhabitants, teaching them agriculture, irrigation and other advances that made their lives easier. But soon the greed of men arose and several of the human leaders wanted more of our technology, technology we would not share with them. They declared war on us and tried to take over the city. Of course our technology was such we could easily have crushed them, but not wishing them harm, we decided to abandon the city and relocate, taking our knowledge with us. The city was destroyed, leaving behind only smashed buildings built by an unknown race. We once again returned to the underwater Complex and remained there for many centuries. During all this time there was no sign of JeffRa or his Terrians."

"Many Oonocks enjoyed living above on land and petitioned Enok and Medaron for another city above. Still believing JeffRa was alive and not wishing for another city to become the center of human activity, Enok and Medaron granted their peoples' wish with the stipulation the new city would be built on land, far from the sea. And in case any legends remained about the advanced cities we once occupied, an area in the southern hemisphere along the Pacific Ocean on the opposite side of the world was selected. An area high on a mountain plateau, surrounded by a dense jungle, inhabited by very primitive people was chosen. It provided us with good surveillance of the land below and the opportunity to see any advancing army. The one drawback of the location was the lack of any large body of water. You may or may not have surmised that, as creatures of water, we must have water available to return to if needed. To rectify this we dug out a huge crater not far from where the city would be built and filled it with saltwater."

"I've never heard of a saltwater lake inside South America," Terrance whispered to Europa.

"Me either," Europa replied.

"No, you wouldn't have," Jeanip said, hearing Terrance's comment. "We made the lake very deep, some places down to over nine hundred feet, and filled it with saltwater so the Oonocks would have a place nearby where they could transform into their true selves. Since we had never lived in an area where water was not readily available, our engineers miscalculated the amount of underground freshwater and freshwater from tributaries which would make their way to the lake and the problems they would cause. They had to constantly work on ways to keep the saline in the water. When we were forced years later to abandon this city, no one remained to correct the saline and eventually the lake became a freshwater lake."

Having solved that mystery, Jeanip continued. "Once the lake was completed, we began building the new city from materials the land provided. We carved huge stones out of a nearby quarry and transported them with our individual fliers, welding the stones together with lasers. In no time our city was constructed complete with a center Complex, individual family houses, irrigation, gardens and livestock. Our purple stones provided us with energy for lights, equipment running and a city wide force field. To minimize human contact, we hid the city behind a fortress of high, red-sandstone walls with a huge double gate barring the entrance. But even though the local inhabitants were primate, humans are curious by nature and it was not long before some of the forest Indians followed our flying craft back to our city. From their reaction to the city and their actions later, we believe they thought their forest gods had come to live amongst them. Not wanting to repeat the previous problems with human interaction, Enok and Medaron ordered we have no direct contact with the natives. I remember even doing a few magic tricks and light shows to keep them away from 'the city of bird men'."

"Bird Men?" Europa asked.

"Yes, that is what the natives came to call us, probably because of our flying machines. In fact, they made such an impression on them they began to make small replicas made of gold. Occasionally we would find a broach or a necklace of these replicas left outside our gate – perhaps a peace offering or a present. I believe your mother has several of them in her jewelry box." A solemn look crossed Jeanip's face as he remembered Minnos had been destroyed and the jewelry box with it. "But now they are lost with the rest of her belongings at Minnos."

"No, Jeanip, one still remains. There was a golden ship broach pinned to Mother's diary. It's still on there." Europa reached down in Terrance's backpack and pulled out her mother's diary and showed Jeanip the attached broach. "I remember playing with several of these when I was young. I always wondered why she had space ships. Whenever I asked her about them, all she would tell me is they were a gift from a friend."

"That they were," Jeanip stated. "An entire tribe of friends who would later warn us of JeffRa's approach. But for now, during this time, we lived content and happy, isolated from the world, hidden high above the canopy. And once more we waited – but this time with a glimmer of hope, a hope that was doomed to fail."

"This next part again is speculation on JeffRa's actions. We believe after destroying Mars, he searched Earth for any signs of Oonocks. For some reason, perhaps he thought he saw something or

310

perhaps we left something behind divulging our existence on Earth, he brought his two remaining ships very close to the planet over the Mediterranean. His ships must have been damaged in his battle on Mars because the ships became caught in Earth's gravitational field and could not break free. The ships crashed in the African desert, marooning JeffRa and his men. Now remember, JeffRa and some of his men were Oonocks so they possessed some of the same powers we did. We believe they used these powers as they advanced across Africa, Europe and the Mediterranean, pillaging and plundering as they searched for us. That would account for the legacy we were given of a superior military race with advanced weaponry that stormed across the continents. After centuries of finding no evidence of our existence, JeffRa turned his eyes toward the continents across the ocean – the Americas. But with his ships destroyed he had no way of crossing the ocean and reaching our landmass. He was not able to obtain the resources, either from the Earth or from his damaged ships, to build an ocean vessel or a flying ship."

"Couldn't they transform into ocean creatures like you do and make the journey?" Terrance asked.

"Luckily for us, they could not," Jeanip answered. "To preserve our true form it is necessary for an Oonock to return to water and transform into their true self every thirty or forty years. That's why Enok and Medaron chose an almost waterless world to exile him too. Evidently, even when it became available, JeffRa and his Oonocks had not returned to the water for thousands of years and therefore were no longer capable of transforming into water beings. Plus the majority of JeffRa's soldiers were Terrians and did not possess the capability of transforming into other creatures. Only Oonocks can transform. We believe he did not wish to leave over half of his army behind. So, unwilling to leave his Terrians behind, along with the fact humans did not possess at that time the technology to build the type of sea vessel JeffRa needed, it would take him hundreds of years to find a way to cross the ocean and step foot on our continent."

"I'm confused," Terrance stated. "You said earlier JeffRa was a natural ship builder, a genius. Plus he possessed many of the same powers and technical knowledge you did. Why didn't he just build his own ships and sail across the ocean?"

"We have speculated on that question many times," Chancee responded. "Perhaps he lost his advanced tools when his ships crashed, perhaps they didn't think they were needed and left them behind, perhaps he just didn't feel like taking the time to build them, which I find very unlikely."

"We believe the real reason is he had brought something with him on his ships he could not leave behind, something numerous and heavy," Jeanip stated. "He could not travel across the Atlantic until he found a way to transport these objects safely because he needed them to destroy us."

"Whatever his reason was it gave us many years of peace and happiness and I personally am thankful he didn't come across earlier," Chancee commented.

"As am I," Jeanip continued. "But he did eventually come across. And Medaron sensed his coming. Terrance, since you know little of our monarch you would not know she had a gift whereby she could sense imminent catastrophes. In fact, I failed to mention she was instrumental in Enok's decision to follow his father's advice and evacuate Europa when he did not return from Ganymede. Shortly after Enoquin and Messor's departure, Medaron started to have an uneasy feeling, a feeling of pending disaster. It grew stronger every day the elder monarchs were gone and she kept Enok apprised of her uneasiness. When his father did not return within the designated time, he added in Medaron's feeling and immediate ordered his people to leave. Just as before, one morning in our newest city Medaron woke feeling something was wrong, but what she could not tell. The feeling persisted and grew stronger each day, a feeling without clarity or substance. Remembering the incident on Europa, Enok put everyone on high alert. Believing in the possibility our enemy was alive and in the vicinity searching for us, and to preserve our concealment, no flying ships were used to patrol the area – everything was done by foot. About a week after Medaron's uneasiness begun one of our patrols came across a native village which had been attacked by jaguars. The inhabitants had been torn to pieces by the animals, yet none of them had been fed upon, which was not in a jaguar's nature. Plus, these people were excellent hunters, yet not one dead jaguar could be found. They searched for survivors but were only able to find one young woman who was clutching a small gold ship in her hand. The patrol tried to help her, but her injuries were too severe. Just before she died she handed her golden ship to one of the soldiers and uttered one word – 'JeffRa'."

"Realizing the severity of the situation, the patrol transformed into horses and galloped back to warn us of the impending attack. However, JeffRa was waiting for them and set up an ambush about half way to the city. As before, the Oonock-Terrians attacked as jaguars while the true Terrians engaged in hand-to-hand combat. They caught our soldiers by complete surprise. Transforming into bears and outnumbered three to one, they engaged our enemy valiantly but took heavy casualties. I believe they all would have died and we would never

312

have known of JeffRa's presence had it not been for our unknown friends. I mentioned before the local forest natives believed we were their forest gods who had come to their land to live. Unbeknown to us, they had taken on the role of our protectors and had been protecting us from other tribes for years – in fact, since the day we arrived there. They viewed this new adversary the same. Using their silent blow guns and camouflaged by the jungle, the natives in death-like-silence attacked JeffRa's men and were able to kill a large majority of them. I don't believe they ever knew what hit them."

"Four of the natives helped our survivors back to the city, physically carrying two of them; the rest remained behind to assure no Terrians followed. When they arrived, Enok invited them in to not only thank them but to also give them sanctuary. They would not hear of it. They returned to their comrades to continue their fight and to protect us from the army that was advancing toward our city."

"The force field was activated and, with the indestructability of the stones we built the city with, we were impenetrable. Years of preparation ensured we could remain behind her walls for years, perhaps even decades. We had an inexhaustible food and water supply, all waste products were recycled, our power source was limitless and contained within the Complex and our new weaponry was ready. We were ready to engage our life long enemy –and again we waited."

"But at least this time we knew he was coming and there would be an end to our wait," Chancee interjected. "No more speculation, no more wondering if he was still alive."

"Yes, we knew," Jeanip replied. "And to his astonishment, JeffRa realized we were aware of his advancement and his element of surprise was lost. Too late he saw the flaw in his plan in regards to the natives. When he realized he would have to deal with them first before he could reach our city, JeffRa delayed his attack and sent his troops out to hunt them down and exterminate them. Luckily, once again JeffRa miscalculated the natives' abilities; having fought amongst themselves for centuries, they were masters at disappearing into the forest, of hiding where they could not be found. After a week of searching JeffRa gave up his search and set his sights once more on our city. As the sun rose on the eighth day we heard what sounded like thunder, but soon saw it was the footsteps of thousands of Terrians marching upon our city from all directions, with JeffRa leading the frontal attack astride a white stallion, a stallion who was one of the transformed Oonocks from our village. Somehow JeffRa's men had captured him and prevented him from transforming into another form. We could also see he had been horribly tortured. JeffRa shouted to Enok that his day of reckoning had arrived as he leaped from the stallion, removed a sword from its sheath and slit the stallion's throat. Helpless to do anything, we watched our soldier fall to the ground and return to his true form as his heart stopped beating. As his body began to dematerialize and our valiant soldier's life flowed out onto the ground, we stared in disbelief as JeffRa did the most horrible thing a being could do - he purposely stomped the soldier's water into the ground, grinding it into the dark brown dirt until all that remained was a circle of black, thick mud. I still to this day remember the look of joy and satisfaction on his face. Shouting the circle of mud was soon to be the fate of all Oonocks, he gave the order to attack. His army stormed the walls, blasting them with their advanced weapons, but unable to cause any damage due to the force field. They next tried catapulting fire bombs but they too were stopped. Everything JeffRa tried failed. We watched attempt after attempt to breach our walls fail for forty-two days. As long as the force field was active JeffRa could not reach us, but we were also prevented from firing upon them, for just as the shield prevented anything from entering the city it also prevented anything from going out. The Terrians stood outside our walls and the front gates, taunting us, yelling obscenities at us as no harm was inflicted upon them. Finally tired of the standoff, on the forty-third day JeffRa's army fell silent and withdrew into the forest."

"We saw nothing of them for fifteen days. And once again we waited, but this time our wait would not be a long one. At noon on the sixteenth day we heard the thunder once again of their advancing footsteps. But this time they advanced only from the front and brought with them a weapon so powerful our blood turned cold as we saw our impending doom. JeffRa had brought up the mountain numerous dark purple boulders of bendicor the size of automobiles, which he must have brought with him on his ships. We believe this was the reason it took him so many years to cross the ocean to reach us; he had to transport the stones and would not have taken any chance they would be lost at sea."

"This was the same purple stone that fueled our space ships, powered our cities, and energized our weapons. We were familiar with the tremendous power our small stones yielded and realized stones of this size, in this quantity, would easily bring down our city walls and end our existence. We knew we had no defense against this destruction and prepared for our city to be entered and hand-to-hand combat. We turned off the force field and began to fire upon the Terrians as they advanced, taking down as many as we could, but their numbers made our killings insignificant. They continued to advance, rolling the bendicor boulders amongst themselves until they had a line of bendicor against the front gate and walls. Seeing their plan, we retreated from the walls and waited at two side entrances planning to exit, swing around and surprise them as soon as the gate was blasted apart."

"The blast was so enormous it not only blew apart the front doors, it also took the front walls with it in addition to part of the side walls. The ground shook severely as huge fissures opened up in the earth outside the fortress, swallowing up many Terrians. Chunks of rock and dirt rained down from the sky, crushing both Oonocks and Terrians alike. Once the shaking subsided, and we were able to regain our footing, we exited the Complex and opened fire on the Terrians, surprising them for only a moment. A huge battle ensued. With the protection shield down and our walls compromised, the Terrians were able to finish blasting apart our structures, eliminating any place for our young ones to hide. The majority of our aircrafts were destroyed in the debris from the blast, but several were able to lift off seconds before the explosion and attack from the air, giving our youth some cover as they ran into the forest. We engaged the Terrians for two days, even fighting through the night as our weaponry lit up the darkness. We killed hundreds, perhaps even thousands of Terrians, but they kept coming. Our ammunition started to run low and our numbers continued to dwindle. We realized we were losing the battle and prepared for our annihilation. But then, as before, out of nowhere appeared hundreds of our Indian friends. They engaged the Terrians and the battle began to turn in our favor."

"Throughout the fighting JeffRa had looked for only one person – Enok. On the third day JeffRa finally spotted his brother and fought his way toward him. Before Enok knew it, JeffRa was behind him and delivered a serious blow. He fell to the ground next to a huge fissure that had opened in the ground. JeffRa stood over Enok while his men surrounded them, fighting off any who came to Enok's defense. JeffRa removed from his belt a special gun he had created just for killing the royal family, identical to the one Terrance gave me on the boat. He aimed it at Enok and prepared to fire, but JeffRa did not realize Medaron and I, along with a handful of others, including Sunam and Misso, had broken through the barrier and had come to Enok's defense. Medaron aimed her weapon at JeffRa's back and discharged her weapon, delivering a direct blow to JeffRa; she did not notice Enok trying to speak in order to prevent her from firing. JeffRa spun around to face Medaron and, to her horror, she saw clenched in his arm was Tiree, hers and Enok's first-born son. I remember the look of satisfaction on JeffRa's face as he smiled and fired his special weapon into Tiree's side. Medaron reached out to grab her son as JeffRa plunged himself and Tiree both over the side and down into the fissure, dropping his gun onto the ground as he fell. Medaron screamed and collapsed. Had Enok not grabbed her foot I fear she would have followed them over the edge."

"Her son?" Earon softly said. "I never knew I had an older brother."

"No, you wouldn't have," Chancee somberly stated. "Medaron never spoke of him, blaming herself for his death. And not wishing to cause her any pain neither Enok nor anyone else ever mentioned him."

"With JeffRa gone his regiment lost heart and withdrew," Jeanip continued. "Runbee was able to put together a small battalion and, with the help of the natives, hunted down the remaining Terrians. We always believed none escaped."

"We lost almost two-thirds of our Oonocks during the battle. Many more were wounded. Our city had been blasted apart and we only had three ships which were still flyable. Medaron was in shock and Enok was gravely injured. Having nowhere else to go, we decided to return to the Ocean Complex. But it was a long way to the ocean and, if Enok was going to have any chance for survival, he had to return to the Complex at once. If we did not get him immersed in our home waters within the next few hours, he was going to die and any home water we had in the city was now blasted away. Leaving Sunam in charge, I flew Enok to the Ocean Complex. Medaron followed in another flier. The third flier carried one of our few living medical personnel. The trip to our Complex took three hours to get there and three to return, plus unloading time. Since the fliers were only capable of carrying one Oonock at a time in addition to the pilot and, the fact it was a seven hour round trip, taking the wounded out by flier was not feasible. We had to come up with another plan or lose a good portion of our wounded."

"We decided Sunam, along with a handful of Oonocks, would put the severely wounded in stasis at the bottom of the saltwater lake where they could remain until we could retrieve them and take them to the Complex. They also needed to search the forest for our youth, who had sought refuge in her undergrowth. Once these two tasks were accomplished, Sunam was to start down the mountain and work his way toward the ocean, taking with him the less wounded and anyone who was able to walk. Their exodus would take four days to complete, and we agreed I would meet them at the ocean's edge to help bring our survivors back to the Complex. With the help of our native friends Sunam was able to quickly find our lost youth and transport the severely wounded to the lake, where he and several other Oonocks took them below. The natives then helped bring the survivors down the mountain and through the jungle, but even with their help it was a horrible journey.

About a fourth of the injured did not make it. We had arrived on this planet with thirty-two hundred Waters. About ninety children had been born since our arrival, ten seniors had died, seventy-two were in stasis at the bottom of the lake and three hundred and eight had remained either at the Ocean Complex or were living apart doing studies or just enjoying themselves. When Sunam met me on the beach, his band of Oonocks totaled eight hundred and thirty-nine. JeffRa's revenge had taken a heavy toll."

"Once everyone from the beach was back at the Ocean Complex, Sunam, Misso, Runbee, Graybin, Swaybuk and I, along with several other Oonocks, returned to the lake to retrieve our injured. Luckily, there had been three fliers left at the Complex thus giving us a total of six ships to transport our severely wounded. When we returned we were surprised and very pleased to discover our native friends had remained there protecting our people below from any possible enemy. We brought up six Oonocks at a time and flew them back to the Complex."

"That's incredible," Europa commented. "I cannot believe the natives continued to guard our people. Did any of the Oonocks you brought from the lake survive?"

"Luckily, they all made it, although some had long recoveries and were permanently disabled," Jeanip continued.

"But not only did they protect our wounded, they had actually caught eight Terrians and held them captive," Chancee added.

"They had Terrians?" Earon asked, amazement clearly visible on his and on the other two listeners' faces.

"Yes," Jeanip replied, smiling. "You can imagine my shock when I saw these eight Terrians hanging from a tree. We were able to interrogate them and learn what JeffRa had been up to the past few hundred years."

"What happened to them?" Europa asked.

Jeanip looked at Europa. "You must remember, Your Highness, we were at war and these Terrians were our mortal enemies. Law dictated their execution. But, as a reward for all they had done for us, I allowed the natives to decide their fate."

"Did they kill them?" Terrance asked, intrigued.

"Let us say they disposed of them according to their way," was all Jeanip said.

"While we transported the injured, several of our soldiers began the task of collecting any fragments of the purple boulders still remaining. This stone is capable of so much energy and power, even in its smallest form, we could not chance it falling into human hands. Their search for fragments produced only a small sack of broken stones because the energy of the blast had vaporized most of the boulders. After collecting the stone, they then began the task of removing any advanced technology from the destroyed city and erasing any indication of our existence. The human world would never know of the battle great war fought between two alien races, other than the fragmented blocks of granite and sandstone and the stories passed down through the centuries by the natives. I understand the humans have in recent years been excavating in the area of our city and have uncovered several pieces of the original front doors and side walls. There has even been some speculation it was built by some alien race." Everyone chuckled at Jeanip's statement.

"I wonder what people would say if they knew their speculation was the actual truth?" Terrance stated.

"Luckily, all they have is speculation," Chancee laughed.

"After the area had been cleaned and proof of our existence erased, Sunam and I returned to do a final inspection and to thank the natives for their tremendous help; we surely would have perished without their intervention. But when we returned they were gone, retreating back into the cover of the forest. The only sign that remained to show they had been there were the hundreds of flower bouquets laying where our gates use to stand."

"Did you ever find them?" Europa asked.

"No, we never saw our friends again and we never got to thank them. My last act before leaving the city for the last time was to gather some of the flowers they had left and throw them into the fissure where Tiree had fallen."

"Enok recovered at the Complex, but his injuries were more serious than any one realized. In fact, it wouldn't be until centuries later the true extent of his injuries would be known. As Enok fought to live, Medaron remained secluded in her habitat in a dangerous state of deep depression, grieving for the son she had lost, blaming herself for his death. She saw no one except Misso and myself and never said a word to either of us during this time. We could not even get her to visit Enok at the medical building. Enok laid on his medical bed fighting for his life, desperately needing to return home to help Medaron deal with the loss of their son, but physically unable to. Medaron laid on her bed, withdrawn into a world of silence and despair, unaware of anything except her sorrow."

"I thought we were going to lose them both," Chancee stated.

"How did they pull through?" Earon asked.

"Somehow Enok found the strength to get well and return home, although he left the medical facility way too early," Jeanip answered. "I have often wondered if he would have stayed longer if he might not be afflicted now with that breathing problem. But recover he did and he saved them both. I believe he willed himself to remain alive because he knew if he flowed out we would also lose your mother."

"A quanish has great power and can even defeat death," Chancee quietly stated, turning his gaze to Terrance.

Jeanip disregarded Chancee's remark and quickly returned to his story; he knew if he paused for even a second there would be all kinds of questions about what a 'quanish' was. "While we waited for Enok's return Misso and I tried to convince Medaron Tiree's death was not her fault, that had she not shot JeffRa Enok would be dead also. I don't know if she heard what we said or not, for she never spoke. She spent her day staring at the purple stone with her face carved on it, the same purple stone that had powered the weapon JeffRa used to kill Tiree."

Terrance reached into his pocket and removed the purple stone Mr. Dark Feather had given him. "Was it like this one, the one you gave me, Mr. Dark Feather?" he asked.

"That IS the stone," Chancee answered, as he remembered back to that day. "I remember the day I got it like it was yesterday. It was the day Enok returned from the medical building and I went to visit him and Medaron. When I entered their habitat I saw a very concerned Enok sitting in the front room with Jeanip. Like Jeanip, I believed he left the medical building too early but knew he felt his place was with Medaron. Enok told me he was not able to get Medaron to break her silence, to come out of her room even though he felt she was glad he was there. I will never forget the look on his face as he asked me if there was anything I could do to help bring her back to him. I agreed to try and asked for permission to enter her room. Upon entering I was shocked to see her; she had lost a lot of weight and there was no life in her eyes. I could see she was walking a very fine line between death and life and understood instantly Enok's concern. Not knowing if I could help or not, I sat down beside her. That's when I saw the stone from JeffRa's gun in her hand. She had worn the edges smooth from turning it over in her hand again and again. I reached over and gently took it, promising her I would keep it safe and, to my dismay, she let me have it. After saying a prayer over her I reminded her she was our monarch, and now, more than ever, her people, and especially Enok, needed her. She looked into my eyes but said nothing. She must have heard me because two days later she emerged from her room and once again became our monarch, putting the needs of her people above her own and nursing Enok back to health. If she continued to grieve she did it privately."

Europa held out her hand. "May I see that, Terrance?" she asked. Terrance placed the stone in her outstretched hand. She turned it over and looked at its carvings. "Why is my mother's face carved on the stone?" she asked, lifting her vision to meet Mr. Dark Feather's. "Why did he not use his own face for the carving?"

"I believe Jeanip has that answer," Chancee stated, nodding toward Jeanip.

"JeffRa fashioned a special weapon to kill the royal family," Jeanip said, looking at Europa. "Its power source was a small purple stone on which we believe he carved Medaron's face – sort of a bullet with your name on it. He would use only this weapon with this marked stone to complete his revenge."

"But why my mother's face? Why not my father's or the person he was going to kill?" Europa asked, still wondering why JeffRa chose her mother as the symbol of his revenge.

"I have my suspicions, but I don't know for sure," Jeanip confessed. "I believe your father may know the reason."

"How did you know, Mr. Dark Feather, to give the stone to Terrance, that we would need it on our journey?" Europa asked, handing the stone back to Terrance and looking directly at Mr. Dark Feather.

"Somethings one just knows," was all Chancee said.

Terrance held the stone out in his hand to give it back to Chancee. "No, Terrance, you keep it," Chancee said. "I feel its power is still needed on your journey. But I do ask one favor of you three," he continued, pointing to the three young beings. "When you arrive at FarCore, place it on one of the tables and leave it there. There it will be safe for all eternity, as I promised Medaron."

"What is FarCore?" Earon asked. "I have heard it mentioned several times over the years."

"FarCore? Mother mentioned in her diary that FarCore is where the Orbs are kept. Has our destination changed? Are we going to FarCore instead of Saint's Isle?" Europa asked.

"No, Saint's Isle is still our destination. As for FarCore, that is another tale," Jeanip answered. "For now, I need to complete this one."

REBUILDING

"We returned to the Ocean Complex with the survivors and wounded. There was not a family who had not lost at least two family members in the battle. Some families were totally wiped out; some had only one or two members remaining. There were children who had lost both parents, parents who had lost their children. The devastation wreaked upon our race was almost unsurvivable, but survive we did. New families were formed. Parents without children took in children with no parents. Families of one or two were incorporated into new, larger families. Those widowed connected with other widowers. During this time Enok continued to recover from his injuries and, somehow together, he and Medaron dealt with the loss of Tiree. They reunited and their love for each became even stronger; and from that great love you were produced, Earon, a true sign of life's renewal. With Enok and Medaron's guidance we began to rebuild our society, but it was a slow process. And while we rebuilt it we remained secured and hidden deep in the ocean depths for over eight hundred years."

"As before, we sent scouts out into the world to search for any signs of Terrians while we remained hidden in the ocean's depths. Occasionally we found a few and immediately eliminated them, but their numbers were small. After the first three hundred years we found no evidence any more existed. As for JeffRa, to the best of our knowledge he died that day Medaron shot him. But since we found no body, we had no way to prove his death. "

"Why would there be a body?" Terrance inquired. "Since he was an Oonock, wouldn't he have flowed out into the dirt?"

"Yes, that is true, Terrance, if JeffRa was still Oonock," Jeanip replied "Remember, he had been living as a Terrian for many millennia and we had no way of knowing if he would retain his human form, a Terrian form or revert back into a Waters and flow out. So as a precaution, we kept open the possibility he was still alive."

"During the first several hundred years of our isolation, as families were being rebuilt, we were blessed with forty male Oonocks, including Earon, and five female Oonocks, two of which were born away from the Complex. Tragically, the three females born at the Complex did not survive past their tenth year. Females are very rare in our society and highly valued; their loss was devastating to the Complex. Their deaths showed us to what extent JeffRa's revenge had extended into our lives. Evidently, JeffRa had spent his years of searching for us to imagine and invent every conceivable way to end our existence and eradicate us from the universe. He had embedded inside his bendicor a silent weapon to interfere with our ability to not only conceive, but it prevented any female child that was born at the Complex from reaching adolescence. Our medical personnel tried to correct the problems but, by the time we discovered JeffRa's trickery, the virus was too ingrained in our systems to be removed; thus meaning that once the current Oonocks have flowed into the water our race on this planet will no longer exist. And if we are the last remaining Oonocks still alive, when we are gone our race will exist no more." Jeanip looked at the trio before him, watching the looks on their faces. Like Chancee and himself, Europa, Earon and Terrance realized the doomed future of the Oonock and the elimination of a great and noble race.

There was a knock at the door as a young female from the galley entered announcing she had brought lunch for them. Jeanip announced it was a good time to take a quick break while the galley personnel brought in salads, sandwiches, fresh fruit and deserts. Twenty minutes later everyone was seated around the table preparing to eat while Jeanip continued his story.

"Now, where did I leave off? I believe I had just explained about our procreation problem."

"Even though our Complex was beautiful, and had anything we needed, it still was confining. It became more difficult to keep up the Oonocks' morale, especially after we learned the devastating truth of our future and inability to conceive. In an attempt to deal with this devastation, Enok and Medaron encouraged everyone to transform into other forms of life and live apart from the Complex. Some returned to the main land as humans, some transformed into Mobies to explore the oceans and some decided to remain in their true form and pursued new areas of study. With the threat of JeffRa and the Terrians gone, some chose to try to contact the other ships that had fled Europa. A group that became known as the 'Callers' transformed into Mobies and began singing high-pitched whale songs into space, hoping their songs would be heard and a rescue would come."

"Enok and Medaron knew our race's only chance of survival was finding the other space ships that left Europa. They hoped their DNA could be synthesized to produce an antidote to correct our reproduction problem. And even if it couldn't, our males might be able to breed with their females since it appeared most of the damage was in our females' genes. Our ships were no longer space worthy, so Enok followed the Callers lead and designed a signal that could be seen from space. He sent a small team up to the surface and instructed them to find a suitable location somewhere close to our last city where a signal could be designed into the earth. They returned within days with news they had found the perfect site about eight hundred miles northwest of the destroyed city. It was close to the ocean, which not only made it easily accessible for the Oonocks, but any Oonock ship that did come to investigate the planet would search along the oceans for signs of surviving Oonocks. The site was also remote, thus assuring the signal could be constructed with little human interference and would remain undisturbed. Enok immediately sent out his engineers to burn a message into the ground."

"What did the message look like?" Earon asked, curious because he had never heard mention of a signal.

"It's only about a mile long," Jeanip explained. "It consists of a number of meter wide holes that are located in a strip eight holes deep. From space the holes look like dots and can be read as a message because of the way they are arranged. From the ground, it looks like nothing except random holes."

"Ingenious," Earon smiled. "What does the message say?"

"It reads 'We are here – the Oonocks'," Chancee replied. "Even though we have had no response yet, we are still hopeful."

"That was one of the reasons Enok had it constructed in stone – it should last for thousands of years so, even if a ship happens to investigate this planet after we are all gone, they will know we were here once," Jeanip explained.

"Let's continue, we have a long way to go yet," Jeanip stated, as he poured himself a cup of coffee. "I believe it was in the early 1600's when Enok decided it was time for Medaron, Earon and himself to return to a life above. Medaron still suffered occasionally from depression and he thought a change of scenery might help her. He sent me and Chancee above to purchase a large parcel of land where a cottage could be constructed. He wanted the land to be on a cliff overlooking the ocean below with scenic mountains in the background, a place blessed by nature, with fields of wildflowers and lots of trees for the wind to blow through for Medaron and Earon. A serene, peaceful location that would remain so as humans evolved."

"We found the perfect location, which was claimed by a band of Native Americans. They were a nation of warriors who valued honor and integrity, a peaceful nation that lived as one with nature. We were the first white men they had ever met and they were intrigued by our skin color. Like the forest natives of South America, they believed we were spirits, but Water Spirits, not Forest Spirits, since we had walked out of the water. They invited us into their camp and Chancee was able to quickly learn their language and their customs. He tried to persuade the chief to sell us a large portion of land at the southern end of their territory, promising those who would come to live there would also be one with nature and honor their traditions. He told the chief the new comers had powers which they would use to protect the tribe from their enemies and allow them to live in peace. Understandably, the chief was cautious and would not commit to giving us the land. Luckily for us, a nearby warring tribe captured the chief's daughter soon after this refusal and took her to their camp. Knowing his beloved daughter would be beaten severely and killed, or worse yet, forced to live her life as a slave, the chief came and pleaded with us to use our powers and save his daughter. Seeing a chance to win the land we wanted, we went to the other village and rescued his daughter. When we returned her to the chief we requested the land we had originally asked for in addition to a good section of land that had belonged to their enemy. He could not refuse."

"That's the story I asked you about, Mr. Dark Feather, the one I found in your book," Terrance stated. "It's the one my father, I mean stepfather, was interested in."

"That is correct," Chancee responded. "However, Jeanip's telling of the story is a more accurate account than the one I wrote in my book. Now that I know JeffRa survived I wish I had never written it."

"What happened to the other tribe?" Earon asked. "I cannot imagine you would have killed them for the land."

"No, we do not kill others so we may possess what they have. That is not our philosophy of life. Chancee thought of a solution which caused them no harm yet granted us the chief's daughter release and our acquisition of their land," Jeanip replied. "It was quite ingenious!"

"What did you do?" asked Europa, as she turned to face Chancee, seeing the look of amusement on his face.

"Since we were spirits of air and water, I thought they should have a trip through the sky. We crammed them into a container and flew them about five hundred miles away and sat them down in a big valley," Chancee stated, chuckling as he remembered the look on their faces when they saw where they were. "To say the least, they never came back to their lands."

"How did Mr. Dark Feather end up staying with the first tribe?" Earon asked.

"The chief was more than willing to give us his enemy's land, but his land came with a condition: that I remain with them," Chancee reported. "I'm not sure if the stipulation was because they feared me or respected me. But, for whatever reason, the chief knew that as long as I remained with the tribe his people could live happily, free from any form of aggression and needing for nothing."

"So, thanks to Chancee, whom the natives called Thomas Dark Feather, we had the land we needed," Jeanip continued.

"So that's how you came to have two names," Europa stated, now understanding why humans referred to him as Thomas Dark Feather but Jeanip and the other Oonocks called him Chancee.

"Yes, he is one of the few Oonocks who has two names," Jeanip smiled, interrupting his story just long enough to answer her question. "I returned to the Complex to advise Enok of our success while Chancee remained in their camp. Enok had been working on the cottage blueprints along with detailed security measures while we were away and, upon my return, immediately assigned me the task of building Minnos. Returning with a small band of engineers and builders, we began construction on the dwelling and were able to complete Enok's plans in several days. But the security measures, including the secret passage, were so extensive and detailed that it took us several weeks to complete them. Even though Enok was almost positive the threat of JeffRa and the Terrians was gone, he was not willing to take a chance with his Medaron and Earon's lives. Thus Minnos was built, a serene place where Medaron could enjoy life while outfitted with the most sophisticated security system in the universe."

"Accompanied by a small elite security detail and myself, Enok sent Medaron to the surface to view their new hideaway. I don't remember what it was, but some urgent business at the Complex kept Enok from coming with her. He told Medaron to decorate the cottage in any fashion she desired and he promised to join her when she was finished. I still remember the look on her face as she took that first step inside – it was the first time I had seen her truly happy since Tiree was killed, except for the day Earon was born. I saw a change in her that day. It was as if all the horrors of the past had been erased. She loved life again and it clearly showed in the twinkle in her eyes."

"Medaron spent the next three months decorating the cottage. I had never seen her so energized, so excited, so dedicated, so committed to a project. She had us paint the walls, build furniture, add a porch that covered the entire circumference of the cottage. She drew up a list of items to bring up from the Complex to enhance the cottage. Each night she sat by the fireplace, hand sewing curtains for the windows. She purchased rugs, baskets and pottery from the natives. To make the cottage a true paradise, she had us gather seeds and plant fields of wildflowers surrounding it. We even planted an extensive vegetable garden. Medaron turned the cottage and its yard into a beautiful home. Finally, she was ready for Enok to join her. But JeffRa's revenge was not finished with her or Enok yet."

"The long awaited day arrived and Enok surfaced to live with Medaron and Earon in the paradise his mate had created for them at Minnos. He was amazed at what she had done with the cottage. He too saw a spark in her he had not seen for a very long time. And he could also see that type of life suited Earon, for he was happy and thriving in the oxygen environment. That night Enok and Medaron slept together in their new bedroom, renewing their deep love for each other, enthralled by their new life and long-denied passions. Their new life had begun and, with it, the promise of a brighter future for their people. But that future was not to be, for when Enok awoke the next morning something was wrong; he had trouble breathing. Each attempt to take air into his lungs became more agonizing than the last. Finally, having no option, Enok was forced to return to the Complex for medical attention and that's when he learned the injury JeffRa had inflicted upon him hundreds of years before had permanently damaged his ability to breathe when transformed into any air-breathing creature. His and Medaron's dreams of living above were destroyed. Although Enok tried his best to persuade her to remain above with Earon for a while and enjoy the home she had so lovingly created, Medaron would not hear of it. She and Earon returned to the Complex to live with Enok. On the day she left she commanded me to add the secret attic and store all her valuables,

327

hoping to return one day with her beloved Enok, a day that never occurred."

"Chancee remained with the natives to fulfill his promise of protection and to manage Minnos. Years later, when a town was built not far from Minnos, he hired a young couple to be caretakers and overseers. Their decedents continued to care for Minnos throughout the years. Medaron would occasionally return to update the cottage, adding the crystal chandeliers, the tapestries and other fine furnishings. During these trips she always made time to visit the native camp to see how they were doing and to inquire if they needed anything."

"Did the natives or townspeople not wonder why she never aged? If I am not mistaken, we are talking a time span of about three hundred years," Europa asked.

"The natives believed she was a water spirit, an eternal being that did not age so they would have been shocked if she HAD looked different," Jeanip explained. "As for the townspeople, Medaron used different names and altered her appearance to look like the descendent of the Waters who came before her. I was always amazed no one ever saw through her disguises."

"And so life for us continued. Then about twenty years ago a miracle happened. Medaron learned she was carrying a female child, the first child to be implanted in over five hundred years, the first female monarch in over eight thousand years. This was joyous news," Jeanip said, looking directly at Europa. He did not want her to misunderstand the next part of his tale. "Oonocks celebrated the news, your parents were ecstatic and Earon reveled in the fact he was to be a big brother. But, with this fantastic news came the remembrance of JeffRa's curse: no female conceived or born at the Complex had survived."

"Enok and Medaron sat down and seriously considered their options. We had been on this planet for over six thousand years and, other than the distress call from Mars, we had never heard from another Oonock. The messages the Callers constantly sang went unanswered, as did our message of holes. We told ourselves perhaps the other ships had traveled too far into space to come back for us, perhaps they had perished on other worlds, or perhaps JeffRa had found them and destroyed them before he came to Mars and Earth. Whatever the reason, Enok decided it was time to resolve ourselves to the fact no rescue was ever coming. We were alone. Having no chance of reproducing we would one day start dying off, leaving fewer and fewer Oonocks until only one would remain – you, Europa. Your parents envisioned you living for centuries, possibly millennia alone and without the companionship of others of your kind. They could not, would not condemn you to that fate."

"But if Medaron became pregnant, couldn't the other women do the same?" Terrance asked.

"We hoped such, but when our medical personnel examined our females they found no change. I said Europa was a miracle. It was never known what changed to allow her mother to conceive her, for she was never able to conceive again."

"But the reality that a rescue was not coming was not the only problem. Humans had made huge advancements in their technology. They now had deep sea submersibles capable of exploring the ocean's depths and robotic submersibles which had almost no limit as to what depth they could explore. Although the humans had explored only about ten percent of the ocean's floor, Enok knew it was just a matter of time before they would search for new discoveries in the vicinity of the Complex. He believed their technological advancements in the next fifty to hundred years would necessitate the abandonment and destruction of the Complex to keep humans from gaining our technology."

Looking at Europa, Jeanip continued. "Knowing these facts, your parents decided your only chance of survival and a happy life was to be born on land – as a human. As a human you would live a normal human life span with no special powers, but you would not be left alone. To ensure you a happy life you were never to know your true identity or where your parents came from. You would never know of the terrible war your people fought or the revenge JeffRa afflicted upon us."

"Also, for your protection, and Earon's too, Enok ordered Sunam to construct Saint's Isle. Enok and Medaron wanted an alternative place of sanctuary in case Terrians still existed and were intent on carrying out JeffRa's oath of revenge. Or worse yet, JeffRa himself was still alive. And, just like our last city, it was totally self-sustaining. Medaron made sure it was filled with everything imaginable to ensure any time spent there would be an enjoyable one. And Enok made sure it was a fortress, a place of sanctuary where neither JeffRa nor any Terrian could ever reach his children."

"While Sunam worked on Saint's Isle, I prepared the cottage for Medaron's return. New security alerts and fences were put in, new security protocols enacted. To ensure your safety Enok ordered that Medaron, Earon and you, Europa, have a guard with them twenty-four hours a day. I was assigned as Medaron's protector while Earon volunteered to be yours. Since your protector had to be someone you could take everywhere with you – school, the beach, dates, etc., Earon chose to transform into a canine, a Rottweiler to be exact; a being no one would question why it was with you."

"I never knew I had a protector," Earon stated, stunned to hear this news. "Who was assigned to protect me?"

"If you never knew then he certainly did the task assigned him," Jeanip smiled. "Tinderoon was your protector. Didn't you ever wonder why he often went places with you, accompanied you when you went out on patrol with Runbee, always rode with you when you went out on horseback? In addition to these times, he often followed you without your knowledge. When you use to accompany Europa to school he was nearby, hidden so you would not see him. You are a monarch, Earon, and as such, security protocol dictates you must be protected at all times. His last act of protection was when he remained in the kitchen at Minnos to keep the Terrians from following you into the cave."

"I had no idea," Earon replied, now sorrowful he had not known. "I just thought he came with me because I was closer to his age. I wish I would have done more with him."

"Like your sister, you cannot know something that is deliberately hidden from you," Jeanip replied.

Europa looked at Earon. "I know how you feel, Earon. I felt the same way when I learned who Sunam and Misso really were."

Jeanip smiled, delighted to see the bond between the two siblings. "I brought Medaron and Earon to the surface along with Birea as Europa's second protector, Misso as Medaron's helper, Tinderoon as Earon's protector and Ebar, Mintoo and Sunam. All were highly trained soldiers. And of course Evonic, our personal medic. Even though we may look human, there are differences a human doctor would not be able to explain, so it was necessary to have our own physician."

"Yeah, like having purple blood," Terrance chimed in, smiling.

"Like having purple blood," Jeanip said, smiling back. "Then, about eight months later, you were born, Europa. Our pasts were fabricated so you would have a normal life. The plan was for you to grow into adulthood, pursue your destiny and then, at the appropriate age, pass on, never knowing who or what your parents truly were. But JeffRa changed all that the day he ambushed your mother. Everything else you pretty well know."

"Mother told me my father died at sea, that he was a treasure hunter," Europa said. "Was that part of the fabrication also? Is my father still alive?"

Jeanip looked at Earon then back at Europa. "In some respects your father was a treasure hunter. And yes, he still resides in the Ocean Complex, although your mother believed he was gone." Jeanip watched Europa's face as she learned the truth her father was alive. After all that had happened he was not sure how she would take it. He quickly looked over to Earon and could see once more the rage beginning to bubble inside him.

"Why did Mother believe he was dead?" Europa asked

"Your parents had a very deep connection, a connection that far exceeds what humans are capable of. Enok could feel her sorrow and pain caused by their separation. When he was given the news our medical personnel could not cure his breathing problem as they hoped and he could never live above in human form, he decided it would be kinder for her to believe he had perished. I think he hoped it would lessen her sorrow," Jeanip answered. "Although he never said it, I believe he regretted this decision years later, but at the time he did what he felt was right."

"He should never have done that," Earon stated.

"As I've said to you before, Earon, it is not for us to judge him," Jeanip replied. "He is our Head Monarch and, as such, his word is law, even if we do not agree with it."

"Jeanip, in the back of my mother's diary are references to bank accounts totaling billions of dollars. Are they accurate?" Europa asked.

"Yes and no. They were accurate about ten years ago. Since then more has been added to them," Jeanip replied. "I would estimate the total has probably doubled, perhaps even tripled."

"But where did all this money come from?" Europa asked.

"From the ocean," Jeanip answered. "Being creatures of the deep we had access to a wealth of sunken ships and their treasures. Over the years the gold and jewels were brought up and sold, the money put into accounts for Oonocks to use whenever they spent time above. So you see, in reality, your father, along with all Oonocks, are treasure hunters."

Once again there was a knock at the door and a young man stepped in to announce dinner would be ready in twenty minutes. He inquired if they wished him to serve dinner there or in the meal room. Jeanip rose from his seat. "It seems we have a bit of dilemma. My tale is basically over but there is still more I have to tell you and you have not gotten to ask your questions. While I believe it would be best for us

331

to eat now, and then get some rest before we leave, I leave this up to you three. We will have time during the next part of our voyage where I can finish my story and answer your questions. Or we can delay dinner and skip the rest period and I can tell it to you now. The choice is yours."

Europa looked at Terrance and Earon. "What do you two think?"

"I know you really want to hear it all, Sis," Earon responded. "As do I. But I think we are all going to need some rest before we head out again. I vote Jeanip tell us later."

Europa looked at Terrance. "I'm in agreement," Terrance replied. "We're not going to be much good out there if we are too tired to stay awake. Just promise me that once he tells you, you will tell me."

Europa nodded at Terrance then turned to Jeanip. "You are right. Right now it is more important we rest and are in top condition for the next part of our journey. We may still have many dangers ahead to face and we will need to think clearly."

"The true decision of a monarch," Jeanip stated. "You have put your own needs behind the needs of those you protect." Jeanip turned and advised the kitchen helper they would dine in the meal room.

"You are going to be a great leader of our people," Chancee said. "I look forward to your rule."

"Jeanip, do I have time to ask a few quick questions?" Europa said, as she stood.

"I believe the young male said we had twenty minutes," Jeanip replied. "Ask your questions."

"You said the Oonocks transform into Mobies when they come to the surface. The day the Terrians attacked Minnos I saw a whale destroy the Terrian vessel. By any chance was that my . . ."

"Your father?" completed Jeanip. "Yes, Europa, that was Enok. Even though he could not be with you, he always watched over you."

"Somehow I knew it was him," Europa stated. "My next question is this: What happened the day my mother was killed? You said you would tell me the truth once we arrived. And Mr. Dark Feather said he would explain why the Orb enabled me to heal you."

"That we did, Europa," Jeanip replied looking at Chancee. "Unfortunately, we do not have enough time for me to explain what happened the day your mother died, but I believe Chancee can give you a condensed version on how you were able to heal me."

"The truth is, Your Majesty, I am not sure how you are doing the things you are doing," Chancee confessed. "But if I were to take an educated guess, I would speculate the Orb is somehow changing you, almost reconstructing your DNA in order to make you into a real Oonock. And by changing you it has awaken long dormant powers asleep for thousands of years in Oonocks. "

"But I thought my Mother was not a healer?" Europa stated.

"That is true, My Child, thus my dilemma on why you are. I believe we will have to wait to see the real reason you were able to heal Jeanip and what else the Orbs have in mind for you."

"May I ask one more quick question?"

"Of course," Jeanip replied.

"The incidents you told us about occurred over hundreds, even thousands of years. May I ask how old you are, Jeanip?"

Jeanip looked at her and smiled. "Time here is different than time on Europa. In earth years we came to this planet over six thousand years ago. I, myself, am just under nine thousand." Jeanip smiled as he saw the astonished look on Europa and Terrance's faces. "Now I believe I have given you more than enough to think about. Let us go and dine, then prepare for the next stage of our voyage."

As the travelers exited the room Europa looked up at Earon and asked, "If Jeanip is almost nine thousand years old, how old are you?"

"I am just a youngster," Earon replied, giving his sister a smile. "In Earth years I am one thousand two hundred and fifty-nine years old."

"That's considered to be the age of a youngster?" Terrance asked. "Guess that makes Europa and I just gleams in our parents' eyes." The three laughed as they walked to the dining area. Jeanip had indeed given them much to think about.

THE VOYAGE CONTINUES

After their meal the four returned to their room where Terrance, Europa and Earon rested for several hours while Jeanip kept watch over them. It was hard for Terrance and Europa to sleep with all Jeanip had told them. They kept going over the story in their minds, thinking of new questions to ask, trying to comprehend everything. Finally sleep overcame them, bringing them dreams of ancient civilizations and flying air ships. As he watched Terrance and his sleeping monarchs, Jeanip's eyes began to grow heavy until he too was fast asleep.

"Europa, Terrance, it is time to wake up," Earon said softly to awaken the two. "But keep your voices low. Jeanip is still sleeping."

Europa opened her eyes and saw Jeanip asleep in a chair not far from her, once again keeping his promise not to leave her side. She looked up at her brother and quietly asked, "Earon, Jeanip said he is almost nine thousand years old. Will you live that long also?"

"Here, you might want to put this on," Earon said handing Europa and Terrance each a thick sweatshirt. "It is going to be pretty cold out on the water." Looking at Europa he answered her question. "No one knows for sure how long we will live here on earth. At home Jeanip would be middle aged, so I suspect we will probably live to be at least eleven to fourteen thousand years old, give or take a century or two." Earon laughed, thinking his comment was humorous. He could see by the astonished looks on the others faces they thought it incredible.

With a serious look on her face, Europa asked her brother, "Earon, how old will I become?"

A somber look spread across Earon's face. "I am not sure, Sis, probably a normal human's life span. I would imagine eighty or ninety years. But I do not think anyone really knows. You are the first Oonock to be born as a human. We have seen what you can do with the Orb, so some of our genetic makeup has to be in you. You too may be able to live for a long time."

"Can I transform like you do?" she asked.

"I have been wondering that myself," Earon responded. "That is something you should ask Jeanip or even Mr. Dark Feather."

"That is something you should ask your father," Jeanip replied, as he began to awaken.

Fed, refreshed and ready to continue their voyage, the four travelers walked down to the docks to board their vessel. As they arrived they saw their white, wooden boat plus three more identical to it. There was also a black fiberglass speed boat in the middle of the four.

"This time we're traveling in the black speed boat," Jeanip stated, pointing to the boat. "Two of the white vessels will exit the channel in front of us and two behind us. Each will then proceed in a different direction separate from our course. If someone IS watching the ocean we hope they will follow the decoys and not us."

"But won't the fact that our boat is the only black one kind of give them a hint which one is ours?" Terrance asked, thinking that's what he would assume if he was a Terrian.

"Although that would be the logical assumption, it is in error," replied Jeanip. "The black boat is designed to blend into the ocean so it is almost invisible to the naked eye in the dark."

Jeanip turned and faced Earon. "Earon, would you please take Europa to the boat and wait for me at the walkway? Europa, I will personally escort you aboard, so please wait for me there. I have something I need to discuss with Terrance before we leave." Turning toward Terrance he gestured for Terrance to follow him. "Terrance, if you would follow me." Noting the worried and concerned look on Europa's face, he turned back to Europa. "Don't worry, Your Majesty. He will join you shortly on the boat. I just need to discuss our trip with him. I will be just a few steps away from you. As promised, I am not leaving you alone."

"I know, Jeanip," Europa answered, giving him a big smile. Europa watched as Jeanip and Terrance took several steps away from the vessel so they could speak privately. "I will wait for you and Terrance here," she announced. She had no intentions of boarding the boat until she was sure Terrance was also coming.

"Terrance, before we leave I need to make sure you understand what is about to happen. The journey we embark on is going to be very dangerous," Jeanip stated, looking directly at Terrance. "Europa and Earon must make it; you do not. You were caught up in this tragedy without any say. Terrance, I want to give you that chance now. If you would like you can end your journey now and remain here with Mr. Dark Feather. Since you know who and what we are, and where we are going, you would have to remain here for a couple of weeks, a month at most. But once Europa is safe you'd be free to go. If you continue this journey with us you must realize there is no coming back for months, perhaps even years. Once we reach our destination you will be a liability and I will not be able to allow you to leave. I know you have a mother and family back in Australia. Are you ready to be separated from them for that length of time? I know you care deeply for Europa, but is this something you really want to do? There is no shame in remaining behind. You have been a great asset to us. Without your help we would not have made it this far. So what is your decision, Son?"

Without hesitation Terrance replied, "If you'll have me, Jeanip, I would like to continue the journey with you. I can't leave Europa; I could never live with myself if I let her continue this journey alone. Plus, I would always be haunted with not knowing if she had made it to safety or not. I feel my presence is still needed, almost as if there is something I am destined to do to assure her continued life. I think Mr. Dark Feather senses it too; that's why he gave me back the purple stone. If he simply wanted it taken to FarCore he could have given it to either Earon or Europa, but he didn't - he purposely gave it to me. You said I have been a great asset to you. I would very much like to continue to be one."

"And what about your family?" Jeanip asked, wanting to be doubly sure Terrance realized what he would be giving up by going with them.

"If I can have a few minutes, I'll write my mother a letter which Mr. Dark Feather can mail when he feels it is safe. I'll let her know I finally decided to join the Secret Service. She'll believe that because I've been talking about doing it for the past few years. I'll tell her I've been assigned to an elite unit battling terrorism and we have been deployed so I won't be able to contact her for some time   And I'll be sure to tell her I love her and not to worry about me."

Terrance could see the look of esteem in Jeanip's eyes. "It would be an honor to have you come along. You are a valiant man, Mr. Landers, worthy of being a Waters." Jeanip held out his hand and shook Terrance's. "You've got ten minutes to write your letter."

Terrance turned and smiled at Europa. "I'll be right back," he said, as he ran with his backpack to a large rock and quickly sat down.

Fearful Jeanip had said or done something to prevent him from coming with them, Europa began to follow Terrance. Jeanip stepped in front of her and gently grabbed her shoulders. "It's okay, Your Majesty. He's not leaving. He has something he has to do and then he'll be right back to finish our journey." Jeanip could see Europa was having trouble believing his words. "I promise you, Europa. He IS coming with us. I swear this to you on my honor as your guardian and faithful servant." Europa knew if Jeanip was using his honor as proof Terrance was going with them, than it had to be true. Seeing Europa believed him at last, Jeanip stepped on to the boat and waited for his young sovereign.

Terrance quickly pulled one of the notebooks from his backpack and scribbled a letter to his mother. When complete, he tore it out of the notebook and wrote his mother's address on the back. Picking up his backpack with note in hand, he ran back to the dock and handed Chancee the note and asked him to mail it when he felt it safe. Chancee handed it to one of his men with instructions to take it to his office for safe keeping.

Europa gave him an inquisitive look as he hurried back to the boat. "What was that all about?" she asked Terrance.

"A letter to my mother so she won't worry too much," he replied, as he stepped onto the boat.

"Oh," Europa said. "That was a good idea."

"Farewell, Your Highnesses," Chancee said, bowing slightly and raising his hand to his forehead. "Farewell, young Terrance. May the Waters give you safe passage and good health."

"You're not coming with us, Mr. Dark Feather?" Europa asked.

"No, My Dear," he answered. "My place is here to protect your back. Plus, there is the possibility JeffRa will try to enter these lands and we must get prepared to fight him if he does." Chancee turned toward Terrance. "Do you still have the purple stone?"

"Yes, Sir," Terrance said, patting his pocket.

"Don't forget to place it in FarCore when you get there," Chancee reminded him. "But until that time never be without it. You may still have need of its powers."

"We won't forget, Sir," Europa said. "And thank you for all your help."

"No thanks are needed," Chancee answered. "Now I will take my leave of you." He turned and walked up the dock toward the Complex. He had only taken a few steps when the sound of an explosion echoed through the cavern followed by yelling, gun fire and the sound of animals. As they turned to look in the direction of the sound, all saw two of Mr. Dark Feather's men running toward them.

"Sir, we're under attack!" yelled one of the soldiers. "Raykin just called in to say they were under attack at the camp and Jepson reports the same at the lodge's perimeter. We've also received word from Runbee that they are trying to come up the channel."

"Sounds like he has a few more men than we assumed," Jeanip said, looking at Chancee.

"The side wall has been breached and Terrians have entered the lodge. Report for battle immediately," came a voice over the speaker.

"I can't believe JeffRa has the audacity to attack the camp or us. He must really want those two," Chancee said, as he nodded toward Europa and Earon. "If he knows you're here we can't take a chance on the boats. He'll be expecting that. You'll have to go by land."

The ground underneath their feet shook as a huge explosion was heard. They could see dust and smoke bellowing in from the east wall. "Looks like besides men, JeffRa still has some of that damn bendicor. He just blasted apart the east wall. You can bet they'll be arriving at the dock shortly," Chancee stated.

"I agree," Jeanip said, as he grabbed Europa's backpack and the two paintings of the Dumbo's and jumped over the side onto the dock. "Quick, Your Majesties and Terrance, off the boat. We'll have to go by land." Handing Europa her backpack and pointing to a wall at the far end of the docks, he ordered, "Earon and Europa, run as fast as you can toward that west wall. When you reach it turn right and follow the tunnel. Do not stop for anyone or anything."

"Jeanip, I don't see a tunnel," Earon said, as he took the backpack from Europa and slipped it over his shoulder. He firmly grabbed Europa's hand and the two took off running.

"Don't worry, you will when you get there." Jeanip yelled. He handed the two paintings to Terrance, "Terrance, I need you to carry the paintings along with your backpack? Can you do that?"

"Yes, Sir."

"Then take them and run with Earon." Terrance grabbed the paintings and took off running as the five boats sped off toward the opening still hoping to confuse the enemy into thinking the monarchs were aboard one of them. Jeanip watched the boats speed off one by one and prepared to follow his monarchs when he heard the sound of yelling behind him. He turned and saw several mountain lions and bears sprinting toward them. Before Jeanip could stop him, Chancee turned into a large grizzly and ran toward the oncoming animals saying only the word, "RUN!" Jeanip watched as several of Chancee's men also transformed and charged the advancing animals. The chamber was mixed with the sounds of fighting animals and blasters. Jeanip followed Chancee's advice and ran after the three travelers. He turned to see if any Terrians were following him and witnessed Chancee go down and get pinned by a Terrian grizzly who was frantically trying to rip out his throat. Jeanip stopped, raised his weapon and fired, hitting the Terrian grizzly and killing it instantly. Seeing his men had taken down the other Terrians, Chancee transformed back into a human and ran toward Jeanip.

"I thought I told you to run," he yelled above the deafening sounds, as he grabbed a coat from the floor and slipped it on.

"That's what I'm doing," Jeanip answered, as he took off running again, Chancee right behind him. They were more than half way to the wall when Jeanip heard commotion behind them. Without missing a step he quickly turned his head and discovered forty Terrian soldiers running toward them. Terrians' bullets began to zing by their bodies as he returned his gaze back to his monarchs. He was relieved to see they had reached the west wall and were turning right as instructed. He watched Europa then Earon disappear behind the wall, but before Terrance could get behind its safety, one of the Terrian bullets struck him. Jeanip and Chancee watched in fear as Terrance dropped the paintings and slumped behind the wall.

"Once I close the door behind us there's no way to open it from this side," shouted Jeanip, as they ran to the fallen Terrance. "You need to come with us."

"No, I'll cover you're back and keep them from blowing apart that door."

"There's too many of them," Jeanip stated, knowing Chancee could not take on forty alone. "You wouldn't have a chance."

"Don't underestimate my capabilities," Chancee laughed.

As they reached the west wall and turned right, Jeanip looked behind again to determine the position of the advancing small army. He was glad to see Chancee's soldiers had descended upon them and only twelve remained, but those twelve were still advancing. Suddenly, a blast sounded behind them to their left deterring everyone's attention to the channel opening. The last white boat had embarked and was blown apart as it emerged from the cave. "May they flow into the Waters and be taken home," Jeanip quietly said.

Chancee bent down to see how badly Terrance was hurt. "I'm okay, Mr. Dark Feather. It just grazed my arm." Terrance held up his left arm to reveal a slice of open flesh in his upper arm, blood freely flowing from it.

"On your feet then," Jeanip ordered, as he picked up the two dropped paintings with one hand and pulled Terrance to his feet with the other. "Can you still carry these with your right arm for a few more minutes?" Jeanip said. "Chancee and I both need our hands free to operate our weapons."

"Yes, I can still carry them, I think." Jeanip slipped the paintings underneath Terrance's right arm. Terrance clenched his arm tightly against his body, pressing them into his side while holding them with his right hand.

"Let's go then. Terrance you first." The three took off running down the tunnel, following the same path Earon and Europa had already gone down.

"Jeanip, why don't you just leave those paintings behind? They're not worth getting shot over."

"I can't leave them, Chancee. They were Medaron's most prized possessions, even more than the Orbs. Plus, Europa wants them."

"They're really no trouble," Terrance said, as he turned his head slightly around to face Jeanip, almost tripping over a rock he did not see.

"Don't talk, Terrance, just keep your eyes on the path ahead," Jeanip ordered.

Finally, they arrived at a steel door where Europa and Earon waited, each trying to catch their breath. Europa noticed the blood trailing down Terrance's arm and ran to his side.

"I'm fine," Terrance said, seeing the worried look upon her face. "Just a small scratch."

Europa reached up and kissed him on the cheek. She removed the paintings from beneath his arm and handed them to Earon. "Earon, would you please carry Mother's paintings?" Earon smiled and nodded his head affirmatively.

"Okay you three, inside the doorway," Jeanip announced. He watched the three step inside then turned to thank Chancee for his assistance. Surprisingly, he saw the dozen remaining Terrians running down the tunnel toward them. Knowing there would be no reinforcements to help Chancee from this end of the tunnel, Jeanip stepped through the doorway, pushed the closure button and grabbed Chancee at the last second and pulled him through. The door closed and sealed them in.

"What did you do that for?" Chancee asked, visibly angry at being pulled inside.

"Hopefully, for the same reason you gave me that shot when we arrived," Jeanip answered, feeling no other explanation was necessary.

Suddenly the ground beneath them began to shake violently, knocking them off their feet. Dirt and rock rained down from above as some of the ceiling began to crumble.

"Looks like he intends to bring the mountain down on top of us," Chancee stated, as he and Jeanip helped the three youngsters to their feet. "If we don't get out of here soon this place will be our tomb."

"Agreed. I guess JeffRa isn't planning on getting Europa and Earon alive anymore. Looks like he simply wants them dead," Jeanip said. The lights illuminating the tunnel blinked, then went dark. "Looks like he got the generator."

Plunged into darkness, the five were forced to stop. "Isn't this going to make it a little hard to proceed?" asked Terrance, as he reached out and took Europa's hand. "Or do you guys possess night-vision too?"

"Unfortunately, as humans, we only see as well as you do, Terrance, but we do plan ahead. Europa, in your backpack are six flashlights. Please give one to each of us." Europa unzipped her backpack, felt around inside for the flashlights and handed one to each member of the party. "Choose your footing carefully but walk as fast as you can down this corridor. It's about a mile to where we need to be. Chancee, you go first, then Earon, Europa and Terrance. I'll bring up the rear. Now go!" The five began to proceed down the corridor shining their flashlights on the ground as they stepped over rocks and debris. Another shock wave spread through the corridor as the mountain was blasted once more. This time they all were able to keep their footing and continue on. After twenty minutes they arrived at a stone wall with a large pool in front of it.

"What happened?" Europa asked. "Was there a cave-in? Are we trapped?"

"No, just another security precaution I believe young Terrance is not going to like," Jeanip stated. "Since Terrians can't swim the last part of our journey has to be through that pool." Everyone saw the frightened look on Terrance's face. Jeanip walked over to him and placed his hand on his uninjured arm. "Terrance, I know you have a fear of water. But I also know you can do this. You can do this for Europa. All I need for you to do is hold your breath. I will bring you through to the other side. I promise. It's not very far."

Terrance looked at Europa, then took a deep breath. "I can do it, Jeanip. I can do it for Europa. Just tell me what to do."

"Good man," Jeanip said. "Europa, in the back section of your backpack are two water proof bags. You and Terrance need to put your backpacks inside them. You will also find in your backpack four water goggles. Please get them out. Unfortunately, I did not bring any extra so someone will have to go without one."

"I will," Chancee said. "I can transform into something so I can see."

"No, I will," announced Terrance. "I'll have my eyes closed the whole time anyways, so what good are goggles?"

"But, Terrance," Europa started to say, then stopped, realizing he was right.

"Okay, everyone strip down to your shirt and underwear. You don't need extra weight weighing you down. Put on your goggles and into the pool. Earon, I need you to carry Terrance's backpack. Chancee, if you would carry the two paintings." Everyone stripped and entered the pool. Terrance clung to the side, already feeling the panic rising.

"Take several deep breaths and fill your lungs with air. Chancee you are number one, Earon you're number two, Europa you're number three and Terrance and I will be number four. When I say your number, submerge and follow the fluorescent yellow rope along the wall to the other side. As I told Terrance, it's not far. None of you should have a problem making it. Ready?" Everyone nodded.

As Jeanip said their number, each took one last deep breath and slipped below the surface and followed the yellow rope. When it was Terrance's turn Jeanip said, "Okay, Terrance, this is it. You can do this. Now take a deep breath and close your eyes." As Terrance heard Jeanip say "four" he felt himself being pulled underwater. The panic he had started to feel earlier was mounting and his mind told him to fight Jeanip, to get back to the surface and air. But he forced himself to envision Europa's face and concentrated on it with every ounce of his being, thus he was able to control his fear. His lungs began to burn for want of air and he didn't know how much longer he could control his panic. He tried focusing harder on his mental image of Europa, but his aching lungs would not allow him to do so. Then it occurred to him that if he began to struggle against Jeanip, Jeanip would not hesitate to let him go. The fear of that was more powerful than his desperate need for air. Just as he could hold his breath no longer they broke through the surface to air and a lighted new chamber.

"Are you okay?" Europa asked, as she swam to Terrance seeing the terrified look upon his face.

"I made it! I really made it!" Terrance said, a big smile spreading across his face.

"That you did," Jeanip said, as leading him to the ledge where Earon and Chancee waited. Jeanip then sank beneath the water and yanked on the rope, disconnecting it from the first chamber. "Just in case the Terrians thought they'd try swimming for a change. Without this they will never navigate the numerous tunnels and make it through."

"How much further is it?" asked Earon.

"Only about five minutes," Jeanip replied.

"Do we have to go through any more pools?" Terrance asked, almost afraid to hear the answer as he began to shiver in the cold.

"No, that was the only one," Chancee answered, as he retrieved several blankets. "Here, this should help with the cold. There are dry clothes aboard the ship for you to change into."

This side of the mountain had not been blasted so the pathway was not littered with rock, thus making it easy for the five to run the rest of the way to their waiting boat. As they rounded the last bend everyone gave a sigh of relief to see a sleek black speedboat waiting. "Jeanip, you never cease to amaze me," Earon said. "You always have a back-up plan for the back-up plan."

"When it comes to yours and your sister's safety, nothing is more important, as you well know, Earon," Jeanip stated, as if his plan for every possible scenario was a common occurrence. "But this time let us hope JeffRa has no more surprises for us. There are no more boats after this one."

"What would have happened if they had destroyed this one too?" Terrance asked.

"Then I'm afraid it would have been the open sea," Jeanip stated looking directly at Terrance. Terrance could see by Jeanip's expression he was not kidding this time; this was fact. It was this boat or nothing. Everyone hurried on board and quickly changed into dry, warm clothing.

"Chancee, would you cover our departure from the lookout?" Jeanip asked. "That is if you still remember how to use one of those blasters!" Jeanip teased.

"When this is all over you and I will have a contest to see who remembers and who doesn't."

Jeanip walked up to Chancee and clasped his hands upon both of his shoulders. "Thank you, Old Friend. We could not have made it without your help. I will not forget to inform Enok of your heroism and your dedication to his children."

"As always, Jeanip, I am here to follow your command. Inform Enok if you wish, but there is no need for thanks or praise. Knowing our sovereigns are safe is all the reward I need," Chancee replied. Turning to the three travelers, he bowed slightly and raised his hand to his forehead. "I must take my leave of you now, Your Majesties". After a short pause he added, "And Terrance."

"Good luck, Mr. Dark Feather," Earon said.

"May the Waters guide you to safety and give you long life," Chancee said, as he turned and left, hurrying up a flight of stairs to the room above. From there he could operate the blaster to keep any Terrians ships from attacking them as they left.

"We have to leave in a few minutes," Jeanip announced. "But before we go I have a few rules to go over with you. I will do the navigating. Each of you will take a shift sitting beside me as my lookout and to help keep me awake. While that person is with me the other two are to remain down in the galley. There's food and drink down there, benches if you want to sleep and some blankets if you get cold. JeffRa will not know if we are traveling by land or sea so he will surely be patrolling both. Therefore, we cannot take the chance of using the lights below, but there is a low light night lantern you can use. But each time before you use it you must check the windows to ensure the blinds are down and secured and the curtains are closed. Be sure the galley door is closed too. Even the smallest flicker of light could give us away. If you need me for something come directly up to me; do not call me from below. Keep your voices low when talking; whispering would be best. Sound does carry out here on the ocean. A lot farther than you imagine."

"It will take us about six or seven hours to reach our next destination." Looking at each one as he said their name, he added, "Earon, you will take the first watch, Europa you have the second and Terrance you get the last. Dress warmly; it's going to be cold tonight. There are several thermoses of coffee down below and several up here. Feel free to drink whatever you need to in order to keep you warm. But remember this – we are running silent so the toilet cannot be flushed while we're at sea."

Jeanip turned to look at Terrance. "Terrance, I know you're not a fan of the water and probably don't have sea legs. There is not much wind tonight, but there still will be swells, probably six to eight feet. The boat is going to rock and it WILL make you sea sick. In the first aid box in the galley you will find Dramamine and ginger capsules. Take two Dramamine now along with one or two ginger capsules. They should keep your stomach quiet. There are also some ginger snaps in the cupboard next to the sink. Keep them handy just in case the pills don't work fast enough. If you start to feel queasy at any time, start eating them and come up on deck. The worst place to be when you're sea sick is below. Know this, young Terrance. If you do get sick I will not hesitate to heave you overboard if I think you are jeopardizing our mission." A look of concern passed over Terrance's face. He wasn't sure if Jeanip was serious or kidding. He hoped kidding.

"Will do," Terrance said, now a little nervous about getting sea sick. It seemed like every obstacle he encountered came with the possibility of Jeanip either ending his life or abandoning him should he fail. Terrance promised himself that if he survived he definitely was going to learn how to swim and get his sea legs.

"There are life jackets below. Terrance and Europa, put one on now. Do not take them off until we reach our next destination. If, for some reason, we have to abandon this vessel you will have to go into the ocean. We will not, under any circumstances, use a raft. Once you are in the water the Waters will protect you."

Jeanip saw Terrance's face turn pale again as he remembered his last ordeal in the water. "But I'm sure, Terrance, that won't be necessary. It's a last resort. But if the thought of being in the water is too terrifying for you, you can still exit the vessel and remain here. Chancee can always use an extra hand. As I told you before, there is no shame in remaining behind."

"No, Sir," Terrance answered. "I'm in. And if something goes wrong and we have to abandon the ship, than please be assured I will not hesitate to go into the water."

"I'll hold you to that," Jeanip answered. "I believe that's it. Does anyone have any questions?"

The three travelers shook their heads negatively.

"Then, Europa and Terrance, you two down below. Put on your life jackets and, Terrance, take those pills. I'll see each of you in several hours. Earon, you might want to grab one of those coats downstairs to help with the chill. And bring one up for me also."

The three went below and did as Jeanip instructed. As Europa and Terrance put on their jackets they could feel the ship moving, pulling away from the dock and beginning its journey to the open ocean. Each of the four travelers wondered what the night would bring – JeffRa or safety.

As they pulled out of the secret harbor Jeanip looked up into the sky to see a bright full moon greeting them, shining its luminous glow upon the dark waters. The moon light was definitely an asset in navigating the dark ocean without lights, but it could also make them easier to spot. Jeanip knew the black camouflage would help them blend in with the surrounding water; he just hoped it was enough.

"So what is the plan, Jeanip?" Earon whispered, taking the co-captain's chair and handing Jeanip his jacket. He watched as Jeanip pushed the throttle forward ever so slightly, coaxing the boat further from shore and out into the open ocean. "Will Runbee and Graybin be guiding us again?"

"No, not this time. JeffRa will assume the dolphins will be guiding us and he'll be looking for them. We thought it best if the dolphins traveled with the decoys. At least that WAS the plan. I saw at least one of the decoy boats destroyed before it emerged from the cove. I don't know if any of the others made it or not."

"So we are on our own at the moment?" Earon asked.

"No, not at all. Unless something happened to them when the Terrians attacked, Runbee and Graybin should be following us at a distance in case they are needed."

"You mean in case we have to bail?"

"Yes."

"So we are going to just navigate blindly?"

"No, I've got the instruments I can read with the help of these," Jeanip said, handing Earon a pair of night-vision binoculars. "I'm able to read the dials. We have a course direction, so we follow it until our guide comes along to lead us the rest of the way."

Before Earon could ask who the mystery guide was he heard Jeanip give him a very quiet "Shhh, listen." Earon strained his ears for any sound but could hear nothing but the ocean waves. He scanned the ocean for any movement, endeavoring to see any lights on the water. Then he saw them; three boats were moving toward their position in an intersecting course. Earon could not determine if they were the remaining decoy boats or if they were Terrian.

"Jeanip, ten o'clock. There are three boats headed this way. They could be Terrian."

"I see them. And you can bet they are Terrian. Our own boats would not approach us for fear of giving away our location. Let's hope Chancee has spotted them too."

Chancee quickly climbed the stairs to the observation deck. He walked over to the blaster he and Niquan had installed the previous day and removed part of its camouflaged covering. As he pressed the button numerous lights turned on and began blinking, making him grateful he had remembered to leave part of the covering on to conceal its illumination. Even with the aid of the full moon to help hide their brightness, blinking lights on shore would be easily seen from the ocean. Putting on his night-vision goggles he watched the boat below slowly pull away from the shore and head out to sea. He aimed the locator at the boat and listened for the "click" when it locked on to the boat's location. He then set the locator to follow the boat, thus allowing him to scan the ocean without fear of losing track of his sovereigns. Jeanip was almost to the one mile marker when Chancee saw lights moving toward his sovereigns. As he magnified his binoculars he saw they were three

Terrian boats. He knew he could destroy one of them with the blaster, possibly two, but there was no way he could get all three before one of them reached the boat. Then to his great relief, Chancee saw just west of the one mile marker several whale blows. He knew instantly it was Enok and several other Waters coming to their aid.

"Enok, if you can get two of them I'll take the other one," Chancee said out loud, smiling broadly. "I should have known you wouldn't be far away from your children tonight."

Chancee watched as the whales dived; he had to time this just right. He aimed the blaster at the farthest boat and calculated the time it would take Enok to reach them. Forty seconds before the whales should be emerging from underneath, he threw off the covering and pulled the trigger, sending a laser stream directly into the last boat. Instantly there was a huge flash as the boat exploded into pieces, raining fire and debris onto the other ships. Seconds later the whales emerged from beneath the other two boats, throwing one into the air and smashing a big hole in the other one. The whales disappeared for a moment, then reappeared as they breached and landed on the boats, destroying the vessels and the Terrians who sailed them. No sooner had Chancee seen the breaching when there was another blinding brightness and he was thrown backwards, chunks of rock falling from the observation deck into the ocean and onto him. He crumbled to the ground under the weight of the falling rocks, pinning him underneath. He turned his head and scanned the ocean for anything he may have missed. Then he saw it – a fourth boat hidden behind the rocks. It had detected his location when he decloaked the blaster and fired it. Fearing another blaster attack, he tried to transform into a bear so he would have the strength to break free of the rock that held him captive; but unconsciousness took over just as he began to transform. As he eyes closed he did not see the two huge whales rise beneath the fourth boat and destroy it just as they had the other two.

———————

"Jeanip, do you think Dark Feather can take out all three with the blaster?" Earon asked.

"Chancee is one of the best marksmen I know," Jeanip stated, "But I don't think even he can destroy three. Let's hope Enok is close enough to help."

Jeanip and Earon watched the three boats grow closer. Suddenly, a blinding burst of light consumed the farthest boat and both watched as it shattered into pieces. They knew Chancee had fired the blaster but would he have time to destroy the other two? As they waited for another light burst they saw one of the boats suddenly rise into the air as a huge Moby came from underneath. They looked at each other and both said simultaneously, "Enok." Wondering what fate was in store for the third boat, a loud sound of breaking wood was heard as Mobies smashed into the third boat, breaking off most of the bow. The whales then breached, smashing down onto the two boats, breaking them apart and drowning the Terrians who had dared approach the monarchs.

"What's going on?" Europa asked, as she and Terrance ran up from the galley. "Are we under attack?"

"Almost," Earon answered. "But Father and Mr. Dark Feather put an end to it." Earon handed Europa his night-vision goggles so she could see for herself. She then handed them to Terrance. As Terrance put them on, there was a blinding flash from behind them, forcing him to close his eyes. He saw the others looking behind him as the light from the blast lit up the sky. In disbelief he watched the cavern they had emerged from minutes before crumble into the sea as the side of the mountain cascaded down, burying everything and everyone on the observation deck.

"There," Earon shouted as he pointed to the fourth boat. "They must have been waiting for Mr. Dark Feather to give away his position."

"Which he did when he fired the blaster," Jeanip replied. "May the Waters find him and take him home."

The light from the explosion began to fade until the four stood in complete darkness once again. Jeanip pushed the throttle forward and began to move the boat out of the area and onto her needed course. "Terrance and Europa, you need to return to the galley," was all Jeanip said.

"But what about the fourth boat?" Europa asked. "Surely they saw us with all that light."

"I'm sure they did, but your father will see to it that they don't follow or give away our position. Now please, Europa, go below."

Mr. Dark Feather had been a great friend and soldier to Jeanip. Even though Europa could not see Jeanip's face, she could tell by the tone of his voice Mr. Dark Feather's death had deeply touched him. Silently she searched for Terrance's hand in the dark and led him back downstairs after giving Earon back his night goggles. Another friend and comrade lost protecting her. Europa wondered if the killing would ever end.

OPEN OCEAN

Earon sat beside Jeanip without saying a word for some time. Like Europa, he knew the death of Mr. Dark Feather had greatly impacted Jeanip. He turned his head to look at the seasoned warrior who was driving them to safety. Once more he wondered how Jeanip managed to endure the death of so many comrades and friends over the centuries. No longer able to withstand the silence, Earon asked, "Jeanip, how did JeffRa know we'd be at the Hunting Lodge? And how was he able to attack us so fast?"

"I don't know, Earon," Jeanip replied. "We had this planned down to the smallest detail. We left absolutely nothing to chance. And only two Waters knew the entire plan. With all the security measures we had in place there is no way JeffRa should have been able to surprise us like he did."

"Do you think there is a spy amongst Mr. Dark Feather's Oonocks?"

"I suppose it is possible. But Chancee and his second in command, Niquan, were the only two who knew the entire plan for the Hunting Lodge. And I trust both of them with my life. No, I don't think there is a spy. Somehow JeffRa has developed a way to discover what we are doing, what we are planning. How else would he have known which window was your sister's or be able to surprise my men at Minnos? Hell, he even surprised me, and that is an impossible task to accomplish. With the security grid we had and all the new advancements in the system, we should have been warned the second a Terrian stepped foot on Minnos. But for now there is no need to dwell on the past events. We need to focus on getting to our next rendezvous."

"You said someone will be showing us the way?" Earon asked, changing the subject as he realized inquiring about how JeffRa found them was pointless for now until more information could be gathered. "Might I ask who that is?"

"I think you already know."

"Father. Father is going to guide us."

"Yes, Enok will be our guide."

"He was also one of the Mobies that destroyed the boats."

"Yes."

"Have the medical personnel finally found a cure for his breathing problems?" A flicker of hope surfaced inside Earon as he entertained the thought his father might at last be able to live on land.

"From what I understand they've made some progress. But I believe it's the sheer size of a Moby's enormous lungs that allows him to breathe the air for longer periods of time." Jeanip answered, wishing the medical personnel had found a cure. If Europa and Earon ever needed their father, it was now. And he had to admit to himself, he needed him too.

With the aid of his night goggles, Earon returned to scanning the ocean looking for any more boats daring to approach them. He thought it eerie how quiet it was; not a sound was audible. Even the boat was silent as it sped across the ocean water. When they boarded the vessel he noticed the bow had been fitted with a special scoop which allowed the water to pass away from the boat causing it to glide across the waters silently. He also suspected the engine was an Oonock design for it too ran without the slightest sound. In this eerie silence they traveled until it was broken by the sound of several whale cries. Suddenly, a large whale emerged alongside the vessel making a startling sound as it blew. Not expecting the whale to be so close, Earon almost bolted out of his seat. Jeanip could barely keep from laughing out loud at the surprised Earon.

"Ha-ha" Earon said sarcastically, as he composed himself. Sliding off his chair, he walked over to the starboard side and saw a large Moby swimming inches from the boat. The whale turned his eye toward Earon and winked. It was Enok. Earon imagined his father was laughing inside also at the fact he had scared his son. Earon watched as his father submerged and resurfaced a few yards ahead of them, taking the lead and steering them in a new direction.

Earon's two hour watch passed quickly and without further event. He knocked on the galley door to advise Europa he would be entering and to turn off the low beam lantern. As he entered he saw Europa snuggled up in Terrance's arms on one of the benches, mugs of coffee and playing cards in front of them on the table.

"Sorry to interrupt your game, Sis, but it is your turn on top", Earon said, removing the night-vision binoculars and handing them to Europa. "Perhaps Terrance and I can finish your card game if he would like."

Europa reached out and took the binoculars, slipping them over her head. "These are the coolest things. It's like living in a green universe. Is this what it looks like down at the Complex?"

"A little bit," Earon answered. "Except we see in color, not monocolor."

Europa leaned over and gave Terrance a kiss. "I will see you in two hours."

Europa went above, closing the galley door behind her. She took a seat next to Jeanip. "Anything I need to know?"

"No, just scan the ocean for anything unusual. And keep an eye on the night sky too." Jeanip replied.

Europa was surprised to hear the blow of the whale. Usually if one can hear the sound of a blow the whale is fairly close. As she searched the ocean ahead she saw the large whale leading their way. She turned to Jeanip and asked, "Jeanip, is that my father ahead of us?"

"Yes, Europa, that is Enok, your father. He is our escort to our next destination." He did not want to avert his eyes from Enok to look at Europa's face to see if she was pleased they followed her father or not, but he believed he heard a tone of excitement in her voice. This pleased him.

"Will I ever be able to meet him?" she asked in a voice so low Jeanip almost didn't hear her.

"Would you like to?"

"Oh, yes," she eagerly replied. "I have fantasized about somehow having the chance to meet my father all of my life. But I never thought it would be possible." She turned to face Jeanip, a hint of fear in her eyes. "Do you think he will want to meet me?"

"Oh my dear, dear Europa," Jeanip replied, amazed at her innocence, astonished that, even after his explanation of why her parents decided she would be born human, she had no concept of how much both Enok and Medaron loved her. "Your father has dreamt of nothing else since the day you were born. Had it not been for the fact the lives of all the Oonocks were in his care he would gladly have sacrificed his life to spend just a few hours with you."

"Really?"

"Really, although if you search your heart you will discover you already knew that. I know Medaron always told you how much your father loved you."

"Yes, she did often. But one never knows if a parent is telling the truth or just something they think the child wants or needs to hear."

"Well, in this case it is definitely the truth." Jeanip thought for a moment then added, "If you have any doubt at all of his and your mother's love for you and how much you meant to them, just think of all they willingly sacrificed for you. They put their life on hold for seventy to eighty years just so your life would be a happy one."

"At lease that was the way my life was supposed to have gone before JeffRa reappeared," Europa stated, remembering all she had lost the past week and a half. Realizing how lonesome her life was going to be without her mother and the others, she turned toward Jeanip and asked, "Jeanip, is there no chance he will ever be able to live on land?"

"I don't know, Your Majesty. Our medical personnel are hopeful."

"Hopefully, it will not take over fifty or sixty years to discover the cure," Europa added quietly.

Jeanip went to ask her why fifty or sixty years, then remembered that, as a human, that was probably how many years she would still live. How tragic it would be, he thought, if they cured Enok after Europa had passed. Not wishing to dwell on her mortality, he changed the subject to a more agreeable one.

"That young man of yours is very impressive, Europa," Jeanip said, glancing quickly at Europa to see the smile on her face.

"How so?" Europa asked, elated at Jeanip's comment. She knew Jeanip held people to a very high standard. Evidently, Terrance had done a few things correctly for Jeanip to approve of him.

"Do you remember when I took Terrance aside just before we were ready to board the boat at the Hunting Lodge?"

"Yes. I thought for a moment you were going to leave him there and make me go without him."

Jeanip smiled. "That would have been a travesty, Your Highness. He is very much needed on this journey."

"What did you talk to him about?"

"Terrance was pulled into this nightmare without his consent. He got dragged along due to his location and to the abruptness of the events. I wanted to give your young man the chance to choose between remaining behind where he would be safe or continue with us. This is not his fight. But he would not even consider it, not even for a second. He said he could never leave you – even if it meant it could be decades before he would be able to return to the real world. And his ability to conquer his fear of the ocean like he did in the cave at the Hunting Lodge and his agreement to go into the ocean if necessary now is commendable. He is a man with honor and dignity. Your father will be impressed by him, as I have been."

"Thank you, Jeanip. That means a lot to me," Europa said. "I was talking with Earon about . . ."

Jeanip's voice became low and serious. "Silence, Your Majesty. You need to go get your brother and Terrance right away. Hurry."

Without hesitation, Europa jumped from her seat and went to the galley door, knocking on it before entering. Earon barely had enough time to turn off the lantern before the door opened. She returned with a confused Earon and Terrance.

"What's up, Jeanip?" Earon asked.

Jeanip pointed to the left. "Possible trouble," he stated. Even without the night binoculars Earon could see silhouetted against the night sky a small dot of light moving. As the light grew larger they began to hear the unmistakable sound of twirling helicopter blades. They watched as a large search light turned on and began to scan the ocean water below searching for something or someone.

"Do you think they're looking for us?" Terrance whispered.

"That is a possibility," Jeanip replied, as he turned off the engine. "Europa, take the wheel. Keep the boat headed in this direction, but leave the engine off. Earon, put on Europa's night binoculars and Terrance, you put on mine." Jeanip removed his night binoculars and handed them to Terrance. "Follow me to the bow. I need your help to pull a cover over the boat." He looked at Europa. "Do not worry, Your Majesty, I still have a few tricks up my sleeve."

Earon and Terrance ran after Jeanip to the front of the boat where they saw a large wooden box. As Jeanip threw the lid off they saw an odd colored, glistening cover with two heavy weights attached. "Earon, take this corner with the weight and lower it overboard on the port side. Terrance, you do the same on the starboard side. Try not to make any sound and be sure the front of the boat is concealed. Then pull it down your side toward the stern," Jeanip instructed, as he handed Earon and Terrance a corner of the drape with a heavy weight. "Be sure the draping completely covers the boat, all the way down to the water's surface. I will take the middle and go across the top of the boat. I will meet you two in the stern."

"But how will you be able to see without the night-vision goggles?" Earon asked, as he took his end.

"I know this boat like the back of my hand," Jeanip replied. "And the moon will give me some light to see by. Plus, I have exceptional feeling in my fingers and will be able to feel my way along. Now hurry, do as I say."

Earon and Terrance lowered their weighted corners into the ocean and watched as the drape concealed the bow of the boat. They then dragged their portion down their respectful sides, making sure it reached the water and concealed the boat completely. Jeanip felt his way down the middle, pulling the drape along the top of the boat, aiding Earon and Terrance on their dispersal. As he reached the end of the wheel house he silently dropped to the deck, pulling the drape with him.

"In each corner of the boat you'll find another weight. Tie it to your corner of the drape and drop it over the stern like you did up front when I tell you" Jeanip ordered, as he reached the stern. Jeanip tied a weight to the middle section and the two tied their weight to their corners. "Okay, on the count of three lower your section into the water. One, two, three." All three silently lowered their weights and drape over the stern completely enclosing the boat.

"What is this covering?" Earon asked before either of the other two could.

"It is something one of Chancee's engineers designed," Jeanip stated. "It should completely conceal the boat and literally make us invisible. If the helicopter does fly over us with its search light, it should see only the ocean's surface."

"Should?" Terrance asked.

"We didn't get a chance to test it out. On paper, that is how it is supposed to work. Let us hope it works that way in reality. Earon and Terrance, sit on the floor by Europa. We need to remain totally quiet with no movement until they leave. And Terrance, if you do not mind, I will need those goggles back now."

Terrance handed the goggles back to Jeanip. As his eyes adjusted to the darkness he wondered how Jeanip was able to see anything even with the moon light, for he could not. Earon took Terrance's arm and led him back into the wheel house. "Okay, Terrance, you are standing right next to Europa. Sit down on the floor," Earon instructed as he sat down also.

The drape was designed to hide the boat from anyone searching for them, yet it allowed them to see though it as if it wasn't even there. As Europa looked up she could see the helicopter with its search light heading in their direction, drawing closer with each one of her heartbeats. The sound of its whirling motor was becoming deafening.

"Can't we shoot it down like we did the one yesterday?" Terrance asked, trying to talk above the helicopter sound without yelling. He put his free hand in his pocket to be sure the purple stone was still safe. Luckily he had grabbed his backpack when they came on deck so he had the blaster close by also.

"No. That would draw attention to our location if it suddenly disappeared. We have to hope it loses interest and moves onto another location. And soon. We can't remain here long or we will not make our destination by daybreak," Jeanip stated, now having to bend down close to the three so he could be heard. "Here they come. Remain still and no talking."

Europa cupped her hands over her ears as the sound of the whirling chopper blades grew in intensity. The drape began to vibrate from the wind of the helicopter blades as it grew nearer, shining its search light upon the surface of the ocean surrounding the boat. Europa held her breath, saying a silent prayer they would not discern Enok swimming ahead of them. The light swung around and returned to shine down on the area where the boat was concealed. The light remained there, as the helicopter hovered above, remaining stationary. Jeanip feared the drape had not worked; they had been discovered. The helicopter moved a few feet from the boat then dropped something into the water. As Jeanip heard the loud splash he feared frogmen had entered the water.

"Something or someone just entered the water. If we are boarded you must immediately jump overboard and swim as far away from the boat as you can," Jeanip ordered, drawing his knife in anticipation of being boarded.

"Should we not get in now?" Earon asked, wondering why they would wait until they were boarded which would make their escape harder.

"No," Jeanip responded. "I need Graybin, Runbee and a few of the other Waters to be here to help with Terrance and Europa. They should be here in about five minutes. Plus, we have no way of knowing from which side they will enter from. If those were divers there can't be more than two, so chances are they will both enter on the same side. Be sure to go overboard on the opposite side; and, if for some reason they board us from both the stern and port side, go off the back." Jeanip paused for a moment and listened, but heard nothing. "Terrance and Europa, be sure your life jacket is secured. Hold on to your backpacks – we need the items you have inside, especially the Orb. I want you three to stand and be ready to exit swiftly."

The three rose and stood there ready to run to a side or to the back if boarded. Earon reached out and took the two backpacks away from Europa and Terrance. "I'll take these for you two," he stated, as he slung them over his shoulder. "After all, I am the better swimmer. Besides, Terrance, you need to concentrate on swimming."

The four remained motionless as the minutes ticked by, but no one tried to board. The helicopter remained hovering over the boat for several more minutes, then moved a few feet away. It again hovered and another object dropped into the water. "How many frogmen are they putting in the water?" Jeanip stated. "Perhaps they are going to try to board from every side thus cutting off any route of escape."

Jeanip quickly began to formulate a new escape route when he heard a silent voice say, "Jeanip and Earon, it's Graybin. Do not worry, you are safe. We have explored the area and there is no one in the water other than ourselves. They are dropping weights into the water to determine if indeed it is water underneath them or a cloaked ship."

"They are only dropping weights in an effort to find us," Jeanip quietly announced to Terrance and Europa. "You three can sit back down." As they sat they watched the helicopter advance a few more feet away and hover. All breathed a sigh of relief as they realized, had the helicopter dropped a weight while they had hovered above the boat, they would have been discovered.

Jeanip looked at his watch. Time was short and they could not wait here much longer if they wanted to reach their next destination on time. But he couldn't with the helicopter so close. "Graybin, is there any way to distract that helicopter? We've got to get going or we will arrive at our next destination too late."

"Help is on its way," came a silent voice belonging to Runbee. "One of the decoy boats is heading this way. I think he plans to get the helicopter to follow him."

"I believe the Calvary has arrived," Jeanip announced, as the four travelers looked out over the ocean and saw a small blue light growing in size and coming toward them. At the same time they began to hear the distant sound of a boat motor. Suddenly, the blue light turned and sped off away from their location, its sound becoming fainter. The helicopter took the bait and sped off in pursuit of the retreating boat.

Seeing their opportunity Jeanip ordered, "Earon and Terrance, pull the stern end of the drape inside the boat. Be sure there's none left overboard that could get caught in the engine. We'll travel for a while with the rest of the drape on just in case they come back."

"Can we do that?" Earon asked, leading Terrance back to the stern. Together they pulled the camouflage drape inside the vessel.

"Guess we'll find out," Jeanip announced, as he threw the throttle forward as soon as the drape was inside. "Hold on," he yelled, as the boat raced forward, away from the helicopter and closer to their destination.

The drape remained in place as they sped across the ocean, following Enok. Once Jeanip was sure it was safe, he stopped for several minutes and uncovered the boat, folding the drape into a pile in the bow in case it would be needed again.

"I believe we are now safe," Jeanip stated. "Earon, you and Terrance can return to the galley. Europa, if you would return to your seat next to me we can continue on our way".

"Do you think we will encounter any more boats or helicopters?" Europa asked, scanning the night sky and ocean.

"One can hope not," Jeanip said, giving her an encouraging smile. "We are quite a ways from the Hunting Lodge, so I don't think we should run into any more Terrians this far out."

"Europa, if you'd like I can take over now," Terrance said, as he paused momentarily at the galley door.

"Thanks, Terrance," Europa stated. "I am fine. I have less than an hour to go on my watch and I would like to remain out here. I love the ocean at night. Plus, I do not think I will ever get tired of watching my father swim ahead of us."

"Your father?" inquired Terrance, looking ahead but not able to see the whale in the dark.

"Yes," Europa answered. "The whale leading us is Enok, Earon's and my father. This is the first time I have ever seen him."

Mostly to himself, as he walked down to the galley, Terrance said, "I don't ever think I'm going to get used to animals not being animals but transformed people, beings."

Although he had not meant them to hear it, both Europa and Jeanip chuckled. "I guess it is a lot for him to comprehend," Europa said. "I know it has been for me. But somehow it is like I already knew it, somewhere in the very deep recesses of my mind I knew I descended from shape shifters even before I found the Orb. I just did not realize I knew it."

"That does not surprise me, Europa," Jeanip said. "Even though you were born human, Oonock DNA still resides in your genetic makeup. Oonocks have exceptional memories and are capable of passing past memories on to others in their lineage. I am sure when you were forming inside your mother some Oonock memories were passed on to you through your mother."

Europa turned her chair so that she could face Jeanip directly. "Jeanip, do you think you could tell me now what happened that day my mother died?" she asked. "Is there enough time?"

"We will make time, Your Highness," Jeanip said. "And if need be we can delay Terrance's watch a bit to assure all your questions are answered." Settling back into his seat, Jeanip began, "As I told you earlier, your mother was still alive when you arrived at the scene of the accident. Tinderoon quickly escorted you over to where I held Medaron in my arms. I believe you were in shock, but somehow you were able to kneel down beside her. Your mother knew she was dying and you would have to face the Terrians, or even JeffRa himself, without her. Medaron believed she had killed JeffRa but she had no way of knowing for sure. And if he still lived she knew he would not stop until you were dead. Knowing she had to somehow protect you, she did the only thing she knew to do; she transferred her powers to you. I placed your hand inside of hers and she initiated the transfer. But the transfer was more than your body could withstand. Your system overloaded and you collapsed into unconsciousness. Earon transformed into his human form and took you back to Minnos while I carried your mother out into the ocean so she could become one with the waters of this world. Then I went below to advise your father of your mother's passing and the fact JeffRa was still alive."

"I do not completely understand, Jeanip," Europa stated. "What is a transfer of powers and why did it affect me so?

"I will try to explain it to you," Jeanip replied. "On Europa, when it is time for the younger monarch to replace the existing monarch, a ceremony is held where the power to lead the people is passed. It is mostly a ceremonial action, something visible the people can see, very similar to when your royalty here on Earth step down from leadership by passing the younger ruler their crown. But instead of a crown we use an amulet, like the one your mother gave you on your birthday. That is our token – only monarchs with the capability to rule may wear them. If the elder monarch chooses, he or she may also pass on a part of themselves; memories, knowledge, customs, etc. And sometimes, if the monarch is an extremely powerful one like your mother was, they can also pass on their powers. That is one of the ways our heritage remains current with the people. "

"How are these powers and knowledge passed on?"

"It's actually a wondrous sight to behold," Jeanip answered. "A special ceremony is held where the elder and younger monarchs face each other, about six inches apart. They outstretch their arms toward each other, the elder holding the younger's hands as a soft white light begins to glow in the elder monarch's abdomen. As the light intensifies, it becomes brighter and turns lilac in color. It completely covers the elder monarch's body and begins to stream out through his/her hands into the younger's body. Soon the younger's body is encased in the light. As the younger's body absorbs the light, it begins to decrease from the elder's until only the light in the younger's body remains. Then that too fades."

"Like what happened when I was able to heal you with the Orb!"

"Yes, that is correct. Since you did not know who you really were, your mother did not transfer any powers to you the night she gave you the amulet." Europa reached up and encircled her fingers around the amulet. She vividly remembered that night, the memory of which brought a warmth of deep love to her heart. "And had JeffRa not appeared, she probably would never have done the transfer. She knew how dangerous it was for you."

"Why do you say that?" Europa asked.

"The transfer of power and memories is a very powerful thing. Even though you are your mother's biological daughter, you are still human. A human body is not made to withstand such a flow of energy and memories as she gave you. On Europa, the future new monarchs are taught from a very early age about the transfer. They are conditioned and prepared for the acceptance of the energy force. You had no preparation, no training. When your mother performed the transfer your body immediately went into shock and you collapsed. It was necessary to keep you in a state of unconsciousness for five days so your body had time to absorb the energy and repair itself. It was a miracle the energy transfer did not kill you."

"Kill me?" Europa asked, as she realized the danger of the transfer and how desperate her mother must have been.

"Evonic said he didn't know how you survived it," Jeanip stated. "But somehow you did. Your body accepted the new energy and powers."

"Is that why I could hear the Orb calling me from mother's attic after she was killed?" Europa asked.

"So it did call to you? I wondered how you knew it was there."

"Actually I found it by mistake," Europa confessed. "I had gone into Mother's room because I missed her and because I was so bored by being upstairs. Remember, this was during the time I was so angry with you and resigned myself to remain upstairs."

"I remember that time well," Jeanip stated quietly under his breath as he recalled those horrible days. "I was afraid you would never forgive me or talk to me again."

"I apologize for my behavior," Europa said, feeling guilty for treating Jeanip the way she did. She should have known to trust him; she should have realized he would never do anything to intentionally hurt her and always did things for her benefit alone.

"I thank you for the apology, but none is needed, Your Majesty," Jeanip replied. "You did not know the truth of who your mother really was and, therefore, reacted in the only way you could. Besides, as a monarch you must remember one never apologizes for one's decisions or actions."

"That may be true but it was still wrong of me," Europa stated.

"That is something we could debate all day," Jeanip smiled. "Please continue your story on how you found the Orb."

"When I went to leave Mother's room I turned off the light not realizing I had turned two switches on. As I closed her door I noticed light shining through Mother's wall. I traced the source of the light and found the secret attic, along with Mother's diary, some paintings and maps and the Orb. To tell you the truth, when I first touched the Orb and it began to glow and hum I was frightened – I thought it was one of your security devices. I actually avoided it while I was up there that day. But that night I dreamt about these beautiful sea creatures and when I awoke the next morning I was consumed with the need to see the Orb again. Does that sound strange?"

"No, not at all. When you touched the Orb it recognized Medaron in you and therefore called out to you," Jeanip replied. "Few Oonocks have been able to communicate with the Orbs. Medaron was one of those few; in fact, she was one of the most gifted Oonocks to interact with them. Whatever it was inside of her that enabled her to communicate with them she passed it on to you during the transfer."

"Since it appears Mother's transfer has given me powers I did not have before, is there the possibility I will be able to transform into other creatures like you and Earon do? Europa asked, hoping Jeanip's answer would be more favorable than Earon's was.

"That I do not know, Your Highness," Jeanip said, dashing Europa's hopes. "Two weeks ago I would have said there was not a chance. But I don't know what the transfer has done to you, how it has changed you or will change you. You have already shown Oonock's powers you should not possess as a human – the ability to heal, as you healed me." Taking his eyes away from the ocean for just a moment, he turned to Europa to say, "Europa, the last Oonock healer died over a hundred and fifty thousand years ago. The fact that you were able to heal is unbelievable, it's . . . well, you should not be able to do it."

"It seemed like such a natural thing to do. You say it is unbelievable, but for me it was like breathing or waving my hand. It took no effort." After a few minutes of silence Europa decided to ask a question she had been curious about. "Jeanip, why does my father choose a sperm whale to transform into?"

"Actually, it is not just your father but all Oonocks do when they want to leave or return to the Complex?"

"Even Runbee and Graybin? Even you?"

"Yes, all Oonocks," Jeanip laughed. "Does it surprise you I can be a whale?"

Europa laughed also. "Somehow I cannot imagine you this huge creature with a tail."

Jeanip laughed loudly seeing the humor in him having an enormous tail. "One day, after you and your brother are safe, I will have to show you. Perhaps I can even take you for a ride on my back. But for now back to your question; the entrance to the Complex is down over eight thousand feet and the water pressure is tremendous. We needed an animal which could both live at the ocean's surface and also withstand that amount of water pressure. There are several animals capable of this but most of them surface only at night. We needed one that could exist above during the day and night; breathe air through lungs, not gills; and it needed to be a large animal. The only animal meeting all our criteria is the sperm whale. Plus, the sperm whale has such tremendous lungs your father is able to stay above longer and breathe with fewer problems."

"What's it like?" Europa asked, a gleam of fascination in her eyes as she thought of the possibilities.

"What is what like, Your Majesty?"

"Being a whale!"

"Big! And powerful!!" Jeanip answered, trying to think of the correct words to describe the feeling. "As you have witnessed, you have enough power to smash a ship to pieces and, due to your enormous size, you virtually have no enemies. Except for humans, that is. We lost several Oonocks to the whale hunters centuries ago before we realized what the humans were up to. We quickly learned how to avoid their boats and, I am glad to report, we never lost another one to their harpoons."

"It must be wonderful to swim so free through the oceans," Europa commented more to herself than to Jeanip.

Jeanip looked down at his watch. "If you have no more questions, Your Majesty, it is time for young Mr. Landers to sit next to me for a while. If you think of any more questions we can continue our discussion when we arrive at our next destination. Thank you for keeping me company, Your Majesty, but it is now time for me to take my leave of you."

"Wow, that went by really fast," Europa replied. "May I ask one more question before I go?" Europa asked, as she stood up. "Do you think there will ever be a way I can visit the Ocean Complex?"

"Humans cannot withstand the pressure existing at that depth in the ocean. As I said, the Complex is down about eight thousand feet. A human cannot go much past eight hundred. Your body would crumble into nothing in seconds. With training and proper decompression, some humans have been able to go deep in their submersibles, but there would be no way to get you from the submersible into the Complex. So, unless you develop the ability to transform into a Moby, I see no way you can ever go there."

"But could I not go down in the transportation capsule my mother came up in?" Europa asked, desperately hoping there was a way for her to visit the Complex and meet her people.

"Yes, I suppose that is a possibility," Jeanip replied, not wanting to dash all her hopes after everything she had lost the past few days. "We could adjust the air pressure in a section of the Complex to accommodate your fragile human body, but I am not sure it would be sufficient. But it is definitely something for us to look into."

"Thank you for all your answers, Jeanip," Europa said, as she stood in front of the galley door, ready to knock to announce her entrance. "And for your honesty." Jeanip could hear the tinge of disappointment in her voice. He knew how much she wanted to visit the Complex.

"But do not despair, Your Majesty. We will discuss your visitation with your father and see what he thinks. If the medical personnel have enabled Enok to breathe air with mammalian lungs finally, perhaps they will also know a way you can exist at the Complex, at least for a short time."

Jeanip saw the smile spread across her face as she thought of the possibility. "You know, Jeanip, I am really not tired. I can stay longer if you would like."

"That is noble of you to offer, but the agreement was each serves two hours," Jeanip said. "Besides, Your Majesty, under other circumstances you never would have been allowed to stand watch with me at all. That is not an undertaking for a female monarch. Besides, I look forward to spending time with young Mr. Landers."

Europa scrutinized Jeanip's face trying to discover his intentions. "You be nice to him," Europa said. "That is an order," she added, just in case Jeanip had plans on interrogating poor Terrance for two hours.

"I assure you, Your Majesty, I will be as nice as I can to the male human who will be living with you on a deserted island for possibly a good number of years," Jeanip said, trying not to let Europa see the glee in his eyes. Yet part of him was telling the truth. This young man could be spending the next year or more with his monarch. And, considering the other two males on the island were her brother and uncle, it put a lot of potential husbandry ideas on Terrance. Jeanip thought he must ask Enok about bringing more Oonocks onto the island.

"He might as well jump overboard now," Europa said, as she turned to go below to get Terrance. As she reached to knock on the door she hesitated once more, then turned back toward Jeanip. There had been one other question that had been haunting her since Jeanip told her their story back at the Hunting Lodge – the subject of fertility. She wondered if JeffRa's curse would also prevent her from having children. Keeping her eyes on the deck floor she softly asked, "Jeanip, will I be able to have children someday? Or will I also be barren like the other female Oonocks?"

Jeanip did not know how to answer her. He wanted to tell her the truth but he also wanted to give her hope. He carefully chose his words and answered, "Europa, I look forward to the day I can hold your children, but the truth is I do not know if JeffRa's revenge of infertility will affect you or not. Since you are human his curse may not affect you. Plus, your mother was able to conceive you somehow. Hopefully, whatever it was that enabled her to have you also lives inside you."

Europa did not say a word in response. She knocked on the cabin door and then entered. Moments later Terrance emerged from the galley with the night goggles and took the seat next to Jeanip. Jeanip could see he was a little nervous about being alone with Jeanip for the next two hours.

"Do not worry, young Terrance. I promised Europa I would not toss you overboard or try to cut out any part of your body," Jeanip said, trying to lighten the mood and ease Terrance's apparent nervousness. "Besides, I would hate for all your splashing to give away our position."

Terrance stared at Jeanip, once again trying to determine if he was serious. He knew Jeanip had a unique sense of humor but he also remembered the day Jeanip almost killed him. When Jeanip winked at him, he breathed a sigh of relief.

"Is that really Europa's father up there?" Terrance asked, wanting to change the subject as swiftly as possible.

"Yes, that is Enok," Jeanip stated. "He hopes to be able to meet you once we get to our final destination."

"Meet ME?"

"Why do you think he would not want to meet you?" Jeanip asked, amazed at Terrance's question. "He knows you have been instrumental in keeping his daughter alive. And even if that were not true, you are the man his only daughter has fallen in love with."

Terrance knew how protective fathers were of their daughters, especially their only daughter. But for that woman to also be the daughter of a king, the future ruler of a nation – the very thought was mind boggling and a little intimidating. "What's he like?" Terrance asked, wondering if his life was safer in Jeanip's hands or Enok's. Neither choice gave him much comfort.

"He is the leader of our people, their protector. He is strong, dedicated, a superb strategist in policies and war. He puts the welfare of everyone before his own and has paid a heavy price because of it. He is confident, assured of who he is. He is tender yet not afraid to make the hard decisions. He brings out the best in each of us and encourages us to reach higher to obtain the things we did not think we could. We follow him not only out of respect but out of a deep love we have for him. He is probably the most magnificent monarch I have ever known or heard of. He is our life and our heart. None of us would be alive today if it were not for Enok." Jeanip turned to look directly at Terrance. "But most of all, young Terrance, he is a loving father who has dreamt of the day when he could meet his daughter and finally hold her in his arms." Jeanip saw a dark cloud come over Terrance's face as he sat there not saying a word. It was not hard to see he was deeply troubled about something. "What is it, Terrance? Did I say something to upset you?"

"No, Sir," Terrance replied. "Enok sounds wonderful, the type of father Europa deserves. I was just thinking about my father, I mean stepfather. If he is this JeffRa then my father is the complete opposite of her father. Where her father is good, mine is evil; where her father is loving and a leader of a people who love him, mine is cold and the killer of thousands."

"Terrance, I want you to listen very carefully to me," Jeanip said in a soft, caring voice. "Who or what your stepfather turns out to be you must realize it is not a reflection upon you. Each of us chooses our own destiny, and I can already tell you are nothing like your stepfather. Yes,

JeffRa is an appalling, evil being who has done horrendous things but I remember a time long ago when JeffRa was a good man, as kind-hearted as Enok and just as loving. His feet were planted on a path not of his choosing, but he is guilty of continuing on that path. Had he had a father who loved him, I do believe he could have been almost as great as his brother."

"Really, Jeanip?" Terrance asked, intrigued by the thought.

"Yes, Terrance," Jeanip replied. "That is one of the reasons why Enok could never bring himself to terminate JeffRa's life. He remembered the good in him and always hoped it would resurface again one day. But when JeffRa killed Medaron he stripped Enok of that hope and Enok was forced to see JeffRa for who he had become, not for who he was when they were young. The next time Enok faces his brother he will sentence him to death and he himself will carry out the order. But enough of such unpleasant things. Let's talk about something more pleasant. Do you have any questions you would like to ask me? "

"I was wondering what it feels like to transform into another creature?" Terrance asked, curious about being a shape shifter. "Does it hurt? I mean, well you know, your bones change shape and you sometimes get hair all over your body. That sounds like it would hurt really bad!"

"You and Europa think alike. She too asked me what it was like. I am not sure it really 'feels' like anything," Jeanip stated. "Have you ever had a beard and mustache for some time, then shaved them off?"

"Yes."

"When you looked into the mirror, did it not feel as if you were looking at a new you, a different you?"

"Yes."

"Well, that is kind of how it feels when you transform into another creature. Your outside appearance is different, but inside you are still the same person you were before."

"And it doesn't hurt?"

"It tingles a little, but it does not hurt. Which, now that I think of it, is quite amazing considering the changes your body goes through; you may even grow a tail," Jeanip stated.

"A tail? I guess I never thought of that. That would be strange." Terrance laughed, as he imagined what it would be like to have a tail he could flick. Or fins to help you sail through the seas. It was most intriguing.

"Do you mind if I ask you a few questions?" Jeanip asked. "You do not have to answer them if you feel uncomfortable."

"It's okay," Terrance stated, as he kept his view on the ocean. "I understand you just met me and know almost nothing about me. And the fact I will be spending a significant amount of time with your niece in the next few months or years may be giving you some anxiety."

"I was wondering if you had any brothers or sisters," Jeanip asked.

Surprised by the questions Terrance answered, "No, I am an only child. Why do you ask?"

"Thought I would ask something more sinister?" Jeanip chuckled. "I was just curious."

"Do you have any siblings?"

"As you may know, Medaron was my sister. I also had two brothers who were killed in our skirmish with JeffRa at the Third City. And a younger sister who chose to stay behind on Europa."

"Stay behind? I forgot that part of your story. You said some of the Oonocks did not believe Europa's grandfather's warning and chose to remain behind. You also said no one has ever heard from them. Do you think they survived when Jupiter exploded?"

"You have a good memory. And just for the record Jupiter imploded, not exploded. There is a big difference. As for the question of survivors on Europa, we have no way of knowing. From what I have seen on your news casts, the protective ice shield is still intact, so it is possible my sister and the others survived. But the implosion happened thousands of years ago; the ice shield would have had ample time to rebuild itself. There is no way to determine what damage was originally done to it. But there is the possibility that in the near future I may learn if my sister or any of the others still live. The other day at Minnos I read an article concerning celestial bodies that may contain life. Scientists feel Jupiter's moon Europa possesses a high probability for having some sort of life. Plans are currently under way to launch an unmanned space probe to Europa in another seven to eight years. The probe will drill a hole through her ice, then plunge into the moon's layer of water in hopes of detecting life in her waters."

"Detecting life?" Boy, are they in for a surprise!" Terrance and Jeanip laughed. For the remainder of his time he and Jeanip talked about nothing of great importance. Soon they noticed the sky growing lighter behind them; dawn was fast approaching.

"There she is," Jeanip stated, pointing to a large object in the distance. "Our destination. Terrance, if you would be so kind as to have Europa and Earon come up," Jeanip instructed.

Terrance went below and returned with the siblings. Again Jeanip pointed to the object on the horizon. "That, Your Majesties, is our destination. And just in time." Jeanip turned to look behind him. "Dawn will be here within the next half hour. Nothing like timing it close."

"That is our destination?" Europa asked. "What is it?"

"You will see," Jeanip smiled.

Jeanip steered the boat toward the object. No longer needing to lead the way, Enok turned and swam to the boat, bringing himself alongside. The three passengers ran over to the starboard side and leaned over the rail to get a better view. Enok raised himself out of the water as far as he could, brushing up against the boat's side. Europa knelt down and reached over and touched her father. She looked into his eye and saw several lilac tears trickle down from the corner. Then she realized she too was crying. For the first time, father and daughter met.

"Father says you look just like Mother," Earon said. "He says he will see you later when we reach Saint's Isle. He cannot wait to finally meet you, but for now he needs to transform into his true self. He sends his love."

Europa looked up at Earon with astonishment. "How do you know that?"

"He told me. Did we forget to tell you we are telepathic?" Earon asked, a big smile across his face. "In our true forms we do not talk like I am now. Remember, we live in a liquid environment where talking is not practical. We talk to each other with our minds, not our mouths."

"Great, you guys can read my mind on top of everything else?" Europa asked, giving a big sigh.

"No, not everything," Jeanip said. "Just the thoughts you direct our way."

Europa's new discovery was interrupted by Terrance as he pointed to the now visible object ahead. "Is that what I think it is?"

Even Earon was astonished as they looked ahead to see a large yellow container ship. "It's the Big D's Banana Boat." He turned and looked at Jeanip. "Our destination is the Banana Boat?"

"Correct," Jeanip answered. "What could be a better hiding place than inside a vessel normally seen on the ocean? No one would expect a Banana Boat to be hiding fugitives."

"This is great!" Terrance said, watching the Banana Boat's stern open to reveal a large holding area below her decks. Jeanip carefully maneuvered the boat through the doors and into the large vessel's belly. As the doors closed behind them, the luminosity of a new day began to bring visibility back to the ocean's surface, revealing nothing except the traveling Banana Boat.

THE BANANA BOAT

Terrance, Europa and Earon looked around in awe of what they saw. The entire bottom half of the ship had been converted into a holding area with forty-foot ceilings filled with recessed blue lighting, thus bathing the area with a soft brightness. At the end of a platform was a moderate dock where two boats were tied. A walkway ran the entire length of the ship. Numerous rooms could be seen branching off from the walkway containing name plates above their doors that read "medical, galley, storage, navigation, security" and several others the new arrivals were too far away from to read. There was a stairway at each end of the walkway which led to a second floor balcony, behind which were numerous doors leading to sleeping quarters. Another stairway at the far end of the second floor led to a narrow third floor walkway. Behind this walkway was a bulletproof glass wall where several soldiers could be seen standing guard with assault rifles. The air inside was surprisingly fresh and cool with just a touch of something that smelled like jasmine.

"This is unbelievable," Europa said, as she surveyed her surroundings.

"Is it not?" Jeanip replied, proud of the Oonock accomplishment. "And the human crew above has no idea this even exits. That was why it was imperative we arrived before dawn so we could enter under the cloak of night. Our arrival would have been hard to conceal once it was light enough for the crew above to see."

Jeanip steered the boat toward the dock where a tall, dark-haired male awaited them. Earon threw him the stern line, which he quickly tied to the dock. After shutting off the engine, Jeanip walked to the bow and threw the bow line to a reddish-haired man waiting there.

"Welcome, Your Majesties," the dark-haired man said, bowing slightly and raising his hand to his forehead. "My name is Altim. I am the Waters in command of this vessel. On behalf of my crew, I welcome you aboard."

"Thank you, Altim," Europa replied, as she and Earon returned the bow. "My brother and I thank you for your assistance and hospitality."

"This is a very impressive vessel," Earon stated, as he continued to take in the spectacle before him. "I do not ever remember hearing of us having such a vessel. Is it fairly new?"

"Actually, this is only her third voyage, but her predecessor has been a familiar sight on the ocean for more than twenty years," Altim replied. "When Medaron was killed and your father learned JeffRa was still alive, he immediately decreed for the vessel to be built. Both Enok and your protector, Jeanip, knew you two would need some kind of secret transport to Saint's Isle. And what better place to hide you in than a ship that has been seen on these waters for decades?"

"Was it your idea to use the Banana Boat, Jeanip?" Europa asked, truly impressed by what she saw.

"It was Runbee's," Jeanip replied. "He has patrolled these waters for many years so he had the best knowledge of the vessels regularly traveling through here."

"We must remember to congratulate him on a marvelous idea the next time we see him," Europa said, trying to stifle a yawn.

Noting Europa's yawn and seeing the tired look upon the young travelers' faces, Altim gestured for the travelers to follow him. "You must be hungry and very tired after your trip. If you would please follow me we will take care of both. Would you prefer to eat or rest first?"

"I suggest we eat first, and then we can rest," Jeanip said. "If that is agreeable with you," he asked Europa and Earon.

"That sounds perfect," Earon replied.

"And perhaps a shower," Terrance added.

"Of course, Mr. Landers," Altim answered. He saw the surprised look on Terrance's face when he addressed him by name. "You are surprised that I know of you? Let me assure you, young Terrance, your name is well known already amongst us Oonocks. Terrance Landers, the young companion and protector of our female monarch, friend of Earon and trusted ally of our Chief Commander, Jeanip. The tales of your heroism and loyalty toward Europa have spread throughout our world, both above and below."

Europa looked over at Terrance. She saw his face quickly flash a bright red from embarrassment. "We never could have made it without him," Europa said, slipping her arm through Terrance's and leaning forward to kiss him on the cheek. Remembering where she was, and how inappropriate it would be to show such affection toward Terrance in public, she immediately straightened and quickly looked over at Jeanip to see his reaction. She was delighted when she saw him smile and give her an affirmative nod.

Giving no indication if he had seen Europa's almost mistake, Altim turned and walked down the walkway. "The dining area is down this way. If you would please follow me." Altim led the way with Jeanip walking at his side. Europa and Terrance followed, then Earon. Terrance turned to see the young man with reddish hair who had tied the bow line bringing up the rear. Terrance noted he had several scratches on his face and his left arm was bandaged up to the elbow. Not sure if he was getting paranoid after all that had happened to them, he was just getting ready to call the man's injuries to Europa's attention when he heard Altim speak.

"Sounds like you had a rough go there, Jeanip," Altim said. "We received word the Hunting Lodge was under attack by the Terrians and they had been able to break through Chancee's defenses."

"They came out of nowhere, just like they did at Minnos. I don't know how JeffRa is doing it," Jeanip replied. "He seems to know every move, every plan we have in place."

"Well, this is one place he won't know about," Altim confidently stated.

"Might you know any information about the decoy boats?" Jeanip inquired. "I saw one destroyed as it left the cavern, but I never saw if any of the others made it."

"We received a communication that only one of the white decoy boats survived."

"And what of the black speed boat we were originally going to take?" Earon asked, as he walked up beside Jeanip.

"That too was destroyed, I'm sorry to report. It was a good thing Jeanip thought of having the spare boat as an alternative escape."

373

"It's always best to anticipate the impossible," Jeanip said.

"Had he not we would not be having this conversation," Terrance quietly stated, remembering all too clearly how close they had come to death.

"Even with the second boat we barely made it out alive," Jeanip reported. "We had barely traveled out onto the ocean before three Terrian boats descended upon us. Thank goodness Chancee had accompanied us and was able to destroy one of the boats while Enok and his team took out the other two." Jeanip paused for a moment, a look of grave concern overshadowing his face as he remembered his fallen comrade. "There was a fourth boat none of us saw. When Chancee destroyed the Terrian vessel they were able to pinpoint his location and blasted the cavern apart. By any chance did the communication say anything about Chancee, if he made it or not?"

"I am sorry to hear that," Altim said. "No, it mentioned nothing about an attack on that part of the cavern or that Chancee was hurt. Perhaps the Hunting Lodge is unaware of the attack and Chancee's need for assistance. I will have one of my soldiers contact them without delay and advise them."

"Thank you, Altim," Europa replied. "The entire cavern appeared to have caved in, burying Mr. Dark Feather. If he is alive he must be severely injured and needing immediate medical attention."

As they continued to walk Altim motioned for one of the guards to approach him. Altim instructed him to contact the Hunting Lodge and advise them the second cavern had been compromised and Chancee may be in need of critical medical attention. After receiving his instructions, the young soldier ran to the security room and immediately contacted the Hunting Lodge to apprise them of the situation. Soon he returned and informed the five the Hunting Lodge was already aware of the attack on the cavern and a rescue party was in route to help Chancee.

Seeing the concerned looks on the four travelers' faces, Altim stated, "I am sure they will reach him in time. He's a pretty spry ol' soldier and capable of surviving about anything."

Without looking at anyone or breaking his stride Jeanip said, "Perhaps not this time."

Altim looked over at Jeanip and realized Jeanip believed Chancee had finally lost his battle with the Terrians. Not wishing to dwell on Chancee's possible passing, he stated, "When we received word you were motionless out in the ocean concealed under the drape with a helicopter above you, we feared you would not be able to make our rendezvous. Or worse yet, the Terrians had narrowed in on your position."

"We would have missed our rendezvous if it had not been for the decoy boat," Jeanip replied. A perplexed look appeared on his face as he realized the decoy boat had not followed orders. "But you said all but one of the decoy boats had been destroyed. I cannot imagine that, in the vastness of the ocean, this one remaining boat just happened to be in the right place at the needed time."

"Actually, Jeanip, that was one of our boats," Altim announced. "When you ran into trouble Enok immediately came here to advise us. Young Cimbor, who's behind us, immediately asked for permission to take out a decoy boat to lead the Terrians away from you. Permission was barely out of my mouth before he was on the boat, speeding toward the doors. We scarcely got them open before he zoomed through. He is the one whom deserves the credit."

Jeanip stopped and turned toward Cimbor. He noticed the man had several new cuts on his face and possibly a broken arm. Jeanip wondered if he had gotten the injuries while attempting to save them. He motioned for Cimbor to come forward. "So, you are the Oonock soldier responsible for leading the Terrians away from us." Jeanip held out his hand to Cimbor. "I would like to shake your hand, Cimbor. I owe you my life, along with the lives of our monarchs' and Terrance's. We could not have gotten away from that helicopter without your help. Thank you."

Cimbor took Jeanip's hand and shook it. "No thanks is needed, Sir. It was all in the line of duty."

Earon stepped forward and extended his hand. "You have my thanks also, Cimbor."

Cimbor lifted his hand to his forehead and slightly bowed, clearly nervous of Earon's display of gratitude. "Your Majesty, I cannot accept your hand. I am a soldier, and therefore in your service."

Earon stepped forward, grabbed Cimbor's hand and placed it into his own. "And a damn fine soldier you are, Cimbor. It is my honor to shake your hand."

Cimbor looked at Jeanip for guidance. "It is acceptable to shake his hand, Cimbor," Jeanip told him. "You will discover our two young monarchs do not always follow the old protocols."

After Cimbor shook Earon's hand, Terrance stepped up and shook it also. Then Europa stepped forward. Although he tried to hide it, Cimbor's uneasiness clearly showed. Cimbor again raised his hand to his forehead and bowed deeper this time to Europa.

"I will not forget your service, Cimbor," Europa stated. "Nor the injuries you sustained while in that service. You saved our lives and you deserve so much more than a handshake. Don't faint on me, but I am going to hug you." With that said, Europa reached out and hugged Cimbor. She could feel his body stiffen as she hugged him. As she withdrew her hug she thought for a brief second she felt something sinister, something evil hidden deep inside Cimbor. Dismissing the idea, she leaned forward and gently kissed him on the cheek. "When the day comes I have a new home, I hope you will consider joining my security detail."

A huge smile covered Cimbor's face as Europa turned around and the group resumed their walk toward the dining room.

Jeanip leaned toward Altim and whispered, "Is he still standing on his feet?"

Altim glanced behind at the smiling Cimbor for a second. "Yes, he's still standing but I think he's walking about six inches off the floor." Jeanip and Altim laughed as they continued to the meal room.

The four weary travelers had a hearty breakfast but were too tired to talk about much. Even Jeanip was silent. Believing his duty to protect his monarchs had not concluded, Cimbor stood at attention several feet behind Europa throughout the meal. Knowing he was injured and probably in need of rest, Europa leaned over to Jeanip and whispered, "Jeanip, he does not have to stand behind me. Should he not be resting or something?"

"I know", Jeanip stated. "I can tell him it is not necessary, but I doubt it will do any good. I have seen this dedication before to duty. Sunam and Misso had the same high degree. Drove me crazy at times. Do you want me to try?"

"Yes, please," Europa answered.

Jeanip turned and addressed Cimbor. "Cimbor, the Majesties are safe here, are they not?"

"Yes, Sir."

"Then it is not necessary for you to stand at attention guarding them," Jeanip said.

376

"That is my assigned duty, Sir, to oversee the protection of Europa," Cimbor replied. "I will not neglect my duty. Plus, as you said, the Terrians came out of nowhere when they breached the wall at the Hunting Lodge. Who is to say that could not happen here also?"

"The difference is we are on a moving boat. But your statement is true and I thank you for your forethought." Jeanip looked at Europa and whispered, "As I said, dedicated to a fault. If it bothers you to have him stand there I can give him a direct order to leave his post."

"No, that is not necessary," Europa replied. "We are almost done with our meal." Then an idea occurred to Europa. "He is not going to stand behind me in my room too, is he?"

"I can definitely say that is a big no," Jeanip replied.

"If you are finished, I will show you to your resting quarters," Altim announced. Addressing Jeanip he said, "I knew you would want to remain with our two monarchs, so I've assembled a room where all four of you can rest. There's a private bathroom for Europa and Earon. Plus, another bathroom with two shower stalls for you and Terrance. The bathrooms have only one entrance, and that is from the sleeping area. I've assigned a female helper to assist Europa," Altim said as he faced Europa. He then turned to Earon. "Earon, if you would like a male helper let me know and I'll have someone assist you too."

"No, I will be fine without one," Earon answered.

Altim led the way to their resting quarters, Cimbor walking a respectable distance behind. Altim opened the door and revealed a beautifully decorated lilac circular room with four beds that were already turned down. They looked so comfortable the four travelers almost forewent the baths and showers. Three bathroom doors were spaced along the wall to the left; to the right was a single door to a sitting room. Standing in the middle of the room was a woman with short cropped hair, lilac eyes, of a muscular build, in her late thirties.

"This is Seemon," Altim said, as Seemon raised her hand to her forehead and bowed. "She is Europa's helper, but she can get any of you anything you need, such as coffee, water, snacks and so forth. Now, if you are no longer in need of my assistance I will take my leave of you and put you in Seemon's capable hands." Altim turned to leave, then stopped, remembering one other thing. "Oh, by the way, Cimbor will be standing guard outside your door."

"How did I know you were going to say that?" Earon asked.

"Were we that dedicated at that age?" Jeanip asked, not sure if he should be annoyed, amused or impressed by Cimbor's dedication.

"From what I've heard, you were worse," Altim chuckled. "And still are. I believe the last indication of such was the killing wound you told no one about that nearly ended your life?" Jeanip stared at Altim, but did not utter a word. Amused at his commander's stare, he chuckled and said as he left, "I'll see you after you've rested."

Addressing Europa, Seemon said, 'Your Majesty, your bathroom is the first door. I have your bath water ready for you. There's an assortment of bath oils and several shampoos." Speaking to Earon she said, "Your Majesty, your bathroom is the second door. I did not run your bath since I was not sure if you would prefer a bath or shower. But if you'd like a bath, I can run one for you."

"No, I prefer showers, thank you," Earon answered.

"Your showers are through the third door," Seemon said to Terrance and Jeanip. "Each of you has a clean set of clothes waiting for you inside. If they are not to your taste, please let me know and I will get you something different to wear. If you have no need of me, I will leave you to your bath and showers. I'll return in twenty minutes to check on you." As Seemon turned to leave Jeanip stopped her and whispered something in her ear. "Yes, Sir, I will bring it right away." She then left the room.

Europa and Terrance entered their bathrooms, both looking forward to a warm bath or shower and soft beds. Earon delayed his entrance wondering what Jeanip was up to, what Seemon was bringing him. He was surprised when Jeanip sat down upon his bed and laid his gun next to him. Bewildered he asked, "Is something wrong, Jeanip?"

"Not at all, Your Majesty. I promised Europa I would never leave her alone again. I am beholding to that promise. I will wait here to assure no one disturbs her or you while you bathe. I have asked Seemon to bring me some warm water and a wash basin so I may wash up out here while I keep guard."

Earon thought of arguing with Jeanip, pointing out Europa was in no danger here on the Banana Boat, but decided against it knowing Jeanip's mind could not be changed. He entered his bathroom and quickly showered, longing for the comforts of his bed. When he returned he noted Jeanip had used the wash basin to freshen up and had changed clothes while never breaking his watch of Europa's door.

"Is she still in there soaking in the tub?" Earon asked, as he looked at Europa's door.

"Yes. Did you forget how long your sister likes to soak?" Both men chuckled. It had been a standing joke at Minnos about the length of Europa's baths. "Don't you remember I nicknamed her 'Prunes' when she was little because she stayed in the water so long? She would come out of the bathroom with her skin all prunish."

"Not this time," said Europ emerging from her bathroom, turning around in a circle with her arms outstretched to show them her smooth skin. "No prune today."

The door suddenly opened startling the four. Cimbor halted his entrance when he saw Jeanip standing in front of Europa with his firearm drawn. "I'm sorry if I startled you. Seemon went back to the kitchen to get the orange juice she forgot. I offered to bring in the coffee and tea she had in her hands." Jeanip lowered his weapon and nodded his approval for Cimbor to enter the room. Cimbor sat the tray down on a small table and carefully surveyed the room.

"Who gave you permission to leave your post, soldier?" Jeanip shouted, anger clearly visible on his face.

"No one, Sir. I was just trying to help Seemon," Cimbor replied, uneasy about Jeanip questioning his departure from his post.

"That is not acceptable." Jeanip stated. "A soldier never leaves his guard post unless there is sufficient reason. Or do you consider a tray of coffee and snacks a sufficient reason?"

Before Cimbor could answer there was a knock at the door, followed several seconds later by Seemon entering carrying a pitcher of fresh orange juice and several glasses. Seeing the anxiety on everyone's faces she asked, "Is something wrong?"

Sensing the tension in the air Europa quickly walked over and took the orange juice and glasses from Seemon. "No, everything is fine. Thank you very much, Seemon, for going back for the orange juice. This is exactly what I am thirsty for." She carried the pitcher and glasses over to the table where the coffee and tea were and poured herself a glass. "Would anyone else like one?"

"I think I would," Terrance said, as he walked over to Europa. He too felt the tension and was impressed at the diplomatic way Europa defused it.

"We need to rest now, so your services will not be needed," Jeanip said, dismissing both Seemon and Cimbor.

Both bowed and raised their hands to their forehead. "Then we will take our leave of you. Good rest, Your Majesties. You are safe here," Seemon stated. "If you desire something before I return, just ring for me. Safe journey." With that said, Seemon lowered the lights and departed the room. Cimbor followed to resume his post outside the door.

Terrance, Europa and Earon crawled into their beds for a needed rest. Jeanip walked to the end of his bed and dragged it across the floor, positioning it in front of the door to assure no one would try to enter the room while they slept. The three young travelers were too tired to question Jeanip on his doings; they snuggled down inside their beds and were soon asleep. Jeanip silently walked over and placed a chair next to Earon's bed, then withdrew a weapon from his boot and laid it on the chair, giving Earon easy access to it should the need arise. He then silently walked over to his bed and laid down, placing his weapon beside him. He fell asleep assured no one could enter the room and endanger his monarchs.

As they slept, the Banana Boat continued on its voyage, bringing the four unseen passengers closer to their destination. Cimbor stood at his post watching over his sleeping monarchs. Enok had gone below to transform back into his true self, gaining strength to surface again to lead his children on their last leg of their journey to Saint's Isle and FarCore.

Jeanip awoke after three hours of sleep. He quietly sat up in his bed and looked at his charges. Earon too was beginning to wake, but Terrance and Europa were still sleeping soundly. Signaling for Earon to be quiet, Jeanip silently walked over to the sitting room. Earon rose and followed.

"Are you not going to move your bed away from the door?" Earon silently asked, using telepathy to assure they did not disturb the two sleeping humans.

"No, I'll leave it there until Europa wakens," he silently replied. "I don't want the noise to awaken her."

"I can help you lift it so it will not make a sound," suggested Earon. "That way when Seemon comes back the door hitting the bed will not startle anyone."

"Very well," Jeanip agreed. Together, he and Earon lifted the bed away from the door, making access to the room once again possible. Jeanip opened the door to have a look at the corridor and saw Cimbor still standing guard. "Europa was right – he would make a fine addition to our new security team," Jeanip thought to himself. "I will have to speak to Altim about transferring him to my command. He would make a good replacement for Tinderoon. I think I'll ask Altim about Seemon also. We will be in need of a good house helper when we resettle."

A soft knock at the door broke Jeanip's thoughts. He opened it to see Seemon standing there with a cart containing coffee and an assortment of other drinks. There was also a tray of sandwiches, cheese, crackers and fresh fruit. Seemon saw Europa and Terrance were still sleeping, so she left the cart just inside the door and walked back out followed by Jeanip. Standing in the doorway with his back to the wall so he could still see Europa sleeping, he addressed Cimbor.

"Cimbor, I didn't get a chance to ask you how you escaped the Terrians," Jeanip quietly said, as he held on to his weapon. "Or how you were injured? How did you get back here without the Terrians knowing where you went?"

Cimbor smiled. "I have learned Terrians are not too bright," he chuckled. "Once I knew they were following me I led them as far away as I could from your location and the Banana Boat. When I had led them as far as I needed to, I put the boat on auto pilot, secured the wheel to head south and jumped overboard. I swam back as a jumper and arrived about fifteen minutes before you did."

"Excellent strategy," Jeanip said.

"I bet they were really pissed when they found out they had been fooled," Cimbor added. "I bet that is one story they will not be telling JeffRa."

"You can be sure of that," Jeanip said.

"As for my injuries, I got them when I let that helicopter get a little too close to me. They opened fired and shot up my boat pretty bad. Pieces of boat were flying everywhere and some flew into my face, cutting it. As for my arm, I was going too fast when I tried to make a sharp turn. The force threw me into the side of the boat and almost broke the arm. Good thing I did not because I do not know if I would have been able to swim back to the Banana Boat."

Jeanip admired the young man's heroism. "Europa asked you to join her security guard whenever we return to land. I would also like to extend that invitation. Would you be interested in joining my team?"

Having trouble finding his voice for a minute, Cimbor cleared his throat and replied, "Oh yes, Sir. I would be honored to. But it is not necessary to wait. If you wish, I can go along with you now and help protect our monarchs."

"That is very noble of you, Cimbor," Jeanip replied. "But I am afraid this trip is only for the four of us. But if something changes before we leave I will definitely reconsider bringing you along with us now." Jeanip saw the smile Cimbor was trying to keep off his face. He looked forward to working with him. "Cimbor, would you go ask Altim to join me here?" Jeanip asked.

"I am sure he is in the security room. I will stand watch if you wish to go speak to him."

Jeanip reached out and placed his hand on Cimbor's shoulder. "Cimbor, I am just like you. I take my security responsibilities very seriously. As long as Europa sleeps in this room I will not step outside this door. Therefore I cannot go to Altim; he needs to come to me."

"Yes, Sir," Cimbor answered. "I should have known that. I will go get him right away." Cimbor turned and ran down the walkway, down the stairs and to the security room. He returned within minutes, panting from running both ways. "He will be right here, Sir."

"Thank you." Jeanip said. "I'll wait for him inside. Tell him to come to the sitting room off the bedroom and advise him Europa is still asleep." Jeanip stepped inside the bedroom, closing the door and locking it. He walked over to the cart Seemon had brought and poured himself and Earon a cup of coffee. He placed several cookies on each saucer and carried them to the sitting room, motioning with his head for Earon to follow. Earon grabbed a banana and followed Jeanip. Jeanip sat Earon's cup of coffee on a small end table next to a chair and then took the seat that gave him easy viewing of the sleeping Europa. Earon sat down and both men drank their coffee and consumed their food without saying a word. They had just finished when they heard another soft knock at the door. Jeanip stood up, firearm in hand and walked over to the door, unlatched the lock and opened the door to see Altim. Altim quietly followed Jeanip back to the sitting room and sat down in the seat next to Earon. Jeanip partially closed the door and sat back down to continue his watch over Europa, placing his weapon on the table next to him.

"I want her to sleep as long as possible," Jeanip telepathically said, holding his finger up to his lips, signaling Altim to speak silently. "We can talk without words."

"As you wish, Commander," Altim responded. Seeing Jeanip's weapon he stated, "Jeanip, there really is no need to carry a weapon in here."

"Hard habit to break. Plus, what is it the humans say, 'Better safe than sorry'? I've eased up on my guard several times this past twenty-four hours and have almost paid a dear price. I will proceed as if she is in danger until I have her and Earon safe at Saint's Isle."

"I assure you, with all our security measures and technology we have, there is no danger here. But, if you feel better keeping your weapon ready to protect her, then so be it. You are the Commander." Altim knew he could not question Jeanip's authority or his commands. If Jeanip felt the need for the weapon and doubt about his security, so be it.

"My compliments on Seemon and Cimbor," Jeanip said, as he continued to watch the bedroom. "They are fine examples of extraordinary soldiers. I may have to take them off your hands when this is over."

"As always, any of my soldiers are yours," Altim replied. "If you prefer, they can go with you now to help out."

"Cimbor mentioned the same thing," Jeanip stated. "I am beginning to get the feeling some of you think I need help getting these three to safety. I am not too old yet to fulfill my obligation, Altim."

"You misunderstand me, Jeanip," Altim quickly said, wanting to clear up any misunderstanding. "I have every confidence in you. You are my Commander, Enok's First in Command. I would never question any of your decisions. I only suggested it so you would not have to bear all the responsibility on your shoulders. How are you going to navigate the boat while you secure the tie lines? Unless you're going to put the three kids into doing physical labor, who is going to unload all those supplies? Even with the unloaders on the island, you can't do it alone. Plus, you must consider the possibility that something could incapacitate you, or even worse, you could be killed. Who will protect them then?"

"He does have a point," Earon said, seeing Jeanip's face tense as his looked away from the bedroom to face him. "Jeanip, you almost died on us once. In fact, if it had not been for Europa you would not be here now. I think it might not be a bad idea to bring these two with us.

Plus, I am sure Europa would appreciate another female if she is going to be on Saint's Isle for an extended period of time. Sometimes a girl needs another female to talk to about things. And had they not been killed, Sunam and Misso would have gone all the way with us."

"If you wish it, Earon, I will bring them along," Jeanip stated, turning back to keep watch over the bedroom.

"Only if you have no objections," clarified Earon. "This is your task. I do not want to do anything to undermine your decisions."

"So what do you say?" Altim asked. "Should I tell them to prepare to go with you?"

Jeanip thought for a moment. Europa would benefit from another female. And Earon was right – Sunam and Misso would have gone with them. Plus, with Cimbor joining them Jeanip would not have to put any of the three on watch and in danger.

"Agreed," Jeanip said. "They will be a great asset to us on this journey and on Saint's Isle. I believe their presence will greatly improve our chances of success."

"I will inform them as soon as I leave here," Altim said. "You will not be sorry that you decided to take them with you. Although I, on the other hand, will greatly miss their expertise and commitment." Altim paused for a moment then added, "I did not get a chance to give you my condolence on the loss of your team," Altim said. "They were some of the finest soldiers I have ever seen. I'm also amazed you were able to make it here alone. The stories of your greatness do not do you justice – you are so much greater."

"Stories?" inquired Earon.

"Jeanip is a legend amongst the military rank," Altim relayed, turning to face Earon. "Everyone wants to work under him. He is our hero, the slayer of more Terrians than any other Oonock. He saved Enok and Medaron countless times. Many feel he should be the next monarch if anything happened to the royal family."

"That's enough, Altim," Jeanip yelled out loud, forgetting for a moment the two sleeping humans in the other room. "I'm not a hero. I deserve no praise, no recognition. I failed at the one main task Enok gave me – to protect Medaron. She died because I was not there when she needed me. I let my guard down and JeffRa took advantage of that. My beloved sister and noble monarch is gone, now part of the water that covers this planet." For the first time Earon saw a vulnerable Jeanip, consumed with grief and guilt as he brushed away tears from his eyes. Seeing his vulnerability only made Earon respect and love him more.

Altim stood and walked to Jeanip, looking him sternly in the eye. "Listen, Sir, because you're only going to let me say this once. You dishonor Medaron's death by saying you failed her. True, her safety was the number one priority Enok assigned you; but Medaron gave you a higher priority - the protection of her daughter. Had Europa been killed instead of Medaron, she would never have forgiven herself – or you – or even Enok. If after all she sacrificed, all the loneliness she endured, had she lost Europa, it would all have been in vain. Don't you remember how we almost lost her when Tiree died? No, Jeanip, you fulfilled Medaron's orders; you're still fulfilling them. Never, ever doubt that. She gladly gave her life in exchange for Europa's safety. Accept her decision. Accept her loss as one soldier accepts another's. Besides, if Enok did not believe in you, trust in you, he would not place the safety of his two most precious things in your hands for safe keeping."

"Are you finished?" Jeanip asked, as he stared at the floor, a tear drop falling from his eyes.

"Yes," Altim simply said. "I meant you no disrespect, Jeanip. But sometimes even Head Commanders need to hear the truth they are not able to see for themselves. For speaking to you in such a manner I will resign my command, if that is your wish." Altim knew it was dangerous to address Jeanip in such a manner, but he felt it was warranted to make Jeanip realize he did not fail Medaron.

"Your resignation is not necessary," Jeanip replied. "Besides, I don't have any one I can reassign to your position."

Understanding Jeanip's reply signified the subject was closed, Altim continued, "This is how the last half of this journey is to proceed."

Altim, Earon and Jeanip went over the final length of their journey for the next hour while Jeanip maintained his vigil, never averting his eyes away from the next room. Finally they heard the two humans beginning to wake. Ending their conversation, Jeanip and Earon returned to the sleeping area to greet Europa and Terrance as they woke while Altim quietly left to tell Seemon and Cimbor his news. Shortly after Altim closed the door Jeanip heard a loud "Yahoo!" outside the door indicating Cimbor had his new assignment.

"Your Highnesses, I would like to keep you secured in this room. I know it will be an inconvenience, but I would feel much better knowing you are safe with me to protect you. The Terrians have gotten through our defenses thrice now and I am no longer confident this place is totally secure. Outside of this room there are too many directions an attack can come from; in here there is only one – the front door."

"Doesn't that mean there's only one way out too?" Terrance asked, concerned they could be trapped inside the room if attacked.

"True, but in here I can fight off an army until reinforcements arrive," Jeanip replied, hoping to ease any of Terrance's concerns.

"How many days before we arrive at Saint's Isle?" Earon asked. He didn't relish the thought of being confined in such small quarters for an extended length of time.

"Unfortunately, we have a two day trip," Jeanip stated. "But I do ask that you honor my request."

"Would we be able to go to the galley to eat?" Terrance asked.

"No, we will have to take all our meals in here too," Jeanip replied. "I can have Seemon bring you anything you may want to eat."

Europa remained silent for a moment as she thought over Jeanip's suggestion. She then turned to face him and said, "Jeanip, I hate the thought of being confined in here for two days. But your overdone security measures and paranoia have saved our lives more than once these past few days. I will not question your decision in matters of our security. If you think it best for us to remain here throughout the voyage, then so be it. I believe I speak for Earon and Terrance also when I say do whatever you feel is necessary to get us to Saint's Isle alive."

"I agree," Earon added.

"Me too," agreed Terrance.

"Thank you, Your Majesties. I am sure we are completely safe here but . . ."

"But," Earon continued, "As you mentioned earlier, the Terrians have somehow known every move we have made. It is possible they know about our voyage on this boat and could try another assault. It is also possible there is an assassin on board already, just waiting for his opportunity to strike."

"A possibility that I have accepted but had no desire to advise you of," Jeanip stated. "After all that has happened and all the security breaches, the only thing we can be sure of is that anything and everything is not only possible but highly probable."

"Paranoia City," whispered Terrance.

"Paranoia City," confirmed Europa.

"Since we are in agreement we will remain in this room for the duration of our voyage. I will ask Cimbor to have Seemon return and take your food order," Jeanip said, as he walked toward the door. When he opened it he was surprised to see Cimbor was not standing at his post. Perhaps Altim had instructed him to wait for them in the galley or perhaps he had gone to get some needed rest. Whatever the reason, he must remember to remind Cimbor he must inform him before he leaves his post. Jeanip reclosed the door and walked over to the bell Seemon had left. He rang it and waited for her to return.

"Is something wrong?" Seemon asked upon entering the room. "I have food ready for you in the galley."

"There's been a change of plans, Seemon," Jeanip stated. "We will be having all of our meals in here for the duration of the voyage."

Upon hearing Jeanip's request Seemon proceeded to the galley and returned with a cart of food. She was accompanied by a confused Altim and a concerned Cimbor.

"I understand you will not be joining us in the galley?" Altim asked. "Seemon informs me you will remain sequestered in here for the duration of the voyage?"

"That is correct," was the only explanation Jeanip gave.

"I can assure you, Your Majesties, the galley is secure," Cimbor stated. "I have checked and rechecked it, plus there are armed guards above the room. You need not worry about going down there."

"We have confidence in Altim's security measures, but we feel it would be best for us to remain in here until our departure," Earon stated, wondering why Cimbor was questioning Jeanip's decision. As a soldier, he should know better than to try to question his commander's orders. Earon believed Cimbor may have just talked himself out of a new duty by doing so.

"Of course, I meant no disrespect," Cimbor quickly said, almost stumbling over his words. "I will have Seemon bring my food down here also so I may dine with you."

Europa and Terrance looked at each other. Even Jeanip did not normally eat with the sovereigns, so why would an unranking soldier assume it was okay for him to do so? There was something strange about this man; he was not following the teachings he would have been taught as a soldier. It was almost as if he considered himself on the same level as the monarchs.

"Cimbor, perhaps I made a mistake in considering you for part of my security team," Jeanip said, as he watched a look of panic cross Cimbor's face. "Soldiers do NOT eat with sovereigns unless invited and I do not remember hearing such a request. Perhaps when I informed you earlier our monarchs were lax on some protocols you wrongly assumed all etiquette protocols were void. Well, they are not, soldier!" Jeanip turned to Altim. "Perhaps there has been something amiss in his training. If he does not know the proper etiquette for dealing with monarchs how can I trust he knows security protocols?"

Before Altim could even answer Cimbor spoke up, again breaking ranking protocol. "Again, I do apologize. I have not slept in over thirty hours and I fear my fatigue has clouded my judgment. I was a member of a lesser royal family on Europa and was accustomed to eating with a royal family. In my fatigue I forgot myself. I will return to my post outside." Without another word, Cimbor turned and left the room, standing in the hallway at his post.

"I am not excusing his behavior, but I have never known him to break protocol before," Altim said, hoping to prevent Jeanip from denying him a place on his team. "In fact, he is probably the best soldier for following proper protocol that I have on this ship."

"We shall see," Jeanip stated, as he looked at Altim. "Go tell him to get some food and some sleep. We'll see how he does after his mind has rested."

"Would you like me to post another guard?" Altim asked. "Or if you prefer, I can stand watch until he returns."

Before Jeanip could answer a voice was heard outside the door. "No need. We're here now." Each turned to see who it was who thought they were capable of guarding the monarchs. To everyone's surprise and delight, through the doorway walked Graybin and Runbee, this time clothed. "We thought you might need some help."

"You are a welcome sight," Jeanip said, as he walked up to them and clasped each on the shoulder. "Runbee, you can stand watch outside. Graybin, this is Seemon," Jeanip said, gesturing toward Seemon who was pouring cups of coffee. "Perhaps you can help her with the meal." He then turned to Altim and added, "Thank you, but I have a guard for the door." Assuming he had just been dismissed, Altim left the room to relay Jeanip's orders to Cimbor.

"Who's the Waters with the angry look outside?" Graybin asked when the door closed behind Altim. "He didn't look too pleased to see us."

"He was supposed to be a new member of our security team," Earon stated. "But he may have allowed his mouth to overstep its bounds. He questioned Jeanip on his methods of securing our safety."

"Oooo, not a good thing to do," Graybin said, smiling teasingly at Jeanip. "That can be a destroyer of one's career to question Jeanip."

"Just do what you've been ordered to do," Jeanip said, as he sat down at the table. He did not dignify her comment with another word. He assumed Runbee would also get a laugh out of her comments when Graybin told him what happened.

Cimbor returned to his post later that day after a needed rest. His demeanor was humble and his attitude greatly changed. Thinking it better to mention nothing of his outburst, he stood at his post in silence, hoping Jeanip would not delete him from the team.

With Cimbor at his post Runbee returned to the room where the four travelers waited, offering assistance in anyway needed. Hoping perhaps he had some news of the Hunting Lodge, Jeanip asked, "Runbee, by any chance have you heard any news about Chancee? Did he survive the cave-in?"

A serious look on his face, Runbee said, "I don't know, Jeanip. I know when they received Altim's message about the Terrian strike on the second chamber, a rescue crew had already been sent to find Chancee. And from what I understand, the cave-in was extensive. There was nothing left of the bottom chamber and the top chamber, where Chancee manned the blaster, was mostly gone also. When Graybin and I left they were still trying to dig him out. If he did somehow survive, he had to be badly injured."

"As I feared," Jeanip stated. He said no more on the subject.

Sitting on her bed Europa listened to the males talk while brushing her hair. She too feared Mr. Dark Feather had not survived his ordeal. As she continued to brush her hair she noticed Graybin walking toward her. "Your Highness, would you allow me to brush your hair?"

"Excuse me?" Europa asked, surprised by Graybin's request. No one had brushed her hair for many years, not since her mother did when she was a little girl.

"It has been many centuries since I have had the privilege of brushing a young woman's hair. I remember with great fondness brushing my own daughter's hair when she was in human form."

Realizing how much it meant to Graybin, and after all she and Runbee had done for them, Europa could not refuse the request. She handed Graybin the brush who immediately sat down beside Europa with a huge grin upon her face. She gently lifted the hair on the side of Europa's face and softly began to brush it.

"Is your daughter a member of your dolphin pod?" Europa asked, intrigued now that she knew Graybin had a child.

"I'm afraid not," Runbee said softly. "She was killed by the Terrians and has flowed into the Waters of Life."

Europa regretted asking the question and wondered how long ago her daughter had been killed. She sat there in silence as Graybin brushed her hair. Then she heard Graybin humming a song, a song she thought her mother had sung to her. As she listened, the song became louder and Europa realized it was the same song. She turned to face Graybin. "My mother use to sing that song to me when I was little. We would sit together and she would hum it while she brushed my hair, just like you are doing."

"Would you like me to stop, Your Highness?" Graybin asked, setting the brush down on her lap.

"No, please continue," Europa answered. "I had forgotten the tune. Is it a Water's song?"

"Yes, it is a Water's lullaby."

"Will you teach it to me?" Europa asked. "I would like to learn it so I can sing it to my children someday, if I am so blessed to have them."

"It will be my pleasure," Graybin replied, as she hummed the song louder, a large smile across both female faces.

Sensing this was a good time to discuss things with the two females occupied, Runbee asked Jeanip, "Have you figured out how JeffRa is getting through our defenses? It's like he knows our every move."

"I've been giving that a lot of thought," Jeanip replied. "I have gone over our strategies again and again and find no flaw in them. Everything was air tight. The only thing I can come up with is he has a spy amongst us, and I know that too is impossible."

"Could someone be impersonating an Oonock?" Terrance asked. Since he knew little about the Oonocks and Terrians he had no idea what they were and were not capable of.

"What do you mean impersonate?" Jeanip asked.

"Since some of them are able to transform like you do, is it possible that one or more of them have transformed into someone you already know and trust? For example, if a Terrian wanted to, could they transform into Earon or Altim?"

"That's an interesting concept," Jeanip said. "And it would definitely explain a lot of things, except for one thing: Oonocks are not capable of transforming into a being that looks different each time. Whatever being we transform into, we always look the same each time we transform into that being." Seeing the confused look on Terrance's face Jeanip explained further. "Earon is a good example for you – you've seen him several times as both a canine and a human. Each time he transformed into Triton you recognized him because he looked identical to the last time you saw him as Triton. And when he transformed into Earon did he not look like the same Earon each time? The reason is we have a predetermined identity based upon our individual genetic makeup and that makeup always keeps us consistent to the last time we transformed into that being. We can alter a few simple things, such as our age, gray in our hair, even our skin color to some degree, but that is all. "

"And thank goodness we cannot," Earon stated. "Can you imagine what it would be like if the Terrians could become anyone they wanted to? We'd never be able to defend ourselves against that."

"That indeed is a scary thought," Runbee commented.

Graybin finished brushing Europa's hair and handed her back the brush. She gently brushed a lock of hair away from Europa's face and smiled. "There, your hair is beautiful. The salty air can dry out your hair before you know it."

Graybin and Runbee remained on board for the next two days helping with guard duty outside the door, watching over the monarchs while Jeanip slept and helping with the meals. Graybin also tried to keep the monarchs and Terrance entertained and busy during their confinement in the room.

Finally, the last day of their voyage arrived. Everyone was excited they would finally be allowed to leave the room that had kept them secure for almost three days. After a light breakfast, Europa and

Terrance packed their backpacks while Jeanip, Earon and Runbee discussed Cimbor's place on the security team. After some discussion Jeanip decided Cimbor had redeemed himself, and since Runbee and Graybin would be returning to the ocean, his presence was needed on the boat. Jeanip instructed Cimbor and Seemon to get their gear and meet them on the dock.

Jeanip, Earon, Terrance and Europa followed several minutes behind them, apprehensive about this final length of their voyage. All knew this part of the voyage would be the most dangerous; if JeffRa wished to fulfill his vow of vengeance he had to assassinate the monarchs between the Banana Boat and the island.

To take her mind off the upcoming danger, Europa fantasized about what type of boat they would be taking this time. As they came down the stairs and walked out onto the walkway she saw tied to the dock the vessel that would hopefully take her to safety. Their black fiberglass boat had been replaced with an ocean blue wooden boat which was larger than either of the two previous ones. It had two complete levels and a cargo hatch on the first deck. She saw several helpers carrying boxes of supplies aboard and placing them in the cargo hold. She then realized they needed to take supplies with them for their long stay on Saint's Isle. She wished she had known that fact because there were a few items she would like to have requested.

Altim stood on the dock waiting to say his goodbyes to his monarchs and the others. As Earon and Europa walked closer, Altim bowed slightly and raised his hand to his forehead. "It has been our pleasure to have you aboard with us, Your Majesties," he said as Earon and Europa returned the bow. "I hope the remainder of your journey is uneventful and we will be able to meet again soon."

"Thank you for your hospitality," Europa said. "I hope we were not too disruptive to your ship."

"Not at all, Your Majesty," Altim replied. "I hope after we eradicate the Terrians you will come back for another voyage – but this time above where you can enjoy all her hospitalities."

"We would like that very much," Europa said. Europa turned to follow Earon and Terrance, who had already stepped on board when she heard Jeanip's voice.

"Europa, if you would please wait, I will personally escort you on board." Europa was going to object then realized Jeanip was once more keeping his promise to never be away from her side; he would not let her step onto a vessel he was not on. She smiled and nodded affirmatively, signaling her willingness to wait.

Altim turned to talk with Jeanip. "I am glad you decided to take Cimbor with you. He really is a first-class soldier. I've never known him to step out of bounds like he did that day. I saw the change in him after he had rested, so he must have told the truth when he said it was due to exhaustion."

"Actually he has Earon and Runbee to thank that he is still a team member," Jeanip said, as he escorted Europa across the plank and onto the boat. "I will not tolerate such behavior for any reason. But Earon and Runbee reminded me the need for another person and, since he comes highly recommended by you, I overlooked the incident. Mind you, I said overlooked, not forgot. If he ever attempts that again or steps that far out of line, I will not hesitate to banish him from this army. And I will advise Enok to have him banished from the Complex."

"I think he understands that," Altim added. "Goodbye, My Friend and Chief Commander. May your journey be less eventful than the last one. May the Waters carry you and our sovereigns to safety and a long life."

"May the Waters bring you a long and good life, My Friend," Jeanip replied, then turned and disappeared with his charges into the vessel.

"Graybin and Runbee, it was nice to see you again. May the Waters guide you safely on your voyage," Altim said, as the two undressed and slipped into the water.

"May the Waters guide you upon your path."

"We'll be leaving in about ten minutes," Jeanip stated, climbing the stairs to the wheel house. "You three will ride with me in here. Europa and Terrance, you will find life preservers under the bench. You need to put one on as before. And Terrance, if you haven't taken anything for sea sickness, please do so now. There is medication in the first aid cupboard."

"Are we going to embark in broad daylight?" Europa asked. "That will allow the crew and any Terrians who are still looking for us to easily spot us, will it not?"

"No," Jeanip replied. "The crew will all be in the dining hall for a special celebration Altim arranged. And a dense curtain of fog will cloak our departure. Even if someone was on deck above or Terrians were ten feet away from this ship, they'd never be able to see us."

"But what if the fog isn't there?" Terrance asked.

"It will be," Jeanip stated. "We make it be there. It's one of the defenses of Saint's Isle - an impenetrable fog no sailor would venture into."

"Except us," Earon added.

"Except us," Jeanip confirmed.

"Jeanip, is there any place in particular you would like Seemon and me?" Cimbor asked. "Is there anything you need us to attend to below?"

"Would you like me to bring up some coffee for you?" Seemon offered. "Or some other drink?"

"Visibility is going to be nonexistent when we emerge," Jeanip replied to both soldiers. "For your safety it would be best for you to stay here in the wheel house with us. I suggest perhaps on the port side bench. As for drinks, I believe we should wait on that until we have arrived at the island."

Cimbor and Seemon sat down on the left while Europa and Terrance took seats on the opposite bench closest to Jeanip. Earon took the seat on Europa's right. Europa opened her backpack and removed her hooded sweatshirt jacket. As she did she saw the Orb resting in the bottom of her backpack, silent and colorless. She hesitated a moment, then lifted the Orb and placed it in her jacket pocket, zipping it securely inside. Earon gave her a puzzled look as to why she was putting the Orb in her jacket.

"Thought I would keep it handy in case we need it again," she said to Earon. "You never know when it is going to be needed or when we could be separated from our backpacks."

"I agree," Earon stated. "You are starting to think like a monarch – always prepared for what may come."

"Or she's learning to think like Jeanip," Terrance added quietly, not wanting Jeanip to hear him. Following Europa's lead, he put on his sweatshirt then his life jacket, placed his and Europa's backpacks on the floor by their feet, then pulled Europa into his arms. Seeing everyone was ready Jeanip started the silent engine and slowly maneuvered the boat away from the dock and toward the exit doors. He signaled to Altim they were ready to depart and the huge cargo doors opened. The boat containing the four adventurers and two new recruits moved forward onto the open ocean, beginning the last stretch of the journey.

SAINT'S ISLE

The boat exited into a dense fog bank so thick the three young travelers could not even see the person sitting next to them. They wondered how Jeanip would be able to navigate in such fog. After a few minutes they felt the boat speed away from the Banana Boat.

"I thought Oonocks couldn't see through fog?" Terrance asked, a little concerned about Jeanip not being able to see where he was going.

"You are correct. Fog is impenetrable to us as long as we're in human form," Jeanip volunteered. "To ease your fears, young Terrance, I know where I'm going because Enok is directing me."

"Father is back?" Europa asked, anxiously wishing she could see through the fog. "How can you tell in this fog? I don't hear his calls."

"I can hear him inside my mind. He is giving me directions on how to navigate so we can pass through the passageway with no problems. Whales operate by sonar and therefore have no trouble navigating through this fog."

"Ingenious," Cimbor said. "An impenetrable fog no one in their right mind would try to sail through. Who thought of such a brilliant camouflage?"

"Actually, it was one of Sunam's ideas," Jeanip said. "He did most of the security work on Saint's Isle while I worked on Minnos. He and his crew built the living quarters and landscaped the grounds. If you are impressed by the fog, what until you see the whole island!"

"He must be a great engineer in addition to an outstanding soldier," Cimbor commented. "I would very much like to meet him someday."

Knowing the sorrow everyone felt over his loss, Earon quickly stated, "We lost him on the first part of our voyage when we came under fire by Terrians in a sea plane. Sunam fashioned a weapon to destroy them, but something happened and part of it flew back into his chest. His wounds were too severe and we lost him."

"I am very sorry to hear that," Cimbor said. "And I am sorry to remind you of such a painful loss. May the Waters take him home and give him an eternity of peace." After a short pause Cimbor added, "I did not know any of the security team had escaped the destruction of Minnos and accompanied you."

"Only two made it," Europa replied. "Sunam and his wife Misso both left with us on the boat. But Misso had been injured in the initial attack and died on route to the Hunting Lodge. And Earon told you how Sunam died."

"I can tell you were very fond of them," Cimbor stated, as he heard the hint of sorrow in her voice. "But remember this, Your Majesty. They died as soldiers, doing their solemn duty of protecting you and they were able to return to the waters from which we came. Few soldiers are fortunate enough to become part of the sea. I only hope my end will be the same." He purposely added a tone of empathy to his voice, hoping it hid his happiness at hearing of their deaths. He was thankful the thick fog prevented her from seeing his smile.

Knowing they died doing their duty and were able to return to the sea did little to ease Europa's sorrow. Misso and Sunam had been with her since the day she was born. She could not remember a morning when Misso was not waiting for her in the kitchen with a glass of milk or juice or, in later years, a cooled cup of coffee. She did not know Sunam as well as she did Misso, but she still had fond memories of him also. He was the one who taught her to ride and how to properly saddle her horse. He was the one who always fixed her truck whenever something went wrong or, sometimes, he would install things just to make it run better or be nicer to ride in; like the time he surprised her with a new sound system. Europa knew Jeanip and Earon also felt their lost. But they had known them as soldiers and were therefore more able to accept their deaths. Since she had never known them as soldiers she could find no solace in their honorable passing. As they moved forward through the fog in silence Europa, along with her three companions, reflected on the events of the past few days, each wondering what the future held.

For the next hour they navigated carefully through the impenetrable fog following Enok's directions. The island was surrounded by many hazards to keep anyone from reaching the island unless they knew the secret path through the labyrinth of jagged rocks, shipwrecks and crashing waves. Europa reached out in the dense fog and grabbed Earon's hand while snuggling even further into Terrance's arms, hoping that would help her with the uneasiness which was beginning to creep into her. Living by the ocean she was used to fog, but not to this extent or duration on a boat. Just as she was about to ask how much further the silence was broken by a sound from Enok signaling they were reaching the end of the fog barrier.

"We're starting to come out of the fog," Jeanip announced almost with a tone of relief, for he too had started to feel uneasy. "Look ahead, Your Majesties, Saint's Isle will be visible in a few minutes."

Europa, Terrance and Earon stood up and looked ahead as the fog began to thin. Within minutes it disappeared totally to reveal an island covered with green foliage and palm trees. A long white sandy beach began at the foliage line and fell down to a deep blue ocean. Gentle waves washed up on the shore, glistening in the sunlight. Rising above the trees on the west side of the island was a large, three-story building made of white marble that sat on a cliff overlooking the ocean. Four large pillars, also of white marble, could be seen gracing its front, reminding one of an ancient Greek temple. A set of double doors made of gold marked the entrance to the habitat. A white marble stairway could be seen rising to the doors with a lilac waterfall cascading down each side before emptying into a large moat. A cloudless blue sky framed the island to complete the picture. Beyond the island the barrier of fog could again be seen, thus assuring the travelers their island was well hidden.

"Welcome to your new home, Your Majesties," Jeanip said. He smiled as he saw the look of awe on his charges' faces.

"I have never seen anything so beautiful," Europa said. "It is unbelievable."

"It was modeled after our first city we had to sink," Jeanip said. "It is totally self-contained. You have electricity, hot and cold running water, air conditioning; basically, all the comforts of home along with gardens. And a security system even more advanced than the one at Minnos, again thanks to Sunam."

"Is this Atlantis?" Terrance asked.

"No, Terrance," Jeanip said, laughing at the human obsession with the lost city. "We did not call our first city Atlantis. That was a name the humans gave it many years later. This is Saint's Isle, a sanctuary designed by Enok and Medaron, built and engineered by Sunam and a handful of talented Oonock engineers."

"How long did it take to build something like this?" Terrance inquired, still not believing his eyes.

"You must remember our technology is far more advanced than Earth's," Jeanip began. "It took Sunam's team a little over three weeks to construct the island and install the barriers we just passed through, and I believe a week to build the house. The house took longer than we anticipated because we had to fly in the white marble for the house and steps."

"A week!" Terrance said in amazement, more to himself than to his fellow travelers. Even with the most sophisticated equipment it would take a human crew months or even years to build such a place.

Europa looked above the island at the beautiful blue sky. "Jeanip, what keeps planes that fly over the island from discovering it?"

"Excellent question," Jeanip commented. "You are definitely beginning to think like a monarch, seeing possible flaws in security matters. There is a security dome that covers the island making it invisible from the air. Anyone flying over it sees only a dense fog bank like the one we passed through. No plane will venture into it since the visibility is zero and, thanks to a magnetic field Sunam installed, their instruments will not function either. No pilot will fly blindly through such a force of nature. Yet from the island you see only blue sky during the day and stars at night. Sometimes when the alignment is just right you can even see Jupiter in the heavens. There's a telescope on the third floor if you ever want to take a closer look. You might even be able to see Europa's shadow as she passes in front of Jupiter."

Cimbor scanned the island looking for security systems to repel any invader that might get through the previous defenses. Seeing none he asked, "Not that I doubt Enok's security measures, but what stops a Terrian from entering the island if they made it this far?"

"That was Medaron's and Sunam's ingenious creation," Jeanip said. "I am not at liberty to say what it is or how it works, but be assured no Terrian will be able to step foot on the island." Europa watched Cimbor's face and body for any change created by Jeanip's words. For a quick second she thought she saw a look of alarm pass over his face, then it was gone.

Up ahead a narrow lagoon appeared, leading into the island. Jeanip began to throttle down the boat as he turned into the lagoon, navigating it up the inlet and into an opening carved in the rock.

"Cimbor and Earon, get the tie lines ready to secure the boat," Jeanip ordered. Cimbor proceeded to the bow and readied the tie line; Earon did the same in the stern. As the boat entered the opening, lights began to turn on revealing a dock and a stone walkway leading to an opening into the estate grounds. Jeanip turned off the engine and brought the boat alongside the dock. Cimbor and Earon jumped off the boat and secured the vessel. Cimbor unhooked the plank and, with Earon's help, swung one end onto the boat so the passengers could disembark. He quickly stepped onto the plank with the intention of helping Europa but was surprised to see Terrance was already escorting her. Stepping back down onto the dock, Cimbor held out his hand to assist Europa in stepping down.

"I'll carry your backpack, Your Majesty," Cimbor said, reaching for the pack in her hand. "Sovereigns are not supposed to carry their own baggage."

Terrance quickly grabbed it. "That's okay, Cimbor. I've got it for her."

"Terrance, as Europa's companion you should not be expected to carry her things either. I insist you allow me to carry it," Cimbor stated, now holding his hand out to Terrance.

Earon walked up to Terrance and jabbed him in his side. He leaned over and whispered in his ear, "Let the poor guy carry her backpack. He feels it is part of his duty." Reluctantly, Terrance handed Cimbor Europa's backpack while keeping his own securely over his shoulder. He wondered what Cimbor's true reason was for wanting to carry it.

"Welcome to Saint's Isle, Your Majesties and Terrance," Jeanip announced. "After you are safe inside, Cimbor, Seemon and I will come back for the supplies." Turning to Cimbor he said, "There is equipment we need from the storage shed to help us bring up the supplies. Once these three are secured, you need to retrieve it." He turned to the two monarchs and Terrance and gestured them forward with his hand, "Now, if you would follow me, I'll show you your new home."

Jeanip led the way down the path, through the opening and out onto the grounds. They were as breathtaking as the first sight of the island had been. Birds of paradise, anthuriums, azaleas and other exotic flowers bloomed everywhere. A pebbled path led through the gardens, leading past several water fountains from which lilac waters flowed. In the trees were parrots, macaws and vividly colored song birds. Butterflies and hummingbirds fluttered amongst the flowers. Several benches and swings with overhead awnings dotted the path where one could sit and enjoy the gardens' beauty. The pebbled path ended at a side stairway that led to the main marble stairs. As they ascended the stairs they were able to see more gardens, fountains and benches spreading across the interior of the island.

As they reached the first level the side stairway ended. Before them stretched the white marble stairway they had seen from the ocean. As they approached the main stairway a plank magically appeared, enabling them to cross over the moat. When the last traveler stepped onto the white stairway, the plank once again disappeared, leaving the upper level secured. As they surveyed the moat they were amazed to see it was filled with large gold fish and lily pads. More exotic flowers ran along the inside wall of the moat.

Upon reaching the top of the stairs Jeanip turned left onto a golden path. They continued down the path until it terminated in front of a pair of large golden doors. At the end of the path on each side stood a large light purple stone column with the same strange symbols Europa had seen on her mother's diary. Beyond the columns was empty space spanning fifteen feet from the end of the path to the door. On the outward side of each column and in front of the door was a sheer drop to the ocean below. Jeanip stopped, unable to proceed.

"How do we get across?" Europa asked when another plank did not materialize.

"I believe your mother gave you the key to extend the path so we can enter," Jeanip said. A puzzled look crossed Europa's face. She didn't recall her mother ever giving her a key. Did she forget something? Suddenly, the amulets around Europa and Earon's necks began to glow as they did the day the Terrians attacked Minnos. Europa and Earon immediately looked at each other, realizing what the glowing amulet meant.

"Jeanip, what is going on?" a frightened Europa asked, as she reached out and grabbed her brother's and Terrance's hands, pulling them close to her. "Why are the amulets glowing?

"I don't know," Jeanip replied, stepping back to position himself before the three, weapon drawn. "The amulets are warning of Terrian presence, but it's impossible for Terrians to enter the island."

"Terrians cannot, but Waters can," Cimbor said, a turning to face the other five, his eyes glowing red. In his hand he held a blaster with a round purple stone in the power chamber.

"JeffRa!" Jeanip exclaimed. "It can't be."

"JeffRa?" Europa repeated, trying to see her enemy in the young soldier standing before her.

"Father?" Terrance asked simultaneously, wondering if this person before him could possibly be his father.

To his horror Terrance heard Cimbor reply, "Hello, son. I was quite surprised to see you accompanying this scum when you arrived at the Banana Boat."

"Oh my gosh, it's true," Terrance said, as he looked into his stepfather's eyes. "You ARE JeffRa. That's why I couldn't find you in the field. You weren't studying the sparrows, you were spying on the Waters, preparing your plan of attack to kill them."

Keeping the blaster pointed at the group, Cimbor's red hair began to turn grey. A deep scar appeared down the right side of his face. His shoulders slumped forward and his fingers became knurled. Now standing before them was Jeffrey Landers, but an older, war weary version showing the many scars and injuries of the battles he had fought. "I guess there is no reason to hide my identity anymore."

Unable to believe her eyes, Europa tightly squeezed Terrance's hand as Cimbor turned into his father, Jeffrey Landers. She knew emotions of love, hate, anger, resentment, astonishment and disbelief had to be racing through Terrance as he tried to come to terms with the now undisputable truth of who his father was.

"So that's how you've been getting through my security," Jeanip said, amazed at JeffRa's supposedly impossible transformation. "How did you do it? We cannot alter our appearance when we transform into a human. And we certainly can't purposely transform to look like someone else. How were you able to completely change your appearance and transform into Cimbor? Plus, you're a Terrian. Even transformed into a Waters, such as Cimbor, you're still a Terrian, not a Waters. The security grid should have picked you up the moment you stepped foot on Water's land."

"What is the matter, Jeanip, worried you are getting too old to install a proper security screening grid? Wondering how I beat your 'unbeatable' security plan?" JeffRa laughed. "I would be delighted to tell you. You might not want to accept this fact, Jeanip, but I am first and foremost a Waters. I am a Waters AND a Terrian. I have had thousands of years to rebuild and strengthen my Waters' DNA. I have devoted my life to it. That, plus fulfilling my oath to eradicate Oonocks and the royal family from the universe. Your security grid did not detect me because I am Waters. And, as such, I can easily step foot upon this sanctuary you and my brother built." JeffRa relished the look of surprise on Jeanip's face. "As for being able to alter my appearance, that took some doing. It took me fifteen hundred years to learn how to trick my cells to transform into someone that did not look like me. I realized after our last battle the only way I could ever get close to the royal family was to look like someone else. I had planned on transforming into one of the Banana Boat's crew, but then young, over-ambitious Cimbor gave me the break I needed. When he came to your rescue I had no trouble capturing him and his boat. The boat's instruments told me from where he came from, so I simply transformed into him and retraced his steps. Luckily, you arrived shortly after I did so I did not have much explaining to do. It did not take much to attach myself to your team. But then, Jeanip, you never left their side and I was unable to be alone with them to finish what I set out to do centuries ago. Can you imagine my amazement and amusement when you actually asked me to join your team and travel with the youngsters to Saint's Isle? I knew all the preparations I had done over the centuries would now pay off and there would be no one to stop me." JeffRa surveyed the structure, pleased at what he believed would be his new home.

"Why do you hate us so much?" Europa asked. "What have I ever done to you?"

"You were born. That is your crime," JeffRa screamed, a deep look of loathing and hatred etched upon his face. "You are the daughter of my brother, Enok and his so-called life's mate."

"Earon, I need you to take Europa and Terrance inside the house. JeffRa cannot reach you there once the door is closed and the walkway withdrawn," Jeanip instructed, keeping his weapon and his gaze upon JeffRa.

"But how?" Europa asked.

"The golden ship inside your mother's diary – that is the key," Jeanip answered, as he maintained his watch on JeffRa. "Insert it in the ship-shaped key hole in the right pillar. A platform will appear. When the door asks you to announce yourselves simply say 'Emergency Waters Tiree'. The doors will open and you can go inside. Seemon and I will keep JeffRa from following you. Hurry!"

Europa had forgotten about Seemon who stood a few feet away from them, her weapon also aimed at JeffRa. Europa looked around for her backpack where the dairy was contained. She didn't see it - and then she remembered; Cimbor had insisted he carry it for her. As she looked at JeffRa she saw her backpack slung over his left shoulder.

"I do not have it, Jeanip," Europa said, almost in a whisper.

"What do you mean you do not have it?" Jeanip yelled. "Where is it?"

"Cimbor took it from me when I got off the boat. He wanted to carry it," Europa replied, continuing to stare at her backpack, realizing she had been tricked.

"My, my, things really are not going your way today, are they My Lady?" JeffRa laughed, raising the backpack into the air. "Looks like I will be going in after you all leave. Thanks for telling me how to get inside, Jeanip. And let me assure you, I will truly enjoy my new home and island. In fact, you have made this place so impenetrable I might just take up the conquest of these puny humans again."

"Saint's Isle will never be yours, JeffRa. And I promise you will not leave here alive," Jeanip shouted.

JeffRa laughed, and then fired his weapon at Jeanip. Pain shot through his body as he fell onto the ground in front of the three, amazed he was still alive. Then he heard a low hum and turned to see Europa holding the Orb. A light was radiating from her and shrouding them in a protective shield. She had not been quick enough to repel all of JeffRa's weapon's charge, but she was able to repel most of it. Her quick actions had once again saved Jeanip's life.

"Our little human is full of surprises, is she not?" JeffRa grinned, his eyes beginning to glow redder. "I see your whore of a mother passed on her powers to you before she died. No matter, I can wait. I have waited thousands of years to get my revenge so a few more hours will not matter. You cannot keep that field up forever. You will grow tired and it will collapse. And since you have put up such a valiant attempt I will allow you to die last. You can watch your brother and your two protectors die before you. But you are not the only one with a trick or two up their sleeve, are they Terrance?" JeffRa looked at his son and smiled. "You have done a great job, Son, pretending to be their friend. I could not have made it this far without your help and surveillance. The identification of which room was Europa's bedroom was especially beneficial since it enabled us to eliminate most of Jeanip's soldiers. Likewise, relaying to me Chancee's message to Jeanip allowed me to know their travel time frames. Come here and join me while I complete my revenge, Terrance. Together we will put an end to their family and then together we will enter our new home."

A horrified look came across Europa's face as she maintained her stare at JeffRa, afraid that if she looked at Terrance she would lose her concentration. "You are with him?" she asked, barely able to say the words.

"No, Europa, he's lying," Terrance quickly yelled. "I'm not part of his plan. He's trying to distract you so you will lose your concentration and the force field will fail." Turning to look directly at JeffRa he said, "Tell her you're lying!"

"Now, Son," JeffRa said in a calm voice. "I would if it were true, but we both know you have been in on this charade since the very beginning."

Suddenly Europa heard a voice inside her mind. It was Jeanip. Somehow he was able to make her hear his words. "Do not listen to JeffRa's lies, Europa. Trust in Terrance. He is your quanish. He has not and will not betray you. Believe in him. He will save you."

"Don't call me 'Son'. I am no son of yours," Terrance yelled. "And you are sadly mistaken if you think I will allow you to kill the woman I love."

"Oh my," JeffRa laughed sarcastically. "You have gone and fallen in love with her. Those Waters' women do have charms that are hard to resist. I know that from experience." The look on JeffRa's face changed from sarcasm to one of disdain. "Terrance, I do not wish to kill you, but if you stand with her I will not hesitate to end your life here today also."

"You will be the only one whose life will end today," came a voice from behind the left column. JeffRa stepped sideways to see who had spoken the words while still keeping an eye on the five behind the shield. As he watched out of the corner of his eye Enok stepped from behind his hiding place and faced JeffRa.

"Why if it is not my big brother," JeffRa said, trying to keep a startled look from showing on his face. "I did not expect you to be here. But I am glad you are. Now you can watch me fulfill that promise I made to you the day you exiled me to Ganymede."

"Why do you not answer Europa's question on why you hate us so much?" Enok asked, staring hard at JeffRa. "Why do you not tell her, and yourself, the truth, Brother? Tell her why you REALLY hate me!"

"Because you do not deserve to live," JeffRa yelled. "I was the better Waters, the better ship builder, but you got all the credit. You got everything and I got nothing"

"That is not the reason, JeffRa, you know it," Enok replied.

"You were father's number one son; I was nothing to him."

"Tell her the REASON," Enok demanded.

"You were my big brother. I looked up to you. And once you became the future monarch you forgot all about me."

"TELL HER!" Enok yelled. "Stop lying to her, to me and to yourself. For once admit the truth!"

"Because you took away from me the only female I ever loved," JeffRa screamed, his face raging with hate, his eyes glowing red as if on fire. "Medaron was to be my life's mate, not yours. When I went to finalize our union with her father I had no knowledge she had been bound to you and you two would soon become life-mates. All that I knew was she had given me her promise of love and commitment. She and I had made plans for our future, for our children. But when you found out about us you could not stand the thought of me having something better than you so you offered her something I could never give her – the title of Supreme Monarch. She wanted power more than she wanted me. So she let me disgrace myself by going to see her father, knowing all along she was bound to you. He laughed in my face!"

"She did not know, JeffRa," Enok said, a sound of regret and sorrow in his voice. "Enoquin and Medaron's father made the agreement without either Medaron or I knowing anything about it. It was you she loved, and you know I had plans to unite with Biireena. We were all sabotaged by our fathers and forced to honor the signed agreement. Medaron had no choice but to become my life's mate."

"You expect me to believe that?" JeffRa asked. "If that is true, why did she not tell me, spare me the disgrace and humiliation?"

"How could she, JeffRa?" Enok answered, hoping his brother would finally see the truth. "As soon as you found out you disappeared and started gathering your army to destroy the two of us. Come on, Little Brother, think! You knew Medaron too well to believe she would have intentionally hurt you. She cared deeply for you. She had a special place in her heart that was reserved only for you. Not even her eventual love for me was able to erase that. It grieved her greatly the day you turned against her."

"I am not a fool, Enok. You do not try to kill someone you love," JeffRa screamed back.

"What else could she do, JeffRa? You led an army against us on Europa. Here on Earth you tried to kill me. Then several weeks ago you tried to assassinate our daughter. You gave her no choice but to end your life."

"If she still loved me or not is of no consequence," JeffRa yelled. "I came to hate you more than her. You always promised me you would watch out for me, you would protect me. You abandoned me and sent me to that hell to live."

"What choice did I have?" Enok asked. "You had just killed our sister and you were plotting our destruction."

"I never killed Quinsong," JeffRa stated, a look of sorrow crossing his face momentarily. "I loved my sister deeply. She surprised us in the hall and one of my soldiers panicked and shot her. I made sure it was the last thing he ever did. I tried to help her, but she ran away, ran away to you and father."

"I gave you a chance at life on Ganymede," Enok stated. "Father wanted me to execute you, to have you flow out onto rock so you would cease to exist for eternity."

"A chance at life?" JeffRa laughed a cold, menacing laugh, his look of sorrow transforming to a look of disdain and loathing. "What kind of life was there on Ganymede? You left us there with little food, no weapons, and no supplies. A quarter of my men were slaughtered by the wildlife in the first two days. Sickness soon took a good share, too. I will not even tell you what the natives did to us."

"You lie! I sent a supply ship with you," Enok stated. "There were knives and simple weapons. I could not trust you with powerful ones but I did not leave you defenseless. There were lanterns, blankets, hammers and tools, cooking supplies plus plenty of food and medicines."

"Now who is lying, Brother?" JeffRa snickered. "The only thing we got when we were dropped on Ganymede was one large sack of food and one jug of water. One jug for hundreds of Oonocks."

"I did not abandon you, Brother," Enok said. "I did order the supplies to go with you. Plus, I sent a supply ship every month for the first three months. I had to stop sending them when none of them returned. We assumed you were attacking them."

"Attacking them?" JeffRa asked. "We could not attack what we never saw. Besides, within the first week of arriving on Ganymede we were captured by the Terrians and placed in torture camps."

"Captured?" Enok repeated, not sure if he should believe his brother or not. JeffRa's account of his exile on Ganymede was very different from what he had been led to believe. "I was under the impression you overthrew their leader and became head Terrian."

JeffRa looked at his brother and laughed. "Does this look like I easily became their leader?" JeffRa asked, ripping his shirt open to reveal thousands of cuts and gashes across his upper body. Enok's eyes filled with tears as he realized the pain and suffering his brother endured at the hands of the Terrians. For the first time he saw the truth.

"As they cut the flesh off my body it was your name I screamed, Enok, not hers. I wanted to never forget who was really responsible for the pain. Each cut rendered made me hate you more, and the more I hated you the more I was determined to survive to have my revenge on you," JeffRa reiterated, his eyes turning red once again. "The only thing that saved my life and the lives of my fellow Oonocks who were still alive was the fact we were able to transform into other creatures. One day when I could take no more pain I somehow found the strength to transform into a Zinbar. I was able to kill several of the Terrians before my strength ran out. When the Terrians saw what I had done we were set free. Evidently, they thought we were their sky gods from their ancient legends. Not wishing to anger their gods, we were exalted above all and from that time on treated very well. Knowing the only way I could seek revenge was to get off Ganymede, my soldiers and I took advantage of the Terrians idolization and led the Terrians to victories over the surrounding tribes. Eventually, I was able to incorporate the tribes into a large army. With their help and our superior knowledge, we built several ships to take us away from that hell of a planet."

"I am so sorry, JeffRa," Enok said, clearly shaken by JeffRa's tale. "I had no idea you endured so much."

"Save your sympathy, Enok," JeffRa yelled at Enok. "I do not want it."

"No, you only want revenge," Earon said, still safe within Europa's shield. "My father was not responsible for what happened to you. You did it to yourself."

"Ah, young Earon. I must say you do look a lot like your brother, Tiree. Did you know I killed him the last time your father and I met? Is it not ironic that after all these years when we meet again I will be able to take his other son's life, along with his daughter's?" JeffRa basked in the thought of killing the two young monarchs, then his thoughts turned to the past. "So you think your father has no responsibility in this matter, young Earon? Let me tell you what your father is responsible for. A time came when I DID abandon my revenge. I had joined with a female Oonock-Terrian who was able to make me forget my former life, who was able to wipe the memory of your mother from my heart for a while and, as a result, my lust for revenge began to subside. Our union was blessed with twin males. On the day of their birth I abandoned my hate and decided to dedicate my life to their happiness and upbringing. For the first time in my life I was content and looked forward to a better life, a life free of hate. But your father was not going to allow me that life. One day when I was away, trying to find a better place for the Terrians to live, your father attacked our village and set off the magnetic pulse from the moon Io we had been working on as a new energy source. Jupiter imploded, destroying itself and blasting Ganymede. When I returned to our village all I found left of my mate and sons were their charred bones." JeffRa turned and stared at Enok. "From that day on, Brother, I lived only to see you suffer the same loss I did – the death of your mate and your children."

"JeffRa, I never attacked your village," Enok said.

"Do not lie, Enok," JeffRa screamed, his rage rising. "We found the remains of an Oonock ship not far from our village, a royal family's ship. Only you have the power to authorize the sailing of that ship."

"Oh my gosh!" Enok said, a horrible realization forming in his mind. "Enoquin." Enok looked directly into JeffRa's eyes. "Father and Mother went to Ganymede to see you at Mother's insistence. She was dying and demanded to see you before she flowed into the waters. Father insisted upon accompanying her. I knew he still hated you tremendously and feared he was up to something, but if he was I could not discover it. He must have gone there with the sole purpose of carrying out your execution and somehow caused Jupiter's destruction in his attempt to do so."

"Is that not convenient to blame it on Father? But I do not care whose fault it was, Enok," JeffRa shouted. "My mate and sons are gone either way. You were the Head Monarch. It was your ship. You and you alone were responsible. And you, along with your people, will pay for it." With that said, JeffRa fired his weapon, hitting a surprised Enok in the chest. Enok was knocked backwards and fell over the cliff to the ocean below.

"No!" screamed Europa, as she watched her father disappear over the edge. The shock of seeing her father shot was enough to break her concentration and the security shield collapsed. JeffRa immediately seized the opportunity and fired his weapon at Europa, Terrance and Earon. Seemon leaped in front of the monarchs and took the blast, dying instantly. Before JeffRa could discharge his weapon again, Terrance fired the Terrian weapon he had removed from his backpack, hitting a startled JeffRa in his bare chest. JeffRa looked down to see purple blood beginning to pour from the hole Terrance's weapon had blasted into his chest. He raised his head to look at his son as he stumbled backwards, tittering on the edge of the cliff.

"Terrance, why?" JeffRa asked, amazed the son he had loved would be the one to end his life.

"Because she is my life," Terrance answered his father, tears beginning to run down his cheeks.

"Then I will meet you in hell," JeffRa said, raising his weapon again to fire at the three young travelers.

Everything happened so fast Europa did not have time to reform the security barrier. She grabbed Earon's and Terrance's hands, closed her eyes and waited for her death. Suddenly, there was the sound of rushing water swirling around them. She opened her eyes to see the water from the basin had covered the four in a protective shield. She could see a stunned JeffRa on the other side staring at the water in terror.

JeffRa stared at the new barrier in disbelief, wondering what was happening. He had fired his weapon but the blast had simply dissipated when it hit the water barrier. As he watched, the front of the water barrier began to swirl and materialize into a figure. To his horror and amazement, standing before him was Medaron.

"Medaron," JeffRa whispered, not believing his eyes. "This cannot be."

"Why not? You created me the day you killed me and I flowed into the waters," came a voice from the water figure. "Enok told you the truth, JeffRa. I had no idea my father promised me to Enok. It was you I loved, that I wanted to spend my life with. But your hate destroyed that love just as it destroyed you. I will not allow it to destroy my children or my brother. Your bloody revenge ends today."

Medaron rushed him, a huge wall of water crashing upon him, knocking him over the cliff's edge. As JeffRa fell, Enok the whale leaped up out of the water and grabbed him securely in his teeth, burying them deep into JeffRa's flesh. As JeffRa screamed in pain, the two brothers plunged into the ocean where Graybin, Runbee and several other Waters waited. They clasped restraining bands onto JeffRa's wrists to keep him from transforming into another being. Then they took the severely injured JeffRa from Enok's mouth and stuffed him into a clear box that was filled with air. Enok transformed into an octopus and wrapped his arms around the box, clutching it securely as he swam down to the bottom of the ocean. Now in his element, Enok transformed into his true self and carried the encased JeffRa to a hole he had secretly carved into the side of the cliff. He placed the box inside the black hole, a hole that was JeffRa's final resting place.

"I cannot allow you to flow out into the waters where you will have access to all that the ocean holds," Enok told his brother. "You have beat death too many times to allow that. The atrocities you have committed against our people and my family are unforgivable. Today I AM your judge and executioner, although it gives me no pleasure. For your crimes I sentence you, Dear Brother, to eternity locked in this box, hidden here in the darkness, alone and forgotten. I sentence you to die in there, retaining the shape of the body you inhabit today. I sentence you to the realization that I live and my children live. You have failed in your quest for vengeance to destroy my family. We live on. The Oonock race lives on. But my brother does not – he died thousands of years ago, the same day my innocent sister did. And know this as you slip away into nothingness - I loved him very much."

With tears in his eyes, Enok picked up several large rocks and covered the hole, cementing them together with a laser tool he had left there for that purpose. Thus JeffRa was entombed for all time at the bottom of the world, sealed behind a wall of rock, alone in darkness. As Enok swam away from JeffRa's tomb, he heard him scream one word: "Enok." And then there was silence.

SAFETY

After the wall of water knocked JeffRa over the cliff, it receded back into the pool it had emerged from and reshaped itself back into Medaron. "Mother, is that really you?" Europa asked, staring at a form of her mother totally made of lilac water. "How can this be?"

"Yes, it is me, Europa," Medaron answered. "When I flowed out into the ocean I became part of her. The power of the Orbs, combined with my love for you three, has enabled me to reassemble the essence of who I was into a water creation of myself in order to protect you and end JeffRa's reign of terror and revenge."

"Will you be able to stay with us?" Earon asked.

"No, I am only able to take this form for a very short time. But know I will always be in the ocean and in the lilac waters of the pools."

"But what do I do now, Mother?" Europa asked. "JeffRa killed Father and Jeanip is gravely injured. I am not able to summon the Orb's power to heal him again. Plus, when JeffRa fell he took my backpack with him and the key to get inside Saint's Isle. How can the three of us survive here alone?"

Medaron looked at her daughter and smiled. "Your father is not dead, My Beloved Child. We knew of JeffRa's plot and it was necessary for JeffRa to believe he had killed his brother. Enok fell over on purpose so he would be ready to seize JeffRa when I pushed him over and take him somewhere from where he can never return." Medaron turned to look at the stairway. "See, here is your father now."

411

As the three young travelers moved their gaze from Medaron to the stairs, they saw Enok walking toward them. Europa and Earon ran to their father, dropping into his outstretched arms. He held them tightly, kissing each on the head. "I'm sorry I scared you," he said. "I had to make JeffRa believe I was dead in order for our plan to work."

"Is he really gone?" Europa asked, tears flowing down her face.

"Yes, My Dear Sweet Child," Enok said. "JeffRa will never enter our lives again."

Enok released his hold of his children and walked over to the water formation of Medaron. "Thank you for your help, My Most Beloved." He raised his hand and gently touched her cheek, being careful not to break the water's surface. "I could not have succeeded without your help. JeffRa's execution has been carried out; something I should have done that day on Europa."

"It is hard to execute the death sentence on someone you love so dearly." Medaron placed her hand next to his on her cheek. "You are and always will be my only true love. I wait for the day when you will join me, but for now care for our children and live on, My Love." Enok watched as the form of Medaron began to dissipate, her shape melting as the water flowed back into the pool it had come from. She was gone once again, returned to the lilac waters from which she had emerged.

Enok hurried over to the crumbled Jeanip and knelt down beside him. Terrance, Europa and Earon were already at his side, Europa having his hand inside of her own as she held the Orb. He was badly injured and having difficulty breathing, a pool of purple blood growing in size beneath him.

"Father," Europa said, looking into her father's eyes. "I cannot make the Orb work in order to heal him. What am I doing wrong?"

"I do not think you are doing anything wrong, Europa," Enok answered. "You used so much of the Orb's and your power to keep the protection shield up you drained it, along with your own energy. You both need time to regenerate."

"Is there nothing we can do for Jeanip?" Earon asked.

"Do not worry about me, Your Highnesses," Jeanip weakly said in a low voice as he looked at Earon and Europa. "I accomplished my mission; I got you here and you are alive. I am ready to join the others in the ocean." Jeanip raised his eyes to look at Enok. "Your Majesty, might I impose upon you to take me down to the ocean so I may complete my journey and flow into the Waters of Life."

A tender look filled Enok's face. "Jeanip, it would not be an imposition. It would be my honor to assist you. But today is not that day. I will take you down to the Ocean Complex where you can receive all the care and rest you need."

"Enok, this is one order I cannot obey. I do not have the strength to transform into a sea creature to make the trip. And I cannot go in this human form."

"My Dearest Friend, I will not allow you to die," Enok said. "I have the box you brought Medaron in twenty years ago waiting for you. You will travel down to the Complex inside it in human form where a medical team is already waiting for you." Enok reached up and lifted Medaron's necklace with her amulet from around his neck. He had been wearing it along with his own since the day Jeanip had given it to him. Knowing Medaron's amulet contained more power than all the other amulets put together, he tenderly lifted Jeanip's head and placed it around Jeanip's neck. "The power and magic inside Medaron's amulet will keep you alive until I can get you down there," Enok said.

"No, Sire," Jeanip protested, his voice even weaker. "That is Medaron's amulet. Only royals may wear the amulets."

"So they may," Enok said. "And, as of this day, you are a member of the royal family in recognition of your accomplishments over the past few weeks. You have saved the royal family and our future."

Jeanip could think of no words to say to express the great pride he felt or the love and respect he had for Enok.

Enok placed one of his hands around his own amulet and laid the other over Europa's hand that held Jeanip's hand. He closed his eyes and somberly spoke the ancient healing words: "Ennay Benu Carif". Immediately the amulet around Jeanip's neck began to glow, as did the ones around Enok, Earon and Europa's necks. Beams of light began to radiate outward from Jeanip's amulet and enter his body, cascading through his veins and arteries, restoring his life force. The amulet was not powerful enough to heal Jeanip, but it would keep him alive until Enok could get him to the Complex.

Seeing Jeanip was breathing a little easier and his bleeding had stopped, Enok scooped Jeanip into his arms and carried him down to the cove, followed by Terrance, Europa and Earon. Graybin and Runbee were waiting there with the transportation box which would carry Jeanip to the Complex. Enok gently placed him inside trying to make him as comfortable as possible. Graybin knelt and gave him an injection of the lilac water to help sustain him.

"Thank you for everything," Europa said, as she knelt next to the transportation capsule, leaned forward and kissed Jeanip on the cheek. "Get well soon and hurry back. Remember, I still need you."

"Same goes for me," Earon said, likewise kneeling down to kiss Jeanip on the forehead. "I still have a lot you need to teach me."

Terrance looked at Jeanip, wondering if he too should kiss him, then decided against it. Instead he just said, "Thank you" and gently touched Jeanip's shoulder.

Too weak to talk, Jeanip looked at his three charges, two tears escaping their hiding place in his eye and sliding down his cheek. Europa gently wiped away his tears with her fingers, then bent over and kissed him once more on the forehead. "I love you," she whispered. She moved back from the capsule and raised her vision to her father's face, nodding an affirmative to let him know he could close the lid. Enok shut the cover, then checked to see the oxygen-enriched atmosphere was working correctly and all seals had engaged. He then jumped into the water, ready to take Jeanip home.

"I will be back in two days," he told the three. "You three wait for me in the house. Be sure to withdraw the walkway once you are inside."

"Father, we have no way of getting inside," Europa stated. "The key inside mother's diary was in my backpack. JeffRa took it with him when he went over the side. How do we get in?"

"Is this what you need?" Terrance asked, as he reached into his backpack and retrieved Europa's mother's diary with the golden ship. "I didn't like the way Cimbor, I mean JeffRa, was always hanging around you, wanting to carry your backpack. There were too many important things in there for us to lose. Plus, I didn't really trust him. So, to ensure they were safe, I took your things out and put them in my backpack. I hope you're not mad; I just wanted to be sure they were safe."

Europa ran to Terrance, grabbing him in her arms, giving him a big hug. "Angry? I could kiss you for doing that." And then she did. She kissed him deeply on the lips, forgetting for a moment her father was watching her. She broke the kiss and looked at her father, trying to figure out what he was thinking. "Sorry, Father. I got a little carried away."

"No need to apologize, Europa," Enok said. "If I was not already in the water I'd probably give him a kiss too." Everyone laughed, even Terrance. "But as Head Monarch I must remind you it is not appropriate for the future ruler of the Oonocks to display such affection toward someone who is not her life's mate in public." He then winked at Europa and dove beneath the water, taking Jeanip with him.

Graybin and Runbee did not transform and follow Enok below but remained in the water inside the cove. "Your Highnesses, we will remain here until we are sure you are inside," Runbee said. "Once we see the walkway retract and the door close, we will exit the water and clothe ourselves."

"Jeanip has explained to us the need for clothing when we are in human form around you," Graybin reported. "Although we still do not understand the reasoning behind it, we will comply with Europa's wishes."

"Once we are clothed we will bring up the supplies from your boat," Runbee continued. "We will advise you when we have everything outside the door and need entry inside."

"There is no need for you to stay," Earon said. "We will be fine, now that JeffRa is no longer a threat. We can bring the supplies up later."

"Forgive me, Your Highness, but we cannot do that. Security protocol states an Oonock may not leave you unprotected when outside a secured environment," Graybin stated. "JeffRa may be gone but there may still be dangers out there. With Jeanip gone it falls upon us to fulfill the obligation of protector. And the carrying in of supplies is not something monarchs are expected to do."

"Since I'm not royalty, perhaps I can help you," Terrance offered.

"You may not be royalty, Terrance, but you are Europa's companion and her very abled protector. Your place is with her, so we ask that you go inside with Europa and Earon."

"Thank you, Graybin," Europa said. "You too Runbee. We welcome your protection and delivery of our supplies."

"Remember, do not reopen the door until we tell you to," Runbee said. "And I must insist on one more precaution. JeffRa was able to transform himself to look like someone else and we have no way of knowing if any of his followers might also possess that ability. Before you allow me entrance into the house you must ask me a question only I or Graybin would know."

"Do you want me to tell you what the question will be now?"

"No, ask me when I am ready to enter," Runbee replied. "That way you will know for sure if it is I or an imposter. Remember, I must answer your question correctly the first time. And do not open the door until after I have given you the correct response. Behind the doors you are unreachable; with the doors open you could be targeted. Do you understand, Your Majesty?"

"Yes, I understand."

Turning to face Earon and Terrance, Runbee asked, "Earon and Terrance, do you understand these instructions and the necessity of Europa assuring our identity BEFORE the doors are opened?"

"Yes," the two responded in unison. Terrance leaned over to Earon and whispered, "I think he may be worse than Jeanip was!"

"Do you really think we could still be in danger?" Europa asked, not sure if she could withstand another attack.

"That is not for me to decide," Runbee said. "Only Enok can say when it is safe for you to be outside the protection of the house. For the moment I must proceed as if you are still in danger. Now, if you please, Your Highnesses, I ask that you go inside as your father asked."

The three reclimbed the marble stairs and soon were standing outside the double golden doors to their home, a chasm barring their way. Terrance handed Europa her diary and she removed the golden ship broach pinned to the inside. She walked over to the keyhole in the column, taking a second look at the lilac pool her mother had occupied hoping perhaps she was watching. She placed the key in the lock, took a step back and waited for the walkway to extend. Nothing happened. She looked at Earon, hoping he might know what was wrong.

"I do not know why it is not working," Earon said. "I have never been here before either."

Terrance took the diary from Europa's hand, opening to the page where the golden ship had been. "Europa, there's a notation here that reads 'All must stand together before the stones and announce their arrival for permission to enter'. Do you remember when Jeanip told us to go inside? He said something too about the door asking us to announce ourselves. Maybe we have to tell it who we are before it will let us in."

"It is worth a try," Europa said. "Earon and Terrance, come stand next to me. Then say your names." Terrance walked over and stood next to Europa. Earon followed and stood on her other side.

"I am Terrance Landers," Terrance said, feeling a little silly at talking to a golden door.

"I am Prince Earon, son of Enok and Medaron, monarchs of the Oonocks," Earon said.

"I am Queen Europa, daughter of Enok and Medaron, monarchs of the Oonocks," Europa stated. "We ask for permission to enter."

"Permission granted," came a voice, as they heard a low rumble sound, then the sound of turning gears. The ground began to tremble slightly beneath their feet as they saw a walkway begin to extend across the chasm. The double, golden doors slowly swung open to allow access to the house.

Upon stepping onto the walkway they heard a voice say, "Welcome Queen Europa and Prince Earon, offspring of Enok and Medaron Waters. Welcome Terrance Landers, companion and protector of Queen Europa and Prince Earon. You are invited to enter."

Europa reached over and removed the golden ship from the keyhole and together the three walked across the walkway and entered the house. As they stepped onto the landing the walkway behind them disappeared once again. Earon and Terrance pushed the doors closed and watched as another keyhole appeared on the inside of the left door. Thinking it might be a lock, Europa placed the golden ship inside the keyhole and watched as the security bolt descended across the doors, securely locking them inside.

The three turned and stepped into what they believed was the entrance to the house. The spectacle that met their eyes was astonishing. The room was massive, with a large fountain of lilac water in the middle of the room made of white marble with a seat of soft yellow cushions circling the fountain. On each side of the fountain were curved white marble staircases leading to the second floor. The walls were a soft lilac, the floor a mosaic of lilac, purple, yellow and blue hues. Overhead, the ceiling was a giant aquarium filled with all kinds of marine life, some of which the three had never seen before. Somehow the water-filled ceiling reflected a warm light that bathed the room in soft illumination. Tall green palms and ferns were pleasingly placed around the room, as were several couches and chairs which looked as if they were the most comfortable furniture every made.

"This is unbelievable," Terrance said, surveying the room.

"You can say that again," Europa agreed. "Is this what the Complex looks like?" she asked Earon.

"It is pretty spectacular, but nothing like this," Earon said. "Remember, the Complex is a water environment, not an air environment. We have furniture and plants, but totally different than those here."

As they began to explore their new home they heard Graybin's voice vibrate through the air, "Your Majesties, this is Graybin. We are ready to bring in the supplies. Please open the door and extend the plank so we may enter."

As they turned around to face the door they were startled to see that, although the door was still there, they were able to see Graybin and Runbee standing at the chasm with two loaders of supplies.

"How do we reopen the doors?" Europa asked.

"Try taking the key back out of the keyhole," Terrance suggested. "But don't forget to ask the security question first."

Europa walked over to remove the golden ship from the door She heard Graybin and Runbee announce themselves to the house just as they had. Then she heard: "Europa, do you wish to verify Graybin's and Runbee's identity?" It seemed the voice came from the door itself.

"Yes."

"Please verify."

Looking through the door at Graybin and Runbee Europa asked, "As a small child of five I had a special ring I would toss you when we played in the ocean. What was the ring and what color was it?"

Without hesitation Runbee answered, "It was a bracelet you wore around your right wrist. It was made of puka beads and shells."

"The shells were alabaster white and the beads were lilac. You had a matching necklace that you also wore sometimes," Graybin added.

"Is that correct?" Terrance asked, hoping their answers were correct and this was not another attempt by the Terrians.

"Yes, that is correct," she replied to Terrance. In a loud voice she stated. "I, Queen Europa, daughter of Enok and Medaron, true monarchs of the Oonocks. verify these two beings to be Graybin and Runbee. Please allow them to enter." She removed the key. Slowly, the doors swung open and the walkway extended itself once again. Graybin and Runbee maneuvered the supply loaders across the walkway and into the house. Terrance and Europa stared at the loaders as they realized they were floating above the ground, void of any wheels. Once Graybin and Runbee were inside, the walkway again disappeared. Graybin and Runbee closed the doors and Europa replaced the golden ship back into the keyhole.

"Your rooms are on the second floor," Graybin announced. "A room has already been selected for each of you, but if it is not to your liking you may select another one. The eating room and kitchen are off to the right of this room. To the left is a flower garden with a pool, if you wish to go swimming. There is a library on the second floor where you can do some reading while you're here. After I put some of the supplies away, I will prepare you something to eat. I'm sure you must be hungry. I'll have coffee ready in about five minutes and will bring you each a cup to your rooms. When dinner is ready I'll announce for you to come downstairs."

The three looked at each other, perplexed at Graybin's announcement. "Are you not returning to the ocean?" Europa asked.

"I'm sorry, Your Majesty, I thought you understood," Runbee said, as he lifted a box off the loader. "We will be your house help until Enok can arrange for a replacement for Misso and Jeanip."

"Is there anything special you would like for dinner?" Graybin asked.

"No, anything will be fine," Earon said, grateful he would not have to try cooking something to eat.

"Then upstairs with the three of you," Graybin said with a big smile. "There are fresh towels in your bathrooms if you wish to freshen up."

The three exhausted three travelers climbed the marble stairs to the second floor. They anticipated there would be elaborate rooms to choose from, but they were not prepared to see each of their names engraved on golden plates mounted on three separate doors.

"Looks like this room is mine," Earon said, placing his hand on the door knob of the door bearing his name. "This should prove interesting. Would you two like to see what someone thinks I might like?" Earon asked as he turned the door knob and opened the door. Upon stepping through the door, the room lights were raised automatically. He stopped as he surveyed the large room, astounded at the sight before his eyes. "I do not believe this," he said in astonishment. "This is my room from the Ocean Complex." He turned to face Europa, a shocked look clearly written on his face. "These are all my things I left down there twenty years ago. Look, here's my old geezba," he said, picking up a weird-looking musical instrument. He strummed the strings and a not-so-beautiful sound emerged from the instrument. "It is meant to be played underwater. Believe it or not, it really has a beautiful tone to it. I will take you two out to the pool one day and play you a song underwater. I guarantee you will be impressed." He paused for a minute as something else caught his eye. "You have got to be kidding me," Earon said, as he ran and jumped on the bed. "This is just like my bed at home, I mean the Complex, except it has been changed to exist in air instead of water. And that is my dresser too." Earon said, continuing to look around the room, recognizing more and more things of his. "Come on, we have to go check your room out," he said to Europa, as he grabbed her hand and ran with her to the door bearing her name, Terrance right behind them.

When they reached her door the three travelers stopped. Earon dropped his sister's hand and anxiously awaited for her to open the door, eager to see what her room looked like. Europa reached out to turn the door knob then stopped, as if frozen in time.

"Is something wrong?" Terrance asked, wondering why she hadn't opened the door.

"No," Europa answered, staring at the door in front of her. "My room and all my belongings, along with Mother's, were destroyed when Minnos was. There is no way any of my things can be inside."

"Come on, Sis," Earon encouraged. "After some of the things we have seen these past few days, anything is possible."

Europa turned the knob and slowly opened the door. As she stepped inside the lights rose just as they had in Earon's room. Earon and Terrance heard her gasp and then she took a step backwards. "This is impossible," she said, almost in a whisper.

"Go in, Europa," Earon said, eager to see what she saw. "I want to see what is inside."

Europa entered followed immediately by Earon and Terrance. Again, none could believe the scene before their eyes. Europa's room was an exact copy of her bedroom at Minnos, the bedroom that had been destroyed in the explosion several days earlier. Her bed contained the same pillows, the same stuffed animals and the same coverlet. On her dresser was the music box her mother had given her on her thirteenth birthday. She walked over to the closet and slid open the door. Duplicates of her lost clothing hung in the closet, along with another red backpack. It was if she had never left her room.

"Look, Europa," Earon said, pointing to two nails on a blank wall. "There are even the nails where you had hung those ugly Dumbo Octopus pictures."

"How is this possible, Earon?" Europa asked her brother.

"I do not know," he answered softly. "I know our technology is far superior to humans, but this is far more advanced than anything I have ever seen."

"Well, after your two rooms I can guarantee you my room is going to be a letdown," Terrance said.

"Let us go see," Earon said, eager to see what the house had to offer for Terrance. "If Europa's room is her room that no longer exists, I am sure your room was a breeze to create."

The three walked down to the door marked 'Terrance'. Terrance opened the door and stepped in expecting to find a nicely furnished room. He too was shocked at what he saw. "What is this place?" Terrance asked. "Are you guys magical or something?"

"Why do you say that?" Europa asked Terrance, as she looked around at the very nicely furnished room, although a little rough for her taste. "It is a very nice room. It suits you."

"It should," Terrance agreed. "It has suited me for ten years. This is a replica of my bedroom back in Australia."

"Australia?" Earon said. "There is no way anyone could have known what your room looked like back there."

"This is freaky," Europa said, now a little uneasy about the house.

"Remember I told you we are telepathic," Earon said, trying to come up with an explanation for the rooms. "Perhaps someone was able to read Terrance's mind and simulate his room."

"Well, that makes me feel better," Terrance stated, now thinking he might have to worry about people reading his mind. "I could have gone my entire life without hearing THAT suggestion."

Just then they heard Graybin coming down the hall with a cart containing three trays of coffee, condiments and a few cookies. She pushed the cart up to Terrance's door, lifted one of the trays off the cart and carried it inside, placing it on a small table. "Are you rooms not to your liking?" she asked, seeing the odd expressions on their faces. "There are other rooms if you would like to select something different."

"No, they are fine," Europa said. "We are just a little, well, shocked at how they look like each of our rooms at home."

"A lot of care was taken to provide you with a room you would feel comfortable in," Graybin explained. "Jeanip was able to give us the details on your room, Europa, several days after your mother died. And Enok supplied us with your things, Earon. Both of your rooms have been ready for over a week. Terrance's room was a bit harder to accomplish."

"Please don't tell me someone read my mind," Terrance said.

Graybin looked at her curiously. "Terrance, we don't read people's minds," Graybin said, wondering why he would think such an odd thought. "Although that would have been easier. The reality is two Waters went down to Australia and visited your mother and recorded detailed notes of what your room looked like."

"They visited my mother?" Terrance asked. "Might I ask what excuse they gave for visiting her?"

"Actually you supplied the excuse," Graybin said. "Your letter to your mother stated you had joined the Secret Service and would be gone on a top secret mission. They told her they were there to do a final background check on you. She accepted the story with no hesitation."

"My letter? But I just wrote that three days ago. There is no way it could have reached her by now," Terrance stated, unable to comprehend how his mother could have already seen the letter.

"We Oonocks do things rapidly," Graybin answered. "She had your letter the day after you wrote it. We talked to her that same evening. Your room was furnished last night." With that said, Graybin turned and left his room, pushing the cart down to Europa's room. She removed another tray from the cart and stood waiting for Europa, feeling her explanation of Terrance's room was more than satisfactory. "Your Highnesses, if I might have you return to your rooms," she said. "Or if you are not ready, may I have your permission to enter?"

"Yes, please feel free to go in." Europa turned toward Terrance and said, "Are you okay?"

"Except for the fact I think I'm about to pass out, yes, I am fine," he replied. "We've been through some really freaky things these past few days, but I have to admit having an exact duplicate of my room may be the freakiest of all."

"It is weird," Europa agreed. "Do you want another room?"

"No, I'll keep this one. If it gets too uncomfortable staying in here then I'll try another one."

"That sounds like a good plan," Europa responded. "I think I am going to freshen up before dinner. I will see you downstairs." She turned and walked down to her room. Graybin had sat the tray on the desk and was pouring Europa a cup of coffee as she entered.

"Would you like me to run you a bath?" Graybin asked. "The water here is very refreshing."

"Perhaps later," Europa answered. "Graybin, may I ask you a question?"

"Anything, Your Highness," Graybin answered.

"Does everyone who stays here get a room that is modeled after something from their past?" Europa asked, intrigued by the possibility of what the other rooms might look like.

"Other people?" Graybin inquired, a little perplexed at the question. "You three are the first to ever stay here."

"No one has ever stayed here before us?" Europa asked, not sure she heard correctly.

"No," Graybin replied. "Saint's Isle was built for you and your brother. It is a sanctuary for the royal family. Your parents ordered it built the day they discovered your mother was carrying you. They were never willing to take a chance JeffRa was dead, so to protect you they had this place built where JeffRa could not reach you."

"But what about the caregivers? Don't they stay here on the property?"

"Caregivers? There are no caregivers."

"But who takes care of the gardens, the fish, and the house?"

"No one, Your Highness. It takes care of itself."

"I see," Europa said, trying to imagine how that was possible.

Graybin stepped back into the hallway and picked up two items from the cart. She carried them into the room and laid them on the bed. "I took the liberty of bringing up your Mother's paintings of the Dumbo Octopus. I will leave them here on the bed for you. If you have no further need of me, I will take my leave of you," Graybin stated. "I still have Earon's coffee to deliver and dinner to complete. Dinner will be ready in two hours."

"Yes, by all means," Europa said, gesturing her hand toward the door so Graybin would know it was okay to leave. "Thank you for bringing up the paintings and your information."

Graybin pushed her cart down to Earon's room and carried the last tray inside and placed it on the large blue speckled rock next to his chair. Earon walked in behind her. Graybin immediately poured Earon a cup of coffee when she saw him enter.

"Would you like me to run you a bath before dinner?" Graybin asked. "Or would you prefer to wait until later?"

"I'll wait until after dinner," Earon replied. Graybin thought how alike the two siblings were.

"Then I take my leave of you, Your Majesty," Graybin stated. "Dinner will be served in one hour and fifty-six minutes." She turned and left the room, closing the door behind her. She pushed her now empty cart over to the elevator and returned to the kitchen to complete dinner.

The three explored their new rooms, then got ready for dinner. As each stepped into the hallway they heard Graybin's voice announce dinner was ready. They looked around to see where the voice was coming from; it was almost as if her voice floated on the air. Unable to determine where the voice came from, they descended the staircase, hand in hand, and headed toward the kitchen. As they entered the kitchen they thought how much it resembled the one at Minnos. There was a large fireplace at the far end with a sitting area. A large wooden table covered with dishes of food stood in the middle of the room with ten chairs; four on each side and one on each end. Several overhead lights hung above the table while a large bouquet of flowers in a lilac crystal vase adorned its middle. The cupboards were made of oak with white marble countertops with waves of lilac swirled through them. The wall opposite the stove and cupboards was made of glass, allowing one to see the gardens and the cascading waterfalls.

"Please have a seat," Graybin stated, as she dished up the last few food items. "I wasn't sure what you liked, so I made a variety of things I hope suits your palates. Once I learn your likes and dislikes I can customize the menu for you."

Europa and Terrance sat down on one side, Earon sat down opposite them. They looked over the massive array of food gracing the table. Graybin had prepared hamburgers, chicken, fish, sushi, several

424

vegetables, French fries and mashed potatoes with gravy. There were plates of sliced tomatoes and cucumbers, several types of breads and two kinds of salad. Several bowls were filled with fresh fruit with a side dish of caramel and chocolate dipping sauces. Pitchers of milk and water were on the table plus two containers of coffee. Several delicious deserts sat on the far counter for indulgence after dinner. Graybin had truly outdone herself. The last bowl of food she carried to the table and placed it next to Earon. "Here you are, Earon. This one is just for you."

Earon looked at it curiously, thinking how much it resembled dog food. He lifted the bowl and took a smell – it even smelt like dog food. "Graybin, would you please tell me what kind of food this is."

"As I mentioned before, I wasn't sure what you three preferred to eat," Graybin responded. "And I knew you lived the past twenty years as a canine, so I thought perhaps you preferred this round, hard nuggets to human food."

"I assure you, I preferred human food over this even when I WAS a canine," Earon said. He looked at Europa who was trying not to laugh, but when she met Earon's eyes she began to laugh hysterically. Earon too began laughing, then Terrance joined in. They were laughing so hard Terrance actually snorted, which made them laugh all the harder. All the stress, anxiety and fear of the past few days that had been held inside them broke free as the sound of laughter filled the house. Perplexed, Graybin and Runbee looked at each other. Humor and laughter were part of an Oonock's character, but neither of them could understand what was so funny.

"Did I do something wrong?" asked a very confused Graybin, as she stared at the three laughing youths.

Unable to answer due to the laughing, Earon waved his hands in the air and shook his head negatively.

"Oh, my sides are hurting," Terrance laughed. "Will you two please stop!"

Finally the siblings were able to get their laughter under control. They debated about explaining to Graybin and Runbee what they were laughing about, but just the thought of telling it started them laughing again.

Europa gave a deep sigh, finally able to stop laughing for the second time. "Oh, that felt good," she said. "Mother always said laughter was the best medicine for what ails you."

"And she was right," Earon added. Turning to look at Graybin he added, "Let me assure you, Graybin, you did nothing wrong. In fact, you could not have done anything more perfect."

"Then we'll leave you to your dinner," Runbee said. "If you need anything please let us know." Runbee followed Graybin to the kitchen sink to start cleaning the pans and skillets she had used in preparing the meal.

"Aren't you going to join us?" Terrance asked, unaware helpers seldom sit at the table with the royal family.

"Yes, please do," Europa said. "I know it is against royal etiquette, but we, I mean I, would really like some company. With Jeanip at the Complex and Mother and Misso gone, it seems so terribly lonely here at the table with just us three. Would you please indulge us tonight and join us like we were a real family?"

Seeing the loneliness in Europa's eyes, Graybin and Runbee agreed to dine with them. "We seldom eat human food," Runbee said, "but we would be honored to sit and dine with you."

"Thank you," Europa said. "It means a lot. Before we start, I would like to give thanks for surviving and making it here to Saint's Isle. And for Jeanip's quick recovery."

"And for Mr. Dark Feather's," Terrance added.

"And for Mr. Dark Feather's," Europa repeated, glad Terrance remembered to add his name to the blessing. "If you would please take the hand of the person next to you." Everyone reached over and held the hand of the person seated next to them and lowered their heads. "Thank you for watching over us these past few days and helping us reach safety. Please watch over Jeanip and Mr. Dark Feather; help them get better quickly. Help the medical personnel find a cure for my father so he can join us here. And please watch over the Oonocks, especially Graybin and Runbee, and bring them long life and happiness. Amen."

"Amen," Terrance and Earon said.

The food looked and smelled delicious. The three travelers sat for the next hour with their two guardians enjoying each other's company and the delicious food Graybin had prepared, talking about the house, its gardens and the beautiful ocean. Thus began their first night on Saint's Isle, safe and secure.

MEDICAL WING

Enok stood behind the glass wall and watched as the medical personnel wheeled Jeanip into the medical room, still encased in the transportation capsule. All hoped that, once he was at the Complex, he would be able to transform into his true self and begin the healing process. "Was he able to transfer into his true form?" Enok asked a young medical assistant who walked up to Enok.

"Yes, Your Highness," the medical assistant replied. "Just as Runbee suggested, once we were able to place Jeanip into an unconscious state and stop his mind from continuing his transformation, Jeanip automatically reverted back to his true form. I am impressed and surprised Runbee knew to advise us to do that. Has Runbee had medical training?"

"No, just a lot of life training," Enok replied, smiling at the young assistant, almost envious of his naiveness, his innocence. Enok surmised this young assistant had been but a youngling when they fought the Terrian wars, so he had no knowledge of life's harsh realities and soul-destroying tragedies. He hoped his ending of JeffRa's life prevented a future war and would thus allow this young man to keep his innocence.

The young assistant looked into his monarch's face and saw the anguish and worry clearly written there. "Without that transformation, I doubt we would have had a chance to save him."

"Does he have a chance?" Enok very softly asked, afraid to hear the young medical assistant's reply.

"Yes, Your Majesty, he has a chance, but I won't lie to you. His injuries are very serious and he has lost a lot of blood. To tell you the truth, I don't know how he even managed to remain alive for the transport down here. All of my life I have heard stories of the great Jeanip and his death-defying deeds, but this is unbelievable even for him, Sire. It is almost as if something kept him alive until we could get to him."

"It was the amulet," Enok stated, again almost in a whisper, as if to speak it aloud would make it not so.

"The amulet, Sire?"

"He wears Medaron's amulet," Enok answered. "She always told me it had magical healing powers that could be invoked whenever they were needed. I knew Jeanip was dying, that he had only a short time to live. After all that had happened I could not lose my dearest friend too, especially not after he saved my children. So in honor and gratitude for his deeds, I made him a member of the royal family and placed Medaron's amulet around his neck." Enok turned and looked into the young assistant's lilac eyes. "Was that wrong of me?"

The young assistant stared back at his Ruling Monarch, slightly confused and unsure of what to say. He was a medical assistant, not a quintot, a spirit healer that you tell your secrets to, yet here was his king telling him what he had done and asking him, HIM, if he did the right thing. As he continued to look into Enok's eyes he understood just a little of what it was like to be Enok; the responsibilities, the weight upon his shoulders, the life and death decisions he had to make for all of them every day. And with that understanding came a deeper love, a deeper respect for this sovereign and for his Chief Commander that was fighting for his life. He reached up and placed his hand on Enok's top shoulder wing and stated, "No, Sire, I do not believe it was wrong."

A smile spread across Enok's lips and it appeared that just a bit of the weight he bore lessened. "Might I ask your name?"

"My name is Gardawyn, Your Majesty," the young medical assistant responded. "My parents are Tiibee and Seeniff from the Star Clan. Both came with you on the ship from Europa."

"I know your parents well, Gardawyn," Enok replied, surprised their young son was now the handsome male floating before him. "Both are well respected in the medical fields. I see you are following in their footsteps."

"Yes, Sire. There were so few medicals left after the war, I felt my place was to fill one of those vacant positions when I grew up. I think Mother was hoping I would become a soldier like my brother, perhaps even join the jumpers' squad and see the world, but I felt I was needed more in medical."

"And I am glad you did," Enok replied, turning his attention back to the motionless being now lying on the table in the working room. "For now you have the task of saving not only my Chief Commander, but my dearest friend, my brother and Europa's second father." Enok turned and looked directly in Gardawyn's lilac eyes. "Can you do that for me, Gardawyn? Can you save Jeanip?"

"I swear upon my life's water I will do everything in my power to save him, Your Majesty. I will take my leave of you so I can begin that process." Gardawyn raised his hand to his forehead then proceeded toward the room where Jeanip awaited.

"Gardawyn," Enok calle,d stopping the assistant from entering the working room.

"Yes, Your Majesty?"

"Thank you for listening."

"Any time, Your Majesty."

"And Gardawyn, tell your colleagues under no circumstance is that amulet to be removed. Tell them I will personally execute anyone who tries to remove it."

"Yes, Your Majesty. I will personally see to it that it remains on Jeanip. I remember the legends my parents told me regarding the ancient healing Orbs and amulets, and we need all the help we can get to save him." Gardawyn turned and hurried into the working room to fulfill his promise to his monarch. He didn't know exactly what had just happened, but he knew it made him determined not to fail.

"Sire, how is he doing?" Enok heard a voice next to him say. He turned to see Gassop floating next to him. He had been so intent on watching Jeanip he had not noticed Gassop enter the room.

"They still do not know if he will make it or not," Enok replied. "We should know more in the next few hours." He turned away from the window and looked directly at the commander before him. "Gassop, I have a very important land assignment that needs immediate attention. Now that we know without a doubt Jeffrey Landers and JeffRa were the same person, it is imperative that we search his dwelling in Michigan for anything relating to us, Europa and the Terrians. Although unlikely, there is the possibility he may have kept a journal, advanced Oonock technology or even some bendicor at his home or office. We cannot take the chance of such items falling into the hands of the humans."

"Or any remaining Terrians," Gassop added.

"Or Terrians."

"I agree, Your Majesty," Gassop replied, suddenly realizing the danger they could still be in. "I can leave right away."

"Thank you for volunteering, Gassop, but I need you here with me. I need someone young, someone who has spent a great deal of time amongst humans and is able to handle an overland trip. In fact, I need two, possibly three such Oonocks. If Jeanip could speak, who would he tell me were the ideal Oonocks from the security squad to send on this assignment?"

"Jeanip would tell you to send Kiijon and Teerdomay," Gassop responded without hesitation. "They are the two Runbee sent to Australia to collect information to construct Mr. Terrance's bedroom. They would have no problems carrying out this assignment."

"Then make it so," Enok replied. "Ask Kiijon and Teerdomay to report to me right away so I can give them their assignment."

"Yes, Your Majesty," Gassop responded. "Right away." Gassop turned to leave then stopped for a moment.

"Yes?" Enok asked, turning his attention to Gassop. "Was there something else?"

"Sire, I know Runbee will be remaining on Saint's Isle to protect our young monarchs for the time being. But I also know he is needed to protect its borders and the waters surrounding the island. If you need someone to fill in for Jeanip as Security Commander, you might want to consider Kiijon," Gassop stated. "Jeanip has mentioned to me several times over the years that when, and if, he ever retired, he thought Kiijon would be a good replacement. He is well versed in all the security rules and protocols, is an excellent combat soldier and has lived amongst humans for extended periods of time. He is at home on land as much as he is in the ocean. And Teerdomay would make an excellent replacement for Birea as Europa's bodyguard. She will need one whenever she resettles on the mainland."

"I will take your suggestion under advisement. But if they come with your recommendation there is no need to doubt their ability." Enok turned back to watch the medical team working on Jeanip.

"I will take my leave, Your Majesty," Gassop said as he turned to leave. "Oh, by the way, I ordered several helpers to bring you something to eat," he announced as he swam away. "It should be arriving in the next few minutes." Food – Enok had forgotten all about eating. He couldn't remember the last time he ate and realized it had to have been several days ago. Thank goodness he had such loyal subjects as Gassop who always kept an eye out for his well-being.

"Sire," Enok heard a soft voice say. "Sire, it is I, Gardawyn. I came to give you an update on Jeanip."

Enok opened his eyes and stretched, feeling somewhat rested. He was surprised to see young Gardawyn floating next to him. He must have fallen asleep, but for how long? Was Jeanip still alive?

"Is he okay?" Enok asked as he stood, the sound of anxiety in his voice. He quickly directed his vision to the room where the medical team had worked on Jeanip all night only to see an empty bed, an empty room. "Where is he, Gardawyn? Have I lost him too?"

"No, Sire, we moved him to another room where he can recover from his surgeries. If you like I can take you to him."

Enok shook his head to clear the sleepiness away. He now remembered the events of the evening. The medical teams had worked on Jeanip all night doing everything in their power to save him. His injuries had been worse than Enok had feared, and twice emergency operations were performed to correct a failing organ. Three times Gardawyn had informed him there was no hope, his injuries beyond their advanced medicine. Each time Enok had gone into the room, placed his hands on his and Jeanip's amulets and said the three words hoping to once again invoke the healing powers of Medaron's amulet. To his dismay and relief, the amulets awoke and sent strands of light into Jeanip's body, giving him just enough energy to remain alive, allowing the Oonock medicine and medical procedures time to heal his body. Each time Enok wished there was a way to bring Europa to his bedside to completely heal his old friend like she did at the Hunting Lodge, but he knew that was impossible. He hoped Medaron's amulet would continue to bring life to Jeanip if needed again.

"Yes, please take me to his room," Enok replied. He followed Gardawyn down a small corridor to a recovery room. Inside he saw Jeanip lying upon a table with tubes and wires connected to him everywhere. He quickly looked to assure himself the amulet still remained around Jeanip's neck, which it did. He scanned the numerous dials and indicators and saw many were just barely in the green, many still in the red, indicating Jeanip was not out of danger yet.

"How is he?" Enok asked.

"It's still anyone's guess if he will survive or not, Your Majesty," Gardawyn stated. "He has a long way to go, but he's a fighter and his body is slowly healing, thanks to the amulet."

"Do not sell yourself or your team short, Young Gardawyn. I am sure your medical talents contributed greatly to his recovery so far."

"That may be, Sire, but without the amulets' healing powers all the expertise in the world would not have saved our Chief Commander," Gardawyn stated. "It will be several hours before we know anything more, Your Highness. Might I suggest you try and get some rest? There is a room down the hall where you can be comfortable and rest for a while. And I might suggest something to eat again."

"Please have a resting bed brought in here for me to use," Enok commanded. "I do not want to be too far from him in case the amulets' powers are needed again. And perhaps someone from the royal kitchen could bring me some breakfast."

"As you wish, Sire," Gardawyn answered. "I will have someone bring you a resting bed immediately and inform the kitchen to bring you something to eat."

While Enok waited he floated over to Jeanip and looked down upon his dearest friend. "Jeanip, you must get better. She needs you and is waiting for you to return to her."

———————

"I am glad to see you got some rest, Your Majesty," Gardawyn said, as he entered Jeanip's room several hours later when he saw Enok beginning to wake. He looked over at the empty dishes sitting on the table. "I am also glad to see you took my advice and ate a little something."

"I guess I did not realize how tired I really was. How is our patient doing?" Enok asked, as he looked down at the still Jeanip.

"Surprisingly well," Gardawyn responded. "His vitals are growing stronger by the minute and we've been able to take him off of several supports already."

Enok looked down and thought how terribly fragile he looked, how battle-worn from his service to Enok. His left arm and the attached wing were encased in an electric tube which was sending energy impulses into his arm to encourage the flesh to regrow. He had lost a great deal of the flesh from his arm when he was hit by the pulse of JeffRa's blaster. When he transformed back into his true form, the damage carried over to his top left wing.

"And what of the damage to his left wing and arm?"

"Both are mending well and the tissue is starting to mend," Gardawyn replied. "We were able to graft new flesh onto his arm. We won't know what permanent damage there is, if any, until both have totally reformed and mended."

Enok floated closer to get a better view of the arm and the wing. He could see the bones had already set themselves in his arm and the grafted flesh was adhering to both appendages. But he worried the damage to the wing was so severe it might impede Jeanip's ability to swim. He realized Jeanip's recovery would be long and difficult. He knew Jeanip would not mind the difficultness, but the length was definitely going to cause a problem. Jeanip would insist on joining the young monarchs as soon as he was able to walk to see to their safety and teachings. Enok admitted he wanted Jeanip at Saint's Isle sooner rather than later also. Enok watched as several small regenerating lights moved, crisscross over his left leg and thigh, filling in the wounds with new tissue.

"And his left leg?" he asked.

"Also doing well," Gardawyn replied, running his medical scanner over Jeanip's body to determine the progression of his recovery. "According to my scanner he is beginning to finally heal. If you have no further need of me, Sire, I will take my leave." Enok nodded his head in approval and Gardawyn left giving Enok time alone with Jeanip.

"Forgive me, Dear Friend, for asking so much of you," Enok thought, as he placed his hand on Jeanip's forehead while once again surveying the extent of Jeanip's broken body. "Perhaps this time I asked too much of you."

"Do I look as bad as I feel?" Enok heard a faint, weak voice say telepathically.

"Actually, I think you probably feel worse than you look," Enok replied, smiling, as he floated over to Jeanip's right side which was free of instruments. Jeanip opened his eyes and look at his monarch's face. "You gave me a pretty good scare, Old Friend. I did not think you would make it through the night."

"Sorry, Your Majesty," Jeanip stated. "I didn't think I would ever see another day either." A serious look crossed his face. "What of my sovereigns and Terrance? Are they okay?"

"Yes, they are secure on Saint's Isle, thanks to you. Runbee and Graybin are with them, so you do not need to worry. You just concentrate on getting well. All three ask me to tell you to get better and return to them soon – they love and miss you."

Jeanip missed them too, but such sentiment was not part of a soldier's character. "And JeffRa?" he asked. He had very little recollection of what had happened after he was hit by the side blast of JeffRa's weapon.

"He is gone forever," Enok said, a sound of relief in his voice. "I finally did what I should have done that day back on Europa. He has been sentenced and executed, put somewhere where he can never return or harm anyone again."

"So you were able to prevent him from flowing out into the waters?" Jeanip asked.

"Yes," Enok answered. "The wrist band held him in human form. And the container you helped me design kept any part of him from coming in contact with the ocean's water. This time we can be assured he will not return."

"And what of his army?"

"Chancee's soldiers were able to eliminate most of them when they tried to attack the Hunter's Lodge. Plus, your blast on Minnos destroyed all the Terrians who had been foolish enough to venture onto the premises. Hopefully, that does not leave a lot left, but we will track down those who did manage to escape. But without JeffRa to lead them, I do not think they will be much of a threat."

"And what of Chancee? Were they able to find his body?" Jeanip somberly asked.

"They not only found his body, they found him alive!" Enok related, seeing the tiniest spark of a smile on Jeanip's face. "That old coot is as stubborn as you are when it comes to dying. He managed to turn himself into a grizzly before the rock ceiling caved in on him. The bear's massive muscular frame enabled him to survive the weight of all that rock. He is still in serious condition in the room next to this one, but the medical personnel say he will be fine."

"I should have known no Terrian would be able to bring him down," Jeanip stated.

"Just as one could not bring you down," Enok added.

"Ah, but we both know that is not true. I would be dead if it were not for Europa. She has twice brought me back from the jaws of death. If it were not for her this bed would be empty." Remembering the events of the voyage, a serious look came across Jeanip's face. "Enok, Europa summoned the power of the Orb to heal me of my injuries when we arrived at the Hunting Lodge. And on Saint's Isle she created that protection shield that saved me. How did she do those things? Only a handful of Oonocks have ever been able to use the Orb's healing powers, and the last one passed a hundred and fifty thousand years ago. And I have NEVER heard of one creating a protective barrier using an Orb. Plus, she is a human and therefore incapable of doing any of those things."

"Yet she did them. A human summoned a Europian's Orb's powers," Enok said. "I too have been trying to determine how she was capable of these feats and the only explanation I find is that when Medaron transferred her powers to her something extraordinary happened to our little princess. Medaron's powers must have joined with human powers that were dormant in Europa and mutated her into a form of Oonock we have never seen before."

"Do you think Europa will be able to transform?" Jeanip asked, wondering what else his queen was capable of.

"Only time will reveal that secret," Enok replied. "That is why it is important for you to rest and get better so you can help her with these new powers and any others that might appear. The medical personnel have been able to make some improvements in my lung problem, but I still am unable to stay above for very long. So, I must continue to rely on you, My Old Friend."

One of the medical personnel floated into the room to administer medication to Jeanip. "Good morning, Your Majesty," he said, as he gave the customary salute. "It is important for Jeanip to rest, so I must ask that you keep your visit brief."

"I was just ready to leave," Enok said. "I promised Europa I would return today to visit with them and I still have to pay Chancee a visit." Enok looked at the medical personnel. "If he gets worse or you need me for anything, contact me immediately."

"Yes, Your Majesty," the young medical personnel replied.

Enok reached down and touched Jeanip's uninjured shoulder. "And Jeanip, leave that amulet on around your neck. That is a direct order. Be assured I will court-martial you if you take it off even if you ARE a member of the royal family now."

Jeanip said nothing but did manage a weak smile. Before Enok was out of the room Jeanip was fast asleep, the medical machines working over his body to heal him.

———————

Enok floated down the hallway to Chancee's room. As he entered he thought how the scene before him was almost identical to the one he had just left. Chancee was lying on a bed in his true form connected to numerous machines with tubes emanating from his body. Several doctors were currently working on him.

"Is this a bad time?" Enok asked the medical personnel.

"Not at all, Your Majesty. We were just checking to see how his recovery was coming."

Enok could see Chancee was still not conscious. "How is it coming?" Enok asked.

"He is pretty bruised and has numerous broken and shattered bones, but thankfully no injury to any of his organs," relayed one of the medical personnel. "He's lucky he thought fast enough to transform into the grizzly, who was able to take a lot more abuse. Had he remained human he would have been crushed to death for sure. From what I was told he had half of the mountain piled on top of him. It took the rescue team hours to dig him out even with our advanced machinery."

"That is one of many things I am thankful for today," Enok replied. "Please tell him I stopped by to see him when he awakens and I will be back in a few days to check on his progress." Enok turned to leave, then stopped and added, "A word of warning: Chancee is known to be pretty cantankerous and will not be happy to learn he is at the Complex. He is going to yell and scream that he immediately be returned to the land above. When he does, please tell him I order him to remain here in the infirmary until I personally tell him he can leave."

"Yes, Your Majesty, we will be glad to pass that order along," the medical assistant said, a big smile on his face. He knew Enok had just made taking care of this patient a lot easier.

"And if he becomes totally unbearable before I return and can be moved, you have my permission and suggestion to move him in the same room with Jeanip," Enok added. "Both are cantankerous old soldiers who hate medical units, so they should be good company for each other. And each will keep the other in line. But, if for some reason Chancee should take a turn for the worse, be sure someone notifies me immediately." Enok turned and left the room not waiting for a response.

From the infirmary Enok floated to the home of Zeeroff, a senior smithy and jeweler. Zeeroff was the only Oonock Enok knew who would be able to make him a copy of the amulet worn by the royal family that he needed. He had sent a messenger to his home yesterday while with Jeanip, requisitioning Zeeroff to make him a copy. He had advised him he would stop by to pick it up before he returned above.

"Good day, Your Majesty," Zeeroff greeted, as he bowed slightly and raised his hand to his forehead. "I was able to comply with your request." He lifted out of a box a round amulet filled with their home's lilac waters. "But I must tell you, it has no power like the real amulets do. It is just a copy, as you asked."

Enok reached out and took the amulet. He turned it over several times as he examined it, pleased with its construction. "This is perfect, Zeeroff. It is exactly what I need. You have done an excellent job and I thank you."

"No thanks is needed, Your Majesty," Zeeroff said, a little embarrassed at his monarch's gratitude.

Seeing that Zeeroff was uneasy about his creation, Enok stated, "Do not worry about it being just a copy. I only need it to look like a real one and to contain our home water plus a tiny piece of bendicor." Holding the amulet in his hand, Enok left leaving a puzzled Zeeroff to wonder what the purpose was of a fake amulet.

THE LIBRARY

Exhausted and emotionally drained, the three retired early to bed, looking forward to a night of rest without the worry of someone hunting them. The sounds of the surf below and the flowing fountain in the foyer lulled the three quickly to sleep. Graybin and Runbee retired to their room to rest, assured the house would watch over its occupants and keep the young monarchs safe.

Each awoke the following morning feeling surprisingly refreshed and ready for a day of new discoveries. Over a wonderful breakfast and several cups of coffee, the three planned out their day. Earon planned to go with Runbee to the saltwater pool on the third floor where they could transform into dolphins and race each other, working off some of Earon's pent up energy. Europa decided to visit the library and spend some quiet time thinking over everything that had happened the past few days. Terrance offered to go with her, but Europa said she really wanted to be alone for a while, so he opted to join Earon and Runbee at the pool where he could toss them objects to retrieve. The three decided to reconnect at dinner, after which everyone, including Graybin and Runbee, would join Earon in the saltwater pool to listen to him play his instrument.

Terrance and Earon escorted Europa to the library, then followed Runbee up the stairs to the third floor saltwater swimming pool. As they reached the top step they could smell the salt air and feel a soft breeze blowing in from the ocean below. Earon closed his eyes and breathed the smell in deeply; he had always loved the smell of the ocean. He followed the smell as it led him through a white marble arch and out onto a large open patio containing a pool the length of one and a half

Olympic size pools, just over two hundred feet long. He looked up to see a beautiful blue sky with just a few small fluffy clouds. Feeling the warmth of the sun on his body, he looked out to see the ocean in all directions. The perimeter of the patio was edged with a green hedge with a white marble stone half-wall behind the hedge. The floor was made of a light lilac stone with specks of gold and lavender swirled through it. Several large potted plants were spaced pleasingly around the patio as well as loungers, chairs and small tables. A small bar extended from the inside wall to complete the picture. It was hard to imagine such a beautiful place could not be seen from above, but he knew the security screen kept it hidden from view.

The pool had been specifically designed for Earon and other invited guests to have a place to transform and enjoy the ocean's waters without ever leaving the security of the house. It was filled with sea water and descended down into the island to a depth of fifty feet. It was more than enough room to allow Earon to transform into a sea creature of his choice and race, jump, swim or flip to his heart's content. At the near end of the pool was a set of stairs and a much shallower portion of the pool; it ranged from three to eight feet. This part of the pool was designed for Europa so she too would have somewhere safe to swim in addition to the freshwater pool on the first floor. It was also hoped Europa would use the saltwater pool to interact with the transformed Oonocks as she had all of her life in the open ocean, although she did not know it.

Terrance watched in amazement as Earon and Runbee transformed effortlessly into dolphins and began to chase each other. After several hours of ball tossing, jumping, racing and ring-catching, Earon had had a good workout and felt rejuvenated and famished. After transforming back into human form and dressing, Earon and Runbee followed Terrance back to the kitchen ready for lunch.

Europa stepped into the library expecting to be amazed at its grandeur, if the rest of the house was any indication of what it would look like. She was not disappointed. The wall on the right was lined with sturdy oak bookshelves holding a large assortment of books. The left wall was made of glass to allow the sun to illuminate the room, while giving the library's occupant a view of the blue sky and gardens below. Positioned in front of the window was an oak desk on which sat a computer. Europa remembered Graybin telling her one had been installed so they could keep abreast of what was happening in the real world during their stay. They could receive information but there was no way to send anything out; a security measure to keep their location secret. On the wall at the far end of the room were four additional oak bookshelves divided in the middle by a huge painting of her parents in their human form. In addition to books, these shelves also contained pictures. The shelves on the right contained pictures of her, covering the ages of infancy through high school. The shelves on the left contained portraits she was not quite able to make out. As she walked toward them for a closer view, she realized they were probably pictures of Earon in his true form spanning numerous years. There was even a picture of her parents in their true form holding a very young Earon. She lifted this family portrait from its place on the shelf and scanned it, mesmerized by their true form's beauty and simplicity. She marveled how breath taking exquisite they were as they floated in a setting of lilac water. She assumed this portrait and the other portraits of Earon had been done while they lived at the Ocean Complex. She wondered how the portraits were made since a water environment would prohibit the use of paints or a camera. She made a mental note to ask Earon or Graybin about how they were created. Looking at their happy faces, Europa imagined herself in the portrait as a Waters and thought about how wonderful it would have been if they had had the opportunity to be a real family. She turned to look at the pictures of herself and noted there was one of her and her mother together when she was about five, but of course there was none of her with her father. Hoping there was some type of photo equipment in the house, she decided to ask Enok if he would take a picture with her that could be placed next to the one of her and her mother. She smiled at the thought, feeling such a picture would make the collection complete.

Europa carefully replaced the family portrait back on its shelf, then walked over to the large painting of her parents. The painting started about six inches off the floor and looked to be about seven feet tall and five feet wide. As she scanned the picture she noticed the painting must have been done at Minnos, for there in the background was the cottage with its circular porch. A simple, but eloquent, carriage stood in front of the cottage with two white horses harnessed to it. More than likely the painting had been done right after Minnos had been completed and her parents still believed they would be living there. That meant the painting was almost four hundred years old and her parents looked no different.

As her eyes scanned the painting she noticed it had an odd appearance, an appearance of a water pool. It shimmered and contained very miniscule waves that rippled down its surface. Intrigued with the possibility it was not a normal painting, she reached out and gently touch it anticipating a hard surface. To her amazement, she watched as ripples circled out from where her fingers touched the painting. She immediately pulled her hand back fearing she might damage it and looked around to see if anyone saw what she saw. She giggled nervously, remembering she was alone in the room. Gently with one finger, she lightly touched the painting again. As before, ripples fanned out across the painting as her finger penetrated the surface. Totally intrigued by this, she pushed her finger deeper into the painting to see how far her hand could penetrate. She was disappointed when her finger stopped just below the watery surface as it struck a hard layer. Evidently the watery effect was superficial.

Afraid to make another attempt to penetrate the painting, Europa walked over to the wall of books. The assortment was amazing. There were classic novels, modern novels, short-stories collections, how-to books, books on nature and the cosmos, comics and even several versions of the bible. As she walked down the bookcases scanning the titles, she came across one bookshelf containing a set of double doors she had not noticed before. She reached up and opened them to reveal a Blu-ray player and a viewing screen. On the shelves beneath the screen was an assortment of her favorite movies and television shows. Whoever had designed this room had thought of everything they might want or need to occupy their time during a long stay on the island.

A soft knock at the door broke the room's silence. After a few seconds the doors opened and Graybin stepped inside. "Forgive me for interrupting you, Your Majesty," she said., "I was wondering if you were going to come downstairs to eat lunch with the males or if you wanted me to bring you something up here?"

"I am not very hungry," Europa replied. "But I would like . . ."

Before Europa could finish her sentence Graybin said," Coffee? I have it right here." Graybin stepped back into the hallway for a moment and reappeared carrying a tray with coffee and some crackers and cheese. "I'll just put it down over here on the table by the sitting chair." After sitting the tray down Graybin poured Europa a large mug of coffee and brought it over to her. "French Roast, your choice of the early afternoon, if I am not mistaken."

"Thank you, Graybin," Europa said. "You are astonishing. You always know what we need; sometimes I think even before we do. You remind me a lot of my mother's helper, Misso. She always seemed to anticipate things. Did you know her?"

"Yes, Your Majesty," Graybin replied, slightly surprised at Europa's question. "Misso was my daughter."

A surprised expression crossed Europa's face. She had no idea Graybin was Misso's mother. It was Misso she had been talking about that day when she told Europa her daughter had been killed by the Terrians and had passed on. "Oh, Graybin, I am sorry. I did not know."

"No need to apologize, Europa," Graybin said. "It is understandable you did not know; you were never told anything about her family life"

"I am sorry we were not able to save her," Europa said, not sure what the Oonock custom was regarding family deaths. "She was a wonderful helper and she is missed very much."

"I miss her too, and Sunam," Graybin said, as her eyes became watery. "But they died valiantly fulfilling their duty. And they were able to flow together into the Waters of Life. No soldier or life-mates could ask for better deaths." Europa could see Graybin was having trouble keeping her emotion under control. "If you have no further need of me, I will take my leave. The males will be expecting their lunch."

"Yes, by all means," Europa said. Then she did something she regretted never doing to Misso; she walked up to Graybin, put her arms around her and hugged her tightly. She whispered in Graybin's ear, "Thank you for all you do for us." When Europa released her and stepped back, she could see Graybin was taken aback by Europa's sign of affection, not accustomed to such actions by royals. As a tear escaped her eye, Graybin turned and quickly left the room without saying another word.

Europa debated if she wanted to check the world news on the internet, read a book or watch a movie, but her attention kept returning to the picture of her parents. She felt there was more to this picture than what she was seeing. After refilling her coffee mug and grabbing a few crackers and pieces of cheese, she returned to the painting. She began to search it, to examine every inch of canvas looking for something she knew was there but not seeing.

Graybin walked into the kitchen several minutes before the three males arrived. She gestured the three hungry males to the table when they entered, keeping her back to them so they would not see the tears in her eyes.

"Has Europa already had her lunch?" Terrance asked Graybin, as she brought him a ham and Swiss sandwich with French fries and coleslaw.

"No," Graybin answered. "Miss Europa said she wasn't hungry, but I did take a small tray up to her in the library in hopes she might nibble a little."

Looking at Earon Terrance asked, "Do you think we should see if she wants to join us?"

"No, I think she needs this time to be alone," Earon answered. "Remember, four days ago she was living at Minnos surrounded by the people who loved her and who cared for her since she was born, secure within the cottage's walls. She was a normal human being with a canine companion and dreams of a human future. Today she is faced with the realization Minnos and everything she loved and owned is gone, almost everyone she cared about is dead, her canine was actually her brother transformed, and he and her parents are aliens from another world. A being she has never known has tried to kill her several times along with her brother and friend. And if that was not enough, she is confined to this island, beautiful as it is, for an undetermined amount of time, away from the world and other human beings except for yourself. I definitely think she has a lot of things to think about."

"Wow, now that you put it all together like that I'm surprised she's not upstairs crying her eyes out," Terrance said.

"She may very well be," Earon stated. "If she is not down for dinner I will go check on her. Besides, the house will let us know if she needs us." Earon picked up his coffee cup and drained it of coffee. He placed it back on the table and said, "Since we have several hours before dinner, how about you and me go explore the house, Terrance? Maybe we can find this FarCore everyone spoke of."

Terrance agreed, but his heart really wasn't in it. He was worried about Europa. Plus, Earon's account of what had transpired lately also reminded him of his own stepfather's death, something he was very much responsible for, and the truth of who he really was. He was never close to his stepfather, but that fact did not erase the sorrow of being a part of what ended his life. Terrance had second thoughts about exploring with Earon, wanting to retire to his room to contemplate his stepfather's end. Yet he realized that keeping busy was the best thing for him to do and followed Earon down the hall, comforted by the fact that the house would watch over Europa.

Earon and Terrance explored the house, looking in every room for any sign of the mysterious FarCore. Even though the house was large, it didn't take long to complete their search. They wished they could go outside the house to explore the entrance cave and the grounds they had first walked through, but that was not allowed. Earon decided to return to his room to prepare his musical geezba for his recital that night. Not knowing what else to do, Terrance retired to his room too. Both agreed to meet in front of Europa's room at six o'clock to accompany her downstairs to dinner.

At six o'clock sharp, both Earon and Terrance emerged from their rooms ready for dinner. Earon knocked on Europa's door but received no answer. "Perhaps she is still getting ready," Earon said, looking at Terrance. He opened the door and called out Europa's name, but only silence was returned.

"Maybe she fell asleep in the library," Terrance suggested. "She looked tired this morning at breakfast."

"She should have joined us at the sea pool," Earon answered ,as they walked down to the library. "A good workout would have energized her."

Earon knocked on the door and entered. Just as Europa had been, they were mesmerized by the beauty of the library. Their eyes scanned the room, taking in all that it had to offer, then they saw Europa standing in front of a painting at the far end of the room. "Europa, it is time for dinner," Earon said, but he received no reply. As he walked closer to his sister he asked, "Europa, are you okay?"

"Is this not fantastic?" Europa asked.

Terrance and Earon stared at the painting. Both felt the term 'fantastic' was an understatement. "What exquisite work," Terrance commented. "I see the Oonocks' advancements over humans extend to the art world also."

"That may be," Earon stated. "But I have never seen anything this detailed, this elaborate."

"Watch this!" Europa said with excitement, as she touched the painting, sending the ripples flowing across the surface. "It is almost as if it was painted with water, but there is a hard surface behind it."

"Can I try that?" Terrance asked, intrigued by a liquid painting.

"Go ahead," Europa said. Terrance reached out his finger and touched it, mesmerized by the ripples his finger created. "This is outstanding."

"I have been standing here most of the afternoon just looking at it," Europa said. "I swear there is more to it than just a painting, but I cannot figure out what."

"We can come back later and see if we can discover its secrets," Earon said. "Right now we need to go down to dinner, after which I had planned on playing my geezba for you two. Remember, Sis?"

"Maybe we could wait until tomorrow to hear you play and come back with Europa here after dinner," Terrance suggested, trying to find a way to postpone him going into the water to hear Earon.

"No way," Europa said, as she turned around, grabbing Terrance's hand as she walked toward the door. "You are not getting out of Earon's concert that easy. You are going to sit next to me, underwater and listen."

"I have everything worked out for you, Terrance," Earon added, following the two down to the kitchen. "You will be in shallow water. You just have to have your ears underwater so you can hear and see the music."

"See the music?" Terrance asked, thinking what an odd thing for Earon to say. "One can't see music."

"You will just have to wait for my performance and see."

As they descended the stairs Europa stopped and turned to face Earon. "Did you know that Misso was Graybin's daughter?"

"No, I did not know that," Earon replied. "But it does not surprise me. There are so few Oonocks left, especially young ones, that everyone is related to someone now."

As they proceeded down, Terrance said, "That's why Graybin can anticipate our needs like Misso. She probably taught her."

After dinner Terrance and Europa went upstairs to change into their swim suits. Earon walked out to the side pool and slipped into the water to check if the geezba needed any tuning. Satisfied it was in perfect tune, he sat at the edge of the pool with his legs hanging in the water, eagerly waiting for Europa and Terrance to return.

"Do you think he will back out?" Runbee asked, as he and Graybin walked across the floor and slipped into the pool.

"No, he promised me he would come," Earon said, his face showing the joy of having an audience to play for. Finally the two appeared, Terrance tightly holding Europa's hand as they walked toward the pool. "Terrance, all you have to do is sit on the steps and put your head under the water so you can hear my geezba as it is meant to be heard. I had Runbee bring snorkels and diving masks for you, so you will be able to see and breathe without any problem," Earon said, pointing to several snorkels lying on a table. "It is totally safe and, if at any time you become uneasy, all you have to do is stand up and your upper body half will be out of the water."

"Come on, Terrance," Europa said, picking up a snorkel and mask for herself and Terrance on their way to the pool. Holding Terrance's hand tightly in her own, she led him to the side of the pool and down the stairs. She explained to him how to use the snorkel and helped him put the diving mask on, assuring him there was nothing to fear and he would be able to breathe with no problem. With some trepidation, Terrance closed his eyes and lowered himself down into the water taking a seat beside Europa. He took a breath through the snorkel ready to jump up if he had any problem breathing. To his surprise and delight, he was actually able to breathe just as Europa had said. He opened his eyes and was amazed to see Graybin and Runbee at the far end of the pool. "I'm doing it," Terrance said to himself. "I'm actually underwater breathing and I can see everything." He turned to look at Europa who gave him a big smile and a 'thumbs up' for his accomplishment.

Earon slipped beneath the water with his geezba. He looked over to Terrance to see how the water phobic human was doing and was relieved to see the smile on his face. He too gave Terrance a 'thumbs up' for conquering his fears. Terrance never ceased to amaze him; when it came to Europa there was nothing Terrance could not overcome if it meant keeping her safe or happy, even his fear of water. His sister had truly found her quanish and Earon was overjoyed. For the first time ever Earon could foresee his sister living a happy life as a human with a good man at her side.

Checking the location of his fingers, Earon began to strum the instrument's strings. The water began to fill with the music of harps, violins, cellos and mandolins as if an entire symphony was playing. As the sound flowed through the water it turned into a visual array of radiant colors, twirling and intersecting as they branched out across the pool, bursting into an explosion of color as the sound diminished. It was beyond anything Europa and Terrance had imagined. Terrance was so enthralled he completely forgot his fear of water and sat there until the last colored note disappeared when Earon finished.

446

Having concluded his song Earon rose and motioned for the other to follow. He sat on the side of the pool eagerly awaited Europa's and Terrance's emergence. "Well, what did you think?" he asked, a large smile framing his face.

"Earon, I have never heard or seen anything so spectacular," Europa said, as she and Terrance stood and removed their masks and snorkels. "I never knew it was possible to SEE sound."

"Anytime you want to play I will certainly take a seat underwater," Terrance said. "I never imagined anything so beautiful. I am so glad you two persuaded me to attend. I actually enjoyed being underwater. I told myself during our voyage here if I survived our journey and arrived alive I would learn how to swim and sail. You're playing tonight makes me even more determined to learn."

Europa leaned over and kissed Terrance. "I am so glad to hear that, Terrance. I love the water – it is like my second home. I now have something extra special to look forward to – showing you all the joys and wonders of a water world."

"Ever think the reason you feel at home in the water is because your family are water beings?" Earon asked, teasing his little sister. "It is undoubtedly part of your emotional makeup."

"You are probably right, Earon," Europa answered. "But I never knew that until the other day. I just assumed I had a weird love for the ocean. Now I know why, thanks to a madman." As soon as Europa said the last sentence she regretted it as she remembered the madman was Terrance's stepfather. She turned toward Terrance, who was still standing next to her and she saw the look on his face. "Oh, Terrance, I'm sorry. I should not have called your father a madman."

Terrance turned toward Europa, trying to put a joyful look upon his face. "Don't worry about it, Europa. Unfortunately, you spoke the truth. Although I never knew him as one, I have to resolve myself to the fact he was a madman, a psychopathic mass murderer."

Earon rose and walked over to where Europa and Terrance stood. He placed his hands on Terrance's shoulder and looked directly into his eyes. "Terrance, never believe that. Your father was not a madman; JeffRa was. Your father was Jeffrey Landers, a decent man from all the accounts you have given of him. That is who you need to remember, Jeffrey Landers the human, not JeffRa the Terrian. They are two separate beings; one good and one evil. Even at the end I could see in your father's eyes his love for you. Never doubt that, okay?"

"I will try," Terrance answered, remembering a few fond memories of Jeffrey Landers.

Feeling enough had been said on the subject, Earon held out his hand to escort his sister to a nearby table. Terrance followed and took the chair next to her. Just as they were sitting down Graybin and Runbee returned from the kitchen with fresh strawberry shortcake and coffee for everyone to enjoy. The five sat around the table enjoying Graybin's delicious treats and watching the pinks, purples and blue colors of the sun set.

"Graybin, these have to be some of the best strawberries I have ever tasted," Terrance commented. "Do you know where they were grown?"

Graybin looked at Terrance, a little amused by his question. "They are from our garden here on the island. I picked them earlier today."

"Garden? We have a vegetable garden?" Europa asked, then realized if her mother helped design the layout of the island she would have insisted on a vegetable garden.

"Yes, Your Highness, we grow all our own vegetables and fruits here on the island. Remember, due to security issues there is no leaving the island for supplies. Other than the supplies you brought with you on your boat and the food we are able to obtain from the sea, everything you eat or use must come from the island."

"We are totally self-contained and can live indefinitely on the food grown and produced here on the island for years, even decades," Runbee added. He too was surprised Terrance and the monarchs had not understood their self-containment. Other than the ocean, where did they think the food came from? "Believe it or not, we even have a few chickens living on the island so we can have eggs for breakfast."

"And Mother always loved her vegetable gardens," Europa said.

"That she did," Graybin replied. "I remember her telling me once it was one of her most favorite things about living above. That and coffee. Speaking of which, would anyone like a warm-up on their coffee?" All three lifted their cups in response to her question.

"Runbee, there is a picture of my parents in the library," Earon said, as he watched Graybin fill his cup. "Do you know where it came from or how it was made? I have never seen anything like it before."

"No, I'm sorry Earon, I don't," Runbee replied. He turned to Graybin. "Do you know?" he asked her.

"I don't know how it was made but I do know it was made by your mother," Graybin stated. "I believe the Orbs which she originally found in the cavern taught her the technique while we still lived on Europa. I believe the knowledge was a gift for the royal family."

"So my mother found the Orbs?" Europa asked.

"Yes," replied Graybin. "She found them shortly after she and your father were joined. It was so long ago I don't remember the particulars, only that the Orbs were from FarCore."

"FarCore?" all three said at once.

"FarCore was on Europa?" Europa asked.

"I thought FarCore was here on Saint's Isle," Earon stated, fearful he was mistaken.

"FarCore exists in many places and has countless entrances, but if there is one on Saint's Isle I do not know about it," Graybin stated. She could see the look of disappointment on the three young travelers' faces. Evidently FarCore was something of interest to them. "If there is an entrance here on the island I am sure your father will know where it is. You must remember to ask him. He would also know the story of how your mother found the Orbs. I am sure he would be delighted to tell you the story when he returns."

"Thank you, we will be sure to ask him," Earon said.

After everyone had finished their desert and coffee, Graybin and Runbee gathered the dishes. "We will take our leave of you now," Runbee said. "We have to prepare for your father's visit tomorrow." With that said the two turned and left, leaving the three travelers alone on the patio.

"I guess we should be turning in too," Europa stated. "Thank you again, Earon, for a wonderful evening. I hope it is the first of many concerts you will entertain us with."

"You can count on it, Sis."

At breakfast the next morning Europa announced she had some things she needed to do before her father arrived, leaving the two men to once again search for FarCore. The little bit of information Graybin had relayed regarding the mysterious location now had Earon more intrigued than ever. Not having much interest in FarCore, but again realizing Europa wanted time alone, Terrance tagged along with Earon trying to look enthused.

Europa watched the two trot off on their exploration. After she was sure they were out of eye sight, she hurried up the stairs and returned to the library to focus on the painting. But this time instead of filling her with awe, a deep sadness overcame her for the life that should have been hers but wasn't.

After a couple of hours of searching, Terrance and Earon became bored with looking for the elusive FarCore. They decided to get Europa and go to the side pool where Earon was going to teach Terrance how to strum the geezba. Earon knocked on her bedroom door but received no answer. He opened the door to an empty room. Thinking she might have returned to the library, they walked down the hall and stood outside the door. Earon hesitated on opening the door when he thought he heard crying inside.

"Terrance, would you kindly go downstairs and ask Graybin if she would mind making another of those delicious deserts she served us last night?" Earon said, now sensing the past weeks' events had finally come crashing down upon his sister. Earon saw the perplexed look on Terrance's face. "I believe my sister and I need to spend some quality sibling time together this morning," he offered as an explanation, although, as monarch, he needed to give none. "You have to trust me on this, Terrance. Please wait for us downstairs."

"Okay," Terrance said, as he turned and walked alone down the staircase and headed toward the kitchen.

Earon knocked on the door and stepped inside. His heart sank as he saw he had been correct. Sitting on the floor in front of the painting was Europa. He could now clearly hear her sobs and see her body shake as she was consumed by a flood of emotions.

"Rough day?" Earon asked, walking over and gently sitting down on the floor beside her. "Care to talk about it?"

"No," he vaguely heard Europa say. "Just things."

"You used to talk to me all the time about everything," Earon said. "What is that you are holding in your hands?" he asked her, reaching over to remove a painting she was holding. He was not surprised when he saw it was the picture of himself with their parents.

"That was when I thought you were a dog and didn't understand what I was saying," she replied, remembering the hours she had poured her heart out to poor Triton.

"Well, maybe it will help if I become Triton for a while again," Earon said, as he took the picture from her hand and lifted her up from the floor. "Let us go sit on the couch." Holding on to her hand tightly, he led her to a nearby couch where he handed her back the picture once she was seated. "Remember, I have to be naked before I can transform, so you will have to close your eyes when I get to my underwear, Sis."

"Stop, Earon," Europa said. "I am not in the mood for games."

"Really, it is no problem," Earon said, beginning to undress. "I will become Triton and lie here beside you and you can pour your heart out to me."

"Earon, stop," Europa repeated, "I have already seen everything once and I do not wish to see it again."

Now in his underwear, Earon looked directly at Europa. "Tell you what, Sis; I will give you a choice. I can take off this underwear and become Triton or I can put them back on and you can talk to me as Earon. The choice is yours."

Earon was surprised when his ultimatum was met with silence. He had assumed Europa would pick Earon immediately. Evidently, she was being stubborn or more upset than he thought. He turned his back to her and pulled his underwear part way down, showing his buttocks. "Here they go," he said.

"Gross!! Pull them back up," Europa yelled, a hint of amusement in her voice. "I will talk to Earon, although I do miss Triton at times."

Earon quickly dressed and sat down next to Europa and pulled her in his arms. "Wise decision!! But you know, Sis, any time you miss ol' Triton it is no problem for me to transform into him."

As he held her he felt another flood of emotion overwhelm her. She began to cry so hard she could barely catch her breath. As Triton, Earon had seen her cry many times, but never like this.

"So what is the matter?" Earon asked, wrapping his arms around her even tighter. "Why are you so upset?"

Finally after several minutes, Europa was able to control her emotions and replied in an almost silent voice, "Oh, Earon, Minnos is gone and almost everyone we knew is dead; Mother, Misso, Sunam and the others. And even Jeanip and Mr. Dark Feather could be dead by now. And it is all because of me. ME. They were protecting me and died as a result."

"They were protecting me too," Earon said.

"Even you were protecting me," she added. "And who was I protecting? No one." She lifted the picture and held it out for Earon to see. "And look at this picture of my family. Who is missing? Me! My whole life has been a lie. Everything I was ever told, who I thought I was, everything I believed – LIES!" Once again her crying became too overpowering for her to talk.

"I do not believe that is true," Earon said, trying to think of what their mother would say if she were there. "Right now you just cannot see the truths in your life. Were you not born to two parents who loved you more than anything, raised by a mother who loved and cherished you and protected by an array of people who likewise loved you? Were you not told that you were from a royal family that had to flee their home country due to a long feud with a warring race? Were you not raised to be strong, independent and a lady with a bright future? I see no lies in any of that?" Earon asked, hoping to get Europa to see the truths in her life.

"You forgot to add the part about my parents being aliens from another world," Europa sobbed. "And that my guard dog was actually my alien brother in disguise."

"A few little technicalities," Earon said, hugging her tightly, resting the side of his face against her head.

"Technicalities?" Europa yelled, raising her head to look Earon directly in the eyes. "I would call them a little more than technicalities, Earon. I am from a race of aliens who have extraordinary capabilities, intelligence and powers, who live for thousands of years and who can shape shift into countless creatures. And can I do any of these things? NO!"

"All families have their black sheep," Earon stated, trying to keep the conversation light.

"But in our family, I AM the black sheep," Europa said, more tears running down her face, soaking Earon's shirt. "Do you not see that? Everyone can transform and do these amazing things except ME. I am human. Our parents made me human. And I do not understand why they did this to me."

Earon leaned down and kissed his sister on top her head. "They did what they thought was best for you," he said softly.

"What kind of life am I going to have?" Europa asked her brother, fearing the future now that she knew the truth. "I am unable to go live with you and father at the Complex. I have to live on land, but the only home I have ever known has been blown to pieces. Where am I going to live? With everyone gone, who will help me find my place in this world?"

Before Earon could answer they both heard a voice say from the doorway, "Your brother and I will help you build that life. And I am pretty sure there is a young man downstairs who plans on doing the same." Europa looked up and saw her father standing in the doorway.

"Oh, it is you," Europa said, as she snuggled back into her brother's arms. "You really did come back."

"As I said I would," Enok replied, aware this time his daughter was not overjoyed to see him.

"Hello, Father," Earon said. Earon sent his father a silent message. "Europa is really upset, Father. She thinks her life has been a lie and she has been robbed of the life that should have been hers as a Waters. And she is feeling guilty about everyone who has died protecting her."

Earon heard his father reply, "She is right. She WAS robbed of the life that should have been hers. But she must realize the robber was not her mother and me, but JeffRa. And thank the Waters not everyone has died."

A glimmer came to Earon's eye as he realized his father was talking about Jeanip and Mr. Dark Feather. Wanting his sister to hear some had survived, Earon asked out load. "Any news on Jeanip or Mr. Dark Feather?"

"Evidently, it takes more than a cave in to end Chancee's existence. He was quick enough to transform into a grizzly and thus prevented his human form from being crushed to death. The rescue crew dug him out and he is recovering at the Complex, a fact that is really going to tick him off when he wakes up."

"Why is that, Father?" Earon inquired.

"The day Chancee became Thomas Dark Feather he promised the chief he would never leave his tribe until the day he flowed out into the ocean. And he never has. Other than an occasional trip into town, he has remained on their land for hundreds of years. So when he awakens to discover he is at the bottom of the ocean at the Complex and off the reservation, he is going to be very, VERY upset."

"And how is Jeanip?" Earon asked. "Were the medical aides able to help him?"

"His injuries were very severe and we were not sure he would survive the night, but old soldiers, such as he, are almost impossible to kill," Enok replied. "He is also recovering at the Complex and is doing well. He has a long road to recovery, but I am sure his stubbornness will have him up and around in several weeks. I would not be surprised if he pays you two a visit within the month."

"That is great news," Earon said. He looked down at Europa. "Did you hear that, Sis? They were able to reach Mr. Dark Feather in time and he is mending at the Complex. And Jeanip is recovering also and will join us soon. Is that not wonderful news? Both are alive!" He heard her sobs subside, assuming the news of Jeanip made her feel better.

"Hurray," Europa said sarcastically. "Should we throw a parade in celebration? Is it not wonderful? Jeanip and Mr. Dark Feather can both return to protect me and someone else can try to kill them and next time succeed."

Enok looked at Earon and motioned his head toward the door. "Earon, I believe your sister and I have some things to discuss. Please keep Terrance company for dinner and ask Graybin to bring Europa and me up a tray."

"I am not hungry," Europa said, clinging onto Earon to prevent him from leaving.

"Ask Graybin to bring up a tray for two, with plenty of coffee," Enok repeated.

"Yes, Sir," Earon said. He released Europa from his arms and lifted her away from his chest, sitting her on the couch. "I need to go, Sis. You need to stay here with Father."

"I do not want to be with him," Europa whispered, keeping her eyes looking down, while she grabbed her brother's shirt to keep him with her. "I want to stay with you."

"No, Sis," Earon replied, removing her grip off his shirt once again. "You need to talk to him. Listen to what he has to say. Ask him what you need to know. He is an unbelievable monarch, but more importantly, he is a wonderful, fantastic father." Earon leaned down and kissed her on top of her forehead, then turned and walked out of the room, closing the door behind him.

Europa glared at Enok as he walked over to a chair across from where she sat curled up. "I know you are upset, Europa. And very upset with the decisions your mother and I made regarding your future. You have every right to your feelings, and I understand why you are confused and even worried. But please let me help you understand."

"Now you want to help?" Europa asked, staring at her father. "Where were you for the past twenty years when I needed your help? Where were you when Mother died?"

"I was being a monarch, protecting my people and you," Enok replied. "I was trying to get better so I could breathe and join you three and we could be a family. But most importantly, I was there watching over you. You just could not see me. I was there through your mother, I was there through Jeanip, and I was there through the security protocols and decrees. And I was there in the waters, patrolling offshore to ensure that you, your brother and mother were safe."

"We all know how well that worked out, protecting us from offshore," Europa said, allowing her bitterness to reflect in her voice. "It helped mother tremendously and kept Minnos in one piece."

Europa's words cut into his heart like a blade. Enok knew Europa spoke the truth – his protection from offshore did not save Minnos or the female he loved more than life itself. Enok rose from his chair and walked over to the large bay window, keeping his back to his daughter so she would not see the tears in his eyes. "Europa, never doubt the fact that had I had an inkling of your mother or you being in danger, I would have immediately come onto land, even though it would have meant my death. We truly believed JeffRa had died that day he went over the cliff. And we became more confident in his demise with every passing century. We had no indication he was still alive, hiding somewhere, plotting our end to fulfill his oath of revenge." Enok paused for a moment as he composed himself, then said, "Europa, do you think a day or even an hour goes by that I do not blame myself for the loss of your mother and Minnos? Your mother was my world, my reason to exist and to be the best monarch I could be. I took some comfort knowing Minnos existed and, as long as it stood, a part of your mother would remain alive and strong, for Minnos was so much a part of her. But then JeffRa took that away from me too. If it were not for the love I have for you and your brother I would have crumbled into nothingness when Minnos was destroyed."

"Was JeffRa telling the truth about loving my mother?" Europa asked, staring at her father's back.

"Yes, he loved her," Enok answered, as he turned and walked back to his chair, taking a seat once more. Europa could see tears in his eyes and realized how much he truly missed her mother and the guilt he felt over her loss. "He loved her very, very much."

"Did she love him?" Europa asked.

"Very much," Enok said truthfully. "And had our fathers not pledged us together, she probably would have become his life's mate instead of mine. But as I told JeffRa, our fathers made the agreement we would join without our knowledge or consent. And once it was made we had no option but to follow their decree. Your mother wanted to explain what had happened to JeffRa, but she never saw him again while we were on Europa."

"Then mother did not love you at first?" Europa asked.

"Your mother was fond of me, as I was of her," Enok replied. "And like your mother, I had another chosen as my life's mate. But something happened to us once we were joined and began to know each other. That fondness grew into a very deep, deep love that still exists today. I cannot imagine loving anyone more than I loved your mother. She made me be a better Waters, a better Oonock, and a better monarch."

"JeffRa's story was a lot different from the one Jeanip told us. Do you think he was lying?"

"I imagine the truth is a combination of the two stories," Enok said. "To us Oonocks, Jeanip's version is the truth. To JeffRa and the Terrians, his version is the truth. Even the Oonocks and Terrians see truth in respect to how it affects them. I believe that is a consistent concept throughout the universe."

"Did you really send JeffRa supplies like you said?" Europa asked.

"Yes, for three months. I never knew he did not receive them," Enok replied. "Now that I know it was my father who caused the destruction of Jupiter, I believe it was also he that secretly prevented the supply shipments."

"Why would your father stop the supplies his son needed?" Europa asked. "He must have known that JeffRa needed them in order to survive on Ganymede."

"I am sure he did. When Quinsong died Father became inconsolable," Enok explained, remembering back to that dark time in his past. "His determination to make JeffRa pay for her death was almost as strong as JeffRa's determination to seek revenge on me. In Enoquin's eyes JeffRa deserved only pain and misery, as did his followers. He would have seen the supplies and medicines as items that would make JeffRa's life easier, something he could not let himself allow. Plus, Father and JeffRa never got along; probably because they were so alike. And I believe he also resented JeffRa because Mother loved him so much. Father often was intentionally cruel and mean to him. There were many times I had to step in between them to keep JeffRa from harm."

"His chest was so badly scarred," Europa said, remembering the many scars of torture JeffRa had shown them. "He must have suffered greatly."

"Yes, I am sorry to say he did," Enok stated, a tone of sadness clearly audible. "Had I known I might have tried to help him, but I am not sure. He was guilty of killing our sister and trying to kill Medaron and me. Would I have had the courage to rescue him knowing he would probably continue his quest to kill my family? I will never know. I loved my brother dearly, but I also had an obligation to protect Medaron and our people. Plus, the intelligence I received told a very different story. I was told he was doing well, had conquered the local tribes and made himself their leader. I was counseled numerous times that he was preparing to destroy not only my family, but the entire planet."

"And he is really gone for good?" Europa asked, not sure if she should believe he truly was.

"Where I have sent him he cannot return," Enok said. "This I promise you. But enough of JeffRa. If you have more questions I will gladly answer them after we discuss the real reason for these tears."

"Oh please tell me Mighty Enok, what is the 'real reason'?" Europa asked, a tone of sarcasm strongly noticeable in her voice, anger building inside her again as she remembered her lost life.

"Europa, I understand you are upset," Enok began. "But I am the Head Monarch and your father. You will treat me with the respect my title and position entitles me to. In return, I will treat you with the respect you deserve as the future Supreme Monarch and I will tell you the truth. Is that understood?"

"Why should I give you any respect?" Europa shouted. "How in your warped mind do you rationalize the thought that I owe you respect?"

"Because I am your father!" Enok replied trying to remain calm.

"My father?" she yelled. "When were you ever my father? Just because you crawled on top my mother one night and planted yourself in her does not make you my father! Jeanip was more of a father to me than you ever have been. At least . . ."

"ENOUGH!" Enok screamed, his voice so loud and forceful the security alarms began to sound. Enok and Europa both heard footsteps on the stairs as Runbee, Graybin, Earon and Terrance ran up the stairs. They watched as the door burst opened revealing the four, Runbee and Graybin both holding assault weapons.

"Are you okay, Your Majesties?" Runbee asked, surveying the room for possible threats.

"Yes, just a little heated argument between father and daughter," Enok replied, reminding Earon and Terrance of a similar argument between Europa and Terrance not long ago. "We are both fine." After taking a calming breathe Enok said loudly, "Security alarms silent, authorization code CJ1-1." The alarms stopped, making the room uncomfortably quiet except for the heavy breathing of Terrance, a result of running up the stairs. Seeing the still-concerned faces Enok stated, "I assure you we are fine. We are in no danger. You can return downstairs."

Runbee grabbed Terrance and Earon and pushed them through the doorway out into the hallway and back to the kitchen. Graybin followed and grasped the door handle to close the library door and give the two monarchs their privacy. Just as it was ready to close she stopped and looked directly at Europa, a stern yet disappointed look on her face. "Today you have shamed your mother, Europa, and acted like a common street tentig. No matter what wrongs you believe he has done, which decisions of your parents you do not agree with, Enok is your father and our king and is NEVER to be talked to in such a manner. You do not have to love him, but his title does demand you respect him." Without another word Graybin closed the door.

"I am sorry for losing my temper, Father," Europa said, knowing Graybin had spoken the truth. She had shamed her mother in addition to disrespecting her parents and her monarchs. She thought how angry and disappointed her mother would have been if she had heard Europa speak to Enok in such a tone. "I am sorry for the things I said and for disrespecting you and Mother."

"I too am sorry, Europa, for raising my voice," Enok said. "But I will allow no one, not even you, to disrespect your mother." He raised himself from the chair and walked over to the couch were Europa sat. He sat down beside her and lifted her hand into his. "My Dearest Daughter," Enok began, looking into her face, "I know Jeanip tried to explain why your mother and I made the decisions we did regarding your life. And I understand you feel you have been robbed and lied to. I am going to try to explain to you your mother's and mine thinking behind our decisions so you can understand better. I do not ask you to forgive us or agree with our decisions, just that you listen. Okay?"

"Okay", Europa softly answered.

"And feel free to ask me any questions you would like," Enok added. "No matter what they are."

"I will," Europa said.

"First, let me say that in our race female births are rare," Enok began., "Especially in the royal family. My sister was the first royal female born in over sixty-three thousand years and the last one until you. So you can see the importance of your conception. Jeanip explained to you about our reproduction capabilities here on Earth being compromised and we, as a race, are no longer able to conceive. No child has been born to us for over five hundred years. And before that,the few female children that were conceived at the Complex did not survive long after birth due to breathing problems. So you can imagine our shock when we learned your mother was pregnant. And the fact she carried a female Waters made it totally unbelievable. We were ecstatic with joy and everyone was celebrating the news. But with that joy came concern, for we knew if you were allowed to develop as an Oonock and be born at the Complex, your chance of survival was almost zero. Our medical personnel advised us your best chance of survival was to be born above as a human who would be capable of breathing air. Considering their advice, and adding in other factors, your mother and I agreed you would be born human. Understand, Europa, this was a mutual decision; both your mother and I were in agreement. To assure your human fetal development progressed as needed, Medaron immediately transformed into a human and lived apart from me in a special oxygenated, low-pressure environment in one of the upper levels of the Complex. There she remained until Jeanip could make the necessary security modifications to Minnos. Once Minnos was ready, Jeanip took Medaron and your brother above to await your birth."

"In the same box you took Jeanip in?" Europa asked, remembering Enok's comment to Jeanip several days before.

"Yes, in the same box," Enok replied. "It was specially created for your mother to allow her to adjust to the extreme pressure changes needed as she went from the deep ocean to the surface. It also allowed her to breathe air rather than water."

"I stated there were several other factors that contributed to our decision besides your almost nonexistent chance of survival. The next factor was and still is totally mine. We had another son before Earon was born. His name was Tiree. He was killed during our last battle with the Terrians."

"Jeanip told us about him," Europa said.

"Did he also tell you your mother blamed herself for our son's death and I nearly lost her to grief? I knew with certainty, if she carried you and then lost you, she would cease to exist; she could not bear the loss of another child. As with you, her only chance to live was above on land. So as a totally selfish act on my part, I agreed for you to be born above as human and for Medaron to live transformed into one too, thus assuring her further existence."

"The third factor was the future of our Complex. With each passing year the human's technology becomes more sophisticated, more advanced. Already they have built submersibles that can descend into the depths of the ocean carrying humans to explore. They have discovered our Complex's exit portal and have tried to pass through it several times. So far they have not found a way to penetrate the dense saline liquid, but we believe it is only a matter of time before they do. Within the next hundred years it is possible humans will develop the technologically advanced enough to pose a threat and discover our home. This is something that cannot and will not be allowed. Therefore, it will soon become necessary for the Complex to be abandoned and destroyed, thus assuring none of our technology will fall into their hands. This means those Oonocks still with us will need to find alternative forms of life to live out their days – either as land or water creatures. There will be no Complex to return to, to rejuvenate when needed, so we assume our life spans will shorten greatly. Plus, other than the one transmission from Mars when they were under attack, we have never heard from any of our other ships that left with us that day and traveled outside our solar system. Have you ever been on the ocean and heard the whales singing?"

"Yes, many times," Europa answered. "Jeanip said some whales are actually Oonocks sending out messages in search of the other ships."

460

"That is correct. These particular Oonocks are from the Song Clan; we named them 'Callers'. To help pass the time when we were hidden below after the war, these particular Oonocks chose to develop a method where they could send a distress signal out into space in an attempt to communicate with our other ships, a signal not detectable to humans. All the humans hear is the whale song, not the high-pitched signal. For over six hundred years our callers have been sending their messages into space hoping to hear from one of the other ships that escaped Europa, but our calls go unanswered. Perhaps they traveled too far out in the universe to hear our signals. Or perhaps the unthinkable happened and JeffRa hunted them down and eradicated them before he came to Mars and Earth. Whatever the reason, your implantation made us finally accept the fact we were alone with no rescue or no reinforcements ever coming to our aid."

"You may be wondering why the Complex's future and the reality we were alone affected our decision. The reason is if you had been born as an Oonock and had survived, chances were you would live hundreds, maybe even thousands of years longer than any Oonock now alive. Add in the factor no new Oonocks would be born, and you would spend your life alone with no one of your own kind to be with. Your mother and I could not condemn you to such a lonely future."

"The last contributing factor was JeffRa's death. We truly believed he died the day he went over the cliff with Tiree. And since our scouts had not seen even one Terrian or any indication of one in almost six hundred years, we felt there was no danger in having your mother, brother or you live above."

"But if you felt there was no danger, why did you have such high security at Minnos and have Saint's Isle built? Why all the security protocols if there was no danger?" Europa asked.

"Even though we believed no Terrians existed we had no way to prove it," Enok answered. "Your mother and I were not willing to take that chance. Although remote, there still was the possibility Terrians still plotted our downfall. I believe the humans have a saying 'better to be safe than sorry'? To be safe we built Saint's Isle and reinforced Minnos to assure your safety while secretly believing and hoping such security measures would never be needed."

Enok looked at Europa. He believed she was starting to understand the reasons for his and Medaron's decisions, but he needed her to understand completely. "Europa, the decision to have you born and raised human was not made lightly. I would have given anything to have you and your mother live with me below. The price we paid for your safety was tremendous, but one we gladly paid. Your mother living above meant we would be separated for decades. Little did we know the day she left the Ocean Complex would be the last day we would ever see each other again. A day has not gone by since she left that I have not missed her terribly, nor has a day gone by since her death that I have not grieved for her loss."

"Why did you have Jeanip tell her you had died?" Europa asked.

"Even though we were separated by hundreds of miles, I could still feel her sorrow, her longing. It tore me apart knowing I was the cause. When the medical personnel told me they could not correct my breathing injury, I knew her suffering would continue for many more years. To ease that pain I decided she be told I had passed on so she could let me go. I thought it was best for her."

"Not a very good decision," Europa said, staring directly at her father. "In fact, I think it was a selfish decision on your part. You eased your pain of causing her sorrow, but mother grieved for you until the day she died."

"I will not debate the merits of my decision nor justify my actions. As a monarch, you make judgments based on what you believe is in the best interest of your people and those you love. If later on you realize it was not the best ruling, as monarch you still must stand by it. This is something you would have learned on Europa when you took over as Supreme Monarch from your mother if JeffRa had not destroyed that reality."

Seeing her father would not discuss his false death Europa asked, "I understand why it was in my best interest to be born above, but why did I have to be born as a human? Why could I not have been born as an Oonock and just lived above? Why was I denied all the fantastic powers and capabilities that Oonocks possess?"

"It was never your mother's or my intention to rob you of anything, Europa," Enok replied. "We simply wanted you to live, to grow up normal and happy and have a long life. Had there been a way for you to be born above as an Oonock we would have done that. But in order for you to be born an Oonock your mother would have to be her true self - a Waters. And Oonocks can only live in their true form in the depths of the ocean, which I have already stated was not a possibility if you were to survive."

"But look what my human life has cost! So many gave up so much to protect me: Earon, Jeanip, Misso and all the others," Europa stated. "Along with Mother, they not only put their lives on hold but many paid a heavy price for doing it – their deaths."

"Europa, you must understand this," Enok said. "The day it was learned your mother carried you the number one priority for every Oonock on Earth was to protect you and keep you safe. From that day on, each Oonock devoted their life to you and would gladly surrender it to save yours. That has been our custom and way of life for millions of years. It would have been no different if you had been born below."

Europa looked at her father's face. "Father, knowing that does not help me deal with all that has happened. I understand what you are saying regarding the Oonocks' customs and their monarchs, but it does put a lot of responsibility upon my shoulders. And on Earon's too. So many have died because of us."

"No more responsibility than other monarchs have had to bear, including those on Earth," Enok answered. "Being born into a royal family and destined to be the next Supreme Ruler comes with obligations and responsibilities. I cannot change the fact you are my daughter or I am the Head Monarch. That is a fact you now have to accept."

"But why did you wait until tragedy struck before I learned who I really was?" Europa asked. "Surely there must have been a time somewhere in my life when Mother could have told me."

"Did she not tell you that you were of royal blood and we had to flee our old country because of war?" Enok asked. "Did she not tell you it was possible that the family, including you, might still be in danger and therefore you must always have a protector with you? Did she not make you follow very strict security rules?"

"Yes, she told me," Europa answered. "But telling someone their parents are of royal birth and their parents are aliens from one of Jupiter's moons are two different things."

"And would you have believed her?" Enok asked, raising his voice slightly as he began to become frustrated once more.

"Yes, I would have," Europa answered, her eyes narrowing some as she too was becoming frustrated. "She could have had Earon transform in front of me or she could have transformed herself. There were ways she could have proven to me who and what she was."

Seeing this line of discussion was not accomplishing what he wanted to achieve, Enok thought he would try a different tactic. "Europa, I am going to ask you two questions. I want you to answer each truthfully with only a 'yes' or a 'no' answer. Nothing else. After you have answered each question you may add your rationalization, but not at first. Agreed?"

"Yes."

"Question number one: Imagine the past few weeks never happen; JeffRa never returned, no one has died, you never met Terrance. You know all about your family's past and the fact they are aliens. You have gone off to college as you had planned and have even met a wonderful man, fallen in love and have decided to get married. Let us even say he is a big science fiction fan and believes there is life on other planets. You bring him to Minnos to meet your mother. Knowing how humans are and how they react to things they do not understand, do you tell him your mother is an alien, that your canine guardian is really your brother, that you are from a race who settled here over six thousand years ago when they fled Europa and that they are shape shifters?"

Europa did not answer right away. She thought over the scenario and wanted desperately to answer 'yes', that she would tell him the truth. But she knew the truth was she would not have told him.

"Would you tell him?" Enok asked again.

"No," Europa replied, looking away from her father.

There was a soft knock at the door. Graybin entered carrying a tray of food and a canister of coffee. Not wishing to disturb her monarchs, she quietly walked over to a small table and swiftly placed the dishes of food on it. She raised the canister of coffee to ask if Europa wanted her to pour the coffee. She shook her head negatively. Graybin placed the coffee canister back on the table and softly walked out of the room.

"Second question," Enok continued, "You married this young man without ever telling him what you were or who your family was. By your definition, your omission to tell him constitutes a lie and your entire marriage is a farce. You have children of your own who also have no idea what their grandparents were or that they are still alive. Your children are growing into adults and soon will start their own families and have their own children who could carry Waters' traits and abilities. Do you tell your children they are part alien?"

"No," Europa answered again, this time her voice very low.

"No," Enok repeated. "You answered 'no' to both questions. Now I would like you to explain to me why you answered negatively. Why would you not tell your future husband?"

Europa thought back to Terrance's reaction when she said her parents were aliens. Without looking at her father, Europa replied, "Because he would have thought I was crazy."

"But you could have had your brother or mother transform into a deer or a bear to prove you were telling the truth," Enok stated.

"That would only have freaked him out," Europa replied. "He would have run screaming all the way to the authorities or to the tabloid papers. They would pay a lot of money for a story like that."

"More than likely," Enok agreed. "And put everyone at Minnos in danger along with all Oonocks everywhere on this planet. Now why would you not tell your children or grandchildren?"

"For the same reason," Europa replied. "They would have thought their mother or grandmother had lost her mind. They would have locked me away. And even if I could convince them, the truth would destroy their futures."

"Do your husband and children not have the right to know?"

"Yes," Europa said, finally realizing what her father wanted her to understand. "They had the right to know but, for their happiness and their future, it would be better if they did not. Just as it was better for me not to know."

"Yes, my Dearest Daughter," Enok said, pulling Europa into his arms, holding her very securely. "We did not tell you what your people were because we saw no benefit in it. Your life would not have been better or happier. But know we both agreed if you ever needed to know the truth we would not hesitate to tell you, just as I am doing now."

"Had JeffRa not reappeared I would have gone off to college and lived my life without knowing," Europa said, trying to imagine what that life would have been like.

"And been happy," Enok added. "That is all your mother and I ever wanted for you. A happy life free of the past horrors JeffRa caused our people." Enok released his hug and gently pushed her into a sitting position so he could look into her eyes. "Always remember, Europa, that your life has not been a lie. You ARE a human being who was born to two parents who loved you very much, born into a royal family that brings you privilege and responsibilities."

"Yes, Father," Europa said. "And I believe it is time I start acting like a monarch and stop feeling sorry for myself."

"After what you have been through, I think you are entitled to a few moments of feeling sorry for yourself," Enok said, giving his daughter a big smile. "Now, how about a little something to eat?"

"That sounds good," Europa said. "I actually am quite hungry." Together they walked over to the table where Graybin had placed their food, eating dinner together for the first time as father and daughter.

As they sat there enjoying each other's company, Europa told her father about her life growing up on Minnos, what it was like, her favorite things and her plans to be an oceanographer. Enok explained how he had traveled to the surface almost every day and swam off the shore of Minnos so he could keep an eye on her, her mother and Earon. He told her how Runbee and Graybin, disguised as Jack and Jill, had also kept tabs on her while she grew up and had traveled to the Complex to give him weekly reports. He knew of the time she fell on her bike and scraped her knee, about Danny Winslow breaking her heart in the fifth grade and how beautiful she looked the night of her prom. With a tear in his eye, he told her of the few times he had been able to see her when at the surface and how much it had meant to him. He also told her of the Complex below, her people who lived there and his duties as Ruling Monarch. Lastly, he told her of Europa, her home world. In great detail he explained what it looked like, the animals and plants that shared that world with them and what existing there entailed. Europa listed to her father, enthralled by his stories, captivated by the possibilities of what her future held.

FARCORE

Seeing the hour was getting late and his time above was almost at an end, Enok announced he would tell her more of the Complex and her home world the next time he visited. As he stood up from the table he noticed a serious look cross Europa's face. "I believe there is something that is still bothering you. Am I correct?"

"Not so much as bothered by," Europa answered, as she refilled her coffee cup. "More like concerned."

"What has you concerned?"

"I was wondering how long I will have to stay here on Saint's Isle," she replied, a little nervous to say what concerned her. "Do not get me wrong, it's a beautiful place, but . . ."

"It is a little short on companionship," Enok finished.

"Yes. Plus, when I do get to leave where am I going to go? Minnos has been destroyed and everyone in town, including my friends, probably think I am dead. I cannot just show back up, just stroll back into town."

"That is very true. And you have already lost so much you should not have to lose your friends back home also. Perhaps once you have resettled we can discover a way where they can be reintroduced into your life." Enok said. "As for where you will live once you leave here, with the wealth we have accumulated over the decades you can rebuild anywhere you would like. You can rebuild Minnos or design something totally new. It is all up to you. You can choose anywhere on this planet to live, Europa. I believe we could even construct a home under the water if that is what you wanted. It would, of course, have to be constructed with the humans knowing of its existence. Humans have dreamt for years of living under the sea. You could be the first one to do so. But if you do build your home on land the only thing I ask is you choose a location close to the ocean so I may visit you."

"I would like that," Europa said, a smile appearing on her face as she thought of the possibilities.

"As for the length of your stay here, I imagine it should not be a long one; perhaps six to nine months," Enok stated. "Definitely less than a year."

"Really?" Europa said surprised. She had thought it would be much longer. "Less than a year? That is wonderful news. I feared I would have to remain here for ten or twenty years."

"You only need to remain here until we are sure all the Terrians have been eliminated," Enok answered. "Once we are sure, you will be free to leave when you like. So you might want to start thinking of where you want to live because, if we allow humans to build your new home, it will take several months to construct."

"Looks like I will have something to help me pass my time here, finding a new place to live."

"Actually I have something to show you and your brother which I believe you will enjoy more. In fact, once you see this you may choose to stay here longer." Enok saw the spark of curiosity spread across his daughter's face. "Now I need for you to go ask Earon and Terrance to join us. And tell Terrance to be sure to bring the stone Mr. Dark Feather gave him. You also need to bring the Orb you found in your mother's attic."

"The stone?" Europa repeated, suddenly remembering what Mr. Dark Feather had asked Terrance to do with it. "Are you taking us to FarCore?"

"Just go get them," Enok smiled. "I will reveal all when you three are here together."

Europa quickly left the room and walked briskly down the stairs as she wiped the tears from her face. She returned within minutes with Earon and Terrance, the Orb securely held in her hand.

"Europa says you have something to show us, Father?" Earon asked, a look of excitement and anticipation clearly visible upon his face.

"Yes," Enok replied. "Terrance, do you have the stone?" Terrance reached into his pocket and removed the round purple stone. "Excellent. Now I need for you to stand before the picture of Medaron and me. That is the gateway to FarCore."

Europa looked at her father, perplexed at his words. "Father, I already tried to put my hand through the painting. There is a solid wall behind it."

"That is true," Enok replied. "It needs to be opened before you can pass through. I believe your mother gave you the key to unlock the gateway."

Earon and Europa looked at each other. "The only key she gave me was the golden ship. And I used it in the front door. Do you want me to go get it?" Europa asked.

"A different key is needed here," Enok replied. "Think back. Your mother gave you a special key the day she died."

Europa thought back to the day she saw her mother for the last time. She replayed the scene over in her mind, but she did not remember her mother giving her anything. Her mother had transferred her powers to Europa and said some words, the same words she used to heal Jeanip with the Orb. THE WORDS!! That was it. Facing the painting and holding the Orb, Europa spoke, "Ennay Benu Carif." The Orb began to hum as swirling rays of light emanated from the Orb and flowed into the painting. The surface of the painting began to trickle, then rain down over the painting.

"The gate is now open," Enok said, standing there as a proud father. "This gateway is from Europa and will allow only Oonocks to pass through, so you need to wear this, Terrance," Enok said, as he slipped a small amulet over his head. "You need to hold Europa's hand as you walk through the gateway to assure you get in. Earon and I will be right behind you. Now you need to announce yourself to the gateway just as you did upon entering the house for the first time."

Europa placed the Orb in her right hand, then took Terrance's hand with her left. "I am Europa Waters, true daughter of Enok and Medaron, monarchs of the Oonocks' Water clan." She turned to look at Terrance.

"I am Terrance Landers, friend and protector of Queen Europa," Terrance said. Together they stepped forward and walked through the painting. Earon and Enok stepped forward and announced themselves, then followed behind them. As soon as all four were through, the gateway reclosed, momentarily plunging them into darkness. Within seconds a light appeared ahead of them over what looked like an archway. Still holding hands, Europa and Terrance walked forward through the archway and entered a large expanse of space.

"Welcome to FarCore," Enok said, as he and Earon followed the two inside.

The three stood there in awe, unable to speak as they tried to comprehend the vision before their eyes, each realizing the panorama before them was an impossibility according to known scientific laws, yet here it was. The area seemed endless with no walls, no ceiling, no end or boundaries. The air had been replaced with the lilac waters of Europa, yet Europa and Terrance had no trouble breathing.

"How is it possible that we're breathing?" Terrance turned and asked Europa. Terrance brought his hand up to his mouth as he gasped in disbelief, chills running down his body. "Europa look at you. You've got WINGS! You're . . ."

"My most beautiful child," Enok said, completing Terrance's statement, as lilac tears filled his eyes and slipped onto his cheek. Three pair of transparent luminous wings could be seen attached to her back, the top pair also attached to her arms, the bottom pair to her legs and the middle pair overlapping the other two pair. Her hair was accented with strings of pearl lights cascading down upon her shoulders. Her eyes were larger and the color of lilac. A soft glow emanated from her body.

Seeing the look on Terrance's face and unaware of her transformation, Europa reached out for Terrance, afraid something was happening. As she lifted her arm she saw wings attached to her arms, gently waving in the lilac water. Instantly she knew they were the wings of an Oonock. "Father, how is this possible?" she asked, turning to her father. Tears began to fill her eye as she saw before her not the elder human Enok but the Enok of Europa, the luminous being she had seen before in her dreams. She saw her father was crying but hoped they were tears of joy when she looked into his eyes. "Father, why are you crying?"

"Because you are so beautiful," he answered, not trying to hide his emotions. "And I never imagined the day would come when I would be able to see the real you." He floated over to Europa and wrapped her in his top wings. He reached out with his second set of wings and pulled Terrance and Earon into his embrace also. The four floated, locked in each other's embrace for several minutes, then broke apart. As they separated, Europa saw Earon also was his true beautiful self, but no transformation had happened to Terrance; he was still a human.

"Father, did FarCore have the power to heal me, to make me an Oonock?" Europa, asked as hope flowed through her body.

"No, I am afraid not," Enok answered. "FarCore is a wondrous place and possesses powers beyond our comprehension. Only time will tell us what transformation, if any, those powers will do to you." Enok paused for a minute. "FarCore has many security devices to protect itself and its contents, one of which you see now. FarCore sees and displays the real you; it strips away any falsehoods of transformations or disguises to reveal your true self. For Earon and me, it sees we are Oonocks and displays us as such. Terrance is human so he remains human. But you, Europa, are part Oonock and part human; since FarCore sees you as both it displays you as each – two complete beings overlapping each other."

"You're all so beautiful," Terrance stated, wiping a tear from his eye also. "Europa told me how utterly lovely the beings in her dreams were, but I had no idea anything could be so beautiful it would bring tears to my eyes."

"Thank you, Terrance," Enok replied. "Thank you for accepting us for who we are and appreciating our beauty. You truly are a remarkable human deserving of my daughter's love and my respect."

"Your Majesty, you said you three transformed into your true selves because of a security device," Terrance stated. "Might I ask why FarCore perceives transformed beings as threats?"

"Yes, Father, why can I not remain transformed into a human?" Earon asked.

"This is the FarCore of Europa," Enok stated. "Only Oonocks pure of heart can enter through the portal. If a Terrian or a human tried to enter, the portal would deny them access because the security device would see they were not pure hearted Oonocks."

"But I got through, Your Majesty," Terrance said quickly.

"Only because you crossed with Europa AND wore the amulet I gave you. Without both you would not have been able to enter." Enok began to float forward. "My time above is short so let me show you a few things before I have to return to the Complex, and hopefully I can answer your questions along the way."

As they floated forward, a replica of the solar system appeared and began to circle around them. It was a replica of what the solar system looked like thousands of years ago before Jupiter had imploded and JeffRa had turned Mars into a barren wasteland.

"Oh my gosh," Europa said, letting go of Terrance's hand and gliding toward the Earth. "There are two earths here," she stated as she saw two blue and green planets.

"No, there's only one," Earon replied. "I believe this other planet is Mars."

"How can that be?" Europa said, looking at Earon. "Mars is barren."

"This is how Mars looked before JeffRa destroyed it," Enok stated. "It was a planet filled with life, with lush forests and blue oceans. That is why the other ships settled there. It was a good place to rebuild, almost identical to Earth in every aspect except for the wildlife. Mars had its own unique wealth of plants and animals."

"It's beautiful," Terrance said, mesmerized by the beauty before him. A somber look came over his face as he realized how close Earth had come to suffering Mar's fate. "What a shame that such a beautiful planet is now void of life."

"Luckily for us Earth was spared her sister's fate," Enok said, as he walked over to Jupiter. "Come here and take a look at this. This is what Jupiter and her moons looked like before the implosion accident." The three moved closer to have a better look at Jupiter. There were no rampant swirling wind storms, no red eye of the great storm that still raged on Jupiter. Although sparse, they could see water and vegetation on the surface. "Even then Jupiter was an inhospitable place, but life did exist there," Enok explained. "It was very different from Earth or Europian life since it developed in a world of methane and hydrogen, but it did exist. You can also see Jupiter's major moons before they were altered by Jupiter's implosion."

"Which one is Ganymede?" Europa asked, remembering it was the place JeffRa and his followers were exiled to.

"This is Ganymede here," Enok said, pointing to the third large moon. "As you can see it too was not the most hospitable place for life, but life was very possible there, although hard. There was sufficient water, vegetation and wildlife for hunting to support JeffRa and his followers."

"Might I ask, Father, why Ganymede was chosen?" Earon asked, curious about the reasons behind the moon's selection. "Would it not have been better to exile them to a location not so close to Europa? Perhaps one of the moons of Saturn or even somewhere outside this system?"

"Now that we know the result of our choice, yes, a location much further away from us would have been a better decision," Enok replied. "But at the time Ganymede seemed like the logical choice. Remember, when I sentenced JeffRa I was still consumed with guilt and felt partially responsible for his actions. I guess I wanted him fairly close so I could be there if he needed me. I still believed he could change and become my little brother again. Since we had discovered Ganymede was already populated with indigenous intelligent life we concluded that, if they could survive there, JeffRa could also. So I chose Ganymede. Plus, the array of supplies and medicines I sent gave him a fighting chance. Or should I say I believed I sent; I now know he never received them, thanks to our father." Europa could see a look of sorrow cross her father's face once again as he remembered the details JeffRa had told them regarding his capture and torture. The look quickly vanished as he turned and floated over to the moon Europa. "And here is Europa, our beloved homeworld. You can see the layer of ice which shielded us from the outside world while keeping us oblivious of the universe beyond our borders for so many millions of years." Enok held out his hand and motioned for his daughter to come closer. "Europa, come here and touch your home world."

Europa glided over to Enok and gently touched the moon Europa. Instantaneously, the orbiting planets disappeared and the scene around them changed to the world beneath the ice layer. Underwater cities appeared filled with the daily activities of Oonocks as they navigated with such grace and beauty through a sea of swirling colors and lights. Sea creatures of every shape and color could be seen swimming through the water, each surrounded by their own luminous light. Huge water ferns of pink, blue and green rose from the ocean floor, some appearing to be hundreds of feet tall. Plants resembling flowers lined the paths of walkways and circled individual dwellings. Sea grass filled in any area not landscaped or containing the large ferns, resulting in a continuous carpet of colors. In the middle of the city was a huge palace constructed of lilac and gold stone, with several large pillars marking the entrance and a golden dome which glistened and shimmered in the light of the ocean.

"So this is what our homeworld looked like?" Earon asked. "It was magnificent. I used to listen to the old ones tell stories of our city when I was young, but I never envisioned it looked like this. The only picture I have ever seen of it is the one in yours and mother's bedroom."

"Yes, it was glorious," Enok replied. "I do not believe there was ever a place more beautiful than Europa."

"Could it have survived, Father?" Earon asked.

473

"One can hope so," Enok replied, hopefully it had endured. "Now I believe Europa and Terrance have a task to complete. If you would please follow me." Once again Enok floated forward and this time a table appeared to their right on which rested hundreds of Orbs identical to the one Europa had found. Some glowed a warm whitish-yellow color and were filled with swirling colors, others were colorless and appeared empty. When he reached the table of Orbs, he turned to face Europa and Terrance. "Europa, place your Orb here on the table with the others. Here it is to remain secured with the records of Europa's past and the memories of Medaron's and my life together."

Europa looked down at the Orb in her hand, afraid to relinquish such a treasure. She raised her vision to look into her father's face as she explained, "But Father, if I leave the Orb here how will I get back in or do the things I have been able to do. Is the Orb not the source of my powers?"

"That is only partly true," Enok said. "Your powers are yours, they are a part of who you are. The Orb only helped you awaken that energy sleeping inside you and they gave you a way to channel and magnify your power through them. With time you will learn, as your mother did, how to use your powers without the aid of the Orbs."

"Since I have not learned how to channel my powers without their aid, should I not keep the Orb?" Europa asked, still uncertain why her father wanted her to leave the Orb. "I feel I still need its help and do not believe it is wise to leave here without it."

"Your Orb is full, like the written pages of a journal," Enok began to explain. "It can hold no more. You need to leave it here with the others and select a new Orb which you may take with you. It will have all the same capabilities as the Orb you have now, but will contain empty pages for you to record your own history."

Thankful she did not have to leave FarCore without an Orb in hand, Europa gently placed her Orb on the table with the others. She looked at the empty Orbs and wondered which one she should select. "May I select any one I wish or is there a specific one?" she asked.

"The Orbs which are not glowing are the ones which need filling. While any of them may accompany you on your life's journey and record your part in Oonock history, often the Orbs will choose which one should go out into the world. To find it you need to cup your hands together and place them over each empty Orb. The Orb will let you know when you have found it."

Trusting her father, Europa cupped her hands and placed them over an empty Orb. Nothing happened. Stepping to the next Orb she again cupped her hands over it and received the same result. She repeated this process three more times and watched in disappointment as the Orbs remained silent. She was beginning to wonder if she was doing something wrong, or if her father was mistaken, when the sixth Orb began to softly hum and emit a low glow even before her hands were over it. Excited this might be the one, she softly put her hands over the Orb and watched as it began to glow along with the amulet around her neck. She quickly looked up at her father and saw his affirmative nod. Smiling, she lifted the new Orb from its resting place, assured she had found the correct Orb.

Turning to Terrance Enok said, "Terrance, I believe Chancee asked you to leave something he gave you here with the Orbs. Please place it on the table with them." Terrance reached into his pocket and removed the stone.

"May I see that one more time?" Europa asked, as Terrance went to lay the stone down on the table. Terrance brought his hand up and dropped the stone into Europa's outstretched hand. She raised it to her eye level and stared at the carving of her mother's face etched into the stone. Keeping her eyes on it she asked Enok, "I asked Jeanip why JeffRa carved only my mother's image on his power stones. Why not his own or even yours, since he said you were the one he hated the most. Why only mother's? Jeanip said he did not know but said perhaps you might." She raised her vision to look directly into her father's eyes. "Father, do you know why?"

Enok returned his daughter's gaze. "I have my suspicions. You must remember that JeffRa loved your mother tremendously and she loved him just as much. Try as he might, he could never stop loving her; a truth he could never accept nor escape from, not even after thousands of years. When my father robbed him of joining with Medaron, I believe JeffRa's very soul was ripped apart. He became consumed in so much torment and agony over her loss. And he desperately needed her to know the great love he still had for her, perhaps even hoping she would go back to him. Of course she did not and he hated her for that too. Thus, to ensure your mother never forgot, he carved her face on a special power stone that would activate the weapon he invented to kill her children and family. That stone would remind her every time it was he whom ended their life and she was the reason why."

"Do you really think that he still loved her that much?" Europa asked, trying to fathom the possibility.

"I know he did," Enok replied. "I know because he did not kill her that day at Minnos. When Jeanip found your mother she laid unconscious in the road, but there was no sign of JeffRa; he had already escaped. That means he regained consciousness while your mother laid helpless on the road. He could have easily killed her while she laid there on the road, and if he truly hated her, he would have. But he could not harm her, could not end her life because he still loved her as much as he always did despite everything that had happened over the millennia. And so that I too would know he still cared for her deeply, he left me this." Enok opened his left hand to reveal a second purple power stone with Medaron's image carved on it. "He left this at the scene of the accident so she would know it was intended for you, Europa, and so I would know he let her live. There was still good in my brother."

"Oh, Father, how tragic, how terribly sad," Europa said, as she picked up the second stone from her father's hand. "To live one's entire life loving someone that much, someone who can never return that love. Now I understand a little bit better why you and Mother could not bring yourselves to execute him on Europa." She softly placed the two stones on the table. "Mr. Dark Feather was right; here in FarCore is where they should be left for all eternity."

Each watched in astonishment as a clear substance bubbled up from the table and covered the two identical stones, encasing each in a protective cover. "Now Chancee's promise to Medaron is fulfilled," Enok softly said. "The power stone that robbed Tiree of his life and stole him away from his mother will stay here at FarCore forever safe, forever existing. It, along with the one he meant for you, will never again cause sorrow or take more lives. It is finally finished."

Enok wiped a tear away from his eyes and turned to his children and Terrance. "Enough of such sorrowful things. I brought you here to bring joy into your lives, not sorrow. Let me show you the wondrous purpose of the Orbs." He picked up one of the Orbs and carried it to a golden ring which suddenly appeared floating in the air just past the table. "The Orbs contain the history and stories of our world and our people, preserved for eternity so all may know what life was like on Europa." He placed the Orb inside the ring and stepped back. A blinding flash of light emanated from the Orb causing the four to immediately close their eyes. When they opened them they saw before them a scene from the memories stored inside the Orb.

Two young male Waters appeared before their eyes sitting on the ocean floor. They were building a large flying ship together, laughing and enjoying themselves. Around their necks each wore an amulet identical to the ones the four visitors wore.

"Who are they?" Europa asked, as she swam closer for a better look at the two.

"That is JeffRa and I when we were young," Enok said, also moving closer to the images of himself and his brother. "This was the day we decided to build a better, faster ship to go explore Jupiter together. Both of us were intrigued by the stories told by those who had already gone there and walked upon her soil. We wanted to see for ourselves what the planet had to offer and explore its wonders."

"You two look like you are having a good time," Earon stated.

"Yes, we were. In our youth, JeffRa and I were very close, almost inseparable," Enok added. "We did everything together in those days. It would be many years before JeffRa's love for Medaron completely tore us apart, although the seed of discontent was planted soon after this day. See the stone JeffRa has in his hand?" They looked closely and could see in young JeffRa's hand a round purple stone made of the same minerals as the stone Mr. Dark Feather had given Terrance.

"Is that bendicor?" Europa asked. "Jeanip told us about it."

"Yes, that is a small stone of bendicor. Even this small of a stone it has tremendous powers. JeffRa engineered and built a special chamber to house the stone and harness more of its power. It was ingenious. He increased our ship's power tenfold. In fact, if JeffRa had not invented the chamber we never would have had the capability to travel to Earth and Mars or outside our system. His ideas changed the future of all Oonocks. See, he is installing the new device now for us to test and see how and if it works."

"Did you two go to Jupiter?" Earon asked.

"No, only I ended up going," Enok said sorrowfully. "Our father intervened and forbade JeffRa from navigating the ship and from having anything to do with the mission. Since I was the eldest son I was to lead the expedition and receive all the honor and credit for the accomplishment. I tried to persuade Father to allow JeffRa to go with me, but he would not hear of it. Nor would he hear of JeffRa receiving recognition for the ship's design, not even as a co-inventor. To Enoquin only one of his sons deserved honor and recognition – that one son was me. His other son deserved nothing, not even an afterthought. I tried to correct Father's wrong by giving JeffRa his due credit when I was renowned for the journey, but father quickly silenced me. Once again JeffRa was excluded and I was exalted above all others." Wishing to see no more, Enok removed the Orb from the golden ring and returned it to its place on the table.

"Did the Orbs record all yours and JeffRa's childhood memories?" Earon asked.

"No, only those events which shaped our history," Enok replied. "I believe the Orb recorded this event for two reasons: JeffRa's idea to use bendicor allowed us to travel outside our solar system and two, it was the day the seed of resentment was planted in JeffRa. This was the day my father succeeded in breaking him and started him down the path of destruction; a path which would change all of our lives, change our world's history and bring about the elimination of the Waters clan and many others."

"You said they recorded events which shaped our history." Europa stated. "So they recorded events outside the royal family?"

"You are correct, Europa. The Orbs record those events which impact upon the world whose memories it is recording, be they large events or tiny moments," Enok replied. "It could be as small as an insect that is blown into a new land and lays eyes. Those eggs hatch and the offspring begin to multiply and devour the foliage in the area. Since they have no predators, the insects go unchecked and soon devour every leaf within thousands of miles resulting in a collapse of the food chain. The result is the death of every living creature. Or it could be as enormous as an asteroid hitting a planet and exploding it into millions of pieces. Only significant events are recorded and they may be about anyone or anything."

"Sir, what are those rock chimneys there?" Terrance asked, as he pointed to thermal vents on the ocean floor.

"Those were the sources of our heat and much of our light," Enok stated. "Our race evolved because of those vents. Their energy enabled the first life forms to develop from the minerals in our waters."

"Can we see more of the Orbs' memories?" Europa asked, eager to see the history of her home world.

"Yes, you may," Enok replied, "But not today. I have little time left and there is still more I need to show you. I will leave the Orbs for you to explore over the next few months while you stay here." He looked down at Europa and smiled. "Remember? I told you I would give you something to occupy your time."

"By the looks of it I would say we could spend the next ten years here and not see everything," Terrance said, looking around the great expanse. "How did you ever create such a place?"

"Actually we did not make it," Enok replied. "Medaron discovered the gateway not long after we were joined while exploring a new cave. She was searching for seenums, a sea creature which very much resembles Earth's Dumbo Octopus. She loved keeping the seenums as pets and had followed several adults into this cave in hopes they would have young ones. Imagine her amazement when she not only discovered numerous young seenums, but several Orbs."

"The Orbs?" Europa asked. "So our race did not create them either?"

"No, the makers of this place did," Enok replied.

"Who were the makers?" Terrance asked.

"We do not know who the makers were or are," Enok replied. "They left no indication of who they were, where they were from or what the real purpose of FarCore was. We think they created expanses like this as a place where they could keep a record of the various worlds in the universes and their histories; their equivalent of what you call a library."

"The universes?" Earon and Europa asked, giggling lightly as they realized they both asked the same question.

"Come over here and marvel at the Librarians' technology," Enok stated as he led them to a large glass-paned window which appeared to be suspended in the water. It was stationary, but there were no walls holding it in place, no support ropes holding it from the ceiling and no legs supporting it from below. Enok purposely led the three completely around the window in a three hundred-sixty degree circle before stopping in front of it. "Now look through the window and behold the universes!" Enok announced with awe in his voice. The three peered through the window and saw an unlimited number of other glass windows suspended in the nothingness. Through some of the closer windows they could see other worlds and other solar systems.

"There must be millions of them," Terrance whispered.

"More like billions," Earon said. "Or trillions. What are they?"

"We believe those are the windows into other worlds, perhaps even other dimensions," Enok stated. "Each solar system, planet, moon, comet and asteroid has a window behind which its history is recorded in the Orbs."

"Can we explore them too?" an eager Earon asked, thinking of the possibilities that lay behind the windows, the unbelievable life forms and worlds that existed.

"No, Son," Enok replied. "One can only enter the history of one's own world, or worlds if you have lived on or were part of more than one. Like the Oonocks; we have history on both our home world of Europa and our new home, Earth."

"So we can't enter the realm of Mars?" Terrance asked.

"That is correct, Terrance, you cannot enter Mar's realm," Enok replied. "But you can study it here within this expanse since it is part of your solar system. If you touch the planet you will be given a panoramic view of what it was and is like, as well as a general history of the planet, but no more. We believe one is prevented from entering other realms as another security measure to prevent beings from possessing the secrets of other worlds and using them to make war and dominate other beings. Can you imagine what would happen if a creature of true evil, true hate had access to an unlimited supply of advance knowledge, weaponry and technology?"

"They could rule or destroy the universe," Terrance said, thinking what could have happened if JeffRa had had such knowledge.

"That they could, Terrance," Enok replied. "The creators of this library wanted to keep a record of the universe; but they did not want that knowledge to be used against others. So they limited who could enter and forbade the entrance into other realms. Even those who are allowed to enter have a very strong restriction placed upon them. The gateway will only show itself to beings of pure spirit, who have a loving heart and possess no ill will toward others."

"But if their security device is able to screen out anyone who would use the knowledge of other worlds for their own gain, that would mean only good people can enter." Europa stated. "So if they are pure at heart, why can they not have access to the other worlds?"

"I believe Terrance has that answer," Enok said, as he turned to look at Terrance, wanting him to see for himself the truth behind JeffRa and the reason why he became the being he was.

Terrance suddenly realized everyone was looking at him. Feeling uneasy and awkward, he wondered why Enok thought he would know the answer. "I'm sorry, Your Highness, but I don't have any idea of what the answer is."

"Yes you do, Son," Enok replied. "You, above anyone here, knows the answer because it is part of your life. Close your eyes and think for just a moment and the answer will come to you."

Terrance closed his eyes, still confused over what Enok said. He began to relive his life in his mind, trying to find the answer when he suddenly realized what it was. He opened his eyes and looked directly at Enok. "Access to the other realms are denied because one never knows what will turn a man of pure heart into an evil beast." Terrance saw Enok nod his head in affirmation. "Just like my father began life as a creature pure in spirit and heart but was turned into a ruthless, hateful murderer because of the combination of his own desires, his ambitions and the cruel treatment by his father."

"Correct," Enok replied. "Any being, no matter how pure, has the capability of being turned to evil."

"And that is another reason why you and Mother could not pronounce the death sentence for him all those millennia ago," Earon said, now realizing another part of the truth behind their actions.

Enok remained silent but confirmed Earon's statement with a nod of his head.

"You said every world has an entrance," Europa said to her father. "Does that mean there is an entrance from Earth?"

"Yes," Enok replied. "But as of yet it has not been discovered. The humans of Earth still wage war against each other, still seek power to dominate the weaker and still have not learned how to live in harmony with each other and nature. Until they do, the human race will be denied access to the Orbs and the gateway. But I believe the human race has many admirable qualities that will one day bring them to global peace and love; and on that day the gateway will make its presence known."

"Father, you said one can only enter their own world, or another world if they have lived there. Since we are on Earth, does that mean we have access to its realm without using a gateway?" Earon asked, excited by the possibility of another area to explore.

"Is that possible?" Europa asked, now very excited by the idea also.

"Yes, since you are of two worlds you have access to both FaCores," Enok said. "Would you like to see Earth's expanse?"

"Would we!" all three answered in unison.

481

Enok laughed and was delighted to hear excitement in the voices. He turned and swam past the Orbs toward a small dot of light. The light grew rapidly in size and then suddenly transformed into an archway from which strange sounds could be heard.

"Welcome to Earth's history," Enok said, as he stretched his hand out, pointing the way through the arch.

After they walked through the archway they discovered they were standing on a large plateau overlooking grassy planes below them. Mountains and active volcanoes could be seen in the distance, with a brilliant blue sky overhead. A large lake glistened in the sun, a light breeze causing small waves to wash upon the shore. Several brachiosaurus emerged from the lake to join the remainder of their herd already grazing on land. Their enormous weight caused the ground to shake as they walked forward. Also grazing on the plains were saurolophus, stegosaurus, several forms of hadrosaurs, a family of gargoyleosaurs and an unfamiliar form of triceratops. In the distant they could see two t-rex with young stalking one of the band of hadrosaurs. As they stared down at the scene before them, a pteranodon flew over their heads and landed several yards away where her young waited for the fish in her mouth.

"This is unbelievable," Terrance said. "I know several paleontologists that would give their right arm to witness this."

"Look, Terrance," Europa shouted, as she pointed toward the t-rex. "They really do have feathers. And look what those tiny arms are for. Who would have guessed it?"

"Remember, you three, nothing you see here in the expanse can ever be revealed to the world," Enok cautioned. "It is forbidden."

"But what harm would there be in announcing a theory about what the t-rex used their short arms for?" Europa asked. "It is already in our past."

"True, but the present must progress according to the scientific discoveries and lifestyles of man," Enok answered. "The creators of this library felt any knowledge removed from here would have the possibility of contaminating the future. If any knowledge is taken from this room the gateway will seal itself and entry will be denied."

"For how long?" asked a concerned Europa.

"Possibly forever," Enok replied.

"But why can I remove the Orb?" Europa asked, as she looked down into the round object in her hands.

"Because it contains no knowledge," Enok replied. "It is blank. You will fill it with your experiences as you go through life."

"Look over there," Earon announced, pointing past the pteranodons. "There's a table of Orbs just like in our realm. Do they contain more of Earth's past?"

"Yes, they are the records of Earth's history," Enok answered. "From the time it formed to today, Earth's history is stored in the Orbs. And since you are a part of this planet you may also explore those Orbs."

"So they can tell me who really killed President Kennedy and if we really walked on the moon?" Terrance asked, intrigued by the possibilities of what he could learn.

"Yes, but use caution when exploring such specific events, Young Terrance," Enok cautioned. "With the answers comes the burden and power of knowledge. Such specific knowledge brings with it a greater chance of sealing the door because of the greater risk of revealing what you have learned outside of the chamber. It is wiser to explore more general subjects or subjects further in the past."

"Do all the realms have Orbs?" Terrance asked.

"We believe so," Enok stated. "I have only been in these two realms. And since I cannot enter any of the others, I can only assume each realm is basically the same, just different histories and scenery. Come, it is time for us to return to our own realm and for me to return to the Complex," Enok said, as he led the way away from Earth's history.

"Father, how do you know all these conditions? And how did mother paint the gateway?" Europa asked.

"Once the Orbs were certain your mother was pure of heart, they revealed to her how to create the gateway and she was given the conditions," Enok replied. "She passed them on to me and I am passing them on to you. When the day comes for you to bring someone here you, in turn, will pass the conditions on to them. Medaron had created the gateway while we were on Europa and was able to bring it with her when we fled our home world. It was very small, about an inch square. She kept it hidden in a golden locket she wore around her neck next to her amulet. When Saint's Isle was completed, she brought the gateway here for safekeeping and was able to reconstruct it as the painting you saw of the two of us. To most beings it is just a painting, but to those who know its secrets, it is the gateway you passed through."

"Will it always remain a picture of you and Mother?" Europa asked, curious as to what would happen to the painting now that her mother was deceased.

"That is another question I do not know the answer to," Enok replied. "But I believe when I have flowed out into the waters and have joined your mother, it will be necessary for the painting to take on the appearance of someone alive. Perhaps it will be a painting of you three."

"That is an interesting theory," Earon stated.

"And a little freaky, too," Terrance added.

The sound of a hall clock began to chime, filling the air with its tone. "We are being told it is time for us to leave," Enok said, seeing the disappointed looks on the three travelers' faces. "Another condition of the expanse: beings tend to get consumed by the knowledge in here and can easily remain for days, weeks or even months without emerging. To assure this does not happen, the expanse has a safety feature: it only allows you access for a specific amount of time. The time limit assures you have a life OUTSIDE of the expanse. But you may return tomorrow, if you like."

"We can come only once a day?" Europa asked, disappointed at the idea.

"Yes, that is the limit for now," Enok replied. "The gateway could change the limit in the future, but we have no way of knowing when that might occur. For now we must abide by its clock. Come, let us go."

Enok led the way back to the gateway entrance. Each one stepped through and onto the floor in the library on Saint's Isle," Enok, Earon and Europa in human form once again. They were surprised to learn they had been in inside the gateway for over two hours. It had seemed like minutes. They understood why the expanse had the stipulation of a time frame that one could spend inside.

Terrance removed the amulet and handed it to Enok. "No, Terrance, you keep the amulet for a while. You will need it if you want to go back inside. Since you are not of Europa you will need to have Europa or Earon go with you at all times. Is that understood?"

"Yes, Sir," Terrance replied, returning the amulet to its place around his neck. He knew what an honor it was to be given something that only a member of the royal family wore.

"Walk with me downstairs," Enok instructed, as he left the library and headed down the staircase. "I will be back in a few days to see how you are doing. Europa, think about where you want your new home to be while I'm gone. We can start building it as soon as you've chosen a location."

"Yes, I will."

"When I return I will be bringing several Oonocks with me to work as helpers and allow Graybin and Runbee to return to the ocean. They have been very generous with their time, but their assignment to watch over you and work as the house staff was only to be temporary until I could bring new helpers aboard. You may be interested to know, Earon, that EeRee has volunteered to work at Minnos."

"EeRee? Really?" Earon asked, a definite tone of excitement in his voice.

Europa noted the immediate joy in Earon's voice and upon his face. She was curious who this EeRee being was. Turning to Earon she asked, "And whom might I ask, Earon, is EeRee?"

"EeRee is probably one of the most beautiful Waters ever born," Earon stated. "We were to be joined as life-mates before Mother found out she was pregnant and I came up to the surface to live. I have not seen her in over twenty years. When I left I released her from any obligation to wait for me and I have always assumed she continued her life without me." Looking at Enok Earon asked, "Will she be coming alone or did she find another Oonock to take my place?"

Enok smiled, stretched out his arm and pulled his son in close to him while they walked down the staircase. "Oh, Earon, you certainly are your father's son. You released her from her obligation to avoid causing her pain just as I did when I instructed Jeanip to tell Medaron I had passed. We were both wrong to do so. The truth is, EeRee only has eyes for you. She has not taken another as her life's mate because she gave away her heart years ago – to you. She waits for you and will not consider another to be joined with."

"Really, Father?" Earon asked, elated to hear his one true love was still waiting for him. "So there is still a chance we can be joined?"

"Most certainly," Enok answered. "And now that your true identity is known to your sister, I see no reason why the joining cannot take place in the near future, perhaps here on the island. That is if you still wish to join with her."

"Most definitely," Earon responded, as his father released him as they reached the downstairs.

"When I return to the Complex I will speak with her parents and make the arrangements for her to accompany me back. Then you two can rekindle your love and decide when you wish to be joined."

Europa watched as Earon began to skip toward the front door. She had never seen her brother so happy, so excited about something or someone. "I cannot wait to meet this EeRee. She definitely has won my brother's heart. And it will be nice to have another female of my own age here on the island." Feeling the weight once again upon her shoulders of her safety interfering with other's lives she added, "I am sorry my conception prevented you from joining with her, Earon."

Earon stopped immediately and turned to face his sister. "Europa, when are you going to stop this? You did not ask to be born, did you? You are not responsible for the changes in all of our lives as a result of your birth. We did what we did not out of necessity but because we loved you and were overjoyed to have a new female monarch, a rare and most precious gift. You must stop blaming yourself for our decisions and for the deaths of those we have lost. If we had it to do over again none of us would have chosen anything different. Besides, even as much as I love EeRee, if I had to choose between joining with her or having a little sister, I would choose the little sister every time."

"Spoken like a true monarch and a big brother," Enok stated, as they reached the front door. He paused for a moment then said, "I believe it is safe for you three to escort me down to the water's edge." He smiled as he saw excitement cross their faces. "During the day, if you wish, you can come out into the gardens. I am sure you are getting a little claustrophobic being cooped up inside the house. Just be sure the doors are locked before dinner and the plank removed. You can unlock the door each morning after breakfast or anytime during the day, if you wish to go outside. If there is any potential danger the security grid will know and the house will not allow the door to be opened. I will be bringing up new security personnel to monitor the grid and see to your safety until Jeanip is able to return. And I have my eye on a young medical personage named Gardawyn that I am considering bringing up also." Enok saw a worried look appear on Terrance's face. He realized the appearance of several young male Oonocks was making Terrance a little nervous. Currently he was the only eligible male on the premises and therefore had exclusive opportunities with Europa. To ease Terrance's fears Enok stated, "And do not worry, Young Terrance. Just as EeRee has eyes only for my son, my daughter has eyes only for you."

Terrance breathed a sigh of relief as he blushed. He looked over at Europa and saw she too was blushing. Neither of them had realized Enok knew of their growing love.

When they reached the ocean Enok turned and hugged each of his children, giving them a kiss on the cheek, then turned and gave Terrance a hug goodbye also. "Now, if you will wait here I will swim by as I leave," Enok announced, as he continued down the path inside the cove and out of sight. Europa started to ask why they could not escort him all the way down to the water's edge when she remembered that, in order to transform, Enok had to disrobe. Although nudity meant nothing to the Oonocks, she understood Enok realized it would be embarrassing and awkward for her to see him that way.

Once he was out of sight Enok undressed and slipped into the water, transforming into a dolphin. He was quickly joined by several others who would escort him back to the Complex. As he promised, he swam over to where the three travelers waited and loudly clattered and clicked his goodbyes. He then dove underneath the surface and disappeared into the ocean's vastness, emerging again in the dense fog bank before transforming into a Moby and returning to the Complex.

That night Europa laid in bed, thinking of all she had seen on the other side of the gateway and all that was left to discover. She also began to think of where she wanted her new house and what it would look like. For the first time in many days she looked forward to her future with excitement and she knew she was going to be okay. She was human, but she was an Oonock of the Waters clan also. She thanked God for both.

For a listing of characters, Oonock terms and updates,

go to prgarcia.com.